In For a Penny

In For a Penny

Kathryn R. Wall (signature)

Kathryn R. Wall

Writers Club Press
San Jose New York Lincoln Shanghai

In For a Penny
All Rights Reserved © 2000 by Kathryn R. Wall

Writers Club Press
an imprint of iUniverse.com, Inc.

For information address:
iUniverse.com, Inc.
5220 S 16th, Ste. 200
Lincoln, NE 68512
www.iuniverse.com

This is a work of fiction. Names, characters, places,
and events are either a product of the author's imagination
or are used fictitiously. Any resemblance to actual persons,
living or dead, events, or locales is entirely coincidental.

Cover design by Ryan Kennedy

ISBN: 0-595-13851-9

Printed in the United States of America

In loving memory of Doris Cooper Everson

1912—2000

Thanks, Mom.

Acknowledgements

While writing is a solitary occupation, the publication of a book always involves many more people than just the author. I wish to thank the following for their special contributions to making this long-held dream a reality:

Erik Woidtke, Beverly Rocher, Shirley Wall, Theresa Bryant, and Allen Wright—first readers whose insights and enthusiasm kept me going.

Fred Bassett and Brewster Robertson—for instruction and guidance.

Bill Merritt—for allowing me a glimpse of the possibilities.

Barbara J. Everson—reader, editor, and sister-in-law *par excellence*.

The Group—Peg Cronin, Vicky Hunnings, and Linda McCabe—wonderful writers, exceptional women, and treasured friends who kept me working .

The rest of my friends and family for their encouragement and support.

And most importantly, this book is for my husband, Norman, who always believed.

1

The blue and white Gulfstream taxies slowly to the end of the private airstrip, then executes a sharp, 180-degree turn. The pitch of its engines climbs to an ear-splitting whine. I can almost feel her yearning to be off, like one of the Judge's golden retrievers straining at the leash.

A fierce August sun, glinting off the sleek metal skin of the plane, nearly blinds me. I raise a hand to shade my eyes just as the pilot releases the brake, and the graceful jet seems to leap into the air. With a final wave, I turn back toward my car.

The explosion knocks me to my knees. Windows in the tiny service building shatter. Flaming debris rains from a smoking sky. Instinctively I throw my arms up over my head.

White-hot pain sears my left shoulder, and I choke on the sickly-sweet smell of burning flesh. Dust swirls in the aftershock, and pieces of the dying plane clatter off the corrugated metal hangar.

Inside my head a voice is screaming, but no sound comes. A deathly stillness blankets me...

I struggled to free myself from the grip of the relentless images. My lungs gasped for air, and my heart thudded against the wall of my ribs. I could feel my head whipping from side to side in frantic denial, and still I could not escape...

Again I lie stunned and helpless under the blazing sun. Again I feel the sharp curve of pebbles beneath my cheek, smell the dank sweat that rolls down my side, as I cower on my face in the dirt and listen to my husband die...

The shrill of the telephone pulled me back. Heavy silk drapes, stretched across French doors that gave onto the deck, kept the room in total darkness. I fumbled for my reading glasses and flipped on the lamp. I drew a deep, calming breath and picked up the receiver.

"Hello?" My throat was still thick with the horror of the dream-memory, and it came out more like a croak.

The clock radio on the nightstand glowed *7:35*. Not exactly an ungodly hour for someone to be calling, but still early enough to send a little shiver of fear skittering down my back. I cleared my throat and tried again. "Hello?"

My hand reached automatically for a cigarette. It was alight, and the first deep, satisfying cloud of smoke had settled into my lungs before I remembered that today was the day I was going to quit. Again.

"Lydia? Is that you, dear?" The tiny voice was barely audible over the pounding of my heart.

No one—*no one*—ever calls me Lydia. At least not to my face. I was born Lydia Baynard Simpson, but I'm Bay to my friends and to anyone who aspires to join their ranks.

"This is Bay Tanner. Who is this?"

"Oh, yes, of course, dear, how silly of me. It's just that your dear mama, rest her soul, always called you Lydia, and so that's how I always think of you. This is Adelaide Boyce Hammond."

Miss Addie! Lord, I hadn't seen her since my mother's funeral more than fifteen years ago. For all I knew, she could have been dead, too. She and Emmaline Simpson had been Braxton girls, inmates of that stuffy academy that had finished so many of their generation of aristocratic Southern debutantes. Her soft, melodious voice conjured up memories of lazy summer afternoons and tea on the verandah.

Unconsciously, I sat up straighter, pulled the sheet tight across my naked breasts, and stubbed out my cigarette. "Miss Addie," I crooned, "how lovely to hear from you. I hope you're well?"

The years of my mother's relentless campaign to turn her tomboy daughter into a proper lady had not been entirely wasted. I could, when pressed, trade social niceties with the best of them.

"Why, yes, dear, I'm quite well, thank you. I was deeply saddened to hear of your poor husband's untimely passin'. So tragic when the young are taken before their time. I hope my note was of some small comfort to you?"

Note? I didn't remember any condolence message from my mother's old childhood friend.

But then, it had been almost a year ago, and the weeks following Rob's murder had been a blur of physical pain and emotional anguish. I had been allowed out of the hospital only long enough to sit huddled in a wheelchair while dignitaries from Columbia and Washington extolled the virtues of my dead husband. The memorial service had been as much media circus as tribute.

There hadn't been enough pieces of him left to warrant a burial.

Absently I fingered the deepest of the shiny-smooth furrows of scar tissue that criss-crossed my left shoulder.

"Yes, Miss Addie, it certainly was a comfort," I lied, "and very kind of you."

"Not at all, dear. I do so admire the brave manner in which you've conducted yourself since your bereavement. Your poor mama, rest her soul, would have been very proud."

I could see I was going to have to pull it out of her, the reason for her call. Otherwise we might be dancing this courtly minuet of pleasantries until lunch time.

"Thank you. Is there something I can do for you, Miss Addie?"

"Oh, yes…well. Oh dear, this is somewhat difficult." I could almost see her tiny octogenarian's hands fluttering, like hummingbirds around a feeder. With a gentle sigh, she got down to business. "I spoke with the Judge yesterday, and he suggested I call you. About a little problem I may have? He was certain you could advise me as to what's best to do."

I should have detected the fine hand of my father in this. Though retired from his law practice, as well as from the bench, Judge Talbot Simpson was still a full-time meddler in my life. "What problem is that, Miss Addie?"

"Oh, just a little investment I made awhile back. Quite safe and certain to be very profitable. The young man assured me. Perhaps you know him, Millicent Anderson's boy, Geoffrey?"

My fingers tightened around the receiver, and I felt a hot flush creeping up my neck. Oh yes, I knew him. Or rather, I *had*. Geoff Anderson had been my hero, my knight, my first, serious love. The fact that I was a gawky adolescent and he a much older Citadel cadet had made no difference. The only saving grace had been his total ignorance of my deep, but undeclared devotion. We'd lost touch after his graduation. I'd heard somewhere that he'd recently abandoned his Miami law firm in favor of real estate development.

"I remember him," I said with studied understatement. "What exactly is it you and the Judge think I can help with?"

I was fairly certain I already knew the answer, or at least the gist of it.

The Judge had an apoplexy when I transferred out of pre-law and into the business school during my junior year at Carolina. He was so angry he refused to pay my tuition bills. I promptly applied for and received a full academic scholarship to Northwestern and marched defiantly across the Mason-Dixon Line into enemy territory. A masters degree in accounting and another in finance had not been enough to earn me his total forgiveness, but he never had any hesitation about sending his friends around for free advice. I did his tax return every year, too, the ungrateful old buzzard.

My mind wandered back in time to catch the last of Miss Addie's reply. "...for lunch today? It would be lovely to see you again, and I'd feel so much easier if we could discuss it in person."

I couldn't think of a graceful way to refuse. I jotted down the directions to her condo and promised to be with her by twelve-thirty.

I plumped up the pillows behind me and lit another cigarette. My second of the day, and my feet hadn't even hit the floor yet.

Damn the Judge and his meddling!

It wasn't that I minded so much advising Adelaide Boyce Hammond about whatever financial problem she imagined she had. There was nothing to keep me from picking up my professional life right where it had left off. Not physically, anyway. The scars would remain, and a slight weakness in my left arm, but I'd learned to camouflage both pretty well. And, even though my mother's trust fund and my own knack for picking stock market dark horses made earning a living optional, I loved my work.

But after Rob was killed, I just had no desire to get back in the race. I had dropped out, scurrying back to the refuge of the beach house to lick my wounds and mourn.

"Baynards are made of sterner stuff." I heard my mother's reproach as clearly as if she towered next to the bed, frowning down on me. I got my height, almost 5' 10", from her side of the family, along with leaf-green eyes a lot of people assumed were colored contacts. The auburn tint to my dark brown hair and a tendency to wisecrack my way through uncomfortable situations came courtesy of the Judge.

Nightmares about Rob, and now visions of my dead mother!

This was exactly the reason I didn't want to sip weak iced tea and pick at mushy shrimp salad across the table from Adelaide Boyce Hammond. She was the past, mine and my mother's. I had expended a large chunk of my adult life trying to shove those painful memories to the farthest recesses of my mind. Miss Addie would bring them all back. Not that she'd mean to. She just wouldn't be able to help herself.

With a sigh, I squashed out the cigarette and flipped back the covers. I pulled on Rob's tattered College of Charleston T-shirt and padded barefoot across the room. Drawing the drapes, I opened the French doors and stepped out onto the deck.

Two ancient live oaks, their twisted limbs dripping Spanish moss, provided dappled shade, but I could already feel the promise of the scorching heat to come. It was low tide. Beyond the dune crowned with sea oats swaying lazily in a light breeze, the ocean retreated from a wide expanse of empty beach. Not quite empty, I realized, as a solitary jogger rounded the headland and trotted into view. Beside his master, a young black Lab, not yet grown into the promise of his oversized paws, loped along in the surf.

The mid-July sun glistened off the runner's golden arms and chest.

Rob always looked like that after a few days at the beach: his unruly shock of light brown hair bleached to the color of ripe wheat; his long, rangy body drinking up the sun.

I buried my face in the shoulder of his T-shirt. Though it had been laundered many times in the year since his death, I could still smell that faint, musky man-odor that had been his alone.

At least that's what I told myself.

A car door slammed somewhere below me. Seconds later the soft voice of Dolores Santiago, my part-time housekeeper, drifted up. Her Spanish endearments, interspersed frequently with *el gato*, told me she was fussing over Mr. Bones, the ragtag tomcat that adopted us not long after I came home from the hospital. The scruffy, battle-scarred tabby had wandered erratically in and out of our lives ever since. Apparently he had decided to grace us with his presence this morning.

I turned my attention back to the beach. The jogger had stooped to pick up a piece of driftwood and fling it out over the water. With a yelp of delight, the black Lab bounded in after it.

Something about the sweet joyfulness of the scene caught at my throat.

We had been happy like that, Rob and I. Carefree, unmindful of how fragile it all was. We had taken so much for granted.

And some bastard had shattered it, blown our joy into a million bits of steel and glass…and flesh.

"*Señora* Tanner?" A soft tap, and the bedroom door slipped open. "*Señora?*"

"Out here, Dolores."

I wiped my eyes on the sleeve of the sacred T-shirt and turned back into the room.

"Your paper, *Señora*." She dropped the *Island Packet* onto the linen chest at the foot of my bed. "Breakfast in twenty minutes?"

Dolores always seemed to be smiling, her white teeth a sharp contrast to the olive skin and blue-black hair pulled up into a tight bun at the back of her head.

"Make it thirty, okay? I haven't showered yet."

"You have the tennis at nine, no?"

"I'll make it. And just fruit this morning, please," I added, heading for the bathroom.

"*Sí, Señora*."

Dolores would undoubtedly cook me eggs or French toast or hotcakes and stand over me just like my mother used to do until I cleaned my plate. But I kept trying.

I snatched up the paper on my way by and glanced briefly at the headline: **Body Pulled From Chicopee River.**

Another drowning, I thought as I peeled off the T-shirt and stepped into the shower. *How can people be so damned careless?*

Only a few hours would pass before I realized just how wrong that snap judgment would turn out to be.

Come Labor Day, the permanent residents of Hilton Head Island, South Carolina breathe a collective sigh of relief, thankful to have our golf courses and beaches, restaurants and roadways returned to us once again. Then, from September to May, the island is almost paradise.

Except for an occasional brush with a hurricane, the weather is temperate, sunny and mild with only a few cold days in the dead of winter.

However, on that steamy July afternoon at the peak of tourist season, at least half of the 100,000 average daily visitors that clog the main island thoroughfare had conspired to make me late for my appointment. Traffic had come to a complete standstill, and the sun beating down at high noon made me wish I hadn't put the top down on my white LeBaron convertible. I kicked the air conditioning up a notch and reached for the newspaper I'd tossed into the front seat beside me.

I skimmed over the drowning story and flipped to the state news section. Although I had been out of the official loop since Rob's death, I still recognized most of the names associated with affairs in Columbia. I had worked with many of these people as a special consultant on financial fraud cases, building evidence and even testifying on occasion. I had thought I was gaining a reputation of my own, outside of Rob's influence, but requests for my professional services had been non-existent since his death.

I knew I hadn't endeared myself to any of them with my relentless demands for action during those first few months. Someone had viciously murdered three men: Rob, his civilian pilot, and a state trooper assigned for protection. Not only had no one been prosecuted, they weren't even close to making an arrest. While everyone—including me— had their suspicions about who had planted the bomb, there was no evidence and no new leads. The trail had gone cold.

A few weeks ago, when it finally dawned on them that I would never resign myself to accepting that, they stopped taking my calls.

A blast from the horn of the big van filling my rearview mirror jerked me back to the present. I dropped the paper and pulled the gearshift into drive.

Fifteen minutes of crawling finally brought me to the Sea Pines Circle, that landmark of the island and bane of drivers uninitiated into its mysteries. I had no doubt this was the origin of the backup. Locals often told tongue-in-cheek stories about tourists stuck for days on the inside lane of the traffic roundabout. I exited at the first right and left them to battle it out.

The Cedars, a fairly new retirement community, nestled among the pines and sweetgums at the edge of the marsh along Broad Creek. Planned for the active senior, most of it was devoted to independent housing designed for those who could take care of themselves. Miss Addie was in the "assisted living" area, a three-story building where residents purchased their own apartments but received cleaning, transportation, and meal service as part of their monthly fee.

I gave my name to the officer at the security gate and pulled up in front of the main building where Miss Addie and I had agreed to meet. A blast of frigid air, in sharp contrast to the stifling heat outside, greeted me as I pulled open the heavy door. I flipped my sunglasses on top of my head and approached the antique reception desk. The woman's smile looked as artificial as her stiff blonde hair. Her beige suit, however, was impeccably cut, and gold bangles clanked on her wrists as she folded her spotted hands primly in front of her. The nameplate to her right read "A. Dixon".

"Good afternoon, and welcome to The Cedars. How may I help you?"

Her perfect diction revealed the hint of an English accent. Her expression held that mixture of arrogance and superiority so common among many expatriate Brits. She glanced disdainfully over my navy blue polo shirt, slightly wrinkled white duck pants, and espadrilles before returning her pinched gaze to my face.

I half expected her to inform me that the servants' entrance was around back.

I brushed a stray lock of hair back off my cheek and pulled myself up to my full height. Two could play this game. "I have a luncheon engagement with Miss Hammond," I replied in my best Southern aristocrat's voice.

"And you are...?"

Lord, this woman was something! You'd think I was trying to sneak into Buckingham Palace.

"Mrs. Tanner. Mrs. Lydia Baynard Simpson Tanner."

There! Match that mouthful, honey, I thought.

"You're expected, Mrs. Tanner," she replied, consulting a list on the desk. "Please proceed straight down this hallway. The dining room will be on your right. Our Mr. Romero will seat you."

I gave her an icy nod, then marched off, shoulders squared, back ramrod straight. I could have balanced the entire Encyclopedia Britannica on my head without losing a volume. Mama would have been proud. Only the slap of my scuffed espadrilles on the polished Mexican tile detracted from my grand exit.

The entrance to the dining room was flanked by two potted ficus trees, a *maitre d's* stand, and Mr. Romero. He was tall, Latin, and gorgeous. If I'd been twenty years older, I'd have had a run at him myself.

"Madame?"

"Mrs. Tanner for Miss Hammond."

"Of course, right this way."

His smile was a knockout, even if the mouthful of gleaming white teeth weren't his own. I followed him to a table set for two in a small alcove by a window. Pulling out the unoccupied wicker chair he seated me with a flourish.

"Enjoy your lunch, ladies."

Almost every pair of female eyes, including mine and Miss Addie's, tracked his progress back to his station at the door.

"Such a charming man," Miss Addie sighed, a look of almost girlish adoration on her wrinkled face. I turned away, slightly embarrassed for her. Miss Addie had never married. Some tragedy in her youth my mother had hinted, but never quite got around to explaining. With an effort, my hostess pulled her attention back to the table.

"Well, Lydia, let me look at you. How lovely you are, dear. Quite lovely. Those green Baynard eyes, so like your mama's. How I've missed her these last years."

Miss Addie raised a delicate lace handkerchief and dabbed at the corners of her faded blue eyes, magnified by thick, wire-framed bifocals. She was dressed formally in an aqua print summer dress she probably still called a frock. Her pure white hair had been recently styled and lay in soft curls around her sunken cheeks. She wore no makeup, and her skin had the pasty-white cast of those who have heeded all the warnings to avoid the sun. Miss Addie's aversion would have come long before the fear of melanoma. In the times in which she and my mother were brought up, girls whose skin became darkened by exposure to the sun were thought "common". A single strand of pearls—real ones, I was sure—lay against her bony chest, and pearl clips adorned her ears.

"Thank you, Miss Addie. You look wonderful, too. You haven't changed at all." I glanced down at my hastily chosen sports clothes. "I wish you'd told me y'all were so formal here, though. I would have dressed up a little."

A sweet smile softened her face. "Nonsense. You young people have the right idea. Comfort should be just as important as those stuffy rules we learned at Braxton. But I'm too old to change now, and it's probably just as well."

She laughed lightly and indicated the other occupants of the dining room with a wave of her delicate hand. I had been right this morning in comparing her to a hummingbird. "Just look at some of these old fools. Why, if I had legs like tree trunks, I certainly wouldn't display them for all the world to see."

Her gaze rested on an overweight woman who had risen a few tables away. The short skirt of the obviously expensive tennis ensemble barely covered her ample rearend. And her legs did resemble some of the gnarled live oaks that dotted the property.

Miss Addie caught my eye and winked conspiratorially. In that moment, I remembered why I had always liked her best of all that group that had danced attendance on my mother: Miss Addie had a sense of humor.

Maybe this wouldn't be so bad after all.

If the company turned out to be a pleasant surprise, the meal was even more so. Miss Addie had "taken the liberty" of choosing the menu: a crisp green salad, followed by an exquisite salmon with fresh asparagus in hollandaise sauce. We waved away the offer of an extensive wine list, both of us opting for freshly brewed iced tea in frosty glasses.

The reminiscences proved less uncomfortable than I'd feared. Even Miss Addie's continual use of my hated first name became almost bearable. Though her chatter scratched against long-buried memories of a childhood I had thought safely repressed, I managed to smile and nod as she recalled with fondness the days when my mother had reigned supreme over local society.

Over thin wedges of *real* key lime pie—with *real* meringue—I tried to edge the conversation around to the reason for her call. "Now then," I said firmly as we both laid our heavy linen napkins on the table next to our plates, "tell me about this investment problem of yours."

Miss Addie fidgeted a little, but finally realized it was time to get down to business. "Well, it has to do with Grayton's Race."

My blank look betrayed my ignorance.

"That old rice plantation on the Chicopee? Oh, surely Emmaline must have talked to you about it, dear? Your mama loved the old place so." Miss Addie's smile melted years off her face. "You should have seen it in its prime. Well, not that we did either, exactly. By the time your mama and I were old enough to attend parties there, it had fallen into some disrepair. But there were paintings of it, as it had been in the last century, a truly imposing greathouse. Wide verandahs, white porticoes, a magnificent avenue of oaks. Quite similar in many ways to your house, Lydia."

"*Presqu'isle* was my mother's house, not mine," I snapped. My hackles had risen again, and I couldn't really say why. Maybe because the Judge and I were always aware that it was my mother, Emmaline Baynard, who had brought the antebellum mansion into the family. My father and their unplanned, change-of-life little girl had always been interlopers. We might live there, but we'd never really *belong*.

"Of course, dear, I know that. Your mother's people have lived there for almost two hundred years. But, like it or not, you are a Baynard. Some day *Presqu'isle* and all its responsibilities will be yours."

I didn't want to talk about this. I hated the house. I wanted no part of it after the Judge was gone, and it had passed to me. They could tear the damned thing down and turn it into a parking lot for all I cared.

"You were saying? About Grayton's Race?" I forced a smile.

"Oh, yes. Well. One of the sons was killed in the First War. Another drank himself to death. Then it all fell to some northern cousins, and they sold off parcels willy-nilly, and…oh dear." Miss Addie applied the lace hanky to her eyes once again. "We had such lovely parties there when I was a girl. It's all so sad."

It was beginning to come back to me now from articles in the local paper, scanned and forgotten, and from gossip around the Club. A real estate investment company had been formed to buy up the surrounding land and restore the old plantation house to its former glory. The Race would become the centerpiece of a planned community with antebellum style homes on large lots, with one or two golf courses thrown in for ambiance. Most of the acreage fronted what locals always referred to as "the pristine" Chicopee River. Those who lived along its unpolluted banks, as well as some outside environmental groups, had protested loudly. I didn't blame them. It was just the kind of desecration I hated. We had already lost too many trees to the greedy axes of the developers.

Miss Addie sniffed delicately, reclaiming my attention.

"So Geoffrey Anderson talked you into investing. How much?" I asked bluntly.

Miss Addie hemmed and hawed, fluttered her hands, and refused to look me in the eye.

I finally managed to pull it out of her. She had plunked down two hundred thousand dollars, almost everything she had left of her inheritance after buying her apartment at The Cedars. Without the income generated by that money, invested in CD's and solid mutual funds, she would soon be hard pressed to meet her monthly fees at the swank retirement home.

I struggled to keep control of my temper.

"Why didn't you call me *before* you made this decision, Miss Addie? Unless you can find someone to buy you out, I don't see how I can help you."

"Well, really Lydia, it seemed so safe. Geoffrey promised we'd have our money back, and with a sizable profit, in just a few months. And he *is* Millicent Anderson's boy. After all, one just has to have faith in one's oldest friends, doesn't one?"

I had my doubts about that. Every family, regardless of how far back its lineage could be traced, had its share of scoundrels and ne'er-do-wells.

"So why the sudden concern?" I asked resignedly. I should have listened to my instincts this morning and found some plausible reason to beg off.

"Well, I've talked with several people, friends from the old days, you understand, and they seem to think it might drag on for a long time. There are rumors circulating, something about a piece of land they need to complete the project. Apparently the owners won't sell. I'm told it could endanger the whole project." The faded eyes behind the thick glasses glistened with unshed tears. "I've called and called, but Geoffrey doesn't seem to get my messages. The Judge thought that maybe you could talk to him and find out when we can expect to get our money…"

"*Our* money?" I jerked upright in my chair, my hand sending the sterling silver salt shaker rolling across the table. "What do you mean, *our* money?"

Miss Addie absently gathered a few grains of the spilled salt in her arthritic fingers and tossed them over her left shoulder. "Why, mine, Lydia. And the Judge's. It was upon his advice that I relied. Well, his and Geoffrey's."

"My father has money in this scheme?" I could feel my voice rising, and other late diners glanced uneasily in our direction.

"Well, dear, of course he does. Didn't I mention that on the telephone? In honor of your dear mama, of course. You see, we local investors are to have bronze plaques with our names embossed on them. A Gallery of Honor in the main hallway of the Race, an eternal memorial to our help in restoring one of the truly great plantation houses of the old South."

I was nearly hyperventilating with anger. I had to get out of there before I embarrassed myself and this dotty old lady.

Bronze plaques, Gallery of Honor! What a crock! Geoffrey Anderson had really been reaching when he came up with gimmicks like that to entice investors into his project. And what would happen if they never got title to this disputed land? The investment would be worthless; the property, unsaleable to another developer. How could my father have been so gullible, a man with his education and experience? And to have pulled Miss Addie down along with him!

I regained my composure long enough to solicit Geoffrey's phone number and mark it in my address book. I thanked Miss Addie for lunch, promised to get back to her soon, and planted a gentle kiss on her paper-thin cheek. I left her staring out the window, a sad smile on her wrinkled face.

Mr. Gorgeous said something as I passed, but I was too upset to respond.

Geoffrey Anderson was going to wish he'd never messed with *my* family and friends. But before I tackled him, my father and I had a few things to discuss. Like, where he had gotten the cash to invest in this harebrained scheme, and exactly when it was that he had taken total leave of his senses.

2

As it turned out, my father beat me to the punch. I arrived home to find the red light on my answering machine blinking furiously. And, fastened to the refrigerator door with a magnet shaped like the Harbour Town lighthouse, was a note from Dolores. While her spoken English is pretty good, she tends to spell things just the way they sound. It took me a few minutes to decipher her meaning:

Juj cald (My father had phoned.)

Vare erjent (It was a matter of some importance.)

U cal kwik (He wanted me to return his call as soon as possible.)

I'll just bet he does, I snorted as I poured myself some lemonade and carried it, along with the portable phone, out onto the deck. The incoming tide brought with it a nice onshore breeze. I'd check my messages later. They were probably all from the Judge, anyway. Patience was not his strong suit.

Miss Addie, sensing my shock at her revelation, had undoubtedly called to warn my father of my extreme displeasure. (She would never be so gauche as to use an expression like "blew her top", although that would have been a more accurate description of my reaction.)

I punched in the number and flopped myself onto the bright cushions of the chaise. I tried to remember when it was that our relationship had changed…when it was that I had become the disapproving parent and my father, the bad-tempered child.

After my mother died, the Judge had seemed to come into his own. *Presqu'isle*, formerly famed for the splendor of its gardens and Emmaline Baynard Simpson's celebrated teas and formal dinners, had become more like a real home for him. The Judge's courthouse cronies, previously *persona non grata* with their loud voices and smelly cigars, now made the old plantation house one of their regular stops.

Thursday night poker. Saturday morning duck hunting. Sunday afternoon barbecues.

Then, his first stroke, mild, but a warning. Kentucky bourbon and contraband Havana panatelas faded into fond memory. The Judge's reformed lifestyle lasted a little less than six months. His second "cerebral vascular incident" had left him a semi-invalid.

Thank God for Lavinia, I thought. I could never have taken over his care, especially after Rob...

It suddenly dawned on me that I had been listening to the phone ring unanswered in my father's house for an unusually long time. I had my finger poised over the redial button when my father snapped, "Yes?" in my ear.

"Judge? It's Bay. Why the hell are you answering the phone? Where's Lavinia?"

"I'm just fine, dear, thank you for inquiring. And you?"

The deep resonance of my father's courtroom baritone thundered down the line. Though partially paralyzed on his left side, his speech had been relatively unaffected. I ignored the sarcasm. Putting your opponent on the defensive was a tactic I had learned at his knee.

"Could you please just answer my question? Where is Lavinia? Are you in your study or did you wheel yourself all the way out in the hall to get the phone?"

"You should never have given up the law, daughter. Your cross-examination technique is classic."

"Thank you, Your Honor."

Why do our conversations always have to go like this? I asked myself. They seemed to start out bad and go downhill from there.

"I got your message," I said into his grumpy silence. "Is something wrong?"

"Of course something's wrong! Why do you think I'm answering the damn phone myself? You need to get over here now, right away. Vinnie's taken off, probably for a few days she said, and it's my night for poker. The boys'll be here at seven-thirty, and they'll expect to be fed. So if you leave now, you'll have time to help me get dressed and then throw something together for us to eat. Better bring some clothes with you, too. If Vinnie doesn't get back…"

"Whoa! Slow down and back up."

"Bay, we don't have time for this. If you don't start out soon…"

"Objection!"

That stopped him. Then I heard his low chuckle. "On what grounds?"

"Confusing the witness."

"Sustained. Sorry, honey, but can't you just get here and leave the explanations until later?"

With a sigh I gave in, as we both knew all along I would. "Okay, okay, I'm coming. But at least tell me where Lavinia is. It's not like her just to take off and leave you alone to fend for yourself."

Lavinia Smalls had been the housekeeper at *Presqu'isle* since shortly after my mother had inherited the house. Long before I was born, the two had established a relationship based on two hundred years of social and racial custom. They addressed each other formally, although Lavinia's title of "Mrs." may have been honorary since no mention of a husband, either past or present, was ever made, at least in my hearing.

As a child I called her Miss Lavinia, dropping the title as I grew up. No one but the Judge, to whom she was devoted, had ever gotten away with "Vinnie".

"Did you read today's paper?" The *non sequitur* brought me up short.

"I glanced at it. Why?"

"See the story about the drowning in the Chicopee?"

"I saw the headline, but I didn't read any farther. What's that got to do with anything?"

"The victim was Vinnie's nephew. You know, her sister Mavis's boy, Derek? She went to be with her family. I told her it would be okay, that you'd come and stay with me. You will, won't you, Bay, honey?"

He was starting to whine. I much preferred his Mr. Hyde personality—the crusty, sarcastic tough guy—to this needy and helpless Dr. Jekyll side.

"How awful for them. Okay, Judge, I'll be there as soon as I can. And if Lavinia calls, tell her how sorry I am, will you?"

I hung up the phone and sat brooding beneath the shade of the live oaks. I felt sad for Lavinia, annoyed by my father's erratic personality shifts, and restless in a vague way that had become all too familiar lately.

I knew what part of it was: I was lonely. I had thought I was getting used to being on my own. After Rob's murder, my friends had been more than supportive. They had rallied around me, fending off the media, trying to give me a chance to heal, both inside and out. But after awhile, their concern became cloying, smothering. At least that's how I perceived it. I pushed them gently away; and, for the most part, they went. Some with regret, others, with relief.

It was their pity I really couldn't handle. Their careful avoidance of Rob's name. That self-conscious lull in any conversation that strayed too close to him…to *us*.

And that was the heart of my problem. I yearned to be part of an *us* again, to feel that shared joy that needed no words, the quick anger more quickly melted in a knowing smile.

I needed love.

I needed Rob.

Enough!

I mentally slapped myself and did the only thing that seemed to work now when I began to sink into pointless grief and self-pity. I got up off my butt and got moving.

I was throwing my overnight bag into the back of the convertible when it struck me that neither my father nor I had mentioned Miss Addie or Grayton's Race.

I had picked the worst possible time of day to leave the island. Rush hour traffic spluttered and crawled, so it was almost five o'clock when I bounced down the rutted avenue of oaks on St. Helena Island and pulled in behind the Beaufort County Sheriff's cruiser parked in *Presqu'isle's* circular drive.

I was annoyed rather than alarmed. The Judge's circle of acquaintance encompassed all branches of the local criminal justice system, so it was not unusual to find solicitors, attorneys, or even old-timers from the sheriff's department trading war stories with my father over cold drinks on the verandah.

I lifted my bag from the back seat and stood for a moment contemplating the deceptively pleasant facade of my childhood home. To an outsider it would certainly have seemed impressive. Its central outside stairway rose from two small side staircases, spilling onto a wide front porch supported by six square columns. The upstairs was deck, rather than porch, and its openness allowed one to admire the central pediment and dormers off each end of the hipped roof.

The foundation was tall, arched, and made from tabby, that mixture of oyster shells and lime that had been the preferred building material in the Lowcountry for more than two centuries. The white frame structure had a rear aspect nearly as pleasing as the front. Situated on a spit of land jutting out into St. Helena Sound, it had taken its name from its location. *Presqu'isle*, the French equivalent of peninsula, revealed the Huguenot ancestry of my mother's family.

As I mounted the sixteen steps and crossed the verandah to the carved oak front door, I tried to shake off my deep-seated antipathy to what many considered one of the finest examples of antebellum architecture on the South Carolina-Georgia coast. After all, the house could hardly be blamed for my unhappiness inside its walls.

As I stepped into the cool dimness of the entry hall, I heard voices coming from my father's study at the rear of the house. After his stroke, we had moved his bed down there and turned an old storage closet into a modern, wheelchair-accessible bathroom. A door led onto the back verandah with a ramp installed so that he could wheel himself outside whenever he got restless.

I set my bag down at the foot of the graceful, free-standing staircase and headed for my father's room. I could smell the cigar smoke when I was still five feet from the doorway. Though they had opened the windows in a hurried attempt to conceal the evidence, the slight breeze off the Sound had only blown it right back into the room.

When I charged into the study, the Judge had that hand-in-the-cookie jar look on his face. He still had almost a full head of thick, white hair, and his broad shoulders were only slightly bowed. His left hand lay useless in his lap. With his right, he made a futile effort to fan away the telltale haze.

"Hello, sweetheart," the Judge boomed, "look who's here."

I had spared only a brief glance at his tall, uniformed co-conspirator whose back was turned to me as I entered the room.

"Hello, Bay. Good to see you."

My heart stopped for a couple of beats, the way it always did when I came unexpectedly face-to-face with my brother-in-law. Sergeant Redmond Tanner was a slightly shorter, slightly younger version of his dead brother. But the strong resemblance always jolted that secret part of me that could still not accept Rob's death.

"Hey, Red. How's it going?"

He had crossed the heart pine floor in three strides and would have engulfed me in a khaki embrace. Instinctively I stepped back, lifting my cheek instead to invite a chaste, brotherly kiss. I regretted the look of hurt that flashed briefly across his rugged face, but I couldn't help myself. He was too much like Rob. It would be too easy to close my eyes and pretend, just for a moment...

Red recovered himself quickly. "You look great, Bay." He settled one haunch onto the arm of the dark green sofa. "The beach life must agree with you."

"Thanks, it's good to see you, too. I never would have guessed it was you, though, aiding and abetting."

His laugh was deep and hearty, just like Rob's. "Hey, when did I ever have any influence over the Judge? He wants a cigar, I say, 'Yes, sir' and grab the matches."

"Well, I'd love to stay and chat, but I understand I'm on KP tonight. I'd better get out to the kitchen and see what I can rustle up for the Bay Street Irregulars."

The name, taken from the main avenue of Beaufort on which most of them had their offices, had been given to the Thursday night poker group by one of its former members. Before his death, Henry Constable had been a devoted Sherlock Holmes fan. Time had whittled the original eight down to five.

"Wait, Bay. I think it would be helpful if you stayed. I was just getting around to the real reason I dropped by."

"This sounds ominous." I crossed the room to flop myself onto the wide seat beneath the bowed window that looked out on the Sound, a favorite spot of mine as a little girl.

The Judge activated the controls on his motorized wheelchair and maneuvered himself closer to my perch.

Red stood alone.

If it was trouble, we had already chosen up sides.

"Did you read about the body we fished out of the Chicopee last night?" In characteristic Tanner fashion, Red had begun to pace.

"I guess everyone in the county but me must have seen it," I replied. "The Judge said the victim was Lavinia's nephew, Derek. That's why she's not here. So what's your interest? It was just another drowning, wasn't it?"

"That was a heartless remark, daughter." My father's eyes were pinched in disapproval. "The boy was only nineteen years old. Try to show a little compassion."

I swallowed hard, embarrassed by his rebuke. Maybe he was right. Maybe my protective wall *was* getting a bit too thick.

"Well, actually, it wasn't just a drowning." Red's face had begun to color up, and his eyes refused to meet mine. My husband always looked like that when he was about to tell me something he knew I didn't want to hear. Red picked up the ivory-handled letter opener off the Judge's desk and studied it as if he'd never seen one before.

"Why don't you just spit it out, Red?" His evasiveness was beginning to get on my nerves.

"The coroner says he was dead before he went into the water. Blunt trauma to the back of the skull, delivered with considerable force. It was no accidental drowning."

"Murder." The judge spoke the word with a strange mixture of repugnance and reverence.

Violent death was rare in our quiet corner of the South. I couldn't remember his ever having been involved in a murder trial. I watched the fantasy play out across his face: The Honorable Judge Talbot Simpson— whole and straight again—presiding over a case that would make head-lines all across the state.

"Nonsense," I said, both to the idea of murder and to my father's wishful thinking. I didn't know why I felt so strongly about the improb-ability of it, I just did. "And even if it wasn't an accident, what does that have to do with us? You said something about the 'real' reason you stopped by. Were you planning on getting to that anytime soon?"

The Judge shot me the kind of look I used to get when I was ten and being bratty.

"Lavinia's grandson, Isaiah, had a fight with the victim yesterday afternoon, outside the school. Isaiah apparently took the worst of it. A lot of threats were exchanged, in front of a lot of witnesses. Pretty much the whole damn football team, far as I can tell."

"And?" I swung my legs off the window seat and sat up straighter.

"And, damn it, the Captain sent me to try and find him. Isaiah, that is. He's not at home. His parents claim they haven't heard from him since last night around supper time."

"So you came here, thinking that Lavinia might have stashed her fugitive grandson somewhere at *Presqu'isle*? Or that she and the Judge had spirited him off?" My voice had turned icy with contempt. "Really, Tanner, it's no wonder you're embarrassed to have to investigate such a screwball theory."

"Knock it off, Bay. It's not that farfetched. The boys had a fistfight. Isaiah said he'd kill Derek if he ever came around practice again. That night, Derek's murdered, and Isaiah disappears. What are we supposed to do, pretend it didn't happen?"

"No, you're supposed to realize that a—what? Sixteen, seventeen year-old...?" I looked to the Judge, who nodded confirmation of my guess.

"So?" Red interrupted. "You think a kid that age couldn't be involved in violence like this? Where the hell have you been, Bay, living on another planet? Don't you watch the news? *Twelve* year-olds are doing hard time for murder these days."

"Maybe in L.A. or Miami or New York. Not in rural Beaufort County," I fired back. "And not someone with the kind of family background Isaiah has. His father grew up here at *Presqu'isle*. Lavinia whupped him as often as she did me. Thaddeus Smalls wouldn't raise up his son to be a murderer."

"Look," Red sighed, running his big hand through his light brown hair in a gesture I found painfully familiar, "let's all calm down a little. We just want to talk to Isaiah, that's all. If he has a good alibi for the time in question, we eliminate him as a suspect and move on. He might even have some idea of who else might have had a beef with Derek."

He bent and picked up his hat from the side table near the doorway.

"It's S.O.P., nothing more. You ought to know how we operate by now."

My indiscriminate rage at the inability of anyone to bring Rob's murderers to justice had spilled out onto every branch of law enforcement in the state. I knew I had sometimes vented my frustration unfairly on Red, simply because he was a cop. I had to keep reminding myself that he, too, wanted justice for his dead brother.

The Judge had been strangely silent during our exchange. His angry voice startled me as much as it did Red.

"You're welcome to have a look around, Redmond," he said stiffly.

Red's face closed down completely. "Not necessary, Judge. I just wanted to talk to Lavinia, see if she had any thoughts on where the boy might be. But thanks for the offer, seein' as how I don't even have a search warrant. Yet."

"She's probably at her sister Mavis's." I spoke softly, hoping he could hear the contrition in my voice as I curled back up on the window seat. "Derek's mother's place. Out by Cherry Point."

"Thanks. I'll try to catch up with her there." Red turned, hesitated, then walked quickly back across to the window seat. He twirled his hat nervously in his hands.

"Can I call you sometime, Bay? Maybe we could have dinner, or something?"

I knew Red had been lonely since his divorce. His schedule didn't leave much time for socializing, one of the big factors in the breakup of his marriage to his high school sweetheart, Sarah. Weekends were reserved for visitation with his two kids, when the rotation allowed him to swing it.

I also knew that dating my dead husband's brother was not a good plan. But I needed to atone for my bad attitude, so I gave him a smile and as non-committal an answer as I could.

"Call me."

"Okay. Thanks."

The Tanner grin lit his face as he nodded to the Judge and strode out of the study. I heard the heavy front door close behind him.

"That wasn't a kindness, Bay, letting him think you might be interested. You aren't, are you? It would be a mistake, daughter, believe me. You can't substitute…"

"Butt out, Your Honor. My love life—or lack of it—is out of your jurisdiction." I bit back the anger that always boiled up whenever my father began dispensing advice…especially about relationships. He and my mother hadn't exactly provided a sterling example of marital bliss. "And speaking of mistakes, I had lunch with Adelaide Boyce Hammond today. Care to explain to me how you got mixed up with this real estate scam? And why you had to drag that poor old lady down with you?"

"It's not a scam. It's a legitimate business investment. But we have more pressing problems right now. Vinnie's going to need our help."

"Why don't we wait until she asks for it? She's a very private person. I don't think she'd appreciate your sticking your nose in before you're invited."

"Don't lecture me about Vinnie." I started to protest, but he cut me off. "And anyway, we don't have time for that now."

As if on cue, the deep-throated *bong* of the antique grandfather clock sounded in the parlor. I glanced at my watch.

6:30.

"Okay. But don't think you're off the hook. We *will* talk about this investment business. Tonight."

As it turned out, we didn't.

By the time I helped my father change into clean clothes and did the same for myself, the front doorbell was chiming. They all arrived together, four men who had known me almost from the day I was born. I braced myself for the inevitable questions about Rob's murder, for the pitying looks I had come to despise. None of that happened. Instead, they all expressed genuine delight at seeing me again and wrapped me in the warmth of their fatherly embraces.

They had their routine down to a science, helping themselves to drinks and setting up the table while I threw together platters of cold meat, cheeses, fresh vegetables, and assorted breads. I set the whole thing out as a buffet on the sideboard in the Judge's study.

They refused to let me sneak off to the novel I had brought along. Before I knew it, I found myself seated in the midst of these contemporaries of the Judge with a pile of red, white, and blue chips in front of me and five cards in my hand.

The death of Derek Johnson provided a hot topic of conversation, as did various minor courthouse scandals and the latest gossip involving local dignitaries. The poker, however, was serious business. No one wanted to go home a loser. So it was past midnight when, twelve dollars richer and stuffed full of Lavinia's homemade blueberry pie, I dragged myself up the stairs and flopped gratefully into my old four-poster. I'd smoked too many cigarettes and eaten way too much, but I had enjoyed every second of it.

It seemed like only a minute later when the phone once again rescued me from the grip of the explosion nightmare only to plunge me headlong into the middle of another.

"Bay? Is that you?" The voice quavered with barely controlled emotion. "It's Lavinia. Please let me speak to the Judge." A shuddering sigh, then a spark of anger broke through. "They've arrested my grandson."

3

The sun had barely risen as I replaced the receiver and threw back the crisp white sheets. I knew the Judge had to be worn out from last night's excitement, so I had taken the sketchy information from Lavinia and let my father sleep. I threw on shorts and a T-shirt, made myself some Earl Grey tea and toast, and got back on the telephone.

My first call caught Dolores just as she was leaving. She didn't sound thrilled about my request, but finally agreed. I asked her to call me back when she got to my place. I made a mental note to make sure my gratitude was reflected in her paycheck.

Next I dialed the sheriff's office in Beaufort. The dispatcher told me that Sergeant Tanner had just gone off his shift and could probably be reached at home in about ten minutes.

Sarah and the kids had remained in the Lowcountry cottage the couple had built shortly after Red's discharge from the Marines. My brother-in-law's "home" was now a one-bedroom apartment in a non-descript building that looked as if it were part of the prison system. His furniture consisted of a card table, three folding chairs, an air mattress, and a 31" rear projection TV that took up one entire wall of the living room.

The phone rang twelve times before I gave up. Apparently an answering machine did not rank high on Red's list of life's necessities. Maybe he'd stopped for breakfast. I'd have to try him later.

I was about to pour myself another cup of tea when the muted *whir* of the Judge's wheelchair sounded in the hallway, and he rolled into the room.

The sight of my father brought a catch to my throat. His hair stood out at odd angles from his head, even though wet comb tracks testified to his attempts to tame it. He had nicked his face in several places, and little bits of Kleenex were stuck to the cuts. His legs, thin and pasty, stuck out of his pajama bottoms. His bare feet were blue-veined and scaly, the nails thick and yellow.

"What the hell's going on?" he growled, maneuvering himself up to the kitchen table. "What are you doing up so early? Who was that on the phone?"

I covered the only way I knew how. "What the hell are *you* doing up? And who said you could shave yourself? God, look at you! It's a wonder you didn't slit your throat."

I rattled another cup out of the cupboard, filled it with tea, and banged it down in front of him. We sat glaring at each other, neither willing to make the first move. The shrill of the telephone next to my elbow saved us the trouble.

I took notes for about five minutes as Dolores relayed the messages I had neglected to take off the machine yesterday. I gave her detailed directions, along with a list of things I wanted from home. She promised to be with us in about an hour. I hung up, determined to stop acting like Mrs. Attila the Hun with my father.

"Want some breakfast? Dolores is on her way, and she'll probably want to cook for you. But how about some toast or cereal to tide you over? I think I can just about manage that."

My uselessness in the kitchen was a family joke. Rob had done most of the cooking at our home in Charleston, and there are more than three hundred restaurants on Hilton Head.

"Any more of that cinnamon raisin bread?"

The cease-fire was holding.

I plucked the bread from the toaster, spread a thin layer of forbidden butter on each slice, and set it down gently before the Judge. The sparkle was back in his deepset gray eyes, and his appearance seemed more silly now than pathetic.

That I could deal with.

"You look like Mag Sauers," I said, and he laughed. The legend of the local crazy woman with wild, tangled hair and mismatched clothes and shoes was a favorite of my father's.

"You're not exactly a fashion plate yourself this morning," he retorted around his old familiar grin. "So who called so damned early this morning?"

I had put the bad news off long enough. A part of me wished I could spare him, but I knew he wouldn't thank me for keeping him in the dark.

"Lavinia." His head snapped up, all semblance of laughter gone from his face. "They've arrested Isaiah. I assume it's to do with Derek Johnson's murder, but Lavinia said they wouldn't tell her anything or let her talk to the boy."

"Damn it, Bay, why didn't you tell me right away? Why didn't you wake me?"

"So you could do what? I've already tried to call Red, but he's between work and home somewhere."

"I could have talked to her, reassured her…"

"I did that. Besides, she knows we'll do whatever we can. Both of us."

The Judge glared at me, unconvinced. Then he used his good right hand to pull the notepad and pencil toward him. "They'll need a good attorney. I'll make a list."

"Lavinia wants Mander Brown."

The Judge raised one bushy white eyebrow.

"I know, she probably wants him because he and Thaddeus are friends, and she's known him since he was six," I replied to his unasked question. "He'll be okay if this turns out to be the stupid, knee-jerk reaction by the cops that I think it is."

"But," the Judge interrupted, picking up my train of thought, "if they have any kind of evidence at all, and it gets to trial, Mander has no experience. He's used to pleading out petty larcenies and car heists."

"Lavinia was pretty adamant about getting him."

"You leave Vinnie to me. Besides, Mander's a good man. He'll be the first to admit it if he gets in over his head."

"Think they'll set bail? I thought I'd take care of that. I don't imagine Thaddeus and Colletta will be able to raise the money if it's too high."

"Hard to say in a capital case. Depends on if they charge him as an adult or a juvenile. But we're getting ahead of ourselves here. Let me make a few calls and see what I can find out."

The front doorbell pealed, and I went to let Dolores in. I relieved her of the garment bag she had packed for me and led her into the kitchen. She and the Judge had met on the few occasions when I had been able to persuade him to attend the parties Rob and I used to throw on a fairly regular basis. Dolores always did the cooking for us, sometimes serving as well.

I heard my father's hearty laugh amidst the clatter of pots and dishes. Dolores would take good care of him. I was off the hook.

I tried to shove that unfamilial thought away as I climbed the staircase to my old room to change.

The Judge was just mopping up the last of the syrup on his plate with a forkful of hotcakes when I made my entrance.

"Ah, *Señora.*" Dolores's smile of approval lit up her black eyes.

The Judge just whistled.

The lifestyle on Hilton Head is decidedly laid-back, so dress tends to be casual except for very formal occasions. Though I had a closet full of beautiful clothes from my working days in Charleston and Columbia, I had pretty much lived in shorts and T-shirts since I moved permanently to the beach. And my social life since Rob's death had been just about non-existent, too. No sense complaining, though. My choice.

So I knew it would be a shock for my father and Dolores to see me for the first time in months in my ivory linen Armani suit, my unruly hair pulled into a smooth coil at the nape of my neck. Cream-colored, sling-back pumps pushed my height close to six feet. I had decided against a blouse. The solid gold cartouche Rob had given me for our tenth anniversary hung suspended from its herringbone chain and nestled against the cleavage exposed where the lapels of the jacket crossed. Thick gold hoops dangled from my ears.

I had to admit it felt good to be dressed like a professional again.

"'Gird up now thy loins like a man' ," the Judge quoted in his best courtroom voice.

I frowned in concentration. Then I had it. "Job," I announced, carried back unwillingly to the rainy days of childhood when my well-read father had first initiated the game.

"Too easy," he said with a grin.

"'Thrice is he armed that hath his quarrel just,'" I fired back.

"Hmmm." The Judge closed his eyes. "Shakespeare, of course. Let me see. *Henry V?*"

"Close. *Henry VI.* I'll give you half a point."

"Your generosity is overwhelming."

"You made the rules."

Dolores had set a fresh cup of tea on a green paisley placemat, so I folded myself carefully into the chair and draped the matching napkin across my lap. My mother would have been appalled to find us eating in the kitchen instead of at the nineteenth-century mahogany table in the heavily paneled dining room.

"So what did you find out? Where are they holding Isaiah?" I reached for the cigarettes I had left lying on the table and lit one. Another day without quitting. Maybe I'd get one of those patches. Or the gum.

"You mean Mustapha Rashid?"

"What? Who the hell is Mustapha Rashid?"

"Isaiah. Seems he's been studying Islam. That's his adopted name. Wanted it put on his record at the sheriff's office." The Judge sighed and shook his head. "Kids."

The word held not contempt, but a sad perplexity. This generation was so far removed from his own experience, they might be visitors from another galaxy.

"Have they charged him?"

"Not yet. They're holding him as a material witness. He's scheduled to be questioned this morning. I got hold of Mander. He'll meet you at the jail. Vinnie, too."

I opened my mouth to question his decision to let Lavinia pick her own lawyer, but he cut me off.

"They can only hold him for six hours without either formally charging him or letting him go." The Judge slapped the armrest of his wheelchair with his good right hand. "Damn! I could be so much more effective if I were there myself."

"So what's stopping you?" I asked and was rewarded with a formidable scowl.

Although the van we had bought him was equipped with a lift and handicapped controls, the Judge refused to use it except for occasional outings with Lavinia at the wheel. Even then he forbade her to stop anywhere, the two of them riding aimlessly around, savoring the sights and smells of his beloved Lowcountry. No one but close friends and family was allowed to see the great man brought low, one useless hand immobile in his lap, a slight droop dragging down the left side of his still striking face.

As I expected, he ignored my challenge.

"I'll keep trying to reach Redmond. He'll be our best bet for inside information."

"If he's not still ticked off at us about yesterday." I was not proud of my performance. The thought of it brought a fresh rush of color to my cheeks.

"Redmond's not one to hold a grudge; you should know that. Besides, one look at you in that getup, and he'll probably spill every secret he's known for the last twenty years."

I stubbed out my cigarette, rose, and lightly brushed his shoulder with my hand as I passed. He looked up, startled. We were not a *touching* family.

"I'll call you if anything comes up I can't handle."

"That'll be the day."

I stuffed my notebook in my handbag, hoping I'd have a chance to return the calls from yesterday. Bitsy Elliott, my best friend since childhood, had phoned three times, once during the day and twice last night. Dolores said she sounded as if she'd been crying.

Probably had another fight with Cal, I thought as I carefully negotiated my way down the sixteen front steps. I'd forgotten how precarious they could be in highheels.

She never should have married the moron, even if he did get her pregnant their senior year at Clemson. Better to raise an illegitimate baby than be stuck with a redneck jock for the rest of your life. My low opinion of Cal Elliott had been formed early, and he'd done nothing in the intervening years to elevate it.

As I settled myself into the convertible, I felt an exhilaration I hadn't known since before Rob's death. Those had been heady days as we schemed against the bad guys, then waited breathlessly to see if they'd step into the trap. As a special investigator for the State Attorney General's office, Rob had engineered dozens of sting operations against organized drug traffickers, and I had been his faithful sidekick and co-conspirator.

Of course, it wasn't the same without him. Nothing would ever be the same again. But today, with a mission to fulfill and right on my side, for the first time in almost a year I felt as if I might just survive without him.

4

Coming upon the city of Beaufort from the crest of the bridge that connects it to the outer islands is one of the most beautiful sights on the Southeast coast.

To the left, Waterfront Park stretches like a tiny jewel along the shore of the Beaufort River. Today its wide esplanade, dotted with wooden benches, was alive with tourists, their bright resort clothes adding splotches of color to the cool green of the live oaks. To the right, the stately mansions of the antebellum Sea Island planters stood in restored splendor. Built high off the ground with wide porches along both floors, they all faced the water, capturing whatever breezes might waft their way.

Before the War of Northern Aggression, wealthy cotton planters had moved their entire households every spring to these summer retreats in an often futile attempt to escape the killing fevers that could strike so suddenly in the low-lying marshes of their island plantations.

I had spent many happy childhood hours wandering the narrow lanes of this area, marveling at the graceful beauty of arches and columns, verandahs and rosy brick. Thankful that the triumphant Union Army had spared them from the torch, my neighbors had lovingly cared for these monuments to a lost way of life, preserving them for future generations to marvel at from the seats of horse-drawn sightseeing carriages.

I crossed over Bay Street with its art galleries, bookstores, and antique shops and fought rush hour traffic up Carteret to where it turned into Boundary at the graceful curve of the river. Passing the high brick wall that protected the hallowed ground of the National Cemetery, I felt a familiar tug. The Judge had early on taught me a reverence for those who had sacrificed their lives in the service of their country. We had spent many brilliant summer afternoons strolling solemnly among the rows of pristine white markers, pausing to read an inscription here and there, and to speculate on the man and the life he might have led had he not given it for the good of others.

I didn't play that game anymore. The speculation would strike too close to home.

The massive complex of the new Government Center loomed up ahead of me. I took a left on Ribaut and a right on Duke Street and pulled into the parking lot across from the Law Enforcement Building which housed the Sheriff's Office. Behind it, and to the left, the walls of the detention center were crowned with coils of barbed wire.

I had just pushed the door of the convertible open when I spotted the group walking slowly along the tree-lined sidewalk between the two buildings. Thaddeus wore his postal worker's uniform. Colletta was also dressed for work, the mustard yellow dress with the SAV-MOR logo embroidered on the pocket stretched tightly across her heavy bosom. Her once pretty face was lost in folds of fat. Her legs beneath the too-short skirt were chunky and solid.

I swung myself out of the car and went to meet them.

They made a handsome trio, these three generations of Smalls. Isaiah stood nearly as tall as his father, just over six feet. He had the body of an athlete: wide shoulders and trim hips beneath a narrow waist, long muscular legs. Sometime in the months since I had last seen him, he'd shaved his head. Some sort of football ritual, I imagined. As I got closer, I marveled at the beautiful shape of his naked skull. He looked like those carvings of ancient African tribal chiefs you see on National Geographic specials on PBS.

The sun glinted off his deep mahogany skin highlighting a swollen right eye and a couple of cuts on his high cheekbones. He wore his battle scars proudly. Altogether an attractive young man. Or he would have been but for the dark scowl that distorted his face as Lavinia waved a long, menacing finger under his nose.

"…a perfectly good Christian name," I heard her say as they stopped to meet me under the sparse shade of a newly-planted pear tree. "It's an honorable name, full of the history of our people. I won't allow you to abandon it as if it were something to be ashamed of. Do I make myself clear?"

Lavinia Smalls spoke in the same quiet, yet forceful voice I remembered from my childhood. She never shouted. She simply fixed you with those piercing black eyes and dared you to ignore her. It was like being a rabbit, frozen in fear, caught in the stony stare of a crouching fox.

Her grandson mumbled something unintelligible and stepped back, dropping his eyes.

"I didn't hear you, Isaiah. And look at me when you're speaking to me, please."

"Yes, ma'am. You've made your feelings perfectly clear."

"Good. Now, there'll be no more of this 'Mustapha' business. I'll expect to see you on Sunday morning. And in a suit and tie. Understood?"

"Yes, ma'am."

"Good. Hello, Bay." Lavinia turned her attention at last to me. "Thank you for coming."

"Yes, thanks a lot, Bay. We appreciate it."

Thaddeus extended a big brown hand that swallowed up my thin, white one. He could have been an athlete, like his son, but his interests had always lain elsewhere. I remembered his spending a lot of time in the Judge's library, his nose planted firmly in a book. He should have gone to college. I know my father had offered to help with the cost. But Thaddeus had settled for a civil service job and marriage to a woman who, while pretty enough in the fresh bloom of her youth, had very little interest in anything more literary than the *National Enquirer*.

"You're welcome, Thad. You know, if the Judge were able, he'd have been here himself."

"I know that. Always been real good to our family, the Judge has. And Miz Simpson, too," he added quickly. My mother would have been furious to be considered merely an afterthought to her socially inferior husband.

"Thad, I got to get to work." Colletta Smalls plucked at her husband's sleeve. Her only greeting to me had been a shy bob of her head.

"So what's the story? Have they released him?"

Isaiah had retreated to the low curb of the semi-circular drive. He sat hunched over, elbows on knees, staring at the ground.

"For the time being. But it's not over. Don't any of you fool yourselves into thinking that it is." Lavinia's frankness was another remembered trait. I had never asked for her opinion unless I was prepared to hear the bald truth as she saw it.

Thaddeus Smalls winced at his mother's harsh words. He wanted desperately to believe their lives could now get back to normal.

"We've got to get the boy over to the school, Mama. And ourselves back to work. What time should we be at Aunt Mavis's?"

"I think it's best to just leave that be for tonight. Under the circumstances. I'll let you know about the funeral. They haven't released Derek… Derek's…body yet."

The full force of her pain resonated in that one word—*body*. A nephew dead and a grandson suspected. I moved closer to her, filled with an unfamiliar need to offer protection to the woman who had always protected me.

Isaiah leaped suddenly to his feet.

"I didn't do it! I didn't kill Derek, Granmama, I swear to God I didn't! I couldn't! You know I couldn't!"

His muscled shoulders shook, and tears spilled over the bruises on his smooth brown cheeks. He looked like what we had all forgotten he really was: a scared boy in a man's body.

Lavinia took his anguished face in her wrinkled hands and gently wiped away his tears. The gesture brought a vivid flashback of skinned knees and other, more subtle pain soothed away by those same tender fingers.

"Of course you didn't, my sweet baby. We all know that."

The uncharacteristic softness of her voice held us all spellbound. Then the old, autocratic Lavinia re-emerged, and we were back on familiar ground.

"Go on, then, all of you. Be about your business. I'll call you later."

"Okay, Mama." Thaddeus brushed his mother's cheek in a hasty kiss, nodded to me, and led his family toward the parking lot. His awkward attempt to put a comforting arm around his son's shoulder was shrugged off impatiently. Apparently the little boy had retreated behind the bravado of the teenager.

"Buy you a coffee?" I asked as Lavinia pulled a ring of keys from her navy blue handbag. I wanted details, and I didn't think standing in the shadow of the detention center was a good place to discuss murder and its aftermath. Although sleek and modern, the place still gave me the creeps.

"I really should check on the Judge."

"He's fine. Dolores is with him."

I recognized the tightening of Lavinia's jaw. The news did not reassure her.

"I hope she doesn't try to feed him any of that spicy, Mexican food. His stomach won't tolerate it. He has very particular tastes. We discuss the next week's menu every Saturday, before I do the shopping. Maybe I should call and…"

"They'll be fine, Lavinia. At least for a couple of days," I added, knowing how proprietary she was about the Judge. "And Dolores is Guatemalan, not Mexican."

Lavinia snorted, unconvinced.

We all have our prejudices, I thought.

We crossed the road together, the older woman matching me stride for stride. We were almost the same height. I was never quite sure just how old she really was, but simple math told me she had to be well into her sixties. She was trim and straight, her tight, gray curls clipped close to her head. Her coffee-colored skin had once led my mother to speculate that Lavinia's father must have been white, since both her younger half-sisters, Mavis and Chloe, were a deep, rich brown.

"The Fig Tree?" she asked as we approached my convertible. The little cafe on the waterfront had been a favorite haunt of the Judge's before his stroke.

"Fine. Meet you there."

A remarkable woman, I thought as I turned the key in the ignition. Like Thaddeus, I, too, wanted to believe this was the end of their troubles. But Lavinia was convinced that it wasn't, and I wanted to know why.

We just managed to beat the local lunch crowd, swelled as usual today by the ever-present mob of tourists. Lavinia had commandeered the last table on the outside deck overlooking the park and the sparkling Beaufort River. I ordered iced tea on my way through the cool, dark bar area and joined her under the welcome shade of the striped awning. Lavinia sipped sweet, black coffee. In the harsh glare of the noonday sun reflecting off the placid blue water, she suddenly looked old.

"Tell me," I said brusquely. She would no more welcome sugar-coating in my questions than I would expect any in her answers.

With a swift glance around to be certain she couldn't be overheard, Lavinia gave me what details she had. According to Isaiah, after his confrontation with Derek he had left football practice and driven home in his beat-up Chevy Nova. He had showered, changed, and packed up his camping gear. He left a hastily scribbled note saying he was going fishing with some friends and would be home by the weekend.

It wasn't until late the next afternoon, when a Beaufort County Sheriff's deputy approached her in the SAV-MOR, that Colletta became aware that her son was in trouble. It was also the first she or her husband had heard of the fight or of its possible connection to Derek's death.

The Smalls had begun calling everyone they could think of that Isaiah might have gone off with. They hit paydirt with CJ Elliott.

Bitsy's son! Was that why she had been trying so frantically to reach me last night?

CJ had told his mother a similar story. Practice had been suspended for the rest of the week while the coaches attended meetings. CJ, the star quarterback, and Isaiah, his favorite wide receiver, had been friends since a love for sports and an uncanny knack for anticipating each other's moves had made them a tandem to be reckoned with in area high school football. They hoped to attend college together, both count-ing on athletic scholarships to help their families with the expense.

A sheriff's deputy had spotted Isaiah's Chevy in the early hours of the morning. A few hundred yards away he had come upon the boys, wrapped in sleeping bags alongside the river, less than a mile from where Derek's body had washed up.

"So they alibied each other," I said as Lavinia accepted a refill from a harried waitress, then emptied three blue packets into the steaming cup. The thought of all that sweetness set my teeth on edge. "That's good, isn't it?"

"Or were in it together. That's what those detectives seemed to be implying. They questioned them separately, but both boys stuck to their stories. Denied knowing anything about it, said they were just fishing and didn't see or hear anything. Mr. Elliott's lawyer had his son out of there inside of an hour. It took Mander Brown a little longer, but they finally had to let Isaiah go, too."

The restaurant was emptying out now, only a few businessmen in dress shirts and loosened ties still lingering over their lunches.

"So why are you being so pessimistic? The police obviously don't have anything concrete, or they wouldn't have let them walk."

"Mander said they have to tread carefully because they're only sixteen and still legally juveniles. But they told both boys to stay close to home and to be available in case they had more questions."

"That sounds pretty standard to me."

"Listen, Bay, I've lived a long time in this town. And all my life in the South. Maybe things have changed on the surface, but underneath… Well, let's just say I won't rest easy until whoever really killed my nephew is locked up for good."

"Do they have any other suspects?" I asked as Lavinia fumbled again for her keys.

"Not that anyone's tellin' *me* about. I thought maybe the Judge…"

She let the sentence hang expectantly between us. For the first time that I could remember, I saw fear in her fearsome black eyes.

"He'll have been on the phone all morning, calling in markers. If there's any inside information to be had, he'll get it."

Lavinia rose and smoothed out the creases in the skirt of her best navy blue suit.

"You'll be at Mavis's?" I asked, suddenly realizing what an awkward position she was in. One member of her family was suspected of killing another. I wondered how Mavis, the dead boy's mother, was dealing with it.

"Yes, I expect I will. For a couple of days, anyway. She's not handling it too well," Lavinia said, answering my unspoken question.

From what I remembered of Mavis Johnson, that probably meant hitting the bottle pretty hard.

"You take care now, hear?" I said.

"You, too. And thanks for coming down." She paused awkwardly. "It was kind of you."

Being obligated to anyone did not sit well with Lavinia Smalls. That brief expression of gratitude cost her some effort. I watched her walk away toward the esplanade, her proud carriage mirroring her inner strength. I had been fortunate to have her as a role model in my growing up.

So, I said to myself as I lit a cigarette and leaned back in my chair, *here I am, all dressed up and no place to go.*

Of course I was glad that my services as bail bondsman had not been required. Yet there was a part of me that was a little disappointed. I had come prepared to do battle in a just cause, only to find that the enemy had surrendered without a shot's having been fired. I could feel the old, familiar lethargy seeping back into my bones.

I'd leave Dolores with the Judge and get on back to the beach. Everything was under control here. CJ Elliott and Isaiah Smalls had competent counsel and caring, involved families. Besides, it was ridiculous to think that either one of them had been in any way involved in the murder of Derek Johnson.

I smiled at the waitress who filled up my iced tea glass and waved away her offer of a menu.

Maybe the coroner had jumped the gun. Who was to say for certain it even *was* a murder? Maybe Derek had been drunk. He was, after all, Mavis's son. Maybe he'd stumbled into the river and hit his head on a rock. Maybe...

The hand that fell heavily on my left shoulder made me wince. The mangled skin there was still tender.

"Now, just give me a peek at those gorgeous green eyes, and I'll know for sure this is who I think it is," a voice boomed behind me. I recognized the wheezing drawl immediately.

I gave a fleeting thought to pressing the lighted end of my cigarette into the pudgy fingers splayed across my injured shoulder. When their owner lumbered around to face me, my worst fears were confirmed.

"I knew it! I said to the boys, I said 'That there's ol' Tally Simpson's gal, settin' there with that nigra woman.' And, sure enough, here you are!"

"Unfortunately." I tried to put as much of my distaste for the man into that one word as I could. I knew, however, from long experience, that he was impervious to insult.

"Mind if I join you?" He didn't wait for permission, but pulled out the chair Lavinia had just vacated and flopped his considerable bulk down across the table from me. "My, my. Just look at you. Your mama was a looker, but she couldn't hold a candle to you, sugar, no siree. Not on her best day."

He raised a fat, stubby finger, and a waitress materialized out of nowhere. "Another gin, honey, and bring the lady whatever she's drinkin'."

He beamed at me, his porky little eyes dancing. His thin, delicate lips were almost lost in quivering jowls that hung in loose folds nearly to his neck. As a teenager I had called him the Pig Man. My father had reproved me while suppressing a smile.

Hadley Bolles. Sometime politician, real estate broker, attorney. Rumor had it that if there was a deal going down anywhere in the county, Hadley was sure to have a hand in it. He proudly referred to himself as a "facilitator".

His beltless tan trousers strained across a vast expanse of ample belly, and wide sweat rings stained his rumpled white shirt. His trademark red bow tie hung slightly askew, like a bright poppy wilted in the heat. His patterned suspenders and exaggerated Southern drawl were straight out of Tennessee Williams.

The Judge tolerated him. I loathed the ground he waddled on.

"Is there a point to this, Hadley, or are you just table crawling?" I lit another cigarette and exhaled the smoke directly into his face. "If you're running for something, I'm voting for your opponent, whoever it is."

His laugh, in contrast to his voice, was high-pitched and feminine, almost a giggle. "You not only got your mama's face, darlin', you got her mouth, too. That woman could flat out cut a man to ribbons when she put her mind to it."

"Why, thank you. I do my best to carry on the old family traditions."

"In the case of your mama, I wouldn't try too hard, suga'. She had a few other habits it wouldn't do for a sweet young thing like you to pick up on."

Bastard!

"Don't let me keep you, Hadley," I sneered. "I'm sure you have some land to despoil or a commissioner to bribe."

Just for a moment Hadley Bolles let his mask of honeyed amiability slip, and the chilling combination of hatred and lust that glowed in the depths of his piggy little eyes sent a current of fear racing up my back. Then it was gone, so fast and so completely I might almost have imagined it.

I hastily crushed out my cigarette, ripped a ten from my wallet, and flung it on the table as I pushed back my chair.

Hadley rose with me, shaking his head as one might over the antics of a naughty child. Then his attention was caught by something over my shoulder.

"Catch up with you boys later," he called, gesturing toward the dim recesses of the bar.

I turned in time to see the retreating back of a medium-sized man in a wrinkled white suit making his way toward the front entrance of the Fig Tree. I had a brief impression of long, oily black hair and an obscenely large diamond sparkling against the olive skin of a hand raised in acknowledgment.

Then the doorway was filled with the broad shoulders of one of the most devastatingly handsome men I had ever seen. He was tall, probably six-foot three at least, and he wore his khaki summer suit and pale blue, button-down collar shirt with casual elegance. His hair, combed smoothly from a high part, was mostly silver with just a few strands of its original dark brown still showing through. He reached a sun-browned hand up to shade his blue eyes from the glare off the river, and I realized with a jolt who he was.

My heart turned sixth-grade flip-flops, even though he was out of uniform.

He recognized me at the same moment.

If it had been night time, the sparks that flew between us would have been visible to the naked eye.

Hadley Bolles stood ignored, his head swiveling back and forth between the two of us. "Well, now, what have we here?" I heard him murmur as Geoffrey Anderson crossed the short space between us and took both my hands in his.

5

"Bay? Is that really you? My God, you went and got gorgeous on me!"

"You didn't turn out so bad yourself," I laughed, stepping back from the intensity in his eyes.

Geoff's answering smile brought back memories of hazy Charleston afternoons, heat rising in waves from the parade ground of the Citadel, as the cadets marched in precise formation. My father, a proud alumnus, had been delighted to introduce his daughter to the storied rituals of the military academy, while at the same time regretting that she could never follow in his footsteps. Now that women had been reluctantly admitted to the once all-male bastion, the Judge was torn between bemoaning the loss of a sacred tradition and wishing it had happened in time for me.

"So y'all know each other already, do you? I don't even get the pleasure of playin' matchmaker?" Hadley insinuated himself between us, and his snide voice dripped with innuendo. "The dashing Lawyer Anderson and the delicious Widow Tanner. Y'all better be careful. It's a small town. Tongues will wag."

"Nice to see you, Hadley. You take care now." Geoff, towering over the fat little weasel, made him seem more ludicrous now than menacing.

Hadley Bolles, totally unaccustomed to being summarily dismissed, covered his anger well. With a knowing leer and a grunt of effort, he turned and waddled off toward the river. Within only a few steps, he had gathered a small group of sycophants around him. His absurd, lilting laugh floated back to us on a welcome breeze as he patted the shoulder of a hopeful favor-seeker.

"I used to call him the Pig Man when I was a kid," I said, breaking what was becoming an awkward silence.

Geoff laughed as he pulled out my chair, then folded himself into the one across the table. "You always were a mouthy little thing, as I recall. It was one of your more endearing qualities."

"I don't know how you figure that. I seem to remember being totally tongue-tied whenever you were around."

"Tongue-tied? You? Not the skinny little tomboy I'm thinking of. I'm talking about the one who always had a bandage stuck on an elbow or a knee, and who followed me around asking a zillion questions whenever I brought my mother over to visit."

I couldn't control the blush that spread across my cheeks. I had been certain the boy-man I'd idolized hadn't even known I existed.

Geoff smiled sweetly and covered my hand with his own. "I'm embarrassing you, aren't I?"

"Just a little."

"Sorry. I'm just so damn glad to see you. I don't even want to think about how many years it's been."

"It has to be twenty-five, or close to it. You went on to law school right out of the Citadel, didn't you? Someplace up north?"

"Yale. Had to follow in my daddy's footsteps, didn't I? That's how it's done around here." A note of bitterness had crept into his voice, and I wondered what he would rather have done with his life. "Hadley called you the Widow Tanner," he went on. "That wasn't your husband in that plane bombing last year, was it?"

I hated talking about Rob's death, especially all the gruesome details that seemed to fascinate people despite their pretended horror. But somehow I found it easy telling Geoff everything, from witnessing the explosion, to my disfiguring injuries, to my gnawing frustration that no one had yet been made to pay. As I talked, his hand tightened around mine, his thumb gently stroking the deep ridge left by my wedding band. He didn't speak, didn't interrupt, just stared intently into my eyes as if trying to absorb the pain into himself. When at last I fell silent, Geoff handed me a clean linen handkerchief, and I wiped away the few tears that, despite all my efforts, had managed to slip down my cheeks.

He never let go of my hand.

And I, who had been virtually untouchable for almost a year, felt comforted by the contact.

"I'm so terribly sorry, Bay. My God, it's a miracle you survived." He paused, giving me a chance to get myself under control. "Did you love him very much?"

I should have been offended, but somehow I wasn't. "Yes, I did. We never had any children, so we were all each other had."

"He sounds like a special kind of man."

"He was. You would have liked each other."

"Probably. But then, I might have resented him when I realized what a beauty my little tomboy had turned into, and that he'd stolen her right out from under my nose."

I welcomed the lightening of our somber mood, and suddenly realized that I was ravenously hungry. We ordered a pound of local shrimp, boiled in the shell, with crusty sourdough rolls still warm from the oven.

We peeled shrimp, dipped them in spicy hot sauce, and talked. Or rather, Geoff talked this time while I attacked the food, pausing only long enough to ask an occasional question. I learned of his two marriages, both ending in divorce, his two sons, both living now with his ex-wives, and his disillusionment with life in south Florida. Estranged from his parents over his decision to set up practice in Miami with two fellow Yale graduates, he had come home when his father's failing health had become too great a burden for his mother to carry alone.

"We eventually had to put him in a home. Alzheimer's or senile dementia, they're not sure which. Either way, he's basically lost his mind." Geoff shook his head sadly. "God, if I ever get like that, I hope someone shoots me. It's not fair when the child has to become the caretaker of a parent. It's unnatural, somehow, that role reversal. But then, I guess you know something about that, huh? The Judge's strokes, and all."

It was my turn to offer comfort. It seemed so natural, my hand in his.

It wasn't until people began to drift onto the deck and the noise level in the bar rose a few decibels that I thought to look at my watch.

Ten past five! This was the after-work crowd beginning to gather.

"Geoff, I can't believe the time. I have to get home. I mean, back to the Judge's. I'm staying there for a few days. Because of Lavinia's nephew... and her grandson's being arrested...Well, not exactly arrested, but...Oh, I don't have time to tell you the whole story now. The Judge will throttle me for not reporting in."

I was frantically stuffing cigarettes and lighter into my bag and groping for car keys when Geoff reached across the table and gently touched the corner of my mouth. The gesture, so strangely intimate, stopped me in my tracks.

"Shrimp sauce," he said, wiping his fingers on a napkin.

"Oh, God," I groaned, grabbing my own crumpled, messy ball of paper and dragging it across my face.

Geoff's grin was infectious, and in a second we were both laughing uncontrollably.

"You can tell me all about it tonight over dinner," he gasped, catching his breath. "I'll pick you up around nine."

"I don't know, Geoff. I mean, I'd love to, but the Judge..."

"Will be glad to see you out enjoying yourself. I'll come a little early, and he and I can swap Citadel stories over a glass of that Kentucky bourbon he's famous for." His smile faded, replaced by an appealing earnestness I couldn't resist. "Say yes, Bay. Please?"

"Yes," I answered, for once acting on impulse instead of weighing the pros and cons of my decision. "Yes. Nine o'clock."

Geoff gave my hand a final squeeze as I reluctantly disengaged my fingers and ran lightly down the steps toward the river. I turned once, sure I would find his eyes still on me. He raised his hand, and I could feel the warmth of his gaze follow me all the way down the walkway to my car.

Lydia Baynard Simpson Tanner, what the hell do you think you're doing? I asked myself as I gunned the LeBaron onto the bridge and headed for *Presqu'isle.* Barely five minutes had passed since I'd accepted a *date,* and already my feet were beginning to ice over.

I had misjudged my father's reaction to my being late. He wasn't upset. He was in a towering rage. He treated me to the kind of tongue-lashing I used to get from my mother when I had committed some social gaffe and embarrassed her in front of her friends. Funny, but I remembered the Judge's taking refuge in his study whenever she launched into one of her tirades. He must have been paying closer attention than I realized.

I let him rail at me as Dolores carried a tray of iced tea and lemonade into his room, left it on the antique cherry coffee table, and scurried off.

I was selfish, ungrateful, inconsiderate. I had no idea what it was like to be stuck in a wheelchair, cut off from the action, always having to rely on others to be your legs, your eyes. I poured my accuser a tall glass of lemonade, added ice, and crossed to the sideboard that served as the drinks cupboard to splash in a generous tot of bourbon before placing it in front of him. A weird combination, but his drink of choice.

I was only half-listening to his enumeration of my shortcomings as a daughter, not to mention my utter uselessness as his surrogate. I was vacillating between trying to decide what to wear and trying to figure out how to get out of going at all; between calculating whether or not I had time to drive back to Hilton Head to raid my little-used closet, or calling Geoff to plead a sudden recurrence of malaria.

My father was winding down. I knew he was getting desperate when he started bringing up things I'd done to aggravate him when I was twelve. Besides, the fact that I refused to defend myself was taking a lot of the sport out of it for him. I knew I had been thoughtless in not calling to let him know about Isaiah's release. But it certainly didn't warrant this kind of virulent attack. I knew it was mostly his frustration talking, probably not all that much to do with me. And he was entitled. Up to a point.

I went to his dresser—a tall, beautifully carved cherry highboy—and pulled open the third drawer from the top. My fingers closed around a slim, wooden case hidden beneath a neatly folded pile of pajamas and handkerchiefs. Turning, I flipped it open, offering my father one of his treasured Cuban cigars.

"Better get in touch with Eddie, or whoever's acting as your procure-ment officer these days," I said, flicking the crystal desk lighter into flame. "Your supply is running low."

The Judge clipped the end from the panatela, sniffed the rich aroma of the tobacco leaf wrapper, and allowed me to hold the lighter as he rolled the cigar in the flame until it was glowing brightly. He refused to give me the satisfaction of asking how I knew where he kept his stash. I lit a cigarette, and we sipped and smoked in companionable silence.

My father offered me no apology for his tirade; but then, I didn't expect one. My own had been made in the form of bourbon and tobacco.

"Vinnie okay?" he finally asked. He avoided my eyes by studying the cloud of blue smoke that rose above his head.

"She seemed to be," I answered in the same calm tone of voice. "She's feeling better about it now that Isaiah's out of jail, but she tossed around some pretty broad hints that he could still get railroaded. The South being what it is, and all."

"That's a load of crap, and she knows it. It's just the stress talking."

"Well, what would really help is another viable suspect."

"Of which there are none, according to Redmond." The Judge tapped ash from his cigar into a cutglass bowl, an heirloom wedding gift from some Baynard cousin or other. I could hear my mother spinning in her grave. "He called this afternoon, looking for you. Said he might stop by later."

His disapproval was evident in his voice, as well as in the lowering of his bushy white eyebrows.

"I ran into Geoff Anderson in town today," I said by way of changing the subject. "We're having dinner tonight, so I'd better get changed."

That got his attention. He took a long swig of bourbon-flavored lemonade. "Business or pleasure?" he asked.

"And what's that supposed to mean?" I snapped, bristling at the smug, know-it-all smile that had replaced the fatherly frown.

"It means, is this a *date* or did you set it up so you could pump the poor boy for information about the Race?"

It wasn't that I had *entirely* forgotten my mission on behalf of Miss Addie. It was just that an afternoon spent in a mutual baring of souls with the alleged perpetrator had softened my suspicion somewhat. I couldn't imagine those intense blue eyes hiding the heart of a con man.

"I'm sure the subject will come up," I said loftily as I gathered my things and headed for the hallway. "I need to let Dolores know I won't be home for dinner."

My father's laugh followed me out of the room. "Hope those two boys don't both show up at the same time. I'm too damned old to be breakin' up fistfights in the parlor."

If there had been a door handy, I would have slammed it.

6

By eleven-thirty, Geoff and I sat alone in the deserted dining room of the popular local seafood restaurant overlooking the Broad River. Judging from the noise level, the bar, however, was still doing a brisk business. I could hear the Braves' play-by-play announcer railing against a questionable call in favor of the Dodgers. Sliding doors stood open wide toward the water, and the soft, heavy stillness of the humid night air was punctuated by alternate cheers and groans from the Atlanta faithful.

We had dined leisurely on sea scallops and scampi, both broiled to perfection in white wine and garlic butter over angel hair pasta. I declined dessert, settling for hot tea and a cigarette.

"Your brother-in-law didn't seem particularly thrilled to meet me," Geoff remarked around a mouthful of hot apple tart dripping with melting vanilla ice cream and caramel. "I hope I didn't step on anyone's toes."

Temptation got the better of resolve—a recurring theme in my life lately—and I swiped a spoonful of warm apples.

"*Mmm*. That's heavenly."

Geoff moved the bowl closer to me, and we polished it off in a few more bites.

"Red just worries about me, that's all," I said. "He's big on family responsibility."

"Trust me, his interest is not brotherly."

I lit another cigarette and turned away from him toward the open doors. I watched as a late night fisherman chugged toward home, the lights of his small boat dancing on the black plane of the water.

"I've made you angry," he said softly. "I'm sorry."

"It's okay. I guess I'm just touchy about Red. He's been through a lot lately—the divorce and then Rob's dying. He's been a good friend to me."

What really gnawed at me was that Geoff was probably right. I had been trying to forget the look of longing I had seen on Red's face yesterday, the schoolboy awkwardness as he asked if he could call me. The fact that I didn't *want* him to feel that way about me wouldn't change anything. And blaming Geoff for pointing it out wouldn't either.

I turned back to find him regarding me anxiously, his eyes full of unasked questions. His face was already becoming familiar to me: the way the light played on his silver hair, the slight bump on his otherwise patrician nose. I hadn't felt this way about anyone since Rob and I had locked eyes across a banquet table at a noisy Chamber of Commerce dinner in Charleston almost fourteen years ago. Corny as it sounds, I had not really looked at another man in all that time.

Geoff had already stirred up feelings I didn't want to examine too closely. I had no interest in any kind of romantic involvement—with him or anyone else. What Rob and I had was a once-in-a-lifetime thing. Trying to duplicate it would only lead to disappointment and more pain.

Keep telling yourself that, Tanner, I admonished myself as Geoff signed the credit card receipt and reached for my hand.

"How about a walk by the water?"

We strolled out onto the boardwalk, our arms occasionally brushing as we left the lights of the restaurant behind. A sharp, dank odor, peculiar to the Lowcountry marshland, rose from the reeds and grasses along the bank as we moved farther away from the docks.

"God, I missed that smell." Geoff paused to stand gazing out across the placid water as he sniffed the air. "I'm going to build my house right on the river, so I can sit out on the porch and feel as if I'm on a boat, right out in the middle of it."

"Which river?" I asked. No sense letting a perfectly good opening like that slip by. Besides, it would be nice to get my amateur sleuthing out of the way, to discharge my responsibility to Miss Addie. That would leave us free for…well, for whatever was coming next.

Geoff turned from his contemplation of the water and reclaimed my hand. He tucked it protectively into the crook of his arm, and we resumed our aimless walk along the shore.

"The Chicopee, of course. Can you think of a more beautiful spot? Actually, it's the old Grayton plantation. We're going to restore the main house, develop the rest. I staked out my lot the first time I walked the property. Lots of live oaks, some pines, and a gradual slope down to the river. I'm going to build on the rise."

Even in the dim light of a quarter moon I could see the enthusiasm in his eyes, sense it in his voice. We came to a wooden bench set alongside the path by the local Audubon Society and settled onto it, our attention fixed on the small chirps and rustles of the nighttime residents of the marsh.

"Wait 'til you see it, Bay," Geoff went on. "It's going to be the finest development this county has ever seen." His arm along the back of the bench moved to encircle my shoulder. His touch warmed me, as if he had absorbed the heat from this afternoon's sun and was radiating it back to me now in the cooling night air.

"Who's 'we'?" I asked, settling comfortably into his casual embrace.

"Well, we have several investors, aside from the original partners. Mostly local folks, or so I'm told. I don't really get into that part of it, except for a couple of presentations I made early on. You know how it goes," he said, easing me closer while his hand absently stroked my bare arm. "My family's well known in the area. Makes people feel more secure when there's a local connection."

It was a jarring note in an otherwise straightforward narrative. I sat up, putting a little distance between us. Geoff sensed the withdrawal was more than physical.

"What?" he asked, concern tingeing his voice.

"I don't know, you make it sound as if you let them believe something that wasn't quite true. Like you were some kind of front man or something. How exactly *are* you involved?"

"There's no mystery here, Bay, nothing sinister, if that's what you're implying. I found the property; I put the deal together. I got some of my contacts in Miami interested, set up the corporation. It's a good, sound investment. Plus we're restoring a part of our heritage that might otherwise be left to fall into total ruin." Geoff laid a finger against my cheek and gently turned my head until I faced him. "You sound concerned. Is this more than just idle curiosity?"

I stood abruptly, fumbling in the pocket of my slacks for a cigarette. It was all perfectly plausible, the kind of deal that went down every day in any rapidly growing resort area like ours. There was just something about Geoff's recitation, smooth and polished, as if he'd said it all before, in exactly the same words.

I waited for him to mention my father's involvement, the investment I knew he could ill afford. He didn't.

"I heard you had a roadblock," I said finally, looking out over the water. "A property owner who won't sell."

Geoff was instantly alert. "Where'd you hear that?"

"Around," I hedged. "Is it true?"

"I'm getting a little confused here. What exactly is it you're accusing me of? Grayton's Race is just what it appears to be—a legitimate investment with solid backers and more than adequate funding. What more can I say?"

"So there's no truth to the rumors? About the possibility of the whole thing going sour?"

Why the hell doesn't he say something about the Judge? Surely he knows?

"Jesus, you're not going to let this go, are you?"

"Why don't you just answer the question?" I asked as I turned slowly to face him.

I flinched at the deep sadness I saw in his eyes.

"I guess I was wrong, but I thought there was something happening here, Bay. Something good between us."

I looked back toward the river, away from the need I saw etched so clearly on his troubled face

"Am I wrong then? Did I misread you so completely?" His voice, full of pain and soft as a caress, floated over me like a gentle breeze.

Deep inside me, unbidden and unwanted, something stirred. Viciously, I pushed it back down and whirled to face him.

"Look, Geoff, I asked a simple question about your business venture, and I don't understand why you refuse to answer it." Anger—at myself, at him, at the whole damn situation—made me stumble over my next words. "And yes, I thought something was happening between us, too, though God knows I'm not ready for it. Maybe I'll never be ready. Maybe I don't even want…"

I could feel tears pooling behind my eyes.

You will not cry, I ordered myself. *You. Will. Not. Cry.*

I drew a deep breath, and exhaled the anger and tears along with it.

"But I'll tell you this, Geoff," I said softly. "If you can't be honest with me about something as trivial as this, then whatever is beginning will end, right here."

For a long moment we stared into each other's eyes. Then a great white heron rose suddenly from the marsh, the beating of its wings sending ripples of sound across the black, humid night. We turned in unison to watch its graceful glide as it caught a warm updraft and floated away, toward the sea.

"Fair enough." Geoff's voice echoed in the empty darkness. He held out his hand to me, palm up, a gesture that seemed part supplication, part surrender. "But you're shivering, darling. Here, come sit down and let me warm you up. And we'll talk."

His smile, so sweet and open, the casual endearment, touched that place within me I had thought dead on the tarmac of a country airstrip. For a moment, I wavered. Then, seemingly without conscious thought, I crossed the space between us and laid my hand in his.

My body had made the decision for me. I settled into the warmth of his arms.

We sat like that for a long while, my head resting on Geoff's shoulder. I could feel his warm breath ruffling my hair, feel the pulse in his throat beating steadily against my cheek. A watershed had been crossed tonight, and it seemed only right to be still and savor it.

Geoff moved first, sighing as he set me upright and removed his arm from around my shoulder. "Okay," he said, the boyish grin I remembered from my childhood back on his face. "Now that we've got *that* settled, it's time for me to keep my end of the bargain." I ran a hand through my rumpled hair and dug the crinkled pack of cigarettes out of my pocket.

"Here, give me those."

Puzzled, I handed them and my lighter over to Geoff. He fumbled around inexpertly, but finally got one going. With a flourish he presented the lighted cigarette to me, filter end first.

"Saw that in an old Cary Grant movie once," he said, his eyes bright with mischief. "I've always wanted to try it."

It was a silly, theatrical gesture. I loved it.

Geoff launched into his explanation with no preliminaries, as if anxious to get it over with. "We did have some trouble with getting title to a piece of land, a vital piece, actually. It had the planned right-of-way for the utilities right smack in the middle of it. We want the Race to be reminiscent of the antebellum South, but I don't think our homeowners want to go back to kerosene lamps and wood stoves."

"Couldn't you go around it, bring the lines in somewhere else?"

"Sure, we could have, but it would have meant redesigning the whole layout, possibly shortening the golf course, or moving the plantation house. Any way you cut it, it would have cost a fortune and set us back months while we waited for new reviews and approvals."

I could see now why rumors of such a holdup would be bad for business. More investors than Miss Addie might have gotten cold feet, wanted out; a domino effect that might have sent the whole project tumbling into collapse.

"Why wouldn't they sell?" I asked, surprised that the planning had gotten to this advanced stage without something as crucial as this having been resolved.

"Initially, it wasn't that they wouldn't. They couldn't." Geoff paused, then dropped the two words that struck fear into the heart of every real estate developer in the Lowcountry. "Heirs property."

When the Union naval forces emerged victorious from the Battle of Port Royal in early November, 1861, the white population of Beaufort, Hilton Head, St. Helena, and the surrounding area fled inland, abandoning their plantations—and their slaves—to the triumphant invaders. The government in Washington, D.C. promptly confiscated this immensely rich farmland (for back taxes, they said, although the rightful owners were never given an opportunity to pay up). Much of it was sold at auction for an average 93 cents an acre. Many freed blacks, aided by abolitionist groups in the north, became landowners.

Over the next century, many of these parcels were divided, subdivided, willed in fractional shares to children, grandchildren, their children, and so on until no one individual had clear title to any specific plot.

The Judge had explained it all to me when he had been involved in trying to probate a will for one of his black clients many years ago, at a time when he was certain I was going to follow him into the law.

"Couldn't you clear it at sheriff's sale?" I asked. Geoff nodded approvingly, as if I had passed a test.

The practice was for whichever member of the family was paying the property taxes to let them lapse. Then, when the land was certified for auction by the county treasurer, it would be declared "heirs" property. Other potential bidders would back off, leaving the family representative to buy it for the back taxes and secure title. Problem solved. At least I was pretty sure that was how the process went.

I gave a Geoff a quick synopsis, and again he beamed his approval.

"Want a job? You've just summarized in thirty seconds what it took a team of attorneys three weeks and a forty-page brief to explain."

"Don't be so hard on your profession," I quipped. "I never knew a lawyer yet who could do things the easy way."

"*Former* profession," Geoff laughed and pulled me to my feet. "We'd better head back, don't you think? I'd hate to find the Judge waiting for us with a shotgun resting across his knees."

"So what happened with your heirs property?" I asked as we strolled along the boardwalk, holding hands like a pair of teenagers.

"We didn't have to go to sheriff's sale because this was a fairly neat one. Only five parties, and three of them were local. We had tracked them all down, and they'd signed off, all except one, but he was committed. Just had to get him in to do the actual signing."

We reached the parking lot, and Geoff paused to open the passenger door of his black Jaguar XJS. I slid into the leather bucket seat as he moved behind the wheel.

"Want the top down, or will you be cold?"

"It's definitely a top-down night. If my teeth start to chatter, we can always turn on the heater."

Geoff resumed as soon as we were underway. "Anyway, we think one of the sleazier members of my former profession latched onto the guy and convinced him to hold out. We assume they wanted to up the price, although what we had agreed on with the others was more than generous. I figure it was the lawyer who leaked it, hoping to put pressure on us to raise the ante. No doubt he had cut himself in for a healthy per centage of whatever the new price turned out to be."

"Sounds like one of Hadley's stunts," I remarked, recalling the thinly veiled animosity I had sensed when the two men had confronted each other earlier in the day.

"Give the little lady a prize."

The wind whipped my hair as the sleek convertible sped along the deserted highway. I loved this feeling of freedom, of being disconnected somehow from the rest of the world, with only a thin slice of moon and a zillion winking stars to light our way.

"But don't quote me on that," Geoff added as he reached over to caress my arm where it lay against the console between us. "I don't have any real proof, and it would be just like the bastard to sue me for slander."

"So what happened?" We were almost at *Presqu'isle*, and I wanted to hear the end of the story so I could report in to Miss Addie and set her mind at ease.

"Well, it's a good news/bad news kind of thing. The guy died, suddenly, a few days ago. His share passes to his mother who has already signed. So…we're back in business."

Geoff took the turn into the driveway too fast and braked to a skidding halt in front of the long stairway, gravel from under the Jag's tires spewing out onto the lawn. Before he could get out, I opened my own door and paused, one foot on the dew-damp grass.

"Call me?" I felt awkward, like the infatuated adolescent I had been the last time Geoff and I had spent so much time together.

"Every hour on the hour, if you think the Judge won't mind the racket."

I laughed, a carefree sound that surprised even me. I was remembering what it was like to be happy. "Don't get out. It's late. I can find my way home from here."

"No goodnight kiss, huh?"

"Not on the first date. I'm not that kind of girl."

Geoff lifted my hand from where it rested on the console and gently pressed his lips against my palm.

"We'll have to work on that. Goodnight, Bay. Sleep well."

"You, too."

I stopped halfway up the steps and watched until the black Jaguar was swallowed up by the night.

The grandfather clock in the parlor struck three as I locked the front door behind me and walked dreamily toward the staircase. The note was taped to the carved newel post at the end of the polished oak banister, just at eye level for someone in a wheelchair. A quotation, *"Be wise with speed. A fool at forty is a fool indeed."*

That little gem was followed by an original admonition, "Don't sleep late. We need to talk."

My first reaction was to rip the damned thing into little pieces and scatter them all over the heart pine floor where my father would be sure to roll over them first thing in the morning. Instead, I grabbed a pen from the hall table and added my own quotation, an appropriate line from the French fablist, La Rochefoucauld: "Old people like to give good advice, as solace for no longer being able to provide bad examples." And my own postscript: "Mind your own business!"

I stayed awake just long enough to peel off my clothes and crawl beneath the cool sheets. For the first time in months, I couldn't remember my dreams.

7

I slept through breakfast but managed to be showered and dressed in time for lunch. I slid into a chair at the kitchen table just as Dolores began ladling steamy fish chowder into earthenware bowls. Although it smelled wonderful, it was not my idea of what to put in an empty stomach. I settled for a buttered sweet-potato roll, one of Dolores's specialties, and a glass of iced tea.

The sky outside the mullioned window over the sink had turned gray and lowering. Black clouds hovered on the horizon. I could hear the slap of the Sound against the pilings of the dock at the back of the property as the wind kicked up.

"Looks like a storm brewing," I said to Dolores who had gone to stand in the doorway out to the hall. "Maybe it'll cool things off a little."

"Your father, he is very angry," she said, glancing anxiously toward the Judge's study.

"At whom?" I asked, helping myself to another warm roll from the napkin-lined basket, and slathering it with butter.

"He talks all morning on the telephone. He shouts. I hear him, even in the kitchen." Dolores frowned at me over her shoulder. "He says words I do not know. Not nice words, I think."

I laughed, imagining Dolores thumbing through the battered English/Spanish dictionary she carried in her car, searching for the translation of some of my father's more colorful expletives.

"You're probably right. And, trust me, you're better off not knowing."

I rubbed my bare arms against the air-conditioned chill of the old house. My mother had spent a fortune on updating the wiring, plumbing, and heating after she inherited *Presqu'isle*, humidity control being vital to the well-being of her precious antiques and paintings. I much preferred the feel of soft breezes through open doors and windows, but I hadn't been around to vote.

"Want me to go get him?" I asked. "Before everything gets cold?"

"No, no, *Señora*. He has a visitor. He says, 'Do not disturb.'"

I didn't like the pinched look of anxiety on Dolores's normally open face.

"Has he been bullying you? No, don't defend him. He has, I can tell. The ungrateful old coot!" I pushed my chair back and jumped to my feet. "Just because Lavinia is willing to put up with his foul moods is no reason…"

Dolores ducked back into the kitchen shaking her head vigorously. "No, *Señora*, is fine. Is no *problema*. *El Juez*…"

Voices drifting up from the back of the house accompanied the soft squeak of motorized wheels on wood floor. I heard my father's booming laugh, followed by a high-pitched giggle that froze me in my tracks.

What the hell was *he* doing here?

I bounded out of the kitchen to confront my father, his hand resting on the polished brass knob of the front door as he prepared to usher out his visitor. Hadley Bolles stopped in mid-waddle as I approached.

"Well, Bay, darlin', what a pleasant surprise. I was just tellin' your daddy what a nice little chat we had yesterday, down at the Fig Tree."

"Lunch is ready," I said, reaching for the handles on the back of the Judge's wheelchair. "Don't let us keep you, Hadley."

My father twisted around to glare at me for that blatant breach of manners. "Care to join us, Hadley?" he asked perversely. His fingers stabbed at the buttons on the armrest in an effort to gain control, but my hands on the chair overrode him.

"Well, now…"

I was suddenly conscious of my bare feet, faded red shorts, and the white cotton T-shirt I had thrown on without bothering with a bra. I knew my nipples had to be standing straight out through the thin fabric because Hadley's piggy eyes were fastened on my chest.

"…depends on what's on the menu," he finished with a nasty little chuckle that made my skin crawl.

"I'm up here, Hadley," I snarled, forcing him to drag his gaze away from my breasts.

The Judge noticed, too. "Another time perhaps," he said stiffly as he pulled the door open wider.

Getting bounced twice in two days couldn't have been a novel experience for someone as obnoxious as Hadley Bolles, but he took this rebuff with less grace that he had Geoff's dismissal of the day before.

"Just remember what I said, Tally," he growled, wagging a thick, well-manicured finger in the Judge's face. He didn't even bother to leer at me as he slapped his stained white fedora onto his head and shuffled across the porch. The first fat drops of rain began to fall as he puffed his way down the steps. I closed the door on the sound of thunder echoing across the open water.

"What the hell was he doing in this house?" I turned and headed down the hallway, not waiting for a reply.

"Business," the Judge said to my retreating back. He rolled behind me into the kitchen and positioned himself at the table.

Dolores had returned the cooling chowder to the kettle, and now began dishing it out again.

"I'll have some, too, please." I flipped the napkin onto my lap and grabbed another roll. What the hell, people ate herring for breakfast, didn't they?

Dolores, who had already eaten, got the Judge settled, then scurried off to check in with her husband. She normally didn't do "overnights", but had made an exception for me in light of Lavinia's trouble and the Judge's special needs. She didn't deserve to be browbeaten for her efforts.

We ate in strained silence for a while, my mind chewing on all the things I wanted to say and knew I shouldn't. The hot soup felt good going down, appropriate somehow with a thunderstorm raging outside. When I had calmed down sufficiently to be pretty sure I wasn't going to bite his head off, I spoke matter-of-factly to the Judge.

"You shouldn't badger Dolores, you know. She's very sensitive, and she's also doing us a tremendous favor. I think you've hurt her feelings."

My father was attempting to butter a roll. I flinched as he tried to anchor it under the rim of his bowl while wielding the knife with his good hand, his face creased in concentration.

How he must hate this, I thought, echoing our conversation of the night before. He was right. I really couldn't imagine what it must be like. I picked up the roll and finished it for him.

"Thanks." He finally looked at me, a sheepish grin on his lined face. "You're right, of course. I'm just used to Vinnie's ignoring me when I get cranky like this. Don't worry about Dolores. I'll make it right with her."

"Good." The rain had stopped while we ate, and a weak sun was beginning to break through the overcast. "What did Hadley want?" I asked conversationally. I lit a cigarette and leaned back into the swatch of checkered sunlight now falling through the window.

"Actually, I called him. He was in his car, on the island, so he stopped by. Look, honey," the Judge said, patting my hand, "I know he's an odious little man. If I weren't a wasted old hulk, I would have pitched him down the steps for the way he looked at you today."

"Don't worry about it. I can handle the Pig Man."

My father chuckled. "Yes, I guess you can. Lord, but you put me in mind of Emmaline, the way you stood there and faced him down."

"So why did you call him?" I asked, ignoring the reference to my mother. My conversation with Geoff last night jumped suddenly into my head. "Something to do with the Race?"

"No," he barked in exasperation. "Because he knows every damned thing that goes on in this town. I thought he might have heard something about Derek Johnson, something we could use to help Isaiah. It's not looking good for the boy."

I got up to fetch the iced tea pitcher from the refrigerator and refill our glasses. "I don't understand. I thought they released him because he had an alibi. He and CJ Elliott were together."

"So they say. After you left with your old flame last night, Redmond stayed for awhile. It seems the detectives aren't entirely satisfied. They're going to talk to young Cal again, see if they can crack his story."

I was reminded with a jolt that I had never called Bitsy. "They're that certain Isaiah is guilty?".

"Means, motive, and opportunity. He appears to have it all."

"Have they found a weapon yet?"

"No, nothing specific. Redmond said it could have been a heavy tree limb, tossed into the river along with the body. They may never come up with it."

We sat quietly, both of us contemplating the ramifications of the detectives' having settled on Lavinia's grandson as their prime suspect. There were plenty of stories around about cops who never looked too much farther once they'd made up their minds.

"So was Hadley any help? And what was all that finger-pointing and dire warning business about?"

"Oh, nothing, really." The Judge spooned up the last of his chowder, wiped his mouth, and maneuvered his chair back from the table. "You know how he likes to throw his weight around."

We smiled at each other, both of us thinking the same unkind thoughts.

"I think I'll take a little rest now," my father said, avoiding my eyes as he rolled toward the door. "See you later."

I sat for a moment, my chin resting in my hands, elbows on the table. Something was going on here, some undercurrent I couldn't quite get hold of. The Judge hadn't answered any of my questions directly. In fact, he'd been downright evasive.

I rose and began to clear the table, stacking the bowls and glasses in the dishwasher. Something else was nagging at me, some question I should have asked, had intended to ask, but had gotten sidetracked from. I wasn't even sure who it was I had meant to put it to.

Can brains rust? I wondered as I set the soup kettle in the stainless steel sink and filled it with soapy water to soak. My head had certainly gotten little use in the past few months. Maybe that was why I couldn't pull the niggling thought into focus from the back of my mind.

It would remain stuck there, needling me like an unscratched itch, until it was almost too late.

My conversation with Miss Addie was short and to the point. I relayed Geoff's assurances that the project was progressing on time, and added my own that everything about Grayton's Race seemed to be legitimate. She was effusive in her gratitude, and I could hear the genuine relief my news had brought her.

The call to Bitsy Elliott was another story.

Elizabeth Quintard, as she had been in the days of our growing up together, was my antithesis in almost every respect. Petite—hence her nickname—blonde and blue-eyed, Bitsy was everything my mother had wanted me to be. More than just conventionally pretty, Bitsy had that wholesome, cheerleader freshness that attracted everyone to her. The most common word used to describe her had been "sweet".

"Elizabeth is a lady," Emmaline Simpson would announce to me about a hundred times a day. "Elizabeth knows how to behave properly."

It always amazed me, thinking back on it, that we had become friends in the first place. It was a downright miracle that we had remained so for over thirty years.

"Bay, honey, thank God!" she exclaimed when we finally made connections that Saturday afternoon. "I thought you had dropped right off the face of the earth!"

Bitsy tends to talk like that, in exclamation points.

"Sorry, Bits. It's been kind of a hectic couple of days." I filled her in on my activities, leaving a few large, intentional gaps around Geoff Anderson. I wasn't ready to *think* about the implications there, let alone talk about them.

"So you know all about the poor Johnson boy? And Isaiah? Imagine them thinkin' he could have had anything to do with such a thing! Ridiculous! I was never so frightened in my entire life as when a deputy showed up at our door in the dead of night and told us CJ was in jail! Thank God it's all cleared up now."

Poor Bitsy! I didn't want to be the one to tell her the cops weren't finished with CJ quite yet.

I was also trying to work out the timing. Her messages had all been left on my answering machine on Thursday; the boys hadn't been picked up until early Friday morning. So that couldn't have been the cause of her tearful urgency.

"So, Bits, what's the problem? Dolores relayed your messages, and she said you sounded pretty upset."

The pause lasted only a few seconds, but I knew my friend well enough to be certain that whatever she was about to say was not going to be the truth. At least, not all of it.

"Oh, you know how I get sometimes, Bay, honey." She kept her voice light, but an undercurrent of *something*—fear, anger?–rippled just below the surface. "Big Cal and I had a little set-to. About money, of all things. He threw a fit over somethin' I bought, but you know I just can't say no when the kids really want something. I just overreacted, that's all. I'm fine now."

"Did he hit you?" I hated asking the question, afraid to hear the answer. But it wouldn't have been the first time "Big" Cal Elliott, former Clemson fullback gone to fat, had smacked his 5'3" wife around. I would have called the cops on him any number of times if Bitsy hadn't gotten hysterical at the mere suggestion of it.

"No! Oh, no, really, Bay, he didn't. Honest! Just yelling. And then he stormed out of the house and didn't come back for two days! I called all over the state and couldn't find him anywhere. I got a little frantic, that's all. I just needed someone to talk to, a shoulder. You know."

I did some more mental arithmetic. "You mean he wasn't home when you got the news about CJ? Where the hell was he? Is he back now?"

"Oh, yes, everything's fine, just fine. Cal met his attorney at the jail and brought CJ home. They're out back now, the two of them, fishin' off the dock."

"And all this over some toy or whatever you bought for one of the kids?" The four Elliott children seemed to grow at such a rate I kept losing track of just how old they were. CJ would be a senior; Mary Alice, called Mally, also in high school, was maybe a couple of years behind. Margaret had to be in junior high; and Brady, the youngest, somewhere around third or fourth grade.

"Yes, can you believe it? Actually, it was a CD player for Margaret. She always seems to get Mally's hand-me-downs, and she wanted a new one, just for herself." Bitsy sighed, and I could almost see her shining, shoulder-length hair flipping back and forth as she shook her head in exasperation. "It was only two hundred dollars!"

Calvin Elliott had inherited a moderately successful used car business from his father and had parlayed it into a string of seven "Big Cal SuperLots" from Greenville to Beaufort. His grinning, pudgy, red-neck countenance beamed down on unsuspecting consumers from billboards all up and down the state.

"He walked out over a couple of hundred bucks?" I asked. "What a jerk! Did he ever say where he was all that time?"

"Well, not exactly. He said he was just drivin' around. Stopped at a couple of bars and lost track of time."

"For two days?"

"I know it sounds feeble. But he's back now, and CJ's home, so I can't raise too much of a ruckus. And to be fair, things have been a little tight lately, I think. Not that Big Cal ever tells *me* anything, at least not directly. But I've overheard him on the phone a few times, shoutin' at someone about some big investment he made that's run into problems."

I could hear tears creeping into Bitsy's voice. She was so damned loyal! My fingers itched to wrap themselves around her husband's flabby neck.

"If only he'd talk to me, maybe I could take some of the burden off him." She swallowed hard. "But he just tells me to mind my own business, take care of the kids, and leave the rest to him."

"Anything I can do to help?"

"You already have. As usual. But don't worry, sweetie, I'm sure everything will be fine. After all, from what I gather, it was the Judge who recommended this investment to Big Cal, so there really isn't anything to fuss about, is there? Your daddy is one of the smartest men I know."

The bottom fell out of my stomach. It had to be Grayton's Race. There couldn't be two projects with rumors flying and investors panicking, both connected to my father.

What the hell is he up to? I wondered as I reassured Bitsy and hung up the phone. Why was the Judge out touting Geoff's development? First Miss Addie and now Big Cal Elliott. And why hadn't Geoff mentioned anything about all this last night? God knows, I'd given him plenty of opportunity. If everything was as up front as Geoff claimed it was, why all the secrecy?

I needed answers. I marched into the study and stopped short. My father lay stretched out in his recliner, his useless legs draped with a light cotton throw. Soft snores bubbled from his partially open mouth. He looked so damned *vulnerable*.

I closed the door softly behind me and took the stairs two at a time.

Last night I had been lulled by the soft river breeze and my own lone-liness…by a tender smile and a girlhood fantasy. In the cold light of day, reality was reasserting itself.

Something was wrong. I could smell it, sense it in the unanswered questions, the averted eyes, the smooth plausibility with which every objection was explained away.

It was time for me to get back to work. Maybe I couldn't get into the courthouse on Saturday afternoon, but my computer could. I would head back to Hilton Head and begin accessing files, checking records. The names of the new owners of the Grayton's Race tract seemed like a logical place to start. Maybe I could find out who else my father had enticed into investing—and why. Rob's clearances had probably been canceled on his death, but he had taught me how to "hack" back in the days when our financial sleuthing had necessitated getting into data-bases we weren't meant to see. Most of those belonged to the bad guys, but the technique was the same. If I could just remember how…

I threw my toothbrush and a few other necessities into my overnight bag and slipped into my well-worn Birkenstock sandals. Dolores had apparently made peace with the Judge. She cheerfully agreed to hold the fort for a couple of days and followed me out onto the porch. As I trot-ted down the front steps, the phone began to ring.

"Remember, you don't know where I am," I shouted over my shoul-der. If it was Geoff, I was glad I'd missed his call. I needed a little dis-tance right now, time to think with my head instead of my glands.

A quiet night in front of the computer screen was what I had planned. It was not exactly what I got.

8

My house smelled stale after being closed up for the last two days. I wandered through the high-ceilinged rooms, opening windows and French doors. The soft susurration of the ocean, just across the dune, was a soothing presence, like a piece of well-loved music playing in the background.

I kicked off my sandals and walked barefooted up three steps onto the highly-polished oak floor of the expansive kitchen. Dolores said she'd left a Caesar salad with grilled shrimp all ready for me in the refrigerator. All I needed to do was dump it in a bowl and add the dressing.

I can handle that. I smiled to myself, remembering Rob's lighthearted teasing about my ineptness in the kitchen. I put everything on a tray and carried it out onto the deck. Although it was still only early evening, I lit some citronella candles to ward off the no-see-ums and sat down at the round, white, wrought iron table.

My nearest neighbors were well hidden behind a cluster of live oaks and pines. The silence was almost complete, broken only occasionally by the bright squawk of a mockingbird perched somewhere over my head. I picked desultorily at my dinner as the sky over the water gradually faded from crystal blue to soft orange.

My head whirled with all the troubling events of the past couple of days: Isaiah and CJ as apparent suspects in a murder investigation, Bitsy's

74

distress at her husband's strange disappearance, my own father's evasiveness about his role in the Grayton's Race development, not to mention all the other inconsistencies in what I had been told about the project.

I pushed the half-finished salad away, lit a cigarette, and propped my bare feet up on the chair next to me. I needed a plan, a roadmap to help me navigate the tangle of conflicting stories. A sharp flash of memory kicked me in the stomach.

Rob. His presence was almost palpable here in the house we had designed and built shortly after our marriage. He used to laugh at me when I called it our beach place. With three bedrooms and as many baths, it was twice the size of the condominium that had been our permanent home in Charleston.

My darling Rob... I could almost hear his soft, upstate drawl. *Make a list, honey, three columns: What do we suspect, what do we know, what can we prove?*

He would pace and talk. I would take notes. We'd bounce ideas off each other, knock down the most outrageous ones, and end up, after several hours of brainstorming, with a blueprint for his investigation. Later he would transcribe it all onto the computer. Even though my participation was unofficial, I always shared in his work. We were a team.

So why did you have to go and die? I silently screamed, the enormity of his loss suddenly crashing in on me. *You had no right to get blown up and leave me alone like this! No right! I need you!*

"I need you," I whispered to the empty night

I lit another cigarette and exhaled slowly. I concentrated on my breathing, the way they'd taught me in therapy. Gradually, the pain receded to the dark corner where I kept it stored.

"Get on with it," I ordered myself. "You need a plan."

But the moment my thoughts turned again to Grayton's Race, another face drifted into that black place behind my closed eyelids. Geoff, his direct blue gaze filled with tenderness, gently kissing my trembling palm. At thirteen, I had dreamed of his touch, my skinny, flat-chested body yearning for the feel of his hands on my skin.

Geoff had been the object of my first, terrifying sexual fantasies.

Last night had shown me the power he still possessed. I had walked without hesitation into his arms, my body somehow believing that was where I belonged. Geoff had dropped miraculously back into my life at the exact moment my heart seemed ready to receive him.

And the doubts? I asked myself ruthlessly. *The seeming half-truths, the smooth evasions? He could be a fraud. What do you really know about him now?*

No! I was a good judge of character—always had been. Geoff couldn't have changed that much. I couldn't be so wrong...

What do we suspect, what do we know, what can we prove?

Sudden movement registered on the edge of my half-lidded vision.

I jumped, fear shooting through me like a lightning strike.

Mr. Bones, my on-again, off-again feline companion, sat perched in the chair to my right. His slim, gray paw shot out and speared another shrimp from the soggy remains of my salad. It disappeared in two quick gulps. He looked like a bear swiping salmon out of a rushing stream.

I blew air out of my lungs and ruffled the fur on the back of his head. "Damn it, Bones, you scared the hell out of me. And who invited you to dinner?"

I had named him for his emaciated appearance the first time I found him sunning himself on my deck. I knew Dolores left a dish out for him every night and the tiny skeletons littering the yard testified to his hunting prowess, so it wasn't that he was hungry. Food was available, and instinct told him to take what was offered when the opportunity presented itself.

The soft pink glow of the fading sun bathed the deck in an eerie light. The cat finished his after-dinner grooming, padded across the table, and curled himself onto my lap. His deep, satisfied purring increased as I stroked his back.

Instinct. Rob always said I could spot the holes in a financial deal from half a mile away. While that was, of course, an exaggeration, I *had* developed a nose for ferreting out a scam. Neither Rob nor I had ever considered ourselves brave. We preferred to do our fighting with brains rather than bullets. We had nailed a number of illegal operations in the state, not by swooping down with SWAT teams to interdict drug shipments, but by following the money.

Instinct. That was what had been gnawing at me for the last couple of days. And it was telling me that something just wasn't right about Grayton's Race.

The sun had finally set over the mainland. The darkness was total, enveloping, except for the feeble flickering of the candles and the glow from the end of my cigarette. Tree frogs squeaked their nightly chorus, and the cat resettled himself across my legs.

Lost in the peace of the soft summer night, I was half-dozing. The screech of an owl, swooping to its prey, jerked me awake. Mr. Bones leaped to the deck. I heard a rustling in the sharp leaves of the palmettos along the dune, then a frenzied squealing, quickly cut off as the owl glided away, dinner clutched in its fierce talons.

Instinct.

I piled the dirty dishes on the tray, carried them back into the kitchen, and loaded the dishwasher. I filled the tea kettle and set it on the stove. I selected a box of Constant Comment tea bags from the cupboard. None of that mild, soothing, herbal stuff. Tonight I was going to need all the caffeine I could get.

Brains could, in fact, rust I decided as I sat frustrated before the bright rectangle of the 17-inch monitor. The desk in the bedroom we had converted into an office was littered with disks and crumpled wads of yellow legal paper.

I couldn't get into the damn courthouse computer! And I couldn't figure out where I was going wrong. It should have been child's play. It had to be something simple, some small command I was forgetting to execute.

In desperation I had finally opened the floor safe concealed in the far corner of my walk-in closet. Against all the rules, Rob had kept duplicates of his case notes here, on three and one-half inch disks. Government corruption was not unknown in the Great State of South Carolina, and Rob preferred to trust no one but himself. And me.

I had retrieved the boxes of disks that held much of the information we had illegally downloaded during our midnight plundering of supposedly secure databases. I was hoping for some clue, a scribbled note, anything to jog my memory and get me past the roadblock of the flashing "Access Denied" messages that filled my screen.

I had sorted through all these files right after my release from the hospital. My hopes of finding something that would lead me to Rob's murderers had been quickly dashed. The number of cases in which he had been involved and the sheer volume of the data defeated me. And my grief had been too new then, too raw. The memories evoked by these tangible reminders of our life together had been more than I could bear.

I turned back to my list making which wasn't meeting with any greater success. I had eliminated the "What can we prove" column from my deliberations. I had no interest in prosecuting anyone even if I were able to make a case. All I wanted was to find out enough about the finances and the backers of the Grayton's Race project to reach an informed opinion about its legitimacy.

Guilt was a hard little knot in the center of my chest.

I had probably jumped the gun in reassuring Adelaide Boyce Hammond about the safety of her investment. I had made similar noises to Bitsy Elliott, though with less fervor.

Moonlight and seductive blue eyes were my only excuse.

I didn't intend to open my mouth again until I knew for sure what I was talking about.

I dumped the overflowing ashtray into the wastebasket next to the desk and headed for the kitchen. The clock above the stove read twenty past two. I'd already gone through two pots of tea and was starting on my third. Even if I decided to hang it up now and go to bed, I'd probably never get to sleep. Caffeine hummed through my veins like electric current through a wire.

I was also starving.

I was leaning over, peering hopefully into the open refrigerator, when a sweep of headlights flashed across the ceiling, freezing me in the glare. They were quickly extinguished, followed a few seconds later by the *thud* of a car door slammed with considerable force.

Soft-soled shoes crunched on the carpet of dead pine needles that covered the driveway. I followed their progress up the wooden stairway.

Two sharp, staccato bursts of the doorbell were followed by a pounding on the stout oak door.

Well, if it's a burglar, I thought, *it's a pretty damned inept one.*

I glanced down at the short cotton nightshirt I'd thrown on before I settled down in front of the computer. I was running for the bedroom to grab a robe when the pounding resumed, punctuated this time by an angry voice I had previously heard speak only with warmth and laughter.

"Bay! I know you're in there. Bay! Open the damned door!"

Anger won out over modesty. I flung myself down the three steps, strode across the white-carpeted great room and flipped on the outside light. When I yanked open the door, I caught him in mid-pound, his fist poised to strike again.

"Will you shut up, for God's sake? You want the neighbors to call the cops?"

I stood with my feet set wide apart, one hand gripping the knob, the other planted firmly against the doorframe. If he wanted in, he was going to have to go through me.

Geoff Anderson lowered his hand and his voice at the same time. "Hi," he said sheepishly.

He wore a white T-shirt with a Salty Dog logo tucked into rumpled khaki shorts, and dark brown deck shoes with no socks. His square jaw was peppered with several hours' growth of beard. He looked like the answer to every single woman's prayer: handsome, boyish, slightly disreputable.

My hand itched to stroke his cheek, to feel the rough stubble beneath my fingers. Or maybe to slap him 'til his teeth rattled. I couldn't decide which.

"What the hell are you doing beating on my door in the middle of the night?" I relaxed my guard dog stance as he shoved both hands into his pockets.

"Can I come in?" He swayed a little, then shook his head as if to clear it.

"You're drunk." I couldn't keep the accusatory tone out of my voice. A familiar hole opened up in the pit of my stomach.

"Am not." He grinned, shaking his head again.

"Geoff, I'm really not in the mood for this. It's late. Why don't you go home and get some sleep." I suddenly realized I didn't even know where he lived. "I'll call you a cab."

"How about some coffee? Please?" Geoff's voice was plaintive, pleading. "I'll just stay a few minutes, I promise. I need to talk to you, Bay."

I hesitated, and he looked directly into my eyes. "Please?"

Fool, I berated myself as I stepped back and swung the door fully open.

A snippet of an old Negro spiritual popped unbidden into my head: "…and the walls came tumblin' down."

I made instant coffee—the only kind I couldn't screw up—and scrambled some eggs for the two of us. While the water was boiling, I ducked into the bedroom to pull on a pair of shorts under the nightshirt. I ran a brush through my hair while I was at it. I thought about makeup, but decided the hell with it. Anyone who came calling after midnight would just have to take me the way I was.

With food and coffee under his belt, Geoff appeared to sober up quickly. I was beginning to wonder if it had all been an act when he seemed to read my mind.

"I only had a couple of beers, you know, and I haven't eaten since lunch. I guess they went right to my head. Sorry."

I waved his apology away. Seated across the kitchen table from each other, we both grew strangely quiet. We sat that way for some time, each of us wrapped in our own thoughts.

For my part, there was a war going on inside. My head demanded confrontation, explanations for all my suspicions. My heart smiled at the quiet joy I felt having him near. I knew I had only to reach out and touch his hand, and I would be in his arms, warm, secure, and safe.

Loved.

I read it in his eyes as they lifted to meet mine. My body yearned toward his, drawn to the desire I saw reflected on his face…

I stepped back from the brink. I slumped in my chair and folded my arms across my breasts. I wasn't sure which of us the familiar defensive posture was meant to protect.

Geoff sagged, too, as the sexual tension drained out of him.

"You said you wanted to talk to me," I said quietly, "so talk."

"Why did you run away from me?"

"I didn't 'run away'. I came home. This is where I live, where I belong."

"Where you hide."

I flinched at the accuracy of his shot. I bought time by lighting a cigarette.

"If that's how you see it. I had things to do here, things I couldn't accomplish on St. Helena. So what's the big deal?"

"The big deal is that you told the Dragon Lady not to let me know where you were."

His characterization of sweet-tempered Dolores as a fire-breathing guardian made me smile in spite of myself.

"I needed a little space. Time to think. I was going to call you."

I suddenly realized that it was true. I would have sought Geoff out in a day or two if he hadn't beaten me to it.

"That's your trouble, Bay. You think too damn much. What's wrong with just feeling?"

"Geoff, there are things…"

"I know, I know. I realized last night after I dropped you off that there was still something bothering you about the project. I don't begin to understand what your problem is, and you don't seem willing to enlighten me."

Geoff took my cigarette from me and stubbed it out in the ashtray. He covered both my hands with his and lightly stroked my fingers.

"Ask me anything you want, Bay, anything. I don't want this hanging over our heads, coming between us. I think I'm falling…"

I stopped him with a finger to his lips. I wasn't ready to hear a declaration of love, not yet. He was right. There were too many questions. But I couldn't bring myself to ask them, not now. Maybe I really didn't want to know the answers. Suddenly, I was overwhelmingly tired.

"You'd better go, Geoff," I said, glancing at the clock as we rose from our chairs. "It's after three. We seem to be making a habit of staying up half the night."

"There's an alternative to staying up, you know." He moved around the table toward me.

"Out!" I pointed sternly at the door, and Geoff backed away, hands held high in mock surrender.

"Okay, okay." He took my hand again as we walked slowly into the hallway. At the door, he turned to face me, that boyish grin back on his face.

"Do you have any hiking boots?" he asked. His fingers smoothed tangled locks of hair back off my cheeks, his touch so gentle I could barely feel it.

"Any what?" I was nearly hypnotized by his soft voice and delicate caress.

"Hiking boots. Or maybe work boots. Something sturdy, anyway, with hightops. There may be snakes."

"Snakes?" I stepped back, batting his arm away. It was much easier to think with his hands no longer on me. "What the hell are you talking about?"

"Tomorrow. I'm picking you up at eleven. We'll have brunch at the Hyatt, then I'm giving you the grand tour of Grayton's Race. I want to show you where I'm building my house."

"But…"

Geoff grasped my shoulders and pulled me gently to him. In my bare feet, I fit perfectly into the curve of his arm, my head just below his chin.

"I can't go to the Hyatt in work boots," I murmured into his neck.

Geoff's laugh echoed in the enclosed space of the hallway.

Then he drew aside the neck of my nightshirt. I flinched as the cool night air touched my injured shoulder. With a tenderness that made my legs nearly fold up under me, Geoff brushed his lips across the shiny ugliness of the grafted skin.

"Tomorrow," he whispered as he released me and slipped quietly out the door.

9

"How did you get into the plantation last night?" I asked. I was stuffing my hair up under a battered Chicago Cubs baseball cap while Geoff secured the boot over the lowered convertible top of the Jaguar.

Although the fierce midday sun bounced shimmering heat waves off the blacktop of the Hyatt parking lot, yesterday's storm had chased most of the humidity south, at least temporarily, and the wind off the ocean felt fresh and relatively cool.

"Magic," Geoff answered, pointing to the array of multi-colored stickers covering the lower left-hand corner of the Jag's windshield. Access to the wooded enclaves of homes and golf courses, like Port Royal where I lived, could be gained only by residents with permanent passes or by temporary paper ones issued to authorized visitors.

"Where'd you get all those?"

"One of the many perks of being in the real estate business," Geoff replied as we eased out of Palmetto Dunes onto Route 278 and headed west.

It was a glorious day, and I was determined to forget everything and simply enjoy it. Last night I had barely enough energy left to log off the computer and sweep the disks into a file cabinet. (I returned them to the safe first thing in the morning.) Except for a brief interruption when I'd thought I'd heard the cat clawing at the French door, I'd slept like the dead.

Conversation was difficult with the wind roaring in our ears, so Geoff and I contented ourselves with exchanging occasional smiles. We crossed over the twin bridges, leaving the island behind. On our right, we passed the glinting metal power line supports that always looked to me like alien giants with huge arms and no heads. Embedded deep in the soft mud of the marsh, they made an ideal nesting spot for ospreys and other birds of prey, the towers a perfect launching pad for them to swoop out over the water, their hawklike talons ready to sink into the tender flesh of unsuspecting fish.

"Music?" Geoff mouthed at me as we swept past Moss Creek. Horses grazed in the paddock near the highway.

I nodded.

Geoff slipped in a tape, and the pure, clear tenor of Pavoratti surrounded us.

The man is amazing, I thought as I closed my eyes and let the sun, the wind, and the "Nessen Dorma" wash over me.

Luciano, of course, for that marvelous voice. But I had been thinking mostly of Geoff who, without asking, had unerringly picked my favorite piece of music.

Past Belfair and Rose Hill, we took the off-ramp and turned right toward Beaufort. A few miles farther on, Geoff flipped on his right turn signal and slowly edged toward the berm. The sandy track he pulled onto was barely discernible among the thick stand of loblolly pines and waist-high weeds.

The sharp blast of a horn made me whirl around in my seat. A scruffy, bearded teenager yelled something out the window of a chrome-laden pickup truck as it roared past us. A gun rack hung in the rear window, and the bumper was plastered with slogans. All I could catch was something about "...Hunting Grounds" before the boy and his friends disappeared around a bend in the road.

"Idiots," Geoff muttered as he slowed the big Jag to a crawl.

Thirty yards in we bounced to a halt before a rusty metal gate secured to weathered wooden posts by a shiny, new padlock. Geoff killed the engine and cut Luciano off in mid-note.

"This is as far as we ride, unless I trade this baby in for one of those four-wheel drive monsters," Geoff said as he slid out of the car. "You game for a hike?"

"I didn't dress like this for the Spring Cotillion. Lead on."

I had ferreted out my old hiking boots from the attic that morning. Rob and I had gone through a short-lived rock climbing phase early in our marriage. Packed away in the same box, I found my heavy woolen socks. An oversized T-shirt and faded jeans completed my ensemble.

Geoff was similarly clad. We'd been a big hit among the starched and suited after-church crowd at the Hyatt brunch.

"Better use this, or you'll get eaten alive."

Geoff tossed a can of insect repellent across the open car. I sloshed it liberally over the exposed skin of my arms, neck and face. It smelled awful, but that was probably good. Where we were going, mosquitoes the size of hummingbirds were not uncommon.

Geoff shrugged a small backpack onto his shoulder, and we set off. We rounded the posts of the gate and headed down the deeply rutted track. It was littered with potholes so large and so numerous we had to walk on either side of the path. Thick woods provided a measure of shade from the merciless afternoon sun, but they also blunted what little breeze ruffled their highest branches. We were soon soaked in sweat.

The silence is never complete where there are trees and plants. Insects buzzed and whirred, for the moment, at least, properly repelled by the smell of the spray. Soft rustlings marked the passage of larger, unseen creatures—squirrels, raccoons, and assorted other rodents. Birdsong filled the quiet spaces with so many varied calls I couldn't begin to identify the singers. Woodpeckers tapped industriously high over our heads as we walked deeper into the woods.

"Want to talk?" Geoff glanced over at me, then quickly away. It was a nervous, edgy gesture.

"Not especially. You?"

"Not if you don't."

We trekked on, our heavy boots making little sound and less impression on the sandy red soil and underbrush. Sweat was trickling between my breasts, pooling around the waistband of my jeans.

"Not much farther," Geoff said as he pulled a handkerchief from his pocket and mopped his face. "This was a pretty stupid idea, wasn't it? We should've waited until evening when it was cooler."

"What's the matter, Cadet Anderson? Didn't those parade ground drills at the dear old Citadel prepare you for a little hike in the woods? Gotten soft, have we?"

"I'm fine. I was worried about you."

"Don't bother. All that rehab at the hospital, plus tennis or golf almost every day have done wonders. I don't think I've ever been in better shape."

"I noticed." He grinned, eyeing the sweaty shirt now plastered to my chest.

I reached down and grabbed a pinecone from among the hundreds littering the forest floor and pitched it underhand at him. He caught it in mid-air and flipped it right back. I ducked, and the battle was on.

We trotted down the track flinging missiles at each other and shrieking like a couple of ten-year-olds. Energy spent, we called a truce at last and flopped breathlessly down onto an outcropping of rock. I sipped gratefully from the bottled water Geoff carried in his pack.

We set out again, more sedately this time. Fifteen minutes later I smelled the river. Nothing identifiable, just a slight change in the taste and feel of the air, the cool, clean ripple of a breeze.

The track petered out at the base of a small rise. Geoff took my hand, and we trudged up the gentle incline. I could feel his eyes on my face as we crested the top.

"It's perfect," I breathed, "absolutely perfect." I felt the tension in his hand relax.

Twenty yards ahead and slightly below, the Chicopee River flowed serenely over wellworn stones along its edge. The color of the water changed from sparkling blue to a soft, rippling green as the wind fluttered the branches reflected in its depths. We stood between two ancient live oaks, their screen of Spanish moss making it seem as if we looked through a shifting veil.

Only one or two pines would have to be cut to assure an unobstructed view to the river. The oaks could stay, guardian sentinels at either side of the house.

"Exactly!" Geoff exclaimed when I voiced my observation.

He began moving back and forth, pacing out the dimensions of the house. This room here, that one there. Porches all around and windows everywhere. His enthusiasm was contagious, and soon I was deep into the game. I knocked out imaginary walls, expanded closets, added skylights.

We discussed, argued, compromised, agreed until I could almost see the magnificent Lowcountry house taking shape before my eyes.

The heat finally got to me, and I dropped gratefully onto the sandy ground, my back resting up against the bole of one of the oaks. I lit a cigarette as Geoff unloaded his pack. More water, apples, a couple of candy bars, along with the bug spray were spread out around us.

"How can you stand to see this developed?" I murmured, almost to myself. Geoff's love for this piece of ground, his passion for the home he would build here, was evident in every word and gesture. "This is what Hilton Head must have been like before Charles Fraser got started on Sea Pines."

What had once been an isolated island, rife with deer and woods and accessible only by boat, had become a world-class resort with its attendant hotels, restaurants, visitors, and traffic. I loved living there, but I knew at what price my enjoyment had been purchased.

"Someone's going to do it. Just like Hilton Head. They were lucky it was a man like Fraser, someone who valued the land and the marshes. He set the standard for all the development that followed, helped to keep it in check."

Geoff rose, took a bite out of one of the apples, and looked once more out across the river. "I want to do the same for Grayton. That's one reason I was so excited when they asked me to head up the project. I can make sure it's done right."

"Look," I began, "I'm not exactly a registered tree-hugger. I understand that people have a right to use their land, make a profit, whatever." I grabbed the other apple and joined him. "I guess it just bothers me to think of all this..." I flung my arm wide to encompass all the quiet beauty that surrounded us. "...all of it torn up, bulldozers and graders everywhere. The birds and wildlife chased God knows where."

Geoff slipped an arm around me and smiled ruefully. "You give a damned good impression of a tree-hugger," he said, and I punched his shoulder. "Maybe you should join our young friends down at the barricades."

"What barricades? What friends?"

"Come on, let's go stick our feet in the water."

He pulled me along down the slope to where a dead pine, toppled by wind and time, lay rotting, its barren trunk jutting out over the river. We shed our heavy socks and boots, rolled up our pantslegs, and straddled the tree. My toes just barely skimmed the water.

"Is this by any chance a clumsy attempt to change the subject?"

Geoff, taller than I and farther out on the log, splashed water up at me with his feet, and ignored my question.

"And what was that you said about being selected to head the project? I thought it was all your idea in the first place."

Geoff picked at the rotten bark, tossed a few pieces aimlessly into the current, and watched them float downstream.

"Hey, wanna go skinny dippin'?" He reached for the waistband of his jeans, and I slapped his hand away.

"Knock it off, Geoff."

"What's the matter, you chicken?"

It was the kind of taunt that, thirty years ago, would have set me to ripping off my clothes in a determined effort to prove I was no such thing.

"Nice try."

I finished off the apple and tossed the core sidearm into the woods. It would make a nice lunch for some lucky animal. Geoff did the same.

"Okay, Anderson, give," I said wiping my sticky hands on my jeans. "What is all this stuff about barricades?"

"The Committee Against the Rape of the Environment. CARE. Ever heard of them?"

"No. Catchy little name, though. Have they been giving you trouble?"

Geoff snorted. "Yeah, you could say that. They've taken to blocking the main entrance to the property, over off the highway. We've cut a driveway and set up a temporary information center in a modular building near the river. These sterling pillars of the community are not happy with our development plans. Let's see, how does their propaganda go? 'We are merely exercising our First Amendment rights to peacefully voice our opposition to the proposed rape of our pristine river and adjacent woodlands.' Or some crap like that."

Geoff shinnied off the log and waded back onto the bank. I followed and flopped down beside him. Little shafts of sunlight filtered through the branches and glinted off the silver of his hair.

"Can't you get a restraining order or something?" I picked up a smooth pebble and tried to skip it across the water. It sank after one bounce. I was sadly out of practice.

"Tried that. No go. They don't actually come onto the property, at least not when anyone's around to catch them at it. They just park their four-wheel drives all up and down the highway so it's nearly impossible for anyone to see the signs, let alone turn into the drive."

He plucked a long-stemmed weed from the ground beside him and chewed on it absently. "I mean, would you want to run a gauntlet of bearded rednecks like that bunch that nearly ran us off the road today just to look at a piece of property?"

"That was them? They didn't look like environmentalists to me. In fact, I've seen that line of pickups parked along the road. I didn't realize it had anything to do with your project. I thought it was a gun club meeting or a duck shoot or something like that."

"Not exactly your usual Sierra Club material, are they? It's really kind of scary when you think about it. Sort of like a marriage between the NRA and Greenpeace. Very strange bedfellows."

"What do you mean 'scary'? I admit they look a little rough around the edges, but they're just kids, right? Surely they're not dangerous?"

Geoff tossed aside the weed and began pulling on his socks. "Come on, we'd better head back. Looks like we're about to get dumped on."

I followed his gaze to the southeast and saw dark storm clouds piling up against each other out over the ocean. Against the backdrop of the blazing sun overhead, they looked alarmingly black and ominous.

We gathered our things together and stuffed them back into the pack. I collected my cigarette butts and slipped them into the pocket of my jeans for later disposal. I may not be a card-carrying environmentalist, but I'm not a litterbug, either.

We took one last look at the view from the top of Geoff's rise, then trotted back down the track. The air had cooled since we'd set out, and the woods seemed less alive with creature-sound. They, too, must have sensed the coming of the storm.

"You never answered my question," I said into the heavy stillness.

"About what?"

"About whether or not there's been any violence."

"Not technically, I guess."

The breeze had picked up, and more of it was reaching the floor of the woods. I lifted the sweaty strands of hair that had escaped my baseball cap and felt a cool rush against my neck.

"What does that mean?"

Geoff shrugged. "There have been incidents."

We picked up the pace as the sky overhead continued to darken. I began to wonder if we would reach the car in time. Not that I'd melt in the rain, but we'd left the top down on the Jag, and I didn't want to have to bail it out.

We almost made it. I caught a glimpse of the Jag's shining chrome just as the first dime-sized drops began to splatter through the leaves. We sprinted the last few yards. I helped Geoff wrestle the boot off and toss it into the back seat. We were completely drenched by the time we got the top and the windows up.

"Timing is everything," I laughed, pulling off my cap and shaking out my hair.

The glass all around us had immediately fogged up, and Geoff flipped on the defroster. Thunder echoed around us as warm air filled the car.

The smell hit us both at the same time.

Sweet, wet, slightly nauseating.

"God, what is that?"

"Those bastards!" Geoff whirled around, his hands scrabbling over the back floor on both sides. "Where the hell is it?"

With another curse he flipped up the crumpled leather top cover we had thrown into the back seat, and I screamed.

One open, glassy eye seemed to be staring right at me as the dead squirrel lay curled in a pool of its own still-warm blood.

10

"You should have let me call the cops."

Two hours later, wrapped in Geoff's fluffy white robe, I was still fuming. I paced back and forth in front of the wide sliding glass door that looked out over the balcony of the penthouse condo in Harbour Town.

Geoff rescued the empty mug from my flailing hand and went to refill it from the pot of tea steeping on the counter. I gazed unseeing as, below me, a tall-masted motor sailer inched its way slowly out of the snug marina, past the famous lighthouse, and out into Calibogue Sound.

"I told you, there's no point. They can't do a damned thing."

"Can't or won't?" I accepted the cup of steaming tea and resumed my pacing.

After his initial outburst, Geoff had dealt calmly and efficiently with the mess in the backseat of his Jaguar. He retrieved the Sunday paper and a couple of beach towels from the trunk while I stood shivering in the pelting rain. He wrapped the mutilated squirrel in several sheets of newspaper and laid it gently at the foot of a towering pine. With one towel, he mopped up the worst of the blood, then covered the stained seat with the other.

I had to be coaxed back into the car. I can tolerate just about anything except cruelty to animals. I lusted for the blood of whoever had slaughtered an innocent squirrel in order to make his point.

93

"Well, at least we could have gone down there ourselves and kicked some redneck butt." My left hand had unconsciously curled into a tight fist, and I was banging it against the side of my leg.

"With what? You may have noticed that I don't have a rifle rack strapped to the trunk of the Jag. I think we'd have been pretty much outgunned as well as outmanned."

I snorted, unconvinced, and turned away from the view. "You said you have some other little souvenirs from the CARE gang?"

"Nothing quite as dramatic as a bloody corpse in the backseat, but the message is pretty much the same."

Geoff patted the sofa beside him, and I settled myself into a corner, my feet drawn up under me. He opened the metal clasp on a legal-sized envelope and slid the contents out onto the coffee table in front of us. There were three Polaroid snapshots and some pieces of brown grocery bag paper folded over several times.

I picked up the first photo. Geoff's beautiful black Jaguar rested on four flat tires.

"What's that sticking out?" I pointed to what looked like sticks, red streamers fluttering on the ends, that protruded from each wheel.

"Surveyor's stakes. You know, what we use to mark out the lot lines? They're wood. It took some effort to drive them into the tires."

The second picture showed the remains of a golf cart that had obviously been dismantled with a sledgehammer. Battered pieces lay scattered across the scrubby grass. In the background, the modular welcome center, as well as the propane storage tank beside it, were covered with red, spray-painted graffiti.

"These guys are a real piece of work. Didn't you call the Sheriff?"

"Sure. But without witnesses, what can the cops do? As they were quick to point out to me."

"Where they'd get your car?"

"On the site. I left it in the drive while I took the golf cart out to my lot. Happened while I was gone, apparently."

"So they were definitely trespassing." I shivered as the implication hit me. "God, Geoff, they had to be following you. Or they have the project staked out."

"Probably both. But remember, a lot of these guys are hunters. They're good at stalking. They could be anywhere in the woods, in camouflage, and I'd never spot them."

I studied the final Polaroid, another shot of the drive. The sun glinted off a shiny carpet stretching for several yards into the property.

"Metal shavings, nails, broken bottles, screws," Geoff answered my puzzled look. "Four inches deep. Took one of my crews almost an entire day to clean it up."

I shook my head in disbelief. These people were playing hardball. While the incidents resembled the sort of actions environmental activists had taken in other parts of the country when endangered habitats were threatened by logging or development, there was a viciousness here that seemed out of character. Nastier. More personal.

Geoff unfolded one of the stiff, brown papers and smoothed the creases as he spread it on the table.

I studied the drawing. It was crude, but effective. The old Grayton plantation house, its dilapidated condition conveyed in a few clever pen strokes, was on fire, realistic flames shooting through its sagging roof. In the foreground, a stick-figure man stood beside an open sports car. Large teardrops fell from his head to the ground. Along the sides and top, thick, red paint had been cleverly drizzled, conveying the impression of dripping blood without obscuring the rest of the drawing.

There was no message, not in words, anyway. The threat seemed clear enough without them.

"Whoever the creep is, he's got talent. You're right, Geoff. This is scary stuff."

"The others are pretty much the same. Variations on a theme. I find them tucked under the windshield wipers of the Jag every few days."

He refolded the paper, replaced everything in the envelope, and tossed it on the table. I picked a cigarette out of the pack, and Geoff lit it for me.

"I can't believe this is the work of legitimate environmentalists," I said. "I know some of them have gone to extremes, like chaining themselves to trees, but this is more like…I don't know, like terrorism, I guess."

Geoff propped his bare feet up on the coffee table and leaned back, his hands clasped behind his head. He had changed into clean shorts and T-shirt after his shower. My clothes were still in the dryer.

"What I think," he said, staring up at the high ceiling, "is that there are some local bad-boy elements mixed up in what started out as a legitimate peaceful protest. I know there are people of good conscience who don't want to see any more development in this area. Hell, you're probably one of them."

Geoff glanced over at me, and I nodded. "Guilty as charged."

"But you wouldn't go to these lengths to stop it, would you? No," he answered for me. "People like us write letters to the editor, attend the review board meetings, talk to officials. We don't trash golf carts or threaten to burn down 150-year old historic buildings."

"You're right. So what are you going to do about it?"

"What can I do? I hired a private security force to patrol the property. I put up a chain link fence all across the front, and a ten-foot high gate across the driveway. But there are any number of ways to get in, if you're really determined. Hell, we walked in today without encountering a soul. Another half hour hike down the river and we would have been at the plantation house."

I shuddered, wondering with a jolt how far we had been from the site of Derek Johnson's murder. The placid Chicopee had been witnessing some less than peaceful events lately.

Geoff sighed and reached to pull me into his arms. I went with only a brief hesitation, my head coming to rest on his shoulder.

"All I can hope for is that, once we break ground and they realize they're not going to stop us, maybe they'll just go away."

"When do think that'll be? Groundbreaking, I mean." The little worms of doubt had begun squirming around in my gut again. I snuggled closer against the solid warmth of his body, trying to shut out the image of Miss Addie's concerned face.

"I can't really say, for sure. A couple of months, maybe. There's still a few glitches to be worked out."

Talk to me, Geoff, I pleaded silently. *Tell me. Don't make me cross-examine you. Offer it, openly. Please.*

"Any problem with the investors?" I forced myself to ask softly, when he didn't elaborate. "About the delays or any of this trouble on the site?"

"I've managed to keep those incidents out of the papers, so it's not common knowledge. And no, I haven't heard any complaints." I felt his tension as his hand tightened on my shoulder. "Why?"

I couldn't do it, couldn't spoil the wonder of being cradled again in strong, loving arms. The late afternoon sun, as brilliant as ever after the passing of the storm, streamed through the glass door. I felt like a child—safe, warm, and drowsy.

"Never mind," I whispered.

He relaxed a little then, running his fingers through my hair where it lay curled against his shoulder. My arm lay loosely across his chest. I fought unsuccessfully to stifle a yawn.

"Why don't you take a little nap? You know, it's mostly my fault you're exhausted. I've kept you up until all hours for the past two nights. And this afternoon was a pretty unnerving experience. You're entitled."

"Yeah, you sure know how to show a girl a good time." I tilted my head back so he could see I was teasing. The look on his face took my breath away. I gulped and tried to wriggle out of his embrace. "I'd better check on my clothes."

"Oh, no you don't. You stay right where you are." Geoff pulled me gently back into his arms. "I've been dreaming about this moment ever since I first touched your hand, first felt your skin on mine."

"Geoff, I…"

I felt the tempo of his breathing change, and the air crackled with that same electricity that had jumped between us on the deck of the restaurant two days ago.

Slowly, tentatively, Geoff lowered his face to mine. He gave me every opportunity to turn away, pull back. I did neither. Our first kiss was everything my teenaged heart had imagined it would be.

His lips brushed my eyes, my cheeks, my neck. He pushed the robe back to caress my shoulders. His fingers gently stroked the puckered skin, traced the scars that criss-crossed my back. Tenderly he made love to my hurt, drawing it into himself, setting me free to give—and to receive.

I helped him pull off his shirt, then ran my hands over the warmth of his chest, felt the swift pounding of his heart, echoing my own.

It was a waltz, a slow, dreamy dance. There was desire, but no urgency. Passion, but no haste. We touched, tasted, explored as the dying sun cast its soft glow across the sofa where we lay.

When Geoff rose and held out his hand to me, I clasped it without hesitation. As we walked slowly toward the bedroom, he paused to tilt my face up toward his own.

"Are you sure?" he whispered. His eyes searched mine, demanding honesty.

Am I? I asked myself. For a moment I wavered, closing my eyes as Rob's sweet face floated up out of my memory. And then he was gone, never to be forgotten, *never*, but stored away in a special place in my heart that would always belong only to him.

Death receded, and life beckoned.

I opened my eyes and laid my hand tenderly against Geoff's cheek as I reached up to brush his lips with mine. My robe dropped to the floor as I pushed the door closed behind us.

I awoke to whistling and the smell of charcoal. There was no momentary disorientation, no *Where am I?* panic. I knew exactly where I was. And why.

My body glowed, my skin alive to the touch of the cool sheet where it lay across my legs. I stretched luxuriantly and sat up. In the dim light cast by a small lamp on the bedside table, I could just make out Geoff's robe draped over the back of a Queen Anne chair. I grabbed it up and headed for the shower.

When I stepped back into the bedroom, toweling my hair, I found my clothes neatly folded on the foot of the bed. I tossed the wet towel over the shower rod, tightened the belt of the robe, and followed the smell of grilling steaks out into the kitchen.

Geoff, wearing only a pair of navy blue sweatpants, was on the balcony flipping T-bones off the grill onto a platter. The glass-topped dining table was set with colorful earthenware plates on woven rattan placemats. Candles in long-stemmed, crystal holders stood incongruously amid an array of mismatched cutlery.

Geoff slid the door open, set the platter on the table, and pulled me into his arms. His kiss against my forehead was sweet and tender.

"Hungry?" he asked, releasing me and pulling out a chair.

"Ravenous. Though maybe I should get dressed first," I added as he opened the drapes wider.

"Not a chance. Besides, we're invisible up here."

The marina below was alive with activity. Harbour Town is a favorite with tourists and islanders alike. Even with the doors closed, the hum of voices and the muted strains of live music drifted up to us.

Geoff reached around me to place a bowl of salad on the table, followed by two brimming wine glasses.

"Gingerale for you," he said before I could ask.

He lit the candles, then turned off the remaining lamps. Suddenly, the marina seemed to leap into life. The boats riding at anchor were outlined by their dock lights against the deep purple of the night sky.

People, silhouetted in the spill of light from the windows of the shops that lined the harbor, crowded the broad esplanade, savoring the soft breeze that floated in off the Sound.

"To us, and to our future." Geoff raised his glass and touched it briefly to the rim of my own. The deep, rich red of his Cabernet Sauvignon glistened in the candlelight.

"To tomorrow," I responded, "and to whatever it brings."

I had learned, in the past year, not to look too far ahead.

A brief frown flitted across Geoff's face and was quickly gone. "Eat," he commanded, grabbing the salad and serving me out a generous helping.

I cut into the steak. It was pink and moist.

"Perfect," I announced around a mouthful of salad. "How did you know?"

"You look like a medium-rare kind of girl."

Geoff reached behind his chair to slide the door partway open. Music and laughter from the crowd below accompanied us as we attacked the food.

"Interesting table setting," I remarked as I sat back, full and satisfied.

Geoff retrieved my cigarettes from the coffee table and did his Cary Grant routine again. " 'Interesting', huh? I prefer to think of it as eclectic. When you've been divorced twice, you tend to end up with the leftovers of the household goods."

"It must be tough being so far away from your kids," I said. "Do you see them often?"

"No, not really. But you know how it is. Teenagers never have time for their parents, even when they live in the same house."

He stood abruptly and began to stack the plates.

"Here, let me do that," I said trying to cover the awkward silence my tactless question had created. I rounded the table and pushed him back into his chair. "The cook shouldn't have to clean up, too."

He reached up and pulled me playfully onto his lap. The robe fell open, and he ran his hand lightly up the outside of my bare leg.

I appeared to have been forgiven.

"The dishes can wait," he murmured into my hair.

His lips traveled down my throat, across the sharp ridge of my collar bone while his fingers fumbled at the belt of my robe. I lay back in his arms, my body already responding to the new familiarity of his touch.

When the doorbell rang, we nearly toppled onto the floor.

Geoff clutched me tightly as we struggled to regain our balance. He looked so dismayed, I had to bite back a fit of the giggles.

"Maybe they'll go away," he whispered, kissing me lightly on the lips.

The bell pealed again, longer this time, as if someone leaned on the button.

"God damn it," Geoff growled. Reluctantly he set me on my feet and ran a hand through his tousled hair.

I couldn't help myself. The suppressed laughter burst out of me. Geoff held onto his scowl until the absurdity of the situation finally struck him, too. We hung on each other, gasping for breath, trying unsuccessfully to control ourselves.

The bell stopped, to be followed by a sharp knocking.

"Persistent little bugger." Geoff gulped and wiped his streaming eyes.

"I'll wait in there," I said, wrapping the robe around me and heading for the bedroom as Geoff approached the door.

I had just slipped from the room when I heard a low exchange that quickly escalated into loud voices. One of them sent a flush of embarrassment washing over the entire length of my half-naked body.

"Look, Tanner," I heard Geoff yell, "you can't just barge in here and throw your weight around. I don't give a damn if you are a cop."

"Where is she?" my brother-in-law barked as I turned and bolted into the bathroom.

11

The silence in the white sheriff's cruiser crackled with unspoken anger. Static and an occasional garbled squawk from the radio broke the quiet, but not the tension.

Sergeant Redmond Tanner and I stared straight ahead as the overhanging limbs of the live oaks and pines along Greenwood Drive flashed by. The uniformed guard at the security gate snapped us a brief salute as we passed out of Sea Pines and negotiated the Circle.

"How did you know where to find me?"

I didn't exactly mean it as an accusation, but it came out sounding like one, anyway.

Red shot me a look that was part anger, part exasperation. The scowl puckering his face had not relaxed since the moment I'd emerged, fully dressed, from the bedroom. Red had delivered his news in a tight voice and few words. Then he'd hustled me out the door of Geoff's condo with the same degree of solicitude he might have shown to an escaped felon.

"Red? I asked you...Oh, this is ridiculous! You're acting like a damned two-year-old."

I snatched my bag off the floor and rummaged for my cigarettes.

"You can't smoke in the cruiser."

"So arrest me."

I rolled down the window and let the humid night air suck the smoke away in lazy spirals.

"I mean it. It's against regulations."

"Tough. I pay a hell of a lot of taxes in this county, so this *my* damn car, bought and paid for. And you have a damn nerve squawking about regulations. Is it regulation for off-duty cops to hunt down ordinary citizens using county property?"

"I didn't *hunt* you down. The Judge asked me to find you, and I did. End of story."

"Did he ask you to embarrass me, threaten my friends, and kidnap me, too? Or was that your own idea?"

I flipped the half-smoked cigarette out the window and wound it back up as we made the turn into Port Royal Plantation.

"And don't start in about littering," I snapped as Red opened his mouth to speak. "This is private property—*my* private property—and I'll throw out whatever I damn well please!"

Red slowed the cruiser and rolled to a stop at the gate. I leaned over, and Harry, the regular night-duty guard, recognized me.

"Evenin', Miz Tanner," he drawled. "No trouble, I hope?"

"No, everything's fine, Harry. Thanks."

The short, chunky black man waved us through. I used the few minutes it took us to wind our way around the golf course and into my driveway to try to get my temper under control.

Red pulled up alongside my LeBaron, put the cruiser in park, and turned off the ignition. I was reaching for the door latch when he laid a tentative hand on my arm.

"Look, I'm sorry, okay?"

The house and grounds were in total darkness, and I couldn't see his face. If his voice was any indication though, the scowl had been replaced by a look of repentance.

"Maybe I got a little carried away," he said.

"A little?"

Red's laugh dropped the tension level several degrees. "Okay, more than a little. But I worry about you, damn it. I know you don't like it, but I can't seem to help myself."

"I know. And I appreciate it. Really. Most of the time."

"Friends again?" he ventured, holding out his hand.

"Friends."

I took the hand, and he quickly covered mine with his other.

"Be careful, Bay, all right? I'm sure you think you know this guy, but that was a long time ago. People change. Anderson may be a different man from the boy you remember."

His echoing of my own thoughts made me squirm just a little. Reluctantly, he let go of my hand as I pulled away. "Thanks for the advice."

"But I should butt out, right?"

I smiled and opened the door. "Thanks for letting me know about Miss Addie. They didn't give you any hint of what happened to her, did they? How serious it is?"

"Nope, sorry. All I know is what the Judge told me, that some English dame from the home called him and said they needed someone down there right away."

"Okay, thanks. I guess I'll find out soon enough. Tell the Judge I'll be in touch when I have some news."

"Want me to drive you to the hospital?"

"No, thanks. I'll probably need my car. See you later."

I hadn't intended to go into the house first, but I was pretty certain Red would hover until I was out of reach. I snapped on lights and waved to him from the kitchen window as he backed slowly out of the drive.

I poured myself a glass of ice water from the jug in the refrigerator, then punched the PLAY button on the answering machine.

The clipped, British voice of Mrs. Dixon resonated off the kitchen walls, and I reached to turn down the volume. She was probably used to talking to folks who were just a bit hard of hearing.

"Mrs. Tanner, this is Ariadne Dixon of The Cedars. Please call me immediately upon your return. I have some urgent news regarding your friend, Miss Hammond. Thank you."

Next came the Judge and Red, both with basically the same *Where the hell are you?* tone. Mrs. Dixon must have called my father after failing to reach me. He, in turn, had sent Red out to track me down.

How did she know to do that? I wondered, as her voice boomed out again from the machine.

"It is imperative that I speak with you immediately. Please meet me at the hospital the moment you return. Miss Hammond has been admitted."

I switched out the lights, locked the door, and jumped in the car. The hospital was only a couple of miles away. I could be there in ten minutes. Though why *I* was being summoned was still a mystery, one I intended to unravel soon.

Ariadne Dixon, immaculate in a navy blue linen dress that screamed Saks, was pacing the tiled floor in front of the nurses' station when I stepped off the elevator. The look of relief that lit her face when she spotted me made my heart sink.

"Mrs. Tanner, thank heavens you're here. I've been quite frantic."

She didn't look frantic. Every hair was glued precisely in place, and her makeup was flawless. She took my arm and guided me to an alcove furnished with two chairs upholstered in teal green cotton and a low table spread with tattered magazines. We sat, and Ariadne Dixon crossed her trim ankles and regarded me solemnly.

"What happened?" Now that I was here, she seemed reluctant to speak. "How's Miss Addie?"

"This is not really my responsibility, you know. The director and his assistant are at a conference in Washington. The Council on Aging, I believe. So dedicated, Mr. Fuenes is. And Miss Grace, as well. Quite respected in their fields. We're very fortunate to have such..."

"About Miss Addie?" I interrupted her without a qualm. I had been virtually hijacked for this supposed errand of mercy, and my patience was pretty well shot.

"Of course, Mrs. Tanner. I was merely trying to explain why it is that *I* am here rather than those more properly in charge."

"I'm sure you've handled everything quite competently. Now, what happened? How badly is she hurt? And why did you call *me*?"

She didn't answer my questions immediately. It was her story, and she was going to tell it in her own way.

"About eight o'clock, Miss Hammond's call button was activated. Briefly, you understand, as if she might have bumped it accidentally. It happens all the time. The staff were busy with other residents, helping them settle in for the night, running errands. The usual. We call it assisted living because we try to help with whatever tasks the residents find difficult to handle themselves. We're not a nursing home. We don't keep 24-hour watch on everyone."

"I understand. Go on."

"I simply want to make clear that we were not ignoring Miss Hammond. The call was not repeated, so staff saw no need for urgency. It was a matter of priorities."

"I'm sure they do an excellent job." I could see the specter of a negligence lawsuit lurking behind all this self-absolving explanation.

"We *all* try to do our best for our residents," she said stiffly.

"So it was some time before anyone went to check on Miss Hammond?" I prompted.

"Fifteen or twenty minutes, no more. It was little Maria, one of our newer aides, who found the poor woman, on the floor next to her bed. Maria quickly summoned senior staff who determined that Miss Hammond was unconscious, but, thank God, not…"

"Dead," I finished for her.

"Quite. The ambulance was ordered, and I accompanied her here. The examination has revealed a badly bruised hip and a broken wrist.

Also, a slight concussion and a cut on her forehead where she apparently hit her head on the bedside table during her fall."

"But she's going to be okay?"

"Of course," Ariadne Dixon nodded.

"But what actually happened? I mean, how did she come to fall in the first place?"

"I really have no idea. Perhaps her doctor can enlighten you."

The irritating woman rose and smoothed out the wrinkles in her linen dress. "Well, then, I shall leave things in your capable hands, Mrs. Tanner. Please keep us informed of Miss Hammond's progress." She turned toward the hallway.

"Hold it!"

My voice echoed off the tiled floor and low ceiling. A nurse, studying charts behind the desk, glared at me over the half-glasses perched on the end of her nose.

Mrs. Dixon paused and raked me with that same disdainful look I had received from her on the day of my first visit to The Cedars. Still in jeans, wrinkled T-shirt and hiking boots, I had once again failed to measure up to her exacting standards.

"What do you mean, you leave everything in my hands?" I lowered my voice and tried to force some of the belligerence out of it. "I don't understand."

"As next of kin, I assumed you would be taking charge of Miss Hammond's care."

"Next of kin? We're not even related. She was...is an old friend of my mother's, that's all."

"How odd. Just yesterday she altered her file, naming you and your father, Judge Simpson, as next of kin to be notified in case of emergency. She even consulted with her attorney about it."

Mrs. Dixon fumbled with her handbag, adjusting the strap more comfortably over her shoulder. For some reason she didn't want to look me in the face.

"I was reluctant to handle such a serious matter myself, it being more properly the place of Mr. Fuenes or Miss Grace to do so. But Miss Hammond was quite insistent that it be done immediately."

"Look, Mrs. Dixon..."

"I'm afraid I may have overstepped my authority." She appeared to be talking more to herself than to me. Then she sighed, the great weight of the bureaucracy of The Cedars apparently too great a burden for her fragile shoulders to bear. "But, what's done is done. You are named as next of kin, so naturally I assumed..."

This made no sense. Surely Miss Addie had family. I remembered sisters and a brother somewhere. Pictures of nieces and nephews...

"Who was on her file before? I mean before she changed it?" I asked.

Ariadne Dixon drew herself up to her full five feet, four inches and raised her chin a fraction. "I really couldn't say. That information is confidential. Good evening, Mrs. Tanner."

The little heels of her navy blue Ferragamo pumps clicked loudly in the charged stillness that permeates hospital corridors in the dead of night. I watched her disappear into the elevator without a backward glance.

I shoved my hands into my pockets and resisted the urge to bolt down the steps, intercept the elevator, and shake her until she got it through her head that I was *not* being saddled with this responsibility. Instead, I flopped myself down onto the soft cushions of the chair and slumped, my long legs stretched out in front of me.

Now what?

I glanced up to see the disapproving nurse eyeing me once again. Her expression had softened, now that I had quieted down. She beckoned to me with a crooked finger.

A sheaf of papers was stacked neatly in front of her, and she held a pen in one hand. She was a big woman, blonde and blue-eyed, fortyish. Her white uniform stretched tightly across impressive breasts and hips. She looked like the kind of nurse who could be both sympathetic to her patients and hell on wheels with anyone who failed to follow procedure.

Reluctantly, I hauled myself up out of the chair. Little clumps of dirt from my mud-caked boots littered the floor around me. I ignored them and approached the desk.

"Sorry, but I couldn't help overhearing," the nurse, whose name tag read *Judy McKay*, said pointedly. "You're the next of kin of Adelaide Hammond?"

"No, actually I'm not. We're not related at all. I think there's been some mistake here."

Nurse McKay consulted some papers attached to a brown clipboard. "You're Lydia Tanner, right?"

"Yes, but…"

"Here's the power of attorney, signed and notarized. There's also one for a Talbot Simpson."

"My father."

"Well, apparently Mrs. Hammond trusted you to look after her. I'll need you to sign some forms."

"It's *Miss* Hammond, and I'm not at all sure about this."

"Medicare is primary, plus she's also got supplemental coverage, so you won't be held personally liable for any payments." The disapproval was back on her face and heavy in her voice.

"It's not that. It's just…Look, is her doctor around? Maybe I should talk to him before I sign anything."

Bad move. I had questioned her authority.

"Dr. Winter has left for the night," Nurse McKay snapped. "And he has nothing to do with the paperwork. Perhaps I should contact your father, as the other power of attorney. Maybe he'll be a little more cooperative."

I was batting a thousand tonight. I had managed to alienate just about everyone I had come in contact with.

I surrendered, picked up the pen, and held it poised over the stack. With a grunt of satisfaction, Nurse McKay pointed and flipped while I scratched my name. Our business concluded, we were pals again.

"Miss Hammond is sedated and resting comfortably," she replied to my request to see Miss Addie. "Come back tomorrow, around ten. You can talk to her doctor then, too. Don't worry," she added, patting my hand in motherly fashion, " we'll take good care of her."

It was after one o'clock when I finally emerged through the double doors of the hospital lobby and into the sweet night air. The next thing to hit my lungs was the smoke from the cigarette I needed so badly my hands actually shook as I lighted it.

I leaned against the warm stone of the building and stared up at an unbelievably clear sky. A thin sliver of new moon lay cradled in the branches of a swaying pine. Tree frogs chorused around me, and the swift beat of an owl's wings ruffled the air overhead.

What the hell is going on here? I asked myself. *Why am I suddenly being dragged into everybody else's problems? Why can't they all just leave me alone?*

Receiving no brilliant flashes of insight into these pointless questions, I crushed out my cigarette in the sand-filled receptacle and plodded wearily across the deserted parking lot to my car. My shoulder ached, and I rubbed it absently as I swung out into the drive. An ambulance, its lights dark and siren quiet, rolled past me and up to the emergency room entrance. The paramedics seemed to be in no great hurry. I tried not to think about what that probably meant for whoever was inside.

Through a haze of weariness that penetrated down to my bones, I headed toward home. My only thoughts were of a hot shower and bed. Despite my nap at Geoff's, I felt as if I could sleep for a week.

Geoff!

My face flushed in embarrassment as I relived the scene in his penthouse living room. My brother-in-law had done everything short of accusing Geoff of rape. It hadn't taken a rocket scientist to figure out what we'd been up to when Red came pounding on the door. And Sergeant Redmond Tanner, his instincts honed by years of being lied to by experts, had surely read the guilt written all over my face.

And why the hell should I feel guilty? I demanded, getting angry all over again as Harry waved me through the security gate, and I turned toward home. It was none of Red's business who I slept with. In fact, it was *nobody's* damn business except mine.

I had forgotten to leave any lights on, and the house looked dark and forbidding. Strange that it should seem so tonight, I thought. I had never been afraid of being alone, at least not in the sense of being the only one in the house, not even after Rob's murder. But so much had happened in the last few days, I was probably just a little edgier than usual.

Far out toward the beach, I saw the faint glow of a flashlight, bobbing up and down as if someone carried it while they ran. Or maybe it was in a boat, riding the soft swells of the ocean.

Probably crabbers, or late-night fishermen, taking advantage of the tide.

I trudged slowly up the steps, my climbing boots feeling as if they weighed forty pounds apiece.

The hell with a shower, I told myself as I dropped my keys on the hall table and headed straight for the bedroom. I'd already had two today, three if you counted getting drenched in the rain.

I thought briefly about calling Geoff and the Judge, both of whom would probably be fretting to hear from me.

Tomorrow is another day, Scarlet whispered in my ear.

I left my clothes in a heap on the floor and dropped naked onto the king-sized sheets. I didn't even bother to close the drapes. The breeze off the ocean was deliciously cool.

Had I been less exhausted, I would probably have been more alert to the signs, subtle though they were. Whether it would have made any difference to the eventual outcome of things, I'll never know for sure.

I try not to think about it. But it's hard.

12

Adelaide Boyce Hammond lay propped up by several pillows, her rose-colored bed jacket a sharp contrast against the snowy hospital linen. Her chalky face looked naked without her thick bifocals.

"Lydia, is that you, dear? How thoughtful of you to come."

Miss Addie's left wrist, encased in plaster, lay immobile against the light cotton blanket tucked in at her waist. Her right hand fumbled for her glasses, just out of reach on the table beside the bed.

"Here, let me." I crossed into the room and fitted the wire-rimmed spectacles onto her face.

It was a semi-private room, but the other bed was unoccupied. The privacy curtains had been pulled back from around Miss Addie's space, and the full force of the morning sun streamed through a tall, wide window.

Though I loathed hospital rooms, this one was better than most. An attempt had been made to bring some civilized touches to its stark utility, with overstuffed chairs flanking the window and soft Monet prints grouped on two of the walls. But the IV stand with its tubes snaking down and the constant beeping of the monitors left no doubt that this was still a far cry from home.

I leaned over and planted a kiss on her forehead, pulled up the straight-backed visitor's chair, and sat down next to the bed.

"How are you feeling?" I heard myself asking.

How I had hated that question, repeated endlessly by every solicitous friend and co-worker who had dutifully trooped up to visit me when *I* had been the one trapped in the grid of tubes and electrodes. Yet here I was, asking this poor old woman that same inane question, in the same soft, lugubrious voice that had driven *me* crazy a few months before.

Miss Addie, however, was a better woman than I. She patted my hand where it lay next to hers on the bed. "Don't you worry about me, dear. We Hammonds are pretty tough old birds. It's in the genes, you know."

"Can I get you anything? Books, magazines, a newspaper?"

"No dear, but thank you all the same. Apparently someone from The Cedars brought me some of my things last night." Miss Addie fingered the bed jacket with her good hand. Suddenly her face clouded over.

"What is it? Are you in pain? I'll get a nurse." I was on my feet, headed for the door, when her voice, surprisingly loud and commanding, stopped me.

"No!" Then, "No, thank you," she said more calmly. "Please, sit back down here, Lydia."

I went meekly back to my chair, puzzled by the change in her demeanor. For some moments, she was silent. Her face pinched in concentration, she seemed to be struggling with some question in her mind. Then she nodded, a decision apparently reached.

"Lydia, something very strange is going on. I really don't want to involve you, but I believe I have no choice."

"What is it? You know I'll help in any way I can."

"You already have, dear, just by being here. I feel much safer already."

"I don't understand. Why wouldn't you feel safe?"

"Lydia, do you think I'm senile? I mean, do I seem to have control of my faculties?"

Loaded question, I thought as the old woman's eyes searched my face. I'd spent only a couple of hours in her presence in the last fifteen years. Who was I to make such a judgment? She *had* been a little vague at lunch the other day, unsure about her investment in Grayton's Race and confused about the details. And she seemed to dwell a lot on the past. But did that make her senile? At eighty-plus, she had a lot of past to remember.

Then I recalled her twinkling eyes and the wry humor she had displayed, and I shook my head. "No, I don't think you're senile. Maybe a little forgetful…"

She smiled at this and nodded.

"…but from what I've observed in the brief time we've spent together, you seem as in control as anyone your age has a right to expect."

"Good. Because what I'm about to tell you will sound crazy, and I wanted to be certain you were inclined to believe me before I begin."

"Let me ask you something first. Why did you have the Judge and me listed as your next of kin? Surely you still have family, don't you?"

"Of course, but they're all so far away. My younger sister, Edwina, is in Natchez and in poor health. The oldest, Daphne, is in a home outside Atlanta. Clarissa passed away twenty years ago. And their children are scattered all over the country. I only hear from them at Christmas."

"Don't you have a brother?"

"You mean Win."

Edwin Hollister Hammond II had been "Win" since the day he was born, or so I'd been told. I remembered him now. A tall, imposing man, approaching middle age, or so it seemed to me, the first time I was aware of him as a visitor at *Presqu'isle*. A cheek-pincher who reeked of rum as I recalled, which was why I tended to avoid him.

"Of course. Win. Where is he?"

"I have no idea. Daddy disinherited him, you know. Win never quite believed he'd actually do it, you see, no matter how many times Daddy threatened, so he hung around, waiting for Daddy to die. After the will was read and he found out he really *had* received nothing, he just disappeared. Walked right out the door of the study and vanished. I heard once he'd gone to South America, but no one really knows for certain."

Miss Addie smiled, a sad, sweet expression that made me swallow hard. "I've always missed Win. He was the baby of the family, you know, and my sisters and Mama spoiled him terribly. Oh, I know what everyone said. That he was a scoundrel, always involved in some shady scheme or other. But he was so dashing, a real charmer. The girls were wild for him. Why, I remember…"

The interruption came in the shape of a formidable black woman whose starched white uniform was dazzling against her ebony skin. She had shoulders like a linebacker. The inevitable question was out of her mouth before she even reached the bed.

"And how are we feelin' this mornin'?"

Miss Addie and I exchanged a knowing look.

The nurse continued her interrogation without waiting for a reply. She inquired about headaches, dizziness, pain, while she fussed with the IV, straightened the bedclothes, and made note of temperature, blood pressure, and pulse.

She had asked me to leave when she first began her examination, but Miss Addie had insisted that I stay. The nurse, who had apparently forgotten her name badge, had grudgingly agreed. Finished prodding at last, she placed a cup with two tiny white pills on the wheeled tray table, swung it across the bed, and poured water from a carafe.

Miss Addie pushed the table away.

"Y'all need to take 'em now, Miz Hammond. They'se for the pain, and they'll make you sleepy. And then we'll have to aks your daughter here to leave, so's y'all can get some rest."

"I'm not…" I began, but was cut off.

"I'll jes wait 'til y'all swallow 'em down."

The nurse stood, arms folded across a surprisingly flat chest, her stance somehow menacing. Miss Addie finally gave in.

"Tha's a good girl," Nurse No-Name crooned as she took the glass from Miss Addie's hand and set it on the bedside table.

I itched to slap her. She made the old woman sound like a puppy being praised for peeing on the newspaper instead of on the rug.

"I'll just sit with her until she falls asleep." I didn't phrase it as a question, and Florence Nightingale got the message. She lumbered out without another word.

I promised myself I would find Dr. Winter as soon as possible and see about getting Miss Addie out of here. I knew from my own experience that she'd recover more quickly in her own surroundings. I would hire a private duty nurse to look after her.

"Lydia, dear, you must listen now. I need to tell you about these incidents."

"Incidents?"

"Yes. Over the past few days, someone has been in my rooms. Not the cleaning staff, you understand. I know all of them, and they're quite trustworthy. No, it's someone else, someone going through my things."

"Are you sure?"

"Yes, I'm afraid I am. First it was my desk—papers and so on. Then some of my little geegaws, figurines and such. Not quite where they should be on the tables, you see. Even my lingerie has been disarranged. Whoever it is, they're very neat and careful. But you see, I'm quite a meticulous person myself. That's how I know."

Miss Addie's eyes were beginning to glaze over as the painkiller took effect. "Mama always insisted on orderliness, everything in its place."

"But why? Do you keep money in your rooms? Jewelry?"

"A little. But nothing is ever taken. Just…disturbed."

She stifled a yawn and slid a little farther down in the bed.

"We'll talk about this another time, all right?" I asked. I could see she was struggling to stay awake. "You just rest now. I'll come back tomorrow."

"No. Please. I want to tell you." Miss Addie's voice was slurred. It reminded me somehow of my mother's. "My fall was not an accident."

"What are you saying?"

"I came back early. Forgot my sweater. Someone was there."

"In your apartment? Who?"

"Didn't see. Pushed me."

Her eyes were closed now, but her face was still scrunched up with the effort to hold on to consciousness.

"Someone did this deliberately? But why? I don't understand."

Miss Addie was fast asleep. Her head rolled gently to one side, pushing her glasses askew. I stood and eased them off her face. I removed one of the pillows from behind her back and pulled the blanket up over her arms.

A wave of tenderness for this vulnerable old lady swept over me. I smoothed a stray lock of white hair off her forehead, and her eyes opened suddenly, startling me. For a brief moment they were clear and aware, her gaze locked on mine as if trying to send a message directly into my brain.

"It was those awful gardenias," she whispered, her lips barely moving.

Or at least that's what I thought she'd said. But that made no more sense than anything else she'd told me that morning.

I had meant it when I'd reassured her that she was not senile. Yet she claimed someone had been rifling her rooms, going through her things. That this someone had pushed her when she surprised him or her in the act, causing her injuries.

It was much more likely that she had suffered a spell, perhaps even a mild stroke, lost her balance, and fallen, striking her head on the nightstand. That made more sense than a deliberate attack by an unseen prowler.

And yet, fantastic as her story seemed, she'd given me no good reason not to believe her.

The last few days, I thought, watching the gentle rise and fall of her thin chest. *Since she had talked to me about her fears for her investment? Surely this couldn't have anything to do with Grayton's Race, could it?*

My decision came swiftly and easily.

With a quick look over my shoulder at the closed door, I eased out the drawer of the bedside table. A spare box of tissues, some straws, and a well-thumbed Bible were all I found. Crossing to the wardrobe, I pulled open the double doors. A soft pink dress in a muted print hung neatly from one of the wooden hangers. On the floor, a pair of low-heeled beige shoes rested precisely side by side. The top shelf yielded a surprisingly delicate lacy white slip, bra, and panties folded in a neat pile. Underneath them, I found the object of my search: a trim, beige leather handbag.

I stepped back into the bathroom and closed the door partway. I didn't want to get into a lengthy explanation of why I was digging through Miss Addie's purse should some officious aide come bustling into the room.

There is no such thing as privacy in a hospital.

Her wallet contained forty-six dollars and change, a gold Visa card, a bank ID card, and a driver's license that had expired four years ago. The rest of the bag held a white handkerchief, her resident's pass to The Cedars, an expensive-looking gold fountain pen, and her keys.

I pocketed the key ring and the pass and returned the bag to the wardrobe shelf. I stole a quick look at Miss Addie, who seemed to be sleeping peacefully.

I'll check it out, I promised her silently. If nothing else, I could reassure her that her fears were groundless.

I picked up my bag and slipped quietly out the door.

I had missed Dr. Winter. He had completed his rounds and returned to his office in nearby Bluffton by the time I checked in again at the nurses' station. The woman on duty gave me his number, and I left mine with her, along with a request for him to call me after he'd examined Miss Addie again later in the day.

The full force of the midday heat struck me like a blow when I emerged from the hospital and headed for my car. I lowered the windows, then the top, and cranked up the air conditioning. My stomach grumbled, reminding me that it was lunchtime. I could stop for a sandwich now, or head on down to The Cedars. This might be a good time to snoop, while everyone was busy eating.

Traffic was heavy, the usual tourist influx swelled by the locals on their lunch hours. Half an hour and a few frayed nerves later, I turned in at the gate of The Cedars, flashed Miss Addie's pass at the guard, and followed the signs through the piney woods to the building marked Marsh Edge. I'd gotten her condo number from her bank ID. I pulled into the designated space and sat, the motor running, my nerve suddenly slipping away.

What do you think you're doing here, Tanner? This isn't one of your detective novels, you know.

I lit a cigarette and ran a hand through my tangled hair.

The annoying voice in my head was right, of course. If there really was anything to Adelaide Boyce Hammond's story, I should call Red—turn it all over to the cops. That would be the logical thing to do.

However, logic—and orderly thinking—had not been governing my life lately. I had been running off in all directions, first getting myself involved in Derek Johnson's death and Isaiah Smalls' arrest, then jumping into the Grayton's Race controversy. I had flung accusations, attempted illegal computer hacking, and, finally, slept with the chief suspect. Now here I was, ready to leap into…what? I couldn't explain what I was looking for, not even to myself.

Not exactly the kind of behavior an obsessive-compulsive *bean-counter* was expected to display. Chaos had always been my enemy. Even as a child I had reveled in neat columns and rows of numbers, their unwavering perfection susceptible to no capricious whim or subjective interpretation.

Two plus two will always equal four.

Truth—constant, predictable, immutable—in a simple equation. Therein lay happiness, safety—and control.

Or so my personal philosophy had always gone.

So what's it gonna be? I asked myself as I crushed out the cigarette.

Two white-haired ladies, trim in tailored slacks and low-heeled shoes, cast suspicious glances in my direction as they strolled past.

Time to fish or cut bait, little girl, the Judge's voice boomed inside my head.

I rummaged in my bag for Miss Addie's keys, turned off the car, and marched purposefully toward the building.

"'In for a penny, in for a pound,'" I mumbled under my breath as I pushed open the door and headed for the elevator.

Empty, the apartment would have been open and spacious. It was a corner unit with tall windows flanking a real brick fireplace. Ten-foot ceilings rested upon carved oak crown moldings. A formal dining room stood opposite a bright, cheery kitchen with a breakfast nook nestled in the curve of a bay window.

Unfortunately—or so it seemed to me—almost every square inch of space was occupied with what must have been the entire contents of the old Hammond estate. Spindly-legged tables were crammed in between massive chests and armoires; overstuffed chairs fought for space with a delicate Empire sofa. One entire wall of the dining area was taken up by a nineteenth-century mahogany sideboard stuffed with several different patterns of china. It looked as if there were at least three complete services for twelve or more.

I edged my way through the maze of furniture along a well-worn path that offered the only unobstructed route across the plush cream carpeting. I paused in the doorway of the master suite and turned back to survey what had to be a fortune in genuine antiques.

Hand-crocheted antimacassars adorned the back of every chair; Queen Anne tables were littered with expensive bric-a-brac: Lalique, Dresden, and Hummel, along with carved jade Chinoiserie, and several squat little figures that looked to my untrained eye like pre-Columbian art.

The walls, a soft ivory, were plastered with paintings of all sizes and periods, most of them oils in heavy gilt frames. I was no expert, but some of my mother's obsession must have seeped unnoticed into my brain. I was sure one was a Holbein, and another looked remarkably like Sargent.

"This stuff belongs in a museum," I told the refrigerated air that circulated gently through unseen vents. Already the place had that dead, flat smell that pervades closed-up, unused rooms.

I turned my attention back to Miss Addie's bedroom. A beautiful cherry rice bed dominated the center of the room, its graceful tapered posts polished to a deep, rich glow. The tops of the matching bureau and nightstand held the same, priceless litter as had the tables in the living room. An inlaid teakwood jewelry case rested on a cutlace runner across the top of the dresser. I lifted the lid and did a cursory examination of its contents. The pearls were there—the ones she had worn at our lunch date—along with a square cut blue topaz ring that I immediately coveted. The rest looked to be costume stuff, nothing remotely worth bashing a little old lady over the head for.

Two heavy crystal perfume bottles caught my eye, and I reached to remove the stoppers, bringing each to my nose. Essence of violets in one. The second was empty, but a faint fragrance lingered...I struggled with the memory...

The soft brush of her sable wrap as she leaned over my bed...the Judge in the background, tall and elegant in his white coat and black tie, checking his watch.

'Now you be a good girl for Miss Lavinia, hear?'

A touch of cheek on cheek. Dazzle of light off the huge diamond as her strong, elegant fingers disengaged my scrawny arms from around her neck.

'Don't mess mama's hair, Lydia. And don't start snivelin'. I swear, you are the most exasperatin' child!'

The click of the light switch. My father's soft, 'Night, darlin'. Sleep tight.'

Then darkness—and more tears. At four, I wasn't sure why she didn't love me. I only knew for certain that she didn't...

Sticky fingers pulled the scratchy, sun-dried sheet up over my head releasing the echo of a scent I would forever associate with loneliness and rejection and my mother...Mint and bourbon and...

"*Evening in Paris,*" I said aloud, choking a little on the lump in my throat.

I returned the stopper to the bottle and resumed my snooping.

I checked out the bathroom, all pearl pink tile and fluffy towels. I even pulled back the shower curtain.

I returned to the bedroom and pulled out the drawers of the bureau, giving each a cursory glance. I couldn't bring myself to rifle through them as Miss Addie's unseen attacker had supposedly done.

What the hell do you think you're accomplishing here? I asked myself and couldn't come up with a reasonable answer.

I glanced toward the bed and spied the call button recessed into the wall, just at the height where Miss Addie might accidentally have pushed it in trying to break her fall. I knelt in front of the nightstand and ran my fingers lightly over the carpet. It was still slightly damp, stiff and discolored in a couple of spots where the effort to wash out the blood had not been entirely successful.

Remembering the thin bandage on Miss Addie's forehead, I guessed that the cut had been small and had probably bled only a little.

But someone had been in here since last night, that much was evident. And now that I thought about it, there had been footprints impressed into the thick carpet, along with the tracks left by the wheels of a vacuum cleaner.

And? What's your point? I flopped down on the floor, leaned against the fluffy down comforter, and crossed my legs, Indian-style.

Housekeeping had been in and done what they got paid for—housekeeping. Nothing sinister in that. In fact, that was probably the logical explanation for everything. Things got moved around when they were being cleaned. And what if something *were* missing? How the hell could *I* tell? It appeared to me that someone could cart off a good-sized truckload of Hammond antiques and still not make a dent in the collection.

There were no obvious blank spaces on the tables, no telltale circles of clear wood surrounded by a thin layer of dust that might have pointed to a missing object.

So if nothing was stolen, what was the point of the attack? Miss Addie had mentioned papers, so I unfolded myself from the floor and crossed to a delicate mahogany writing desk tucked into the far corner of the room. Its tiny drawers could hardly hold much. They appeared to be more for decoration than utility. I pulled out the matching chair and sat down.

A few receipts, a savings passbook showing a little over twelve thousand dollars, and a box of heavy, embossed stationery were all they yielded up. A black, lacquered Chinese box embellished with bright red poppies held odd buttons, bits of colored thread, a cloth tape measure, and several business cards. I leafed through them. Local businesses—a dry cleaner, hairdresser, and so on. Nothing of interest.

What could this shadowy someone have been looking for?

I rested my chin in my hands and gazed out the window across the marsh. A pair of snowy egrets, their white wings brilliant against the soft blue of the sky, glided gracefully in to land on the trunk of a dead tree lying exposed in the mud at low tide. Behind the marsh, Broad Creek ran sluggishly into Calibogue Sound. One span of the new cross-island highway bridge was just visible between the sweet gums, pines, and palmettos.

A not-too subtle reminder of what some folks thought of as progress and others, as desecration. We would always be at odds here, I thought, the preservationists and the developers.

Which led me to Geoff, a subject I had been trying to avoid thinking about all day.

He had called early that morning, full of questions about last night, his concern for Miss Addie's condition sounding genuine enough. He was off to Miami, an urgent meeting with his backers. They were sending a plane for him. He wished I could go with him, but he understood my need to stay close to home in case Miss Addie needed me. He should be back tonight, but would call if he got delayed.

He missed me.

He loved me.

There. It was out.

I knew what he wanted to hear from me, and I sidestepped as best I could. In the cold light of day, the niggling doubts were creeping back. Red had been right. What did I really know about Geoff—except that he was handsome, a tender and skillful lover, and apparently crazy about me?

As Neddie Halloran, my old college roommate, would have said, three out of three ain't bad.

So what was my problem?

A low growl rumbled in my stomach, reminding me it was way past time for lunch. Even Holmes and Watson had to eat. Unfortunately, I had no Mrs. Hudson to carry in a tray laden with tea and goodies and the best Victorian silver.

Well, this has been a fool's errand, I chided myself as I rose and retrieved my bag from the bed where I had tossed it. As I flung its strap across my shoulder, a picture popped into my head.

Beige shoes, beige purse.

I generally lugged this same, oversized canvas tote with me no matter what I was wearing. Rob used to joke that I could live out of its contents for months, even if I were marooned on a deserted island. But someone of Miss Addie's generation and upbringing would always have a bag to match her shoes. Braxton rules.

I approached the doors of the walk-in closet and flung them wide. She didn't have many clothes, but what she had was of top quality. Shoes were neatly hung on racks along one wall, and above them, a shelf with several handbags in colors ranging from black to navy blue to brown to white. I lifted down the latter, a medium-sized straw with two handles. It was festooned with bright flowers and shells. I recognized it as the bag that had sat next to her chair in the dining room the day we had lunch.

I could tell from the heft of it as I pulled it from the shelf that this was where I would find all the flotsam and jetsam that had been missing from the neat little beige number in the hospital wardrobe. I carried it back into the bedroom and dumped the contents onto the white comforter.

A couple of hankies, one clean, one not. A package of tissues, comb, compact, loose change. The address book it had not occurred to me to miss from the desk, as well as a checkbook with the last few checks not deducted from the balance. I did a quick calculation and figured she had something more than fifteen hundred dollars in her account.

There were several envelopes among the jumble, all opened, most advertisements and credit card offers. I removed the enclosure from the one with The Cedars as the return address. It was an invoice for her fees for the month of August, due on the first, now just a few days away. The sum was staggering. No wonder she had been so upset about the delays in Grayton's Race. At this rate, Miss Addie's savings would be gone by Christmas.

The last item was a sheet of plain white paper, folded over several times into a small rectangle. I had just opened it out and realized it was a photocopy of a handwritten letter, when I heard the click of a key in the front door lock.

Hastily I scooped up the address book and checkbook and dropped them into my own capacious bag. The rest I stuffed back into the straw purse, crossed swiftly to the closet, and replaced it on the shelf. I was heading for the hall when I realized I still had the photocopy in my hand. I quickly refolded it and stuffed it into the pocket of my slacks just as Mrs. Dixon stepped into the room.

We nearly collided in the doorway.

"Mrs. Tanner!" she cried, her hand flying to her chest. "My God, you nearly frightened me half out of my wits!"

"What is it, Ari?" a voice boomed from the living room. "Who's here?"

I recognized the Spanish lilt of the dashing Mr. Romero even before he joined Mrs. Dixon in the doorway. I had no choice but to retreat. They were blocking my only avenue of escape.

"Mr. Romero, how nice to see you again. I just popped in to pick up a few things for Miss Hammond. One always feels so much more at home if one has one's own things at hand, don't you find?"

God, I was prattling like an idiot! What was the matter with me? Why should I feel so intimidated by two resthome employees?

"Quite." Ariadne Dixon's face hardened into its habitual sneer of disapproval. "However, I personally sent over what I thought Miss Hammond would require in the way of necessities last night. Did I miss something?"

It was probably only my lurid imagination that read a *double-entendre* into the question.

I smiled sweetly and moved toward the door. Neither of them budged.

"If you'll excuse me now, I really should be getting back to the hospital."

"And did you get what you came for?" Mrs. Dixon asked archly as she reluctantly moved aside, allowing me to pass.

"Yes, thanks so much," I bubbled.

I clutched my tote bag tightly against my side and nearly sprinted for the front door.

"Visitors are required to register at the reception desk." Romero's voice was low and accusatory. "I did not see your name."

Okay, buster, that's enough. I wheeled to face them.

"Oh, but I'm not a *visitor*. I'm the next of kin. Isn't that right, Ari?" I dangled Miss Addie's keys in front of her nose.

She bristled at my use of her pet name. Maybe it was reserved for friends—or lovers?

"And, besides which," I went on, the arrogance bred of my Southern aristocratic ancestors dripping from every word, "I fail to see why my comings and goings should be of concern to a *maitre d'* and a part-time receptionist."

Ari looked as if she'd like to rip me to shreds with her well-manicured nails. Mr. Macho-Romero betrayed his anger only by a tightening of his fists at his sides. The supercilious smile never left his face.

I was appalled that I had ever found him attractive.

I wrenched open the door and stepped aside, a pointed invitation for them to precede me. With a quick glance at each other, they filed out, pausing in the hallway while I locked the door behind me. I waited them out, determined that they would not re-enter the apartment the minute my back was turned.

"Was there something else?"

Again they consulted each other with their eyes. It was Mrs. Dixon who spoke.

"We merely came to be certain that everything was in order. In Miss Hammond's absence, we felt it our duty to safeguard her possessions."

"How very commendable of you. However," I sneered back, "that will no longer be necessary. I live very close by, so I'll be dropping in from time to time to check on things myself. Until such time as Miss Hammond can return."

"As you wish." Ariadne Dixon stepped into the elevator alongside her accomplice, and the three of us rode down in strained silence.

We parted at the outside door, and the two of them moved off toward the main building. They stopped a short way down the sidewalk and stood watching me, their heads together in earnest conversation.

My hands shook a little as I leaned against my car and lit a cigarette. This time it wasn't from nicotine deprivation. There was something scary about those two. I had no trouble picturing either one of them pushing Miss Addie down, then slithering away, leaving her to be found by someone else.

And the other thing that made my knees wobbly was that trip down in the elevator. In the enclosed space, I had become aware of a smell, sweet and flowery. Whether it was his aftershave or her perfume, I couldn't tell. Neither could I identify it for certain as gardenia. But it could have been.

The paper I had thrust hurriedly into my pocket crackled against my leg as I slid behind the wheel. All I had been able to see before Dixon and Romero had come barging in was the start of the inside address, written in a formal, spidery script that had to be Miss Addie's.

Mr. J. Lawton Merriweather, Attorney.

I knew Law Merriweather. In fact, I had scolded him for recklessly drawing to an inside straight last Thursday night in the Judge's study. I had taken that pot with a full house—aces over eights, as I recalled.

I couldn't pull the letter out with my two antagonists glaring at me from just a few feet away, but I would examine it the minute I got home.

I hoped it was only a coincidence that Law Merriweather shared office space with Hadley Bolles.

13

I stopped long enough to grab a cold sub sandwich to carry back to the house with me. The confrontation at The Cedars had decided me—I was calling Red as soon as I got in the door.

I didn't know exactly what was going on, but that little scene had convinced me that Miss Addie's fears had to be taken seriously. I wanted Red there to hear her story first-hand as soon as she woke up.

There was a strange car parked in the drive as I pulled in. I didn't know anyone with a red Mustang convertible, so far as I could remember. Then I spotted the dealer tag and realized who it had to be, just as Bitsy Elliott trotted down the steps to intercept me.

"Bay! Thank God! I thought I was goin' to have to sit here on your stairway for *days* waitin' for y'all to get home!"

"How'd you get into the plantation?"

It wasn't the friendliest of greetings, but I was getting a little irritated at people dropping in on me with no warning. What was the point of having a security gate if the whole world could just wander in unannounced?

"Well, when I couldn't reach you, I called your daddy, and he told me about Miss Hammond. How is the old dear? Lord, I haven't seen her in dog's years. I'll have to call Mama and let her know. I'm sure she'll want to send some flowers and a note. I remember Miss Hammond was especially kind to us when Daddy passed."

One good thing about a conversation with Bitsy was that you didn't have to contribute if you didn't want to.

"So anyway, I called the hospital, and they told me that Miss Hammond was doin' as well as could be expected and that you had already left."

The running monologue continued as I unlocked the door and headed for the kitchen. If I didn't eat soon, I was going to be sick.

Bitsy helped herself to iced tea and poured one for me while I unwrapped the sandwich.

"So then I thought, who do I know in Port Royal? Besides you, of course. And Jane Anne Bingham's name just popped right into my head. And she very kindly called me in a pass and here I am!"

I was wolfing down the sub, nodding at Bitsy and wiping occasional dribbles of oil and vinegar off my chin with a paper napkin. About halfway through, I had taken enough of the edge off my hunger to give my friend my full attention, and I realized with a start that she looked awful.

Her eyes seemed bruised, the soft skin beneath them puffy from crying. The smile was forced, as was the chatter. It was overdone, even for Bitsy. She twirled the tall, frosty glass around in her hands, ice cubes rattling against the sides while she studied the flower pattern on the blue place mat with more attention than it deserved. Her sudden silence was a sure-fire clue that she had something on her mind.

I stuffed the last of the sandwich in my mouth, washed it down with tea, and reached for her hand.

"Bits, what is it? What's wrong?"

The tears came in a flood, cascading down her face. She made no attempt to wipe them away. I snatched tissues from the box on the counter and laid them in front of her, but she made no move to pick them up.

"Come on, tell me," I implored, moving around to the chair next to hers. I put an arm around her shoulder, and she collapsed against me. The sobs shook her entire body.

"Is it Cal again? What has he done?" I tightened my embrace and stroked her hair, the same way Lavinia used to comfort me when I was little. "I swear, if he hit you again, I'll take the Judge's .22 and shoot the bastard myself."

I felt the barely perceptible shake of her head against my shoulder.

Well, she'd deny it anyway, even if he had, I thought. I would never understand how a woman could stay with a man who beat her. Never.

I continued patting and crooning meaningless reassurances until soft hiccups and snuffles signaled the end of the storm. Bitsy sat up and offered me a watery smile, then reached for the wad of tissues on the table. She scrubbed at her face and blew her nose.

"I'm okay now, Bay, honey. Really."

"Sure?"

"Uh-huh." She took a sip of tea and rose to deposit the soggy tissues in the trash. "Got a cigarette?" she asked as she flopped back down at the table, and I returned to my chair across from her.

"A cigarette? Elizabeth Quintard Elliott, you haven't smoked since high school! And it always made you sick. You only did it to try to prove you were as cool as I was."

The real Bitsy smile was back on her gamin face. "It's a cigarette or a bourbon. Your choice."

I dug the pack out of my tote bag and shook two out. I leaned across to light it for her. She inhaled expertly and blew smoke toward the ceiling.

"You've been practicing," I accused, pushing the ashtray between us.

Her laugh was rueful. "What is it the kids say nowadays? Busted?"

We smoked in silence for awhile, Bitsy seeming to grow calmer with each puff.

That's why it's so damned hard to quit, I thought. *Sometimes there's just nothing so comforting.*

"Okay, girl, let's have it," I said at last.

Bitsy stubbed out the cigarette and gathered herself as if preparing for battle. "I think CJ is doin' drugs."

This was the last thing I'd expected her to blurt out, and I was momentarily stunned.

CJ? The star quarterback?

"That's crazy," I finally managed to splutter. "He's an athlete! He wouldn't do anything so stupid to his body."

Then names—famous ones—professional ballplayers in the headlines, flashed through my mind, and I realized what a thoroughly asinine statement that had been. It reminded me of Red the other day at the Judge's, ridiculing me for denying that teenagers could commit murder.

"That's what Big Cal said," Bitsy replied. "I tried to talk to him about it, and he just blew up. That's what we were really fightin' about last week, not just money like I told you. Sorry."

"That's okay. I knew you weren't telling me the whole story. You always were a lousy liar." I walked to the refrigerator and poured us out some more tea. "Want to sit out on the deck?"

The sun was behind the trees now, and the breeze would be kicking in from the ocean.

"Sure."

We carried our glasses and the cigarettes and stretched out on two chaises. The air was heavy with the smell of pine and salt, the light slanting through the oaks dappling the weathered wood of the railing.

"So what makes you think CJ is using?" I asked quietly. The very thought of that perfect young body riddled with drugs made me shudder.

"I think Mally knows. That was the first I really forced myself to look at it. But I think I'd been suspectin' somethin' for quite awhile without havin' the nerve to put a name to it."

"Mally told you?"

"Not exactly. She'd never rat out her brother. But she's been leavin' pamphlets—you know, the kind of thing they pass out at school?–lyin' around where I'll be sure to see them. How to spot the signs, where to get help. That sort of thing."

Bitsy reached for the cigarettes and lit this one herself.

"So what are the signs?" For all the media blitz about teenagers and drugs, I realized I was woefully ignorant of the specifics. It was totally outside my experience.

"Well, to back up a little, I think he may have started out with steroids. You remember how scrawny he was goin' into high school?"

"Yeah, I guess I do. He was always built more like you than Cal, though, except for the height."

"I've been doin' some readin', and I see now that it wasn't natural the way he just bulked up so fast. The summer between his freshman and sophomore years, he suddenly filled right out, got muscles, put on weight. I thought it was because he and Isaiah were workin' out all the time, liftin' weights and all."

Isaiah Smalls! Please, God, I thought, *don't let* him *be involved in this, too.* It would flat out kill Lavinia and his parents.

"Anyway," Bitsy continued, "he developed skin problems later on that year, too. That's another sign. I assumed it was just the typical teenage thing, although neither Cal or I ever had a problem with acne."

That was true enough. Bitsy's flawless complexion had been the envy of every girl in high school.

"But steroids aren't that bad, are they? I mean, it's not like crack or heroin."

Bitsy picked a fallen twig up off the deck and began to strip the bark from it. "I think he's graduated up to some of those other things. Marijuana, for one. On the rare occasions when he lets me close enough to actually hug him, I can smell it. Sort of sweet and cloyin', isn't that how it smells?"

Leave it to my best friend to assume that *I* would be an expert on the aroma of a joint. Not that I hadn't tried it once or twice in college, but she didn't know that for sure. Actually, I hadn't been all that impressed with the whole thing. Being high meant being out of control.

"Yes, that's a pretty accurate description," I admitted. "But is that all you have to go on? I mean, don't you think you might be jumping to conclusions a little here?"

"Why else would Mally be leavin' all those drug brochures around? And CJ's grades did drop at the end of last year. He used to be a solid 'B' student."

"What does Cal think?"

"That I'm nuts. You know how he feels about CJ. He's been primin' our son to carry on the Elliott tradition at Clemson almost from the day he was born. If he thought for a minute it was true, he'd probably kill CJ and whoever he thought was supplyin' him. In fact, he said so the night he stormed out of the house."

"Have you asked Mally about it?"

"Oh, I couldn't do that! I couldn't put her in the position of havin' to betray her brother's confidence."

It was at times like these I was happy that Rob and I had decided against starting a family right away. We always meant to, one day, but the time just never seemed to be right.

"Look, Bits, do you want me to talk to Mally, see what she knows? It wouldn't be the same thing as telling you. It might be easier for me to persuade her that she was helping rather than squealing on him."

Bitsy rolled onto her side and regarded me expectantly. "What I'd really like you to do is talk to your friend, the psychologist. I think maybe she could help us. Do you think she might?"

"You mean Neddie? What a good idea! She's a specialist on kids and drugs."

Nedra Halloran had been my college roommate for two years at Northwestern. We'd met in a computer class when she was still a business major. We were as different as Bitsy and I were, and again that somehow seemed to form the basis for a lasting friendship.

Neddie, Boston-Irish, with flaming red hair and sea-green eyes, had switched to psychology in our final year, right after her adored younger brother had died of a heroin overdose at the age of eighteen. She'd had to stay on and start nearly from scratch, but she was determined to do something with her life that could help to spare other families from the agony her own had suffered.

She had visited me on breaks and had fallen in love with the South. After completing her training, she'd made the move, setting up her practice in nearby Savannah. We kept in touch sporadically, but Neddie deserved a lot of the credit for getting me through this last year. Her sound, no-nonsense advice, offered only when I solicited it, had helped to keep me sane when the world around me seemed to have gone crazy.

"I thought maybe y'all could come to dinner, observe CJ in his natural habitat, so to speak. What do you think?"

"I still think you might be overreacting, but maybe Neddie could put your mind at rest. Want me to call her?"

"Do you think she'd do it? I mean, come to the house? Big Cal would never agree to take CJ to a psychologist. He doesn't hold with that kinda thing."

I nearly snorted out loud. I just bet Big Cal didn't want anything to do with a shrink. One of them might just figure out why *he* was so screwed up.

"I'm sure she will if I ask her to." I patted Bitsy's arm reassuringly and was rewarded with a dazzling grin.

"You're the best, Bay, honey, the absolute best." Bitsy glanced down at her watch and jumped to her feet. "Lord, look at the time! If I don't get on home, the kids will be tearin' the kitchen apart. I swear, those four can leave a place stripped of food faster 'n a swarm of locusts!"

I walked her out to the car, and we exchanged hugs.

"I'll call you and set up a time, shall I? Then you can check with your friend and see if it suits. I'll try to pick a night when Big Cal is visitin' one of the dealerships upstate." She slipped her sunglasses on and squeezed my hand. "That way I won't have to hire an off-duty policeman to keep you and my husband from murderin' each other."

"Good plan," I acknowledged as she backed the Mustang around and sped out of the driveway. I watched her take the turn too fast and kick up gravel from the side of the road. Her spirits had apparently been restored. Bitsy in a good humor was literally hell on wheels.

My indulgent smile faded as I turned and trudged back up the steps. Another complication in a week that was already threatening to swamp me. Just what I needed.

I picked up the phone and dialed the sheriff's office.

By the time Red finally called me back, late that night, so much else had happened in between, I'd almost forgotten why I wanted to talk to him.

I had spent so much of the day on the telephone the receiver had seemingly become an extension of my arm. None of the news had been good…

Dr. Winter's call, not long after Bitsy left, had started the flood of bad tidings. Miss Addie could not be awakened, and he feared she had slipped into a coma. He was surprised, because the bump on her head had been minor, and she'd seemed to be making good progress.

"I can be there in ten minutes," I'd told him, my heart sinking into my shoes. I'd grown attached to Miss Addie in the last few days. The thought that she might die was almost more than I could bear.

Dr. Winter forestalled me. He was moving her into intensive care, and no visitors would be allowed until she was stabilized. Apparently my legal status as next of kin didn't cut any ice with the good doctor. He promised to keep me informed.

I retreated back onto the deck, a portable phone and Miss Addie's address book in hand. Edwina, the invalid sister in Natchez, was upset, but unable to travel. She told me she was nearly paralyzed by arthritis. Her children and grandchildren were scattered over California, Nevada, and Montana. She didn't feel she could impose on any of them to make such a long trip when there was really nothing anyone could do right now.

"Adelaide is fortunate to have such good friends as you and your father," Edwina drawled.

I hung up, frustrated and more than a little angry at the cavalier manner in which she'd passed her sister's welfare over into the hands of virtual strangers.

Daphne was having one of her "bad" days, or so the sympathetic director of the nursing home outside Atlanta informed me. There was no point in my talking to her, since she didn't even know who *she* was at the moment.

"Late-stage Alzheimer's, you know." The woman spoke in a whisper, as if naming the dread disease might somehow provoke it into claiming the minds of still more of her elderly residents.

I left it to her to break the news, should a period of relative lucidity overtake Miss Addie's sister.

I had no idea how to go about finding Win, the disinherited scoundrel who had fled for parts unknown more that twenty years ago. Who even knew if he was still alive?

I sat for awhile, staring out at nothing, as shadows overtook the deck. On impulse, I stuffed the cigarettes in my pocket and trotted barefoot down the steps that gave onto the path to the beach. The sun was setting over the mainland, and streaks of mauve and orange spread through high, wispy clouds, diffusing the splendor from shore to horizon. I wandered along in the surf, kicking up little sprays of water. We were somewhere between low and high tides, so there was still plenty of beach left between the ocean and the dune.

I encountered a jogger, headphones firmly in place. The wire disappeared into the pocket of her shorts where the Walkman bounced against her leg with every stride. She nodded as we passed, the look of grim determination never leaving her face. An overweight couple, their matching neon-yellow T-shirts a bright splash against the darkening sky, bicycled by me. Tourists from the nearby Westin Hotel, I guessed, anxious to wring every last second of enjoyment from their limited vacation days. I hoped their red faces were a result of too much sun and not from the unaccustomed effort of pedaling beach bikes through loose sand.

I walked on toward the narrow spit of land that jutted out into the water. Beyond it, a long sand bank rose, barely visible now in the mid-tide shift. Farther out, I could just discern the outline of Bay Point off the tip of St. Helena Island. *Presqu'isle* lay at the other end. It was hard to believe that this narrow strip of water was all that separated me from my childhood home. It would take an hour to drive it going by land.

I sat below the dune and smoked, marveling as the faint, pinkish glow was finally overtaken by the deepening purple twilight. The sweep and grandeur of the ocean had its usual calming effect. I rose and strolled back toward the house.

I would never be able to live far from the water again.

The portable phone was ringing as I climbed the stairs. My soggy pantslegs clung to my ankles as I sprinted up the steps and grabbed it up before the machine could kick on.

"Hello?" I gasped, collapsing onto the chaise. My feet were caked with sand, and I had left powdery footprints all along the deck.

"Bay, honey, you okay? You sound out of breath."

My father's voice was soft and low, his usual bluff heartiness missing.

"I was down at the beach. I had to run to get the phone. What's up? You sound kind of done-in yourself."

"Oh, I'm fine, sweetheart, don't you worry. Just a little tired, is all. Vinnie was just here. Left a few minutes ago. She asked me to call you."

"I knew she'd never be able to trust Dolores to look after you. She probably had visions of your being force-fed tacos and burritos and refried beans."

"No, no. Nothin' like that. In fact the two of them seemed to get on pretty good. Spent more 'n half an hour gabbin' in the kitchen when Vinnie first got here."

The Judge sounded more than tired. He seemed weighed down by a weariness that would take more than a good night's sleep to cure. At that moment I decided to hold off telling him about Miss Addie's relapse. He had enough on his plate already.

"How is Lavinia holding up?"

"She's fine, just fine. Listen, Bay, they've released Derek's body to the family. The funeral is tomorrow, ten o'clock, at the AME church outside Bluffton. You know the one, don't you? On 278?"

"Yes, I know it. It's got that little fenced-in cemetery right next to it."

So this was the cause of his gravity. He would be feeling Lavinia's distress, sharing it.

"Aren't they going to have a viewing?"

"Under the circumstances, they thought it best not to. There's been enough publicity already. It will be a small, private ceremony. Family only. Vinnie just wants to get it behind them, let them get on with their lives."

I thought about Thaddeus and Colletta. And Isaiah. They, too, would undoubtedly like to see closure on what must be extremely painful for them all.

The silence lengthened, my father and I both wrapped in our own thoughts.

"I would like to attend the service, Bay." His voice, firm and strong again, startled me. "Vinnie has invited us, and I want you to take me."

This was another shock, to add to the many I'd had already today. My father rarely left the house. He never appeared in public.

"Are you sure?"

"Of course I'm sure. Do you think I'd let Vinnie go through an ordeal like this alone?"

"She's not alone. She has her family."

"*We* are her family, too," he bellowed, all trace of melancholy gone. "I'll expect you here by nine."

The slam of the receiver was loud in the damp night stillness.

Damn it all, I thought, reaching shakily for a cigarette, *why am I always the bad guy? I'm thirty-eight years old, and I haven't been able to please him my entire damned life. Why the hell do I keep on trying?*

I set the phone on the deck beside me and lay back in the chaise. Dew was beginning to settle as the air cooled, and the moisture had seeped into the cushions. I watched the stars wink on through the haze of the smoke I blew up toward the sky.

A soft, plaintive *meow* drifted up from the ground below me, and I called softly to Mr. Bones. He bounded up the steps and leaped eagerly onto my stomach. He was purring loudly even before he had settled himself. I stroked his night-damp fur and gave myself up to the pain.

I had struggled for almost a year to overcome the belief that life had cheated me, to rise above the despondency that had settled like a pall over my spirit after Rob was killed. I had denied myself the luxury of surrendering to the deep, wrenching grief. I had known instinctively that, given free rein, it would have crushed me.

Instead I had tried to heed the "Baynards are made of sterner stuff" crap my mother used to preach at me. I had sucked it up and gone on as best I could.

So that night, with the cat making soothing, kneading motions against my chest, I allowed myself to wallow in all the self-pity I had so long denied.

It felt good.

It didn't solve anything, but it felt good.

If Geoff Anderson hadn't picked that moment to call, things might have gone differently.

He wanted to let me know he wouldn't be back until later the next day, business having held him up longer than he'd anticipated.

I was confused, unsure what to say, how to act, and it came through loud and clear.

Geoff was hurt, bewildered by my lack of response to his warmth, his expressions of love. I didn't blame him. I'd certainly led him to expect more from me than the curt, one-word replies he was receiving.

But he didn't get the message. He pressed. "What's wrong, Bay? What have I done?"

"Nothing."

"What do you mean, nothing? Something's bugging you. Tell me."

"I'm just tired."

"It's more than that. Is it your friend in the hospital? Or are you having second thoughts about last night?"

Damn him! I blushed, remembering that smug little speech I'd made to myself outside Geoff's bedroom door. The one about consigning Rob to a special place in my heart and getting on with my life. What a handy little piece of self-deception that had been!

"Bay? Are you? Having second thoughts?"

"No. Maybe. I don't know."

By the time we hung up, Geoff's hurt had blossomed into anger. I knew I could expect to find him pounding on my door as soon as he got back onto the island.

I disengaged the cat's claws from my cotton sweater and dragged myself inside. I needed food and sleep, in that order...

So I was scrounging in the cupboards when Red's call came in, bringing the disastrous day full circle. At first I let the machine answer and would have ignored him altogether, if my brother-in-law hadn't sounded so concerned. Next thing I knew, *he* would be over here, demanding explanations.

So I picked up the phone and made him wish he hadn't been so insistent. Red got the full brunt of my anger, guilt, and frustration. It wasn't fair, but, hey—that's what families are for. He took it well.

"Let's talk tomorrow, after you've had a chance to calm down a little, okay?"

Red spoke in that perfectly reasonable tone that made me want to strangle him.

I replaced the receiver for the final time that night without mentioning Miss Addie. There seemed no point now that she was comatose. Then I went back to foraging. I finally settled on two slices of toast piled with chunky peanut butter and a banana whose peel was more black than yellow.

Too keyed up to go to bed, I flipped on the television and stretched out on the couch. I fell asleep with the Braves trailing the Padres, four to one in the bottom of the sixth.

14

It was too perfect a day to be dealing with death.

A cool front had lowered the humidity and the temperature to the mid-seventies, making it feel more like April than late July. Fat, cottony clouds, wandering aimlessly in a delft-blue sky, provided welcome patches of shade in the stark, treeless cemetery.

I stood beside the Judge's wheelchair, one hand resting on the rubber-tipped handle, as much for reassurance as for balance. The heels of my navy blue pumps were sinking into the loose, sandy soil.

Ours were the only white faces in the group gathered loosely around the splendid oak coffin. Draped in lavish sprays of lilies, roses, and carnations, it rested on a plain wood bier next to the yawning hole in the ground. Not for the first time in my life, I shuddered at the barbarism of funeral customs.

The gaunt, graying Reverend Gregory Jackson read the service. His voice rose and fell in a sing-song cadence that gave the clichéd words an unusual beauty. A soft chorus of murmured *amens* could be heard now and then in the background. Many of the well-dressed women, eyes closed, faces uplifted, swayed from side to side, as if to the strains of an unearthly music only they could hear.

I looked across the tarp-covered mound of dirt next to the grave at the three women who huddled together at the foot of the coffin. Lavinia

Smalls stood ramrod straight, her dry-eyed gaze fastened on the empty field beyond the church. One arm encircled the heaving shoulder of her sister, Mavis, whose son was about to be consigned to the ground. Chloe, the other half-sister, sobbed uncontrollably on Mavis's right, her brown face mottled by grief.

They were a strange contrast, these three products of a common mother and obviously different fathers.

Behind them and off to one side, the rest of the Smalls family stood tall and proud. Thaddeus looked strikingly handsome in a dark gray suit that lent him a dignity his postal worker's uniform could never achieve. He and Colletta flanked their only child, their stance at once protective and defiant. Their posture dared anyone to cast a glance of suspicion on the son whose head was bowed in respectful silence.

A mourning dove was cooing somewhere off to my left, a soft, measured refrain that seemed a fitting accompaniment to the close of the service. Reverend Jackson scooped up a handful of loose dirt and solemnly offered it to Mavis as the coffin was lowered into the grave. With a trembling hand, she sprinkled it over the rich gloss of the polished oak. As the mourners began to disperse, most pausing to offer a word of comfort to the weeping Mavis, someone began to hum the melody of an old, cherished hymn. Others picked it up, and soon the sad, sweet strains filled the tiny cemetery, rising unfettered in the clear air.

Around a surprisingly large lump in my throat, I found myself joining in, the words rising unbidden from some long-dormant corner of my memory:

> ...*ye who are weary come home.*
> *Earnestly, tenderly Jesus is calling,*
> *Calling, O Sinner, come home.*

The Judge added his clear baritone, and I wanted the peace I felt at that moment to go on forever.

When the song ended, my father and I exchanged wistful smiles, shared memory heavy between us. If only my mother's religious fervor had had room for such sweetness, such spontaneity, maybe…

Lavinia approached us, and the spell was broken.

"Thank you," she said simply, her gratitude encompassing us both. "Will you join us at Mavis's?"

"I think not," my father replied. "We'll just pay our respects here and get on back to the house. That'll be best, don't you reckon?"

"Of course. Whatever you think best." She took my hand and patted it gently. "It meant a lot to us that you were here today. Both of you."

Lavinia turned away and led us up to the small knot of family gathered around Mavis. The Judge shook her hand solemnly and offered his formal condolences. I added my own, and she thanked us for the flowers.

I helped the Judge maneuver his chair across the rough gravel parking lot and onto the ramp that would lift him into the van.

Got to give the old buzzard credit, I thought, hitching up the straight skirt of my navy blue dress and climbing into the driver's seat. He had sat tall through the whole service, his infirmity displayed to a group of almost total strangers. Maybe there was hope for him yet.

"You look pretty handsome today, Your Honor," I remarked as I backed the big van around and headed down the drive. I hadn't seen him in a suit and starched shirt since…I couldn't remember when.

My father snorted, a self-deprecatory little grunt, closed his eyes, and settled back in his chair.

"Okay, fine," I said. I fiddled with the unfamiliar air conditioning controls, got the vents adjusted, and pulled out onto the highway toward Beaufort.

The tune of the hymn kept running through my head, and I found myself humming it softly, trying to hold onto the serenity the music had brought me. It lasted until I pulled around a slow-moving green Bronco in the right-hand lane and glanced idly over at the driver.

Red Tanner, in civilian clothes and his own car, looked sheepishly back at me and waved. The stern, ebony face of Matt Gibson, chief death investigator for the Sheriff's Department, regarded me sternly from the passenger seat. His nod of recognition was curt and something less than cordial, although we'd known each other since grade school.

So you were staking out the funeral, I thought, accelerating past them and nearly cutting Red off as I whipped back into the inside lane.

The bastards! Why couldn't they leave Lavinia and her family in peace, at least on this one day?

"And just when I was beginning to like you again, Tanner," I mumbled as I reached for my cigarettes and stabbed in the lighter, "you have to go acting like a cop."

The Judge studied me for a second, one bushy white eyebrow raised, then settled back into his nap.

Dolores, no doubt in honor of the solemnity of the occasion, had set lunch out on the long mahogany table in the dining room. The second-best china—the Royal Doulton with the deep blue border—reflected the glow of the crystal chandelier, lighted in an effort to dispel the gloom of the dark paneled walls. Waterford goblets and highly polished heavy silver sparkled against the white damask cloth.

That'll teach them to underestimate Dolores, I thought as I walked around the perfectly proportioned room, idly touching these treasures that had been so important to my mother. Neither she nor Lavinia would have been able to find a single flaw in the perfection of the table. Even the flowers, picked that morning from the garden Lavinia maintained along with all her other duties, were artfully arranged in a low Chinese vase.

"It looks wonderful," I told a hovering Dolores.

"*Gracias, Señora.* Your mother had many beautiful things."

"Yes, she did."

I was about to ask why there were three places set when a timer *dinged* in the kitchen, and Dolores scuttled off. I was pretty certain I knew who our guest was going to be, and it was not going to make for a companionable meal.

What I really wanted to do was get the hell out of these clothes, throw on a ratty T-shirt and rattier shorts, and flop myself on the beach for about three days. No phones, no problems—mine or anyone else's. Just me and the ocean and the sun.

But I couldn't let all of Dolores's efforts go to waste. Besides, I needed to be where the hospital could reach me. I had called this morning, before leaving home, but there had been no change in Miss Addie's condition.

The doorbell chimed, and I went to let Red in.

We eyed each other warily. I left him to close the door himself, and he followed me silently into the front parlor. This was one of my favorite rooms, small and elegantly decorated with claw-footed Empire furniture and pale yellow walls.

"Drink?" I offered as Red moved across the straw-colored carpet. He stopped in front of a glass-fronted highboy and studied my mother's collection of antique salts. "Oops, sorry," I sneered, sounding anything but, "I forgot. You're still on duty."

Red turned slowly to face me. "You know, it amazes me that my brother never beat you."

I could tell by the tilt of one corner of his generous mouth that he was joking, but it was a subject I couldn't take lightly. I'd applied too many ice packs to too many of Bitsy's bruises to find domestic violence amusing.

"If you're trying to piss me off more than I already am, you're making a damned good start."

"Profanity is the refuge of a limited vocabulary," my father announced from the hall. This doorway was too narrow to allow the wheelchair through. It had been my mother's room, anyway. The Judge had rarely entered it even when he could walk.

"Samuel Pepys. Or Ben Johnson. One or the other of them," I said as I pushed his chair toward the dining room. Red trailed along behind.

"Neither," the Judge tossed over his shoulder.

I settled him at the head of the table and walked around to the place on his right. Red, his face still crinkled in amusement, held the chair for me.

"Christopher Marlowe. John Donne." I fired names at him as I unfolded the damask napkin and draped it across my lap.

"Not even close."

"Okay, you win. I'm stumped. Who said it?"

The Judge lifted the cover on a silver chafing dish, releasing a pungent steam redolent of garlic, wine, and seafood. He smiled in triumph.

"My mama."

"Granny Simpson? That's cheating! She's not in Bartlett's."

"No, but she was a very wise and wonderful woman. You'd do well to heed her advice."

My only memories of my grandmother were of painfully twisted, arthritic fingers, a deeply lined face, and a soft, breathless voice that never failed to soothe. But I had been spellbound by all the stories about her. She had been a Southern lady in the truest sense of both those words. Even my mother hadn't argued with that.

We helped ourselves to the perfectly prepared filet of sole that fell apart in tender chunks at the slightest touch of the fork. Fluffy rice laced with baby peas and pearl onions was accompanied by crisp, green snap beans, blanched just enough to bring out their fresh-picked sweetness.

We spoke of inconsequential things, our concentration reserved for appreciation of the meal. By the time Red, the last to finish, finally leaned back in his chair, the atmosphere had mellowed considerably. I poured coffee for the men from a tall, antique pot.

"I can't believe you still do that." My father stirred cream into his cup and pointed at my plate.

A small row of peas lay off to one side of the otherwise empty dish. They were arranged in a neat semicircle, the green half-moon precisely symmetrical and evenly spaced.

"You know I hate the damned things, but Dolores keeps trying to slip them by me."

"Bay is the only person I've ever known," my father said, turning to Red, "who could eat a helping of vegetable soup and leave a pile of peas in the bottom of the bowl."

"A truly talented woman," my brother-in-law replied with a grin. "I've always said so."

I rose and began clearing the table, ignoring their little jokes at my expense. Dolores was just pulling a bubbling peach pie out of the oven as I stacked the dishes on the counter.

"That was a fabulous meal, *mi' amiga.* Thank you."

The flush of her olive skin might have been from the heat of the kitchen, but I suspected it was more from my calling her "my friend". We had long ago passed out of the stage of employer and servant, so far as I was concerned. But it made Dolores uncomfortable, for some inexplicable reason, and she preferred to maintain a certain formality in our relationship.

"Will I serve the dessert now, *Señora*? There is also the iced cream. It is the peach, too. Your favorite, no?"

"My favorite, yes," I answered, pulling out the racks of the dishwasher.

"No, no, *Señora*! You must see to the guest. I will do."

She shooed me out of the kitchen, and I followed the smell of cigar smoke down the hall to the Judge's room.

"...so it keeps coming back to Isaiah Smalls and the Elliott kid," I heard Red say as I walked into the blue haze. I slipped off my shoes and curled up on my favorite window seat. Red passed me an ashtray as I lit a cigarette.

"Why?" I asked, adding my own stream of smoke to the cloud hanging close to the ceiling. Even the combined efforts of the air conditioning and an oak ceiling fan whirling at full speed couldn't clear the air.

Red opened a window in self-defense, then looked at the Judge as if for permission to speak.

"What?" I demanded, suppressed anger rising again in my chest. "I have as much right as *he* does to know what's going on."

Again the two men exchanged glances, Red looking as uncomfortable as he had the day he came hunting for Lavinia.

Was that really less than a week ago? I asked myself incredulously. It seemed as if enough had happened in the past few days to fill at least a couple of months.

I rose and replaced the ashtray on the Judge's desk. I picked up a round glass paperweight and tossed it back and forth between my hands

"Well? So what's the big secret? Don't make me charm it out of you. I'm really not up to it."

My attempt to lighten the mood fell flat. The heavy silence lengthened, and I could hear the measured beats of the grandfather clock down the hall.

Finally, Red ran a hand through his thick, brown hair and mumbled, "You're not gonna like it."

"I don't like being kept out of the loop, either, so it's a toss-up. Come on, give."

"We've been investigating Geoffrey Anderson as a possible suspect in the murder of Derek Johnson."

The words came out in a rush. Red actually flinched as if he were afraid I was going to pitch the paperweight at him.

"And before you start beratin' poor Redmond as six kinds of a fool, sit down and listen to what he has to say."

The Judge's defense of Red shocked me into silence. I couldn't figure out whose side he was on anymore. I walked across the room and resettled myself on the window seat.

"I'm listening."

"Well, as I was tellin' the Judge, we turned up some very interesting information that made us want to take a closer look at Anderson. You know about this development deal he's got goin'?"

I nodded and shook a cigarette out of the pack.

"What isn't common knowledge is that there was a glitch—a big one. One of the sellers of a vital piece of property backed out. The whole thing was about to go down the tubes."

"Is that supposed to be a news flash? Geoff told me that the first night we went out. I know all about it." I didn't even try to keep the smugness out of my voice.

Red looked startled. "Why didn't you say something?"

"Why should I?" I countered, looking at my father His face was flushed, and his eyes slid quickly away from mine. What the hell was his game? Surely he had known about this, too. Why else send Miss Addie to me for help? I was thoroughly confused.

This would have been the perfect opportunity to demand an explanation from him about the extent of his involvement with Grayton's Race and with Geoff. But it was a private matter, between him and me. Red might be family, in the loose construction of that concept, but he wasn't *blood*.

"Anyway," I went on, turning back to Red, "it's a moot point. The deal's going through as planned."

"Sure it is," Red snapped, the color rising in his face, "because the troublemaker conveniently died. Pretty damned coincidental, don't you think?"

"Right. And the CIA killed Kennedy, and the underground militia planted the bomb in Oklahoma City, and the Navy accidentally shot down TWA 800. Any of your pet conspiracy theories I've missed?"

Red and I were on our feet now, shouting at each other across a yard of highly polished heart pine floor.

"And Geoff told me about *that*, too. Sorry to disappoint you, but I'm not 'shocked' by your less than startling revelations," I yelled.

"Did he also happen to mention that this conveniently dead problem was named Derek Johnson? Or didn't your pillow talk get that far?"

"You son-of-a…"

"That's enough! Both of you!"

The Judge's stern command was like a dash of cold water. I retreated back to my refuge under the window. Red took a deep breath, expelled it, and collapsed into the red leather wing chair next to the fireplace.

I was too shocked to speak.

Derek Johnson had been the heirs property holdout? Why hadn't Geoff told me that? He knew about my concern for Adelaide Boyce Hammond's investment, my involvement with Isaiah Smalls and CJ Elliott.

I'd told him. Hadn't I?

I tried to reconstruct our conversations—on the river after dinner, in my kitchen at three in the morning, on our outing to Geoff's homesite. And afterwards. In his bed.

I'd *meant* to tell him, but had I?

I dropped my head and studied my hands, clenched tightly in my lap. A deep flush rose from my throat to stain my cheeks. My mind couldn't recall everything we'd said, but my body remembered all too well. The electric touch of his hands on my flesh…the reawakening of the desire I'd thought dead along with my husband.

"Look, Bay…" Red's voice, pitched low and steady, was still a shock in the strained silence that had followed our shouting. "Look," he began again, "I'm sorry. I didn't mean to blurt it out like that."

I raised my head and met his eyes. "No, *I'm* sorry," I said, swallowing my shame. "You and I don't seem to bring out the best in each other lately, do we?"

He winced at that, and I could have bitten my tongue.

"Tell her the rest of it, Redmond," the Judge commanded from across the room. That presence that had quelled even the most rambunctious of attorneys still emanated from my father, despite his useless hand and withered legs.

Red looked apprehensive, his eyes darting between the Judge and me.

"Go ahead," I sighed, "let's get it over with." I was tired of fighting. I just wanted to escape to the sanctuary of my beach house and shut out the whole damned world again.

"Well, we talked with Anderson. Matt Gibson and I. Asked him about his whereabouts on the night in question. And—bottom line—he had an alibi. A good one. We checked it out. So, he's clear. End of story."

I should have been relieved, but somehow I wasn't. I had a feeling I hadn't heard it all yet.

"And we've got a couple of other angles we're looking at. Mrs. Johnson says Derek was hanging out with a pretty rough crowd lately. Some of his friends have had a few minor scrapes with the law. But so far, I'm afraid Isaiah is still at the top of Gibson's hit parade."

I shook my head as Red Tanner rose and approached me. "I'll never believe that, Red. Not unless he confesses."

"I know. It's okay."

He seemed about to say something more, thought better of it, and turned to the Judge. "Thanks for lunch, Your Honor. I'll be in touch."

"Aren't you staying for dessert?" I asked as Dolores appeared in the doorway.

"No, thanks. My *official* shift starts at three. Got to get home and change."

He seemed very anxious to make his getaway. "Great meal," he said to Dolores who smiled her thanks. With a wave, he was gone.

My father and I demolished the slices of warm peach pie and smooth mounds of ice cream in silence. When Dolores had reclaimed the empty plates and left us with frosted glasses of lemonade, I broke the stillness.

"What was it that Red didn't want to tell me?" I asked.

The sharp lift of the Judge's chin confirmed my suspicions: there *was* more to come.

"You've been hurt so much already," he murmured, so low I almost missed it.

I knew he would get to it in his own way, so I lit a cigarette and waited.

"It's about Geoffrey Anderson's alibi," he said at last, looking directly at me. "He was in Miami. With his wife."

For a moment I didn't get it.

"You mean his *ex*-wife," I said stupidly. "He has two of them, you know."

The Judge shook his head sadly.

"No, sweetheart. He has *one* ex-wife. And one current one. I'm afraid your Geoff is still very much a married man."

15

The brand-new courthouse, squatting behind the Law Enforcement Center and adjacent to the jail, baked unshaded in the afternoon sun. A triangular pediment rose over the wide double doors. Fake columns flanked the shallow steps that led up from a circular, brick-paved courtyard. It was an attempt to imitate the classic Georgian architecture that typified older halls of justice, the kind that dominated village greens in so many Southern county seats. The effort fell flat. It looked exactly like what it was: a cheap imitation of the original, set down in a barren landscape, a functional building without grace or beauty.

I had come straight from the Judge's. All I really wanted was to go home and forget about this entire day. But I needed information, and this was the place to get it.

I trotted briskly up the steps, anxious to escape the merciless heat. Inside, a uniformed officer dropped my bag onto a conveyor belt that rolled it through an x-ray scanner. I stepped through the arched metal detector and retrieved it on the other side.

Not exactly a scene out of *To Kill a Mockingbird*, I thought as I skirted the curved, balustraded staircase that led to the three courtrooms on the second floor. It was split into two sweeping sections, another abortive attempt at antebellum splendor. I located the county tax assessor's office, handed over my request, and was told to come back in about half an hour.

I plunked two quarters into the soda machine and carried my Diet Coke out onto the relative shade under the front overhang. I wanted a cigarette and some solitude. Neither was permitted inside the bustling courthouse.

The Judge's revelation had hit me like a blow to the stomach.

Geoff was still married.

He had held my hand, looked me straight in the eye, and lied through his teeth. And I had bought it. He had even aroused my sympathy—intentionally, I was now convinced—with his tale of alienation from his sons because of his divorces from their mothers.

Divorces. *Plural.*

There was no way I had misunderstood *that.*

So the next logical question was, what else had he lied about?

That was what I was here to find out. My frustrated attempts at computer hacking had gotten sidetracked by my infatuation with the object of the search. I checked my watch. In a few minutes I would know who the owners of record of Grayton's Race were, how much they had paid, and, possibly, how deeply in debt they were. And to whom.

Sergeant Red Tanner and Matt Gibson seemed to think there was motive for murder somewhere in the Grayton's Race deal. I wasn't buying it. My concern was for Adelaide Boyce Hammond, still comatose in the intensive care unit, and for the viability of her investment. Unless something drastic happened to make me change my mind, I was going to recommend that she sell out as quickly as she could, even if it meant taking a loss.

I'd tell Big Cal Elliott the same thing, if in fact, as I suspected, he too was an investor.

My father, whose pitying glances after his disclosure about Geoff had sent me bolting out of the house, would hear my advice, too. Whether or not he chose to take it was out of my hands. Though he had so far sidestepped my attempts to pin him down, I was certain he had another agenda that he was keeping to himself. It would only be revealed when he was damned good and ready to share it.

I downed the last of the soda, now sickeningly warm in the near ninety-degree heat. The day, which had begun with such cool promise, had turned into another mid-summer scorcher. The breeze had dropped, and the temperature soared. I deposited the empty can in an overflowing trash container and submitted to the security check once again before making my way back to the tax office.

I pushed through the heavy door to confront the pudgy, white-clad form of Hadley Bolles leaning proprietarily against the counter. He clutched several pages of computer printouts in his sausage-like fingers.

"Well, Bay, darlin', we meet again. I don't see you for months, and then—wham! We run into each other three times in one week. It must be fate, it surely must."

I ignored him and addressed the matronly woman behind the counter. "Do you have my information ready? It's been half an hour."

Her kindly, lined face colored up, from the end of her pointed chin to the roots of her gray-brown hair. She cast a quick, fearful glance at Hadley.

I didn't need to ask. I ripped the papers out of his hand, flipped them back into order, and found my handwritten request paperclipped neatly on the front.

"You really are a snake, Hadley," I snapped, folding the sheaf of print-outs and stuffing them into my bag. "You've got all the moral rectitude of a pit viper."

"Now, now, little girl, don't get your back up. Nothing secret about those ol' documents. Information in the public domain, ain't that right, Doris?"

The county employee ducked her head and scurried back to her desk.

"Besides, you don't wanna go makin' slanderous comparisons like that in front of witnesses. That wouldn't be smart, darlin'," he sneered, "not smart at all.".

"You're right, Hadley," I replied, one hand on the door. "The snake might sue me for defamation of character."

I probably hadn't left him speechless. Hadley so rarely was. But I was out the door and down the hallway before he could summon up a suitably scathing comeback.

The smarmy bastard, I fumed as I gunned the LeBaron into evening rush hour traffic and crawled my way back toward the island. Now everyone in the county would know about my interest in the particulars of Grayton's Race.

Well, so what? It wasn't as if *I* had anything to hide. Geoff and I were definitely through, although he didn't know it yet. So if my snooping around pissed him off, too bad. The sooner my involvement in this whole mess was history, the better.

I crossed over the Broad River bridge, pausing in my internal monologue long enough to admire the incredible beauty of sun, sky, and water reflecting back on each other in a dazzling shimmer of light.

Why couldn't people just leave well enough alone? It wasn't as if we *needed* any more houses or golf courses. Maybe the protesters were right. Maybe I'd take Geoff's tongue-in-cheek advice and join them at the barricades. *After* I'd extricated my family and friends from any financial involvement, of course.

I tapped my horn lightly and waved as I sped by the afternoon shift of picketers. Three of them sat on the hoods of their pickup trucks with "SAVE OUR RIVER" placards resting on their shoulders.

Almost an hour later, I rolled onto the bridge over the Intracoastal Waterway and breathed a sigh of relief. I was nearly home. Lavinia would be back with the Judge tonight, Dolores free to return to her family.

Tomorrow things could start getting back to normal for all of us.

I roundly cursed whoever had invented the answering machine, and myself for buying one. For the first half hour after I walked into the house, I ignored the little red light. It blinked accusingly—four times in rapid succession, then a pause, then the sequence repeated itself.

I stripped down to my pink lace underwear and added my dress and stockings to the pile already on the floor. I thought back to this morning, when, of course, I had overslept. I had awakened to the cheerful chatter of Katie Couric coming from the TV I had left on all night long. It had been a race to get myself showered, shampooed, dressed and out the door in time to make my father's deadline of nine a.m. The clothes I had slept in had fallen where they lay as I flung them off on my mad dash to the bathroom.

Laundry tomorrow, I decided as I dropped my frothy lace bra onto the heap.

I hated wearing a bra, and I avoided it whenever decency allowed. No matter how wide or soft the straps, they seemed to cut into the tender flesh around the grafted skin on my left shoulder.

I clasped my hands together high over my head and went through a series of stretches designed to work out the kinks I had acquired from sleeping on the sofa last night. I followed that up by dashing cold water over my arms, neck, and breasts, and toweling myself briskly dry.

I scrubbed my face clean of the minimal makeup I had put on that morning. My eyes looked tired, I thought, as I met my own gaze in the mirror, and I had been spending too much time indoors. The rosy glow had faded from my cheeks. I brushed my hair into a ponytail on the top of my head and secured it with an elastic band.

In Rob's old C of C T-shirt and my grungiest cutoff jeans, I felt ready to face the machine. I lit a cigarette and punched the button.

The first two calls were from Geoff. His anger of the night before had reverted back to pained confusion.

Why was I acting like this? What had gone wrong? He felt sure we could work it out if only I would talk to him. He was certain I was there, screening calls, and refusing to pick up. He cursed the business that would keep him in Miami for at least two more days.

Yeah right, buster, I thought, stabbing the cigarette out viciously. *Is that what they're calling it these days? Business?*

He ended both messages with protestations of love.

I was hard pressed not to pick the damn machine up and fling it across the room. It was a relief when his honeyed, hypocritical voice was replaced by the bright babble of Bitsy Elliott.

"Bay, honey, are you there? Pick up if you are. It's me." A pause, during which I could hear the click of a lighter and the soft rush of exhaled smoke. "Okay, I guess you're not. You probably went to the Johnson boy's funeral. CJ wanted to go, but his daddy and I told him it wasn't a good idea. Besides, it was just for family, right? Anyway, how about this Friday night for dinner? Big Cal will be in Greenville from Thursday 'til Sunday. Some problem up there with the bookkeeper. Anyway, if you could get Dr. Halloran to come, she could stay over with you and y'all could have a good long visit over the weekend. Course, we *could* do it Saturday, but the older kids are gonna scream bloody murder if they have to stay home on a Saturday night! Anyway, let me know. Love ya! Bye!"

I smiled despite my annoyance at myself for having forgotten to call Neddie. You couldn't help but smile at Bitsy's nonstop chatter.

The last message was another from Geoff. He would definitely be back on Friday, probably late. He would come straight over from the airport. He had things he needed to tell me. We had to talk.

We'll see about that, Mr. Geoffrey Snake-in-the-Grass Anderson, I thought childishly.

If everything worked out right, I wouldn't be here Friday evening. And if I came back from Bitsy's to find him lying in wait for me, I'd have an ally. Neddie Halloran had an Irish temper to match her frizzy red hair. Geoff wouldn't stand a chance.

I left messages on both Neddie's office and home machines, asking her to call me the next day. I had a nagging feeling there was something else I was supposed to do, but I couldn't remember what it was. I rummaged through the clutter of the junk drawer with its matchbooks, shoelaces, pencil stubs, and old grocery receipts and finally came up with a small, spiral-bound notebook with three pages left in it.

Since premature senility seemed to be overtaking me at a rapid rate, I was going to have to start writing things down. I set the pad next to the phone, found a pencil end that was still long enough to get my fingers around, and wrote, "Neddie at Bitsy's—Fri" followed by "time" and a question mark.

It wasn't much of a list. But the way things had been going lately, I would probably be adding to it soon.

My stomach growled, and I surveyed the pristine kitchen. I knew from last night's foray into the cupboards that I would find little to eat behind their gleaming, light oak doors. Thank God Dolores would be back tomorrow.

I lifted the receiver and dialed two numbers I knew by heart: the guard gate, to leave a pass, and the pizza delivery place that could find their way to my house blindfolded. A medium mushroom and pepperoni would be here in twenty minutes.

I slid on my reading glasses and spread the papers from the tax office out on the kitchen table. I grabbed a legal pad from the office and my favorite Waterford pen from my bag.

By the time the doorbell announced the arrival of my dinner, I was already deep into the tangled web of corporations and holding companies that masked the real names of Geoff's associates—and alarm bells were going off in my head.

I awoke the next morning to a cacophony of birdsong and the tart smell of the ocean. I squinted at the bedside clock through bright sunshine pouring through the open French doors. I couldn't tell if the first numeral on the digital face was an eight or a nine, only that it was round.

I rolled over and thought about going back to sleep. Then the memory of last night's discoveries—or lack of them, actually—wormed its way into my consciousness, and I decided I'd better get up.

I stretched out my sleep-cramped muscles and concluded that I also needed some exercise. My body had become used to a daily routine of tennis or golf, and it was starting to rebel. And besides, it looked like too glorious a morning to spend it all indoors.

I brushed my teeth, tied up my hair, and selected a dark turquoise bathing suit from among the several I'd had made after the explosion. One-piece, cut daringly low in the front, the back was solid material that covered almost all my scars. Only the slightest hint of the skin graft could be seen at the top of my shoulder. I slathered it with SPF 30 sun screen, threw on a T-shirt and sandals and headed for the kitchen.

Dolores was humming softly to herself as she brought order out of the mess I'd left last night. I'd meant to clean it up before she got there, but exhaustion had won out.

"*Buenas dias, Señora*," she chirped, stuffing the greasy pizza box into the trash.

"Good morning, Dolores. I'm really sorry about all this."

She smiled and shrugged. "*Es nada.*"

"And don't worry about the bedroom," I added, remembering the mound of discarded clothes on the floor. "I'll get the laundry together later."

I drank a quick cup of tea, waved off Dolores's offer of breakfast, and walked briskly toward the ocean. The beach was deserted except for a couple of locals and their dogs. I pulled off the T-shirt and plunged into the surf.

I'm not a strong swimmer, but I've got stamina, despite the smoking. As I stroked back and forth in the warm salt water, I again resolved to give up the habit. *How*, I wasn't sure, but I'd do it. Soon.

Back at the house, refreshed and more relaxed than I'd been in days, I found a note from Dolores on the kitchen table.

Stor was all it said.

When I entered my room, I found the bed neatly made and the pile of dirty clothes gone from the floor. She'd taken the laundry, too.

I emerged from the shower determined to get my act back together and stop letting other people pick up after me. As I pulled on white shorts and a hot pink cotton golf shirt, I spied the day's *Island Packet* on the chest at the foot of the bed. On top of it was a folded piece of plain white paper.

I recognized it immediately. It was the photocopy of the letter I had found in Miss Addie's apartment and stuffed hurriedly into my slacks. I had forgotten all about it. Dolores must have come across it when she gathered the laundry and went through the pockets.

I sat down on the bed, reached for my cigarettes, and opened the letter.

As I had suspected, it was from Miss Addie. J. Lawton Merriweather was apparently her attorney, although I thought I remembered that her family had used a big firm in Charleston. It had been written last Thursday, the day Miss Addie called me and began the whole weird chain of events that had disrupted my quiet, reclusive life.

The letter confirmed that Law was to meet her at The Cedars last Saturday morning to effect the changes they had discussed earlier. She also wished to consult him on the possible liquidation of some assets. Adelaide Boyce Hammond expressed her appreciation for his coming to her, since she had been unable to drive for some years.

Miss Addie must have real clout, I thought as I refolded the letter and carried it into the office. Anyone who could get a lawyer to make a house call—and on a Saturday morning in the middle of the summer— must have pushed some serious buttons. I tucked the paper under the desk pad, unsure of exactly what it meant, but certain Miss Addie would want me to keep it.

I spent the rest of the morning on the phone.

My first call was to Columbia. My hands shook a little as I punched in the once-familiar number.

It had taken them a long time after the bombing to appoint a replacement for Rob. The Special Investigations unit of the State Attorney General's office had been his baby, conceived, staffed, and administered pretty much by my husband himself. His background as a lawyer with the Justice Department had given him contacts in Washington that made him uniquely qualified for the job.

Belinda St. John, a tall, willowy black woman of Haitian descent, had been his hand-picked assistant. Her stunning good looks often caused those around her to underestimate her keen, incisive mind. But for a scheduling snafu that had forced her to be in court that day, Belinda would have been on the plane with Rob.

When she had been passed over for his job in favor of the inexperienced college pal of a prominent political hack, Belinda St. John had threatened to take her sharp wits and voluminous knowledge into private practice. Instead she had accepted the newly-created post of Special Counsel to the Governor. I had seen her smooth, high cheek-boned face in the background of many news conferences and photo ops, always just behind the handsome, boyish figure of our state's Chief Executive.

Belinda wouldn't have the information I needed, but she could get it for me. Discreetly.

I'd had some time to think about the *coincidence* of Hadley Bolles showing up at the tax office at precisely the right time to intercept my request for the owners of record of the Grayton's Race tract. I didn't believe in coincidences. Someone had alerted him, and that made me very nervous. I decided the fewer people who were aware of my continued interest, the better.

The conversation with Belinda St. John was strained, punctuated by uncomfortable silences. After she had inquired into the progress of my recovery and I had asked after the well-being of her two children, we seemed at a loss for something to say. So I got quickly down to the reason for my call: I needed the names of the stockholders and incorporators of the various corporations and holding companies that were listed on the tax records as the owners of Grayton's Race.

"You can get that from the Secretary of State's office," Belinda told me, her voice full of unasked questions. "It's all public record."

"I know. It's just that I don't want to make a formal request, have a record of it anywhere. It's a long story, and I'll give it to you if you want. But right now I'm just operating on hunches and suspicions. I don't really have anything concrete to go on."

"Sounds like the old days," she said, a catch in her voice. A lot of the tension between us dissipated.

"Yeah, you're right. I even tried hacking into the computer system, but I'm afraid I've lost my touch."

"I didn't hear that."

"Gotcha."

"Bay, is this something the SI unit should be advised about?" Her tone had turned serious. "The guys Rob and I used to investigate play for keeps. You of all people should know that. This doesn't have anything to do with one of his old cases, does it?"

"No, no. It's strictly a local thing, Bel. Just doing a favor for some old friends."

"No one's called me 'Bel' since Rob was killed. God, I'd like to nail those bastards!"

When I didn't reply, she backed off. "Sorry. Bad memories. I'm sure you don't need to be reminded."

"Why haven't they? Nailed them, I mean." I tried hard to keep the quaver out of my voice. "How can they just let it go, all those deaths?"

"Politics, honey. In this town, it's always politics." Then her tone turned to steel. "But don't think we've forgotten. There are a lot of us here who will never forget. The game's not over."

Belinda would be out of town on a junket with the Governor for the next few days, she said, but she'd give my request to her aide, Dennis Morgan. He was absolutely trustworthy, she assured me, and could be relied upon to operate with complete discretion. I gave her my fax number, and she said I should have the information in the next couple of days. I thanked her, and we hung up with mutual promises to stay in touch that neither of us believed we'd keep. Our connection had been severed with Rob's death.

Dolores returned with the groceries, and I helped her unload the car and restock the larder. I chided her for dealing with the laundry, but she shrugged it off.

"You have many things on your mind, *Señora,* many troubles. I do small thing to help is all."

Impulsively I hugged this little woman who only came up to my shoulder. She wriggled away in embarrassment and chased me out of the kitchen. Now that there was food in the house, lunch was her first order of business.

I gathered up my notes and the phone and moved my base of operations out onto the shade of the deck.

I spoke to the intensive care nurse's station, and they managed to track down Dr. Winter. He was a little more optimistic than he'd been the day before. He was exploring the possibility that Miss Addie had had a reaction to one of her medications. He had changed the entire course of her drug therapy. He assured me that my friend was in no immediate danger, although she was still unconscious. One of the many knots in my stomach relaxed a little at the news. He still didn't want her to have visitors, so there was little I could do but wait. Dr. Winter promised to call me the minute there was any change.

I left a message for Law Merriweather to call me when he got back to the office. I didn't think he'd tell me anything about his discussions with Miss Addie—privilege and all that—but I at least wanted to inform him about her condition. As her attorney, he had a right—and a need—to know.

I bullied Dolores into sitting down at the kitchen table and sharing the huge mound of pasta with clam sauce she'd whipped up for me. She caught me up on the news of her family. She was very proud of her three kids, all of whom spoke perfect English and did well in school. Then she launched into a catalogue of the wonders of *Presqu'isle.*

Dolores had been extremely impressed with the beauty of my mother's antiques and with the splendor of the house itself.

I tried to match her enthusiasm, but the place held no charm for me. Growing up there had been like living in a museum, everything untouchable and off limits. Had there been love, it might have been bearable. As it was...

I sent a protesting Dolores off for a well-deserved free afternoon and cleaned up the kitchen myself. I was wiping down the green marble counters, happy to be doing something useful, when Neddie finally returned my calls.

"Hey there, Tanner, how the hell are ya?" she greeted me in her booming voice. "Long time, no hear."

Despite her many years in the South, Dr. Nedra Halloran had kept her broad New England accent. That last word had come out "heah-uh."

"Hey, Neddie. I'm okay. How's the wonderful world of mental medicine?"

"The kids are great. I swear, though, most of the parents could use a brain transplant. They oughta make you get a permit to get knocked up. It's tougher to get a driver's license than it is to drag some poor, unsuspecting kid kicking and screaming into the world."

It was a familiar, recurring theme. Neddie believed that bad kids were generally made, not born. While I wasn't a wholehearted subscriber to her theory, she had a lot of experience to back it up.

"Good thing you and I skipped the motherhood thing," I said. "Imagine what kind of screwed up offspring *we* might have produced."

"Speak for yourself, Tanner. I would have made a *fabulous* mother. Too bad my ovaries had other plans."

Neddie's inability to have children had contributed to the breakup of her short-lived marriage to a popular Savannah newscaster. But in typical Neddie fashion, she had faced the disappointment and moved on.

"So, what's up?" she asked. "You really doing okay?"

"Yeah, I'm fine. Well, not really *fine*, but all right. Listen, I've got a proposition for you."

"If he's tall, rich, and Catholic—and not *absolutely* repulsive looking—I'm available."

"Try to control yourself, Nedra. Aren't there any guys left in Savannah?"

"Not many single, straight ones. At least none that are looking for a strictly carnal relationship with a slightly overweight, shanty-Irish redheaded shrink."

"With a resume like that, they should be beating down your door. Listen," I said, dropping the banter, "remember my friend, Bitsy?"

"That disgustingly petite little thing with the gorgeous blond hair and no butt? Of course I remember her. I hate her."

"She's got problems, Neddie, and I think you could help."

I detailed Bitsy's concerns about CJ, her belief that he was exhibiting the signs of drug abuse, and her inability to get any support from her husband. I had Neddie's attention now, and I could hear her scribbling notes while we talked. All business now, she asked a couple of probing questions I didn't have the answers to.

"So the old man won't let her bring the kid in for evaluation, huh? The classic ostrich syndrome—if I don't know about it, I don't have to deal with it. Boy, parents like that really piss me off."

"So how about it? Want to spend a couple of glorious, fun-filled days at this fabulous beach resort without cost or obligation? Say yes, Neddie. I'd really love to see you."

"Sure. On one condition."

"What's that?"

"You don't cook. Nothing. Not even an egg. I'm in the kitchen, or we eat out."

"You're so good for my ego, Halloran. No wonder you're such a successful psychologist."

"Hey, I usually get ninety bucks an hour for this routine. You want charm, it costs extra."

As usual after a conversation with my irreverent ex-roomie, I hung up laughing. Neddie's last patient on Friday was at two o'clock, so she should be here sometime before five. I called Bitsy and set dinner for seven. I told her to save her gratitude until we heard what Neddie had to say.

I figured that was enough work for one day, so I called the Club to see if I could scare up a tennis match. Brad, the young pro, told me to come by about four. If no one was looking for an opponent, he'd play me himself.

As I stripped off my clothes and stepped into my tennis whites, I realized that I hadn't thought about Geoff Anderson all day.

Things were definitely looking up.

16

Neddie and I had just enough time for a quick swim on Friday after-noon before we had to dress for dinner at the Elliotts. My friend turned heads all up and down the beach when she peeled off her white mesh cover-up to reveal a scandalously skimpy, emerald green bikini.

"My God, Halloran, why did you bother? I mean, why not just go naked?" I asked as a couple of gawking college guys nearly ran their bikes into the ocean.

"You don't like it?"

Neddie surveyed herself critically, turning to look over one shoulder at the thin strip of fabric covering barely a third of her rounded bottom. She had a lush figure, full-breasted, with long legs and generous hips. With her shoulder-length, frizzy hair blowing in the slight breeze off the water, she reminded me of Bette Midler in "Beaches".

"Of course I like it. It is quintessentially *you*. I'm just insanely jealous of your body, that's all."

"Yeah, right. There's not an ounce of flab on you. And that gor-geous tan! I look like a fat, white slug that just crawled out from under some rock."

Neddie has that creamy, softly freckled skin that frequently blesses Irish redheads.

"Come on, Halloran, quit bitching. Let's get in the water before someone jumps your bones right here in front of all the tourists."

"Promises, promises."

Back at the house, we dressed casually, Neddie in white slacks and a shimmering silk blouse in her favorite green. I chose cream colored linen trousers and a soft peach sweater. Neddie tied a brightly patterned scarf over her wild tangle of hair as we climbed into the convertible.

"I can put the top up if you want," I offered as we pulled out of the driveway.

"No, this is great. I love the feel of the wind. It's just that this mop will look even more like I just stuck my finger in a light socket if I don't tie it down."

Traffic was light, the locals already home from work, and the tourists nursing their sunburns before heading out to dinner.

"Anything else I should know about this bunch before we charge into battle?" Neddie asked as we eased over the speedbump at the entrance to Spanish Wells. It was one of the few areas of exclusive homes on the island with no security gate.

"No, I think you're pretty much up to speed. I really haven't spent that much time with the kids, at least not since they've gotten older."

I turned into the long drive and pulled up in front of Bitsy's massive, Spanish-style home. Its red tile roof gleamed in the rays of the waning sun, towering live oaks casting long shadows across the creamy adobe walls.

"Wow, this is kind of out of character for Hilton Head, isn't it?" Neddie marveled. "Looks like it belongs in California."

"Big Cal's choice. He thinks it has 'class'. Bitsy would have been happy with something smaller and more regional, architecturally; but, as usual, she didn't have much to say about it."

"Not your favorite guy, is he?" Neddie commented as we mounted the steps and rang the bell.

"Look up 'pond scum' in the dictionary, and you'll find his picture." The door opened, and we were engulfed in the warmth of Bitsy's welcome.

After the obligatory tour of the house, during which Neddie made the appropriate *oohs* and *aahs*, we sat down to a Lowcountry feast of oysters, crab, shrimp, and corn with new potatoes and homemade rolls. Unlike me, Bitsy is a whiz in the kitchen and had done all the cooking herself.

The four kids, scrubbed and shining, were well-behaved and surprisingly good company. Neddie, her easy rapport with them evident from the start, drew them into the conversation. Even Brady, the youngest, his slight stammer more endearing than annoying, had us laughing at his convoluted tales of life in the third grade.

I kept stealing glances at CJ whose muscular frame occupied his father's place at the head of the table. He alone seemed ill at ease, responding to Neddie's gently probing questions with monosyllabic answers. Not until she got onto football—an area she was surprisingly knowledgeable about—did any animation light his somber, almost sullen, expression.

"Yeah, the Panthers are awesome, aren't they? They could have a shot at the Super Bowl this year."

"You think so? I'd bet Dallas will have something to say about that. Or the Forty-Niners."

Mally, who, at fifteen, was almost a carbon copy of her mother at that age, nattered away about school, friends, boys, and getting her driver's permit. She had helped Bitsy serve and clear and was now placing thin wedges of dark pecan pie in front of each of us.

"If this is homemade, I'm going to have to arm wrestle you for the recipe," Neddie said around a mouthful of the sweet, rich dessert.

"Actually, Mally made it." Bitsy beamed with pride.

"I'd be happy to copy off the recipe for you, Dr. Halloran. It's my Grandmomma Quintard's." She lowered her voice conspiratorially. "It's got *bourbon* in it."

"Just a dash," Bitsy hastened to add, glancing at me.

The two youngest kids, Brady and Margaret, wolfed down the pie and asked to be excused. They distributed exuberant hugs all around the table before scampering off toward the family room.

"They want to watch 'Jurassic Park,'" Bitsy explained, smiling fondly at the retreating backs of her children.

"Yeah, for about the hundred and fiftieth time." The sarcasm brought the scowl back to CJ's face. "Can I be excused, too? I got things I gotta do." He rocked back on two legs of the heavy oak chair and stared at his mother.

"No!" Bitsy cast a panicky look at Neddie, who made an almost imperceptible *stop* motion with her hand, as if to say, *Cool it. Go easy.*

"I'd rather you stayed," Bitsy said more calmly, "just for a while longer, okay?"

The front two legs of CJ's chair landed with a *thump* that sounded unnaturally loud in the strained silence.

"Why don't you go bring in the coffee," Bitsy suggested to her glowering son, "and some tea for your Aunt Bay? Mally will help you."

"I don't need any help." CJ flung his balled up napkin on the table and stalked off to the kitchen.

Bitsy shrugged an apology.

Neddie smiled and shook her head. "Don't worry about it. I've seen much worse."

"CJ can be *such* a creep," Mally offered from the wisdom of her fifteen years. "Honestly. Boys!"

By ten o'clock it was obvious that CJ was not going to participate in any more attempts at conversation, so we rose to take our leave. Mally, on the other hand, had chattered almost non-stop, asking Neddie pointed questions about her work and seeming absorbed by the answers. She had left the table only long enough to refill the coffee pot.

"How about lunch tomorrow?" I asked Bitsy as the five of us stood alongside my car in the soft, humid darkness. We'd had no opportunity to talk alone, and I knew she'd be anxious to hear Neddie's preliminary diagnosis.

"What a great idea." Neddie had picked up on my train of thought. "Doesn't your club do a brunch on weekends?"

"Yes, and it's wonderful. Twelve-thirty okay with you, Bits?"

I hoped Bitsy could read my eyes, that she was getting the message. "Uh, sure. Yes. That sounds good," she said.

"Oh, can I come, too, Aunt Bay? Please?"

Mally's rudeness was so out of character I was momentarily at a loss.

"Mally!" her mother snapped, obviously embarrassed.

"Oh, please, Mom? Can I?"

"You don't want to spend your Saturday hanging out with a bunch of old ladies," I said. "You'll be bored to tears."

"Don't you have Ashley and Jennifer coming over tomorrow to swim in the pool? Besides," her mother added as Mally opened her mouth to protest, "I need you to look after Brady and Margaret for me."

"Mo—om." It was the lament of every thwarted teenager.

"Next time, okay, honey?" Neddie held out her hand. "Nice to have met you, Mally. And don't forget about that pecan pie recipe, okay?"

Mally reluctantly shook hands with Nedra and gave me a brief hug before flouncing back into the house.

Neddie was thanking Bitsy for the wonderful meal when CJ mumbled, " 'Night, Aunt Bay," and engulfed me in an unexpected bear hug. With his lips just inches from my ear he whispered, "I need to talk to you. Can I come over? Tomorrow morning?"

"Sure," I murmured, completely taken aback. "Sure."

"What are you two whisperin' about over there?" Bitsy sounded edgy and suspicious.

"I was just apologizing for being such a dud tonight." CJ lied with a practiced ease that made me nervous. "Too much football practice, I guess. It really wears me out."

He turned the full force of his considerable charm on Nedra. "It was nice to meet you, Dr. Halloran. I hope you'll come back real soon. I promise to be better company next time."

"I'll look forward to it."

As we rolled down the driveway, I turned back to wave. CJ had draped his arm across his mother's shoulder, and hers was wrapped around his waist.

"Well," I asked while Neddie retied the scarf around her hair, "what do you think?"

We turned onto the parkway and picked up speed.

"What did he really say to you just now?"

I cocked an eyebrow at her, and she smiled knowingly.

"Honey, I've been lied to by my patients in every conceivable way known to man. You think I can't spot bullshit when I hear it?"

"He's coming over tomorrow morning. He wants to talk to me."

"Good."

"What do you mean 'good'? I don't know how to deal with someone with a drug problem. He should be talking to you."

"It's not him."

"What do you mean, it's not him? What the hell are you talking about?"

"It's not him. With the drug problem."

I had to stop for the light at Mathews Drive, and I turned to face Neddie.

"What exactly are you saying?"

Neddie shrugged and looked me squarely in the eye.

"It's the girl. It's Mally."

We were still arguing about it at midnight as we got ready for bed.

"I don't get it, Tanner," Neddie mumbled around a mouthful of toothpaste.

I sprawled on the bed in the guest room trying unsuccessfully to blow smoke rings. I heard her rinse and spit, then the light clicked off in the adjoining bath. Neddie, whose oversized T-shirt was even rattier than mine, flopped down beside me.

"Give me one of those," she said, pointing at the cigarette.

Reluctantly, I tossed her the pack. "God, I'm corrupting everyone around me. First Bitsy, now you."

"Don't flatter yourself, girl. I can navigate the road to hell very nicely on my own, thank you."

"What don't you get?" I asked as she lay down on her back and blew a perfect circle on her first try.

"You, that's what."

"Why?"

"Well, you drag me up here to find out if one of your friend's kids is on the stuff. I confirm your worst fears, and then you argue with me. Who's the expert here, anyway?"

"I know, I know. It was just such a shock to hear you say it was Mally. I still can't believe it."

Neddie stubbed out the cigarette and rolled over onto her stomach. "Look, kid, it doesn't give me any joy to be right, you know? But she's definitely on uppers of some kind. I think CJ knows it, too. That's why he was so hostile."

"What am I supposed to say to him tomorrow? I mean, I don't want to make things worse."

"Just play it by ear. Listen closely, hear him out. Most of all, don't make judgments. He's feeling very protective of his little sister. He could be a big help in getting her into therapy voluntarily."

"Make judgments? *Moi?*" I asked in mock surprise.

"Yeah, you." Neddie flung the comforter back and pulled the pillow out from under my head. "Now get the hell out of here, will you, and let me get some sleep?"

I clambered off the bed and paused in the doorway when she called my name.

"What were you so nervous about when we drove back in tonight? You looked as if you expected someone to jump out of the bushes and grab you."

I *had* been surprised—and more than a little relieved— not to find Geoff Anderson waiting in the driveway. I hadn't been aware that it showed. But then Neddie was trained to see below the surface of the faces we all put on for each other. Trying to fool her was pointless.

"There was that possibility," I admitted.

Neddie was instantly alert. "Are you in some kind of danger?"

"No, it's nothing like that. Just someone I didn't particularly want to deal with tonight."

"Would this by any chance be a *male* someone?"

"Goodnight, Nedra." I flipped off the overhead light.

"Okay, but don't think you're gonna worm your way out of telling me. Tomorrow I expect to hear the whole sordid story, including the intimate and prurient details."

"You're a sick, perverted woman, Halloran."

"I know. That's why you love me. G' night."

I closed the door and walked across the hall into the office. Sometime between the time we went out for our swim and the time we got back from the Elliotts, Belinda St. John's assistant had come through. Several pages of printing lay in a neat stack at the base of the fax machine.

I was surprised, because the fax had been acting up the last time I'd used it, spewing paper out onto the floor. Since I am extremely mechanically challenged, I'd made no attempt to find the problem. It must have fixed itself in that mysterious way that machines sometimes do, I decided as I stood and glanced down the list of names.

Nothing leaped right out at me, but one or two were vaguely familiar. As I'd suspected, some of the incorporators were themselves corporations and partnerships. Dennis Morgan was good. He'd anticipated my needs and done additional research so that every entry was cross-referenced to the *individuals* involved, where possible.

In a handwritten cover sheet, he said that some of the businesses were out-of-state, mostly from Florida. He had some friends in the statehouse there, he wrote, and I should let him know if I wanted those stockholder names, too.

I decided it could all wait until tomorrow. My head was already stuffed with enough things to worry about.

"'Sufficient unto the day is the evil thereof' ", I muttered as I crawled in between the freshly laundered sheets.

Old St. Matthew sure had that right, I thought as I drifted off.

17

The sound of Nedra Halloran's deep, husky laugh drifted in through the open French doors. A second voice, obviously male, responded. I finished dressing quickly, embarrassed that CJ Elliott had apparently arrived while I was in the shower.

I stepped out onto the deck and followed the hum of conversation around the corner to the screened-in area off the greatroom. Neddie and CJ were sprawled in my deep-cushioned wicker chairs, empty coffee mugs dangling from their hands. Egg-smeared plates and forks lay on the round table. Toast crumbs peppered the bright yellow tablecloth.

"Hey, she rises!" Neddie greeted me with a grin and hooked her foot under another chair, pulling it up to the table. "Want some breakfast?"

"No, thanks. You know I never eat before noon if I can help it. Sorry I overslept, CJ," I said to my honorary nephew.

"Hey, no problem, Aunt Bay. I got here awful early. I just hung around in the driveway until Dr. Halloran came out for the paper and found me."

"Sure I can't fix you something?" Neddie asked again. "Toast or a bagel?"

"You should have one of the Doc's omelets. They're awesome." CJ poured himself more coffee.

"I made tea for you. It should still be hot. Wanna grab the pot for me, CJ?"

"Sure," he said, leaping from his chair.

"Looks like you've made another conquest," I remarked under my breath as CJ bounded up the steps to the kitchen.

"He's a real good kid," Neddie replied, "but he certainly has something on his mind. I'm gonna disappear in a minute and leave you two alone."

She correctly read the apprehension on my face. "Don't worry. Just listen. That's all you need to do right now."

"Okay, if you say so."

CJ slid the screen open with his foot and set the teapot and a clean mug down on the table in front of me.

"Well, I'm off to the beach," Neddie announced. I could see through the mesh of her cover-up that she wore a more modest, one-piece suit today. "Catch you guys later."

"See ya, Doc." CJ's eyes followed her as she trotted down the stairs and disappeared among the trees.

I busied myself stirring sweetener into my tea and lighting a cigarette. CJ studied the generic seaside prints on the back wall, the collection of shells and dried sand dollars on the end table, even the woven rush mats on the floor.

He looked everywhere except at me.

"So. What's on your mind?" I finally prodded him.

CJ gulped a mouthful of coffee and countered my question with one of his own. "Why did you and the Doc come over last night? My mother set it up, didn't she?"

"She invited us, yes," I hedged.

"She thinks I'm doin' drugs, doesn't she." He delivered it as a statement of fact in a wry, almost patronizing voice.

I wasn't sure how much I was supposed to contribute, so I waited for CJ to continue. When he didn't, I said quietly, "She *has* expressed some concern about you."

"Damn it! How could she think *I'd* be so stupid? I'm an athlete. I wouldn't put that crap in my body!"

It was almost a word-for-word rendition of what I had said to Bitsy a couple of days ago. Up until last night, I would have been overjoyed at CJ's convincing denial. As it was, I already knew that *he* was not the problem. I took Neddie's advice and kept silent.

"Well, as usual, she's got it all screwed up," he scoffed.

"Should she be more concerned about your sister?"

His head snapped up at that. "Who said anything about Mally? Who told you it was her?" He paused, then nodded knowingly. "The Doc, right?"

I poured more tea and gave CJ an opportunity to digest this information. "Aunt Bay," he said at last, "you have to promise that you won't tell anyone about any of this, okay?"

"If Mally has a drug abuse problem, your parents have a right to know. They have to get her some kind of help."

He looked at me oddly, as if I weren't getting it. "I know that. It's already taken care of. I talked to Mally last night, after you guys left. She really liked Dr. Halloran. She said she'll go into treatment if Mom and Dad will let her go to the Doc. We're going to talk to them tomorrow when Dad gets back."

CJ's casual dismissal of his sister's drug problem rankled me more than a little. CJ didn't seem to notice.

"That's good. See that you follow through. This is not something to be taken lightly. Neddie—Dr. Halloran—is the best. I know she'll be able to help Mally." I lit another cigarette and relaxed back into the chair. "And don't worry. None of what we've said here will leave this room."

"Thanks, but that's not why I really came over. I wanted to talk to you about Zay."

"Who's Zay?"

"You know, Isaiah. That's what all the guys call him."

"Oh, right."

"Anyway, it's about me and Zay. And Derek. And you promise you won't tell anyone about it, right?"

For a moment I was too shocked to answer.

Derek? This was about Derek Johnson?

I had no idea what he was going to say, but I wouldn't lie to him. This was too important.

"I can't promise that, CJ. If you know something about Derek's murder, you have to tell the police. Come on, you know that as well as I do," I snapped as he jumped up and began pacing. "Just sit down and tell me. We'll decide together who else has to get involved. I promise I won't do anything without checking with you first. Deal?"

"Okay," he finally conceded after a short pause. "But, see, Zay told me not to say anything, and I gave him my word. But the cops want to talk to me again, on Monday. That guy Gibson called yesterday. And I'm afraid Zay is still a suspect, and I don't know what to do."

CJ looked close to panic, and I wanted to put my arms around him, offer comfort. Instead, I let him fight his own battle for control. When he had it back, he jumped right in.

"See, Derek was a dealer. Everyone at school knew you could get just about anything you wanted from him. Uppers, downers, crack, dust. Even heroin and coke, if you had the money."

My God, I thought, stunned. *Poor Lavinia. And Mavis.*

I shook my head in disbelief. "Was he supplying your sister?"

CJ nodded. "She's not hooked real bad, you know? Just pills, and she knows she has to get off them. She'll be okay."

"Why the hell didn't anyone turn him in? Why didn't you?"

"He was Zay's cousin, sort of. Besides, nobody narcs, not if you want to keep your friends."

It was a perverted code of teenage ethics that I would never understand. "Go on," I urged him.

"Well, that day at football practice—you know, the day Derek...died?"

I nodded.

"Derek was hangin' around, like he did sometimes. He got steroids and growth hormone for some of the guys on the team, stuff to build up muscles. But lately he'd been offering free samples of the 'good' stuff—crack and like that. Trying to get kids hooked. And Zay told him to take a hike, to leave the guys alone."

"And that's what the fight was about," I interrupted. There it was. The answer to the question that had been nibbling at my subconscious was suddenly staring me right in the face.

You're an idiot, Tanner, I berated myself silently. It was so obvious. In all the discussions of the day of Derek's death, I had never once asked what the big argument with Isaiah had been about.

"Yeah," CJ said, jerking me back, "Zay hates that drug shit. He told Derek if he came around practice again—or around Mally—he'd kill him. Derek laughed at him, made some crack about Zay bein' a pussy. Then they started throwin' punches."

"So what happened next?"

"Well, Zay said we had to teach Derek a lesson. Make sure he got the message. Derek's got that little fishin' shack on the river, you know? On that land his granddaddy left him and his momma? He hangs out there a lot."

The heirs property. So Red had been right about that, too.

A lot of things were beginning to make sense.

"So you and Isaiah went looking for him?"

CJ hung his head. "Yeah," he muttered. "We told our folks we were going campin', and we pitched a tent down river from the shack. After it got dark, we headed up that way. Zay had…" CJ faltered and looked away.

"What? What did he have?" I demanded.

"A baseball bat."

"Oh, God!"

'Blunt trauma to the back of the head' I could hear Red saying. 'He was dead before he went into the water.'

"We were just gonna threaten Derek, honest. He's…he was a lot bigger'n Zay. We were just tryin' to even things up a little."

Two against one was more than even, I thought, but kept it to myself.

"So what happened when you found him?"

"We didn't, that's just it. He wasn't there. We waited, but he never showed up. We went back to camp, ate some sandwiches, and went to sleep."

"And that's it?"

The boy squirmed and bit at his right thumbnail.

"Come on, CJ. You've gone this far. Let's have the rest of it."

"I woke up about two o'clock. Zay wasn't in his sleeping bag. And the bat was gone. So I got worried and started down the path to the shack, and Zay and I nearly ran smack into each other. He looked real scared and told me to shut up and get back to the tent."

The words were pouring out. CJ had wrestled alone with this dilemma for more than a week. I couldn't have stopped him now if I'd wanted to.

"When we got back, Zay said he went off on his own because he didn't want to get me in any trouble. But when he got close to the shack, he heard voices, loud, like people arguing. He waited behind a tree. There was a boat tied up at the old dock, and two guys were yellin' at Derek."

"Could Isaiah see who they were?"

"No. Just that there were two of 'em—white guys—and they were big. A lot bigger 'n Derek. Zay turned to sneak away, and he must've made some kind of noise, 'cause one of the guys yelled, 'Who's there?' and started walking toward where Zay was hidin'. The guy had a gun. Some kind of automatic rifle, Zay said, like maybe an Uzi or somethin'. He could see it in the light from the lanterns in the shack."

I was on the edge of my chair. "What did he do? How did he get away?"

"He just crawled back into the brush and hid. They didn't look real hard. Probably figured it was a raccoon or a deer. Anyway, Zay finally made it back to the path, and that's when we ran into each other." CJ sat back, exhausted. "Could I have a Coke or somethin', Aunt Bay? My throat's really dry."

"Sure, honey." The childish endearment slipped out before I could stop myself.

I walked up the steps to the kitchen, torn between keeping my promise to CJ and grabbing up the phone and getting Bitsy over here on the double.

Honor won out. I carried glasses of ice and two cans of soda back onto the deck.

"Sorry, all I've got is diet."

"That's okay. Thanks."

I listened to the rest of CJ's incredible tale in stunned silence.

The boys had stayed awake the rest of the night, trying to decide what to do. They didn't want to start up the car for fear of advertising their presence to whoever was threatening Derek. At first light, they crept back up the trail. The boat was gone, and Derek was nowhere around. But lying along the bank, not far from the dock, they found Isaiah's baseball bat. He'd dropped it in the woods when he'd fled the night before.

"And it had stuff all over it. Blood and hair and…stuff."

Derek Johnson's brains, I thought, and shuddered.

"And Derek's place was trashed, like there'd been a big fight. So we figured somebody had gotten hurt, maybe even killed. And it was Zay's bat. His name was scratched in the handle. So if it was Derek that was dead, they'd be sure to think Zay did it. Because of the fight at school."

"What did you do with the bat?" If the police had found it, Red would have told me.

"We buried it in the woods and went back to camp and waited for someone to come."

Leaving your prints all over, and screwing up any other evidence that might have been on it, I thought bitterly.

"Why didn't you just get the hell out of there?" I asked.

"We figured it would look bad if we ran. We'd told our parents we'd be gone a couple of days, and it'd seem funny if we came back early. Besides, on TV the cops can always find clues to prove you were somewhere even if you think you've cleaned everything up. Or someone could have seen us turn off the highway. So we just decided to stay put for another day, and, if they came, we'd just play dumb and stick to it."

I had to admit there was a certain convoluted logic in their thinking. What a load these two kids had been carrying around! But there was still a question I needed to ask, and I wasn't sure I wanted to hear the answer.

"*You* never actually saw these two men at Derek's dock, right? You only know what Isaiah told you about them."

CJ jumped to his feet, his fists balled at his sides. "You think Zay's lying? You think he killed Derek and made that other stuff up?"

"I'm just trying to make sure I have it all straight," I lied. Because that was exactly the scenario that had leaped into my mind, much as I tried to suppress it. For the first time since Red Tanner first suggested that Isaiah Smalls might be involved in his cousin's murder, doubt was gnawing at my belief in the boy's innocence.

"So what should I do, Aunt Bay?"

CJ's earnest young face looked trustingly down at me. I felt a sudden surge of that maternal instinct that must kick in when an animal's offspring are threatened. Even though he wasn't my kid, I wanted to give him money, ship him out of the country, whisk him far away from this awful mess.

I couldn't do that, and I knew it.

So did he.

"I think you already know what you have to do, CJ," I said softly. "You just wanted me to confirm it, right?"

After a long pause during which we stared silently at each other, CJ Elliott nodded.

"Good boy. I'll help you talk to your parents and your lawyer. Who is it, by the way?"

"Mr. Merriweather. From Beaufort."

Well, that's handy, I thought. At least it wasn't some stranger who might question my right to get involved. Law would understand my loyalty to both families.

"And then we'll contact Mander Brown. That's Isaiah's attorney. I'll also run this by my father and Isaiah's grandmother. We can trust them."

"Isaiah's gonna think I narced on him."

"He probably will, at first, but it has to be done. You could be in real trouble, CJ. Didn't you ever hear of an accessory-after-the-fact to murder? You two were crazy to lie to the police. Anyway, once we're all on the same page, we'll go to the sheriff. Together."

"That won't be necessary."

The disembodied voice sent me rocketing to my feet. Then the tall, wiry frame of my brother-in-law made its way slowly up the back steps and onto the deck. The sun glinted off the brass nameplate pinned to the pocket of Red Tanner's beige uniform.

CJ shot me a panicky look that quickly hardened into one of betrayal.

"Sorry. I didn't plan it this way." Red looked at me and shrugged.

"You son-of-a-bitch! How much of that did you hear?"

"Enough," he said softly.

18

"CJ, sit down and don't say another word."

"No way. I'm outta here." He grabbed his car keys off the table.

"I'm afraid I can't let you do that, son."

Red Tanner had his thumbs hooked into the belt of his sharply-creased trousers. All traces of my shy, bumbling brother-in-law were gone. He looked every inch the tough, implacable law officer I often forgot he was.

"I'm not your son. And you can't make me stay if I don't want to."

"CJ, sit down!" I yelled. "Shut up and let me handle this!"

His teenage bravado was an act. A closer look revealed a frightened kid on the verge of tears. He dropped into the chair and stared at his feet.

"I'm calling your lawyer and your mother. And you don't have to talk to him," I said, gesturing at Red. "Don't answer any questions, got it?"

"Bay, why don't you stay out of this? You know he's going to have to talk to me, sooner or later."

"Probably. But it's only going to be with his attorney present. And his parents. Or did you forget he's still a juvenile?"

I turned and dashed into the house, grabbed the portable phone, and was back on the deck in less than a minute. No one spoke as I punched in Bitsy's number.

"Bits? It's Bay. Listen, we've got a problem here."

I gave her a quick synopsis of the situation, leaving out the details of her son's startling revelations about the night of the murder.

"Get hold of Law Merriweather, and the two of you get over…Hold on." I covered the mouthpiece with my hand. "Are you arresting him?" I snapped at Red.

"He's gonna have to come in for questioning."

"Damn it, answer me straight. Are you taking him in now?"

"I can wait for his mother and his lawyer. There's no rush. I'm not trying to railroad the kid."

I gave him a look that said what I thought of his assurances. "Bitsy? Come over here. Both of you. What? No, I won't let him say anything more. Okay. Right. Hurry."

I hit the OFF button and immediately dialed again. With trembling hands I lit a cigarette. Red reached for the coffee pot, picked up my empty tea mug, and poured himself a cup. His eyes traveled back and forth between CJ and me as if he expected one of us to bolt.

In the fifteen years we'd known each other, I had never been so angry at him.

"Lavinia, let me talk to the Judge. It's urgent."

I repeated the story I'd told CJ's mother while my father listened intently.

"No, he didn't Mirandize him. I've been present the whole time," I replied to his first question. "No, he doesn't have a warrant, either. He was just sneaking around my house, eavesdropping on a private conversation." I glared at Red who met my stare unflinchingly. "Okay. I'll keep you posted."

I dropped the phone onto the table. "Everything's under control, CJ. The cavalry's on the way."

The boy jangled his keys in his hand. His right leg had started to jump in jerky little spasms that betrayed his fear.

"Stay put, okay? We'll be right back."

I jerked my head toward the deck, and Red followed me out. I walked a few feet down the porch, out of earshot of CJ. Red positioned himself so that the boy was in his line of sight.

"What the hell are you doing here, Tanner? How did you know the kid was going to spill his guts to me? Of all the underhanded, sneaky…"

Trying to keep my voice low and explode with anger at the same time was making me shake with frustration.

"Calm down, Bay. It was an accident, I swear to God. I just dropped over to talk to you. I heard voices, so I walked around back. When I caught the gist of the conversation, I had no choice but to listen. I'm a cop, damn it, and we're talking about murder here. Can't you get that through your head?"

"I know exactly what we're talking about—a sixteen-year-old kid who's scared out of his mind. He came to me for help, and thanks to you, I've betrayed him."

"Bay…" Red laid his hand on my shoulder, and I slapped it away.

"No. I don't want your apologies. Maybe you didn't plan this, I don't know. But the damage is done anyway, isn't it?"

He didn't have an answer for that.

We stood silently for several moments.

"You know, this might not be a bad thing, my takin' him into custody. If the kid's story is true—and I'm not saying I'm buying it all— then he and his buddy could be in danger. If one of them actually saw the real killers."

I hadn't thought about that. He could be right. Although CJ said that Isaiah hadn't seen the two men clearly, he might remember enough.

"Hey, what's up?" Neddie's voice from the path below startled us both. "Something wrong?"

As she trotted up the stairs, CJ jumped to his feet. "Hey, Doc!" he called. "Doctor Halloran!"

Neddie paused, one foot on the top step. "Bay? What's going on? I saw the sheriff's car in the driveway. What's he doing here?"

She glared at Red, and I realized that, though I had spoken often of Rob's brother, the cop, he and Neddie had never actually met.

The doorbell saved me from awkward introductions and explanations.

Within fifteen minutes, the house had emptied. At Bitsy's urging, Neddie accompanied the group to the sheriff's office. Her statement that Neddie was CJ's therapist wasn't strictly true, but Red was beyond arguing. They'd sort it all out down there.

I had been pointedly requested to stay out of it by everyone involved.

It wasn't until I called to report in that the Judge finally revealed what Red had apparently come to tell me: early that morning Isaiah Smalls had been formally charged with the first-degree murder of Derek Johnson. They would seek to try him as an adult.

And CJ and I had just unwittingly handed them all the ammunition they would need to make it stick.

I spent the rest of the morning pacing and chain-smoking. The Judge had assured me they couldn't use anything CJ had said against him since he hadn't been advised of his rights. Red couldn't testify to it either. Hearsay.

It sounded right, but I was still afraid. I kicked myself for not paying better attention in the few law courses I'd taken before changing majors. Regardless, I was pretty sure they could—and *would*—use what CJ had revealed to pry the truth out of Isaiah Smalls.

Since Dolores didn't come on weekends unless I had something special going on, I cleaned up the kitchen, made the beds, and ran the vacuum cleaner over an already spotless carpet. It was something to do.

I resisted the urge to call Red's office and find out what was going on. My father had advised me to stay out of it and, for once, I intended to take his advice.

To keep my mind from running around in fruitless circles, I finally flopped myself down at the desk and studied the list Dennis Morgan had faxed to me the day before. The same two names that had caught my eye in my first cursory glance last night, again set off bells in my memory: Southland Real Estate Investment and Meridian Partners Group.

Both were among the several Florida companies whose stockholders Morgan had been unable to provide me. I accessed my word processing program, and composed a letter asking him to check it out at his earliest opportunity. I faxed it to the private number Belinda St. John had given me.

Then I went to the kitchen, wolfed down a bagel to pacify my rumbling stomach, and settled myself in a shady corner of the deck.

Back in our college days, Neddie Halloran had taught me the benefits of meditation. I'd never really been able to "empty" my mind completely, but I had learned to quiet it. I had used the technique to help me through some of my more painful rehabilitation after the explosion.

I closed my eyes, rested my hands, palms up, loosely on my thighs, and breathed slowly. I focused on pushing out of my consciousness all the conflicts and anxieties that had beset my life in the past week. I concentrated instead on the constancy of my own steady breathing, felt the ebb and flow of the blood through my veins as my heart sent it out and back…out and back. The sweet songs of a dozen different birds faded into the background until there was only the peace and solitude of a tranquil mind and the measured rhythms of my own body…

When I came back, almost twenty minutes later according to my watch, I felt calm and refreshed. A lot of the confusion that had muddied my thinking had been blown away, leaving a clear, sharp certainty that I would find the pieces I needed to complete the puzzle.

And I now knew why the two names on the list of the Grayton's Race incorporators had seemed so familiar. I had held the solution in my hands just a few days ago and had failed to recognize it.

I strode purposefully into the bedroom closet and pulled up the false floorboard that concealed the safe.

When Red Tanner dropped off Neddie Halloran, shortly after four that afternoon, he sent her in as point man to see if I had calmed down enough to talk to him. She found me in the office amid a clutter of computer disks, cigarette butts, and several pages of yellow legal paper filled with scribbled notes and numbers.

"What happened?" I demanded when she appeared in the doorway. "How are the kids?"

"I need a drink." She turned and headed for the kitchen, calling back over her shoulder, "And don't give me any shit about it either, Tanner. I'm not in the mood."

Neddie made straight for the cupboard over the refrigerator and rummaged through the bottles I hadn't touched since the last time Rob and I had entertained. She pulled down a half-empty fifth of tequila and busied herself with limes, ice, and salt. Glass in hand, she sat down at the kitchen table and motioned me to join her.

"That was a cheap shot, Neddie," I said as she sipped gratefully at the clear liquid. "I've never tried to impose my hangups on you or anyone else."

"Yeah, you're right. Sorry. It's just that you always look so damned disapproving when anyone drinks around you. Your face gets all puckery—like you just ate a pickle."

She demonstrated, and I had to laugh. "I couldn't possibly look that bad. Besides, my faces are more a reaction to watching you gulp that stuff than to anything else. How can you stand it? It smells like bad cough medicine."

"Red wants to talk to you," she said, changing the subject abruptly.

It hadn't taken the two of them long to get on a first-name basis, I thought angrily, then stopped, surprised at myself. Where had that come from?

"Tough," I said, touching the flame of my lighter to a cigarette. "Talking to my brother-in-law can be hazardous to your health, or hadn't you noticed?"

"Seems like a nice enough guy to me." Neddie regarded me over the rim of her glass. "And there's no use beating a man up for doing his job. He feels bad enough as it is, without you dumping any more guilt on him."

"Is this free advice, Dr. Halloran, or is the meter running?"

Neddie downed the last of her drink. "I'm going to ignore that last crack, Tanner, because I know from experience how your mouth can get away from your brain."

We stared at each other for a long minute. I wasn't sure which one of us started to smile first, but we were both grinning when Neddie got up from the table and came around to give my shoulder a quick squeeze.

"Okay, we're even," I said.

"No, I think I'm one up, but I won't argue with you." Neddie moved toward the hallway. When she turned, her face was once again sober.

"Isaiah Smalls is still in jail. They can't have a bail hearing until Monday, or so Mr. Merriweather said. They questioned CJ for about an hour, but he was pretty cool. He only answered when his lawyer told him to and didn't volunteer any information. I said the kid was under tremendous stress—which is true—and that keeping him any longer could be injurious to his emotional well-being. Which is also true. He's riding a fine line between doing what he knows is right and maybe helping put his best friend on death row. A lot tougher people have cracked under a lot less pressure."

"So they let CJ go?" I asked.

"Yes. His father showed up right at the end of everything. He may be a loudmouthed s.o.b., but he gets results. We were out of there about five minutes after he started throwing his weight around."

"Big Cal doesn't make all those campaign contributions for nothing."

"Whatever he does, it works. His kid's at home. The other boy's lawyer—the one with the strange name—is going to interview CJ at the house tonight. Get his version of the story."

"Mander Brown."

"Yeah, that's the one. So anyway, that's where it stands. Except that I'm so damned confused I don't know which end's up. Somebody needs to explain this whole thing to me. All I've gotten so far are bits and pieces."

"I know. We really pitched you under the bus, didn't we? Thanks, Neddie. Not just for what you did for CJ and his family. But for being there for *me* every time I need you."

Neddie waved my gratitude away. "You'll pay. Starting tonight. I want a very large, very rare steak and a bottle of excellent wine which I intend to drink entirely by myself. Your treat."

"You're on. I've got so much to tell you. I think a lot of things about this mess may be coming together. I want to run it all by you, see what you think."

"You mean there's more to this Derek Johnson thing than meets the eye?"

I nodded. "Lots."

"Anything that could get these kids off the hook?"

"Maybe," I said, "if they're telling the truth. Their story's so fantastic, I'm inclined to believe them. It's almost too bizarre for them to have invented it. And there are some other connections I don't think even the cops are aware of. I just need to work it all out, make sure of my facts. We'll talk after dinner."

"Boy, you sure do lead an exciting life for a reclusive widow-lady. I should hang out with you more often." Neddie began to unbutton her blouse. "Now get out there and make nice with that handsome brother-in-law of yours. He's waiting in the cruiser. I'm going to have a swim, a shower, and a nap, in that order. Okay?"

"Enjoy," I said. I rose and tucked my cigarettes and lighter into the pocket of my shorts and went to get some answers from Sergeant Redmond Tanner.

19

I let Neddie pick the restaurant. She opted for a local favorite that specialized in both beef and seafood. Tucked away in a small marina on Broad Creek, its wide windows overlooked the salt marshes glowing golden-red in the setting sun.

Neddie poured the last of the Cabernet into her long-stemmed wine glass and leaned back in her chair. "I'm not sure I'm following any of this, Bay. Some of your conclusions seem to be based on pretty flimsy evidence."

"I know there are still holes in it. That's why I need to do some more digging into Rob's files when we get home. But those two names—Southland Real Estate and Meridian Partners—came up in one of his investigations, I'm sure of it. That's why they sounded familiar to me. And with what Red told me this afternoon, it's all starting to hang together."

"But what's the connection with what's been going on here? The murder of the Johnson kid and this land deal business? And your friend, Miss Hammond? I still don't get it."

"Keep it down, Neddie." Her voice had risen steadily with each glass of wine. "Let's not announce it to the whole world yet, okay?"

"Sorry." Neddie covered her mouth with her hand and looked guiltily around.

The restaurant, off the beaten trail but still jammed with tourists at the height of the season, had filled steadily while we ate our leisurely meal. Seven o'clock reservations had been a good idea. Now, just before nine, there wasn't an empty table in the place. Even the long bar, adjacent to the smoking section where we sat, was crowded with people waiting to be seated.

"Look, let me run through it again," I began. "First…"

The tall, tan body of our college-age waiter materialized at my elbow. He wore a bright blue Hawaiian print shirt and white shorts. He was a good-looking kid, clean shaven and muscular. He and Neddie had been flirting lightly all night long.

"What else can I get for you ladies? Another bottle of wine? How about a peek at the dessert menu?"

"Nothing for me, thanks. Neddie?"

"I'll have a Bailey's, on the rocks. And bring my friend here some hot tea. Constant Comment, if you have it." She winked at the boy, then whispered loudly, "It's okay. She's the designated teetotaler."

He laughed dutifully and moved away.

I lit a cigarette and stared out into the deepening twilight.

"You have to learn to lighten up a little, Tanner. Everyone who takes a drink isn't on the slippery slope to alcoholism." Neddie's voice had lost its bantering tone. She was deadly serious now.

"I'm aware of that. But what is that old expression? Something like, 'Blood will out'? I've got enough proof right here of my addictive tendencies, don't I."

I stubbed out the half-smoked cigarette as the waiter reappeared with my tea and Neddie's liqueur.

"Sure I can't interest you ladies in some dessert? The New York cheesecake looks really good tonight."

"No, thanks. Just the check please." I reached for my bag.

"That's already been taken care of."

"What do you mean? By whom?"

The young man gestured toward the bar. "By that gentleman over there. The tall one with the silver hair. Blue oxford shirt, navy slacks. See him?"

I turned and looked in the direction he was pointing. Geoff Anderson leaned back on his barstool and touched one finger to his forehead in a mock salute.

"That won't be necessary," I snapped, ignoring Geoff's tentative smile. I pulled out my wallet and slapped my gold card on the table.

"Sorry, ma'am. Like I said, it's already taken care of. You ladies have a nice evening." The waiter moved off before I could mount an argument.

"Damn him!" I spluttered, shoving my credit card back in my wallet. "Come on, let's get out of here."

"What's the rush? Let me finish my drink. And what are you so ticked off about, anyway? I can't remember the last time a handsome stranger picked up my tab. Probably never, now that I think about it."

I pushed back my chair and slung my bag over my shoulder. "Are you coming?"

Neddie folded her napkin and placed it deliberately on the table. "He's not a stranger, is he? This wouldn't by any chance be the mysterious 'someone' you wanted to avoid last night, would it?"

I stood and dug the car keys out of my bag.

"Okay, you win." Neddie rose and followed me toward the exit. "But I want an explanation, and I want it soon. You're acting pretty weird here, even for you."

I ignored her as I took the long way around, avoiding the bar. My precautions were pointless. As we crossed the crowded parking lot, I could see Geoff Anderson slouching nonchalantly against the side of my car.

"Bay, I want to talk to you."

"Get out of my way, Geoff."

I edged around him toward the driver's side, but he moved to block my path.

"No. Look, this is making me crazy. You have to tell me what's the matter. Everything was so great Sunday. *We* were great. And now you won't even take my calls. What's happened? What have I done?"

"Oh, quit playing the wounded lover, Geoff. That routine's getting old. Now get out of the way, or I'm going to call the cops."

"Who, the ever-present Sergeant Tanner? He'd love that, wouldn't he? Riding to the aid of the damsel in distress. He's the cause of all this, isn't he? He's finally succeeded in turning you against me."

Geoff's face twisted into an ugly sneer, his voice low and nasty. It was a side of him I hadn't seen before, not even when we were kids. Red had been right about one thing. I didn't know this man at all. Maybe I never had.

"How's the wife?"

My words dropped into the charged stillness like rocks into a pond. The bluster went out of Geoff Anderson like air out of a slashed tire.

"Who told you? Never mind, I can guess," he said resignedly. He moved away from the car and closed the door gently as I slid behind the wheel. The slam of the door on the other side made me jump in surprise.

I had totally forgotten about Neddie, an unexpectedly silent witness to this humiliating scene.

As I cranked the engine, Geoff leaned over, his breath warm on my face.

"It's not what it looks like, Bay. There are reasons, ones I couldn't tell you about before. If I lied about some things, it was because I had to. But I never lied about my feelings for you. And they haven't changed. If you ever want to hear my side, you know where to find me."

I stared straight ahead as Geoff gently kissed the side of my face, then walked away. A minute later, I heard the guttural roar of the Jaguar as he sped off into the night.

"You okay?" Neddie touched my shoulder as I dropped my head onto my hands. I had the steering wheel locked in a death grip. "What in the hell was that all about?"

"I've really made a mess of it this time," I whispered.

"Want to talk about it?"

"Yeah, I do. But not here, all right?"

"Sure. But let me drive. You just relax and get yourself back together."

"Are you sure you're okay to drive?"

"You mean am I sober enough? I won't even dignify that with an answer. Move over."

We switched places. I lay back against the headrest and watched the stars overhead stream by.

"I had a crush on him when I was a kid," I began. "I must have told you about him when we were roommates."

"I seem to recall your mentioning something about it. Military, wasn't he?"

"The Citadel."

"That explains it then."

"What?"

"The arrogance. Subtle, but apparent. Your father has it, too."

I smiled into the darkness. "They prefer to call it 'confidence.'"

"Right."

I told Neddie the story of our accidental reunion a week ago, our mutual instant attraction. How Geoff seemed able to overcome my reluctance and indecision with a look or a touch.

How I had gone willingly to his bed only three days after our first meeting.

"Lust at first sight," Neddie said wryly.

I squirmed uncomfortably and didn't reply.

"Nothing wrong with that," she added as we turned into the plantation. "And besides, it's not as if you picked up some stranger in a bar. This was someone you had a history with. Look," she went on, "you and Rob had a damned near-perfect marriage. I always envied you that. It's a rare thing these days…And then he died."

We pulled into the driveway, and Neddie shut off the car. She made no move to get out, turning instead to look at me slumped down in the seat.

"After you recovered from your injuries, you hid out here. No dates, no involvement, no men, period. You even avoided your father. Just as you're feeling ready to get back into the world, wham! Along comes a man you had feelings for a long time ago, someone you always thought of as unattainable. And he wants *you*! You, the scrawny little nuisance he never had time for before. How am I doin' so far?"

"Let's go for a walk on the beach."

I got the flashlight out of the glovebox. We left our shoes in the driveway, and I led the way down the path.

We wandered awhile in silence, the *sshsshing* of the ocean our only accompaniment.

"So you slept with him. Big deal. Quit beating yourself up about it. You were lonely, vulnerable, and celibate for too damn long. You didn't know he was married. When you found out, you ended it."

I kicked up water with my bare feet as we waded through the shallows.

"You did end it? I mean, that's what tonight's little scene was all about, right?"

"Yes, it's over. I just hadn't gotten around to telling him yet."

Neddie laughed. "So I gathered."

She couldn't see my answering smile in the darkness. I was beginning to feel better.

"You did the right thing, honey. You made a mistake—a totally understandable one. Forgive yourself, learn from it, and move on. But most importantly, don't let this sour you. Now that you've gotten out into the world again, don't go crawling back into that hole you dug for yourself."

"You're pretty damn good at this, you know?"

"That's why I get the big bucks. Come one, let's head back. I promised the Elliotts I'd call and see how it went with CJ and the other kid's lawyer."

We turned around and retraced our steps. As we approached the house, movement on the deck made me stiffen. Then the plaintive *meow* of Mr. Bones drifted down, and I let out a sigh of relief.

We mounted the steps, and Neddie scooped up the purring cat. "Oh, you're a lover, aren't you, you mangy old thing?"

The cat rubbed his head under her chin.

"What are you so jumpy about?" Neddie asked, her attention still focused on the cat.

"I'm not sure," I answered, flopping down on the chaise. "It's just a feeling, like something's…I don't know, not quite right. Out of place, like I'm looking at something and not really *seeing* it. It started the night I came home late from the hospital, the night Miss Addie got hurt."

I folded my hands behind my head and tried to put my vague unease into words.

"There were lights on the beach that night. They were moving away from the path, now that I think about it. Fast. As if someone were running. And then there's the fax pages."

"Fax pages?"

"Yes. They were in a neat pile. Before that, the machine was spitting them out onto the floor. And how did Geoff know where to find us tonight?"

"Are you saying you think someone's been in the house? Geoff? Why?" She set the cat back on the deck and perched on the edge of the chaise. "Are you sure you're not getting just a little paranoid here?"

"I don't know, maybe. But Geoff is involved in this land business up to his eyeballs, and he's lied to me at every turn. He's certainly proved he can't be trusted. I wrote the number of the restaurant on the pad by the phone when I called to make the reservation. He could have seen it there and followed us."

"I think you're reaching. All this digging into Rob's files is bringing back bad memories, old fears. You're transferring. It's almost classic."

"Thank you, Mrs. Freud. So how do you explain Geoff's showing up where we were eating? There are hundreds of restaurants on the island. Are you telling me it was a coincidence?"

"They do happen, you know." Neddie rose and stretched. The cat immediately jumped up and began winding himself around her legs. "You got anything to feed this little hobo?"

She reached down to scratch him behind his ears.

"Lower cupboard to the right of the stove. Dolores always gets a few cans of catfood when she shops."

Neddie picked up the cat and started toward the door.

"So you think I'm getting all spooked over nothing?" I called, and she turned around to face me.

"I always believe in listening to your own instincts, so I'm not dismissing your fear out of hand. Why don't you wait a couple of days, see how you feel? If you still think it's not just a reaction to all the turmoil of the last week, then call a locksmith. Get the locks changed, install an alarm. That's the sensible approach, don't you think?"

Neddie and Mr. Bones disappeared into the house. Through the screen I could hear the cat's loud mewing accompanied by the whir of the electric can opener. I sat for awhile and let the tranquillity of the night wash over me.

I was relieved to have the confrontation with Geoff behind me. It was good it had happened the way it did, spontaneously and without warning. With no time to prepare or rehearse what I wanted to say, the break had been much cleaner, much easier than I'd feared.

I would probably never be sure exactly what my feelings for Geoff might have been. I knew it was all mixed up with my grief for Rob, my self-imposed isolation, and a fond remembrance of a childhood crush. What if he really were single, if he hadn't lied? Would I ever have come to care for him as he claimed he did for me? Or was it simply as Neddie had observed, lust and nothing more?

I decided to be thankful I had found out the truth before I became so emotionally entangled that the pain of it would have been worse than it already was.

But to be fair, I owed Geoff something, too. He had shown me that it was possible for me to give of myself, to be open to the possibility of finding love again. I'd made a bad choice, but in doing so I'd been reminded that I still needed trust and honesty in a relationship for it to have any hope of succeeding.

Forgive yourself, learn from it, and move on.

Neddie's words wrapped themselves around me in a soft blanket of comfort.

When I walked into the house, she was sitting cross-legged on the kitchen floor stroking an obviously contented Mr. Bones. The whole room smelled like tuna fish.

"You talk to Bitsy?" I asked. I got the iced tea pitcher from the refrigerator and poured myself a glass.

"The line was busy. I'll try again in a few minutes. You want to finish what you started telling me over dinner? About how this is all coming together?"

"No, not yet. You were right. I have some big holes to fill in. If you don't mind, I think I'll go work on my research some more. I have a couple of ideas I want to check out on the Internet."

"No problem. I'm going to put on a CD and get through a couple of articles I brought along. I never seem to find time to keep up with the literature when I'm at home. Then I think I'll hit the sack. It's been a busy day."

"Great. See you in the morning then. And make sure you put the cat out, okay? I don't want fleas all over the house."

"She's a hard woman, isn't she, Bonesy?"

The cat pricked up his ears, then went back to grooming his paws.

It took me only a few minutes to lose myself again in the intriguing paper trail that was the Grayton's Race development. What had first alerted me to the possibility that things might not be strictly on the up-and-up was the list of owners I'd gotten from the tax office. Every one of them had been a corporation. No individuals had been listed. When the shareholders of these companies turned out to be other corporations, I knew I was onto something. This was a classic method of concealing the real money men behind a project, especially if the disclosure of their identities would somehow adversely affect the deal. Such as, if the investors were convicted felons. Or had known ties to organized crime.

This was what Rob and I had encountered time and again in his investigations into drug trafficking in the state of South Carolina. He had brought down more than one of these "paper" organizations through persistent digging of the kind I was engaged in now.

Money laundering was the "white collar" end of the drug trade, but a vital one, nonetheless. Cut off the money and you cut off the supply. Rob had never gotten to the roots of this diseased tree, but he'd managed to hack off quite a few branches. He had been getting closer, though, and he was certain it was only a matter of time before he had enough proof to nail the big boys.

So was I. In fact, I was convinced he'd died for it.

None of the individuals' names that Belinda St. John's assistant had turned up had meant anything to me. They were likely just fronts, small-fry attorneys in big law offices or cousins of the wives of the real investors. This, too, was typical of a shady operation. It always drove Rob crazy because these "red herrings" were so hard to track down. That was what had made me remember another recurring name on the documents Dennis Morgan had faxed to me.

It was a law firm out of Palm Beach, Florida, and they had prepared most of the articles of incorporation for the bogus companies, even the South Carolina ones: Winningham, Masur, LeBrand, and Holt.

I logged onto the Internet and tried several websites before I hit on the right one. The Florida Bar Association had thoughtfully provided a listing of their member firms with officers, partners, and associates arranged in alphabetical order. I scrolled down the screen until the Winningham firm popped up. The roster of its staff attorneys followed the bios of its managing partners.

The first name on the list was Geoffrey Anderson.

20

I don't know how long I sat chewing on the implications of my discovery.

At first, Geoff had told me he had been the initiator of the project; that he had found the land, put the deal together. Later, as we sat on the gentle rise where he planned to build his house, he had talked about feeling "lucky" to have been chosen to head up the development. He'd also claimed to have given up his law practice. So why was he still on the payroll of the firm whose name kept popping up on every legal document connected with Grayton's Race?

If I called him right now and demanded an explanation, I was certain he'd have a plausible story all ready to refute every one of my accusations. But since he'd already proved he could lie with conviction, confronting him would be pointless.

When Neddie stopped in the doorway on her way to bed, I decided to withhold this troubling new information until I was sure where it fit in. Instead, I asked her how the Elliotts were doing.

"Well, it's good news for CJ, bad news for his friend. Isaiah's attorney said that Isaiah has pretty much substantiated the story that CJ told you and that Red overheard. Which means that CJ's out of it as a suspect. And he can't testify to anything other than what he actually saw."

"Which also means that he can't be Isaiah's alibi, either."

"Right. They'll be taking Isaiah out to the river tomorrow so he can show them where he buried the baseball bat."

My thoughts went to Lavinia Smalls. I hoped her fierce pride and love for her family would see her through this terrible time.

"Oh, I almost forgot," Neddie went on. "Bitsy said to tell you that she and her husband will help with Isaiah's bail, if it's granted. She said you'd offered before, but they want to do it themselves. Sort of a gesture of their faith in their son's friend."

"I thought they were having money problems. At least that's what Bitsy led me to believe."

"Apparently not. Big Cal said they'd be at the hearing Monday morning, ready to do whatever was needed. Maybe he's not as bad as you think he is."

"Trust me on this, Neddie. I've known the man for twenty years. There's something in this for him, even if it's only to bolster his image and get his name in the paper. Big Cal Elliott never does anything that isn't to his own personal or business advantage."

"You're probably right. As you say, you know him better than I do. Anyway, I'm off to bed. Don't stay up all night with that stuff, okay? I'm going for a swim first thing in the morning, and then we can do brunch. I want to head back to Savannah before the traffic gets too heavy."

I nodded absently, my mind suddenly struck with an idea I wasn't sure I wanted to explore.

"Bay?"

"Huh? Okay, sure. G'night," I mumbled.

"You're really out of it, girl. I put the cat out and locked up, so you quit worrying about whatever it is you're worrying about and get to bed, you hear?" she called and closed the bedroom door behind her.

Big Cal never does anything that isn't to his own personal advantage.

My own words kept ricocheting around inside my head. Why would Cal Elliott be willing to put up the bail for Isaiah Smalls? What would it gain him?

Nothing, I decided, at least nothing I could make sense of. I discounted altruism right up front. Besides, Isaiah had almost gotten CJ thrown in jail as an accessory. That couldn't have endeared him to Big Cal's heart.

What if he found out about Derek Johnson's being the holdout on the Grayton's Race project? If he had a lot of money tied up—money he couldn't afford to lose—would that be enough of a motive for murder? Maybe not. But what if he also knew that Derek was the one supplying his daughter with drugs? Mally didn't rank as high on Big Cal's list of priorities as CJ, but still…

I racked my memory trying to recall exactly when Bitsy said he'd disappeared. Hadn't she told me he wasn't there when the police came to tell her about CJ's arrest?

"This is crazy," I said out loud. Here I was, trying to construct a case against my best friend's husband. Granted I didn't like the guy, but could I really see him bashing some kid over the head with a baseball bat, then throwing his body in the river, knowing full well that Isaiah would be blamed?

No, I answered myself, I couldn't believe that.

Hiring somebody else to do it? Big Cal had a lot of connections. It wouldn't be hard for him to find out how to…

Enough! This is getting you nowhere. Leave it to the police.

I forced the whole wild scenario out of my mind and turned back to the computer.

I had been making a handwritten key to help me organize the dozens of disks Rob had compiled over the years of his investigations into drugs and organized crime in the state. For security reasons, none of them was labeled, and all were passworded. I knew Rob's favorite security codes, but not which one applied to which disc. It made for slow going.

But I was determined to keep at it. I had a theory. All I needed was one link between Southland Real Estate or Meridian Partners and the Palm Beach law firm that Geoff was apparently still affiliated with.

If Rob had turned up any evidence that Southland or Meridian was a front, I could blow the whole Grayton's Race project out of the water. I would expose it for what I was now sure it really was: a money-laundering scheme run by south Florida drug traffickers.

I wasn't yet sure where Derek Johnson's murder fit into the whole picture, but my instincts told me it might be connected.

Sergeant Red Tanner had confirmed CJ's claim that Derek was a pusher when I'd talked with him that afternoon. Red had checked the story out with the Narcotics unit. He'd shown them the morgue photos, and they'd identified Derek as a small-time street dealer they knew only as "Boomer". No connection had been made with the dead boy until CJ had put it together for them.

"Boomer" had been suspected of being a member of a gang calling themselves the Sunshine Boys, a local distribution network for illegal drugs flowing in from Florida. It was an ongoing investigation, but the understaffed unit hadn't gathered enough hard evidence to make any arrests. Apparently, Derek–"Boomer"–kept a low profile, avoiding the periodic sweeps that netted the occasional user or his immediate supplier. Most were pled out, and the offenders back on the streets in a matter of months.

At any rate, the Sunshine Boys were considered small potatoes compared to the organizations targeted by Rob's SI unit and by the State Law Enforcement Division.

It was almost two o'clock when my eyes forced me to take a break. The tightly packed words on the computer screen were beginning to run together. I took off my glasses and leaned back in the chair.

In less than a minute, I was sound asleep.

Mr. Bones probably saved my life.

When the cat, claws extended, leaped onto my lap, I shot straight up out of the chair. Disks, papers, and an overflowing ashtray went flying in all directions.

"Jesus, Mary, and Joseph, cat!"

I had the presence of mind to keep my voice down, but I was sure the hammering of my heart was more than loud enough to wake Neddie. The poor cat, as startled as I, cowered under the desk.

"Come on, kitty, I'm sorry. It's okay. You can come out now," I coaxed.

I crawled around on my hands and knees picking up the computer disks and trying to scoop the cigarette butts back into the ashtray. Now that the initial shock had passed, I was beginning to see the humor.

"Come on, baby, I'm not going to hurt you. You scared me, too, you know. Come on, you have to go back outside."

I paused and sat back on my haunches. "And how the hell did you get *in?* Neddie said she put you out."

Suddenly the situation was no longer amusing.

My hand shook as I reached up and turned off the goose-necked lamp on the desk. The only illumination now came from the bright rectangle of the computer screen. I crouched on the floor and listened intently.

The soft hum of the air conditioner masked any sounds an intruder might have made. Besides, thick carpet would help muffle footsteps, and there were no creaking stairs or groaning floorboards to betray a stealthy misstep.

But someone was in the house. I knew it. Someone had opened a door, allowing the cat to streak in unnoticed. I could feel the ocean breeze drifting in through the open doorway of the office.

I cowered there in the dark, my brain frozen in fear. *Think!* I ordered myself, *think!*

There was only the modem line in this room—no phone. The closest one sat on my bedside table down the hall. I didn't have a gun, wouldn't have known how to use one if I had. But if someone meant me harm, why hadn't he struck while I was asleep in the chair? And what the hell did he want?

When I finally reached a decision, it seemed as if an hour had passed. In reality it couldn't have been more than a couple of minutes. Neddie had a cellular phone in her purse. We'd use that to call the cops after we locked ourselves in the guestroom. It was a cowardly solution and might put Neddie at greater risk, but I couldn't help it. I needed the comfort of another human presence.

I rose up onto my hands and knees and crawled toward the doorway. My eyes had grown accustomed to the dark, and I risked a quick look up and down the hallway. No one lurked in the shadows, at least as far as I could tell. Neddie's door was slightly ajar. I crept cautiously across what seemed like an acre of carpet, eased the door open with my shoulder, and slipped inside. I scrambled quickly to my feet, pushed the door closed, and twisted home the lock.

My sense of relief was out of all proportion to the safety I had achieved. A determined thug could splinter the hollow door with a couple of well-placed kicks. I tip-toed across the room and tentatively approached the bed.

"Neddie!" I whispered urgently, "Neddie! Wake up!"

I knelt by the bed, my face inches from hers. I put my hand on her arm and shook it gently. Her eyes fluttered open.

"Wha-a-a-t...," she mumbled, and I clamped my hand over her mouth.

"Ssshh! Someone's in the house!"

Neddie came instantly awake, her eyes darting around the room. When I was sure she recognized me, I took my hand away.

"The cat's inside, and there's a door open somewhere. I could feel the draft. Get your cell phone and call 911."

"What? What are you saying?"

"Get your cell phone!"

"I can't! It's in my bag. I left it in the living room by the sofa."

"Damn! Now what?" I couldn't think, couldn't focus on anything but my fear.

Neddie sat up and ran her hands over her face and through her tangled hair. "Wait a minute. Let's stay calm. Did you actually see anyone?"

"No! I didn't go exploring, damn it! But if you locked up, then someone had to break in, didn't they? I don't think it's probably a social visit at three a.m."

"Maybe they've taken whatever they came for and left."

"Then why is the door still open?"

"I don't know! Let me think."

I slid to the floor, my hands clasped tightly around my knees, while Neddie crawled quietly out of bed and pulled on a pair of sweatpants under her nightshirt.

The moon moved out from behind high, drifting clouds and bathed the room in a soft, eerie light.

"The window!" I hissed. "We'll go out the window, over to the neighbors and call the cops."

Neddie hesitated for a second, then reached down to pull me to my feet. "Let's do it."

I slid open the wide window next to the bed and checked the ground below. With the garage built underneath, the house sat up high. The drop looked to be about twelve feet.

"Let me go first, then I can help you down."

I slung one leg over the sill.

"Bay, wait." Neddie grabbed my arm and moved close to my ear. "Is this a good idea? I mean, maybe we should wait. We're not even sure there's anybody here."

"*I'm* sure. Come on. We can do this."

I got my other leg out, squirmed around until both my hands gripped the ledge, then "walked" myself down the cedar siding. I let go and landed, knees bent, in a soft pile of pinestraw the landscapers replenished regularly.

Neddie poked her head out the window, and I gave her the thumbs up. Shorter than I, she had a longer fall, and I tried to cushion her landing as she dropped. We were both breathing heavily, more from fear than from exertion. Even so, I couldn't suppress a "we did it" grin. Neddie clapped me lightly on the shoulder.

It was then I heard the soft, metallic *clink* from the front of the house. We both froze. Then Neddie gestured frantically toward the back and turned in the direction of the path that led through the trees to the house next door. I grabbed her hand and shook my head.

Now that I was no longer trapped inside, fear was giving way to anger. Out here in the open, I felt less vulnerable. Someone had violated my sanctuary, not once, but several times if my instincts were correct.

I wanted to know who it was. And why.

Neddie plucked at my arm and tried to pull me toward the path. I turned and put my mouth close to her ear.

"You go. Call the cops. I'll stay here in case he tries to run for it. Go!"

I pushed her gently. She looked as if she wanted to argue with me. "Go!" I hissed again, and she disappeared around the corner of the house.

The pinestraw muffled my footsteps as I crept cautiously forward, my back pressed up against the side of the house. I inched toward the driveway, held my breath, and darted a quick look around the corner.

I might have missed him if it hadn't been for the soft glint of the moonlight off the tool he held in his gloved hand. Dressed entirely in black, his face was covered with a dark ski mask.

He was sliding out from underneath my car.

I pulled back, my heart thudding wildly.

A bomb! He was wiring my car with a bomb!

Nightmare memories of a rain of hot metal—and scorched flesh— flashed through my paralyzed brain. It took every ounce of self-control I had left not to run blindly down the path, away from this terrifying scene.

I should have realized there would be two of them. I never heard his accomplice creep up behind me, but some sixth sense made me turn just as the blow was delivered. It glanced off the side of my head. My injured shoulder took the worst of it.

With a cry of agony, I crumpled to the ground. Through a gray haze, I felt strong hands under my armpits, knew I was being dragged toward the driveway. My brain told my body to resist, but the messages weren't getting through.

The sharp blare of sirens, approaching fast, penetrated my half-conscious mind. My attacker dropped me, face down in the pinestraw, and sprinted away. I heard muttered curses, then two sets of footsteps receding in the direction of the beach.

I had just managed to struggle to my hands and knees when the night was shattered by a blast so loud it seemed to come from inside my head. I had barely a second for the smoke and flame to register on my numbed senses.

Then choking darkness enveloped me.

21

The first person I saw when I opened my eyes was Rob.

At least, in those first confused moments after my return to consciousness, I was sure it was his well-loved face, furrowed with concern, hovering just a few inches above mine. Then a puff of breeze blew some of the lingering smoke away, and I realized it was only Red.

My throat closed with the bitter pain of remembrance, and I turned my head to hide the tears I couldn't control.

"It's all right, Bay. You're safe now."

Red smoothed my matted hair back off my forehead, touched the wetness on my cheeks. I let him think they were tears of relief.

Gradually, the sounds of the chaos around me penetrated the muted roar that still reverberated inside my head: the shouts of the firemen as they directed hoses toward the twisted wreckage that had been my car; the excited babble of my neighbors gathered in a tight knot at the end of the driveway, kept at bay by a uniformed officer.

Then a single voice, raised high in indignation, made my lips twitch in the beginnings of a smile.

"God damn it, let me through! I'll have your ass, buddy!"

Red looked up. "Hey, Mike," he called, "it's okay. Let her through."

Neddie Halloran shouldered her way past the deputy and was at my side in seconds.

"Oh, my God! Bay, are you all right? Is she all right?" Neddie grabbed the shirt of a blue-clad paramedic who had been hovering just out of my line of vision. For the first time I realized I was lying on a gurney.

"She appears to be, ma'am, from an initial examination." He gently pried Neddie's fingers from his pocket. "We need to get her transported, though. We'll know more once we get her to emergency."

"No!" I struggled to sit up before I realized I was strapped down. "Neddie!"

My friend turned and clutched the trembling hand I held out to her.

"Don't let them take me to the hospital! Please!"

"*Ssshh*, honey, take it easy." I watched her cast a helpless look at Red.

"Bay, don't be ridiculous." My brother-in-law moved around to the other side of the gurney. "You have to go to the hospital. You were unconscious. You could have a concussion. And it looks like you took a hell of a whack on that shoulder."

Some of the shock must have been wearing off. At the mention of my shoulder, I suddenly became aware of the deep, aching pain concentrated just below my neck on the left side. Tentatively I rotated the joint and winced. It was bad, but not nearly as bad as it had been after my first close encounter with a bomb.

"Is it broken or anything?" I asked the young paramedic who stood observing me from a short distance away.

"No, ma'am, doesn't appear to be. Especially since you have motion. But it really should be x-rayed, just to be sure."

"Then I'm not going to the hospital. Get me off this thing."

Red and the paramedic exchanged exasperated looks. I counted on Neddie to understand.

"They can't make me, can they?" I asked her. My red-rimmed eyes implored her to help me, to be on my side.

"No, they can't make you, honey. But I think you should. I really do think you should."

"You can take care of me, can't you? You're a doctor."

"For crissake, Bay, I'm a shrink, not an internist."

"I'll go in tomorrow—or later today," I amended as I realized that dawn had broken, the sky above me lightening with each passing minute. "I promise. I just want to go under my own power, in my own time. Neddie?"

The paramedic threw up his hands and walked away toward the ambulance. Neddie undid the straps that held me, and she and Red eased me into a sitting position. It was probably intentional that they faced me away from the smoking ruin in the driveway.

They couldn't do anything about the smell. The air was heavy with gasoline and oil fumes, and the unmistakable stench of burned rubber.

"How bad is the house?" I asked, afraid to look.

"The garage and the kitchen took the worst of it. Most of the windows on this side are gone, and there'll be some water damage. The firemen hosed it all down, just in case."

Red's recitation was blunt and emotionless. I knew he was angry at me for refusing to go to the hospital and shaken by my narrow escape. Just how close it had been made me shudder.

The paramedic, whose name tag proclaimed him to be Andy Petrocelli, approached and handed me a clipboard with some papers on it.

"We'll need you to sign these releases if you're really serious about not going to the hospital." He sounded aggrieved and just a little ticked off.

I took the pen he offered me and scratched my signature where he pointed.

"No offense, Andy, okay?" I asked as he turned to go. "I know you guys are the best. It's just a personal quirk."

"No offense taken, ma'am," he drawled. His smile made him look younger, more like the twenty-something he probably was. "You just make sure you get to a doctor and get checked over, hear?"

"You bet. Thanks for everything."

Andy Petrocelli touched his forehead in a little salute, then climbed into the ambulance. Red and Neddie supported me as I climbed off the gurney. The rescue squad collapsed the stretcher and loaded it into the back. Then the vehicle moved slowly down the drive. My gawking neighbors stepped aside long enough to let it pass, then reformed.

None of them knew me well enough to be genuinely concerned, I thought. It was just the ghoulish curiosity that affects us all in the face of a disaster.

"Well, now what?" Red's voice was tinged with exasperation and weariness. "Want me to run you over to the Judge's? You sure as hell can't stay here."

"I don't see why…" I began when we were interrupted by another sheriff's deputy.

"What is it, Woody?" Red asked.

"Sarge, we got a lotta press out here. Papers and TV. What should I tell 'em?"

I turned to look toward the end of the driveway, and immediately the lights of several video-cams clicked on. I could hear shouts of "What happened?" and "What's the story?" coming from the crowd that seemed to be growing rather than diminishing. "Anybody dead?" was my personal favorite.

"Tell them this is a crime scene and to stay the hell out. Better get some tape up, by the way. I want this whole area sealed off. And post a man on the beach path so we don't get a lot of gawkers or reporters wandering up from there. I want everything secure when the detectives get here."

The patrolman hurried off to carry out his orders. Red watched him go for a minute, then turned abruptly back to me.

"And I suppose you were about to say you're staying here, right?"

"If my bedroom's still intact, yes. You got a problem with that?"

"Jesus! For someone who's supposed to be smart and savvy, you sure can come up with some stupid ideas. Of course I have a problem with that. Somebody just tried to blow you up! Has that even registered in that stubborn head of yours?"

"Could I sit down?" I asked meekly. My legs were getting wobbly, and I had a headache that threatened to explode out of my eyes.

Instantly Red's strong right arm was around my waist. He and Neddie practically carried me to his cruiser where I collapsed gratefully onto the front seat.

"I'm sorry, Bay. I didn't mean to yell at you. If you want to stay here, I'll post a couple of men. I'm sure the Captain will okay it. I'm off duty in a couple of hours, and I'll come and relieve them myself. Just let me check with the firemen and make sure it's safe to go in, okay?"

"Red…"

"You just rest here. I'll check it…"

"Red, shut up!"

He stopped then, his handsome face an agony of regret and confusion.

"It's okay, Red. I know you're just trying to protect me. Like you always do. And I'm an ungrateful bitch. Wait!" I commanded as he began to protest. "I know my staying makes it more difficult for you guys, and I'm sorry about that. But I can't run, not anymore."

I looked across at Neddie who had slid into the seat on the other side. Again, I counted on her to understand. "If I let them force me out, I might never have the courage to come back."

"She's right," Neddie said softly. "It has to be Bay's decision."

I raised my face to look anxiously up at Red. He smiled and laid a hand gently against my cheek.

"When could any of us Tanner men ever say no to you?"

He wheeled and strode off in search of the fire captain.

"You sure about this?" Neddie asked as I leaned back against the seat. "We could go to a hotel or bunk in with the Elliotts."

"We?" My eyes, gritty from the smoke and ash, were getting heavier by the minute. It was all I could do to stay awake.

"You don't think I'm leaving you alone, do you? I'll call my service and have them reschedule my appointments for the next couple of days."

"Neddie, I don't want you involved in this. I think you should go home. If anything happened to you…"

"Shut up, Tanner. If you're staying, I'm staying. You're stuck with me, so get used to it."

I squeezed her hand and managed a shaky smile. "Okay."

"Besides," she went on, her natural quirky humor never suppressed for long, "I intend to help you pick out your new car."

I dozed a little then, I think. When Red returned, he and Neddie escorted me, one on either side, up the outside steps, across the deck, and directly into my bedroom. Except for the lingering smell, the room was exactly as it had been when I'd changed for dinner the night before.

Neddie led me straight into the bathroom, turned the taps in the shower on full blast, and helped me peel off my filthy, tattered clothes.

"I think we'll just burn these," she said, wrinkling her nose as she dropped my slacks and sweater into the wastebasket. "Now don't come out of there until the hot water runs out." She steered me toward the tub. "I'll just leave the door open a little. Call me if you need help."

The steam rose around me in soothing clouds. I soaped myself three times before the water stopped running black. I let the stinging spray pound on my neck and back, working the deep soreness out of the spot where my assailant's blow had landed. By the time my hair was squeaking through my fingers, I felt a thousand per cent better. But I was still bone-weary, anxious only to crawl into bed and sleep for a week. If the cops had questions, they'd have to wait. I didn't have that much to tell, anyway.

As I toweled myself dry and slipped into the nightgown Neddie had left for me on the vanity, the fear and the horror were almost gone. I would sleep, give my body a chance to heal. But I would no longer cower in the shadows as I had done for the past year. This time, I would fight back.

As I pulled the sheet up around me and slowly drifted off, my thoughts were not of fire and noise and death. If I dreamed at all, I knew it would not be of the dark pit of terror, but the hot, sweet light of revenge.

As it turned out, I slept without dreams, at least none I remembered. I rolled over onto my back and stretched, wincing a little at the tightness in my shoulder. I flexed my elbow, then the fingers of my left hand. Everything seemed to be working the way it was supposed to.

Gradually I became aware of activity at the front of the house: the *clang* of hammers on nail heads, the buzzing of an electric saw, and the voices of what sounded like a hell of a lot of people.

It was just after two in the afternoon, and harsh sunlight pushed around the edges of the closed drapes. I got up then and dressed in shorts and a T-shirt. I was just running a brush through the rat's nest of my hair when Neddie stuck her head around the door.

"Hey, you're up! How're you feeling?"

I pondered the question for a few seconds. "Surprisingly good," I said, and meant it. "What's all the racket out front?"

"Some guys are here boarding up the windows. It's gonna be a few days before they can get all the glass cut and replaced. And I called a locksmith. All the locks have been changed except for this one in the bedroom. They were waiting for you to wake up."

Neddie pulled three sets of keys from her pocket and set them on the nightstand. "Thought you might want these, too," she said and pitched a fresh pack of cigarettes at me. I caught them in mid-air with my left hand.

"Thanks."

"Well, you ready to meet your adoring public?"

"What does that mean?" I dug a book of matches out of the night-stand drawer, lit up, and inhaled gratefully. "I'm not talking to the press. Period. No exceptions."

"Oh, they're long gone. Red's boys wouldn't even let them on the property. 'Victim under doctor's care, all official statements to come from the press liaison officer at the department', etc., etc. Just like on TV."

"Then who wants to see me?"

"Only the rest of the immediate world. Let's see, there's your father, Lavinia, a black couple I believe are her son and daughter-in-law, and the entire Elliott clan. Red, of course, and a big black cop named Gleason or Gibson, or something like that. Plus the head of the arson squad of the fire department and a couple of 'suits' with very impressive-looking credentials from SLED. Oh, and our friend from the restaurant last night. Geoff, isn't it?"

"They're all here *now*?" I sank down on the bed, unsure of my ability to face such a mob.

"I can't be sure. I haven't taken attendance recently. Some have come and gone and come back. Dolores and Lavinia and I have been hopping trying to keep them all fed and watered."

"Sounds like you've been having a damned party!" I snapped.

"Well, it *has* been sort of like an Irish wake—without the corpse, of course."

I knew Neddie's gallows humor was meant to help me deal with the horror of last night, not minimize it. The wicked grin on her face brought a grudging smile to my own.

"You're somethin' else, you know?"

"Want me to clear some of them out? I think the cops are gonna want first crack at you. I've already told them everything *I* know, which isn't much. Red says they've picked up a few clues, but they're counting on you to fill in a lot of the blanks."

"They're going to be disappointed. The one guy had a ski mask on. The other one was just a…presence, I guess. He hit me from behind. I never got a look at him. Except…"

"What? What do you remember?"

I closed my eyes and let the nightmare images click through my mind like slides in a projector. "Nothing specific. Probably nothing at all, really. I just got the impression that he was big. I mean, *really* big. I'm five foot ten, and when he hit me, it came from above. I think that's what made me turn. I caught a flash of the—whatever it was—out of the corner of my eye on its way down."

The memory of how close it had been to being my head that took the full force of that blow made me shiver.

"And another thing. When he was dragging me. He didn't grunt or anything. Just hauled me along as if I weighed nothing at all."

"Be sure you tell all that to Red. You never know what could help."

I leaned back against the headboard, reluctant to move out of the sanctuary of my bedroom to face a crowd of people, no matter how well-meaning. I had hated being the center of attention from the time I was a kid, and nothing had changed. Neddie, curled on the end of the bed, regarded me with a professional eye.

"What are you thinking?" I asked.

"I guess I've been waiting for you to show some effects from nearly getting blown up last night. You're too damned calm. It's worrying me."

"Would you feel better if I went screaming around the house tearing at my hair?"

"It might be a more natural reaction than this 'hey, no problem' mode you seem to be in."

I lit another cigarette and watched the smoke drift upward toward the ceiling fan. "Neddie, this isn't an act. Believe me, I'm as surprised as you are. But you know what my overwhelming emotion is right now? It's anger. And determination. I'm going to find out who did this and make sure they pay. No more cringing and hiding. Does that make me crazy?"

"We don't use the term 'crazy', honey. At least not in public. I just want to be sure that you're not deluding yourself, putting up a good front. I don't want a delayed reaction to sneak up and smack you right between the eyes."

"I honestly don't think you need to worry." I stubbed out the cigarette and dug my sandals out from under the bed.

"Well, shall we do it?" Neddie moved toward the door.

"Wait a sec. Before I talk to the cops, what did you tell them about what's been going on? I mean, about my feeling that someone had been in the house before last night?"

Neddie raised an eyebrow. "Why?"

"Just answer the question."

"Nothing. I didn't think it was my story to tell."

"Good. Okay, let's go." I ran my hands through my thick, dark brown hair. "Do I look all right?"

Neddie's head was cocked to one side. I knew she wanted to pursue the subject, but then thought better of it and pulled the door open. "A tad bit singed around the edges," she mocked, "but otherwise as homely as ever."

"Go to hell," I laughed.

They were clustered in little knots, organized by age, race, occupation, and relationship to me. Or something loosely approximating that. Only Geoff Anderson, leaning on the rail of the deck and staring out at the ocean, stood alone.

A pariah to everyone, apparently.

I hesitated on the edge of the greatroom. Suddenly I was sixteen again and unsure of what was expected of me. It reminded me of the night of my first cotillion, floating self-consciously down the great oak staircase at *Presqu'isle*. My parents, Lavinia, and my date all waited at the foot of the steps, their faces turned expectantly up at me. I remembered three of those faces smiling in approval. Only my mother's had been pinched in apprehension as if she expected me to trip and fall and disgrace her once again.

It was a few seconds before anyone realized I was standing there. The whir as the Judge activated his wheelchair and rolled in my direction seemed to galvanize everyone else to action. Soon I was engulfed in the embraces of people who seemed genuinely to care about me, wrapped in the warmth of their concern.

I was touched more than I cared to admit.

Eight-year-old Brady Elliott saved me from the humiliation of bursting into tears.

"Hey, Aunt B-Bay," he stammered, yanking on the leg of my shorts to get my attention, "can I ride in your new t-t-tank? Daddy said you n-needed one."

The general laughter broke the tension, and I could feel the whole room relax.

"Tell him to find me a good deal on one, kiddo, and I'll consider it," I said, tousling his short blond hair.

I caught Big Cal's eye, and he looked quickly away.

My neighbors must have scurried straight from the end of my driveway back to their own kitchens that morning. The table in the dining area sagged under the weight of casseroles, desserts, and assorted trays of meats and vegetables. The series of folding doors that allowed the kitchen to be closed off were pulled shut. I wasn't ready to deal with that yet, but I could tell by the pained expression on Dolores's face as she bustled back and forth that it was bad.

The kitchen was much more her room than mine. I decided right then to let her redesign it to suit herself when it came time to get the repairs done. I had so few opportunities to repay her for her care of me. Perhaps this would be a gesture she would accept.

As people finally drifted off to replenish empty plates and glasses, I glanced out toward the deck. Geoff's soft blue eyes were boring into mine. I couldn't read his face. It seemed to have been wiped clean of all expression. When he realized I was looking at him, he held something up in his right hand. I couldn't tell what it was from that distance. He made an exaggerated motion of placing whatever it was on the wrought iron table.

He said something, then turned and disappeared down the outside steps. A few seconds later I heard the roar of the Jaguar receding down the road.

"What was that all about?" Bitsy's voice at my side made me jump. "What did he say?"

I shrugged and moved away. I'd wait until I was alone to find out what Geoff Anderson had left for me on the deck.

And I wasn't entirely certain my lip-reading had been accurate, but I'd thought he'd said, "I'm sorry."

22

Except for my father and the "official" guests at this impromptu party, Dolores was the last to leave. For once I didn't have to force her to take the leftover food with her. I had no place to keep it.

I'd finally braved a look at the kitchen, and there wasn't much left of it. Part of the ceiling had fallen in, probably from the weight of the water that had been poured onto it. Although most of the mess had been cleared away and the windows secured with huge sheets of plywood, the room was definitely unusable. The only good news was that the structural integrity of the house seemed to be intact, although the garage underneath was pretty much gutted. The electricity, knocked out in the explosion, was back on, but it would be tomorrow before my phone service could be restored.

Having nothing more of substance to add to the statement she'd already given, Neddie had retreated to the guest room for a well-deserved rest. I sat in one corner of the off-white sofa, my legs tucked up under me, surveying the solemn faces of the men arrayed in a semicircle in front of me. It shouldn't have been an adversarial situation, but it felt like one.

My father confirmed my feeling the second Neddie had left the room. "What an incredibly stupid thing that was to do, Lydia," he growled around the cigar clamped tightly in his teeth.

I knew he was really angry. I was never "Lydia" except when he was seriously ticked off at me.

"What on earth possessed you to try to apprehend these people on your own?" he continued, shaking his head at my supposed recklessness. "What were you thinking of? That any child of mine could be so…"

"Mind if the accused gets a word in edgewise?" I snapped. "First, I didn't try to 'apprehend' anybody. I was just watching to make sure they didn't skip before the cops arrived. And secondly," I said, more reasonably than I felt, "I don't think these gentlemen are here to listen to you scold me as if I were some naughty four year-old, okay?"

He shut up then and busied himself with adding bourbon to the drink sitting next to him on the end table. I glanced at Red and saw his lips twitch before he got his face under control again.

"Okay, let's get this over with," I said firmly. "Who wants to go first? Or should I just tell it, and let you ask questions after?"

Red, Matt Gibson, and the two men from the State Law Enforcement Division exchanged looks. Silver and—for a moment I drew a blank on the other one's name. Neither was anyone I knew from the "old" days. Heywood, that was it. Silver and Heywood, in almost identical gray suits and red striped ties, conferred with their eyes, then Silver spoke.

"This is your case, gentlemen. We're just here to observe and to help in any way we can. However you guys want to play it."

Red pulled a mini tape recorder out of his breast pocket and set it on the coffee table. "This will save time," he said to me, pushing the *Record* button. "This way they can get your statement typed up, and you can just come in and sign it tomorrow. Any objections?"

I shook my head and lit a cigarette while Red identified himself, the date, time and those present. I was beginning to feel more like the suspect than the victim.

Matt Gibson, the death investigator, took over. "Why don't you just give it to us in your own words first. If anyone needs clarification we'll wait until after you've finished. Agreed?"

He looked at his fellow officers and got nods all around.

I'd had plenty of time to decide just how much I was going to reveal about the events of last night and my suspicions about what had led up to them. I tried to stick only to the facts, starting with the cat's jolting me awake and my realization that someone must be in the house. I took them through it step by step, ending with my impressions of the size of my attacker.

There was only one logical question left to be asked, at least from their perspective, and I wasn't prepared to answer it. They would want to know *why*. I intended to keep my thoughts about that to myself, at least for now.

"Do you have any idea why someone would try to kill you, Bay? And by this particular method?" Matt Gibson spoke quietly, his face grave as he waited for my reaction.

I'm a terrible liar. You can usually see it in my eyes, so I try not to look directly at people when I'm about to tell a whopper. I studied my hands as I spoke. "I don't know, Matt, unless it has some connection with what happened to Rob. Am I right in assuming they were pros?"

The law enforcement officers looked pointedly at each other. No one spoke. Finally, Agent Heywood cleared his throat and pulled a notebook from his pocket.

"The device was wired to the ignition of your car. It would have detonated when you turned the key. It's a standard technique of the mob, among others. Forensics have been over what pieces we were able to recover." He consulted his notes and continued, "Apparently you interrupted the perp before he had a chance to finish, and it went off prematurely."

Silver jumped in. "Or, your coming on the scene like that may have caused them to alter their plans. This big guy you describe may have been trying to drag you to the car so they could be certain you were in it when the bomb exploded. Either way, you're damn lucky."

What Neddie had called my unnatural calm was beginning to fray a little around the edges. Somehow, hearing my close brush with death being discussed with such bland detachment, made it all the more horrifying. I could feel a nerve in the corner of my right eye begin to jump.

"But that still doesn't answer why," Matt Gibson persisted. "If it had anything to do with your husband or his work, why wait almost a year to do something about it? What could have spooked them into acting now?"

I felt the blood rush out of my head as the answer struck me like last night's blow. Of course! That had to be it!

Red, who knew me better than anyone there, except my father, leaned forward in his chair. "What is it, Bay? You've remembered something."

"No, no, it's just…" I stammered. I fumbled for a cigarette and lowered my head to the flame of the lighter. I needed those few seconds to get myself under control. I had to think this out before I said anything more. When I looked up, five pairs of eyes— my father's included— were staring at me intently. I exhaled and ran a hand through my hair.

"It's just that…I'm really tired, I guess," I finished lamely.

The faces of Red and the Judge clearly said they weren't buying it, but both let me slide.

"Neddie said you'd picked up some clues," I said, hoping to shift the attention away from myself. "Anything I should know about?"

Red sat back in his chair, appearing to relax. His eyes never left my face.

"A partial tire track—probably from one of those ATV's—and a heel print. On the beach near the end of your path. We were able to get photos, but the tide came in and wiped them out before we could get casts. They won't be much help unless we get something to compare them with."

Heywood flipped his notebook closed and replaced it in his pocket. "We'll send the bomb fragments up to the FBI lab, see if they can get any signature from it."

"Signature?" I asked, "what's that?"

"The people who make these devices generally do it the same way every time," Agent Silver offered. "Use the same kind of tape and wire, construct them in the same configuration. If the feds have this particular pattern on file, we may get a hit. They have the fragments from the other…incident, the one involving Mr. Tanner. They'll certainly compare those two."

"I think my daughter should rest now, gentlemen." The Judge spoke for the first time since I had politely told him to butt out. "If she thinks of anything else that might assist you with your investigation, we'll be in touch with your office."

I was about to protest his highhanded interference when he quelled me with a look. I got the message and uncoiled myself from the sofa. I shook hands with the two SLED agents and thanked them for their help.

Matt Gibson covered my hand with both of his chocolate brown ones and nodded encouragingly. "We've got men, front and back. They'll be here 'round the clock until we nail these bastards. So you sleep easy, hear?"

"Thanks, Matt. I'll be fine."

Red walked with them out to their cars, but I knew he'd be back. He and my father had exchanged a few whispered words while I was saying my good-byes. By the time I had cleared away the dirty glasses and stacked them in the sink of the half-bath that had become the makeshift kitchen, I heard the front screen door bang, and my brother-in-law was dropping a gym bag in the entryway.

"Before you start yelling, I'm sleeping on your couch tonight. Your father agrees; and, even if he didn't, I'd do it anyway. So save your breath."

"Good," I said, curling up in my corner again. "I was going to suggest it. I'll feel a lot better with you in the house."

He looked a little stunned at not getting an argument, but recovered quickly and crossed to resume his seat.

"Now, daughter," my father began, "let's hear what it was that Matt Gibson's question triggered. You remembered something. I could almost hear the light bulb click on in your head." He glanced over at Red. "Redmond is off duty, so you can speak freely. It won't go any farther."

There was no point equivocating with my father. My own stubbornness was a trait passed directly from his genes to mine. I would not be able to wiggle out from under his stern gaze with lame excuses of fatigue and confusion. But it had to be on my terms.

"Okay, you're right. I think I'm onto something. But before I lay it out for you, I have to get it straight in my own head. I need proof, and I'm close to having it. I'm not making any accusations or involving either of you until I'm certain. When I am, you'll both hear it. Immediately, I swear."

"This is crazy." Red jumped up and paced back and forth in front of the empty fireplace. "It's not your place to get proof, damn it! You're not the cops, *I* am. You tell me what you know, and we'll take it from there. Isn't almost getting killed twice enough for you? You want to go for three?"

"Want to keep it down a little in here?" Neddie appeared at the end of the hallway, her eyes heavy with sleep. "How's a girl supposed to rest with people shouting at the top of their lungs?"

"Sorry. But maybe you can talk some sense into this thickheaded friend of yours. I sure as hell can't."

Neddie mostly listened as the battle raged for another fifteen minutes. In the end, the Judge and Red had to admit defeat. I wasn't sharing my theories until I was damned good and ready.

"Don't worry about me, Judge. Red's here, and the other cops. I know what I'm doing," I reassured my father as I stood beside the open passenger window of his van. An off-duty patrolman had volunteered to drive him home.

"I hope so," he said, refusing to look at me.

I finally convinced Red and Neddie that I would be perfectly safe while they went out to pick up some dinner for us. It was still light outside, and there were three deputies stationed near the house. And I desperately needed to be alone. Reluctantly, they went.

I felt as if I had been cooped up inside for days. I stepped through the French doors and out onto the deck, breathing deeply of the salt-laden, pine-sweet air. A mockingbird squawked at me from the end of the railing.

I crossed to the round table, reached down, and picked up a set of keys fastened to a business card. The logo was from the local luxury import car dealer, and the embossed name printed underneath was *Buck James, Sales Professional.*

I turned the card over. The block letters were neat and compact. Geoff had written, *If you don't like this one, Buck will give you the same deal on whatever you choose.* It was signed simply "G.A.".

Oh, Geoff, I thought, clutching the keys tightly to my chest, *why can't you just let it go? Let me go?*

I walked slowly back into the house, making certain to lock the door behind me. I moved down the hallway toward the office. In all the excitement of last night and this afternoon, I had forgotten all about my notes and Rob's computer disks. It was past time I got them back in the safe.

I stood in the doorway for a full minute before it finally registered.

I didn't have to worry about putting anything away.

It was gone. All of it.

23

The breeze off the ocean was blessedly cool. It rattled in the fronds of the palmettos whose long, sharp leaves clacking against each other sounded like fingernails tapping on a window. Had I been inside, it would probably have scared the hell out of me.

But, at three a.m., I had slipped out onto the deck and settled myself in a chaise longue. I'd made my presence known to one of the deputies who'd nodded at me sympathetically, then continued his patrol.

Now, at somewhere around five-thirty, I watched the sky beginning to glow pink and gold with the first hint of dawn. Bluejays, cardinals, mockingbirds, and grackles began to call to one another from the moss-laden live oaks and towering pines. Soon the whole island would stretch itself awake.

And I still had no answers.

Who had stolen the disks? And why?

Those were the questions that had plagued my rest, kept me tossing in tangled sheets until I had finally given up and wandered outside. I knew I hadn't checked the office after the explosion. All I was sure of was that the disks were there when I crawled fearfully across the hallway into Neddie's room last night. That my assailant had taken them made the most sense, although the house *had* been crowded with people while I slept. In the confusion, anyone could have slipped into the office, shoved the disks into a bag, and walked unchallenged across the deck to deposit them in a trunk or a glovebox for later disposal.

But who? And again, why? The clear, blue eyes of Geoffrey Anderson materialized before me in the hazy predawn stillness. He alone of my many visitors had an interest in stopping me from delving farther into the intricately constructed house of cards that was the Grayton's Race ownership. But could I picture him sneaking around, ransacking my house while I slept peacefully in the room next door? While my friends and family waited anxiously just a few feet away?

No, I decided, no more that I could buy Red's insinuations that Geoff might have been involved in Derek Johnson's murder, regardless of how fortuitous it had been for the viability of his project. He wasn't capable of it. Deceit? Definitely. Fraud, probably. But murder and robbery? I just couldn't see it.

No, the theft—and the attempt to silence my curiosity permanently— were the obvious motives for last night's bizarre chain of events.

And the likely suspects? That was easy. The men who had murdered my husband were the same ones who were involved in the construction project headed by Geoff Anderson. I knew it as surely as I knew the sun would come up this morning. So I was doubly dangerous to them. A bomb had worked before, and they'd walked away scot-free. So why not try it again? Killing me would be the proverbial two birds with one stone.

And how had they known I was a danger to them?

When Matt Gibson asked the question, "What spooked them?" I knew immediately what they had done.

Stanley Wojeckewski could have told me in a minute, not only what type of device, but how long it had been in place and probably the location of the terminal that was intercepting. My phone might even be tapped, too. Stanley was an electronics whiz, one of those nerdy computer guys that lived for a chance to dive into boards and chips. Rob had employed him to "sweep" our terminal and the phones once a week to prevent just such a thing as this from happening. I was convinced that, on one of their forays into my house, someone had wired my computer so that everything I brought up was "mirrored" onto another terminal. What I saw, they saw.

It was the only explanation that made any sense. No one else but Neddie was aware of the existence of the disks, or that I had been searching them for a connection between the Miami drug underworld and Grayton's Race. If the phone was indeed tapped, that had only been a bonus for them.

I could feel the warmth through the back of my shirt as the sun climbed over the horizon. I lit a cigarette and stretched out full-length on the chaise.

I could call Stanley, have him run a diagnostic on my computer, check out the phone, but it would have been pointless. Locking the old barn door after the horse had galloped away.

But without the disks, I had little hope of proving my theory about Grayton's Race. If I laid it all out for Red, he might buy it simply because it came from me. Without evidence, though—something other than my unsubstantiated recollections of a couple of names *maybe* glimpsed briefly over a year ago—he would be unable to take it any farther. Even if he could convince someone to investigate my claims, all it would accomplish would be to alert those I suspected that I had not given up. They could run to ground, cover their tracks. Even have another crack at me.

Which is probably what they're planning right now, thanks to your incredible carelessness, I berated myself. I shifted onto my side and drew up my knees.

Or maybe they weren't. Maybe getting their hands on the only evidence that could possibly link the drug cartel, the money-laundering scheme, and Grayton's Race was enough for them. Maybe they felt safe now.

"Men willingly believe what they wish", Julius Caesar had written a couple of millennia ago. Apparently the same held true for women.

And philosophizing was pretty pointless at this stage of the game. What I had to do was decide where to go next. Accompanied by Red Tanner's soft snores from the living room couch, I chased my options around in my head. In the end, there were really only two choices: pursue it with everything I had, or back off. There was no middle ground.

If I went forward with my efforts to discredit the development project and extricate my family and friends from their unwitting involvement with drug money, I would have to find an alternate source of information. Belinda St. John, Rob's former assistant, seemed the logical place to start.

But, as much as I wanted to believe her fierce insistence that Rob had not been forgotten by his colleagues, where was the proof? The investigation my husband had begun was as dead as he was. Nothing had been done, no progress made in the long months since his plane exploded. Not only was that probe going nowhere, there had apparently been no concerted effort to find his murderers. The whole incident was an ugly stain on the reputation of the state and those charged with its administration. I couldn't picture any branch of the government, unless it might be SLED, stirring up the whole mess again.

So what did I expect Belinda to do? Her career and her children's well-being were tied to her ability to keep the boys in Columbia out of the headlines, except for the ones they wanted to be in. How much rocking of the ship of state would she be prepared to do on behalf of a man who'd been dead for almost a year, and his widow who had been, at best, a marginal friend? Her loyalties were no longer owed to Rob and the SI unit, her success no longer tied to them.

Pursuing would also mean dealing with Geoff Anderson, the one tangible link I had between the project here and the Miami drug lords I was sure were behind it. How much could I count on his professed feelings for me? Or were they, too, a sham, a calculated attempt to get close to me, to find out how much I knew or suspected? How deeply dented was the armor of my childhood knight?

Backing off, on the other hand, would be the sensible thing to do. I had built a good life for myself here, despite the continuing pain of Rob's death. At thirty-eight, I was financially secure. I could retire for good, if that's what I wanted to do. Even before the first explosion, I had been gradually extricating myself from the CPA practice I shared with two scions of old, moneyed families in Charleston. They would have no trouble finding someone to buy me out.

I had friends—good ones. They had proven that yesterday. Geoff Anderson had shown me that it was possible for me to give of myself again, when the time—and the man—were right. If they never were, well, I'd learn to deal with that, too.

But where did this option leave me? Back in the old, sheltered existence, avoiding involvement, responsible to and for no one but myself. I sure as hell didn't want to die. There had been times, after Rob's murder, when I thought I did. Last night had proved to me that my will to survive was alive and kicking. But wasn't the safe, self-indulgent life I'd been leading a kind of death, too?

Besides, I owed something to the people who mattered to me. For better or worse, I had become intimately involved in the lives of Adelaide Boyce Hammond, CJ Elliott, and Isaiah Smalls, not to mention my father, Bitsy, Mally, even Neddie. How could I walk away from that? From them?

And, if I were being perfectly honest with myself, a part of me was savoring the chase. Despite the danger, I itched to pursue the bastards who had most likely killed my husband and then tried to murder me. I wanted their asses in the slammer, and I wanted to be the one who put them there.

By the time Red, wearing only a pair of sweatpants, stumbled blearily out onto the deck, I realized I had already made up my mind.

"What are you doin' out here?" Red mumbled as he stretched and wandered over to lean on the railing. "It's not even six yet."

"Pondering the meaning of life," I said airily, trying to make light of the real battle that had been raging inside my head in the last, dark hours before sunrise.

"Heavy." Red looked over his shoulder at me and grinned. "Is that what almost getting blown up does to you?"

I padded over to join him at the railing. We stood silently, each of us marveling at the soft, luminescent quality of the light as it spread slowly across the vast expanse of the ocean.

"I guess I should be an expert by now, huh?"

"Do me a favor and don't go getting any more experience, okay?"

When I didn't answer, his face lost its teasing brightness.

"Red, there are some things I have to do that you're not going to like. But you have to trust me not to put myself in any unnecessary danger. You can't protect me for the rest of my life. Sooner or later I was going to have to step out of the shadows and into the sunlight. I've just decided that today's the day."

Red knew that opposition would only harden my resolve, so he kept silent. I turned away from the mixture of fear and longing I read in his eyes.

"So, here's the deal. I'm gonna go roust Neddie out and then have a shower. I'll use the guest bath and you can use mine. And make it snappy. We're going out to breakfast, and I'm starving. And you know how cranky I get when I'm hungry."

Red watched me gather up my things from the deck beside the chaise and turn toward the door. "Bay? What is this all about?" he asked as he moved swiftly across the boards and grasped both my upper arms. "What are you up to?"

"I'm back in the game, Tanner," I said, twisting gently out of his grip, "and anybody who doesn't want to play better get the hell out of my way."

We took two cars.

Red dropped us off at the visitor's lot where—luckily, as it turned out—Neddie had left her pearl gray Mercedes on Friday afternoon. We rendezvoused at an unpretentious little diner set back off the main highway. It usually escaped the notice of the tourists who tended to congregate at the more well-known franchise place across the road.

Seated at the counter on high barstools, we put away over-easy eggs and piles of redskin home fries hot off the grill. I mopped up the last of the eggs on my plate with a piece of whole wheat toast and sat back.

"Boy, for someone who doesn't eat breakfast, you sure inhaled that." Neddie sipped coffee and shook her head at me.

Conversation had been minimal and mostly concerned with trivia. There was no privacy in Frank's, which was one reason I'd picked it. Red had been pushing me about my intentions ever since our exchange on the deck. I hadn't formulated any definite plan yet, just a couple of vague ideas about who I needed to talk to.

Red's disapproval was evident in the long crease down the middle of his forehead as he scowled at me over his coffee cup. "I'm scheduled for the four-to-midnight shift this week, but I'm going to try to switch. I'd rather be at your place and settled in before it gets dark," he said.

"You really don't have to. I don't think I'll have any more trouble."

With the disks gone, my attackers had to think I was no longer a threat to them. Without evidence I was just another hysterical female. Having failed once, they would probably be reluctant to draw attention to themselves with another attempt, at least for awhile. I figured I had some breathing room, and I meant to take full advantage of it. By the time they thought about having another crack at me, I intended to have their butts nailed to the wall.

Besides, any normal woman would have gone screaming back into hiding, or left the state. I was counting on their assuming I was just such a normal woman.

Red wanted to argue, but was reluctant to make a scene in the close confines of the narrow diner. When his beeper went off, he cursed and strode angrily out to the cruiser to call in. I paid the check and hustled

Neddie out the door. We waved at Red as we pulled out into the thickening Monday morning traffic.

The car dealership was nestled back in the trees about halfway up the island. I'm generally a "Buy American" consumer, but I'm not fanatic about it. I had to admit the gleaming chrome and sleek, fluid bodies of the foreign cars arrayed at the front of the lot had me salivating just a little. I jiggled the keys Geoff Anderson had left on my deck and wondered what had given him the idea I would let him pick out a car for me. Still, I had to start somewhere. I needed the independence of my own wheels if I were to get my half-formulated plans off the ground.

Buck James turned out to be a pleasant surprise. Far from a slick, stereotypical young hustler, Buck was fiftyish, balding, and soft-spoken. If he knew the reason for my sudden need for a new car, he didn't refer to it. He simply led us to the back of the lot, chatting genially about what a good guy his friend, Geoff, was, and how he hoped I'd approve of his choice.

When I spotted the little two-seater convertible tucked in among the trees, it was love at first sight. A soft, pale aqua, the color reminded me of the ocean on a sunny day. I checked the sticker and gulped a little; but, when Buck named the price he had agreed on with Geoff, I knew I had to have it. I glanced at Neddie who was grinning as widely as I.

"If you don't buy it, I'm going to," she said, running her hand over the creamy top and matching leather interior.

Buck called a lot boy to wash it up and put on the temporary plate while he escorted Neddie and me into the dealership to take care of the paperwork. I wrote a check out of my investment account, and, in less than half an hour, I was on my way.

Neddie had agreed to go back to the house and await the arrival of the phone company. I instructed her to have them replace all the phones, even the undamaged ones. She looked a little askance at my request, but I didn't explain. The less Neddie knew about my suspicions, the better it would be for her. I also asked her to oversee Dolores's meeting with the contractor who was coming to give us an estimate on restoring the kitchen.

So, with the top down and my hair streaming out behind me, it was just past ten when I whipped into the parking lot of the hospital and began my quest for answers where the questions had all begun: with Adelaide Boyce Hammond.

Judy McKay, the nurse who had been on duty the night Miss Addie was brought in, looked up from behind the desk as I stepped off the elevator. Her face registered shock, then softened into sympathy as I walked up to her.

"My God, Mrs. Tanner, are you all right? I couldn't believe it when I read in the *Packet* about the explosion."

She wanted to ask me about what I had done to earn myself a murder attempt by a mad bomber, but was too well brought up to voice the question.

"At least I have some good news for you," she said, removing her glasses. "Your friend woke up yesterday, and she appears to be fine. We've moved her back into her old room. Dr. Winter tried to call you yesterday, but your phone was out of order. I guess..."

She stopped guiltily and let the thought trail off. We both knew why my telephones were inoperative.

"That's great," I said. It was the best possible news, far more than I'd hoped for. "Can I see her?"

"Sure. If you hurry, you might catch the doctor. He just went in a few minutes ago."

"Thanks." I moved off down the hallway. I could feel Judy McKay's eyes following me speculatively. I guessed I would have to get used to that. The survivor of an attempted professional hit was bound to arouse people's curiosity.

Dr. Winter, leaning over the bed, blocked my view as I entered the room. He straightened at my approach and greeted me with a grin.

"Well, Miss Hammond, looks like you've got a visitor."

Miss Addie was thinner and paler than the last time I had stood here. Her lacy pink bed jacket hung on her as if it were made for someone twice her size. But a hint of the old sparkle shone out of her faded eyes, and someone had brushed her hair into a soft, white halo.

"Welcome back," I said as I bent to brush her sunken cheek with my lips. Tears welled up and threatened to spill over before I got myself under control.

"Thank you, dear." Her voice was creaky with disuse.

"How is she?" I turned to Dr. Winter who gave me an almost imperceptible nod of his head.

"Oh, we just need to fatten her up a little, and then we'll chase her out of here and make room for someone who's really sick. How about it, Miss Hammond?"

"Whatever you say, Doctor, but I don't seem to have much appetite."

"I've given the kitchen orders to whip you up some goodies that'll be irresistible, gooey things guaranteed to pile on the calories. Starting with lunch today."

Miss Addie nodded. She was trying hard to keep her eyes open.

"You go ahead and rest now," he went on in his hearty bedside voice. "I'll look in on you again this afternoon. A word, Mrs. Tanner?" Dr. Winter took my arm, and we stepped into the hallway.

"Is she really all right?" I asked as soon as we were out of earshot. "She looks so…shrunken."

"It was touch and go for awhile, but, yes, she'll recover. It was a strange reaction, one I've never encountered with that particular painkiller before."

My mind shot back to the pushy nurse with no name tag who had administered the pills to Miss Addie the day she lapsed into a coma. All my suspicions about her "accident" came screaming back into my mind. Was this another result of her sending me poking into the Grayton's

Race project? Had Miss Addie, too, been the victim of an abortive attempt on her life?

"Are you sure it was the right drug? Could she have been given the wrong medication by mistake?"

Or by design? I couldn't bring myself to say it out loud.

I related the events of last Monday morning. Even before I finished, Dr. Winter was shaking his head.

"No, no. The woman you're describing is Edie Benson. I know her well. She frequently forgets her name badge. She's been written up about it several times. No, we did a tox screen as a matter of course. Miss Hammond just happened to be allergic to this particular drug. Because of her age, her reaction was intensified."

His pager beeped, and he pulled it from his belt. "I'm needed in emergency. Miss Hammond is going to require some special care until she's completely back on her feet," he said, edging away from me.

"Don't worry. I'll take care of whatever she needs."

"Good. We'll keep her a few more days. That'll give you time to get something set up."

"Thank you, Doctor," I called as he turned and hurried off.

When I walked back into the room, Miss Addie was awake and looking much more alert. "There you are, Lydia. I hoped you hadn't left for good. I'm sorry about nodding off like that. I just seem to need these little catnaps. I'm feeling quite refreshed now."

"No problem. Whatever it takes to help you get better." I pulled up the bedside chair and sat down. "Up to a few questions? Just say so if you're not."

"Heavens, yes, child. I've been itching with curiosity about what you've been up to." Her eyes were dancing, and a little color had returned to her cheeks.

"Well, I went over to your condo last Monday right after you fell asleep."

She waved aside my apology for lifting her keys and pass from her handbag. "I was going to give them to you anyway, dear."

I told her about my encounter with Ariadne Dixon and the suave Mr.
Romero, and about my feeling that they had lied about what they were
doing in her apartment.

"Do you think it could be one of them who pushed you?"

"Gracious, I really don't know. I never saw anyone, you see. But I
think whoever it was must have been hiding in the bathroom. I had my
back to it when I felt the hands."

Miss Addie shivered then, a tiny *frisson* of remembered fear that
made me want to kick myself for reminding her.

"You mentioned gardenias the other day. At least I think that's what
you said."

"Did I? How odd! I've always hated gardenias."

"Did you smell them that night?"

"I really can't remember. It all seems so long ago now."

"Did you ever notice the fragrance before? On Dixon or Romero?"

"I don't think so dear. I've had them both to tea a few times, and they
seemed quite pleasant. I really can't believe either of them would do anything so…well, *uncivilized*. And what reason could they possibly have?"

I didn't have an answer for that.

We talked for a few more minutes, but nothing else revealed itself as
bearing on the identity or motive of Miss Addie's attacker. Try as I
might, I couldn't get hold of any connection between this assault and all
the other strange occurrences of the past two weeks. Maybe it had just
been a sneak thief, surprised in the act by Miss Addie's unexpected
return. Maybe I should just call Red, turn it all over to the cops.

Adelaide Boyce Hammond's eyes were beginning to droop when I
reached into my bag for my keys, and my fingers brushed up against a
much-creased paper. It was the copy of the letter I had found in Miss
Addie's handbag. Shoved underneath my desk pad, it had been overlooked by whoever had rifled my office. I'd retrieved it last night and
stuffed it in my tote.

"Miss Addie," I ventured, and her eyes snapped open. "One more question. What did you meet with Law Merriweather about?"

I unfolded the letter and held it out to her. She glanced briefly at it, then turned away, her face flushed.

"What is it?" I pressed. "It might be important."

"Well, dear, I talked to Lawton about a number of things. The powers of attorney, for one. I hope you didn't mind about that." I shook my head. "Then, there was my will, and I wanted his advice about...Oh, dear. I'm afraid the Judge will be quite upset with me."

My ears pricked up at the mention of my father. "Why would the Judge be upset with you?"

""Well, dear, it's not that I didn't have faith in him. Or in you. And after your call that Saturday, to let me know that everything was fine with Grayton's Race, I did feel rather foolish."

"I don't understand."

"You see, I asked Lawton to look into selling some of my things. Mother's and Father's things, actually, that I'd inherited. Maybe one or two paintings or some of the porcelain." Her voice had sunk to an embarrassed whisper. "In case I needed the money."

I did my best to reassure her that neither the Judge nor I had taken offense. She was nodding off again as I tucked the blanket around her and tiptoed out the door.

I was no closer to finding the answers to my questions, but the conversation had served one useful purpose. It had reminded me that it was my father who had actually set the wheels in motion; first, by convincing Miss Addie and others to invest in Grayton's Race, but, more inexplicably, by urging her to contact *me* about her fears of losing her money.

Why had he done that? I would have been blissfully ignorant of the whole sordid mess if he had just kept his mouth shut. For some reason, he'd wanted me involved. Now he wanted me out. And he had yet to explain his own entanglement with Hadley Bolles and with Geoff Anderson.

Time for some answers. If I had to tie him down until he leveled with me this time, that's exactly what I'd do.

Spirits somewhat restored, I hopped in my new Z3 and turned her loose in the direction of Beaufort.

24

If all the picketers had been gone from in front of Grayton's Race, everything might have turned out a lot differently. But, as I made the turn toward Beaufort, I spotted a lone pickup truck still parked at the entrance to the property. On impulse, I pulled in behind it.

The lanky young man who climbed down out of the cab to greet me was quite a surprise. Far from the stained T-shirts, ripped bluejeans, and baseball caps of the others I had encountered, he was dressed in well-pressed khaki slacks, a crisp blue denim shirt, and Bass loafers. He looked to be in his early twenties. He reminded me more of a college student from some impressive eastern university than an eco-freak.

"Hi," he said as I approached the truck. "Something I can help you with?"

His smile was open, his brown eyes under thick blond hair, direct and non-threatening. I had a tough time picturing this guy dropping bloody squirrel carcasses into the backseats of open Jaguars or demolishing golf carts with a sledgehammer.

"Are you associated with CARE?" I asked, stopping a few feet from his open door.

"Founder, president, and chief cook and bottle washer. Nathan Spellman. My friends call me Nat."

I took the offered hand. His grip was firm, but not crushing.

"Bay Tanner. I wonder if I could ask you a few questions?"

"You from the press? Not that that's a problem," he added quickly, "but you're a little late. I could have used some publicity a few weeks ago."

I shook my head. "Sorry. Just a concerned citizen, I guess you'd say."

"Concerned citizens are always welcome, too. What can I do for you?"

"Well, I wanted to know about the group—your aims, your philosophy. How you recruit new members, things like that."

"You interested in joining? A little late for that, too, but I've got some literature here." He reached into the front seat of the truck and extracted a computer-generated flyer from a thick stack bound by a rubber band. While obviously homemade, the artwork and layout were surprisingly professional.

"Thanks, I'll look this over. But could you give me a short rundown of what you're all about?"

"Sure. See, I've been working on my master's thesis on eco-system management. This was part of my research. I picked this area because it has such a dichotomy—rapid development in a relatively fragile natural environment. You from around here?"

"Born and raised," I said.

"So you know all about Hilton Head."

"As a matter of fact, I live there. But I always thought they'd done a pretty good job of keeping the sprawl under control."

"Oh, they have," he rushed to assure me, "don't get me wrong. I was going to use them as an example of how you can have the best of both worlds. Planned development that's also compatible with the environment. At least in the beginning."

I smiled to let him know I had taken no offense on behalf of my adopted island home.

"But this," he went on, his hand sweeping a wide arc toward the entrance to Grayton's Race, "and all the stuff springing up on the 278 corridor, that's another story. It's all happening too fast. Not enough studies have been done to determine what the long-term effects are likely to be. This is old-growth forest in here, some really spectacular trees. And you've seen the river, of course. Incredibly clean and unpolluted."

This was all fascinating, but not the kind of information I'd been hoping to get. Part of my half-formed theory rested on a connection between the incidents at Grayton's Race and Derek Johnson's sudden refusal to sign off on his property. I tried to steer Nat back toward my real area of interest.

"So how did you get all the guys I saw out here to join up? Are they researchers, too?"

A flash of suspicion darkened his wide-set brown eyes. "Are you a cop?"

"Me? No, of course not. Why?"

"Well, we've had some trouble with some of our...members. Vandalism, that kind of stuff. I never condoned any of it. In fact, I threatened to turn them in when I heard about it. I thought maybe you were undercover or something. See, a lot of the guys that jumped on the bandwagon are locals. Hunters, fishermen, like that. It took me awhile to realize they had their own agenda."

Nat Spellman did something then that completely won me over. He blushed. "I'm a city boy, you see. Baltimore. This was my first experience with..."

"Rednecks," I supplied, and he laughed.

"Yeah. But that's all over with. As you can see, they've disappeared now that they got what they were after."

"What's that?"

"The head of the project—a guy named Anderson—met with some of them last weekend. At his office over there in the welcome center. They worked out a deal where part of the land will be set aside as a sort of game preserve where they can hunt and fish. He even promised to build them a gun club, with a target range and everything. So they've gone away happy. And me—I'm just goin' away, period. I was just getting ready to pack it in when you pulled up."

"You've accomplished what you wanted to then?" I asked.

Though his words were upbeat, his face told me otherwise. "Enough, I guess. At least I'll be able to start writing my thesis when I get back to Maryland. And it's been a great learning experience. I just wish I could have made more of a difference. Looks like the development will be going through as planned."

"Hold on a sec," I said, turning back toward my car. I grabbed my checkbook out of my bag and hastily scribbled out a check. "Here." I handed it to him. "A donation for the cause."

His mouth dropped open when he looked at the amount. "Gosh, Ms. Tanner, I'm not sure I can accept this."

"Sure you can." I held out my hand. "It was nice to meet you, Nat Spellman. Good luck with your paper, and keep the faith, okay?"

"Thank you. Thanks a lot." He folded the check and stuck it in his shirt pocket.

I sat in the car and lit a cigarette while the earnest young grad student started up his truck and pulled out onto the highway. He waved as he passed me, heading north.

Sometimes I actually have hope for the next generation.

And his casual remark about a meeting in Geoff's office had been worth twice what I had given him. I backed the Z3 slowly along the shoulder of the road, then turned into the driveway of the Grayton's Race welcome center.

The modular building was larger than it appeared from the highway, about the size of a double-wide trailer. It sported a fresh coat of white paint, although here and there a faint shadow of the graffiti I'd seen in the snapshots Geoff had shown me still bled through.

There was no sign of the Jaguar. An older Pontiac Grand Am was the only car in the graveled lot. I parked and got out before I could change my mind. I had no real idea what I was going to say—or even what I thought I might accomplish here. But sometimes the best plan is no plan. I walked up three wooden steps and pushed open the door.

The air inside was frigid, which was probably why the red-haired receptionist was huddled inside a bulky cardigan sweater. She looked up and quickly closed the magazine she'd been reading. Deftly she slid it into the center desk drawer and gave me a practiced smile.

"Hey, there," she chirped, "welcome to Grayton's Race. What can I do for ya?"

It was the kind of drawl I probably would have retained if I hadn't spent a lot of my college years surrounded by flat, Midwestern twangs.

"I'd like to see Mr. Anderson, please."

"Oh, gosh, I'm sorry, he's not in. Could I help you with somethin'?"

She was so young and eager, I almost felt bad about scamming her. I made a show of checking my watch.

"I was supposed to meet him here at noon," I lied, "to take a tour of the property. Do you expect him back soon?"

"You had an appointment? Oh, lord, he didn't say anythin' to me." She reached for a leather-bound datebook and flipped pages. "I don't see anythin' here. Let me check the desk calendar in his office."

The receptionist swiveled out of her chair and started down a narrow hallway toward a closed door at the back. I stepped around a large laminated map of the project with the golf courses, streets, and lots marked out in bright colors, and followed right behind her. She looked startled when she glanced up from the desk to see me standing in the doorway.

"He doesn't have it written on his calendar, either. What did you say your name was?"

I hadn't, nor had I given any thought to needing a fake one, until she asked.

"Smythe," I improvised, and spelled it. "Mrs. Marian Smythe."

It was a little better than *Mary Smith*, but not much.

"Hi, I'm Tiffani. With an 'i.'"

I could have guessed that.

"Gosh, I'm really sorry, Mrs. Smythe," she chattered on. "It's not like Mr. Anderson to forget an appointment. I could try to reach him on his car phone, but he was goin' to a couple of meetings today, and I'm not really sure where he is."

"Perhaps he'll be back soon. Why don't I just wait awhile?" I crossed into the room and settled in one of the club chairs facing the desk. I gave "Tiffani-with-an-i" my most reassuring smile.

"Oh, gosh, I don't know, Mrs. Smythe. Mr. Anderson's real particular about his office. *I'm* not even supposed to be in here when he's gone. He usually keeps it locked. He must've been in a rush this morning."

The desk was standard office issue, the chairs comfortable, but inexpensive. The white-framed prints of familiar beach scenes were churned out by the thousands. They decorated every wall in every waiting room in the Lowcountry. The only things that could make this room worth locking were the three four-drawer filing cabinets ranged against the far wall. Heavy and gray, they sat beneath two small windows set high in the fake oak paneling.

This was precisely what I'd been hoping for. If Geoff had records pertaining to the project, this was where they'd be. The cabinets had locks, but they weren't pushed in. If I could get little blonde Tiffani out of there for five or ten minutes, I could at least see if they contained anything worth my while.

We were at an impasse, though, as Geoff's receptionist and I smiled woodenly across the desk at each other.

"I wonder if I might have a glass of water?" It was a tired ploy, but I was counting on innate Southern manners to win out over suspicion and job security. "Or maybe some coffee?"

I'd noticed a small kitchen on the opposite end of the building, an empty pot sitting in the bottom of a coffee maker on the counter.

"Well, sure, I'd be glad to. Would you like to wait out front?" Tiffani asked hopefully.

"Oh, I'm just fine right here, thanks. The sun feels so good."

I pointed toward the windows and gave her my best everything-will-be-just-fine face. With a shrug of defeat, she walked past me and down the hall.

When I heard the water start to run, I jumped up and pulled open the top drawer of the first cabinet. It appeared to hold paid invoices, arranged alphabetically. With a quick glance over my shoulder, I tried the next two. Nothing looked promising. I stooped and slid open the bottom drawer. The folders here were unmarked. The first one held what seemed to be legal documents. Before I had a chance to check any of them out, I heard the clack of Tiffani's high-heeled pumps on the uncarpeted hallway.

When she stepped into the room, I was leaning casually against the file cabinet, apparently admiring one of the bland pictures.

"Here we go," she announced in her cheerful little voice.

"Thanks so much." I took the offered mug from her and pretended to sip.

"I'm getting ready to go to lunch in a few minutes," Tiffani said apologetically, "and I have to lock up Mr. Anderson's office. But you're welcome to wait in the reception area if you like."

"Oh, no, that's okay, dear. I've decided I'll just get on out of your way. I'll call Mr. Anderson and set up another appointment. You've been so kind. Bye-bye now."

I pushed the mug into her hand and fairly trotted out the door. The wheels of the Z threw up a little gravel in my haste to get out of there.

Out on the highway, I took a deep breath to calm my racing heart. I pulled into the first commercial driveway I came to. With trembling fingers I lit a cigarette, then reached into my bag for the document I had pilfered. It was a copy of the Articles of Incorporation, the same ones I had received over the fax from Belinda St. John's assistant. It wasn't exactly news, but it was like finding a gold doubloon on the floor of the ocean. Where there was one, there were probably more.

Who knew what treasure that bottom drawer might hold? I was convinced it was my best chance for the evidence I needed. But how to get at it? I needed a really good scheme this time.

But first I had to settle things with my father. With that behind me, I could concentrate on just exactly how I was going to get my hands on the papers in that cabinet.

25

Lavinia insisted on fixing me lunch even though she and the Judge had just finished. My father had retired to his recliner for his customary afternoon nap, so I sat at the kitchen table while she reheated the pork and stuffing and brewed fresh tea.

Living up north, I had gotten away from the old Southern tradition of taking the heaviest meal of the day at noon. The custom dated back to the plantation era when work in the fields began at daybreak. It had made more sense for the cooking ovens to be fired up in the morning before the heat of the sultry afternoons descended.

Lavinia moved about the kitchen with a brisk economy of motion acquired over decades of preparing meals in this room for me and my parents. No clatter of pans or clank of dishes disturbed the companionable silence we had shared countless times before. Ever since I had gotten old enough to sit on my own at the worn oak table, I had loved to watch her. She moved as gracefully now as she had when I was too young to appreciate such things.

Lavinia put the casserole dish in the oven to warm, poured us both iced tea, and joined me at the table. It wasn't until her deep brown eyes looked directly into mine that I remembered what had taken place this morning in the courthouse just a few miles away.

"What happened at the hearing? Did Isaiah get bail?" I asked.

Her face told me that she knew I had forgotten. I felt the blush of shame at my thoughtlessness creep up my throat.

"It's all right, Bay. You've had your own troubles to tend to. Yes, he's home now, the Lord be praised. Mr. Brown said bail wasn't as high as it could have been, probably because so many folks came and spoke for him."

Lavinia brushed a hand across her eyes. I had never seen her look so weary.

"Your father even sent a letter to the court, vouching for Isaiah's character. Mr. Elliott put up the money. And he's going to pay for the lawyers, too. Lawton Merriweather will be working with Mander Brown when the trial starts."

"When do they think that'll be?" I asked, wondering again about Big Cal's motives.

Lavinia's worn fingers picked nervously at the fringed edges of the placemat. Her skin was almost the same color as the pale oak of the table. "At least a couple of months, so they say."

My father was still asleep when I finished what I could of the heavy lunch. When Lavinia refused my offer to help clean up, I wandered out the back door and settled into a rocking chair on the verandah. The Sound was unruffled by the light breeze that rattled the palmettos. Here and there its smooth surface was dotted with floating pelicans, their ungainly brown bodies rocking gently in the slight swells kicked up by passing pleasure boats. The air was alive with birdsong, and, in the sporadic silences, the sharp *tap-tap* of a woodpecker high in a loblolly pine sounded unnaturally loud.

This was the true beauty of *Presqu'isle*, I thought, not the polished tables and proud antiques. This part of my home I could love, and always had.

I kicked off my shoes and pushed the chair into motion. In the drowsy peace of the summer afternoon, I rocked and smoked and thought. It wasn't quite meditation, but it served the purpose. By the time I heard Lavinia stirring about the kitchen, squeezing fruit, no doubt, for my father's bourbon and lemonade, I felt calm and in control. It wasn't to last.

When I strolled back into the house, Lavinia looked as if she wanted to say something to me, then, with a shrug, changed her mind. I took the tray from her and carried it into the study.

If my father was surprised to see me, he didn't show it. I set the drinks on the low table next to his wheelchair, retrieved a cigar from the dresser drawer, and again held the crystal desk lighter for him as he performed the ritual. I settled myself in a corner of the sofa with my bare feet tucked up under me.

"You want to talk about the project, about Grayton's Race," the Judge began abruptly. "You're right. It's time."

My father's clear, gray eyes regarded me steadily as he blew smoke toward the ceiling. If he'd hoped to throw me off balance by taking the initiative, he'd miscalculated. I'd seen him in action from the bar as well as from the bench from the time I was in grade school. I'd spent many summer afternoons tucked quietly into a corner of the old courthouse, watching in rapt fascination as my father mesmerized with the sheer power of his voice, manipulated with clever argument, intimidated with a frosty stare.

Oh, yes, I knew all his tactics.

"Whatever you think," I said in the same reasonable tone.

I held his eyes, and slowly a smile began to twitch at the corners of his mouth.

"Damn, you should have stayed in law school, daughter. You've got the touch. With your looks and your brains, you could have stood this ol' county on its ear."

"Irrelevant, Your Honor."

My father took a sip of bourbon and settled back in his chair. The smile faded. "About six months ago, Hadley Bolles came to me with a proposition."

"I knew that fat weasel was involved in this somehow."

My father ignored me and went on. "He represented a group of investors who wanted to get in on the development boom goin' on around here. Before the environmentalists and the preservationists got their way with the County Council and the Legislature and shut it all down. Hadley seemed to think it was only a matter of time before those groups got together and began litigating. Even if they eventually lost, they could tie things up in court for years. In the meantime, there was money to be made—serious money—if his clients could get up and runnin' before all this hit the fan."

I lit a cigarette and leaned forward. "What did he want from you?"

"My name. And my influence, little as it is anymore."

I heard the wistful longing in his voice, a lament for the days when a word from Judge Talbot Simpson could sway any negotiation, make or break any deal.

"To what purpose?" I asked.

"Hadley's clients were outsiders, from out of state, actually. They figured the backing of a few prominent, local citizens would be helpful in greasing the wheels, getting approvals, permits, and so on. There's a lot of sentiment around here about the Race, you know. A lot of old-timers remember it in its glory years."

I thought about Adelaide Boyce Hammond and her teary nostalgia for the parties and cotillions of her youth. It wouldn't have been difficult to convince her and others that they were contributing to the preservation of local history while turning a nice profit in the process.

"How does Geoff fit into the picture?"

"Pretty much the same way. His father, Carter Anderson, was one of the most respected attorneys in this town, and you know Millicent's family were among the original settlers. She never tired of reminding your mother about that."

I shook my head at the remembered intensity of their competition, the constant jockeying for prominence among the DAR and Daughters of the Confederacy members. Millicent Bowdoin Anderson had my mother beat by a generation and never let her forget it.

"Plus he was affiliated with the Florida firm that represented the investors," my father continued. "Hadley figured he was a gift from the gods, and persuaded them to put him in charge of the project."

"So you knew all about Geoff before I ever accepted that date with him."

"Not everything," he said and refilled his glass.

And suddenly I wondered how "accidental" my meeting with Geoff on the verandah of the Fig Tree had really been. Hadley had been there, too. Coincidence? He'd been meeting with someone, I remembered now, the stranger in the white suit with the large diamond glittering against his olive skin. Was *he* the Miami connection?

But why would any of them have been interested in me then? It didn't make any sense. I had only become involved, and in the most peripheral manner, the day before. In fact, I had been in Beaufort only because of the questioning of Isaiah Smalls about the murder of Derek Johnson. Unless...

"Tell me about Derek Johnson," I said.

"What about him?" The calm, steady voice now shook a little, and my father looked everywhere except at me.

"Did you know he was the holdout on the heirs property? That his backing out endangered the entire project?"

"What are you implying?"

"I'm not implying anything. I'm trying to get at the truth here. Isn't that what you always taught me to do? I've had a gut feeling all along that Derek's murder was somehow connected to Grayton's Race. Tell me I'm wrong."

His silence was my answer. It lengthened as he continued to avoid my eyes.

Finally, he said, "I can't prove anything."

"But you have your suspicions, haven't you? My God, Father, what have you gotten yourself involved in?"

The Judge activated his wheelchair and steered himself up the ramp and out onto the verandah. The screen door banged shut behind him.

I lit a cigarette and smoked it down to the filter before I followed him out into the blistering heat. What little breeze there was failed to move the wet, heavy air. I pulled a rocking chair up next to where he sat staring out at the placid Sound.

"Okay," I began, "you don't have to say anything, just listen. If I'm way off base, just shake your head."

"No, Bay. I want you out of this now. Drop it. Stop your meddling."

"Don't be ridiculous," I snapped. "You know I can't do that. I won't. *You* may be able to sit by and let Lavinia's grandson take the fall for a murder you know he didn't commit, but I sure as hell can't."

He whirled his chair around to face me then, his mouth a grim line of deep anger. "How dare you! You honestly think I would let that happen? The boy will never be convicted. Never! In fact, I fully expect the charges to be dropped. Law Merriweather will see to that. The state has a very weak case. All the evidence is circumstantial."

"Even the baseball bat with Derek's brains all over it?" I asked, and he flinched. "You're amazing, you know that? You and your cronies? You think you own the whole damn county, don't you? 'The boy will never be convicted.' You say it with such smug authority. From your lips to God's ear, huh? Well, what if he is? What if the Sheriff decides not to play ball? What if a jury of just regular folks decides to ship him off to death row and let them stick a needle in his arm?"

"You don't know what you're talking about, daughter." He dismissed my concern with a wave of his hand. "Now just do as I say. It was a mistake to involve you in the first place. I'm ordering you to stay out of my business."

"Too late, Your Honor. You should have thought of that before you sicced Miss Addie onto me. What did you think I'd do, hold her hand

and make soothing noises about everything being just fine, then crawl back into my hole and disappear again?"

The Judge turned his chair back around and gazed out over the sloping lawn down to the water. I had been dismissed.

"Well, as usual, Father, you've underestimated me. I have it pretty well figured out now, except for one thing. What could Hadley Bolles possibly have on you to force you into pimping for a bunch of drug dealers and covering up a murder?"

The broad shoulders that had carried me, literally and figuratively, all my life, slumped as all the defiance and anger went out of him. The blazing orator had vanished, leaving a helpless, crippled old man hunched in a wheelchair.

For a long time my question hung unanswered in the humid afternoon air. Then my father raised his weary face to mine and smiled, a sad, bittersweet look that made my heart turn over.

"I've never underestimated you, Lydia Baynard Simpson. Never."

"You're not going to tell me, are you?"

He shook his head sadly. "No, I'm not."

"But why? I can help, Father, I want to. We can fight this. You can't just sit by and let that bastard get away with blackmailing you! We can…"

"Hush, child, hush. You don't know what you're saying. There are others involved here…people who can be hurt, damaged. People who can no longer defend themselves."

"I don't…?" I began when the real meaning of his words hit me. *People who can no longer defend themselves.* "It's about Mother, isn't it? Hadley has something on my mother."

I clambered out of the rocker and knelt in front of his wheelchair.

"But for God's sake, Father, she's dead! What can he possibly reveal that could hurt her now?" I took his good hand in mine and forced him to look at me.

"Leave it, Bay," he whispered, "please. I'll handle this in my own way. It's not your burden to carry."

The deep, long-suppressed fury found a crack in my defenses and erupted.

"Not my burden?" I shouted, jumping to my feet. "Not *my* burden? The woman has been a stone around my neck my entire ██████damn life!"

I watched the pain flicker across his eyes, but I couldn't stop now. Nothing mattered but my need to spew it all out—the anger, the hurt, the humiliation of a lifetime of silence.

"What secret could she possibly have that would be worth sacrificing your honor for? My mother was a lush! Miss Emmaline Tattnall Baynard of *Presqu'isle*, DAR, Daughter of the Confederacy, socialite, philanthropist, and pillar of the Episcopal Church was a drunk! Did she think everyone didn't know it? Do *you*?"

I laughed, a harsh, choking sound and slapped my hand on the railing. "God, that would be almost funny if it weren't so pathetic. My third grade classmates knew she was a drunk. They used to call me 'Bay Rum' and snicker, did you know that? No, you probably didn't," I answered for him. "You were too busy making excuses for her. 'Mother's not feeling well.' 'Mother has a headache, go play outside.' 'Mother didn't mean to slap you so hard.'"

I could feel my mocking words slice into him, but I couldn't seem to stop myself. Maybe it all needed to be said, finally, for both of us.

"She hated me and despised you." I cut off my father's attempt to interrupt. "Oh, yes, don't deny it. I used to hear her shouting at you in the middle of the night. How she'd married beneath her—*everyone* said so—and that's why she had to bear the shame of a *common* child without one redeeming social grace. 'An unfortunate accident' she used to call me, didn't she? Well didn't she?" I screamed.

"That's enough, Bay! Leave him alone."

Lavinia stood in the doorway at the top of the ramp. Her words were sharp, but her face held only a deep sadness.

I didn't know how long she'd been there. I prayed she hadn't heard anything about my father's passive complicity in the railroading of her grandson. I didn't think he could survive without Lavinia's respect.

"How can you defend her?" I asked, my anger ebbing under her calm gaze. "She treated you like an indentured servant. You of all people saw what she was capable of."

Lavinia stepped onto the porch, a light cotton throw draped over her arm. She approached the wheelchair and spread the blanket gently across my father's useless legs. He raised his face to her, and their eyes locked. The look that passed between them took my breath away.

And in that moment, I knew.

As I watched, stunned by the enormity of the realization, her pale brown fingers reached out to brush his spotted white hand in a gesture of tender reassurance. Then, without a word or a glance at me, she turned and walked back into the house. The door closed softly behind her.

I stood for a long time staring after her, this woman who had sheltered and protected me as best she could. There was a lot I didn't understand. Perhaps I never would.

I turned back to find my father gazing searchingly up into my face. I couldn't meet his eyes, couldn't let him see the knowledge of his long-held secret reflected in my own. I dropped into the rocking chair, my entire body trembling with the aftermath of spent emotion.

"Bay, I want you to listen to me now. Please." His voice held a strange mixture of determination and defeat. "You must leave this alone. I want you to go away, take a trip somewhere. These are dangerous men. You must prove to them that they've succeeded in scaring you off. I swear no harm will come to Isaiah."

He reached out with his good hand and clasped my arm. "I've been a selfish, arrogant old fool, and you almost had to pay the price for it. I couldn't live if anything happened to you, Bay." His voice cracked, and his fingers tightened around my wrist. "Promise me you'll go. Promise me."

I wanted to throw myself at his feet then and lay my head in his lap. To let him stroke my hair and tell me everything would all right. But we had too much history between us, too many years of crouching behind our protective walls. In building a barrier against the pain of my mother's rejection, I finally realized that I had shut him out, too.

I couldn't change that now, but I could give him some measure of peace. I covered his wrinkled hand with my own. "Okay, Daddy, I'll go. Whatever you want."

I rose and left him there. I let myself quietly out of the house and down the sixteen steps. I stood for a moment, the splendor of the antebellum mansion shimmering proudly through the haze of my unshed tears.

Maybe I will *live here again someday,* I thought as I drew a deep, shuddering breath and pulled slowly away from *Presqu'isle.*

Then, eyes straight ahead, I forced myself to concentrate on adding the finishing touches to my plan for tonight. I had a lot to do, and time was running out.

26

It took a lot longer than I expected to get everything down. Because I didn't want to risk using the computer, I wrote it out longhand on a yellow legal pad. When I was finished, I used the fax machine to make copies. The original I would lock in the floor safe. I put the other two sets in big manila envelopes and addressed one to Belinda St. John at the Statehouse. I'd mail it on my way out. On the other I printed Red Tanner's name in big block letters and left it propped up against my computer screen.

Mr. Bones, my feline security system, rose from his place on the floor and rubbed his head up against my legs as I pushed back my chair from the desk. I figured he had earned permanent resident status for his work on my behalf last Saturday night.

Persuading Neddie to leave had been less difficult that I'd anticipated. Without divulging the specifics of our conversation, I finally convinced her that I was taking my father's advice and going on a trip. I even went through the charade of packing a couple of bags.

I was aided by the fact that, with the phones now restored, her service had finally gotten through to her with a message that one of her teenaged patients had been hospitalized. A drug overdose, she told me, shaking her head sadly. She really should go.

We threw together a salad and shared an early dinner before she tossed her bags in the Mercedes and turned to hug me tightly.

"I feel funny about leaving you here alone. Are you sure you'll be okay?" she asked, concern wrinkling her face.

"I'll be fine. I have a nine o'clock flight to Miami, then direct to St. Thomas," I lied.

"How long do you expect to be gone?"

"I don't know, a month probably. I might as well stay away until all the mess is cleared up with the kitchen. Dolores says it'll take that long for the remodelers to finish up."

"Well, have a wonderful time, and try not to worry. I'll call and check up on the Judge from time to time."

"Thanks for everything, Neddie," I said. "I couldn't have gotten through this without you."

"Hey, that's what friends are for, kiddo. Any time you need company climbing out your windows, I'm your girl." She settled herself behind the wheel and reached for my hand. "Be careful now, you hear?"

"God, Halloran," I laughed, "that was almost a *drawl*! We'll make a Southern belle out of you yet."

"Not in this lifetime. See ya." She backed the car around and headed out. About halfway down the driveway, she stuck her head out the window and shouted, "Thanks for everything, Tanner. It was a blast!"

I picked up a pine cone and threw it at her retreating taillights. I could hear her hoot of laughter as she pulled out into the road.

After she left, I emptied my suitcases, then made a show of loading them into the tiny trunk, just in case Red decided to check up on me. I'd spun him the same tale about leaving town, and I was pretty sure he'd bought it. At least he made appropriate noises about being glad I'd finally come to my senses. He agreed to reduce the armed patrol around my house to one man, starting tonight.

The most difficult part was calling Geoff Anderson. I finally reached him at home just after Neddie left. He sounded relieved to hear from me.

Geoff asked after my health ("I'm fine), the house ("It's not as bad as it could have been"), and my new car ("It's perfect. I love it.").

The amenities completed, an awkward silence settled over us. I lit a cigarette, inhaled deeply, and plunged in.

"Geoff, I've been thinking about what you said, in the parking lot the other night. About there being reasons for what you told me? Or rather, what you *didn't* tell me."

"I never meant to lie to you, Bay, you have to believe that. It's just..."

"I understand that, Geoff." I didn't want him to start explaining now. That wasn't part of the plan. "I'm ready to listen now. But I think we should do it face to face, don't you?"

"I can be there in no time at all."

"No! I mean, I have another idea."

I gave him my well rehearsed lie about leaving the country, to get away for awhile and recover. He, too, thought it an excellent idea.

"I'm leaving tonight, an eleven o'clock flight out of Savannah. I was wondering if you could meet me there, earlier. For dinner."

"Why don't I just drive you in myself? That way you won't have to worry about your car."

It was the one flaw in my scenario that I'd had to think really hard about. Of course, his suggestion made the most sense, but it certainly wasn't what I wanted. It defeated my whole purpose.

"No, thanks. See, I'm having a security system installed on the Zeemer while I'm gone, and I've already arranged for the shop to pick up the car from the airport lot."

It sounded feeble, even to me, but Geoff was apparently so eager to justify his string of lies to me that he accepted it without question. We arranged to meet at the Delta ticket counter at eight-thirty. I told him I might be a little late, what with packing and all, and he promised to wait for me.

He didn't have the nerve to tell me he loved me, but he tried hard to put meaning into his voice as we said goodbye.

So, if the gods smiled, that should keep Geoffrey Anderson far away from the welcome center during my covert rifling of his office files. When I failed to show up, he'd probably go back to Hilton Head or call my father in St. Helena. Either way, he would have no reason to look for me at Grayton's Race.

I spent the next hour practicing unlocking doors with a credit card. When Red had taught his brother and me, several years ago, it had been more of a parlor trick than anything else. We'd only done it for real once, when Rob and I had locked ourselves out of the apartment in Charleston. The ease with which we'd gained entry using Rob's American Express card convinced us to install deadbolts the next day.

Deadbolts hadn't stopped the creeps who had broken into my house here, I thought ruefully, but then they undoubtedly had a lot more experience at it than I.

As near as I could remember, there were no special locks on the welcome center, nor on Geoff's office door. I sent up a silent prayer to the patron saint of breakers and enterers, whoever he might be, that I hadn't missed spotting a padlock—or an alarm system.

The last thing I had done was to sit down at the desk and record my version of the events of the past two weeks and my interpretation of how they fit together. There was no reason to believe that I wouldn't be there to relate them in person. I should be in and out of Geoff's office in less than an hour, and everyone who might possibly come looking for me believed me to be safely on my way out of the country.

Still, I had nearly died twice in the last twelve months, and Rob...I reopened the envelope to Red and hastily scribbled instructions for Miss Addie's care once she was released from the hospital, adding a power of attorney that would enable him to access whatever funds he might need.

Nothing is going to go wrong, I told myself. I was merely taking the old computer mantra to heart: Backup, backup, backup.

Finally, at eight o'clock, I emerged from the bedroom, as confident as I could be for a total novice at this cloak-and-dagger stuff that I had covered all the bases. I was dressed in loose black slacks, a matching sweater, and low heeled pumps. It was the closest I could come to a cat burglar outfit without arousing the suspicions of my solitary sentry.

I found him standing by my car when I trotted down the front steps with my oversized tote bag slung across my shoulders.

"You have a safe trip, ma'am," he said, touching his cap. "We'll look after things here."

"Thank you, deputy," I replied, sliding behind the wheel.

I pulled out onto the roadway and never looked back.

I had planned on arriving at the welcome center around nine, about the time it got fully dark. It was 8:58 by the digital clock on the dashboard as I eased past the Grayton's Race sign and pulled into the driveway of the nursery just down the road.

I cut the lights and coasted on around the building to the loading area in the back. I got out of the car and slipped off my pumps, replacing them with a pair of black Nikes I'd carried in my bag. I also extracted my dark Braves' baseball cap and stuffed my hair up under it. I took my Platinum Visa card from my wallet, tucked the keys and a mini-flashlight in my pocket, and locked my totebag in the trunk.

I set off in the direction of Grayton's Race, following the road but keeping well back in the trees. There was very little traffic on this Monday night, but I stopped and turned my face away whenever approaching lights signaled an oncoming vehicle.

It took me a little over ten minutes to reach the drive. I skirted around its sharp bend and stopped dead.

The fence! I had forgotten about the goddamned fence!

The gate, seven or eight feet high at least, rose in front of me. It was secured with a huge padlock. The fence itself stretched away on both sides and disappeared into the trees.

I moved back into the brush and sat down in a pile of soft pine needles, my back against the scratchy bark of a gum tree.

How could I have been so stupid? How could I have missed the fence this morning? I had driven through the gate twice, and its presence had never even registered on my feeble brain. Besides which, Geoff had *told* me about it the night we…were together at his apartment.

Think! I ordered myself. *Calm down and think*!

What had he told me? Did the fence encircle the entire property?

No, of course not. That would be impossible, given the vastness of the place. Geoff had implied that its purpose was to keep out vehicles rather than people. So, all I had to do was follow it to the end, round the corner, and I was in.

But then another part of that conversation popped into my head. A security force! Geoff had hired private security to patrol the grounds!

I half-stood then, ready to bolt back to my car and get the hell out of there. This had been a harebrained scheme from the start. I had no business playing James Bond. I was totally out of my depth here. I took one step away from the tree and stopped.

If I turned tail and ran now, what would happen to my father? To Lavinia? The original point of this exercise had been to find proof of the drug connection. Once I had that safely tucked away, I could force Geoff Anderson and his pals to return the cash the Judge and his friends had unwittingly contributed to their little money-laundering scheme. If I could manage to come up with something that would help get Isaiah Smalls off the hook, that would be an added bonus.

Now, however, the stakes had been raised considerably. The only way to stop Hadley Bolles from continuing to blackmail my father was to get the proof of his criminal involvement in this whole scam and negotiate a trade: my information for his. It would probably keep the slimy bastard out of jail, but it just might be enough to keep him from trying anything like this again.

I sat back down, dying for a cigarette, but I had left them in the car. Besides, it would be the height of stupidity to provide the light that could lead a security patrol right to me.

I took a few deep breaths and willed my heart to slow down. I pushed the button to illuminate my watch face. *9:21.* Time was indeed running out.

Nat Spellman, the founder of CARE, had told me that Geoff had reached an agreement with the destructive wing of the organization. So, no more vandalism, no need for security. It made sense, but could I count on that? I decided to wait and see if anyone made an appearance. Even if they were on foot, there would be no need for stealth. They were the good guys. I should be able to hear them coming long before they could spot me.

By nine-forty, my nerves were stretched to the breaking point. Only the rustle of night creatures and the occasional *whoosh* of a passing car had disturbed the silence. I rose, dusted off the seat of my pants, and followed the fence into the woods.

I had gone about thirty yards when the chain link I had been brushing with my fingers to keep me on line ended abruptly. I eased through the tightly-packed trees and reversed my course. I didn't hesitate when I came once again to the driveway. I walked swiftly across the open space and up to the building. A stranded motorist looking for a phone was my new cover story, and I would stick to it come hell or high water.

Maybe there is a patron saint of burglars, I thought, as I mounted the three wooden steps. A light fixture flanked the door on the left-hand side, but the bulb was burned out. And there was no deadbolt.

Moonlight glinting off the silver propane tank gave me just enough illumination. I dropped the card once, but it took me less than three minutes to pop the lock. The door creaking closed behind me sounded like a woman's scream in the heavy stillness. I shivered and clicked on the flashlight. Shielding it with my hand, I followed its feeble glow down the hallway to Geoff's office. That door was locked, too, but my confidence was running high. I got it on the first try.

I crossed immediately to the windows and closed the half-open blinds tightly. I risked a quick peek around the edge at the parking lot outside. All remained quiet.

The filing cabinet was unlocked. I pulled open the bottom drawer and sat cross-legged on the floor. I trained the flashlight on the first folder and began digging.

It was indeed a gold mine. Southland Real Estate Development. Meridian Partners Group. The familiar names leaped out at me. Correspondence, financial statements. I nearly shouted with the joy of it.

I pulled off the baseball cap and tossed it on the floor beside me. I kept the documents in order as I carried each pile out to the big Canon copier in the outer office. It was a beauty, with all the latest bells and whistles, cranking out copies as fast as I could feed in the originals. I kept glancing at my watch, conscious of the time I had wasted crouching in the woods in fear. No sense pressing my luck. I'd just copy everything the files contained and sort through them when I was safely away from Grayton's Race.

I did take care when I put the documents back, keeping everything in order so no one would know they had been compromised. I didn't want to spook them into running.

I had just shoved the last batch of copies into a big manila envelope I'd pilfered from Tiffani's desk when the overhead light snapped on, and Geoff Anderson walked into his office.

"I think you're going to miss your flight," he said.

27

For one terrifying moment, I thought my heart had stopped. I couldn't seem to draw enough air into my lungs. My whole body trembled as I stood frozen in the glare, my eyes riveted on Geoff Anderson leaning casually against the door frame. His arms were folded across his chest, one leg crossed over the other. His wide shoulders filled the doorway. Even if I could force my legs to move, there was nowhere to run.

Slowly I placed the envelope of photocopies I'd been clutching to my chest onto the desk. With my right foot I gently eased the bottom drawer closed. My eyes never left his face.

I took a deep breath and leaned against the wall, mimicking his stance. "What tipped you off?" I asked in as calm a voice as I could manage.

"You didn't really expect me to buy that 'come back, all is forgiven' routine, did you? So out of character. I knew I'd lost you the minute you found out I was still married. Nice try, but you're not that good an actress."

Geoff strolled across the cheap brown carpet and perched himself on the corner of his desk. He was still between me and the door.

"You were pretty good, though," I answered, eyeing the distance between myself and possible freedom. "That was a very convincing performance. I was sure you'd be cooling your heels at the airport about now. So how did you figure out I'd be here?"

Geoff smiled and shook his head. "Mistake number two. If you're going to try and case a joint, you ought to wear a disguise. You're a very memorable woman, *Mrs. Smythe.*"

So Tiffani-with-an-i hadn't been the empty-headed little twit I'd taken her for.

"Plus," he went on, apparently relishing his role of knowledgeable expert, "if you're going to let someone you don't entirely trust pick out a new car for you, it might be a good idea to check it over before you drive it off the lot."

"You bugged my car," I said. Why hadn't I thought of that possibility before?

Geoff reached into the left pocket of his tan linen blazer and removed a small, rectangular box, about the size of a Walkman. "Cutting-edge electronics. It's really amazing what they can do these days," he said.

The tension of this cat-and-mouse game had made my legs begin to wobble. I edged around in front of Geoff and collapsed into the same chair I'd occupied just a few hours before.

"You wouldn't happen to have a cigarette, would you?" I asked.

"Those thing are gonna kill you one of these days. Tiffani probably has some in her desk. Hold on."

He backed out of the office. I glanced longingly at the two windows flanking the filing cabinets. I would need a stool to reach them, and they were both so small I wasn't sure I could squeeze through even if I could get up there. Besides, Geoff could be back in here in three strides the second he heard me move.

"Sorry, they're not menthol," he said at my elbow.

Damn! The man moves like a cat, I thought as my heart settled back into some semblance of its normal rhythm.

My fingers shook only a little as I fumbled a cigarette out of the pack. Geoff struck a match and leaned over to light it for me. I was ashamed at how much better I felt when that first blast of nicotine hit my bloodstream.

Much calmer now than I had any right to feel, I exhaled and leaned back in the chair, resuming my pose of nonchalance.

"So what happens now?"

"That's entirely up to you. They're going to succeed in killing you, you know, unless you back off and somehow convince them you're no longer a threat."

His matter-of-fact delivery chilled me.

"Who's 'they'?"

"Come off it, Bay. Don't play dumb with me, please." He gestured toward the envelope of documents spilling out onto the top of the desk. "That was only for confirmation, right? You'd already found the evidence you needed."

How much did he know, and how much was guesswork? Maybe I could still bluff my way out of this.

"It's true I had some suspicions, but that's all. Nothing concrete. Once you stole the disks from my office, I had nothing. If you destroy the records you have here, all my proof will be gone."

I thought fleetingly of the envelope I had dropped in the mail box on my way off the island tonight. If I didn't manage to survive this, would Belinda St. John have enough to act on? Would she have the courage to do it?

Geoff shook his head as if at an obtuse child, and straightened his jacket. For the first time I noticed the bulge in his other pocket. Another electronic device, or a weapon?

"They've been one step ahead of you all the way along the line. For a smart woman, you sure have been slow to catch on," he said.

That stung. "Catch on to what?" I snapped. I knew it was pointless to bait him, but maybe if I could keep him talking, some brilliant plan to extricate myself from this nightmare would pop into my head. "That you wired up my computer, tapped my phone? I figured that out the day after the explosion. It was the only way you could have known about my digging into the records. Did you enjoy creeping around my house in the dark? Get off on that, did you?"

"You really are an amateur. You don't actually think I do that kind of thing myself, do you? I'm an attorney, Bay, and a damned good one. That's what I do."

"And that's how you sleep at night?" I yelled, control finally deserting me. "How you live with yourself? You're just the middleman, hands squeaky clean, right? You think just because your finger isn't on the button, you're not responsible? Can you really be that delusional?"

That one hit home. Geoff tensed, the muscles tightening along his jaw. He rose then and began to pace, his steps taking him farther away from the door. I bent my head to light another cigarette and measured my chances of escape. I had him rattled now. Maybe I could use it to my advantage.

"What happened to you, Geoff?" I asked. "How did you ever get mixed up with people like this? Drug dealers, mobsters, murderers! How many people have you had killed?"

"You're not listening to me, Bay!" He whirled angrily, one finger stabbing the air, punctuating his shouted words. "I don't break into people's houses! I don't have people killed!"

"What about Derek Johnson, your holdout on the land deal? Are you telling me he just conveniently died?" Without realizing it, I had parroted Red's accusations, flung at me in anger in the Judge's study, what now seemed like a lifetime ago.

"Johnson? Was that his name? I had no control over that. The stupid kid thought he could hustle the system, thought he could hold out for more money. I hear he even threatened to blow the whistle on the drug operation he'd been running on the river. He signed his own death warrant the minute he put the squeeze on."

My hand trembled as I reached to stub out my cigarette in the round, metal ashtray on Geoff's desk. *My God*, I thought, *who is this man?*

Where had he gone, the boy I'd idolized, standing tall and proud in his cadet's uniform?

"And I suppose you didn't try to have Miss Addie killed. Or me either, for that matter." As long as Geoff was willing to talk, I might as well get all the information I could. If somehow I managed to get out of this, I'd need all the ammunition against them I could gather.

"Of course not," Geoff said, his voice rife with scorn that I could think such a thing. "You can't seriously believe I had anything to do with that bungled attempt on your car, can you? I told them it wasn't necessary. I told them I had the situation under control."

His casual dismissal of my near brush with death stunned me. Could he really be that callous?

"What about Miss Addie? Were they trying to silence her, too?"

"The Hammond woman? You're saying someone tried to kill her?" I almost believed his perplexity was genuine. "I have no idea what you're talking about," he said.

"She was attacked in her apartment at The Cedars. She's one of your investors in Grayton's Race."

The one that got me into this mess, I thought, but didn't say.

"Why would they do that? I know they have some contacts there, a couple they use from time to time. Foreigners, I think. But they're strictly smalltime players, nothing to do with the project. I hear they've got their own little scam going, something to do with ripping off valuable works of art and replacing them with cheap copies." Geoff ran his hands over his sleek, silver hair and came to perch on the edge of the desk once more. "What's the point of all this, Bay? You're not going to believe me anyway, are you? You're determined to think the worst. Besides," he added, checking his watch, "we're running out of time."

His hand slid toward his coat pocket, and my body tensed.

"Geoff, wait!" I cried. "Please! One more question."

His hand moved back to the desk, and I let my breath out slowly.

Stall! I told myself. *Keep him talking.* What other choice did I have?

"I've already said more than I should. You see how much I've come to trust you."

His open smile, suddenly soft, indulgent, transformed his face. For a moment, the man who had awakened my body, nearly captured my heart, gazed fondly at me as if our talk of murder and larceny had never taken place. Was he so out of touch with reality that he believed I could overlook everything he'd revealed?

"How did you ever get involved in all this? What happened to you? What went wrong?" I didn't have to feign the sincerity in my voice. "Make me understand," I said softly.

"So you can do what? Save me? Turn me from my life of crime? Oh, Bay, you really are wonderfully naive."

I had to force myself not to shrink away when he reached out to cup my cheek in his hand. The look he turned on me then was bittersweet, a hint of the boy I used to know shining out from jaded eyes.

"You really want an answer? Let's just say that when I set up practice in Miami with my two buddies from Yale, we weren't too choosy about who we took on as clients. One morning we woke up to find out we'd become attorneys to the kind of people you just don't walk away from."

"Did you try?"

"Truthfully? No. After a while you get used to living well."

"But why go to Miami in the first place? You could have come home…"

"Back here? And done what? Gone into business with my father? The thought of it makes me shudder. You know what this town is like. It never changes. Everyone's still living in the last century, upholding their sacred traditions, pining for the glory days of 'The Cause'. Here I'd be forever known as Carter and Millicent Anderson's 'boy', forced to endure the same people, the same parties at the same clubs, year after dreary year. God, I'd rather be dead! You can understand that, can't you? You refused to live the life the Judge had laid out for you. You got out, too."

That Geoff could find our two life choices comparable finally convinced me that I was not dealing with a rational man. I needed him angry again, pacing, if I were to have any chance of making a break. Despite all his talk about my fate being in my own hands, I didn't believe him for a second.

"And this—what you have now—this is better?" I didn't have to force the disgust into my voice. "Look at yourself, Geoff. You're a drug dealer, even if you don't hang out on the corner and slip the bag into someone's hand. Your Saville Row suits and hand-stitched loafers only make you better dressed than the Derek Johnsons of the world, not any less despicable."

His reaction surprised me. "You've been watching too many gangster movies, Bay. It's a business, just like General Motors or IBM, one that's made me a very wealthy and powerful man. I can live with that."

Geoff stood then, and slipped his hand into the right-hand pocket of his blazer. My heart jumped in terror. But he withdrew, not a weapon, but a slim, blue passport. He tossed it into my lap. With shaking fingers, I opened the cover.

Mine.

"Where did you…?"

"That's not important. What matters is that you're getting out of the country. Now. Tonight."

"You mean you're not going to…?"

"Shoot you? I told you, Bay, I don't kill people. But others aren't so fastidious. You're booked on the last flight out to Atlanta, connecting to Barbados. You can buy whatever you need when you get there. Money doesn't seem to be a problem for you either, does it?" he added snidely. "From there, I want you to lose yourself. There's lots of little islands nobody's ever heard of. Find one and disappear."

"Disappear? But what about…?"

"The Judge? Your precious brother-in-law? They all think you're on the run anyway, don't they? Hopefully you were more convincing with them than you were with me."

"Why are you doing this, Geoff?" Could he really be willing to let me go, let me just walk away?

He went on as if I'd never spoken.

"Of course, I'll have to cover my own ass, give them a good story. They aren't going to be happy that I let you escape. But I'll manage. They need me. I can convince them you're no longer a threat."

He had lost his mind. That had to be it. Or else it was a trap. Maybe they wanted me far away, out of contact with my family and friends, where a convenient accident could go unchallenged by anyone who cared about me. My mind raced. Could I trust him? Would I have a better chance out in the open? At the airport? Or would someone be watching, shadowing me, until I was isolated enough to make the job easier?

"After everything you've told me, you're willing to let me go? I have to know why, Geoff. I have to understand."

"Because I love you." He smiled and reached for my hand. "And after awhile, when all this has blown over and the project is well under way, I'll find you. I have contacts in the islands, people I can trust. When you've had time to think it over, I feel sure you'll come to your senses, come to realize that we belong together. We always have."

I ripped my hand away and jumped to my feet. "You're insane!" I screamed, mindless of the consequences. "Do you seriously believe I could ever love a man who trades in misery and death? That I could ever bear to have you touch me again? You and your mobster friends killed my husband, you miserable bastard! You killed Rob!"

Geoff grabbed my wrist and twisted hard, forcing me back down into the chair. "Rob!" he spat at me. "I'm sick of him, do you hear me? Sick of listening to your endless whining, your constant worshipping at the feet of the almighty Rob!"

The vehemence of his attack took my breath away.

"What did he ever do for you? What? He pushed and pried into things that were none of his business and got himself blown away for it. He left you alone and vulnerable. Look at everything that's happened to you! It's all his fault, all of it. *He* put you in this position. And who's here to get you out of it? Who's the only one that can save you? Me! Not your precious Rob. Me! He didn't deserve you. You're lucky he's dead!"

My scream of rage caught him completely by surprise, giving me the few extra seconds I needed. I threw all my weight at his shoulder, sending him toppling to the floor. I snatched the envelope off the desk and flew past him, slamming the door behind me.

The first bullets thudded into the wall just over my head. I ducked, skidding around the corner as a fusillade from the automatic weapon shredded the cheap plywood and shattered the windows around me. My fingers were scrabbling frantically for the doorknob when a giant *whoosh* seemed to suck all the air out of the building, and the propane storage tank exploded in a huge rush of flame.

The percussion knocked me to the floor. I sprawled there, stunned and breathless, while debris bounced off the building. I heard a loud ripping sound and managed to pull myself to my feet just as the roof over Geoff's office collapsed in a shower of sparks. Clouds of heavy, black smoke rolled toward me. I flung open the door and threw myself down the steps, missing the last one and landing hard on my shoulder. I rolled away from the building, stopping only when I encountered the blessed coolness of dew-damp grass.

I lay there coughing, trying to draw oxygen into my lungs, when I heard his shouts.

"Bay! Help me! I'm trapped!"

Without conscious thought, I stumbled back toward the steps. Flaming tree limbs popped and snapped, crashing down around me as I ran. Smoke pouring through the open door made visibility impossible. I stepped back then, terrified of re-entering the raging blaze. Geoff's cries, hoarse and choking, were barely audible now above the crackling of the flames.

I pulled my sweater up over my face and charged into the burning building.

I tried desperately to remember everything I'd ever heard about sur-
viving in a fire. I fell to my knees and crawled toward the sound of his
voice. The floor felt hot and sticky, the heat already beginning to melt
the carpet. I yanked the sleeves of the sweater down over my hands. I
collided with the receptionist's desk as I rounded the corner.

"Geoff!" I screamed. "The door's blocked!"

A beam, one end already glowing, lay jammed against the twisted
door. I would never be able to move it! Sparks dropped from the ceiling,
and I beat at my hair and clothes. A window exploded, showering my
head with shards of glass. I felt a warm rivulet of blood trickle down
into my eyes.

I forced myself forward and threw all my weight against the beam. It
moved a fraction, and a flicker of hope leaped within me. Again I
attacked the obstruction, wedging my good shoulder under it, and
again I managed to shift it slightly before it fell back into place.
Frantically I searched for something to use as a lever, but my hands
encountered only useless, smoldering debris.

I was coughing continuously now, my lungs bursting with the need
for air.

Flames were breaking through the floor behind me when I finally
realized it was no use.

"Geoff!" I cried. "I can't do it! I'm going for help!"

I dragged myself across the burning carpet and threw myself once
more out into the cool night. I could hear sirens wailing in the distance
as I scrambled to my feet.

Through eyes nearly blinded by smoke and blood, I looked back at
the inferno. Through the shimmering heat-haze I saw Geoff's black-
ened hands clawing desperately at the high, narrow window. I will hear
his screams until I die.

The first fire engine was just blasting through the chain-link fence
when the entire building erupted in a wall of flame and disappeared
from sight.

28

Two weeks later, on a sultry August morning, one year to the day from Rob's murder, I sat across the desk from Hadley Bolles, prepared to play the most important poker game of my life.

The cards I held, tucked neatly into the soft leather briefcase resting at my feet, were copies of the documents I'd duplicated and rescued from the welcome center at Grayton's Race. What kind of hand Hadley was holding was what I'd come to find out.

Once again I was dressed for battle. The sleeves of my white Armani suit failed to cover the matching gauze bandages that wound around both my hands. They were healing well, most of the burns only the first- or second-degree variety. Thank God the skirt was long enough to hide similar dressings on my knees.

I had barged in unannounced, hoping to catch the Pig Man off guard. Wearing his usual wrinkled shirt, plaid suspenders, and red bow tie, Hadley had barely acknowledged me as I walked into his office and seated myself, uninvited, in the spartan visitor's chair in front of his desk. He was studying a brief, the pale blue cover clutched in his pudgy hands. It might have been my imagination that the tissue-thin papers quavered just a little.

An antiquated air conditioner labored in the window that looked out onto Bay Street, but did little to dispel the layer of heat that blanketed the room. Without thinking, I reached to lift my mass of hair up off my neck, forgetting that most of it was gone, shorn off in the emergency room the night of the fire. The cut on my head had been ugly and deep, requiring seven stitches to close it. Having only a few inches of soft curls framing my face would take some getting used to.

I shifted in my seat, uncomfortable at not being able to cross my legs. My wounds were beginning to itch, and I resisted the temptation to dig at them. Hadley glanced up, I assumed to check if I were still there. If he thought he could wait me out, he had sadly miscalculated.

My eyes roved over the framed artwork on his wall, several quite good pencil sketches of local plantation houses along with a couple of oils in heavy gilt frames. The pictures sent my mind back to the day, just over a week ago, when Miss Addie and I had stood arm in arm in the shade of a towering live oak and watched three sheriff's deputies lead Ariadne Dixon and her Latin lover away in handcuffs.

Armed with the sketchy information I'd gotten from Geoff Anderson, Red had launched an investigation into the pair that netted surprising results. Dixon and Romero, who turned out to be husband and wife, were wanted by the authorities in several states. They had run their scam of substituting clever fakes for the genuine artworks of elderly residents in upscale retirement homes from California to Florida. Ironically, it had been Miss Addie's meeting with Law Merriweather to discuss disposing of some of her treasures that had triggered their panic. They had been attempting to *replace* the original pieces when her unexpected return had surprised them. A professional appraisal would have blown their entire operation sky-high.

I smiled, remembering how eager each had been to blame the other for Miss Addie's injuries. I hoped it turned out to be the haughty Ariadne who took the fall for that. At any rate, where she was going, there would be no Saks or Ferragamo. I wondered how she'd look in penitentiary orange, and who would do her nails.

Adelaide Boyce Hammond was recovering nicely, the cast due to be removed from her wrist in a few days. Though she tried to hide it, I knew she still fretted about her investment. Her cause, as well as that of the other locals sucked into the Grayton's Race debacle, was one of the primary reasons I was here.

My own safety was the other.

"Hadley, put that damned thing down," I finally said. "Quit stalling and find me an ashtray."

Lighting a cigarette had become a major operation with my hands wrapped like a prizefighter's, but I'd managed to work out a pretty good system.

"I'd prefer it if y'all didn't smoke in here." Hadley looked earnestly into my eyes, and I laughed.

"Get off it, Hadley," I said, exhaling smoke toward the ceiling. "This whole place reeks of cigars."

He pulled open a drawer and slapped a cheap plastic ashtray onto the desk.

"Thanks."

"Well, missy, to what do I owe the pleasure?" He folded his dimpled hands in front of him, his thick thumbs working against each other in a gesture that betrayed his nervousness.

Good, I thought, *keep him off balance. He must have some inkling of why I'm here.*

"I want to negotiate a trade." I reached down and picked up the brief-case, settling it onto my lap.

"That presumes you have somethin' I'm interested in acquirin', which I very seriously doubt." His smirk didn't carry quite the confidence it normally did.

"Oh, I think you'll be interested in what I have to offer," I said. I pulled out a handful of the photocopies and spread them, fan-like, in my hand. "Your name is mentioned very prominently in this little bundle, and not exactly in a flattering light, I might add. I can't imagine what the Bar Association might make of them, let alone some of your stodgier clients."

His pudgy fingers itched to snatch the papers out of my hand, but for once he exercised restraint.

"I don't know what you're talkin' about, darlin', but I fear you have been seriously misinformed. If those papers refer to the few little legal matters I handled in regards to the Grayton's Race project, why I can't imagine what would make you think anyone would care a fig about 'em one way or the other."

The smarmy smile was back on his face, but his eyes gave him away. I hadn't seen fear reflected in them too many times, but I knew enough about the emotion to recognize it when I saw it. I stubbed out my cigarette and laid my bandaged left hand flat on the desk where he couldn't fail to get the message it implied.

Everyone in the county had read about the fire and Geoff Anderson's death. Only I knew the extent of the revelations that had preceded it. Or the exact contents of the documents I now waved under his nose.

"Look, Hadley, let's cut the crap, okay? Here's the deal, and it's not open for discussion. The Grayton's Race project is dead as of today. Not one bulldozer rolls onto that property, not one tree gets cut. And every one of the locals you forced my father to entice into investing gets their money back, with interest."

"Who the hell do you think…"

"Be quiet! I'm not finished. Then, you're going to retire. I've heard you bought yourself a nice little place down in the Keys. Go fishing. Enjoy the rest of your life."

"Is that all?" The bravado rang false, and he knew it as well as I did.

"No. You'll also bury whatever it is you think you have on the Judge. Not one whisper, not even a hint, or all bets are off."

"I could ruin the high-and-mighty Judge Talbot Simpson like that." He snapped his sausage-like fingers, and tried to stare me down.

"You could try," I said, holding his eyes steadily. "But who do you think they'd believe in the long run? One of the most respected men this town has ever known, caught, perhaps, in a little indiscretion? Or the man tied to organized crime who blackmailed his friends into lending their names to drug dealing, money laundering, and murder?" I shook the papers at him for emphasis. "What's it going to be?"

The acrid smell of his sweat-stained shirt mingled with old cigar smoke and fear. But you had to give him credit. He didn't go down easily.

"What do I get out of it? Always supposin', that is, there's one grain of truth in anythin' you've been goin' on about."

I straightened the papers and shoved them back in my briefcase. "You get to live, Hadley, to a ripe old age probably, if you can convince your pals that all this wasn't your fault. And you get to do it in relative comfort, instead of rotting in some federal prison until you're old enough to need someone to wipe the drool off your chin." I paused, calling on every ounce of self-control I possessed not to blink. "So, do we have a deal?"

I held my breath. Even now, it could go either way. If he called my bluff, I would have to fold. I'd played every card I had.

"You'll leave the papers with me, of course." He held out his hand, and I nearly fainted with relief. I rose from the chair, willing my knees not to wobble as I headed for the door.

"I don't think so, Hadley. The originals and two other sets are already in safe places. As long as you keep your end of the bargain, that's where they'll stay. But if I hear one word of gossip about my father and Lavinia, or Miss Addie and the others aren't cashing their checks within thirty days, the documents will be in the hands of every newspaper in the state, not to mention the Attorney General and the FBI. And one more thing." I turned, my hand on the doorknob. "Tell your associates the same thing goes if I should meet with any unfortunate 'accident'. You tell them to leave me and my family alone, and they'll have nothing to fear from me."

"We're just supposed to trust you?" he shouted, his round face mottled in anger.

"Yes, you are. Contrary to your life experience, Hadley, there are actually people in this world who keep their word. I'm one of them. So long as you play straight with me, you have nothing to worry about. Have a nice day."

I marched through the door, head high, trotted down the steps, and out into the blazing sunshine of Bay Street. I threw the briefcase into the front seat of the Zeemer and slid behind the wheel. I revved the powerful engine and laid a little rubber as I whipped out into a break in the traffic, just on the off chance that the Pig Man was watching from his window on the second floor. Two blocks down, I pulled into the parking lot along the waterfront. I threw the gearshift into park and let my head fall forward onto the leather-covered steering wheel.

And for the next ten minutes I wept with the sheer relief of having pulled off the biggest con of my life.

Later that same afternoon I sat rocking on the back verandah, staring out over the water, when I heard the screen door swing open, followed by the soft *whir* of the Judge's wheelchair as it rolled up the ramp. He maneuvered himself in beside me and joined in my contemplation of the Sound.

These long silences had become commonplace during my recuperation at *Presqu'isle*. Until my house was restored and the kitchen once again useable, I had given Dolores a paid vacation and moved in here. Lavinia plied me with favorite foods from my childhood and refused to meet my eyes. About the only genuine contact we'd enjoyed had been our exuberant high-fives on the Saturday morning we turned to the sports page and learned that the previous night's football game had been won in the final seconds on a forty-yard touchdown pass from CJ Elliott to Isaiah Smalls.

I reached out for the cigarettes lying beside me on a low table, but the Judge was there before me. He shook one out of the pack, placed it between my bandaged fingers, and struck the disposable lighter. I smiled at him over the flame.

"You'd think I'd had enough of fire, one way and another, wouldn't you?"

"You'd think," my father said, looking back out to the water.

A great blue heron rose suddenly on silent wings, startled into flight from the shallows where he had been fishing daintily on long, spindly legs.

I'd been torn, almost from the moment the rescue squad had hustled me into the ambulance, about how much to reveal of the awful events of that tragic night. No one asked why I'd been so insistent about returning to my car to retrieve my bag, nor why I refused to let anyone take it from me, even in the emergency room. Once the envelope I had managed to stuff into the back of my slacks was safely in my purse, I didn't let it out of my possession.

I had to tell them about Geoff, of course, even though I knew there was no hope that he had survived. When the fire had finally been extinguished, they'd found his charred body curled in a fetal position beneath the narrow windows.

I was hailed as a heroine for my valiant rescue attempt, though I tried my best to downplay it. Even now, I couldn't explain why I had risked my life to save the man who had been trying to kill me. Maybe I never would.

If anyone ever figured out that it was Geoff's wild gunfire that had triggered the explosion, I never heard of it. Why we were there in the first place never came up.

In the end, I decided to keep my own counsel, giving Red and the Judge just enough bits of the truth so that they could help right the many wrongs Geoff Anderson had caused. No one but me would ever know the whole story.

"Talked to Law Merriweather this morning, while you were out," my father said, and I turned to look at him. "The solicitor has decided he doesn't have much of a case against Isaiah. They found other prints on the baseball bat, unidentified ones, and a lot of smudges that might have come from someone wearing gloves, laid over top of the boy's. They've decided to drop the charges, pending further investigation. They'll hold an open indictment against 'person or persons unknown.'"

I breathed a deep sigh of relief. The last of the lives nearly destroyed by the madness of the past few weeks had been salvaged. I smiled and touched his arm. "That's good news," I said. "Lavinia will be relieved."

"Yes, I'm sure she will. So where did you go this morning, all decked out in your battle armor?" he asked, the twinkle back in his soft, gray eyes.

"Business," I said, and he laughed.

Then he turned his chair to face me, and his smile faded. "It's been one hell of a year for you, daughter. I hope the next one is a little kinder."

"Thank you, Daddy, me, too."

He nodded once, then rolled down the ramp into the house.

I pulled up a wicker stool, propped my feet on it, and gazed out over the railing toward the Sound. The heron had returned to the shore. His long, pointed beak dug into the mud as he picked his way gracefully through the tufted grass. The shimmering haze of the late afternoon light, reflecting off the water, mesmerized me, held me, as if in a trance. Birdsong and the rustle of a light breeze high up in the branches faded. And in the depths of that sweet silence I felt the hard knot of grief and fear dissolve within me.

The heron rose then, in silent majesty, his great, gray wings barely ruffling the air. I watched until he disappeared, into the sun.

Parties, Politics, and
Public Policy in America
Sixth Edition

William J. Keefe
University of Pittsburgh

PRESS

A Division of Congressional Quarterly
1414 22nd Street, N.W., Washington, D.C. 20037

Printed in the United States of America

Library of Congress Cataloging-in-Publication Data

Keefe, William J.
    Parties, politics, and public policy in America / William J. Keefe. -- 6th ed.
      p. cm.
    Includes index.
    ISBN 0-87187-597-7
    1. Political parties--United States. I. Title.
JK2265.K44 1991   90-22350
324.273--dc20   CIP

For Martha, Kathy, Nancy, Jodi, and John

Table of Contents

c h a p t e r   t h r e e

Political Parties and the Electoral Process: Nominations   87

c h a p t e r   f o u r

Political Parties and the Electoral Process: Campaigns and Campaign Finance   137

c h a p t e r   f i v e

Political Parties and the Electorate   183

Tables and Figures

Tables

on this interesting literature. The scholarship tracks that I followed are amply reflected in the footnotes.

The fifth edition of this book, published in 1988, differed in many ways from the previous one. This sixth edition represents an even more extensive revision, including the addition of a new chapter. Coverage of parties in the electorate has been broadened—contributing to a more comprehensive analysis of the nominating process, campaigns, campaign finance, and elections. New material has been introduced throughout the book. Among the topics to receive expanded treatment are the media, television's impact on campaigning, campaign finance, political action committees, public-party linkages, party in Congress, party organization, change and continuity in voting behavior, party differences during the Bush administration, party reform, southern politics, congressional campaigns and elections, political participation, and party responsibility.

The American party system may need to be rescued from its detractors, but that is not the main purpose of this book. Nor is it to sketch a blueprint showing where the best opportunities lie for making further changes. The central purpose is rather one of exegesis: to bring into focus the major features of the parties, to account for party form and functions, and to examine and interpret the parties' present condition.

For helping on one or more of the first five editions, I thank Herbert E. Alexander, Paul A. Beck, Keith Burris, Holbert N. Carroll, Edward F. Cooke, Stephen Craig, William J. Crotty, Robert L. Donaldson, John Havick, Brooke Harlow, Jon Hurwitz, Charles O. Jones, Jodi Keefe-McCurdy, David C. Kozak, Paul Lopatto, Thomas E. Mann, Roger McGill, James M. Malloy, Michael Margolis, Russell Moses, Morris S. Ogul, David M. Olson, Raymond E. Owen, Josie Raleigh, Bert A. Rockman, Robert S. Walters, Donna Woodward, and Sidney Wise.

For the sixth edition, I especially acknowledge the assistance of Holbert N. Carroll, Robert L. Donaldson, David Fitz, Jon Hurwitz, Leslie McAneny of the Gallup Organization, Morris S. Ogul, and Guy Peters. I am indebted to David M. Olson of the University of North Carolina at Greensboro for a wide range of thoughtful suggestions for revising the book. Everyone mentioned in this and the previous paragraph should know how much I appreciate their advice and friendship. But they are not perfect, not by a long shot. Despite their assistance and good intentions, errors of fact and interpretation may somehow have crept into a page here and there. If this turns out to be the case,

I hope they will come forward and acknowledge their responsibility for them.

I want to thank David R. Tarr, director of the CQ Book Department, and Margaret Seawell Benjaminson, developmental editor, for their support and encouragement. I was fortunate that Colleen McGuiness, who edited the fifth edition, could also edit this one. She is a superb editor, and the book is much better for her efforts.

Finally, I owe special thanks to my wife, Martha, who typed the manuscript of this edition as well as the earlier ones. Her help was indispensable.

Parties, Politics, and
Public Policy in America

chapter   one

Political Parties and
the Political System

THE AMERICAN political party system is not an insoluble puzzle.
But it does have more than its share of mysteries. The main one,
arguably, is how it has survived for so long or, perhaps, how it survived
at all, in a difficult and complicated environment. The broad explanation, arguably as well, is that the party system survives because parties
are an inevitable outgrowth of civil society ("factions . . . sown in the
nature of man," thought James Madison[1]); because parties perform
functions important to democratic polities ("democracy is unthinkable
save in terms of parties," wrote E. E. Schattschneider[2]); and because the
American public has never held particularly high expectations of parties
or made particularly rigorous demands upon them—thus in truth their
survival has not been contingent on performance.

A logical starting point for understanding the political party system,
an enduring institution of American society, is to recognize that parties
are less what they make of themselves than what their environment makes of
them.[3] Put another way, in language social scientists sometimes invoke,
parties typically are the dependent variable. That is, to a marked extent
the party owes its character and form to the impact of four external
elements: the legal-political system, the election system, the political
culture, and the heterogeneous quality of American life. Singly and in
combination, these elements contribute in significant and indelible ways to
the organizational characteristics of the parties, to the manner in which
they carry on their activities, to their internal discipline, to the behavior of

1

both their elite and rank-and-file members, and to their capacity to control the political system and to perform as policy-making agencies.

The Parties and Their Environment

The Legal-Political System

The Constitution of the United States was written by men who were apprehensive of the power of popular majorities and who had scant sympathy for the existence of party. Their basic intent, evident in the broad thrust of the Constitution and in line after line of its text, was to establish a government that could not easily be brought under the control of any one element, whatever its size, that might be present in the country. The underlying theory of the founders was both simple and pervasive: power was to check power, and the ambitions of some men were to check the ambitions of other men.* The two main features in this design were federalism and the separation of powers—the first to distribute power among different levels of government; the second to distribute power among the legislative, executive, and judicial branches. Division of the legislature into two houses, with their memberships elected for different terms and by differing methods, was thought to reduce further the risk that a single faction (or party) might gain ascendancy. Schattschneider developed the argument in this way:

> The theory of the Constitution, inherited from the time of the Glorious Revolution in England, was legalistic and preparty in its assumptions. Great reliance was placed in a system of separation of powers, a legalistic concept of government incompatible with a satisfactory system of party government. No place was made for the parties in the system, party government was not clearly foreseen or well understood, government by parties was thought to be impossible or impracticable and was feared and regarded as something to be avoided. . . . The Convention at Philadelphia produced a constitution with a dual attitude: it was proparty in one sense and antiparty in another. The authors of the Constitution refused to suppress the parties by destroying the fundamental liberties in which parties originate. They or their immediate successors accepted amendments

---

* In addition to using terms such as "candidate," "legislator," "member," and "representative" to apply to men and women in politics, I have referred to them in the masculine gender—"he," "him," "his." This is simply a matter of style. These pronouns are employed generically.

that guaranteed civil rights and thus established a system of party tolerance, *i.e.,* the right to agitate and to organize. This is the proparty aspect of the system. On the other hand, the authors of the Constitution set up an elaborate division and balance of powers within an intricate governmental structure designed to make parties ineffective. It was hoped that the parties would lose and exhaust themselves in futile attempts to fight their way through the labyrinthine framework of the government, much as an attacking army is expected to spend itself against the defensive works of a fortress. This is the antiparty part of the constitutional scheme. To quote Madison, the "great object" of the Constitution was "to preserve the public good and private rights against the danger of such a faction [party] and at the same time to preserve the spirit and form of popular government." [4]

Federalism also works at cross purposes with the development of centralized parties. As an organizational form, federalism guarantees that there will be not only fifty state governmental systems but also fifty state party systems. No two states are exactly alike. No two state party systems are exactly alike. The prevailing ideology in one state party may be sharply different from that of another state—contrast the state Democratic party of Mississippi with its counterpart in New York, the state Republican party of Utah with its counterpart in Connecticut. And within each state all manner of local party organizations exist, sometimes functioning in harmony with state and national party elements and sometimes not. There are states (and localities) where the party organizations are well financed and active and those where they are not, those where the organizations are easily penetrated by outsiders and those where they are not, those where factions compete persistently within a party and those where factional organization is nonexistent, those where the parties seem to consist mainly of the personal followings of individual politicians and those where traditional party organizations and their leaders exercise significant influence.[5] Parties differ from state to state and from community to community, and the laws that govern their activities and shape their influence also differ. A great variety of state laws, for example, governs nominating procedures, ballot form, access to the ballot, campaign finance, and elections. On the whole, northeastern states are most likely to have statutes that foster stronger parties, while southern states tend to have statutes that weaken them.[6] Similarly, strong ("monopolistic") local party organizations have been

What Is a Political Party?

"A political party is first of all an organized attempt to get power."

—E. E. Schattschneider

"[A party is] any group, however loosely organized, seeking to elect governmental office-holders under a given label."

—Leon Epstein

"Party is a body of men united, for promulgating by their joint endeavors the national interest, upon some particular principle in which they are all agreed."

—Edmund Burke

"A party isn't a fraternity. It isn't something that you join because you like the old school tie they wear. It is a gathering together of people who basically share the same political philosophy."

—Ronald Reagan

"We Democrats are all under one tent. In any other country we'd be five splinter parties."

—Thomas P. ("Tip") O'Neill, Jr.

"A party is not . . . a group of men who intend to promote public welfare 'upon some principle in which they are all agreed. . . .' A party is a group whose members propose to act in concert in the competitive struggle for political power."

—Joseph A. Schumpeter

SOURCES: E. E. Schattschneider, *Party Government* (New York: Holt, Rinehart and Winston, 1942), 37; Leon Epstein, *Political Parties in Western Democracies* (New York: Praeger Publishers, 1967), 9; Edmund Burke, *Works,* vol. I (London: G. Bell and Sons, 1897), 375; *Pittsburgh Post Gazette,* March 20, 1980, 9; *Washington Post,* June 17, 1975, 12; and Joseph A. Schumpeter, *Capitalism, Socialism and Democracy* (New York: Harper and Row, 1942), 283.

more prominent and durable in the East than anywhere else.[7] The broad point is that the thrust of federalism is dispersive and parochial, permitting numerous forms of political organizations to thrive and inhibiting the emergence of cohesive and disciplined national parties.

The Election System

The election system is another element in the environment of political parties. So closely linked are parties and elections that it is difficult to understand much about one without understanding a great deal about the other. Parties are in business to win elections. Election systems shape the way the parties compete for power and the success with which they do it. Several examples will help to illustrate this point.

Although a state's election calendar may appear neutral, even innocuous, it has a substantial bearing on party fortunes. Many state constitutions establish election calendars that separate state elections from national elections—for example, gubernatorial from presidential elections. The singular effect of this arrangement is to insulate state politics from national politics. Similarly, the behavior of voters also weakens state and national political linkages. Even in those states in which governors are elected at the same time as the president, the chances are better than three out of ten that the party that carries the state in the presidential contest will lose at the gubernatorial level. (The outcomes in presidential-gubernatorial voting from 1964 to 1988 are indicated in Table 1-1.) Meanwhile, the national tides that sweep one party into the presidency may be no more than ripples by the time a state election is held two years later. Although the Democratic party won presidential election after presidential election during the 1930s and 1940s, a great many governorships and state legislatures remained safely Republican. Recent Republican success in presidential elections (1968, 1972, 1980, 1984, 1988) was not translated into major gains for the party at the state level. Prior to the 1988 presidential election, for example, the Democratic party held majorities in sixty-seven state legislative chambers. Despite George Bush's comfortable victory over Michael S. Dukakis, the Democrats won majorities in sixty-eight individual legislative chambers. And at the same time, the Democrats gained an additional governorship in the twelve gubernatorial races, bringing their total to twenty-eight.

The use of staggered terms for executive and legislative offices diminishes the probability that one party will control both branches of government at any given time. When the governor is elected for four years and the lower house is elected for two years—the common pattern—chances are that the governor's party will lose legislative seats, and sometimes its majority, in the off-year election. The same is true for the

TABLE 1-1   Split Outcomes in Presidential-Gubernatorial Voting: States Carried by Presidential Candidate of One Major Party and by Gubernatorial Candidate of Other Major Party, 1964-1988

Year	Gubernatorial elections	Split outcomes	Percentage
1964	25	9	36
1968	21	8	38
1972	18	10	56
1976	14	5	36
1980	13	4	31
1984	13	5	38
1988	12	4	33

president and Congress. Whatever the virtues of staggered terms and off-year elections, they increase the likelihood of divided control of government.

The use of single-member districts with plurality elections for the election of legislators carries important ramifications for the parties. When an election is held within a single-member district, only one party can win; the winning candidate need receive only one more vote than the second-place candidate, and all votes for candidates other than the victor are lost. Although the single-member district system discriminates against the second-place party in each district, its principal impact is virtually to rule out the possibility that a minor party can win legislative representation. Indeed, only a handful of minor party candidates have ever held seats either in Congress or in the state legislatures. The device of single-member districts with plurality elections has long been a major bulwark of the two-party system.[8]

Single-member districts distort the relationship between the overall vote for legislative candidates within a state and the number of seats won by each party. The discrepancy may be sizable. The majority party in the state legislature nearly always profits from its ingenuity in drawing district lines. Gerrymandering, in other words, is effective. Consider the 1988 congressional elections in California, a state well known for gerrymandering. Republican House candidates won 46 percent of the statewide congressional vote but only 40 percent of the seats. Even so, the party fared better than in 1984 when its House candidates won a majority of the statewide vote (50.5 percent) but only 40 percent of the seats.

Extreme partisan gerrymandering may be on the way out. In 1986 the Supreme Court refused to invalidate an Indiana reapportionment act that favored the Republican party, stating that this particular gerrymander of state legislative districts was not sufficiently offensive to warrant judicial intervention. At the same time, the Court warned that gerrymanders will be held unconstitutional "when the electoral system is arranged in a manner that will consistently degrade a voter's or a group of voters' influence on the political process as a whole." [9] Thus, solutions to the problem of gerrymandering may be found in the courts. The lasting impact of the Supreme Court's opinion should become apparent following the census of 1990. State legislators, who will redraw district lines then, have been served notice that egregious gerrymandering, which entrenches the dominant party, will not pass constitutional muster.

Few, if any, electoral arrangements have had a greater impact on political parties than the direct primary, an innovation of the reform era of the early twentieth century. The primary was introduced to combat the power of party oligarchs who, insulated from popular influences, dominated the selection of nominees in state and local party conventions. The primary was designed to democratize the nominating process by empowering the voters to choose the party's nominees. Today, all states employ some form of primary system, although mixed convention-primary arrangements are used in a handful of states. In New York, for example, a candidate for a statewide office must receive at least 25 percent of the party convention vote to win a place on the primary ballot. Access to the primary ballot in Colorado requires a candidate to obtain 20 percent of the convention vote, while a 15 percent vote is required by the Massachusetts Democratic party.[10]

The convention method survives for the nomination of presidential and vice-presidential candidates. But convention decisions are heavily influenced by the outcomes of presidential primaries. In 1988 nearly two-thirds of the states selected their delegates in presidential primaries.

The precise impact of the primary on the parties is difficult to establish. Its effects nevertheless appear to be substantial. First, by transferring the choice of nominees from party assemblies to the voters, the primary has increased the probability that candidates with different views on public policy will be brought together in the same party. Whatever their policy orientations, the victors in primary elections become the party's nominees, perhaps to the embarrassment of other party candidates. In 1986, to take an unusual example, two disciples of

Lyndon H. LaRouche captured the Democratic nominations for lieutenant governor and secretary of state in Illinois. Citing the views of LaRouche followers as "abhorrent, racist, anti-Semitic, anti-democratic, and irrational," and unwilling to run on the same ticket with them, Adlai E. Stevenson III resigned as the Democratic candidate for governor. After being barred from running as an independent (since he had missed the filing deadline), Stevenson created a third party, the Illinois Solidarity party, for the November election—and lost decisively.

Second, observers contend that primaries have contributed to a decline in party responsibility. Candidates who win office largely on their own, who have their own distinctive followings within local electorates, have less reason to defer to party leaders or to adhere to traditional party positions. Their party membership is simply what they choose to make it. Third, the primary has contributed to numerous intraparty clashes; particularly bitter primary fights sometimes render the party incapable of generating a united campaign in the general election.[11] Finally, primaries apparently contribute to the consolidation of one-party politics. In an area where one party ordinarily dominates, its primaries tend to become the arena for political battles. The growth of the second party is inhibited not only by the lack of voter interest in its primaries but also by its inability to attract strong candidates to its colors. One-party domination reveals little about the party's organizational strength—indeed, one-party political systems likely will be characterized more by factionalism and internecine warfare than by unity, harmony, and ideological agreement.

"The cumulative effect of the direct primary," in the view of David B. Truman,

> is in the direction of organizational atrophy. The direct primary has been the most potent in a complex of forces pushing toward the disintegration of the party.... Even in those states using a closed primary and some reasonably restrictive form of enrollment to qualify as a voter in the primary, the thrust of the direct primary is disintegrative. In states that have embraced the full spirit of the direct primary by providing for an open system in one or another of its forms, where in effect anyone can wander in off the street to vote in the primary election of any party or where any organized interest group can colonize any party, the likelihood of any organization controlling nominations on a continuing basis is small.[12]

Such are the arguments developed against the primary. Of course, others can be made on its behalf.[13] In some jurisdictions, moreover, the dominant party organization is sufficiently strong that nonendorsed candidates have little or no chance of upsetting the organization slate. Potential challengers may abandon their campaigns once the party leaders or the organization have made known their choices. Other candidacies may not materialize because the prospects for getting the nod from party leaders appear unpromising. Taking the country as a whole, nevertheless, the evidence is persuasive that the primary weakens party organization. Unable to control its nominations, a party forfeits some portion of its claim to be known as a party, some portion of its raison d'être. The loose, freewheeling character of American parties owes much to the advent, consolidation, and extension of the direct primary.

For an additional illustration of the relationship between the election system and the party system, consider the use and impact of nonpartisan elections. While searching for a formula to improve city government early in the twentieth century, reformers hit upon the idea of the nonpartisan ballot—one in which party labels would not be present. The purpose of the plan was to free local government from the issues and divisiveness of national and state party politics and from the grip of local party bosses, which in turn, it was thought, would contribute to the effectiveness of local units. The nonpartisan ballot immediately gained favor and, once established, has been hard to dislodge; indeed, the plan has grown in popularity over the years. Today, substantially more than half of the American cities with populations of more than five thousand have nonpartisan elections.[14]

A large variety of political patterns is found in nonpartisan election systems. In some cities with nonpartisan ballots, the party presence is nonetheless quite visible, and there is no doubt which candidates are affiliated with which parties. Elections in these cities are partisan in everything but label. In other cities, local party organizations compete against slates of candidates sponsored by various nonparty groups. In still other cities, the local parties are virtually without power, having lost it to interest groups that recruit, sponsor, and finance candidates for office. Finally, in some nonpartisan elections neither party nor nonparty groups slate candidates, thus leaving individual candidates to their own devices. This type is particularly prevalent in small cities.

It is difficult to say how much nonpartisan elections have diminished the vitality of local party organizations. Here and there the answer is plainly, "very little if at all"; elsewhere, the impact appears to have been substantial. Whatever the case, where parties are shut out of the local election process, other kinds of politics enter—possibly centered around interest groups (including the press), celebrity or name politics (the latter favoring incumbents), or the idiosyncratic appeals of individual office seekers. Where party labels are absent, power is up for grabs. Whether the voters in any real sense can hold their representatives accountable, lacking the guidance that party labels furnish, is problematical at best.

Myths to the contrary, election systems are never designed to be neutral and never are neutral. Some election laws and constitutional provisions, such as the single-member district system or the rigorous requirements that minor parties must meet to gain a place on the ballot, provide general support for the two-party system. Of the seventeen minor parties that ran candidates for the presidency in 1988, for example, only the New Alliance party managed to get on the ballot in all fifty states. Altogether, minor party candidates for the presidency received a mere 898,168 votes (1.2 percent) out of a total of 91,584,820 cast. Leading the way for this varied assortment were the Libertarians, whose presidential candidate, Ron Paul, received 431,616 votes.

Other laws and constitutional provisions make party government difficult and sometimes impossible—included here are such system features as staggered terms of office, off-year elections, direct primaries, and nonpartisan ballots. The major parties are not always passive witnesses to existing electoral arrangements. At times they simply endure them because it is easier to live with conventional arrangements than to try to change them or because they recognize their benefits. At other times major parties seek new arrangements because the prospects for party advantage are sufficiently promising to warrant the effort. It is a good bet that no one understands or appreciates American election systems better than those party leaders responsible for defending party interests and winning elections.

The Political Culture and the Parties

A third important element in the environment of American political parties is the political culture—"the system of empirical beliefs, expressive symbols, and values which defines the situation in which political action takes place." [15] As commonly represented, the political culture of a nation is the amalgam of public attitudes toward the political system, its subunits, and the role of the individual within the system. It includes the knowledge and beliefs people have about the political system, their feelings toward it, their identification with it, and their evaluations of it.

Although there is little comprehensive information on the public's political orientations toward the party system, scattered evidence indicates that large segments of the public do not evaluate parties or party functions in a favorable light. Studies of the Wisconsin electorate between 1964 and 1984 by Jack Dennis bear on this point.[16] The range of public attitudes on a series of propositions about American parties, including those that reveal diffuse or generalized support for the party system as a whole and for the norm of partisanship and those that reveal acceptance of the ideas or practices congruent with a system of responsible parties, is presented in Table 1-2.

The principal conclusion to be drawn from the data provided in the table is that the public is highly skeptical of the parties and their activities. In 1964, 90 percent of the Wisconsin electorate endorsed the idea that "the best rule in voting is to pick the best candidate, regardless of party label." By 1984, 94 percent accepted this idea. An overwhelming majority of the public believes that the parties do more to confuse issues than to clarify them and that they often provoke unnecessary conflict. Less than half of the electorate sees any merit to even having party labels on the ballot.

Also of interest, the Wisconsin data reveal that support for cohesive and disciplined parties is extremely limited. Only about one out of five persons believes that a legislator "should follow his or her party leaders even if he or she doesn't want to." Overall, little in this profile of popular attitudes suggests that the public understands or accepts the tenets of a responsible party system.[17]

Whether the orientations of the Wisconsin voters to the parties are representative of popular attitudes elsewhere is hard to say. But it seems likely that this is the case. In nationwide surveys of voter attitudes toward control of the presidency and Congress by the same party, typically only about one-third of the voters believe that the country is better off when the same party controls both branches. The public clearly prefers divided control of government.

Popular dissatisfaction with the party system is also reflected in the trends concerning party identification and split-ticket voting. In 1937, 84 percent of all people identified themselves as Democrats and Republi-

TABLE 1-2   Trends in Popular Support for the Party System, 1964-1984
(Shown as Percentage Supportive)

	1964	1966	1970	1972	1974	1976	1984
Diffuse support							
The parties do more to confuse the issues than to provide a clear choice on issues. (disagree)	21	19	21	28	24	19	29
The political parties more often than not create conflicts where none really exists. (disagree)	15	14	19	18	18	17	29
It would be better if, in all elections, we put no party labels on the ballot. (disagree)	67	56	44	42	38	36	45
Support for responsible party government							
A senator or representative should follow his or her party leaders even if he or she doesn't want to.	23					10	19
Contributor support							
People who work for political parties during political campaigns do our nation a great service.	68					53	77
The best rule in voting is to pick the best candidate, regardless of party label.	10				5	6	6
Cleavage function support							
Democracy works best where competition between political parties is strong.	74				73	66	73

SOURCE: Jack Dennis, "Public Support for the Party System, 1964-1984" (Paper delivered at the annual meeting of the American Political Science Association, Washington, D.C., August 28-31, 1986), 19. Also see his earlier study, "Support for the Party System by the Mass Public," *American Political Science Review* 60 (September 1966): 600-615.

cans. Several times during the 1970s only 67 percent of the voters professed to be partisans. By the early 1990s, according to Gallup surveys, the proportion of partisans hovered around 72 percent. Put another way, self-professed independents now compose between one-fourth and one-third of the electorate, as contrasted with one-sixth half a century earlier.

TABLE 1-3   Ticket Splitting: Percentage of Voters Casting Votes for President of
One Party and for House Member of Other Party

Election year	Voters splitting ticket (in percent)
1960	14
1964	15
1968	18
1972	30
1976	25
1980	28
1984	26
1988	31

SOURCE: Center for Political Studies, University of Michigan; and, for 1988, ABC News/*Washington Post* survey, as reported in *Public Opinion,* January-February 1989, 27.

Trends in split-ticket voting (voting for candidates of more than one party in the same election) show similar erosion of citizen linkage to the parties. Consider the voting behavior of the public for the offices of president and member of the U.S. House of Representatives (see Table 1-3). In the 1960 Kennedy-Nixon race, only 14 percent of all voters split their tickets to vote for a presidential candidate of one party and for a House candidate of the other party. In 1988 an extraordinary 31 percent of the voters split their tickets between these offices. Defections from the Republican presidential ticket are more likely to occur than from the Democratic ticket. According to an ABC News/*Washington Post* survey in 1988, 11 percent of those who voted for Dukakis/Bentsen voted for a Republican House candidate, while 20 percent of those who voted for Bush/Quayle voted for a Democratic House candidate.

Ticket splitting is a major explanation for the frequent appearance of a truncated political system, characterized by Republican control of the presidency and Democratic control of Congress. Numerous voters, in other words, regularly support Republican presidential candidates and Democratic congressional candidates. Their preference for Democratic congressional candidates is, in part, a preference for incumbents.

Adding to the party problem, many voters see little or no difference in the effectiveness of the parties in governing. Surveys by the Gallup poll, starting as long ago as the 1940s, have asked voters to identify the most important problem facing the nation and to select the party best able to handle it. The results are instructive (see Figure 1-1). Over most of the period 1945-1985, the Democratic party received much higher

FIGURE 1-1 The Public's Perception of the Party Best Able to Handle the Most Important Problem Facing the Nation, 1945-1988

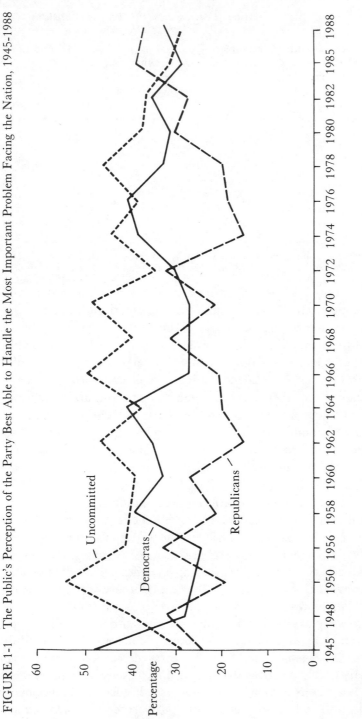

SOURCE: Developed from data appearing in *Gallup Report*, April 1985, 23; October 1988, 8.

marks than the Republican party. But beginning with Ronald Reagan's second term, the public came to view the Republican party as best able to deal with public problems. In some ways the most important fact revealed by the data is that voters who cannot distinguish between the parties' capacity to handle major problems (or who have no opinion) often outnumber those who select either party. Rarely does the proportion of uncommitted voters fall below 35 percent in these surveys. At least one-third of all voters take a neutral stance when asked to judge the two parties as agencies for solving major public problems.[18]

The evidence thus indicates that American political parties rest on a relatively narrow and uncertain base of popular support. Scarcely anyone can fail to notice the widespread skepticism of politics and politicians that pervades popular thought. Few vocations stir so little interest as that of the politician. The language of American politics is itself laced with suspicion and hostility. In the argot of popular appraisal, political organizations turn into "machines," party workers emerge as "hacks," political leaders become "bosses," and campaign appeals degenerate into "empty promises" or "sheer demagoguery." That some politicians have contributed to this state of affairs, by debasing the language of political discourse or by their behavior, as in the Watergate affair, is perhaps beside the point. The critical fact is that the American political culture contains a strong suspicion of the political process and the agencies that try to dominate it, the political parties.

A Heterogeneous Nation

To complete the analysis of the environment of American parties, it is necessary to say something about the characteristics of the nation as a whole. No array of statistics is required to make the point that the United States is a nation of extraordinary diversity. The American community is composed of a great variety of economic and social interests, class configurations, ethnic and religious groups, occupations, regional and subregional interests, and loyalties, values, and beliefs. There are citizens who are deeply attached to inherited patterns and those who are impatient advocates of change, those who care intensely about politics and those who can take it or leave it, and those who elude labeling—those who are active on one occasion and passive on another. There are citizens who think mainly in terms of farm policy, some who seek advantage for urban elements, others whose lives and political

Parties and . . .

Political systems and political parties come and go. The American two-party system, however, is a survivor. It has been around, in more or less its present form, for well over a century. How does the public view it? Data from national surveys by the Los Angeles Times Mirror, presented below, suggest these conclusions: First, a significant majority of the public believes that the two parties are not as alike as "two peas in a pod"—one out of four voters perceives "a great deal" of difference between the parties. Second, much of the public correctly perceives the parties' ideological thrusts: a conservative, business-oriented Republican party versus a liberal, working-class, labor-oriented Democratic party.

Thinking of the Democratic and Republican parties, would you say there is a great difference in what they stand for, a fair amount of difference, or hardly any difference at all?

	1987
A great deal	25%
A fair amount	45
Hardly at all	25
No opinion/don't know	5

SOURCE: *The People, the Press, and Politics* (Los Angeles: Times Mirror, 1987), 125; and *The People, the Press, and Politics* (Washington, D.C.: Times Mirror Center for the People and the Press, 1990), 50.

interests revolve around business or professions. Diversity abounds. Sometimes deep, sometimes shallow, the differences that separate one group from another and one region from another make the formation of public policy that suits everyone all but impossible.

For the major parties the essential requirement is that they accommodate themselves to the vast diversity of the nation. And they have done this remarkably well. Each party attracts and depends upon a wide range of interests. Voting behavior in the 1988 presidential election (Bush vs. Dukakis) illustrates this point (see Figure 1-2). Most groups divided their vote between the parties in a ratio fairly close to that of the electorate as a whole (46 percent Democratic, 54 percent Republican). The most distinctive vote distributions on the Democratic side were those of blacks, Hispanics, Jews, and persons with annual incomes under $10,000; for the Republicans the most distinctive clus-

... *the Public*

What does it mean to you when someone says he or she is a Republican?

	1987	1990
Conservative	21%	22%
Rich, powerful, monied interest	18	21
Business-oriented	13	10
Not for the people	5	4
Against government spending	5	6

What does it mean to you when someone says he or she is a Democrat?

	1987	1990
For working people	21%	18%
Liberal	18	18
Too much government spending	7	3
Cares for poor, disadvantaged	7	7
For social programs	7	9

NOTE: For the second and third questions, only the leading answers are listed. Also, the replies were unprompted, with some respondents offering more than one answer. About half of the sample consists of "other" and "don't know" responses.

ters were those of white born-again Christians, white Protestants, voters under 30 years of age, and persons with incomes over $40,000. An important point to recognize is that neither party excludes any group from its calculations for winning elections. On the contrary, each party expects to do reasonably well among virtually all groups. And ordinarily the parties do.

The heterogeneity of the nation is one explanation for the enduring parochial cast of American politics. As Herbert Agar has explained:

Most politics will be parochial, most politicians will have small horizons, seeking the good of the state or the district rather than of the Union; yet by diplomacy and compromise, never by force, the government must water down the selfish demands of regions, races, classes, business associations, into a national policy which will alien-

FIGURE 1-2 The Voting Behavior of Groups in the 1988 Presidential Election, in Percentages

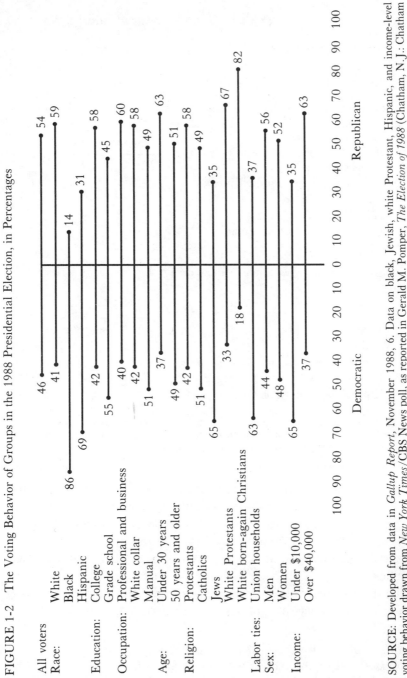

SOURCE: Developed from data in *Gallup Report*, November 1988, 6. Data on black, Jewish, white Protestant, Hispanic, and income-level voting behavior drawn from *New York Times*/CBS News poll, as reported in Gerald M. Pomper, *The Election of 1988* (Chatham, N.J.: Chatham House Publishers, 1989), 133-134.

ate no major groups and which will contain at least a plum for everybody. This is the price of unity in a continentwide federation.[19]

Party Organization

Party organization has two common features in all parts of the United States. First, parties are organized in a series of committees, reaching from the precinct level to the national committee. Second, party committee organization parallels the arrangement of electoral districts. With the exception of heavily one-party areas, party committees will be found in virtually all jurisdictions within which important government officials are elected. The presence of party committees, however, reveals little about their activities or their vitality in campaigns.

A familiar description of American parties begins by likening their organizational structure to that of a pyramid. At the top of the pyramid rests the national committee, at the bottom the precinct organizations, with various ward, city, county, and state committees lodged in between. Although it is convenient to view party organization within this pattern, it is misleading if it suggests that power flows steadily from top to bottom, from major national leaders to local leaders and local rank and file. Subnational committees actually have substantial autonomy, particularly in the crucial matters of selecting and slating candidates for public office (including federal office), raising and spending money, and conducting campaigns. (See a sketch of party organization in Figure 1-3.)

The National Committee

The most prestigious and visible of all party committees is the national committee.[20] The people who serve on the national committee of each party are prominent state politicians, chosen in a variety of ways and under a number of constraints. Their official tenure begins when they are accepted by the national convention of each party.

The selection of national committee members is not a simple matter. The Democratic party, operating under its 1974 charter, has elaborate provisions governing the composition of its national committee. Among its membership are the chairperson and the highest ranking official of the opposite sex of each recognized state party, two hundred

FIGURE 1-3   Party Organization in the United States: Layers of Committees and Their Chairpersons

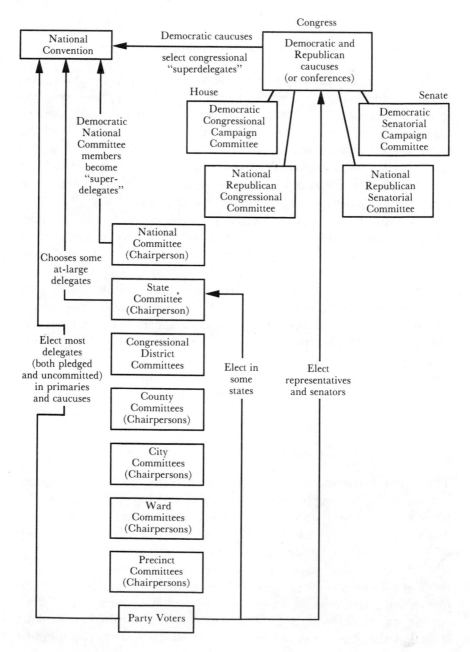

additional members allotted to the states on the same basis as delegates are apportioned to the national convention, and a number of delegates representing such organizations as the Democratic Governors' Conference, the U.S. Congress, the National Finance Council, the Conference of Democratic Mayors, the National Federation of Democratic Women, the Democratic County Officials Conference, the State Legislative Leaders Caucus, and the Young Democrats of America. As in the case of delegates to the party's national convention, members of the national committee must be selected "through processes which assure full, timely, and equal opportunity to participate" and with due attention to affirmative action standards.

To know what the national committee is, it is necessary to look at what it does.[21] One of its principal responsibilities is to make arrangements for the national convention every four years. In this capacity it chooses the convention site, prepares a temporary roster of convention delegates, and selects convention speakers and temporary officers who will manage the assembly in its opening phase. The committee is especially active during presidential campaigns in coordinating campaign efforts, publicizing the party and its candidates, and raising money. Following the election, the committee often faces the task of raising the necessary funds to pay off campaign debts.

The influence of the president on his party's national committee is substantial. "I don't think the Republican National Committee can ever really be independent," a longtime committee staff member has said. "[The committee has] a responsibility to the leader. Policy is always made at the White House, not here. We accept it and support it." [22] The same is true for the Democratic National Committee (DNC). "The president likes a party that serves as a supportive tool for the president," observed a state party chairperson during the Carter administration. "An independent organization is looked upon as a nuisance. That is inevitable." Or, as a White House aide remarked, President Carter "is turned on to the DNC as a service institution." [23]

The national committees come to life during presidential election years because their major efforts are directed toward the election of their party's presidential candidate. During nonpresidential years most of the national committee's work is carried on by committees or the national chairperson. Study groups occasionally are created by the committee (perhaps under instructions from the national convention) to examine certain problems, such as party organization, party policy, or convention management. In 1969, for example, the DNC created the Commission on Party Structure and Delegate Selection, known as the McGovern-Fraser Commission, to hold hearings and to suggest proposals for changes in party procedures. Included in its wide-ranging report were recommendations urging state parties (and, in certain cases, state legislatures) to eliminate discrimination of all kinds in party rules; to open party meetings and processes to participation by all members of the party; to remove or moderate restrictive voter registration laws or practices; and to provide for the fair representation of blacks, women, and young persons in state delegations to the national convention.

Four subsequent reform commissions—the Mikulski Commission (1972-1973), the Winograd Commission (1975-1978), the Hunt Commission (1981-1982), and the Fairness Commission (1984-1985)—further refined party rules. The broad thrust of the 1969-1978 reforms was to increase popular participation in the presidential nominating process while at the same time diluting the power of party professionals. In counterpoise, the recommendations of the Hunt Commission were directed toward restoring the influence of party regulars and officeholders in the presidential nominating process and relaxing certain other party rules introduced in the 1970s. Adopted by the DNC in 1986, the recommendations of the Fairness Commission largely reaffirmed the system used in 1984, though the commission made several changes regarding delegate positions for party and elected officials, eligibility for participation in primaries and caucuses, and the allocation of delegates. (See Chapter 3.)

Although the Democratic party resisted the temptation to establish a new rules commission for the 1992 election, it did continue to tinker with its presidential nominating process. In 1990, for example, the DNC adopted a major rules change to require all states to follow proportional representation in the distribution of delegates among presidential candidates. Under this rule, any presidential candidate who receives at least 15 percent of a state's primary or caucus vote is entitled to a fair (proportionate) share of delegates. Systems that award winners extra delegates were thus outlawed. The DNC also moved up the start of the 1992 presidential primary season by one week, to the first Tuesday in March—an action that was viewed as an invitation to populous California to switch its primary from June to March. But California declined to do so.

The national committees of the two parties are by no means alike.

In recent years, the Republican National Committee (RNC) has been much more effective than its Democratic counterpart in raising campaign funds (especially through direct-mail methods) and in providing services for candidates. Operating with a large field staff, the RNC makes a variety of technical services available to national and state candidates; these services include public opinion surveys and computer analyses of voting patterns. Extending its reach, the RNC even makes financial contributions to party candidates in key state legislative races.[24] National and state organizations have become more interdependent in the Republican party than they have in the Democratic party.[25] With a less elaborate organization and a much less successful fund-raising operation, the DNC concentrates its efforts on the presidential election. And many Democratic party politicians find fault with its emphasis. "There is no sense that the Democratic state parties are part of a national whole," observed one leader. "The DNC is viewed by the state parties as a foreign power that does not dispense foreign aid." [26]

The National Chairperson

The head of the national party is the national chairperson.[27] Although the chairperson is officially selected by the members of the national committee, in practice he or she is chosen by the party's presidential candidate shortly after the national convention has adjourned. Very few leaders in either party have held the position for an extended period— the chairperson of the party winning the presidency usually receives a major appointment in the new administration, and the chairperson of the losing party is replaced by a new face. When a vacancy in the chairmanship of the out party occurs, selection of the new leader is made by the national committee. Factional conflicts may come to the surface when the committee is faced with the responsibility of finding a replacement, since the leading candidates will usually be identified with certain wings of the party.

The central problem the national chairperson must come to terms with in presidential years is the direction and coordination of the national campaign. The Republican national organization has far outstripped its Democratic rival in the task. One major reason is that such national chairmen as Ray C. Bliss (1965-1969) and Bill Brock (1977-1981) concentrated their efforts on organizational reform, seeking in particular to strengthen state and local Republican organizations by providing them with all kinds of "electioneering" assistance.[28] A successful fund-raising program, based on more than two million small contributors, makes these efforts possible.[29]

On the Democratic side, the position of the national chairperson has been particularly frustrating. No recent Democratic president has made a significant effort to strengthen the national party apparatus; indeed, each has tended to downgrade it.[30] The difficulties that face the national chairperson were aptly described by Kenneth M. Curtis, who resigned in 1978 after only one year in office:

> Have you ever tried to meet the payroll every two weeks of a bankrupt organization and deal with 363 bosses [national committee members] and 50 state chairs? . . . I tried it for a year and simply decided I'd like to do something else with my life. It's not the sort of job that you lay down in the street and bleed to keep.[31]

Congressional and Senatorial Campaign Committees

The other principal units of the national party organization are the congressional and senatorial campaign committees, one committee for each party in each house. These committees, composed of members of Congress, are independent of the national committees. The campaign committees are an outgrowth of the need of members of Congress to have organizations concerned exclusively with their political welfare. As such, the committees raise campaign funds for members, help to develop campaign strategies, conduct research, and otherwise provide assistance to members running for reelection.[32] In addition, the committees may make funds available for party candidates in states or districts where the party has no incumbent. A certain degree of informal cooperation occurs between the party committees of Congress and the national committees, but for the most part they go their separate ways: the former bent on securing reelection of incumbent legislators and on improving the party's prospects for winning or retaining control of Congress, the latter preoccupied with the presidential race.

The Republican campaign committees are the most active and best financed. In 1988 the National Republican Senatorial Committee spent about six times as much money on Republican senatorial candidates as the Democratic Senatorial Campaign Committee did on its candidates. On the House side, the National Republican Congressional Committee

(NRCC) outspent its rival by about two to one.[33] Nevertheless, the spending gap between the parties is not as large today as it was in the early and middle 1980s. Occasionally, the NRCC enters congressional primary fights, supporting one Republican over another.[34] Overall, the influence of the national Republican party committees on House and Senate elections has grown substantially in recent years. Democrats have much to learn from the Republicans about party building.[35]

State Committees

Midway between the national party apparatus and local party organizations are the state party committees, often called state central committees. So great are the differences between these committees from state to state—in membership selection, size, and function—that it is difficult to generalize about them. In some states the membership is made up of county chairpersons; more commonly, state committee members are chosen in primaries or by local party conventions. Their number ranges from less than a hundred members to several hundred. In some states the state central committee is a genuinely powerful party unit and is charged by custom with drafting the party platform, slating statewide candidates, and waging an intensive fund-raising campaign. In other states the committee's impact on state politics is scarcely perceptible. In a fashion similar to that found at the national level, the state chairperson is ordinarily selected by the party's gubernatorial candidate. And like the national chairperson, the state leader is usually a key adviser to the governor on party affairs, particularly on matters involving the distribution of patronage.[36]

Local Party Organization

Below the state committee of the party is the county committee, ordinarily a very large organization composed of all the precinct officials within the county. At the head of this committee is the county chairperson, who is usually elected by the members of the county committee. Often a key figure in local party organization, the county chairperson is active in the campaign planning, in the recruitment and slating of party candidates, in the supervision of campaign financing, and in the allocation of patronage to the party faithful. In many counties, the leader's power is enhanced by his active recruitment of candidates for precinct committee members—the very people who in turn elect him to office. Some states have congressional district party organizations, developed around the office of U.S. representative. Where these committees exist, they function essentially as the member's personal organization, set off from the rest of the party and preoccupied with errand running for constituents and the election of the member. Although local party officials, such as the county chairperson, may be instrumental in controlling the original congressional nomination, their influence on the representative's policy orientations is virtually nil. Indeed, one of the dominant characteristics of congressional district organization is its autonomy. Further down the line are the city and ward committees, which vary in size and importance throughout the country. Their activities, like those of other committees, are centered around campaigns and elections.

The cornerstone of American party organization is the precinct committee, organized within the tens of thousands of election or voting districts of the nation. In metropolitan areas a precinct is likely to number one thousand or two thousand voters; in open-country areas, perhaps only a dozen. The complexity of party organization at the precinct level is mainly a function of precinct size. The precinct committee member is chosen in one of two ways: by the voters in a primary election or by the vote of party members attending a precinct caucus.

In the lore of American politics, elections are won or lost at the precinct level. A strong precinct organization, the argument runs, is essential to party victory, and the key to a strong organization is a precinct leader bent on carrying his precinct. In attempting to advance their party's fortunes, the committee members engage in four main activities: those associated with the campaign itself, party organizational work (for example, recruitment and organization of workers), promulgation of political information, and identification and recruitment of candidates for local office. For most jurisdictions, it appears, the most important activities are those related to the campaign, such as inducing and helping people to register, contacting voters, raising money, campaigning for votes, and transporting voters to the polls. Undoubtedly differences exist in the role perceptions of party officials. A study of precinct leaders in Massachusetts and North Carolina, for example, found that about 60 percent saw their principal task as that of mobilizing voters.[37] In Connecticut and Michigan the leading activities of

precinct officials are fund raising, canvassing, and distributing literature.[38] And in Pittsburgh, about two-thirds of the committee members
describe their most important task as electoral—but here they tend to be
indifferent to organizational goals and more supportive of particular
candidates than of the party slate as a whole.[39] One study has shown that
the organizational vitality of local parties (as measured by such things as
the presence of officials, allocation of time to party business, regular
meetings, the existence of a budget, and participation in various kinds of
campaign activities) is highest in the East (for example, New Jersey,
New York, Pennsylvania, and Delaware) and Midwest (for example,
Indiana, Ohio, and Illinois) and lowest in the South (for example,
Louisiana, Georgia, Florida, Kentucky, and Texas).[40]

Does the strength of local party organizations make a difference in
electoral politics? A study by John P. Frendreis, James L. Gibson, and
Laura L. Vertz provides a two-part answer. First, the presence of well-
organized and active local party organizations does not have a significant
direct effect on the persuasion of voters and thus on election results. That
appears to be the domain of candidate organizations. But second, and of
overlooked importance, in jurisdictions where a party organization is
active, the party more likely will be involved in recruitment and therefore able to field a full slate of candidates. Party building, in other
words, comes a step at a time. The structural strength of the party, this
study suggests, provides a base for the eventual development of competitive party politics.[41]

The Changing Parties: "Old Style" and "New Style" Politics

In the late nineteenth and early twentieth centuries the best examples of
strong party organization could be found in the large cities of the
Northeast and Midwest—New York City, Boston, Philadelphia, Jersey
City, Kansas City, and Chicago. Well-organized and strongly disciplined, the urban machine during this era was virtually invincible.
Precinct and ward officials maintained steady contacts with their party
constituencies—finding jobs for people out of work; helping those who
were in trouble with the law; aiding others to secure government benefits
such as welfare payments; assisting neighborhoods to secure government
services; helping immigrants to cope with a new society; and helping
merchants and tradespeople in their efforts to obtain contracts, licenses,
and the like. The party organization was at the center of community life,

an effective mediator between the people and their government. Party officials were "brokers," exchanging information, access, and influence for loyalty and support at the polls.

Today the picture is much different. Although the party organizations continue to provide social services in certain large cities, the volume of such exchanges has declined sharply. Numerous factors have contributed to this loss of function, including (1) the growth of civil service systems and the corresponding decline in patronage; (2) the relative decline in the value of patronage jobs; (3) the arrival of the welfare state with its various benefits for low-income groups; (4) the steady assimilation of immigrants; (5) the growing disillusionment among better educated voters over many features of machine politics; and (6) the coming of age of the mass media with its potential for contacts between candidates and their publics. Many disadvantaged citizens remain, particularly in large cities, who continue to rely on local party leaders for assistance in solving the problems in their lives. But most Americans scarcely give a thought to using party officials in this way. Where the parties have suffered a loss of functions, it is reasonable to assume that they have also suffered a loss of vitality. The result has been a decline in their ability to deliver the vote on election day.

Except for certain local offices here and there, party organizations have much less influence on election outcomes now than in the past. Relatively few voters rely on the parties for information on campaigns or for voting cues. "Controlling" votes, except perhaps in a few big city wards, is a lost art. Today the most important players are the media, and what counts in campaigns is the candidate's image. As Peter Hart, a well-known poll taker observed, "A campaign is not played out anymore so much for people or voters; it's played out for the media." [42] Assisted by their advisers, candidates plan steadily for ways to gain media attention, to establish good relationships with print and broadcast media, and to generate favorable newspaper stories or acquire a few seconds of exposure on television. An "old style" party leader of the 1930s or 1940s would be left incredulous at the scope of today's campaign activities that fall outside the purview of the party organization.

Television is central to major campaigns because "retail" politics has given way to "wholesale" politics.[43] Candidates no longer rely as much on precinct organization, and they have less time to stand at mill gates, march in parades, or visit an array of plants, businesses, farms, or halls. Another city or state (or airport) is on the day's agenda. As opportunities for personal visits with voters (including party, civic, labor, and business leaders) have diminished, emphasis has shifted to the wholesale politics of the television commercial, the 15- or 30-second political spot. The mediating function of local leaders, reflected in their assessments of candidates and their interpretations of issues for rank-and-file voters, has atrophied in the face of television dominance.

The key feature of this new style of politics is the growth of *candidate-centered* campaigns.[44] Nowhere is the campaign apparatus of the parties as important as the personal organizations of individual candidates. Candidates—for minor offices and major ones, incumbents and challengers—all have their own organizations for managing the activities of campaigns. Within these units the key decisions are made on campaign strategies, issues, worker recruitment, voter mobilization, and the raising and spending of funds. Candidates often hire campaign management firms, public relations specialists, and political consultants to assist them. These professionals conduct public opinion surveys; prepare films and advertising; raise money; buy radio and television time; write speeches; provide computer analyses of voting behavior; and develop strategies, issues, and images. Less and less of campaign management is left to chance, hunch, or the party organizations.

Candidate-centered campaigns revolve around candidate-centered fund raising. Although the national parties continue to supply funds to candidates and to spend money on their behalf—especially important on the Republican side—their role in campaign finance is not as decisive as that of political interest groups or of individual contributors. Typically, House candidates obtain about half of their funds from individual contributors while Senate candidates receive almost two-thirds of their funds from this source. Political action committees (PACs) rank next in importance. House incumbents in 1988 received 47 percent of all their campaign funds from PACs; Senate incumbents, 29 percent. Interest groups have outpaced the parties in funding campaigns for Congress. Their prominence helps to account for the candidate-centeredness of contemporary American politics.

The role of independent expenditures in campaigns also needs to be understood. Under the Federal Election Campaign Act (FECA) passed in 1971 and amended several times since then, limits are placed on the amount of money an individual or political action committee can give to

PAC Contributions to Congressional Candidates, 1978-1988

Under the terms of the Federal Election Campaign Act adopted in 1971, corporations and unions are permitted to use funds from their treasuries to establish and administer political action committees (PACs) and to solicit financial contributions to them. Amendments to the act in 1974 further encouraged the development of PACs and their financial participation in partisan campaigns. In 1974 there were about six hundred PACs; in 1991 they numbered more than four thousand. Their contributions to House and Senate candidates have grown apace:

Year	Total contributions to congressional candidates (in millions)	Percentage to incumbents
1978	$ 34.1	57
1980	55.2	61
1982	83.6	66
1984	105.3	73
1986	132.7	68
1988	147.9	74

SOURCE: Assorted press releases, Federal Election Commission.

a federal candidate. In addition, a presidential candidate who accepts federal funds for the general election campaign cannot accept private contributions. But no limit exists on the amount of money that supporters of federal candidates can spend to aid their campaigns as long as the funds are spent *independently*—that is, without contact with the candidates or their campaign organizations. As a result, groups of all kinds spend heavily, especially in media advertising, opposing as well as supporting presidential and congressional candidates. In the 1988 presidential race, independent expenditures exceeded $21 million, two-thirds of which focused on presidential candidates.[45] The intense involvement of groups in campaigns has changed the nation's political ambiance and its political structures, serving to promote the independence of candidates and officeholders from party controls, while making them even more reliant on interest groups.

The Activities of Parties

A principal thesis in the scholarship on political parties is that they are indispensable to the functioning of democratic political systems. Scholars have differed sharply in their approaches to the study of parties and in their appraisals of the functions or activities of parties, but they are in striking agreement on the linkage between parties and democracy. Representative of a wide band of analysis, the following statements by V. O. Key, Jr., and E. E. Schattschneider, respectively, sketch the broad outlines of the argument:

> Governments operated, of course, long before political parties in the modern sense came into existence. . . . The proclamation of the right of men to have a hand in their own governing did not create institutions by which they might exercise that right. Nor did the machinery of popular government come into existence overnight. By a tortuous process party systems came into being to implement democratic ideas. As democratic ideas corroded the old foundations of authority, members of the old governing elite reached out to legitimize their positions under the new notions by appealing for popular support. That appeal compelled deference to popular views, but it also required the development of organization to communicate with and to manage the electorate. . . . In a sense, government, left suspended in mid-air by the erosion of the old justifications for its authority, had to build new foundations in the new environment of a democratic ideology. In short, it had to have machinery to win votes.[46]

> The rise of political parties is indubitably one of the principal distinguishing marks of modern government. The parties, in fact, have played a major role as *makers* of governments, more especially they have been the makers of democratic government. . . . [Political] parties created democracy and . . . modern democracy is unthinkable save in terms of the parties. . . . The parties are not . . . merely appendages of modern government; they are in the center of it and play a determinative and creative role in it.[47]

The contributions of political parties to the maintenance of democratic politics can be judged in a rough way by examining the principal activities in which they engage. Of particular importance are those activities associated with the recruitment and selection of leadership, the representation and integration of interests, and the control and direction of government.

Recruitment and Selection of Leaders

The processes by which political leaders are recruited, elected, and appointed to office form the central core of party activity.[48] The party interest, moreover, extends to the appointment of administrative and judicial officers—for example, cabinet members and judges—once the party has captured the executive branch of government.[49] As observed earlier, the party organizations do not necessarily dominate the process by which candidates are recruited or nominated. Increasingly, candidates are self-starters, choosing to enter primaries without waiting for approval from party leaders. With their own personal followings and sources of campaign money, they often pay scant heed to party leaders or party politics. Some candidates are recruited and groomed by political interest groups. Many candidates find interest groups a particularly lucrative source of campaign funds. The looseness of the American party system creates conditions under which party control over many of the candidates who run under its banner is thin or nonexistent.

What do the candidates say about the importance of parties in their decision to run for office? A study by Thomas A. Kazee and Mary C. Thornberry of thirty-six candidates who ran for Congress in competitive districts found that twenty-two (61 percent) were self-starters, six (17 percent) were party-recruited, and eight (22 percent) were of a "mixed" variety (self-starters encouraged to some extent by party activists). Many self-starters had participated in party affairs prior to their decision to run, which suggests that the party role in the recruitment of members of Congress is more important than the above percentages suggest.[50] And other studies have found that county party chairpersons often report that they participate in the recruitment of congressional candidates.[51]

Although no longer a dominant force in electoral politics, the parties still play an important role in finding candidates and in electing them to office. It is difficult to see how hundreds of thousands of elective offices could be filled in the absence of parties without turning each election into a free-for-all, conspicuous by the presence of numerous candidates holding all varieties of set, shifting, and undisclosed views. Composing a government out of an odd mélange of officials, especially at the national level, would be very difficult. Any form of collective accountability to the voters would vanish. Hence, whatever their shortcomings, by proposing alternative lists of candidates and campaigning on their behalf, the parties bring certain measures of order, routine, and predictability to the electoral process.

The constant factors in party politics are the pursuit of power, office, and advantage. Yet, in serving their own interest in winning office, parties make other contributions to the public at large and to the political system. For example, they help to educate the voters concerning issues and mobilize them for political action, provide a linkage between the people and the government, and simplify the choices to be made in elections. The parties do what voters cannot do by themselves: from the totality of interests and issues in politics, they choose those that will become "the agenda of formal public discourse." [52] In the process of shaping the agenda, they provide a mechanism by which voters not only can make sense out of what government does but also can relate to the government itself. The role of the parties in educating voters and in structuring opinion has been described by Robert MacIver in this way:

> Public opinion is too variant and dispersive to be effective unless it is organized. It must be canalized on the broad lines of some major division of opinion. Party focuses the issues, sharpens the differences between contending sides, eliminates confusing crosscurrents of opinion. . . . The party educates the public while seeking merely to influence it, for it must appeal on grounds of policy. For the same reason it helps to remove the inertia of the public and thus to broaden the range of public opinion. In short the party, in its endeavors to win the public to its side, however unscrupulous it may be in its modes of appeal, is making the democratic system workable. It is the agency by which public opinion is translated into public policy.[53]

Representation and Integration of Group Interests

The United States is a complex and heterogeneous nation. An extraordinary variety of political interest groups, organized around particularistic objectives, exists within it. Conflicts between one group and another, between coalitions of groups, and between various groups and the government are inevitable. Since one of the major functions of government is to take sides in private disputes, what it decides and does is of high importance to groups. When at their creative best, parties and their leaders help to keep group conflicts within tolerable limits. Viewed from a wider perspective, the relationship between parties and private organizations is one of bargaining and accommodation—groups need the parties as much as the parties need them. No group can expect to move far toward the attainment of its objectives without coming to terms with the realities of party power; the parties, through their public officeholders, can advance or obstruct the policy objectives of any group. At the same time, no party can expect to achieve widespread electoral success without significant group support. Quid pro quo, Latin's most useful political expression, explains this nexus.

Bargaining and compromise are key elements in the strategy of American parties. The doctrinal flexibility of the parties means that almost everything is up for grabs—each party can make at least some effort to satisfy virtually any group's demands. Through their public officials, the parties serve as brokers among the organized interests of American society, weighing the claims of one group against those of another, accepting some programs, and modifying or rejecting others.[54] The steady bargaining that takes place between interest groups and key party leaders (in the executive and legislative branches) tends to produce settlements the participants can live with for a time, even though these compromises may not be wholly satisfactory to anyone. In addition, of deeper significance, the legitimacy of government itself depends in part on the capacity of the parties to represent diverse interests and to integrate the claims of competing groups in a broad program of public policy. Their ability to do this is certain to bear on their electoral success.

The thesis that the major parties are unusually sensitive to the representation of group interests cannot be advanced without a caveat or two. Parties are far more solicitous toward the claims of organized interests than toward those of unorganized interests. The groups that regularly engage the attention of parties and their representatives in government are those whose support (or opposition) can make a difference at the polls. Organized labor, organized business, organized agriculture, organized medicine—all have multiple channels for gaining access to decision makers. Indeed, party politicians are about as likely to search out the views of these interests as to wait to hear from them. In recent years, special cause groups—those passionate and uncompromising lobbies concerned with single issues such as gun control, abortion, tax rollbacks, equal rights, nuclear power, and the environment—have kept legislators' feet to the fire, exerting extraordinary influence as they judge members on the "correctness" of their positions. By contrast, many millions of Americans are all but shut out of the political system. The political power of such groups as agricultural workers, sharecroppers, migrants, and unorganized labor has never been commensurate with their numbers or, for that matter, with their contribution to society. With low participation in elections, weak organizations, low status, and poor access to political communications, their voices are often drowned out in the din produced by organized interests.[55]

No problem of representation in America is more important than that of finding ways to move the claims of the unorganized public onto the agenda of politics. But the task is formidable: "All power is organization and all organization is power. . . . A man who has no share in any form of organized power is not independent of organized power. He is at the mercy of it." [56]

Control and Direction of Government

A third major activity of the parties involves the control and direction of government. Parties recruit candidates and organize campaigns to win political power, gain public office, and take control of government. Given the character of the political system and the parties themselves, it is unrealistic to suppose that party management of government will be altogether successful. In the first place, the separate branches of government may not be captured by the same party. In more than two-thirds of the elections from 1950 to 1992, the party that won the presidency was unable to win control of both houses of Congress. Every Republican president since Dwight D. Eisenhower has faced this problem. Division of party control complicates the process of governing, forcing the president to work not only with his own party in Congress but also with elements of the other party. The legislative success of Republican presidents usually depends on gaining the support of conservative Democrats, mainly from the South. The result is that party achievements in majority building tend to be blurred in the mix of coalition votes, and party accountability to the voters suffers. In the second place, even though one party may control both the legislative and executive branches, its margin of seats in the legislature may be too thin to permit it to govern effectively. Disagreement within the majority party, moreover, may be so great on certain issues that the party finds it virtually impossible to pull its ranks together to develop coherent positions. When majority party lines are shattered, opportunities arise for the minority party to assert itself in the policy-making process. In the third place, midterm (or off-year) elections invariably complicate the plans of the administration

TABLE 1-4   Off-year Gains and Losses in Congress by the President's Party, 1946-1990

Year	House		Senate	
1946	D	−55	D	−12
1950	D	−29	D	−6
1954	R	−18	R	−1
1958	R	−47	R	−13
1962	D	−4	D	+4
1966	D	−47	D	−3
1970	R	−12	R	+2
1974	R	−48	R	−5
1978	D	−15	D	−3
1982	R	−26	R	0
1986	R	−5	R	−8
1990	R	−8	R	−1

NOTE: R = Republican; D = Democrat.

party. The president's party almost always loses seats in both houses. The Republican party lost five House seats and eight Senate seats in 1986, after losing twenty-six House seats and breaking even in the Senate in 1982. Since 1946 the administration party at midterm has suffered an average loss of twenty-six seats in the House and four in the Senate (see Table 1-4). Very few events are as predictable in American elections or as dispiriting for administrations as the chilly midterm verdict of the voters. And finally, the problems the majority party has in managing the federal government about equal the problems it has in managing most state governments.

The upshot is that although the parties organize governments, they do not wholly control decision-making activities. In some measure they compete with political interest groups bent on securing public policies advantageous to their clienteles, and sometimes certain groups have fully as much influence on the behavior of legislators and bureaucrats as legislative party leaders, national and subnational party leaders, or the president. Yet, to identify the difficulties that confront the parties in seeking to manage the government is not to suggest that the parties' impact on public policy is insubstantial. Not even a casual examination of party platforms, candidates' and officeholders' speeches, or legislative voting can fail to detect the contributions of the parties to shaping the direction of government or can ignore the differences that separate the parties on public policy matters.

An understanding of American parties begins with recognizing that party politicians are more likely to set great store in the notion of winning elections than in using election outcomes to achieve a broad range of policy goals. Candidates have interests and commitments in policy questions, but rarely do they rule out bargaining and compromise in order to achieve half a "party loaf." Politicians tend to be intensely pragmatic and adaptable persons. For the most part, they are attracted to a particular party more because of its promise as a mechanism for moving into government than as a mechanism for governing itself. Party is a way of organizing activists and supporters to make a bid for office.[57] This is the elemental truth of party politics. That the election of one aggregation of politicians as against another has policy significance, as indeed it does, comes closer to representing an unanticipated dividend than a triumph for the idea of responsible party government.

Notes

1. Alexander Hamilton, John Jay, and James Madison, *The Federalist* (New York: Modern Library, 1937), 55.
2. E. E. Schattschneider, *Party Government* (New York: Holt, Rinehart and Winston, 1942), 1.
3. This proposition is debatable. For the counterposition—one that stresses the capacity of parties to shape themselves—see Austin Ranney, *Curing the Mischiefs of Faction: Party Reform in America* (Berkeley: University of California Press, 1975), especially Chapter 1; and Jeane Jordan Kirkpatrick, *Dismantling the Parties: Reflections on Party Reform and Party Decomposition* (Washington, D.C.: American Enterprise Institute for Public Policy Research, 1978). For a wide-ranging analysis of the proposition presented in the text, see Robert Harmel and Kenneth Janda, *Parties and Their Environments* (New York: Longmans, 1982).
4. Schattschneider, *Party Government,* 6-7.
5. David R. Mayhew, *Placing Parties in American Politics* (Princeton, N.J.: Princeton University Press, 1986).
6. David E. Price, *Bringing Back the Parties* (Washington, D.C.: CQ Press, 1984), particularly Chapter 5.
7. Mayhew, *Placing Parties in American Politics,* particularly Chapters 2 and 7.
8. For a careful exposition of this argument, see Schattschneider, *Party Government,* 67-84.
9. *Davis v. Bandemer,* 106 S. Ct. 2810 (1986). For a comprehensive examination of legislative reapportionment, see Bernard Grofman, "Criteria for Districting: A Social Science Perspective," *UCLA Law Review* 33 (October 1985): 77-184. The political considerations in reapportionment are explored in Q. Whitfield Ayres and David Whiteman, "Congressional Reapportionment in the 1980s: Types and Determinants of Policy Outcomes," *Political Science Quarterly* 99

(Summer 1984): 303-314.

10. Price, *Bringing Back the Parties*, 126.

11. For studies of the effects of divisive primaries on party unity and election outcomes, see Donald B. Johnson and James R. Gibson, "The Divisive Primary Revisited: Party Activists in Iowa," *American Political Science Review* 68 (March 1974): 67-77; Patrick J. Kenney and Tom W. Rice, "The Relationship between Divisive Primaries and General Election Outcomes," *American Journal of Political Science* 31 (February 1987): 31-44; and Patrick J. Kenney, "Sorting Out the Effects of Primary Divisiveness in Congressional and Senatorial Elections," *Western Political Quarterly* 41 (September 1988): 765-777.

12. David B. Truman, "Party Reform, Party Atrophy, and Constitutional Change: Some Reflections," *Political Science Quarterly* 99 (Winter 1984-1985): 649-650.

13. For a more extensive analysis of the primary, see Chapter 3.

14. The introduction of partisan information in nonpartisan elections has the effect of turning them into partisan contests. See a study by Peverill Squire and Eric R. A. N. Smith, "The Effect of Partisan Information on Voters in Nonpartisan Elections," *Journal of Politics* 50 (February 1988): 169-179.

15. Lucian W. Pye and Sidney Verba, eds., *Political Culture and Political Development* (Princeton, N.J.: Princeton University Press, 1965), 513.

16. The data and general line of argument developed in these paragraphs are derived from Jack Dennis, "Support for the Party System by the Mass Public," *American Political Science Review* 60 (September 1966): 600-615; Dennis, "Changing Support for the American Party System," in *Paths to Political Reform,* ed. William J. Crotty (Lexington, Mass.: Heath, 1980), 35-66; and Dennis, "Public Support for the Party System, 1964-1984" (Paper delivered at the annual meeting of the American Political Science Association, Washington, D.C., August 28-31, 1986), 19. Also see Thomas M. Konda and Lee Sigelman, "Public Evaluations of the American Parties, 1952-1984," *Journal of Politics* 49 (August 1987): 814-829.

17. A system of "responsible parties" would be characterized by centralized, unified, and disciplined parties committed to the execution of programs and promises offered at elections and held accountable by the voters for their performance. For an analysis of this model, see Chapter 7.

18. For a careful analysis of the meaning of data such as presented here, see Martin P. Wattenberg, *The Decline of American Political Parties, 1952-1984* (Cambridge, Mass.: Harvard University Press, 1986), especially Chapter 4, and his earlier study, "The Decline of Political Partisanship in the United States: Negativity or Neutrality?" *American Political Science Review* 75 (December 1981): 941-950. Wattenberg finds that negative attitudes toward the parties have not increased significantly since the 1950s. Instead, the public has become more neutral in its evaluation of them. For a challenge to the "neutrality hypothesis," see Stephen C. Craig, "The Decline of Partisanship in the United States: A Reexamination of the Neutrality Hypothesis," *Political Behavior* 7, no. 1 (1985): 57-78.

19. Herbert Agar, *The Price of Union* (Boston: Houghton Mifflin, 1950), xiv.

20. For an instructive study of the national committee and the national chairperson, see Cornelius P. Cotter and Bernard C. Hennessy, *Politics without Power: The National Party Committees* (New York: Atherton Press, 1964).

21. See two studies that trace the growing importance of the national party: Charles

H. Longley, "National Party Renewal," and John F. Bibby, "Party Renewal in the National Republican Party," in *Party Renewal in America: Theory and Practice,* ed. Gerald M. Pomper (New York: Praeger Special Studies, 1980), 69-86 and 102-115.

22. *Congressional Quarterly Weekly Report,* February 16, 1974, 352.
23. *Congressional Quarterly Weekly Report,* January 14, 1978, 61.
24. *Congressional Quarterly Weekly Report,* October 25, 1982, 3188-3192.
25. See an excellent study of the institutionalization of the parties by Cornelius P. Cotter and John F. Bibby, "Institutional Development of Parties and the Thesis of Party Decline," *Political Science Quarterly* 95 (Spring 1980): 1-27.
26. *Congressional Quarterly Weekly Report,* January 17, 1982, 140.
27. See Cotter and Hennessy, *Politics without Power,* 67-80. They see the roles of the national chairperson as "image-maker, hell-raiser, fund-raiser, campaign manager, and administrator."
28. Robert J. Huckshorn and John F. Bibby, "State Parties in an Era of Political Change," in *The Future of American Political Parties,* ed. Joel L. Fleishman (Englewood Cliffs, N.J.: Prentice Hall, 1982), 82.
29. F. Christopher Arterton, "Political Money and Party Strength," in *The Future of American Political Parties,* ed. Joel L. Fleishman, 105.
30. Huckshorn and Bibby, "State Parties in an Era of Political Change," 83.
31. *Congressional Quarterly Weekly Report,* January 14, 1978, 58.
32. The chairmanship of a congressional campaign committee is a major political plum. The chairman has numerous opportunities to help party candidates be elected and, more important, to help incumbents be reelected. The chairman concentrates on fund raising, "signs the checks" for the party's candidates, and inevitably gains the gratitude of winners.
33. Press release, Federal Election Commission, August 15, 1989.
34. *Congressional Quarterly Weekly Report,* November 1, 1980, 3234-3239.
35. See an instructive study of the expanded role of the national parties in congressional elections by Paul S. Herrnson, *Party Campaigning in the 1980s* (Cambridge, Mass.: Harvard University Press, 1988). Along the same lines, see Paul S. Herrnson, "Reemergent National Party Organizations," in *The Parties Respond,* ed. L. Sandy Maisel (Boulder, Colo.: Westview Press, 1990), 41-66.
36. For an examination of the strength of party organizations at the state level, see John F. Bibby, Cornelius P. Cotter, James L. Gibson, and Robert J. Huckshorn, "Trends in Party Organizational Strength, 1960-1980," *International Political Science Review* 4 (January 1983): 21-27, and "Assessing Party Organizational Strength," *American Journal of Political Science* 27 (May 1983): 193-222.
37. Lewis Bowman and G. R. Boynton, "Activities and Role Definitions of Grass-roots Party Officials," *Journal of Politics* 28 (February 1966): 121-143. Also see Lee S. Weinberg, "Stability and Change among Pittsburgh Precinct Politicians," *Social Science* (Winter 1975): 10-16.
38. Barbara C. Burrell, "Local Political Party Committees, Task Performance and Organizational Vitality," *Western Political Quarterly* 39 (March 1986): 48-66.
39. Michael Margolis and Raymond E. Owen, "From Organization to Personalism: A Note on the Transmogrification of the Local Political Party," *Polity* 18 (Winter 1985): 313-328.
40. James L. Gibson, Cornelius P. Cotter, John F. Bibby, and Robert J. Huckshorn, "Whither the Local Parties?: A Cross-Sectional and Longitudinal

Analysis of the Strength of Party Organizations," *American Journal of Political Science* 29 (February 1985): 139-160.

41. John P. Frendreis, James L. Gibson, and Laura L. Vertz, "The Electoral Relevance of Local Party Organizations," *American Political Science Review* 84 (March 1990): 225-235. Indicators of the structural strength of a party organization include the presence of a constitution and by-laws, a complete set of officers, an active chairperson, bimonthly meetings, year-round office, staff, and budget.

42. Quoted in Albert R. Hunt, "The Media and Presidential Campaigns," in *Elections American Style,* ed. A. James Reichley (Washington, D.C.: Brookings Institution, 1987), 53.

43. See a column by R. W. Apple, Jr., in the *New York Times,* February 11, 1988.

44. See an analysis of President Reagan's popularity and an accompanying argument regarding the decline of partisanship and the growing candidate-centeredness of presidential elections in Martin P. Wattenberg, "The Reagan Polarization Phenomenon and the Continuing Downward Slide in Presidential Candidate Popularity," *American Politics Quarterly* 14 (July 1986): 219-245.

45. Press release, Federal Election Commission, May 19, 1989.

46. V. O. Key, Jr., *Politics, Parties, and Pressure Groups* (New York: Crowell, 1964), 200-201.

47. Schattschneider, *Party Government,* 1.

48. Agreement among students of political parties on the nature of party functions, their relative significance, and the consequences of functional performance for the political system is far from complete. Frank J. Sorauf points out that among the functions attributed to American parties have been simplifying political issues and alternatives, producing automatic majorities, recruiting political leadership and personnel, organizing minorities and opposition, moderating and compromising political conflict, organizing the machinery of government, promoting political consensus and legitimacy, and bridging the separation of powers. The principal difficulty with listings of this sort, according to Sorauf, is that "it involves making functional statements about party activity without necessarily relating them to functional requisites or needs of the system." He suggests that, at this stage of research on parties, emphasis should be given to the activities performed by parties, thus avoiding the confusion arising from the lack of clarity about the meaning of function, the absence of consensus on functional categories, and the problem of measuring the performance of functions. See his instructive essay, "Political Parties and Political Analysis," in *The American Party Systems: Stages of Political Development,* ed. William Nisbet Chambers and Walter Dean Burnham (New York: Oxford, 1967), 33-53.

49. In about four-fifths of the states, judges are chosen in some form of partisan or nonpartisan election. In the remaining states they come to office through appointment. A few states employ the so-called Missouri Plan of judge selection, under which the governor makes judicial appointments from a list of names supplied by a nonpartisan judicial commission composed of judges, lawyers, and laymen. Under this plan, designed to take judges out of politics, each judge, after a trial period, runs for reelection without opposition; voters may vote either to retain or to remove him from office. If a majority of voters cast affirmative ballots, the judge is continued in office for a full term; if the vote is negative, the judge loses office and the governor makes another appointment in the same manner. But even under this plan, the governor may give preference

to aspirants of his own party. Irrespective of the system used to choose judges, party leaders and party interest will nearly always be involved.

50. Thomas A. Kazee and Mary C. Thornberry, "Where's the Party? Congressional Candidate Recruitment and American Party Organizations," *Western Political Quarterly* 43 (March 1990): 61-80. For a discussion of the role of the national parties in recruiting candidates for Congress, see Herrnson, *Party Campaigning in the 1980s,* 48-56.

51. See Cornelius P. Cotter, James L. Gibson, John F. Bibby, and Robert J. Huckshorn, *Party Organization in American Politics* (New York: Praeger, 1984); and Gibson, Cotter, Bibby, and Huckshorn, "Whither the Local Parties?" 139-160. And for additional evidence on the vitality of local parties, see Kay Lawson, Gerald Pomper, and Maureen Moakley, "Local Party Activists and Electoral Linkage," *American Politics Quarterly* 14 (October 1986): 345-375.

52. Theodore J. Lowi, "Party, Policy, and Constitution in America," in *The American Party Systems,* ed. William Nisbet Chambers and Walter Dean Burnham, 263.

53. Robert MacIver, *The Web of Government* (New York: Macmillan, 1947), 213.

54. See a discussion of the party role in "the aggregation of interests" in Gerald M. Pomper, "The Contributions of Political Parties to American Democracy," in *Party Renewal in America: Theory and Practice,* ed. Gerald M. Pomper, 5-7.

55. Few facts about the political participation of Americans are of greater significance than those that reveal its social class bias. A disproportionate number of the people who are highly active in politics are drawn from the upper reaches of the social order, from among those who hold higher status occupations, are more affluent, and are better educated. Citizens from lower socioeconomic levels constitute only about 10 percent of the participants who are highly active in politics. See Sidney Verba and Norman H. Nie, *Participation in America: Political Democracy and Social Equality* (New York: Harper and Row, 1972), especially Chapter 20.

56. Harvey Fergusson, *People and Power* (New York: Morrow, 1947), 101-102.

57. Consider the development and components of a party model based on the idea that the only standard useful in evaluating the vitality of American parties is simply the ability of the party to win office. Using this standard, Joseph Schlesinger argues that the major parties are healthier now than ever in the past. See his "On the Theory of Party Organization," *Journal of Politics* 46 (May 1984): 369-400.

chapter two

The Characteristics
of American Parties

THE MAJOR parties are firm landmarks on the American political scene. In existence for more than a century, the parties have made important contributions to the development and maintenance of a democratic political culture and to democratic institutions and practices. In essence, the parties form the principal institution for popular control of government, and this achievement is remarkable given the limitations under which they function. This chapter examines the chief characteristics of the American party system.

The Primary Characteristic: Dispersed Power

Viewed at some distance, the party organizations may appear to be neatly ordered and hierarchical—committees are piled, one atop another, from the precinct to the national level, conveying the impression that power flows from the top to the bottom. In reality, however, the American party is not nearly so hierarchical. State and local organizations have substantial independence on most party matters. The practices that state and local parties follow, the candidates they recruit or help to recruit, the campaign money they raise, the auxiliary groups they form and re-form, the innovations they introduce, the organized interests to which they respond, the campaign strategies and issues they create, and, most important, the policy orientations of the candidates who run under their label—all bear the distinctive imprints of local and state political cultures, leaders, traditions, and interests.[1]

Although there is no mistaking the overall decentralization of American parties, the power of the national party to control the presidential nominating process has grown immensely—particularly for the Democratic party. The Democratic reform movement, begun in the late 1960s, drastically altered the rules and practices of state parties in matters related to the selection of national convention delegates. In 1974 the Democratic party held a midterm convention to draft a charter—the first in the history of either major party—to provide for the governance of the party. The charter formally establishes the Democratic national convention as the highest authority of the party and requires state parties to observe numerous standards in the selection of convention delegates. Moreover, as a result of a 1975 Supreme Court decision, national party rules must govern if a conflict arises between national and state party rules concerning the selection of delegates. "The convention serves the pervasive national interest in the selection of candidates for national office," the Supreme Court ruled, "and this national interest is greater than any interest of an individual state." [2]

The centralizing reforms of the Democratic party, however, need to be kept in perspective. On the whole, they have contributed more to the devitalization of the national party organizations than to their strengthening. The reforms have not increased the probability that candidates who are nominated will win the election. Furthermore, the spread of presidential primaries and the opening up of party caucuses have transformed the national convention, diminishing its independent role in choosing the presidential nominee. In recent conventions the delegates have done little more than ratify the choices made earlier in party primaries and caucuses. In effect, the average party voter, joined by candidate enthusiasts, not the convention, picks the nominee. And in reality the choice may be limited simply to the candidates who have somehow survived the Iowa caucuses and the New Hampshire primary. The party conventions themselves are less and less party gatherings. Rather, they are assemblies dominated by the leading candidate, his organization, his entourage of advisers, and the activists drawn to his preconvention campaign. Public officials and party leaders draw power from their relationship to the candidate whose nomination the convention will confirm. Those aligned with candidates rejected in the preconvention period are of minimal interest, even to television reporters in search of an angle that can be parlayed into a story. All recent conventions have been dominated by the leading candidate and his organization. The same can be said for state delegations—where all the action takes place in candidate caucuses. When the preconvention struggle produces a nominee, the party presence in the convention is scarcely more than a backdrop.

In the Democratic party, the influence of national party agencies on state and local organizations is confined mainly to the presidential nominating process.[3] National party rules thoroughly regulate the processes by which national convention delegates are chosen. The influence of Republican national party agencies on subnational parties, by contrast, shows up most clearly in matters of campaign finance. In 1988, for example, national Republican party committees' contributions to House and Senate candidates and expenditures on their behalf totaled about $18 million, as contrasted with about $11 million for national Democratic party committees.[4] In addition, Republican national committees spend vastly more money than their rivals in national advertising campaigns and in the provision of other services (for example, polls, registration drives) beneficial to all the party's candidates. Despite an improved performance in fund raising, the Democrats are still no match for the Republicans.[5]

National party leaders do not have a great impact on the nomination of candidates for Congress. Ordinarily, these nominations are treated as local matters, even though members of Congress are national officials. Furthermore, congressional party leaders rarely attempt to discipline fellow party members who stray from the reservation—who vote with the other party on key legislative issues or otherwise fail to come to the aid of their party. (In an unusual action in 1983, the House Democratic Caucus removed a Texas representative, Phil Gramm, from the Budget Committee because he had played a major role in shaping President Reagan's budget strategy in the previous Congress. In response, Gramm resigned his seat, switched parties, and was reelected as a Republican. Other conservative "Boll Weevil" Democrats who had supported Reagan's economic program suffered no penalties, however.) Members who ignore their party typically escape sanctions and, by dramatizing their capacity to resist party claims, sometimes improve their standing with the voters.

The position of the national party apparatus is also revealed in the character and activities of the national committee. For the party in power, the national committee is predominantly an arm of the president. Neither national committee has significant influence on fellow party members in

Congress, on the party's governors, or on the party's public officials further down the line. The shaping of party positions on major questions of public policy is thus well beyond the capacity of the committee.

Factors Contributing to the Dispersal of Party Power

The position of the national party is strongly affected by the legal and constitutional characteristics of the American political system. American parties must find their place within a federal system where powers and responsibilities lie with fifty states as well as with the national government. The basic responsibility for the design of the electoral system in which the parties compete is given to the states, not to the nation. Not surprisingly, party organizations have been molded by the electoral laws under which they contest for power. State and local power centers have naturally developed around the thousands of governmental units and elective offices found in the states and the localities. With his distinctive constituency (frequently a safe district), his own coterie of supporters, and his own channels to campaign money, the typical officeholder has a remarkable amount of freedom in defining his relationship to his party. His well-being and the organization's well-being are not identical. To press this point, it is not too much to say that officeholders are continuously evaluating party claims and objectives in the light of their own career aspirations. When the party's claims and the officeholder's aspirations diverge, the party ordinarily loses out. A federal system, with numerous elective offices, opens up an extraordinary range of political choices to subnational parties and, especially, to individual candidates.

For all of its significance for the party system and the distinctiveness of American politics, however, federalism is but one of several explanations for the fragmentation of party power. Another constitutional provision, separation of powers, also contributes to this condition. A frequent by-product of separation of powers is a truncated party majority—when one party controls one or both houses of the legislature and the other party controls the executive. At worst, the result is a dreary succession of narrow partisan clashes between the branches; at best, a clarification of differences between the parties occasionally may come about. At no time, however, does a truncated majority help in the development and maintenance of party responsibility for a program of public policy. The dimensions of this party problem in the states are revealed by the data provided in Table 2-1. Currently, well over half of all gubernatorial-

TABLE 2-1   Incidence of Party Division (Governor versus Legislature)
Following 1984, 1986, and 1988 Elections

Relation between governor and legislature	Following 1984 election		Following 1986 election		Following 1988 election	
	Number	Percent	Number	Percent	Number	Percent
Governor opposed [a]	27	55	29	59	31 [b]	63
Governor unopposed	22	45	20	41	18	37

SOURCE: Developed from data in *Congressional Quarterly Weekly Report,* November 17, 1984, 2944-2945; November 15, 1986, 2894-2895; and November 19, 1988, 3372-3373.

NOTE: Nebraska is excluded because it has a nonpartisan legislature.

[a] At least one house is controlled by a majority of the other party.
[b] As a result of the 1988 election, 18 of these 31 governors faced opposition party majorities in both houses. Fourteen of the 18 were Republicans.

legislative elections lead to divided party control of the branches. Republican governors in particular are likely to confront this situation. The pattern at the national level is just about the same.

A third factor helping to disperse party power is the method used to make nominations. It was noted earlier that nominations for national office are sorted out and settled at the local level, ordinarily without interference from national party functionaries. One of the principal supports of local control over nominations is the direct primary. Its use virtually guarantees that candidates for national office will be tailored to the measure of local specifications. Consider this analysis by Austin Ranney and Willmoore Kendall:

A party's *national* leaders can affect the kind of representatives and senators who come to Washington bearing the party's label only by enlisting the support of the state and local party organizations concerned; and they cannot be sure of doing so even then. Assume, for example, that the local leaders have decided to support the national leaders in an attempt to block the renomination of a maverick congressman, and are doing all they can. There is still nothing to prevent the rank and file, who may admire the incumbent's "independence," from ignoring the leaders' wishes and renominating him. The direct primary, in other words, is *par excellence* a system for maintaining *local* control of nominations; and as long as American localities continue to be so different from one another in economic interests, culture, and political attitudes, the national parties are likely to retain their present ideological heterogeneity and their tendency to show differing degrees of cohesion from issue to issue.[6]

Fourth, the distribution of power within the parties is affected by patterns of campaign finance. Few, if any, campaign resources are more important than money. A large proportion of the political money donated in any year is given directly to the campaign organizations of individual candidates instead of to the party organizations. Candidates with access to campaign money are automatically in a strong position vis-à-vis the party organization. Not having to rely heavily on the party for campaign funds, candidates can stake out their independence from it. Whether candidates can remain independent from the interest groups that pour money into their campaigns is another question.

Fifth, a pervasive spirit of localism dominates American politics and adds to the decentralization of political power. Local interests find expression in national politics in countless ways. Even the presidential nominating process may become critical for the settlement of local and state political struggles. A prominent political leader who aligns with the candidate who eventually wins the presidential nomination, particularly if his support comes early in the race, can put new life into his own career. He gains access to the nominee and increased visibility. If his party wins the presidency, an appointment in the new administration may be offered to him. Or if he chooses to run for a major public office, he is likely to secure the support of the president. National conventions settle more than national matters.

Congress has always shown a remarkable hospitality to the idea that governmental power should be decentralized. A great deal of the major legislation that has been passed in recent decades, for example, has been designed to make state and local governments participants in the development and implementation of public policies. Locally based political organizations profit from these arrangements. A basic explanation for Congress's defense of state and local governments lies in the backgrounds of the members themselves. Many of them were elected to state or local office prior to their election to Congress. They are steeped in local lore, think in local terms, meet frequently with local representatives, and work for local advantage. Their steady attention to the local dimensions of national policy helps to safeguard their own careers and to promote the interests of those local politicians who look to Washington for assistance in solving community problems. The former Speaker of the House, Thomas P. ("Tip") O'Neill, Jr. (D-Mass.), had it right when he said, "All politics is local." [7]

Finally, the fragmentation of party power owes much to the growing importance of outsiders in the political process. Chief among them are the media, campaign management firms, and political interest groups. Increasingly, candidates hire expert consultants to organize their campaigns, to shape their strategies, and to mold their images. And they use the media to present themselves to the voters—what counts, modern candidates know, is how they are perceived by the voters. As for political interest groups, their role in campaigns, particularly in their financing, probably has never been more important than it is right now. In 1988 PACs contributed about $148 million to the campaigns of candidates for Congress—roughly five times as much as they gave in 1978. Interest group money has become a major force—some would say an overwhelming force—in American politics, particularly in congressional elections. And the heightened prominence of interest groups in election campaigns has increased their influence on officeholders.[8]

The Power of Officeholders

Writing in the 1960s, James M. Burns sketched the organizational strength of state parties:

> At no level, except in a handful of industrial states, do state parties have the attributes of organization. They lack extensive dues-paying memberships; hence they number many captains and sergeants but few foot soldiers. They do a poor job of raising money for themselves as organizations, or even for their candidates. They lack strong and imaginative leadership of their own. They cannot control their most vital function—the nomination of their candidates. Except in a few states, such as Ohio, Connecticut, and Michigan, our parties are essentially collections of small cliques and they are often shunted aside by the politicians who understand political power. Most of the state parties are at best mere jousting grounds for embattled politicians; at worst they simply do not exist, as in the case of Republicans in the rural South or Democrats in the rural Midwest.[9]

Is the situation different today? Yes, in some respects. Recent research has shown that the parties are stronger organizationally than they were in the 1960s. At the state level, for example, most parties now maintain a permanent state headquarters in the state capital with a professional staff. State party budgets have grown in size, and systematic fund raising has become a more important activity. Party organizations are better equipped to provide candidates with services, including research assistance and campaign money. They are also more effective in recruiting candidates for public office in many jurisdictions. Organizational vitality is particularly evident in the Republican party. About three-fourths of all Republican state parties and one-fourth of all Democratic state parties can be classified as "strong" or "moderately strong" from an organizational standpoint.[10] But this still leaves a number of states where one or both parties are weak and inconspicuous.

Strong everywhere, however, are independent candidate and officeholder organizations. They dominate the campaign and election process. Candidates and officeholders—aided by hired consultants and assorted handlers—at all levels develop strategies and issues, raise funds, recruit workers, interact with interest groups, assemble coalitions, cultivate the media, make news, and mobilize voters. The party organization may provide useful services to the candidates, facilitating their campaigns, but that is about it. Candidates shape their own campaigns and win largely on their own efforts and on their own terms. The perspective of Barbara G. Salmore and Stephen A. Salmore is instructive:

> Technology is the development most responsible for ending party primacy in campaigns. . . . What made the advent of television and the computer unique was that they provided candidates everywhere with an effective alternative means of getting information about themselves to the voters. Newspapers, magazines, and radio paled in comparison with what television offered—a powerful combination of visual and aural messages. Candidates could enter voters' homes and give party organizations competition they had never had before. . . . Once candidates learned that they could independently compete with party organizations and that they had the direct primary as the vehicle to do it, why should they give up their independence and control of their messages to the party organizations?[11]

In the candidate- and media-centered politics of the late twentieth century, the party may be only an afterthought in the career calculation of members. Consider these observations about contemporary members of Congress—the first by a political scientist, Burdett A. Loomis; the second by Rep. Thomas S. Foley (D-Wash.):

Policy entrepreneurs. Free-lance artists. Independent operators. Idea merchants. Central to almost all characterizations of a new political style is a sense of independence. Congressmen and senators can depend on their own enterprises for reelection, for legislative initiatives, for publicity, for a sense of certainty in their uncertain lives.[12]

Nobody in the United States Congress ever talks about the Democratic or Republican party. . . . I have never heard a member of the Congress refer to a colleague and urge a vote for him because he was in the same party. Most Democrats and Republicans could not recall three items in the platform of their party. . . . We have 435 parties in the House.[13]

Law and the Parties

One of the major features of American parties is that their organization and activities are extensively regulated by law—state law in particular. David E. Price has distinguished two general bodies of state law: statutes that relate to *nominations and elections* and statutes that affect *party cohesion in government.*[14]

Laws affecting nominations and elections differ from state to state. A few examples will help to illustrate their diversity. Although the direct primary system is used everywhere, some states still permit party conventions to participate in the choice of nominees. For example, state law or party rules may stipulate that a candidate for a statewide office must receive a certain percentage of the party's state convention vote to qualify for a place on the primary ballot. In some states, law or practice encourages the parties to make preprimary endorsements; in other states such gatekeeping action is prohibited. States vary sharply in the extent to which they seek to protect the integrity of the parties by limiting primary voting to persons preregistered by party. The best (or at least most benign) arrangement, from the standpoint of the parties, is the closed primary. (See Table 2-2 for data on regional differences in party influence on nominations as promoted by state laws or practices.) States also differ significantly in how their laws protect the parties from independent candidates and "sore losers" (candidates who lose their party's nomination and then run under another banner in the general election). As a final example, law in eight states helps to promote the parties through public funding of campaigns, channeled through the parties.

TABLE 2-2   Party Capacity for Influencing Nominations, as Reflected in State Laws and Practices

Region	Number of states in region	Number of states in which party conventions help choose major state-level nominees	Number of states in which parties regularly make preprimary endorsements	Number of states in which primary voting is limited to persons preregistered by party	Total	Average per state
Northeast	10	3	6	8	17	1.7
Border	4	0	0	4	4	1.0
South	11	0	0	2	2	0.2
Midwest	12	1	7	4	12	1.0
West	13	3	3	7	13	1.0
Regular party organization states	8	2	6	5	13	1.6

SOURCE: Developed from data in David E. Price, *Bringing Back the Parties* (Washington, D.C.: CQ Press, 1984), 128-129 (as adapted). Price examines eleven party-strengthening laws and practices in the states, three of which, referred to here, are central to party influence on nominations. The table also reflects the presence of party-strengthening laws and practices in states where local parties traditionally have been strongest. As identified by David R. Mayhew, who examined the structure of American parties at the local level, these "regular party organization states" are Connecticut, Delaware, Illinois, New Jersey, New York, Ohio, Pennsylvania, and Rhode Island. Local party organizations in these states have been distinguished by hierarchy, substantial autonomy, lasting power, an active role in the nominating process, significant patronage, and an absence of factional conflict. See Mayhew, *Placing Parties in American Politics* (Princeton, N.J.: Princeton University Press, 1986), Chapter 2.

The impact of state law on party cohesion in government is sizable. Laws may make it easy for the parties to function as collectivities or they may make it difficult. Where ballots facilitate straight-ticket voting, for example, as they do in twenty-one states, the probability increases for gubernatorial-legislative coattailing and thus for the election of candidates who share the same party label. The election calendar may also affect party control of government. Election of the governor and the legislature at the same time promotes party control, while elections held at different times encourage divided control of government. Finally, states differ in the degree to which they consolidate executive power. Short terms for the governor, prohibition against reelection, and provision for a multiplicity of statewide elective offices all contribute to the weakness of executive authority and, ultimately, to the fragmentation of party power.

State laws can be either a boon or a barrier to strong parties. Party-strengthening laws are most likely to be found in the northeastern states. Southern states are least likely to have laws favorable to the parties, their leaders, and their organizations. Intraregional variation is particularly noticeable in the Midwest and West. In the Midwest, Kansas and Nebraska do not have nearly as many proparty laws as Michigan and North Dakota. In the West, California is largely antiparty in its statutes, while Utah is considerably more proparty. On the whole, state law is more likely to have a negative than positive impact on the strength of the parties. Can the parties be trusted? Are they worth preserving? In most states the law seems to say no, probably not, or, at best, perhaps.

Variations in Party Competition from State to State and from Office to Office

Familiar and conventional interpretations in American politics are never easy to abandon. Old labels persist even though their descriptive power has been sharply eroded. Such is the case in the designation of the American two-party system. Vigorous two-party competition in all jurisdictions is clearly unattainable. Surprisingly little two-party competition is found, however, in certain electoral districts of the nation. The American party system is in some places and at some times strongly two-party, and in other places and at other times, dominantly one-party. In some states and localities factional politics within one or both major parties is so pervasive and persistent as to suggest the presence of a multiple-party system. Competition between the parties is a condition not to be taken for granted, despite the popular tendency to bestow the two-party label on American politics.

Competitiveness in Presidential and Congressional Elections

Although in many states and localities little more than a veneer of competitiveness exists between the parties, this is not the case in presidential elections. Contests for the presidency provide the best single example of authentic two-party competition, particularly in recent decades.[15] With but three exceptions in all two-party presidential contests since 1940, the losing presidential candidate has received at least 45 percent of the popular vote; the exceptions occurred in 1964 (Barry Goldwater received 39 percent of the vote), 1972 (George McGovern, 38 percent), and 1984 (Walter F. Mondale, 41 percent). Several elections in the modern era have been extraordinarily close: in 1960 John F. Kennedy received 49.7 percent of the popular vote to Richard Nixon's 49.5 percent, and in 1968 Nixon obtained 43.4 percent to Hubert H. Humphrey's 42.7 percent (with George C. Wallace receiving 13.5 percent). In another extremely close race in 1976, Jimmy Carter received 50.1 percent of the vote, while Gerald R. Ford received 48.0 percent.

A view of presidential elections from the states is worth examining. In the last two decades the number of one-party states and regions in presidential elections has declined precipitously. The tempo of Republican growth in the once-solid Democratic South has quickened (see Figure 2-1). The watershed in southern political history appears to have been 1952. Dwight D. Eisenhower carried four southern states (Florida, Tennessee, Texas, and Virginia), narrowly missing victories in several others, while receiving more than 48 percent of the popular vote throughout the South. Nixon's victory in 1968 was similarly impressive. In the District of Columbia and in thirty-nine states outside the South, Humphrey led Nixon by about 30,000 votes; in the eleven southern states Nixon led Humphrey by more than 500,000 votes. The high point of Republican appeal was reached in 1972, when Nixon received 70 percent of the southern vote, a much larger proportion than he received in 1968. One result of the 1976 nomination by the Democrats of Jimmy Carter, a native of Georgia, was that the Republican surge in the South was arrested; although Gerald Ford ran well in nearly all states of the Confederacy, he carried only Virginia. In 1980 the Republicans again did well in the South. Reagan received 53.6 percent of the major party vote in the South, winning all of this region's states except Georgia. In 1984 his percentage jumped to 62.6, a level well above his national average of 58.8. In 1988 George Bush also substantially exceeded his national showing in winning 58.8 percent of the southern vote.

At the other end of the scale, certain traditionally Republican strongholds have become more competitive. At one time immoderately Republican, such states as Maine, New Hampshire, and Vermont are no longer in the bag. Each election puts a further strain on old party loyalties. Landslide elections occur from time to time, as in 1964 (Johnson over Goldwater), 1972 (Nixon over McGovern), and 1984 (Reagan over

FIGURE 2-1   Republican Percentage of Two-Party Presidential Vote in
Eleven Southern States, 1940-1988

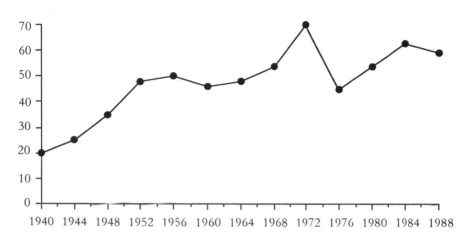

Mondale), but they are often followed by cliffhangers, as in 1968 (Nixon over Humphrey) and 1976 (Carter over Ford). What is more, some presidential elections are much closer than they appear at first glance. In 1988, for example, a switch of less than 600,000 votes from Bush to Dukakis (out of 91.5 million cast) in eleven states would have led to the election of Dukakis. (Bush narrowly carried such big states as Illinois, Pennsylvania, and California.) It is a good guess that most future presidential elections will be closely competitive—decided by thin margins in a handful of states—especially when no incumbent is in the race.

Congressional elections are another story. Many congressional districts have a long history of one-party or incumbent domination. The diversion of House and Senate elections from the mainstream of competitive politics is obvious (see Table 2-3). In no election during the 1980s did as many as 20 percent of the House elections turn up in the marginal (or competitive) category—that is, elections in which the winning candidate receives less than 55 percent of the vote. In 1988 a mere 8.8 percent of all House elections were marginal—the smallest number in history. Though more competitive than those of the House, Senate elections usually result in control by the same party. Incumbency is the key factor in limiting turnover of congressional seats. As would be expected, party control is most likely to shift when a seat is open—when no incumbent is running.

House elections have become so noncompetitive (and predictable) that the 55-45 division may no longer constitute a good measure of

TABLE 2-3 Marginal, Safer, and Uncontested Seats in House and Senate
Elections, 1982-1988, by Percentage of Total Seats

	House				Senate			
Election margin	1982	1984	1986	1988	1982	1984	1986	1988
Seats won by Democrats by less than 55 percent of the vote (Marginal)	9.2	7.4	4.3	5.1	9.1	12.1	29.4	12.1
Seats won by Republicans by less than 55 percent of the vote (Marginal)	8.3	5.7	5.0	3.7	27.3	6.1	11.8	21.2
Seats won by Democrats by 55 percent or more of the vote (Safer)	42.8	38.9	42.6	40.7	51.5	33.3	29.4	45.5
Seats won by Republicans by 55 percent or more of the vote (Safer)	27.3	33.6	31.5	31.9	12.1	45.5	29.4	21.2
Uncontested seats	12.4	14.4	16.6	18.6	2.9	0.0	3.0	0.0

SOURCE: Data drawn from various issues of *Congressional Quarterly Weekly Report.*

marginality. If a marginal district is defined as one won by less than 60 percent of the vote, the results are still not much different. Even under this loose definition, only 16 percent of all House elections were marginal in 1988. A whopping 84 percent were thus won by 60 percent or more of the vote (see Table 2-4). Both parties thrive on safe-district politics. Between 1982 and 1988, only fifty House seats switched party hands. Evidence of this sort recently prompted the *Congressional Quarterly Weekly Report* to run an article entitled "Is Competition in Elections Becoming Obsolete?" [16]

Decisive party victories are not confined to any particular locales. In every region in 1988, more than 90 percent of the House elections were won by 55 percent or more of the vote (see Table 2-5). Many elections in southern and eastern states were uncontested. This analysis, of course, is after the fact. Many members of Congress view each election with trepidation, feeling that their constituencies are never as secure as postelection analyses stamp them.[17] Yet in light of the findings on one-sided House elections, one really has to wonder whether members' anxiety is well founded.

Filling out this account of noncompetitiveness at the congressional

TABLE 2-4   Noncompetitiveness in House Elections, 1988

	Districts won by 60 percent or more of the vote		Uncontested [a]		Total of easily won (60 percent or more) and uncontested House elections	
Party	Number	Percent	Number	Percent	Number	Percent
Democratic	163	37.5	63	14.5	226	52.0
Republican	120	27.6	18	4.1	138	31.7
Total	283	65.1	81	18.6	364	83.7

SOURCE: Developed from data in *Congressional Quarterly Weekly Report,* May 6, 1989, 1060-1065.

NOTE: The party breakdown following the 1988 election was 260 Democrats and 175 Republicans. Eighty-seven percent of all Democratic candidates and 79 percent of all Republican candidates won by at least 60 percent of the vote (including those elections that were uncontested).

[a] Winning candidate had no major party opposition.

level is evidence on the advantage of incumbency (see Table 2-6). In the usual election, more than 90 percent of the House incumbents on the ballot are returned to Washington. A record for House incumbents was established in 1988, when more than 98.5 percent were reelected. In 1990, 96 percent of House incumbents were returned to Washington— but some by closer margins than usual in this election marked by considerable anti-incumbent sentiment. Senate incumbents face stiffer opposition, but they also ordinarily do well. Only one of thirty-two incumbent senators seeking reelection lost in 1990. Few incumbents fall by the wayside in the primaries. So overwhelming is the advantage of incumbents that it is rare for more than 1 percent to lose in their bids for renomination. Congress is an arena for two-party politics not because its members are produced by competitive environments but because both parties have managed to develop and maintain large blocs of noncompetitive seats. Incumbency is a major factor in each party's success in reducing competition.[18]

Competitiveness at the State Level

A wide range of competitiveness exists in the fifty states, as shown by the data of Figure 2-2. In devising this figure, the degree of interparty

TABLE 2-5   House and Senate Electoral Margins by Region, 1988

Chamber and region	Seats won by less than 55 percent of the vote	Seats won by 55 percent or more of the vote		
		Contested	Uncontested [a]	Total
House				
South	10%	54%	36%	90%
East	5	75	20	95
Midwest	9	87	4	91
West	9	82	9	91
Senate				
South	40	60	0	60
East	27	73	0	73
Midwest	12	88	0	88
West	56	44	0	44

SOURCE: Developed from data in *Congressional Quarterly Weekly Report,* May 6, 1989, 1060-1065.

NOTE: *South:* Ala., Ark., Fla., Ga., Ky., La., Miss., N.C., Okla., S.C., Tenn., Texas, and Va.; *East:* Conn., Del., Maine, Md., Mass., N.H., N.J., N.Y., Pa., R.I., Vt., and W.Va.; *Midwest:* Ill., Ind., Iowa, Kan., Mich., Minn., Mo., Neb., N.D., Ohio, S.D., and Wis.; *West:* Alaska, Ariz., Calif., Colo., Hawaii, Idaho, Mont., Nev., N.M., Ore., Utah, Wash., and Wyo.

[a] Includes some elections in which the only opposition was that of a minor party candidate.

competition was calculated for each state by blending four separate state scores: the average percentage of the popular vote received by Democratic gubernatorial candidates; the average percentage of Democratic seats in the state senate; the average percentage of Democratic seats in the state house of representatives; and the percentage of all terms for governor, senate, and house in which the Democrats were in control. Taken together, these percentages constitute an "index of competitiveness" for each state.

In more than one-half of the states, party competition for state offices lacks an authentic ring. Over the period of this study, 1974-1980, eight states (six southern plus Maryland and Rhode Island) were classified as one-party Democratic; another twenty states were designated as either modified one-party Democratic or modified one-party Republican (only North Dakota). Twenty-two states met the test of two-party competition.

Two particularly interesting correlations with competitiveness appear. One concerns the relationship between one-party domination and

TABLE 2-6   The Advantage of Incumbency in House and Senate Elections, 1968-1990

Year	Total number of incumbents				Percentage of incumbents running in general election elected
	Defeated in primary	Running in general election	Elected in general election	Defeated in general election	
1968					
House	3	401	396	5	98.75
Senate	4	24	20	4	83.33
1970					
House	7	391	379	12	96.93
Senate	1	29	23	6	79.31
1972					
House	13	380	367	13	96.58
Senate	2	25	20	5	80.00
1974					
House	8	383	343	40	89.56
Senate	2	25	23	2	92.00
1976					
House	3	381	368	13	96.59
Senate	0	25	16	9	64.00
1978					
House	5	377	358	19	94.96
Senate	3	22	15	7	68.18
1980					
House	6	392	361	31	92.09
Senate	4	25	16	9	64.00
1982					
House	4	383	354	29	92.42
Senate	0	30	28	2	93.33
1984					
House	3	408	392	16	96.07
Senate	0	29	26	3	89.65
1986					
House	2	391	385	6	98.46
Senate	0	28	21	7	75.00
1988					
House	1	408	402	6	98.53
Senate	0	27	23	4	85.18
1990					
House	1	406	391	15	96.31
Senate	0	32	31	1	96.88

SOURCE: *Congressional Quarterly Weekly Report,* March 25, 1978, 755; November 15, 1986, 2891; November 12, 1988, 3267; and November 10, 1990, 3797.

FIGURE 2-2 The Fifty States Classified According to Degree of Interparty
Competition, 1974-1980

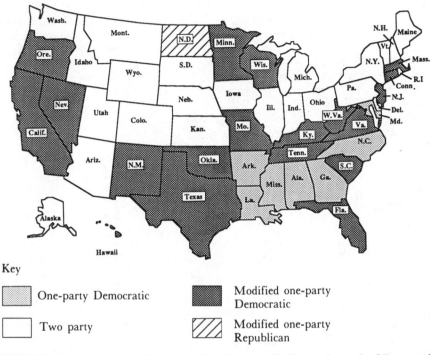

Key

One-party Democratic

Two party

Modified one-party
Democratic

Modified one-party
Republican

SOURCE: Based on data in John F. Bibby, Cornelius P. Cotter, James L. Gibson, and
Robert J. Huckshorn, "Parties in State Politics," in *Politics in the American States,* ed.
Herbert Jacob and Virginia Gray (Boston: Little, Brown, 1983), 66. The classification
scheme was developed by Austin Ranney.

membership in the Confederacy—all of the southern one-party Democratic states withdrew from the Union, as did South Carolina, Texas,
Florida, Tennessee, and Virginia (all modified one-party Democratic
states). For many of the states that today have a low level of party
competition (in particular for state offices), the Civil War was the great
divide. The second correlation is related to urbanization: not surprisingly, the two-party states are significantly more urbanized than the
other states. Many of these states are also distinguished by having high
per capita incomes, a significant proportion of recent immigrants, a high
proportion of labor devoted to manufacturing, and a low proportion of
labor devoted to agriculture. In general, however, there are fewer social
and economic differences between these four categories of states now

than in the past.[19]

The degree of interparty competitiveness cannot be measured only in terms of the struggle for state offices. Some of the states in the one-party or modified one-party categories exhibit vigorous two-party competition in national elections. Virginia, for example, classified as a modified one-party Democratic state, has long had a number of voters who support Republican presidential candidates. Indeed this nominally Democratic state voted Republican in nine of the eleven presidential elections between 1948 and 1988. Competitiveness must therefore be explored along several dimensions.

Competitiveness at the Office Level

Party competition differs greatly not only between states but also between offices in the same state. The complexity inherent in the concept of competitiveness is revealed in Figure 2-3. To unravel the figure, examine the location of each state office on the horizontal and vertical axes. The horizontal axis shows the extent to which the parties have controlled each office over the period of the study; the vertical axis shows the rate of turnover in control of the office between the parties. Some offices are steadfastly held by one party, and other offices are genuinely competitive. Wide variations exist within each state. Taking the northern states as a group, there is less competition for seats in the House than for any other office. By contrast, the offices of governor and senator are the most competitive—even these offices, however, are not significantly competitive.

Overall, the pattern of competition depicted by the data in Figure 2-3 testifies to the inability of state parties to compete for and to control a range of offices. To emphasize a point made earlier, the figure suggests, albeit subtly, that the successful officeholder is one who develops and maintains his own campaign resources, knowing that the party organization is about as likely to be a spectator to his career as a guardian of it.

The Persistent Two-Party System in America

Despite the existence of one-party systems here and there, political competition in the United States usually comes down to competition between the two major parties, Democratic and Republican. The reason American politics has been receptive to a two-party rather than a multiple-party system, as in many European democracies, is not plain.

FIGURE 2-3   Party Competition for Individual Offices (Selected States)

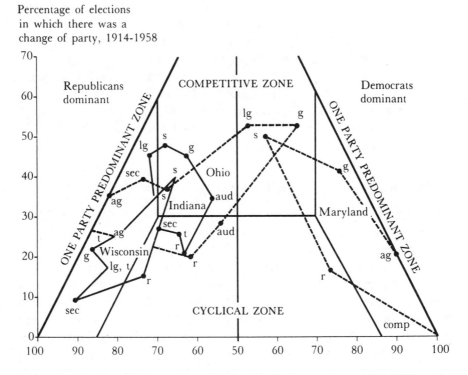

Percentage of elections
in which there was a
change of party, 1914-1958

Percentage of electoral victories for the dominant party, 1914-1958

SOURCE: Joseph A. Schlesinger, "The Structure of Competition for Office in the American States," *Behavioral Science* 5 (July 1960): 203. "The more centrally located on the horizontal axis the more competitive an office was in overall terms; the higher on the diagram the more rapid the rate of turnover; and correspondingly, the lower on the diagram an office falls, the longer the cycles of one-party control, regardless of the degree of overall competition."

NOTE: g = governor; s = senator; r = congressman; lg = lieutenant governor; sec = secretary of state; ag = attorney general; aud = auditor; t = treasurer; comp = comptroller.

What follows is a summary of the principal hypotheses, less than laws and more than hunches, that have been offered as explanations.

A familiar explanation is that electing House members from single-member districts by plurality vote helps to support the two-party pattern. Under this arrangement a single candidate is elected in each district, and he needs to receive only a plurality of the vote. Third party candidates have slight inducement to run, since the prospects are poor that they could defeat the candidates of the two major parties. On the

Single-Member Districts and Party Representation, 101st Congress (1989-1990)

Members of the U.S. House of Representatives (and of most state legislatures) are elected from single-member districts. (For the small states of Alaska, Delaware, North Dakota, South Dakota, Vermont, and Wyoming—each of which elects one U.S. representative—the entire state is a single-member district.) The single-member district system is a distorting mirror for popular preferences. It inflates the number of seats won by the majority party while reducing the number won by the minority party. Since only one candidate can win in each district, all votes for the losing candidate are wasted. The relationship between votes (statewide congressional vote for each party) and seats won in a variety of states in 1988 is reflected in the table below.

| State | Democratic | | Republican | |
	Statewide congressional vote	Seats won	Statewide congressional vote	Seats won
West Virginia (4)	77%	100%	23%	0%
Georgia (10)	67	90	33	10
Maryland (8)	60	75	40	25
Mississippi (5)	66	80	34	20
Utah (3)	43	33	57	67
Michigan (18)	53	61	47	39
North Carolina (11)	56	64	44	36
California (45)	54	60	46	40
Minnesota (8)	59	63	41	37
Nebraska (3)	35	33	65	67
Iowa (6)	49	50	51	50

SOURCE: Developed from data in *Congressional Quarterly Weekly Report*, May 6, 1989, 1074-1080.

NOTE: Number of House members for each state shown in parentheses.

other hand, if members of Congress were elected under a proportional representation scheme, with several members chosen in each district, third party candidates would undoubtedly have a better chance of winning some seats. Third parties are up against the same obstacle in presidential elections as they are in congressional races: only one party can win. For the office of the presidency, the entire nation takes on the cast of a single-member district. Each state's electoral votes are awarded as a unit to the candidate receiving a plurality of the popular vote; all other popular votes are in effect wasted. In 1968, for example, George Wallace, candidate of the American Independent party, received about five million popular votes in states outside the South but won electoral votes only in the five southern states he carried. Running as an independent in 1980, John B. Anderson received nearly six million popular votes (6.6 percent of the total vote) but no electoral votes. If electoral votes were divided in proportion to popular votes in each state, third party candidates would likely make a bigger dent in the electoral vote totals of the major parties. Electoral practices in the United States are hard on third parties.

The diversity and flexibility that characterize the two major parties also contribute to the preservation of the two-party system. The policy orientations of the parties are rarely so firmly fixed as to preclude a shift in emphasis or direction to attract emerging interests within the electorate. Moreover, each party is made up of officeholders with different views. Almost any political group, as a result, can discover some officials who share its values and predilections and who are willing to represent its point of view. The adaptability of the parties and the officeholders not only permits them to siphon off support that otherwise might contribute to the development of third parties but also creates a great deal of slack in the political system. Groups pressing for change know that there is always some chance that they can win acceptance for their positions within the existing party framework.

Another central explanation for the durability of the two-party system in America is found in a tradition of dualism.[20] Early political conflict occurred between those who favored adoption of the Constitution and those who opposed it. Subsequently, dualism was reflected in struggles between Federalists and Anti-Federalists and, later still, between Democrats and Whigs. Since the Civil War, the main party battle has been fought between Democrats and Republicans. In sum, the main elements of conflict within the American political system have ordinarily found expression in competition between two dominant groups of politicians and their followings. This, in a nutshell, is the essence of American party history. Third parties have cropped up from time to time to challenge the major parties, but their lives ordinarily have been short

TABLE 2-7 Third Party and Independent Presidential Candidates Receiving 5 Percent or More of Popular Vote

Candidate (party)	Year	Percentage of popular vote	Electoral votes
John B. Anderson (Independent)	1980	6.6	0
George C. Wallace (American Independent)	1968	13.5	46
Robert M. LaFollette (Progressive)	1924	16.6	13
Theodore Roosevelt (Progressive)	1912	27.4	88
Eugene V. Debs (Socialist)	1912	6.0	0
James B. Weaver (Populist)	1892	8.5	22
John C. Breckinridge (Southern Democrat)	1860	18.1	72
John Bell (Constitutional Union)	1860	12.6	39
Millard Fillmore (Whig-American)	1856	21.5	8
Martin Van Buren (Free Soil)	1848	10.1	0
William Wirt (Anti-Masonic)	1832	7.8	7

SOURCE: *Congressional Quarterly Weekly Report,* October 18, 1980, 3147 (as adapted).

and uneventful—so deep-seated is the attachment of a majority of Americans to inherited institutions and practices. Third parties or independent candidates rarely receive as much as 5 percent of the popular vote; this has occurred only eleven times since 1832 (see Table 2-7).

A profusion of other themes might be explored in seeking to account for the two-party character of American politics. Election law, for example, makes it difficult for all but the most well-organized and well-financed third parties to gain a place on the ballot. In presidential elections they must struggle in state after state to recruit campaign workers and funds and to collect signatures for their nominating petitions.[21] Even audiences may be hard to come by. In addition, because the risk of failure looms so large, new political organizations must strain to find acceptable candidates to run under their banner. Aspiring politicians are not notable for their willingness to take quixotic risks for the sake of

The Voting Behavior of Southern Whites . . .

	1976		1980		1984		1988	
	D	R	D	R	D	R	D	R
Vote for president	47%	53%	35%	62%	28%	72%	33%	67%

SOURCE: Developed from data in *Public Opinion*, December/January 1985, 4; and *The '88 Vote* (New York: Capital Cities/ABC Inc., 1989), 55.

NOTE: D = Democrat; R = Republican.

From shortly after the Civil War to mid-twentieth century, the Democratic party maintained a virtual monopoly of power in the states of the Confederacy. In party language, the confederate states were the "Solid South," since in election after election citizens voted overwhelmingly for Democratic candidates. The cohesion of the South stemmed from the experience of secession and the collective bitterness over the loss of the war, from the durable economic interests of an agricultural society, and, most important, from a widespread desire to maintain segregation and white supremacy by excluding blacks from the political system.

But historical cohesion has its limits. The Solid South was destined for destruction when the national Democratic party became active in the 1940s in promoting policies, economic as well as racial, that were anathema to the party's conservative southern wing. In 1948 southern Democrats rebelled and created a "bolter" party, the Dixiecrats. Although this insurgent party failed—the Dixiecratic candidates carried

ideology or principle, particularly if there is some chance that a career in one of the major parties is available. The extraordinary costs of organizing and conducting major campaigns, the difficulties that attend the search for men and women to assume party outposts, and the frustrations that plague efforts to cut the cords that bind American voters to the traditional parties all serve to inhibit the formation and maintenance of third parties. It also appears that the restless impulse for new alternatives that often dominates other nations, thus leading to the formation of new political parties, is found less commonly in the United States.

Finally, strange as it may seem, one-partyism enhances the two-party system. Each party has a number of areas (states or districts) that vote consistently and heavily for its candidates, irrespective of the inten-

... in Presidential and Congressional Elections

only four states—it served as an instrument of transition for many southern whites disillusioned with the liberal thrust of the national Democratic party. Thus southern whites who had voted for the Dixiecrats in 1948 found it possible in 1952 to do the unthinkable, to vote for a Republican, Dwight D. Eisenhower. And as a result of the support of these "Presidential Republicans," Eisenhower carried four southern states and only narrowly lost several others.

Throughout the 1950s and 1960s, Republican strength in the South was largely confined to presidential elections. Republican congressional candidates generally fared poorly. The pattern of southern politics is sharply different today. Southern whites are almost as likely to vote for Republican congressional candidates as they are for Republican presidential candidates. According to the 1988 ABC exit poll, for example, 43 percent of all southern voters voted for George Bush for president and a Republican House candidate. Another 8 percent split their tickets to vote for Michael S. Dukakis and a Republican House candidate. The shift has been so substantial that it is now common for the Republicans to elect at least one-third of all southern members of Congress.

The South has moved a long way toward development of a genuine two-party system for national offices. State and local offices continue to be dominated by the Democratic party. The South's last fling with a minor party candidate was in 1968, when Alabama's George C. Wallace ran for the presidency. Today's two-party competition in the South is the natural extension of a secular trend begun some four decades ago.

---

sity of forces that play upon voters there and elsewhere. Even when one of the major parties has a particularly bad election year, it is never threatened with extinction. Republicans may clean up in outstate and downstate Illinois, but Chicago will remain safely Democratic. Most of the rural, less-populous counties of Pennsylvania will vote Republican "til the cows come home," but Pittsburgh, Philadelphia, and other industrial areas will vote to elect Democratic candidates. Year in and year out, for most offices, Maryland and Rhode Island turn to the Democrats, while Utah and South Dakota faithfully vote Republican. One-party areas remove some of the mystery that surrounds American elections. Each major party owes something to them, counts on them, and is not often disappointed.

Parties as Coalitions

Viewed from afar, the American major party is likely to appear as a miscellaneous collection of individual activists and voters, banded together in some fashion to attempt to gain control of government. But there is more shadow than substance in that view; when the party is brought into focus, its basic coalitional character is revealed. The point is simple but important: the party is much less a collection of individuals than it is a collection of social interests and groups. In the words of Maurice Duverger, "A party is not a community but a collection of communities, a union of small groups dispersed throughout the country." [22]

Functioning within a vastly heterogeneous society, the major parties have naturally assumed a coalitional form. Groups of all kinds—social, economic, religious, and ethnic—are organized to press demands on the political order. In the course of defending or advancing their interests, they contribute substantial energy to the political process—through generating innovations, posing alternative policies, recruiting and endorsing candidates, conducting campaigns, and so on. No party seriously contesting for office could ignore the constellation of groups in American political life.

Traditionally, each party has had relatively distinct followings in the electorate. The urban working classes, union families, blacks, Catholics, Jews, persons at the lower end of the educational scale, and the poor have been mainstays of the Democratic party since the early days of the New Deal. Southerners and various nationality groups have also played major roles in the Democratic party. In counterpoise, the Republican coalition has had a disproportionate number of supporters from such groups as big business, industry, farmers, small-town and rural dwellers, whites, Protestants, upper-income and better-educated persons, non-union families, and "old stock" Americans. Coalition politics has been a major feature of successful election campaigns.

Today, these coalitions are clearly in flux, particularly on the Democratic side. For example, although the vast majority of state and local offices in the South continue to be controlled by the Democratic party, the Republicans have made major gains at the national level and especially in presidential elections. Consider recent history. Disillusioned over the liberal thrust of the party, many lifelong southern Democrats bolted in 1964 to support Barry Goldwater, the Republican nominee. In even greater number they moved into the ranks of the American Inde-

The Most Loyal Groups in the Party Coalitions

Groups	Presidential election year		
	1980	1984	1988
Percentage points more Democratic than the nation as a whole			
Black	40	48	40
Hispanic	11	20	23
Unemployed	6	26	16
Jewish	0	26	18
Large cities	9	21	12
Low income	6	13	16
Union household	3	12	11
Percentage points more Republican than the nation as a whole			
White fundamentalist or evangelical Christian	8	19	27
White Protestant	8	13	12
Southern white	6	12	13
High income	8	10	8
White	5	5	5

SOURCE: Developed from data in *New York Times*/CBS News surveys as reported in *New York Times*, November 10, 1988; and Gerald M. Pomper, *The Election of 1988: Reports and Interpretations* (Chatham, N.J.: Chatham House Publishers, 1989), 133-134.

NOTE: In 1980, 15 percent of the Jewish vote was cast for John B. Anderson. Low income is defined as under $12,500 annually, high income as $50,000 and over. Of the total vote in 1988, Hispanics made up 3 percent; Jews, 4 percent; and unemployed, 5 percent. The largest groups were whites with 85 percent of the total vote; white Protestants, 48 percent; southern whites, 23 percent; and high income, 24 percent. Blacks made up 10 percent of the total vote and low income, 12 percent.

pendent party in 1968, voting for George Wallace in preference to the Democratic and Republican nominees, Hubert Humphrey and Richard Nixon, respectively. In 1972 southern voters switched to Nixon. With a Georgian, Jimmy Carter, at the head of the Democratic ticket in 1976, they abandoned their newly found Republicanism and returned to the Democratic fold. But their stay was brief. In 1980 and 1984 they voted decisively for Ronald Reagan, and he swept the region (losing only Georgia in his first election). And in 1988 George Bush ran stronger in this region (receiving 58.8 percent of the vote) than anywhere else and carried every southern state.

Distinctiveness in the voting behavior of religious groups in presidential elections has also eroded in recent years (see Figure 2-4). In 1960 Catholics voted 28 percentage points less Republican than the entire electorate. Protestants, in contrast, voted 12 percentage points more Republican than the national average. Since then, Catholic support for Democratic presidential candidates has declined substantially. In 1984, according to most surveys, the Catholic vote closely paralleled the national vote. In 1988 it was 5 percentage points less Republican than the national average but still much closer to it than in the past. At the same time, the overall Protestant vote has become less firmly tied to the Republican party. (But it should be noted that *white* Protestants voted overwhelmingly for both Reagan and Bush.)

Union members have become a less predictable element in the Democratic coalition than they were in the past, particularly during the Kennedy and Johnson years. In 1984 union families favored Walter Mondale over Ronald Reagan by a margin of only 52 to 48 percent. In 1988 they preferred Michael Dukakis to George Bush by a hefty margin of 63 to 37—a party division about the same as in the 1976 race between Jimmy Carter and Gerald Ford. Overall, the voting behavior of group members is more volatile today, especially in presidential elections—a fact consistent with a period of *dealignment* in which group attachments to the parties become weaker.

American parties are fragile because they are coalitions. At times they seem to be held together by nothing more than generality, personality, and promise. Perhaps what is surprising, all things considered, is that they hold together as well as they do.

The chief threat to party cohesion develops once the election is over and the party is placed in government. It is at this point that coalitions split apart. The behavior of the Democratic party in Congress illustrates this phenomenon. The party unity data in Table 2-8 show how often northern and southern House Democrats voted in agreement with a majority of their party in the first session of the 101st Congress (1989).[23] For northern Democrats, party unity was highly important. More than

FIGURE 2-4   The Growing Similarity in Voting Behavior of Catholics and
Protestants in Presidential Elections

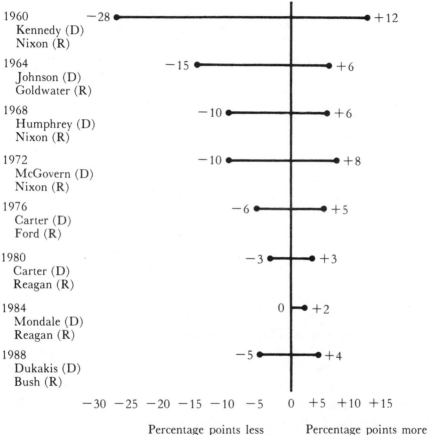

SOURCE: For 1960-1980 data, Everett Carll Ladd, "The Brittle Mandate: Electoral
Dealignment and the 1980 Presidential Election," *Political Science Quarterly* 96 (Spring
1981): 13. For 1984, the exit poll of the *Los Angeles Times* (November 6, 1984) reported the
Catholic vote at 59 percent Republican, the same as the national Republican average, and the
Protestant vote at 61 percent Republican. The Gallup poll showed the groups at 61 percent
Republican and 39 percent Democratic, respectively. *Gallup Report,* November 1984, 13.
The 1988 data are drawn from the *Gallup Report,* November 1988, 7.

NOTE: D = Democrat; R = Republican.

TABLE 2-8   Intraparty Conflict in House Roll-Call Voting, 101st Congress, First Session

Region	Percentage of northern and southern Democrats voting with a majority of their own party					
	90 percent or more	80-89.9 percent	70-79.9 percent	60-69.9 percent	50-59.9 percent	Under 50 percent
Northern Democrats	38	40	14	4	2	2
Southern Democrats	9	24	31	22	9	5

SOURCE: Developed from party unity data compiled in *Congressional Quarterly Weekly Report,* December 30, 1989, 3564-3565.

NOTE: Failures to vote lower party unity scores.

three-fourths of this large bloc voted with a majority of their party 80 percent or more of the time. But only 33 percent of all southern Democrats met this standard. At the other pole, among those Democratic House members least likely to support their party, southerners substantially outnumber northerners. Although intraparty conflict is an important feature of congressional politics, there is less of it today than in the past. Specifically, southern Democrats are now less inclined to bolt from their northern colleagues than they were in the 1970s and early 1980s.

The facts presented in Table 2-8 are evidence that significant disagreement hides behind the party label, especially in the case of congressional Democrats. When party coalitions come apart in Congress, biparty coalitions are often brought to life. The most persistent and successful biparty coalition in the history of Congress has been the conservative coalition, formed by a majority of southern Democrats and a majority of Republicans. In existence in one form or another since the late 1930s, this coalition comes together on essentially the same policy issues that divide northern from southern Democrats. During the early 1980s, the conservative coalition played a key role in the adoption of the Reagan administration's legislative program. Since then, the coalition's influence has declined somewhat. Currently, it comes together on about 10 percent of all recorded votes (as contrasted with more than 20 percent in the 1970s). When it does form, however, it usually wins. In 1989, for example, the coalition appeared on 11 percent of the recorded votes of both chambers and won 87 percent of the time.[24]

Parties of Ideological Heterogeneity

To win elections and gain power is the unabashedly practical aim of the major party. As suggested previously, this calls for a strategy of coalition building in which the policy goals of the groups and candidates brought under the party umbrella are subordinated to their capacity to contribute to party victory. The key to party success is its adaptability, its willingness to do business with groups and individuals holding all manner of views on public policy questions. The natural outcome of a campaign strategy designed to attract all groups (and to repel none) is that the party's ideology is not easily brought into sharp focus. It is, in a sense, up for grabs, to be interpreted as individual party members and officeholders see fit.

The data provided in Figure 2-5 illuminate the ideological distance that separates Senate members of the same party on proposals of key interest to the Americans for Democratic Action (ADA)—a group well known for its identification with liberal causes and policies. Those senators voting in harmony with ADA objectives in the 101st Congress supported such policies as reduced funding for the strategic defense initiative (SDI) and the MX missile, reallocation of certain defense funds to education and social services, limitations on military aid to El Salvador, elimination of all funds to procure additional B-2 bombers, and increased liabilities for oil spills from tankers and onshore and offshore facilities. In addition, members voting in line with the ADA opposed President Bush's proposal for a smaller increase in the minimum wage ($4.25 instead of $4.55), military aid for the noncommunist Cambodia resistance, provision for dependent child care through tax credits and block grants instead of subsidies, circumvention of prevailing wage laws by contractors in hiring tenants and homeless people, a constitutional amendment to grant Congress and the states the power to prohibit the physical desecration of the U.S. flag, and joint U.S.-Japanese development of the F-16 fighter plane. This sketch of ideological conflict in the Senate, presented in Figure 2-5, shows that each party is a mass of tensions and contradictions, with the party members marching to different drums.

The divisions within each major party can be easily identified. Southern Democrats do not view the world in the same light as northern Democrats, nor do they respond to the same cues and constituency clienteles as their northern colleagues. Some eastern Republicans have

FIGURE 2-5   Democratic and Republican Support of Americans for Democratic Action (ADA) Positions, by Region and Certain Individual Senate Members, 101st Congress, First Session

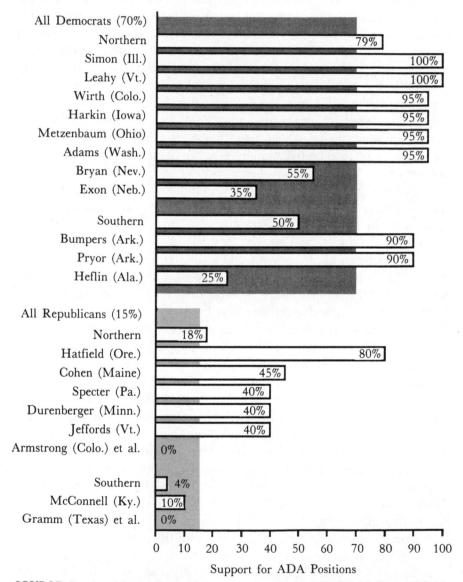

Support for ADA Positions

SOURCE: Developed from data provided in *Congressional Quarterly Weekly Report,* March 3, 1990, 705.

NOTE: The eleven states of the Confederacy plus Kentucky and Oklahoma are classified as southern; all others are classified as northern. Nine Republican senators had ratings of 0.

more in common with northern Democrats than they do with fellow party members from the South or the Midwest.[25] But tempting as it is to fasten on intraparty differences as a way of explaining the performance of the parties in policy-making arenas, the argument can easily get out of hand. In truth, the parties are far from identical, and each has more unity than is commonly supposed.

Although the structure of voting in Congress does not exhibit a high degree of ideological coherence within each party, it nevertheless does show important and continuing policy differences between the parties— at least, between majorities of each party. Democratic members of Congress and Democratic congressional candidates are much more likely to support social welfare legislation and an expanded role for federal government, for example, than are Republican officeholders and Republican candidates. Programs to advance minority rights, to assist public education, to improve the lot of the poverty stricken, to provide medical care for the elderly, or to promote the interests of organized labor typically produce substantial disagreement between the parties, with most Democrats aligned on the liberal side and most Republicans aligned on the conservative side. General differences between party majorities also exist on defense policy and on aid to anticommunist rebels. Hence, to return to the metaphor used earlier, even though party members may be marching to different drums, most of them are playing the same tune.

Parties of Moderation and Inclusivity

Another way to view American parties emphasizes their moderation and inclusivity. They are, in fact, "catchall" parties in which all but the most extreme and intractable elements in society can find a place and, in the process, stake a claim to a piece of the action.

The American party is anything but clannish. It will devote a friendly ear to just about any request. All groups are invited to support the party, and in some measure all do. Almost everything about the major party at election time represents a triumph for those who press for accommodation in American politics. Platforms and candidate speeches, offering something to virtually everyone, provide the hard evidence that the parties attempt to be inclusive rather than exclusive in their appeals and to draw in a wide rather than a narrow band of voters. "No matter how devoted a party leadership may be to its bedrock elements," V. O. Key, Jr., observed, "it attempts to picture itself as a gifted synthesizer of concord among the elements of society. A party must act as if it were all the people rather than some of them; it must fiercely deny that it speaks for a single interest." [26]

The inclusivity of American parties means that they occupy virtually all of the political space in the political system. Minor parties are forced to search for distinctiveness. Some fashion narrow appeals. Others press bizarre or hopeless causes. Still others maneuver only at the ideological fringes, seeking to address extreme left wing or right wing audiences. Their dilemma is that only a relative handful of voters are at each ideological pole and only a few will be attracted to a narrow or single-issue appeal. The net result is that most minor parties struggle to secure candidates, financing, media attention, and credibility. The bottom line is that they struggle simply to stay in business.

The founders established an intricate system of divided powers, checks and balances, and auxiliary precautions to reduce the government's vulnerability to factions. The "Madisonian system"—separation of powers, staggered terms of office, bicameralism, federalism, life appointments for federal judges, fixed terms of office for the president and members of Congress, among other things—makes it difficult for any group (faction or party) to gain firm control of the political system. Today's parties qualify as Madison's factions, but with an unexpected twist. They are in no way a factional threat. Their inclusivity and moderation represent at least as great an obstacle to factional domination of government as formal constitutional arrangements. Because the major parties include all kinds of interests, they are not free to favor a single interest or a small cluster of interests to the exclusion of others. Standing party policies are an expression of earlier settlements among divergent interests. Virtually every new policy can be contested by interested party elements. Every affected interest expects a hearing, bargaining occurs as a matter of course, and accommodation typically takes place. The broad consequences, ordinarily, are, first, that policy making is a slow process and, second, that policy changes are introduced incrementally. The parties' moderation ordinarily means that no one wins completely, no one loses completely. (One consequence of this is that the public often has difficulty in deciding which party to single out for credit, which party to blame.) This argument is sketched in Figure 2-6.

FIGURE 2-6   Moderate Parties and Policy Making

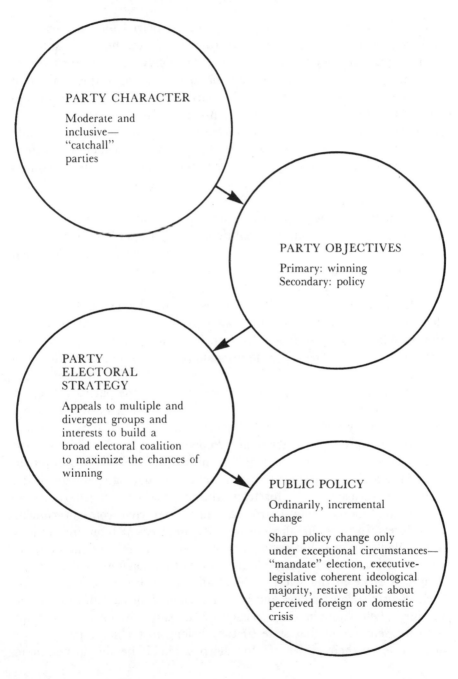

The Party as an Interest Group

Although American parties are sometimes criticized for their cool detachment from important social and economic issues, the same cannot be said for their attitude toward a band of issues having high relevance for the party, *qua* party. Certain kinds of issues, or policy questions, that come before legislatures present the party with an opportunity to advance its interests as an organization—in much the same fashion as political interest groups attempt to secure or block legislation that would improve or impair their fortunes. As E. E. Schattschneider wrote some years ago, within each party is both a "public" and a "private" personality.[27] The public dimension of the party is on display when larger questions of public policy are brought before the legislature. As often occurs on these questions, party lines fail to hold; factions ease away from the party; and biparty coalitions are born, empowered for the moment as the majority. The party's public appearance, in the judgment of many critics, leaves much to be desired. The fundamental flaw is that the party nominally in control of government, but rent by factionalism and fragmentation, cannot be held responsible by the public for its decisions. The problem is not that party unity collapses on all issues but that it collapses with sufficient frequency to make it less than a dependable agent for carrying out commitments presumably made to the electorate.

In sharp contrast is the private personality of the party. Though it is an exaggeration to argue that the party is engaged in steady introspection, it is surely true, as Schattschneider has observed, that "the party knows its private mind better than it knows its public mind." [28] It has a sharp sense of where the best opportunities lie for partisan advantage and of the perils and pitfalls that can threaten or damage party interests. Numerous occasions arise for transmitting benefits to the party organization and its members. Patronage can be extracted from government at all levels. In some jurisdictions literally hundreds or thousands of jobs are available for distribution to party stalwarts. At the national level, the custom of "senatorial courtesy" guarantees that senators will have the dominant voice in the selection of candidates to fill various positions, such as district court judges and U.S. marshals. This custom calls on the president, before nominating a person for a position in a state, to consult with the senators of that state (if they belong to the same party as he does) to learn their preference for the position. If he should nominate someone objectionable to the senators of that state, the prospects are strong that the full Senate will reject the nominee, irrespective of his qualifications. On questions of this sort—those that touch the careers and political fortunes of members—party unity is both high and predictable.

Legislators have never won reputations for queuing up behind proposals that might limit maneuvering in the interest of their careers or their party's welfare. With only a few exceptions, for example, they have opposed plans to extend the merit system, to take judges out of politics, and to empower independent boards or commissions to assume responsibility for reapportionment and redistricting. There is a private side to such public questions—to extend the merit system is to cut back party patronage, to remove judges from the election process is to cut off a career avenue for legislators with their sights on the court, and to give a nonlegislative commission control over redistricting is to run the risk of a major rearrangement of legislative districts and a resultant loss of offices. Legislators and the parties they represent take seriously their role as guardians of the welfare of the organization and the personal interests of its members. As a collectivity, the American party is most resourceful and cohesive when it is monitoring party business. And party business is about as likely to intrude on the great public questions as it is on those of narrow or parochial concern. Opportunities to advance the party cause—through debate, legislation, or investigations—are limited only by a failure of imagination.

The Ambiguity of Party Membership

For those people who set great store by neat and orderly arrangements, the American major party is vastly disappointing. There are numerous examples of the party in disarray. A particularly good one, in the judgment of some students of American politics, involves the concept of party membership.

Who is a party member in the United States? The answer is not clear, though a stab at the question can be made by considering the legal aspects of party membership. Closed primary states have tests of membership. Legal party membership in these states is determined by self-classification at the stage of registration. The significance of establishing membership is that each party's primary is open only to members registered in that party.[29] About one-half of the states have authentic closed primary systems. By contrast, open primary states have no test of party affiliation. Gaining membership consists merely of the voter's request for the ballot of the party in whose primary he wishes to participate. In certain open primary states the voter is automatically given the ballots of all the parties, with instructions to mark one and discard the rest.

Apart from primary voting in closed primary states, membership in a major party is of slight moment. In effect, anyone who considers himself a Democrat is a Democrat; anyone who considers himself a Republican is a Republican. A citizen may register one way and vote another or not vote at all. No obligations intrude on the party member. He can be a member without applying for admission, a beneficiary without paying dues or contributing to campaigns, a critic without attending meetings, an interpreter without knowing party vocabulary, an apostate without fearing discipline. To the citizen who takes politics casually, it may be the best of all worlds. The typical American is insensitive to the claims, problems, and doctrine of his party. His principal participation in party life is through the act of voting— sometimes for his party and sometimes not.

The Indomitable Party?

The party in America is at the center of the political process. Nonetheless, its grip on political power is far from secure. To be sure, the people who are recruited for party and public offices, the issues that they bring before the electorate, the campaigns in which they participate, and the government that they help to organize and direct—all are influenced by party. The basic problem remains, however, that the party is unable to control all the routes to political power. In some jurisdictions, nonpartisan election systems have been developed to try to remove parties from politics, and to a degree they have succeeded. Moreover, so thoroughly are some states and localities dominated by one party that party itself has come to have little relevance for the kinds of men and women recruited for office or for the voters in need of cues for casting their votes. Devices such as the direct primary have also cut into the power of the party organization, serving in particular to discourage national party agencies from attempting to influence nominations, including those for national office, and to open up the nominating process to all kinds of candidates. In addition, divided party control of government has become a chronic problem of both state and national governments. Typically one party winds up controlling the executive branch and the other party one or both houses of the legislative branch. Determining which party is the majority party has become increasingly difficult.

The party-in-the-electorate—voters who regard themselves as party members—probably has never been weaker than it is right now. Between one-fourth and one-third of all voters profess to be independents. Strong partisans are less numerous than in the past. More than half of all voters regularly cast split ballots in presidential elections. Most voters do not view parties in a favorable light or believe that party control over government is desirable. On the whole, the nation's political culture is a hostile environment for parties. The absence of citizen interest in elections also takes a toll on party vitality. It is a spectacular fact that more than 100 million citizens who might have voted in the 1986 congressional elections chose to stay home, and voter turnout (33.4 percent of the voting-age population) was the third-lowest in the nation's history. And in the election of 1988, only 50.16 percent of the voting-age population cast ballots—the lowest level of participation in any presidential election since 1924. In the midst of the signs of party deterioration, it is not surprising that the influence of the mass media, public relations experts, campaign management firms, and political action committees has grown markedly in virtually all phases of campaigns and elections.

Perhaps the wonder of American politics is that the party system functions as well as it does. From the perspective of party leaders, the Constitution is a vast wasteland, scarcely capable of supporting vigorous parties; federalism, separation of powers, checks and balances, and staggered elections all have proved inimical to the organization of strong parties. National and state constitutions apparently were drafted by those who were suspicious of the concentration of power in any hands; their designs have served to fracture or immobilize party power. The party itself is an uneasy coalition of individuals and groups brought together for limited purposes. Within government, power is about as likely to be lodged in nooks and crannies as it is in central party agencies. Conflict within the parties is sometimes as intense as it is between the parties. As for the individual party member, he has a great many rights but virtually no responsibilities for the well-being of the party.

Public disillusionment over the parties places a further strain on their capacities. Many voters believe that the parties have not posed imaginative solutions for such nagging issues as racial injustice, urban decay, inflation, unemployment, and poverty. Similarly, citizens are concerned about the "old" politics that seems to dominate the parties, manifested in a preoccupation with patronage, perquisites, and the welfare of the organization instead of public policy. The parties are also subject to harsh criticism for their apparent willingness to yield to the blandishments of pressure groups and local interests, while too frequently ignoring broad national interests and problems. For many citizens, parties appear as starkly conservative institutions, fearful of innovation and unable to shape intelligent responses to contemporary dilemmas.

Negative attitudes toward government, politics, and parties have increased. A 1990 survey by the Times Mirror Center for the People and the Press found that one-third of the electorate "completely agrees" with the proposition that "elected officials in Washington lose touch with the people pretty quickly." "Despite the personal popularity of President Bush," the study concludes, "cynicism toward the political system in general is growing as the public in unprecedented numbers associates Republicans with wealth and greed, Democrats with fecklessness and incompetence." [30]

The party reforms of the modern period have done more to weaken the parties than to strengthen them. The spread of presidential primaries, the opening up of caucuses, the ideology of popular participation, and the federal campaign finance law (and Supreme Court rulings concerning it) have diminished the role of parties and party leaders in presidential elections. All too often, parties are nothing more than spectators to the campaign clashes of candidate organizations. As for the members of Congress, they have never been more independent; party is what they choose to make of it. In the current state of free-floating politics, interest groups have gained increasing influence over election outcomes and public policies. Their role in financing congressional campaigns is one of the main reasons that campaign expenditures are out of control, increasing at a rate that far outstrips inflation. In sum, the politics of today looks much different from that of the 1960s.

For those citizens who believe that democratic politics depends on the presence of viable parties, conditions must surely appear grim. Even so, it is by no means clear that the major parties are in the process of withering away, to be replaced by government without parties or government by multiple-party coalitions. Survival in this weakened state seems much more likely. And finally, it is useful to remember that, whatever else may be said of American parties, they have never been particularly strong.

Notes

1. On the decentralization of American parties, see Robert Harmel and Kenneth Janda, *Parties and Their Environment* (New York: Longmans, 1982), especially Chapter 5.
2. *Cousins v. Wigoda,* 419 U.S. 477 (1975). This case involved the seating of the Illinois delegation to the 1972 Democratic National Convention. The Court upheld the right of the Democratic convention to refuse to seat the Illinois delegation, which, according to findings of the credentials committee, had violated national party rules concerning the selection process for delegates and whose makeup inadequately represented youth, women, and minorities. The right of the national party to establish rules concerning delegate selection was further strengthened by the Court in a case involving Wisconsin's open presidential primary: *Democratic Party of the U.S. v. LaFollette,* 101 S. Ct. 1010 (1981).
3. The centralizing reforms in the delegate selection process of the Democratic party have not altered the basic decentralization of the party. See William J. Crotty, "The Philosophies of Party Reform," in *Party Renewal in America: Theory and Practice,* ed. Gerald M. Pomper (New York: Praeger Special Studies, 1980), especially 45-48.
4. Press release, Federal Election Commission, March 27, 1989.
5. See Paul S. Herrnson's analysis of the growing role of national party committees in providing services, such as fund raising and advertising, for House candidates. The Republican party has been much more active in this respect. "Do Parties Make a Difference?: The Role of Party Organizations in Congressional Elections," *Journal of Politics* 48 (August 1986): 589-615; and *Party Campaigning in the 1980s* (Cambridge, Mass.: Harvard University Press, 1988). And see an earlier article by Elizabeth Drew, "Politics and Money," *New Yorker,* December 6, 1982, 64.
6. Austin Ranney and Willmoore Kendall, *Democracy and the American Party System* (New York: Harcourt, 1956), 497.
7. Thomas P. O'Neill with William Novak, *Man of the House: The Life and Political Memoirs of Speaker Tip O'Neill* (New York: Random House, 1987), 26.
8. See the interesting evidence of the influence of moneyed interests on congressional decision making marshalled by Richard L. Hall and Frank M. Wayman, "Buying Time: Moneyed Interests and the Mobilization of Bias in Congressional Committees," *American Political Science Review* 84 (September 1990): 797-820.
9. James M. Burns, *The Deadlock of Democracy: Four Party Politics in America* (Englewood Cliffs, N.J.: Prentice Hall, 1963), 236-237. For an instructive study of state party organizations and leaders, see Robert J. Huckshorn, *Party*

Leadership in the States (Amherst: University of Massachusetts Press, 1976).

10. See Cornelius P. Cotter, James L. Gibson, John F. Bibby, and Robert J. Huckshorn, *Party Organizations in American Politics* (New York: Praeger, 1984); and Bibby, Cotter, Gibson, and Huckshorn, "Parties in State Politics," in *Politics in the American States: A Comparative Analysis*, ed. Virginia Gray, Herbert Jacob, and Kenneth Vines (Boston: Little, Brown, 1983).

11. Barbara G. Salmore and Stephen A. Salmore, *Candidates, Parties, and Campaigns: Electoral Politics in America* (Washington, D.C.: CQ Press, 1989), 255-256.

12. Burdett Loomis, *The New American Politician: Ambition, Entrepreneurship, and the Changing Face of Political Life* (New York: Basic Books, 1988), 244.

13. Representative Foley made this statement prior to becoming Speaker; he is quoted in Austin Ranney, *The Referendum Device* (Washington, D.C.: American Enterprise Institute for Public Policy Research, 1981), 70. Ranney is cited in Salmore and Salmore, *Candidates, Parties, and Campaigns,* 248.

14. This section on law and the parties is based primarily on the findings of David E. Price, *Bringing Back the Parties* (Washington, D.C.: CQ Press, 1984), especially Chapter 5. Contrast the heavily regulated parties of today with those of half a century ago described by E. E. Schattschneider in *Party Government* (New York: Holt, Rinehart and Winston, 1942), 11: "The extralegal character of political parties is one of their most notable qualities."

15. The competitiveness of presidential elections also can be examined from the perspective of the electoral college. Of the forty-six presidential elections held between 1876 and 1968, twenty-one can be classified as "hairbreadth elections"—those in which a slight shift in popular votes in a few states would have changed the outcome in the electoral college. See Lawrence D. Longley and Alan G. Braun, *The Politics of Electoral College Reform* (New Haven, Conn.: Yale University Press, 1972), especially 37-41.

16. *Congressional Quarterly Weekly Report*, May 6, 1989, 1060-1065.

17. On this point, see especially Richard F. Fenno, Jr., *Home Style: House Members in Their Districts* (Boston: Little, Brown, 1978), 10-18; and Thomas E. Mann, *Unsafe at Any Margin: Interpreting Congressional Elections* (Washington, D.C.: American Enterprise Institute for Public Policy Research, 1978).

18. The literature on legislative-constituency relations, which includes examination of the incumbency factor in elections, is impressive. Anyone who takes the time to read the following studies on the subject will know vastly more than any normal person should know: David R. Mayhew, "Congressional Elections: The Case of the Vanishing Marginals," *Polity* 6 (Spring 1974): 295-317; Gary C. Jacobson, "The Effects of Campaign Spending in Congressional Elections," *American Political Science Review* 72 (June 1978): 469-491; Jon R. Bond, Gary Covington, and Richard Fleisher, "Explaining Challenger Quality in Congressional Elections," *Journal of Politics* 47 (May 1985): 510-529; Donald A. Gross and James C. Garrand, "The Vanishing Marginals, 1824-1980," *Journal of Politics* 46 (February 1984): 224-237; Robert S. Erikson and Gerald C. Wright, "Voters, Candidates, and Issues in Congressional Elections," in *Congress Reconsidered*, 3d ed., ed. Lawrence C. Dodd and Bruce I. Oppenheimer (Washington, D.C.: CQ Press, 1985), 87-108; John C. McAdams and John R. Johannes, "Constituency Attentiveness in the House: 1977-1982," *Journal of Politics* 47 (November 1985): 1108-1139; Glenn R. Parker and Suzanne L. Parker, "Correlates and Effects of Attention to District by U.S.

House Members," *Legislative Studies Quarterly* 10 (May 1985): 223-242; Melissa P. Collie, "Incumbency, Electoral Safety, and Turnover in the House of Representatives, 1952-1976," *American Political Science Review* 75 (March 1981): 119-131; John R. Alford and John R. Hibbing, "Increased Incumbency Advantage in the House," *Journal of Politics* 43 (November 1981): 1042-1061; James E. Campbell, "The Return of the Incumbents: The Nature of the Incumbency Advantage," *Western Political Quarterly* 36 (September 1983): 434-444; Diana Evans Yiannakis, "The Grateful Electorate: Casework and Congressional Elections," *American Journal of Political Science* 25 (August 1981): 568-580; Richard Born, "Generational Replacement and the Growth of Incumbent Reelection Margins in the U.S. House," *American Political Science Review* 73 (September 1979): 811-817; Candice J. Nelson, "The Effect of Incumbency on Voting in Congressional Elections, 1964-1974," *Political Science Quarterly* 93 (Winter 1978-1979): 665-678; John R. Johannes and John C. McAdams, "The Congressional Incumbency Effect: Is it Casework, Policy Compatibility, or Something Else?" *American Journal of Political Science* 25 (August 1981): 512-542; Warren Lee Kostroski, "Party and Constituency in Postwar Senate Elections," *American Political Science Review* 67 (December 1973): 1213-1234; and Lyn Ragsdale, "Incumbent Popularity, Challenger Invisibility, and Congressional Voters," *Legislative Studies Quarterly* 6 (May 1981): 201-218. And see these books: David R. Mayhew, *Congress: The Electoral Connection* (New Haven, Conn.: Yale University Press, 1974); Fenno, *Home Style*; Gary C. Jacobson and Samuel Kernell, *Strategy and Choice in Congressional Elections* (New Haven, Conn.: Yale University Press, 1981); and Gary C. Jacobson, *The Politics of Congressional Elections* (Boston: Little, Brown, 1987), especially Chapter 3.

19. See Austin Ranney, "Parties in State Politics," in *Politics in the American States*, ed. Herbert Jacob and Kenneth Vines (Boston: Little, Brown, 1976), 63-65; and Bibby, Cotter, Gibson, and Huckshorn, "Parties in State Politics," 59-96.

20. For analysis of the dualism theme, see V. O. Key, Jr., *Politics, Parties, and Pressure Groups* (New York: Crowell, 1964), 207-208.

21. Major party nominees are automatically given access to the general election ballot. Minor, new party, and independent candidates have to qualify for the ballot by establishing a certain level of support, which is set by state law. For an analysis of ballot access laws, see Bruce W. Robeck and James A. Dyer, "Ballot Access Requirements in Congressional Elections," *American Politics Quarterly* 10 (January 1982): 31-45.

22. Maurice Duverger, *Political Parties* (New York: Wiley, 1965), 17.

23. As provided by the Constitution, each of the two regular sessions that make up a Congress convenes at noon on January 3, unless a different day is appointed. Thus, the 101st Congress actually runs from 1989 to 1991; the first session from 1989 to 1990, the second session from 1990 to 1991. For the sake of clarity, however, this technicality will be sidestepped. Congress usually adjourns some time before the new year. So, in effect, the life of the 101st Congress, for example, is from 1989 to 1990; the first session covering the year 1989, the second session 1990.

24. *Congressional Quarterly Weekly Report*, December 30, 1989, 3551-3555.

25. For a study of the decline of party unity in both parties in the lower house of Congress, see Barbara Deckard Sinclair and John Stanley, "Party Decomposi-

tion and Region: The House of Representatives, 1945-1970," *Western Political Quarterly* 27 (June 1974): 249-264. A major explanation for the decline has been the growth of regional and ideological cleavages within the parties. Most notable for their declining party unity scores from 1945 to 1970 were eastern Republicans (more liberal than their party colleagues) and southern Democrats (more conservative than their party colleagues). For the most part, regional cleavages within the parties are due to ideological differences.

26. Key, *Politics, Parties, and Pressure Groups*, 221.
27. Schattschneider, *Party Government*, 133-137.
28. Schattschneider, *Party Government*, 134.
29. In 1973 the United States Supreme Court upheld, in a 5-4 decision, a New York state law that requires a voter to register his party affiliation thirty days in advance of a general election to be eligible to vote in that party's next primary election. Had the Court not upheld this "closed" provision, nothing would prevent voters from switching parties as often as they like, permitting Democrats to vote in Republican primaries and Republicans to vote in Democratic primaries. *Rosario v. Rockefeller*, 410 U.S. 752 (1973).
30. *The People, the Press, and Politics, 1990* (Washington, D.C.: Times Mirror Center for the People and the Press, 1990), 32, 2.

Political Parties and
the Electoral Process:
Nominations

IT IS PROBABLE that no nation has ever experimented as fully or as fitfully with mechanisms for making nominations as has the United States. The principal sponsor of this experimentation is the federal system itself. Under it, responsibility for the development of election law lies with the states. Their ingenuity, given free rein, has often been remarkable. A wide variety of caucuses, conventions, and primaries—the three principal methods of making nominations—has been tried out in the states. The devices that have lasted owe their survival not so much to a widespread agreement on their merits as to the inability of opponents to settle on alternative arrangements and to the general indifference of the public at large to major institutional change.

Nominating Methods

Caucus

The oldest device for making nominations in the United States is the caucus. In use prior to the adoption of the Constitution, the caucus is an informal meeting of political leaders held to decide questions concerning candidates, strategies, and policies. The essence of the caucus idea, when applied to nominations, is that by sifting, sorting, and weeding out candidates before the election, leaders can assemble substantial support behind a single candidate, thus decreasing the prospect that the votes of like-minded citizens will be split among several candidates. Historically, the most important form of caucus was the legislative caucus, which, until 1824, was used successfully for the nomination of candidates for state and national offices, including the presidency. The major drawback to the legislative caucus was that membership was limited to the party members in the legislature, thereby exposing the caucus to the charge that it was unrepresentative and undemocratic. A modest reform in the legislative caucus occurred when provisions were made for seating delegates from districts held by the opposition party. Nevertheless, when the (Jeffersonian) Republican caucus failed to nominate Andrew Jackson for the presidency in 1824, it came under severe criticism from many quarters and shortly thereafter was abandoned for the selection of presidential nominees. (But another form of caucus survives in the presidential nominating process. See the subsequent analysis of the caucus-convention system for choosing delegates to the parties' national nominating conventions.)

Party Conventions

Advocates of reform in the nominating process turned to the party convention, already in use in some localities, as a substitute for the legislative caucus. The great merit of the convention system, it was argued, was that it could provide for representation, on a geographical basis, of all elements within the party. The secrecy of the caucus was displaced in favor of a more public arena, with nominations made by conventions composed of delegates drawn from various levels of the party organizations. As the convention method gained in prominence, so did the party organizations; state and local party leaders came to play a dominant role in the selection of candidates.

The convention system, however, failed to live up to its early promise. Although it has been used for the nomination of presidential candidates from the 1830s to the present, it has given way to the direct primary for most other offices. Critics found that it suffered from essentially the same disabling properties as the caucus. In their view, it was sheer pretense to contend that the conventions were representative of the parties as a whole; instead, they were run by party bosses without regard either for the views of the delegates or for the rules of fair play. A great many charges involving corruption in voting practices and procedures were made, and there was much truth in them. Growing regulation of conventions by the legislatures failed to assuage the doubts of the public. The direct primary came into favor as reformers came to understand its potential as a device for dismantling the structure of boss and machine influence and for introducing popular control over nominations.

Direct Primary

Popular control of the political process has always been an important issue in the dogma of reformers. The direct primary, with its emphasis on voters instead of on party organization, was hard to resist. Once Wisconsin adopted it for nomination of candidates for state elective offices in 1903, its use spread steadily throughout the country. Connecticut became the last state to adopt it, in 1955, but only after much tampering with the idea. The Connecticut model (the challenge primary) combines convention and primary under an arrangement in which the party convention continues to make nominations, but with this proviso: if the party nominee at the convention is challenged by another candidate who receives as much as 20 percent of the convention votes, a primary must be held later. Otherwise, no primary is required, and the name of the convention nominee is automatically certified for the general election.

Part of the attractiveness of the primary is its apparent simplicity. From one perspective, it is a device for transferring control of nominations from the party leadership to the rank-and-file voters; from another, it shifts this control from the party organization to the state. The primary rests on state law: it is an official election held at public expense, on a date set by the legislature, and supervised by public officials. It has often been interpreted as an attempt to institutionalize intraparty democracy.

It is not surprising that the direct primary has had a better reception in reformist circles than anywhere else. For the party organization, it poses problems, not opportunities. If the organization becomes involved in a contested primary for a major office, it probably will have to raise large sums of money for the campaign of its candidate. If it remains neutral, it may wind up with a candidate who either is hostile to the organization or is unsympathetic toward its programs and policies. Even if it abandons neutrality, there is no guarantee that its candidate will win; indeed, a good many political careers have been launched in primaries in which the nonendorsed candidate has convinced the voters that a vote for him is a vote to crush the machine. Finally, the primary often works at cross purposes with the basic party objective of harmonizing its diverse elements by creating a balanced ticket for the general election. The voters are much less likely to nominate a representative slate of candidates, one that recognizes all major groups within the party, than is the party leadership. Moreover, if the primary battle turns out to be bitter, the winner may enter the general election campaign with a sharply divided party behind him.[1] It is no wonder that some political leaders have viewed the primary as a systematically conceived effort to bring down the party itself.

Types of Primaries

Four basic types of state primaries are in use: *closed, open, blanket,* and *nonpartisan.* Two special forms of primaries are also used: *runoff* and *presidential* (the latter is analyzed in the section on the presidential nominating process).

Closed Primary

Twenty-six states use a closed primary to make nominations.[2] The key feature of this primary is that the voter can participate in the nomination of candidates only in the party to which he belongs—and this is established through registration as a party member.[3] State laws vary substantially in the ease with which voters can switch back and forth between the parties. Voters in the closed primary states of Iowa, Ohio, and Wyoming, for example, can change their party registration on election day—a provision that makes their systems palpably open. Other closed primary states establish a deadline for changing parties sometime prior to primary election day. South Dakota sets this deadline at a mere fifteen days and Oregon at twenty days, while New York and Kentucky set it at about eleven months. The mean requirement is roughly two months. Some closed primary states prohibit voters from switching parties once the candidates have filed declarations of candidacies, while other less restrictive states encourage "voter floating" by permitting changes in party registration after candidates have declared themselves. Sharp differences exist among closed primary states in how they foster or protect party efficacy and integrity.[4]

Other differences in closed primary systems may result from the 1986 Supreme Court ruling in *Tashjian v. Republican Party of Connecticut*. The case arose from the efforts of the Connecticut state Republican party to attract independents by permitting them to vote in its primary elections. Unable to change the state's closed primary law in the legislature, the party successfully challenged it in court. By a 5-4 vote, the Supreme Court ruled that states may not require political parties to hold closed primaries that permit only voters previously enrolled in a party to vote. This ruling leaves the choice of primary system to the parties instead of to state legislatures. Hence, a state party may choose to open its primary to unaffiliated (or independent) voters or it may choose to bar their participation. Within a year of the Court's decision, seven other states enacted enabling legislation under which a party could permit unaffiliated voters to vote in its primary. The *Tashjian* decision does not outlaw closed primaries, and presumably many state parties will continue to permit only registered party members to vote in their primaries.[5]

Open Primary

From the point of view of the party organization, the open primary is less desirable than the closed primary. Twenty-one states (not counting states that use blanket or nonpartisan primaries) have some form of open primary—defined as one in which the voter is not required to register as a party member to vote in a party primary. Provisions for open primaries differ from state to state. In nine states the voter is given the ballots of all parties, with instructions to vote for the candidates of only one party and to discard the other ballots.[6] Nothing can prevent Democrats from voting to nominate Republican candidates or Republicans from voting to nominate Democratic candidates. The strongest appeal of this form of open primary is that it preserves the secrecy of the voter's affiliation or preference.

In the other twelve open primary states, voters are required to declare a party preference at the polls to obtain a ballot. In some states the declaration is recorded by election officials and in other states it is not. A voter's right to participate in a particular primary may be challenged. Interestingly, switching parties from one primary to the next in certain open primary states, such as Rhode Island, is more difficult than switching in certain closed primary states, such as Iowa.

Party leaders suffer from a special anxiety in open primary states: the possibility that voters of the competing party will raid their primary, hoping to nominate a weak candidate who would be easy to defeat in the general election. Whether raiding occurs with any frequency is difficult to say, but in some states large numbers of voters do cross over to vote in the other party's primary when an exciting contest is present. One of the central arguments used by the state of Connecticut in the *Tashjian* case was the party's need to protect itself from raiding by members of the other party. The Supreme Court found this defense of the closed primary "insubstantial."

The use of open (crossover) primaries in the presidential nominating process has been a continuing source of aggravation for some party leaders, since these primaries permit nonparty members to influence the choice of a party's nominee. In Wisconsin, one study has shown, roughly 8 to 11 percent of all voters in presidential primaries are partisan crossovers—that is, Democrats voting in the Republican primary or Republicans voting in the Democratic primary. And a surprising one-third of each party's primary participants are self-styled independents. In a close race, the presence of these outsiders can make a difference in the outcome.[7]

To combat crossover voting, the charter of the Democratic party, adopted in 1974, specified that delegates to the party's national convention be chosen through procedures that limit participation to Democratic voters. Despite this provision, Wisconsin continued to permit voters to participate in the state's Democratic presidential primary without regard to party affiliation. When delegates were later chosen in the Democratic caucus system, they were obligated to vote in accordance with the voters' presidential preferences as revealed in the open primary. In a decision designed to protect party processes, the Supreme Court ruled in 1981 that states could continue to hold open presidential primaries, but that the results did not have to be recognized in selecting state party delegates to the convention.[8] The effect of this decision was to require Wisconsin in 1984 to select its delegates in closed caucuses—that is, caucuses limited to Democrats only. This restriction did not last long. In the belief that the "Democrats only" provision had produced considerable ill will and had narrowed the party's base, the Democratic National Committee (DNC) voted in 1986 to permit Wisconsin Democrats to return to their traditional open primary, in which independents and Republicans can participate. This new rule thus accepts the open-primary heritage of states such as Wisconsin and Montana, but it does not permit other states to change their systems by opening their delegate selection processes to members of other parties.

Blanket Primary

The states of Alaska and Washington complete the circle of open primary systems with what is known as a blanket primary. No primary is quite so open. Nor does any other provide voters with a greater range of choice. Under its provisions the voter is given a ballot listing all candidates of all parties under each office. Voters may vote for a Democrat for one office and for a Republican for another office. Or they may vote for the candidate of a third party. They cannot vote for more than one candidate per office. The blanket primary is an invitation to ticket splitting.

Nonpartisan Primary

In a number of states, judges, school board members, and other local government officials are selected in nonpartisan primaries. State legislators in Nebraska are also selected on this basis. The scheme itself is simple: the two candidates receiving the greatest number of votes are nominated; in turn, they oppose each other in the general election. No party labels appear on the ballot in either election. The nonpartisan primary is defended on the grounds that partisanship should not be permitted to intrude on the selection of certain officials, such as judges. By eliminating the party label, runs the assumption, the issues and divisiveness that dominate national and state party politics can be kept out of local elections and local offices. Although nonpartisan primaries muffle the sounds of party, they do not eliminate them. It is not uncommon for the party organizations to slip quietly into the political process and to recruit and support candidates in these primaries; in such cases, about all that is missing is the party label on the ballot.

Since 1975 Louisiana has had an "open elections" law that renders its primaries nonpartisan. Under this system, all candidates for an office are grouped together in a primary election. A candidate who receives a majority of the primary vote is elected, thus eliminating the need for a general election. If no candidate obtains a majority of the votes cast, the top two, irrespective of party affiliation, face each other in a runoff general election. Among the apparent effects of the open elections law have been a pronounced advantage for incumbents, new difficulties for the Republican party, a growing number of candidates who have no party affiliation, costlier campaigns, and, perhaps most important, the development of institutionalized multifactionalism—marked by intensified campaigning at the primary stage with numerous candidates competing for the same office. Party obviously counts for little in the Louisiana setting. Even the ballot has been modified, changing from party column to office block as a means of inhibiting straight party voting.[9]

Runoff Primary

The runoff or second primary is a by-product of a one-party political environment. As used in southern states, this primary provides that if no candidate obtains a majority of the votes cast for an office, a runoff is held between the two leading candidates. The runoff primary is an attempt to come to terms with a chronic problem of a one-party system—essentially all competition is jammed into the primary of the dominant party. With numerous candidates seeking the nomination for the same office, the vote is likely to be sharply split, with no candidate receiving a majority. A runoff between the top two candidates in the first primary provides a guarantee, if only statistical, that one candidate will emerge as the choice of a majority of voters. This is no small consideration in those southern states where the Democratic primary has long been the real election and where factionalism within the party has been so intense that no candidate would stand much of a chance of consolidating his party position without two primaries—the first to weed out the losers, and the second to endow the winner with the legitimacy a majority can offer.

An Overview of the Primary

The great virtue of the direct primary, from the perspective of its early Progressive sponsors, was its democratic component, its promise for changing the accent and scope of popular participation in the political system. Its immediate effect, it was hoped, would be to diminish the influence of political organization on political life. What is the evidence that the primary has accomplished its mission? What impact has it had on political party organization?

An important outcome of having the primary system is that party leaders have been sensitized to the interests and feelings of the most active rank-and-file members. Fewer nominations are cut and dried. Even though candidates who secure the organization's endorsement win more frequently than they lose, their prospects often are uncertain.[10] The possibility of a revolt against the organization, carried out in the primary, forces party leaders to take account of the elements that make up the party and to pay attention to the claims of potential candidates. There is always a chance—in some jurisdictions, a strong possibility— that an aspirant overlooked by the leadership will decide to challenge the party's choice in the primary. The primary thus induces caution among party leaders. A hands-off policy—one in which the party makes no endorsement—is sometimes the party's only response. If it has no candidate, it cannot lose; some party leaders have been able to stay in business by avoiding the embarrassment that comes from primary defeats. In some jurisdictions, party intervention in the primary is never even considered, so accustomed is the electorate to party-free contests. For the public at large, the main contribution of the primary is that it opens up the political process.

The primary has not immobilized party organizations, but it has caused a number of problems for them. Party leaders' lack of enthusiasm for primaries is not hard to understand knowing that, among other things, the primary (1) greatly increases party campaign costs (if the party backs a candidate in a contested primary); (2) diminishes the capacity of the organization to reward its supporters through nominations; (3) makes it difficult for the party to influence nominees who establish their own power bases in the primary electorate; (4) creates opportunities for people hostile to party leadership and party policies to capture nominations; (5) permits anyone to wear the party label and opens the possibility that the party will have to repudiate a candidate who has been thrust upon it; and (6) increases intraparty strife and factionalism.[11] It seems no institution is better designed than the primary to stultify party organization and party processes.

On the whole, the primary has not fulfilled the expectations of its sponsors. Several things have gone awry. To begin, competitiveness has been absent in primaries. The surprising number of nominations won by default may be because of any of several reasons. For one, uncontested primaries may be evidence of party strength—that is, potential candidates stop short of entering the primary because their prospects appear slim for defeating the organization's choice. Second, the deserted primary simply may demonstrate the pragmatism of politicians: they do not struggle to win nominations that are unlikely to lead anywhere. As V. O. Key and others have shown, primaries are most likely to be contested when the chances are strong that the winner will be elected to office in the general election and will be least likely to be contested when the nomination appears to have little value.[12] Thus, the tendency is for electoral battles to occur in competitive districts or in the primary of the dominant party. Third, the presence of an incumbent reduces competition for a nomination. In House elections between 1956 and 1974, Harvey L. Schantz has shown, 55 percent of all Democratic primaries were contested when no incumbent was running, and only 37 percent when an incumbent was in the race; for Republican primaries, the percentages were 44 and 20, respectively. Overall, the prospects for primary contests are greatest in districts in which a party has no incumbent but has a reasonable chance to win in November.[13]

Experience with the primary has also shown that it is one thing to shape an institution so as to induce popular participation and quite another to realize it. No fact about primaries is more familiar than that large numbers of voters assiduously ignore them. A majority of voters usually stay away from the polls on primary day, even when major statewide races are to be settled. A turnout of 25 to 30 percent of the eligible electorate is the norm in many jurisdictions. The promise of the primary is thus only partially fulfilled. The reality is that the public is not keenly interested in the nominating process.

The National Convention

The American national convention is surely one of the most remarkable institutions in the world for making nominations. In use since the Jacksonian Era, it is the official agency for the selection of each party's candidates for president and vice president and for the ratification of each party's platform. At the same time, it is the party's supreme policy-making authority, empowered to make the rules that govern party affairs.

The national convention historically has served another function of prime importance to the parties. It has been a meeting ground for the party itself, one where leaders could tap rank-and-file sentiments and where the divergent interests that make up each party could, at least in some fashion, be accommodated. In its classic role, the national convention presents an opportunity for the national party—the fifty state parties assembled—to come to terms with itself, permitting leading politicians to strike the necessary balances and to settle temporarily the continuing questions of leadership and policy. Under the press of other changes in the presidential nominating process, however, the party role in conventions has recently been diminished.

Until the 1970s, national convention decisions could best be explained by examining the central role of national, state, and local party leaders and the behavior of state delegations. These were the "power points" in the classic model of convention politics, aptly described by the authors of *Explorations in Convention Decision Making:*

> Historically, state delegations have been thought to be the key units for bargaining in conventions; operating under the unit rule, they bargain with each other and with candidate organizations. The rank-and-file delegates are manipulated by hierarchical leaders holding important positions in national, state, and local party organizations. In order to enhance their bargaining position, these leaders often try to stay uncommitted to any candidate until the moment that their endorsement is crucial to victory for the ultimate nominee. After the presidential balloting is over, the vice presidential nomination is awarded to a person whose selection will mollify those elements of the party who did not support the presidential choice. At the end of the convention, all groups rally around the ticket and the party receives a boost in starting the fall campaign.[14]

The classic model of convention decision making bears only modest resemblance to the patterns of influence at play in the most recent party conventions. In broad terms, decentralization of power is now the chief characteristic of the struggle for the presidential nomination. State delegations have given way to candidate blocs in importance, and party leaders have been displaced by the leaders of candidate organizations. Party leaders have few resources with which to bargain in those state delegations that are split among candidates. The governor who heads a state delegation may be nothing more than a figurehead; meetings of many state delegations are concerned more with announcements (for example, bus departures for the convention site) and ceremonies than with strategy. In contrast, the action is found in the candidate caucuses, where the strategy sessions on candidates, rules, and platform planks occur. Uncommitted delegates have become less numerous than in the past. (But see the subsequent discussion of a change that increases the number of uncommitted delegates at the Democratic convention.) Today's party conventions are dominated by candidates and their organizations. Accordingly, the influence that party and elected officials wield in conventions is largely a product of their affiliation with one of the candidate organizations.

The decline of the party presence in national conventions results from a confluence of forces: the new delegate selection rules that both opened up the parties to amateur activists and contributed to the spread of presidential primaries, the capacity of candidates to dominate campaign fund raising (using government subsidies under a matching system since 1976), and the general weakness of state and local party organizations.[15] The reliance of candidates on party leaders in the preconvention period has never been less—in most states, party leaders cannot do much either to help or to hurt a candidate's chances to win delegates. What matters to the candidate is winning the immediate primary or placing well (as judged by the mass media) to attract new funds and to build momentum for the next contest. In the modern scheme of campaigning, expert consultants, an active personal organization spread out around the state, and the mass media loom much more important to the candidates than the party structures and party leaders.

Selection of Delegates

National convention delegates are chosen by two methods: presidential primaries and caucus-conventions. Each state chooses its own system, and it is not unusual for a state to switch from one method to another between elections in response to criticisms by the press, by the public, and by politicians unhappy about recent outcomes.

Loosely managed by the parties, the caucus-convention system provides for the election of delegates by rank-and-file members (mixed with candidate enthusiasts) from one level of the party to the next— ordinarily from precinct caucuses to county conventions to the state convention and from there to the national convention. The first-tier caucuses (mass meetings at the precinct level) are crucial, since they establish the delegate strength of each candidate in the subsequent conventions, including the national. Candidates and their organizations must turn out their supporters for these initial party meetings; a loss at this stage cannot be reversed.

At one time the chief criticism of the caucus-convention system was that it was essentially closed, dominated by a few party leaders who selected themselves, key public officials, "fat cats" (major financial contributors), and lesser party officials as delegates. The democratizing reforms of the 1970s changed all this, opening up the caucuses to participation by average party members and short-term activists willing to spend an afternoon or evening in discussion and voting. Today, the delegate-selection caucuses are dominated by competing candidate organizations and their enthusiasts, and prominent party officials may or may not be found in their ranks. Preoccupied with the struggle for delegates, the media pay scant attention to the caucus as a party event.

In 1988 about one-third of the states, mainly small and medium-sized ones, used the caucus-convention system for the selection of their delegates. Although party leaders no longer dominate caucus decisions and vastly more people now participate in the caucus process, caucus turnout is still not high in comparison with primary states. Only about 800,000 voters took part in the states' first-round Democratic caucuses in 1988; on the Republican side, caucus participation was even spottier. (For the Republicans, about 200,000 first-round caucus votes were tabulated in ten states; in the remaining states, no votes were even recorded.)[16]

The enthusiasm among party regulars for the caucus-convention system appears to be waning. This method poses major problems for them. In some caucus states party regulars have been reduced to by-standers as candidate organizations, bolstered by amateur enthusiasts, vie with one another for votes and delegates. Intraparty conflict has also erupted more frequently in caucus than in primary states. Finally, party leaders are sensitive to the charge that caucus results may not be representative of voter sentiment generally. For these reasons, particularly the last one, more states likely will adopt presidential primaries in the 1990s.[17]

Used by almost all of the populous states, presidential primaries are easier for the public to understand. A large majority of each state's delegates is chosen on primary day by the direct vote of the people; the remaining delegates are chosen through party processes following the primary. This method was introduced in the early twentieth century. Like the direct primary used to nominate national, state, and local officials, the presidential primary was designed to wrest control of nominations from the bosses (the party professionals) and to place it in the hands of the people by permitting them to choose the delegates to the nominating conventions in a public election. In 1904 Florida became the first state to adopt a presidential primary law. In little more than a decade, about half of the states had adopted some version of it. Its use since then has fluctuated. Only sixteen states and the District of Columbia held presidential primaries in 1968. The popularity of this device grew in the 1970s, and thirty-five states, plus Puerto Rico and the District of Columbia, held primaries in 1980. The number fell again in 1984, when the Democratic party held primaries in twenty-eight states, the District of Columbia, and Puerto Rico, and the Republican party held them in twenty-four states. In 1988 each party held primaries in thirty-five states, the District of Columbia, and Puerto Rico. In several of these states the results were nonbinding, with delegates chosen separately in party caucuses. No Democratic candidates even filed to be on the North Dakota primary ballot. Altogether, for the 1988 conventions, 67 percent of the Democratic delegates and 77 percent of the Republican delegates were chosen in primaries.[18]

The broad objective of presidential primaries is to encourage popular participation in the presidential nominating process.[19] In 1988 twenty-three million people voted in Democratic primaries and some twelve million in Republican primaries, an increase of about one-third over 1984. About one million voters participated in caucuses.[20] Thus about thirty-six million voters took part in the presidential nominating process, as contrasted with nearly ninety-two million people who voted in the general election. Neither participation in the nominating process nor in the general election is impressive, but it is at least improving in the former.

Prior to the 1970s, the manner in which national convention delegates were selected was left to the states. Today, the Democratic party in particular tightly regulates the methods of delegate selection. The dimensions of national party control can best be appreciated by examining Table 3-1, which includes certain major rules in effect for the 1992 Democratic National Convention. In the selection of delegates, the rules make clear, not much is left to chance or to the discretion of individual state parties.

An amalgam of recommendations by five party study commissions, stretching from 1969 to 1985, the rules were designed to serve several major objectives: (1) to stimulate the participation of rank-and-file Democratic voters in the presidential nominating process; (2) to increase the representation of certain demographic groups (particularly women, blacks, and young people) in the convention through the use of guidelines on delegate selection; (3) to eliminate procedures held to be undemocratic (such as the unit rule, under which a majority of a state delegation could cast the state's total vote for a single candidate); (4) to enhance the local character of delegate elections (by requiring 75 percent of the delegates in each state to be elected at the congressional district level or lower); and (5) to provide through proportional representation that elected delegates fairly reflect the presidential candidate preferences of Democratic voters in primary states and Democratic participants in caucus-convention states. (The proportional representation rule was relaxed in the 1980s but reinstituted for 1992.)

For many members of the first commission, the McGovern-Fraser Commission, the underlying objective was to diminish the power of party professionals in the convention, while at the same time increasing that of party members and activists at the local level. They succeeded in extraordinary degree. A new type of participant, to whom candidates and issues were central, came to predominate in the Democratic convention. Party professionals were thoroughly overshadowed in the 1972 and 1976 conventions.[21] Party leaders and public officials gradually have been readmitted since then. Following a recommendation of the Winograd Commission, the Democratic National Committee adopted a provision to expand each 1980 state delegation by 10 percent to include prominent party and elected officials. That provision set the stage for further change. In 1982 the Democratic party again revised its rules to augment the influence of professional politicians in the convention. Adopting a recommendation of the Hunt Commission, the DNC added a bloc of 568 uncommitted party and elected officials as delegates to the 1984 convention. Members of this group—sometimes referred to as superdelegates— were chosen by virtue of the public or party office that they held; nearly two hundred Democratic members of Congress, for example, were selected by House and Senate party caucuses. Continuing to grope for the proper balance in the 1988 convention, the Fairness Commission (the fifth such reform commission in a decade and a half) recommended an increase in the number of superdelegates to about 650. This increase was approved by the Democratic National Committee in 1986.

But that did not end the matter. To satisfy Jesse Jackson's objec-

TABLE 3-1   Principal Delegate Selection Rules for the 1992 Democratic National Convention

---

Rule 1A: State parties shall adopt affirmative action and delegate selection plans which contain explicit rules and procedures governing all aspects of the delegate selection process. . . .

1C: State delegate selection and affirmative action plans shall be submitted to the DNC [Democratic National Committee] Rules and Bylaws Committee for approval. . . .

2A: Participation in the delegate selection process shall be open to all voters who wish to participate as Democrats.

2C: Nothing in these rules shall be interpreted to encourage or permit states with party registration and enrollment, or states that limit participation to Democrats only, to amend their systems to open participation to members of other parties.

3A: All official party meetings and events related to the national convention delegate selection process . . . shall be scheduled for dates, times, and public places which would be most likely to encourage the participation of all Democrats, and must begin and end at reasonable hours.

5C: In order to achieve full participation by groups that are significantly underrepresented in our party's affairs, each state party shall develop and submit party outreach programs, including recruitment, education and training, in order to achieve full participation by such groups in the delegate selection process and at all levels of party affairs.

6A: In order to encourage full participation by all Democrats in the delegate selection process and in all party affairs, the national and state Democratic parties shall adopt and implement affirmative action programs with specific goals and timetables for African Americans, Hispanics, Native Americans, Asian/Pacific Americans and women.

6C: State delegate selection plans shall provide for equal division between delegate men and delegate women. . . .

6G: Each state affirmative action program shall include outreach provisions to encourage the participation and representation of persons of low and moderate income. . . .

7C: Seventy-five percent (75%) of each state's base delegation shall be elected at the congressional district level or lower. Twenty-five percent (25%) of each state's base delegation shall be elected at large.

7D: In those states with more than one congressional district, after the election of district-level delegates and prior to the selection of at-large delegates, each state Democratic Chair shall certify pledged party leader and elected official delegates equal to 15% of the state's base delegation. . . .

8A: [Unpledged party leader and elected official delegates shall include] members of the DNC . . . Democratic governors . . . all former Democratic presidents, all former Democratic vice presidents, all former Democratic majority leaders of the U.S. Senate, and all former Democratic Speakers of the U.S. House of Representatives . . . four-fifths of the U.S. House of Representatives and U.S. Senate . . . big city mayors and state-wide elected officials ... state legislative leaders ... state legislators ... members of Congress not previously selected and other state, county and local elected officials and party leaders.

9A: The selection of at-large delegates shall be used, if necessary, to achieve the equal division of positions between men and women and the representation goals established in the state party's affirmative action plan.

10A: No meetings, caucuses, conventions or primaries which constitute the first determining stage in the presidential nomination process ... may be held prior to the first Tuesday in March or after the second Tuesday in June in the calendar year of the national convention. Provided, however, that the Iowa precinct caucuses may be held no earlier than 15 days before the first Tuesday in March; that the New Hampshire primary may be held no earlier than 7 days before the first Tuesday in March; that the Maine first tier caucuses may be held no earlier than 2 days before the first Tuesday in March.

11A: All candidates for delegate in caucuses, conventions, committees and on primary ballots shall be identified as to presidential preference, uncommitted or unpledged status at all levels of a process which determines presidential preference.

11H: Delegates elected to the national convention pledged to a presidential candidate shall in all good conscience reflect the sentiments of those who elected them.

12A: Delegates shall be allocated in a fashion that fairly reflects the expressed presidential preference or uncommitted status of the primary voters or, if there is no binding primary, the convention and caucus participants. States shall allocate district level delegates and alternates in proportion to the percentage of the primary or caucus vote won in that district by each preference, except that preferences falling below a 15% threshold shall not be awarded any delegates.

12E: Under no circumstance shall the use of single-delegate districts be permitted.

16A: The unit rule, or any rule or practice whereby all members of a party unit or delegation may be required to cast their votes in accordance with the will of a majority of the body, shall not be used at any stage of the delegate selection process.

19C: In the event the delegate selection plan of a state party provides or permits a meeting, caucus, convention or primary which constitutes the first determining stage ... to be held prior to or after the dates for the state as provided in Rule 10 ... [the number of the state's delegates] shall be reduced by 25 percent. In addition, none of the members of the DNC from that state shall be permitted to vote as members of the state's delegation. ... [If a state violates proportional representation as provided in Rule 12] the delegation of the state shall be reduced [by 25 percent]. ... [If a state permits a threshold other than 15 percent] the delegation of the state shall be reduced [by 25 percent].

SOURCE: *Delegate Selection Rules for the 1992 Democratic National Convention* (Washington, D.C.: Democratic National Committee, 1990).

tions to superdelegates, few of whom were in his corner, Michael S. Dukakis agreed to cut their number sharply for the 1992 convention, eliminating almost all slots for Democratic National Committee members. Although this harmony pact between the candidates, designed to produce a united party, was easily ratified by the delegates, it did not survive for long. In 1989 the Democratic National Committee voted to restore superdelegate status to all DNC members. Hence, the party's 1992 convention will again have about 650 superdelegates—including the party's governors, members of Congress, DNC members, and numerous state and local officials. (See Rule 8A, Table 3-1.)

The manner in which delegates are allocated to candidates has been a persistent problem for the Democrats. Tinkering and temporizing, the party has vascillated between winner-take-all and proportional representation since the early 1970s. A close look at recent behavior is worthwhile—because in all probability the party has not concluded its experiments.

In 1988 the national Democratic rules permitted state parties to choose from among three broad plans. First, states could select the *proportional representation* method, under which any Democratic candidate who reached the threshold of the primary or caucus vote (15 percent, lowered from the 20 percent level used in most states in 1984) was entitled to a proportionate share of the delegates; candidates who failed to reach the threshold did not qualify for any delegates. Second, states could adopt what amounts to a *winner-take-all* system. In this direct-election form, voters cast ballots for individual delegates who were pledged to candidates or uncommitted. The candidate who came in first in a district could win all or most of the delegates instead of sharing them with the trailing candidates. Third, states could choose a *winner-take-more* plan. Here, the winning candidate in each district was given a bonus delegate before the rest were divided proportionally.

In 1988 the Democrats used strict proportional representation in thirty-five states, the district winner-take-all system in five states (Illinois, Maryland, New Jersey, Pennsylvania, and West Virginia), and the bonus system in ten states.[22] Either nonproportional scheme has been an attractive option for a populous state, since by permitting a candidate to claim a disproportionate number of delegates a state could magnify the importance of its contest. An impressive victory in Illinois or Pennsylvania was likely to yield more delegates and garner more media attention than modest victories in half a dozen smaller states where delegates were allocated proportionally and hence scattered among several candidates.

For the time being, in the Democratic party, nonproportional systems are banned. In 1992 all states are required to allocate their publicly elected delegates on a proportionate basis, giving each candidate who reaches the 15 percent threshold of the primary or caucus vote a fair share. This controversial change stemmed from the Jackson-Dukakis agreement in 1988; Jackson's delegate share had been adversely affected in winner-take-all states. In 1992 states that fail to comply with the proportional representation rule face the loss of 25 percent of their national convention delegates.

Proportional representation has had two controversial side effects. First, it permits the candidate who builds an early lead, the front-runner, to continue to pile up numerous delegates even in those states won by another candidate. It still takes a long time to nail down the nomination, however, since some other contenders will always reach the threshold and thus share in the distribution of delegates. Second, proportional representation prevents a trailing candidate from winning big— capturing a large share of the delegates in a populous state, as could occur under a winner-take-all arrangement.

The Republican party was considerably less active than the Democratic party in the 1970s and 1980s in restructuring its delegate selection rules, but it did make a few changes. Its current rules require open meetings for delegate selection; ban automatic (ex officio) delegates; and provide for the election, not the selection, of congressional district and at-large delegates (unless otherwise provided by state law). State Republican parties are urged to develop plans for increasing the participation of women, young people, minorities, and other groups in the presidential nominating process, but they are not required to do so. The push to nationalize party rules, pronounced among Democratic reformers for the past two decades, finds only limited support among Republicans. Rather, Republicans continue to stress the federal character of their party; the basic authority to reshape delegate selection rules rests accordingly with state parties.[23]

Republican delegate selection practices differ in several major respects from those of the Democrats. In the first place, Republicans have resisted the allure of proportionality in delegate allocation, placing much more emphasis on some version of winner-take-all. As observed by the chief counsel of the Republican National Committee, "the allocation of delegates to our convention has always been based in part on the

Democratic Party's Delegate Selection Rules . . .

In the Democratic party, national rules prescribe in detail how delegates to the national nominating convention are to be chosen. Initially, the reformers focused on means to make the party more open, the delegate selection process more democratic, and the delegates themselves more representative of major demographic groups. The recent commissions, by contrast, have sought chiefly to restore the influence of professional politicians in the convention and to give state parties somewhat wider latitude to formulate methods for selecting delegates.

For party officials, rule making is no day at the beach. Candidates, interests, party blocs, and state politicians must be accommodated. New rules, moreover, produce unanticipated consequences as well as winners and losers.

The one constant in Democratic presidential selection politics is change.

Intraparty Democracy

McGovern-Fraser Commission (1969-1972)

Developed rules to permit all Democratic voters a "full, meaningful, and timely" opportunity to take part in the presidential nominating process.

Required each state party to include in its delegation blacks, women, and young people in numbers roughly proportionate to their presence in the state population.

Required at least 75 percent of each state delegation to be selected at a level no higher than the congressional district.

Eliminated practices held to be undemocratic, such as the unit rule.

Mikulski Commission (1972-1973)

Reaffirmed many McGovern-Fraser guidelines.

Dropped "quotas" but required states to establish affirmative action plans to encourage full participation by all Democrats, with special efforts required to include minority groups, native Americans, women, and youth.

Required a fair reflection of voters' presidential preferences (thus proportional representation) at all levels of the delegate selection process, with a few exceptions.

Created a national party compliance review commission to monitor implementation of state affirmative action and delegate selection programs.

...*Key Provisions of Reform Commissions*

Intraparty Democracy and Party Renewal

Winograd Commission (1975-1978)

Specifically identified women, blacks, Hispanics, and native Americans as the objects of "remedial action to overcome the effects of past discrimination."

Shortened the period for delegate selection from six to three months.

Eliminated last vestiges of winner-take-all systems.

Outlawed "crossover" primaries.

Increased the size of state delegations by 10 percent to augment representation of top party leaders and elected officials.

Required delegates to vote for the presidential candidate they were elected to support for at least first ballot.

Voted not to require each state to have an equal number of men and women in its delegation, but the Democratic National Committee later adopted equal-division rule.

Party Renewal

Hunt Commission (1981-1982)

Retreated from proportional representation by permitting state parties to adopt winner-take-all or winner-take-more systems.

Provided that 14 percent of the delegates to the 1984 convention be chosen on the basis of their public office or party status ("superdelegates").

Tightened the primary-caucus "window" by reducing the period between the Iowa caucuses and the New Hampshire primary from thirty-six days to eight.

Eliminated binding first ballot for delegates.

Fairness Commission (1984-1985)

Increased number of superdelegates from 568 to about 650 for the 1988 convention.

Lowered threshold from 20 to 15 percent, thus making it easier for trailing candidates to share in the distribution of delegates.

Permitted Wisconsin and Montana to conduct open (or crossover) primaries, banned earlier by the Winograd Commission.

electoral college, which is winner-take-all. People who don't like that should argue with James Madison or Thomas Jefferson." [24] Second, the Republican party has no provision for the automatic selection of party or party officials—superdelegates in Democratic nomenclature. Third, the party has no requirement that state delegations be evenly divided between men and women, a rule imposed on state Democratic parties beginning in 1980. (Women delegates are nonetheless numerous in Republican conventions.) And finally, each state Republican party is free to schedule its presidential primary or caucus as it sees fit. The Michigan Republican party, for example, begins its delegate selection process almost two years in advance of the party's national convention.[25] On the Democratic side, the primary-caucus calendar is tightly governed by national party rules. Party differences in delegate selection reflect basic party differences in philosophy and organization that can be summed up in the appellations "federal" Republicans and "national" Democrats.

Evaluating Presidential Primary and Caucus-Convention Systems

Sometimes it appears as though the only persons who are satisfied with the presidential nominating process are the winners—the nominees and their supporters. Everyone else, it seems, can find reasons to be unhappy or frustrated about the process.

To the initiated and uninitiated voter alike, the primaries and caucuses are a mass of oppositions and paradoxes. Unpredictability reigns. Victory in a single state can be the key to the nomination. And victories in the early primaries and caucuses are usually crucial. Consider recent outcomes. In the judgment of many observers, on the day that John F. Kennedy defeated Hubert H. Humphrey in the West Virginia primary in 1960—a Catholic winning in an overwhelmingly Protestant state—he sewed up the nomination. In 1964 the critical Republican primary took place in California, where Barry Goldwater narrowly defeated Nelson Rockefeller. In 1972 George McGovern's nomination seemed to be guaranteed by his win in California. Jimmy Carter's string of early primary victories in 1976, beginning with his narrow win in New Hampshire, gave him a commanding lead. His weakness in late primaries, marked by several losses to California governor Jerry Brown, had no effect on the nomination. Challenged by Edward M. Kennedy and Jerry Brown in 1980, Carter again won the New Hampshire primary and five of the next six primaries, forcing Brown out of the race. Kennedy won ten of thirty-four primaries, but half of those victories came on the last day of the primary season, too late to matter. Although the Democratic struggle in 1984 was much different, a case can be made that Walter F. Mondale's successes in Alabama and Georgia on "Super Tuesday," the second Tuesday in March, were indispensable, serving to keep him from elimination after a series of media and real victories by Gary Hart. In 1988 Michael Dukakis's victory in New Hampshire was critical, following his third-place finish in Iowa. His clear-cut victory over Jesse Jackson in Wisconsin, seven weeks later and following many inconclusive primaries in a multi-candidate field, appeared to seal the nomination for him. On the Republican side, George Bush's victory over Kansas senator Robert Dole in New Hampshire and his sweep of the South on "Super Tuesday" three weeks later for all intents and purposes settled the nomination.

Where the key state victories occur makes a difference. When a major state emerges as the focus in the preconvention struggle, no one thinks much about it. When Iowa and New Hampshire vault a dark horse into prominence or otherwise dominate the selection process, it is another matter. Both George McGovern in 1972 and Jimmy Carter in 1976 owed their nominations to their strong showings in these states. And Gary Hart, another outsider, almost parlayed a better-than-anticipated vote in the Iowa caucuses in 1984 (15 percent to Mondale's 45 percent) and a victory in New Hampshire into the nomination. For Bush and Dukakis in 1988, New Hampshire's results obliterated their poor showings in Iowa and, most important, made them the clear-cut front-runners. The most important result of an early victory or unanticipated good showing is the extraordinary free media time it produces. It is simply mind-boggling to learn that Iowa and New Hampshire, with about 3 percent of the nation's population, receive about 30 percent of the media coverage given the entire campaign for the presidential nomination.[26]

At bottom, the issue is the representativeness of Iowa and New Hampshire of the entire Democratic electorate. Neither state has a major metropolitan area, a large urban (unionized) workforce, or a sizable minority population. The voters in these states are patently not a cross section of the majorities[27] that elect Democratic presidents, and they are more likely to vote Republican than Democratic in November. (In the six presidential elections between 1968 and 1988, Iowa voted Republican four times, New Hampshire five times.) Their prominence in eliminating contenders, in turning long shots into viable candidates, and in controlling the route to the nomination leaves attentive Democrats in the other forty-eight states and the District of Columbia baffled, if not wholly incredulous.

Regional variation in candidate strength also can be decisive. If, in 1976, the western primaries and caucuses had been held at the beginning of the nominating season instead of near the end, both Jimmy Carter and Ronald Reagan might have fared differently.[28] In 1980 both Carter and Reagan gained critical momentum—the bandwagon effect—by winning a string of early southern primaries. And in 1984 Mondale's virtual sweep of the industrial Northeast gave him a lead that Hart's later victories in western states could not overcome. George Bush's massive victory in the South on "Super Tuesday" effectively ended the contest for the nomination. Sequence makes a difference.

The electoral results in the early caucus-convention and primary states are the peculiar dynamic of the presidential nominating process. And overemphasis of the results by the media is the norm. Often speaking with greater finality than the voters themselves, the media create winners and losers, front-runners and also-rans, candidates who should "bail out" and candidates who have earned "another shot." Voters learn who did better than expected and who did worse than expected. Winning or placing well is translated into a major political resource, with the psychological impact greater than the body count of delegates won. The rewards for capturing the media's attention are heightened visibility, an expanded and more attentive journalistic corps, television news time, interest group cynosure, endorsements, campaign funds, and a leg up on the next contest.

In the nominating process the media have become the new parties:

> The television news organizations in this country are an enormously dominant force in primary elections. They're every Tuesday night, not only counting the votes, but, in some cases, setting the tone. (A member of the Jimmy Carter organization)
>
> . . . [if] you're short of delegates, the real determining factor's going to be the psychological momentum the press creates. Is he a winner? Can he get the nomination? (A member of the Fred Harris organization)

You go into a place like New Hampshire and you've got two things in mind. Primarily is winning New Hampshire. Secondly is getting out the stories about your candidate and where he stands and all that to the rest of the country. (A member of the Ronald Reagan organization)

Everywhere we go, we're on a media trip; I mean we're attempting to generate as much free television and print, as much free radio, as we can get. Any angle can play. (A member of the Morris Udall organization)[29]

If you're not first or second in New Hampshire, you might as well pack your bags. (John Sears, Republican political consultant)[30]

The task of a presidential hopeful, threading a path through the minefield of successive primary elections, is not to win a majority but rather to survive. Survival means gaining as high as possible a rank among the candidates running for election. Coming in first in early primaries means achieving the visibility that ensures that a candidate will be taken seriously by the news media. (Nelson W. Polsby, *Consequences of Party Reform*)[31]

Were it not for the media, the Iowa caucuses and the New Hampshire primary results would be about as relevant to the presidential nomination as opening-day baseball scores are to a pennant race. (David L. Paletz and Robert M. Entman, *Media Power Politics*)[32]

What really matters is the interpretation of election results by the print and broadcast media. Christopher Arterton writes:

Those who manage presidential campaigns uniformly believe that interpretations placed upon campaign events are frequently more important than the events themselves. In other words, the political contest is shaped primarily by the perceptual environment within which campaigns compete. *Particularly in the early nomination stages, perceptions outweigh reality in terms of their political impact.* Since journalists communicate these perceptions to voters and party activists and since part of the reporter's job is creating these interpretations, campaigners believe that journalists can and do affect whether their campaign is viewed as succeeding or failing, and that this perception in turn will determine their ability to mobilize political resources in the future: endorsements, volunteers, money, and hence, votes.[33]

Primaries and Caucuses in 1988

Candidates	Primaries on ballot	Primaries won	Percentage of primary vote	First-round caucuses won
Democratic				
Michael S. Dukakis	36	22	42.4	12
Jesse Jackson	36	7	29.1	7
Albert Gore	35	5	13.7	2
Richard A. Gephardt	30	2	6.0	1
Paul Simon	35	1	4.7	0
Others and uncommitted	—	0	4.1	0
Republican				
George Bush	37	36	67.9	12
Robert Dole	33	1	19.1	3
Pat Robertson	34	0	9.1	3
Jack F. Kemp	25	0	2.7	0
Others and uncommitted	—	0	1.2	0

SOURCE: Developed from data in *Congressional Quarterly Weekly Report,* July 9, 1988, 1892-1897.

NOTE: Some states hold both a primary and caucuses. In Texas, for example, Dukakis won the primary while Jackson won the caucuses. Included in the Democratic caucus listing are American Samoa, Democrats Abroad, and the Virgin Islands; included in the Republican caucus listing are Guam and the Virgin Islands. Twenty-three million votes were cast in the Democratic primaries and twelve million in the Republican primaries. Turnout data and official vote tabulations for candidates in caucus states are incomplete. For example, in some states that held caucuses late in the nominating season, after Bush had nailed down the nomination, no effort was made to tabulate votes for individual candidates. Some state parties simply make estimations of turnout for their caucuses.

The opening weeks of the nominating process are critical, since more and more states have shifted the dates of their primaries or caucuses to the early part of the season—front loading, in the argot of analysts and political junkies. In 1988 nearly every southern and border state had its delegate-selection event on the same day in early March in a move to enhance southern influence in the nominating process and, on the Democratic side at least, to improve the prospects of moderate or conservative candidates. But with Jesse Jackson in the race, the "Super Tuesday" strategy backfired, and the southern vote was split about evenly among Jackson, Dukakis, and Tennessee senator Albert Gore (ostensibly the southern candidate). Some southern states thus lost enthusiasm for the Dixie event in 1992 and scheduled other primary dates. Most, however, decided to remain a part of this de facto regional primary. To encourage California to abandon its June primary and to adopt an early date, the Democratic National Committee in 1990 moved up the start of the primary season to the first Tuesday in March. Holding a major state primary at this early date, the DNC reasoned, would inevitably reduce the importance of the Iowa and New Hampshire results. Well-known candidates, moreover, would have less reason to commit themselves to endless campaigning in these small states. After prolonged consideration, however, the California legislature in late 1990 defeated the plan to make the state's presidential primary one of the nation's earliest. The measure failed when lawmakers could not agree on whether to permit referendums on the primary ballot. (Most Republicans wanted to bar referendums from the presidential primary ballot— fearing a low turnout in an uncontested primary—while certain key Democratic leaders favored their inclusion.)

Front loading requires candidates to get out of the blocks fast. Slow starters usually find themselves out of the race before most of the nation's voters have had a chance to express their preferences. Inconclusive results in the early caucuses and primaries mean that the struggle for the nomination may continue to the end of the season (second Tuesday in June) and perhaps beyond to the convention itself. Trying to predict how the calendar will affect individual candidacies, state or regional influence, or voting patterns is impossible. Too many imponderables, including the peculiar mix of candidacies, are present. And what serves certain interests in one election, moreover, may not in the next.

The Democratic party has sought, thus far without great success, to diminish the significance of the early phase of the presidential nominating process. In 1982 the Democratic National Committee adopted a rule proposed by the Hunt Commission to restrict the nominating season (the caucus-primary "window") to the period of early March to early June, with a few exceptions. Under the rule in effect for 1992, Iowa opens the nominating season in February (but no earlier than fifteen days before the first Tuesday in March), followed by New Hampshire (no earlier than seven days before the window). Maine's first-tier caucuses slip in two days before the formal opening. (See Rule 10A, Table 3-1.) Despite these exceptions, the overall schedule is more compact. In 1976 the Iowa caucuses were held in January, more than five weeks before the New Hampshire primary. This long interval permitted unknown Jimmy Carter to capitalize on his strong Iowa showing, giving him increased media attention, new supporters, and additional campaign funds that were vital for the New Hampshire primary and elsewhere.

The rule narrowing the window may be an advantage for well-known candidates with campaign organizations in place and significant national followings. But not too much should be made of that. The major development is front loading. For most candidates, doing poorly and running out of funds, the end of the race comes early. If a clear-cut front-runner has emerged by mid-March, the last three months of the season may be nothing more than the mop-up stage. But if two or more strong candidates survive after the southern primaries, as happened in 1988 on the Democratic side, the race has just begun (and the front-loading states have miscalculated).

A realistic campaign for the presidential nomination is expensive. Money is the sine qua non. It separates the serious candidate from the dilettante or the rank outsider. Of course there is never enough of it, and the law does not make it easy to raise. Under the Federal Election Campaign Act, no individual can contribute more than $1,000 to any campaign. Moreover, candidates can qualify for matching federal funds only after they have raised $100,000 in small sums ($250 or less, $5,000 per state) in twenty states. Political action committees may contribute up to $5,000 to a candidate, but their gifts are not eligible for matching public money. Candidates are thus compelled to develop a large network of small contributors, spread around the country—making fund raising a chore for all candidates and a major obstacle for some. Plans and activities to raise money must be launched long in advance of the election year. It is thus easy to mark the opening of a new campaign. It begins with the creation of fund-raising committees and the scramble for money. The money hustle is aptly described by the press secretary to Fred Harris, who sought the Democratic nomination in 1976:

> You're caught in a kind of vicious circle. In order to raise money, especially money from more than twenty states, then you have to have national media attention, not just good local media that Fred has been able to generate. . . . But in order to raise that kind of money dispersed among twenty states then you need national media exposure. You need it because people do judge by national media exposure as to whether the campaign is serious or not and, believe

me, they hesitate before they give money. . . . They're going to wait
until they see Fred's smiling face on national television.[34]

The system of caucus-conventions and presidential primaries is a
crazy quilt of activity. Candidates fly from one end of the country to the
other, then back again, emphasizing certain states, deemphasizing others, and doing their best to impose their interpretation on the most recent
results. Candidates are never wholly confident about how or where they
should spend their time or money; voters are not quite sure what is going
on. Yet there is more to the system than its awkwardness, complexity,
and unpredictability.

Popular participation in the presidential nominating process generally was not of much consequence prior to the reforms of the 1970s.
Candidates, following their instincts and the advice of assorted national
and state politicians, chose to enter primaries, to avoid them, or to
participate in certain ones while skipping others. As recently as 1968,
only sixteen states even held primaries. And Hubert Humphrey captured the Democratic nomination that year even though he did not
contest any primaries (which were dominated by Eugene McCarthy and
Robert F. Kennedy). In states using the caucus-convention system, the
chief method of nomination, one or a few leaders typically controlled the
selection of delegates and thus the outcome. To win the nomination,
candidates spent much of their time cultivating key state party leaders.
Only a few candidates at any time, moreover, were thought to be
"available" for the office—that is, possessed of attributes that would
prompt party leaders around the country and the media to take them
seriously. Presidential nominees were chosen in a relatively closed system from among a very select group.

That ambiance and the rules and practices that fostered it have
disappeared. Today the system is remarkably open. The impact of party
leaders and organizations is minimal in the process. No leader can
"deliver" a state. Candidates rarely write off a primary or caucus,
though they often downplay the significance of certain ones. And most
important, the rank-and-file voters now play a central role in the
presidential nominating process.[35] In 1976 nearly twenty-nine million
voters cast ballots in both parties' primaries. The number rose to about
thirty-two million in 1980 and, with fewer primaries and no contest on
the Republican side, declined to about twenty-four million in 1984. A
record was established when thirty-five million voters took part in the

1988 presidential primaries. Overall, about one-fourth of the eligible electorate now votes in presidential primary states.[36] Perhaps one million voters turn out for the first-tier caucuses in the caucus-convention states.[37] The presidential nominating process is much more responsive to popular preferences than ever in the past. It is a new participatory system. Nothing looks quite the same. Even an incumbent president may have reason to fear a challenge to renomination (for example, Carter versus Kennedy in 1980) in the free-for-all of primaries and caucuses. Whether the new system produces better candidates (or better presidents) than those previously chosen in smoke-filled rooms is another matter.

Presidential primaries, because they tap voters' preferences in a more direct fashion than caucuses, and at the same time involve a much larger sector of the electorate, present a particularly good opportunity for testing candidates, policies, and issues in a variety of states.[38] Consider evidence of the past two decades. The Vietnam War was the pivotal issue in both the 1968 and 1972 Democratic primaries. It contributed to President Johnson's decision not to seek reelection in 1968 and, four years later, was central to George McGovern's nomination. When an outsider, Jimmy Carter, won a large majority of the Democratic primaries in 1976, the intensity of voters' resentment toward the "Washington establishment" was revealed. Voter attitudes toward conservatism were brought to light in 1980. Ronald Reagan easily won the first primary in New Hampshire (following a narrow loss to George Bush in Iowa, the first caucus-convention state), lost narrowly to Bush in Massachusetts, and then won six primaries in a row—all by large margins. Most of the other contenders for the Republican nomination, faring poorly in the early primaries, soon withdrew. Reagan lost only four of the thirty-two primaries he entered. On the Democratic side in 1984, an intense struggle culminated in a close victory for Walter Mondale—one that he gained without either a majority of the national primary (or caucus) vote and one that revealed both the party's contradictions and its bleak prospects in the November election. Much the same could be said for Michael Dukakis in 1988. Primaries make and break politicians' careers, while illuminating the problems of the party, in particular factional conflict and an absence of consensus on program and policy.

What has been the overall impact of the preconvention struggle on the choice of nominees? The primary and convention-caucus process has become decisive, sharply constricting the significance of the national conventions in the selection of presidential nominees. John Kennedy owed his nomination in 1960 to, more than anything else, his successes in primary states. Numerous state and local Democratic candidates would have preferred a safer candidate, but they found it impossible to withstand the surge of public support behind Kennedy. Democratic party professionals were again confounded in 1972 and 1976 when party outsiders, George McGovern and Jimmy Carter, respectively, won numerous primary victories and, coupled with their successes in nonprimary states, the nominations. On the Republican side, despite the advantage of the presidency, Gerald R. Ford barely escaped with the nomination in 1976 after an extraordinary preconvention challenge by Ronald Reagan, who won ten primaries. President Ford won seventeen. After the first wave of primaries in 1980, there was not much doubt concerning the eventual winners. Carter won nine of the first thirteen Democratic primaries, and Reagan won ten of the first thirteen Republican primaries. In 1984, benefiting from delegate selection and delegate distribution rules that diminished the chances of outsiders and winning where it counted, Mondale had captured the nomination by the end of the primary and caucus season. Reagan had virtually no opposition. In 1988 Bush had the Republican nomination sewed up by early March, Dukakis the Democratic nomination by mid-April.

The preconvention struggle, however, may not always settle the choice of the nominee. If it does not, the selection will turn on convention bargaining. A brokered convention, characterized by sparring between leading candidates (perhaps including some who avoided the primaries and caucuses) and by a more important role for party leaders and public officials, is thus still a possibility. Sooner or later, doubtlessly, there will be one.

The Convention Delegates

The ramifications of political reforms are often much larger than anticipated. The new emphasis on popular participation in the delegate selection process, coupled with the requirements for affirmative action plans to promote the representation of disadvantaged groups, has sharply changed the composition of Democratic national conventions. Prior to the 1970s, Democratic delegates were preponderantly male, middle-aged, and white. And they were usually party regulars—officials of the party, important contributors, and reliable rank-and-file members. Public officeholders were prominent in all state delegations. The selection process itself was dominated by state and local party leaders.

The reforms produced a new breed of delegate. As a result of the guidelines adopted by the McGovern-Fraser Commission, the representation of women, blacks, and young persons in the national convention increased dramatically. For example, the proportion of women delegates grew from 13 percent in 1968 to 40 percent in 1972, and of blacks from 5.5 to 15 percent. Under current rules, each Democratic state party is required to develop outreach programs to increase the number of delegates from groups that have been significantly underrepresented in the past, such as persons over sixty-five years old, the physically handicapped, and persons of low and moderate income. Another affirmative action rule specifies that in the selection of at-large delegates, preference shall be given to blacks, Hispanics, native Americans, Asian/Pacific Americans, and women. Moreover, all state delegation selection plans must provide for an equal division of delegates between men and women. These mandated changes have had a profound impact on the composition of state delegations.

The chief losers in the reordering of the 1970s were Democratic party professionals and public officeholders, as issue and candidate enthusiast delegates ("amateurs," in broad terms) replaced them in state after state. Recent changes in party rules—marked by adding superdelegates in 1984, 1988, and 1992—have altered the composition of the convention. A survey of Democratic delegates in 1988 found that 43 percent held some party office and 26 percent held an elective (or public) office. Seventy-four percent of the delegates reported that they were engaged in party activities on a year-round basis. Twenty-two percent of the delegates, by contrast, said that they engage in party work only when the issues or candidates are important to them.[39] Clearly, professional politicians have reemerged after being sidelined by various party reform commissions. Whether their presence will make much difference remains to be seen. Recent conventions have been cut and dried, the presidential nominees having been chosen earlier by primary voters and caucus participants.

Changes in the composition of Republican convention delegations have come more gradually. Even so, a larger proportion of women, blacks, and young people are being elected as Republican delegates than ever before. Amateur activists are also more numerous in Republican

The Characteristics of Democratic and Republican National Convention Delegates in 1988

	Democrats	Republicans
Sex		
Male	50%	65%
Female	50	35
Race/ethnicity		
White	69	91
Black	22	4
Hispanic	6	2
Asian	2	1
Native American	1	1
Education		
Some high school	1	1
High school graduate	8	7
Some college	18	22
College graduate	28	34
Law degree	16	18
Medical degree	0	1
Other advanced degree	27	15
Religion		
Protestant	51	70
White Protestant	31	67
Catholic	30	24
Jewish	6	2
Household income		
$0-$9,999	1	0
$10,000-$19,999	4	2
$20,000-$34,999	16	8
$35,000-$49,999	22	16
$50,000-$99,999	35	35
$100,000-$999,999	14	24
$1 million and more	0	1

SOURCE: Adapted from survey data in *USA Today,* August 15, 1988, and *New York Times,* August 14, 1988. Percentages may not total to 100 because of rounding and because a few delegates failed to respond to certain questions.

conventions, but not on the scale found on the Democratic side. Party leaders, longtime party members, and public officials have steadily played key roles in Republican conventions.

Convention delegates do not reflect a cross section of the population or a cross section of the party membership. Two demographic characteristics in particular differentiate delegates from the wider public and rank-and-file party members: high income and substantial education. In 1988, 71 percent of the Democratic delegates and 68 percent of the Republican delegates had completed four years of college; a surprising 43 percent of the Democrats and 34 percent of the Republicans had undertaken graduate work. Among Democratic delegates, 49 percent had incomes in excess of $50,000; among Republicans, 60 percent. In addition, Protestants were more numerous in the Republican convention (70 percent) while Catholics and Jews were more fully represented in the Democratic convention (30 percent and 6 percent, respectively). Blacks made up 22 percent of the Democratic membership but only 4 percent of the Republican membership, while the percentages for Hispanics were 6 and 2, respectively.[40]

Liberals regularly are overrepresented in the Democratic convention, conservatives in the Republican convention. Thirty-nine percent of the Democratic delegates in 1988 described themselves as liberals, as contrasted with 27 percent for the Democratic party membership as a whole. And while 43 percent of rank-and-file Republicans saw themselves as conservatives, 60 percent of the Republican delegates described themselves in that fashion. Only 1 percent of the Republican delegates viewed themselves as liberals and only 4 percent of the Democrats emerged as conservatives.[41] Ideological distinctiveness is more characteristic of delegates than of average party members.

The Politics of the Convention

Three practical aims dominate the proceedings of the national convention: to nominate presidential and vice-presidential candidates, to draft the party platform, and to lay the groundwork for party unity in the campaign. The way in which the party addresses itself to the tasks of nominating the candidates and drafting the platform is likely to determine how well it achieves its third objective, that of healing party rifts and forging a cohesive party. To put together a presidential ticket and a platform that satisfies the principal elements of the party is difficult. The task of reconciling divergent interests within the party occupies the convention from its earliest moments until the final gavel—at least in most conventions. By and large, convention leaders have been successful in shaping the compromises necessary to keep the national party, such as it is, from flying apart.

The Convention Committees

The initial business of the convention is handled mainly by four committees. The committee on credentials is given the responsibility for determining the permanent roll (official membership) of the convention. Its specific function is to ascertain the members' legal right to seats in the convention. In the absence of challenges to the right of certain delegates to be seated or of contests between two delegations from the same state, each trying to be seated, the review is handled routinely and with dispatch. Most state delegations are seated without difficulty. When disputes arise, the committee holds hearings and takes testimony; its recommendations for seating delegates are then reported to the convention, which ordinarily (but not invariably) sustains them. The committee on permanent organization is charged with selecting the permanent officers of the convention, including the permanent chairperson, the clerks, and the sergeant at arms. The committee on rules devises the rules under which the convention will operate and establishes the order of business.

Ordinarily the most important convention committee is the committee on resolutions, which is in charge of drafting the party platform. The actual work of this committee begins many weeks in advance of the convention, so that usually a draft of the document exists by the time the convention opens and the formal committee hearings begin. When a president seeks reelection, the platform is likely to be prepared under his direction and accepted by the committees (and later by the floor) without major changes.

A fight over the nomination may influence the drafting of the platform, since the leading candidates have an interest in securing planks that are compatible with their views. Indeed, the outcomes of clashes over planks may provide a good indication of which candidate will capture the nomination. In the 1968 Democratic convention, for example, it was all but certain that Hubert Humphrey would win the nomination when the convention, after a lengthy and emotional floor debate, adopted by a comfortable margin a plank that reflected the Johnson administration's position on the Vietnam War. Humphrey's two principal opponents, senators Eugene McCarthy and George McGovern, were the most prominent supporters of the losing minority plank, which called for an unconditional halt to the bombing of North Vietnam. In the 1976 Republican convention, intense struggles occurred in the platform committee between the forces of President Ford and those of Ronald Reagan. Almost all the planks adopted represented victories for the supporters of Ford, thus auguring well for his nomination.

The 1980 Republican and Democratic platforms were fashioned in sharply different ways. Harmony prevailed at the Republican convention, and the members quickly approved a platform with planks that meshed comfortably with the views of its nominee, Ronald Reagan. The document of the platform committee was adopted without change. Debate over the Democratic platform, by contrast, was acrimonious and protracted. Numerous minority reports were adopted on the floor. In the end, the delegates adopted a platform that in major respects (particularly in its economic and human needs planks) was more in line with the liberal views of Senator Kennedy and his partisans than with those of President Carter. The high level of conflict over the platform was surprising given that an incumbent president, the certain nominee, was seeking reelection. No one expects the president's forces to lose on key convention votes. In 1984 scarcely a discordant note was struck at the Republican convention as it renominated President Reagan and approved the platform without debate. On the Democratic side, compromises on the platform among the Walter Mondale, Jesse Jackson, and Gary Hart forces were sufficient to avert divisive floor fights, and the party, stressing family and eschewing tradition, chose Geraldine A. Ferraro as its vice-presidential nominee.[42]

In 1988 Jesse Jackson won numerous platform concessions from Dukakis as party leaders worked hard to unify the party for the campaign. On the few planks that were controversial—for example, the Jackson-inspired planks on tax increases for the wealthy and Palestinian self-determination—Dukakis's forces prevailed. Adopted with a minimum of controversy, the 1988 Republican platform followed the conservative doctrines set down in the Reagan platforms of 1980 and 1984.

Selecting the Presidential Ticket

To some party leaders, the best convention is the one that opens with significant uncertainties and imponderables—a good, though not sure-fire, prescription for generating public interest in the convention, the party, and its nominees. In the usual convention, however, uncertainties are far from numerous. Doubts are much more likely to surround the choice of the vice-presidential nominee than the presidential nominee. So many presidential candidates are screened out during the primary-caucus season that by the time the convention opens the range of choice has become sharply narrowed, perhaps nonexistent.

The early stages of the nominating process are especially important for the selection of presidential candidates (see Table 3-2). Typically, the candidate leading the public opinion polls at the start of the year (before the first delegate has even been chosen) winds up with the nomination. New opportunities for challenging leading candidates in primaries and caucuses may alter this pattern. In 1972 and 1976 the Democratic nomination was won by an outsider whose poll standings were unimpressive at the start of the year. And in 1980 Ronald Reagan won the Republican nomination, although he trailed in the early polls. Walter Mondale had a wide lead in the initial polls in 1984 and, after an early scare, nailed down the nomination before the Democratic convention opened. In 1988 George Bush's nomination went according to form, as he led from the outset. On the Democratic side, the early polls had Michael Dukakis trailing Gary Hart, Jesse Jackson, and Paul Simon. He did not wrap up the nomination until well into the primary season.

The experience of recent conventions is worth noting. In the 1960, 1968, and 1972 Republican conventions, Richard Nixon's nomination occurred on the first ballot, without significant opposition. In 1964, in the judgment of most party professionals, Barry Goldwater's nomination was assured by his victory over Nelson Rockefeller in the California primary. The great bulk of the Goldwater delegates had been captured earlier in state conventions. The Democratic experience is about the same. Lyndon Johnson's nomination in 1964 was a foregone conclusion, following the custom (at that time) that incumbent presidents were entitled to another term if they chose to run. In 1968, with the forces opposed to the Johnson administration in disarray following the assassination of Robert F. Kennedy, scarcely any doubt existed that Vice President Hubert Humphrey would become the party standard-bearer.

TABLE 3-2   Continuity and Change in Presidential Nominating Politics, 1936-1988

Year	Leading candidate at beginning of election year	Nominee
Party in power		
1936 (D)	Roosevelt	Roosevelt
1940 (D)	Roosevelt	Roosevelt
1944 (D)	Roosevelt	Roosevelt
1948 (D)	Truman	Truman
1952 (D)	Truman	Stevenson
1956 (R)	Eisenhower	Eisenhower
1960 (R)	Nixon	Nixon
1964 (D)	Johnson	Johnson
1968 (D)	Johnson	Humphrey
1972 (R)	Nixon	Nixon
1976 (R)	Ford	Ford
1980 (D)	Carter	Carter
1984 (R)	Reagan	Reagan
1988 (R)	Bush	Bush
Party out of power		
1936 (R)	Landon	Landon
1940 (R)	?	Willkie
1944 (R)	Dewey	Dewey
1948 (R)	Dewey-Taft	Dewey
1952 (R)	Eisenhower-Taft	Eisenhower
1956 (D)	Stevenson	Stevenson
1960 (D)	Kennedy	Kennedy
1964 (R)	?	Goldwater
1968 (R)	Nixon	Nixon
1972 (D)	Muskie	McGovern
1976 (D)	Kennedy-Humphrey	Carter
1980 (R)	Ford	Reagan
1984 (D)	Mondale	Mondale
1988 (D)	Hart	Dukakis

SOURCE: Donald R. Matthews, "Presidential Nominations: Process and Outcome," in *Choosing the President*, ed. James David Barber (Englewood Cliffs, N.J.: Prentice Hall, 1974), 54 (as updated).

NOTE: D = Democrat; R = Republican.

In 1972 George McGovern arrived at the Democratic convention with more than twice as many delegate votes as any other candidate, and his nomination on the first ballot, though it could not have been predicted a few months earlier, was anything but a surprise at the convention. In

1976 Jimmy Carter came to the Democratic convention in Madison Square Garden with the nomination locked up. Some months earlier, that feat could not have been predicted either. First-ballot nominations occurred at both conventions in 1980, 1984, and 1988.

In only a few conventions in the last four decades has there been substantial doubt about the ultimate winner: both conventions in 1952 (Dwight D. Eisenhower versus Robert A. Taft in the Republican convention and a wide-open contest in the Democratic convention), the Democratic convention in 1960 (John F. Kennedy, who won the presidential primaries, versus the field), and the 1976 Republican convention (Gerald R. Ford versus Ronald Reagan). It is unusual for a front-runner—the candidate holding the most delegate votes prior to the convention—to lose out at the convention. Often the front-runner is nominated on the first ballot.

The final major item of convention business is the selection of the party's vice-presidential nominee. Here the task of the party is to come up with the right political formula—the candidate who can add the most to the ticket and detract the least. The presidential nominee most often makes the choice, following rounds of consultation with various party and candidate organization leaders.[43] Although a great deal of suspense is usually created over the vice-presidential nomination, convention ratification comes easily once the presidential nominee has decided and cleared the selection with key leaders. Unless the presidential nominee is inclined to take a major risk to serve the interest of his own faction or ideology (as Barry Goldwater did in choosing Republican national chairman William E. Miller in 1964), he selects a candidate who can help to balance the ticket and unify the party.[44] Jimmy Carter's choice of Walter Mondale in 1976 fits neatly into this category, as does Ronald Reagan's choice of George Bush in 1980. Mondale's selection of Geraldine A. Ferraro in 1984 broke with major party tradition in more ways than one: Representative Ferraro was the first woman to be nominated for the vice presidency, the first Italian-American to be nominated for national office, and the first nominee to be anointed prior to the opening of the convention.

The choice of Sen. Lloyd Bentsen, a conservative Texan, by Michael Dukakis in 1988 was designed to bring ideological balance to the ticket and to attract voters in the South (and particularly in Texas with its large block of 29 electoral votes). Dukakis's "mini" southern strategy, centered around Bentsen, plainly failed, as he lost every southern state.

George Bush's surprising selection of a younger, telegenic U.S. senator, Dan Quayle of Indiana, reflected his desire to merge conservative and generational appeals. He hoped to satisfy the party's powerful conservative wing, win the attention of the postwar "baby boomers," improve the party's lagging position with women voters, and strengthen its prospects in the Middle West. Many conservatives were pleased with Quayle's selection, but undoubtedly he hurt the ticket as a result of prolonged controversies involving his qualifications and National Guard service during the Vietnam War. The broad point is that the presidential nominee ordinarily has a great deal of leeway in choosing a running mate, although the need to reward or placate a particular party element can drastically reduce the list of possible candidates.[45]

A National Primary? Regional Primaries?

Dissatisfaction with the current system has led some politicians and analysts to prefer a single, one-day national primary. Under a typical proposal, to win the nomination a candidate would be required to obtain a majority of the popular vote cast in his party primary; if no candidate received a majority, a runoff election would be held between the top two finishers. A separate vote would be held for vice-presidential candidates. The national convention would be retained for writing the platform and fashioning party rules.

Another plan calls for regional primaries—all those states holding primaries within a region would be required to hold them on the same day.[46] A total of perhaps five regional primaries would be conducted, one each month from March through July in the presidential year, their order to be determined by lot. The national convention would continue, at least formally, to select the presidential candidate. When the primaries failed to produce a clear-cut winner, the actual choice would be made by the convention.

Still another proposal would require all states using primaries to choose one of four dates (in March, April, May, or June) on which to hold them—thus bringing a measure of order to the system and diminishing the significance of a single state's early primary. Left to the decision of each state, a caucus-convention system could be used in place of a primary. The national convention would continue in its present form.

Public Opinion on Proposals to Change Election System

Proposal: A nationwide primary election to replace political party conventions

Year	Favor	Oppose	No opinion
1952	73%	12%	15%
1956	58	27	15
1964	62	25	13
1968	76	13	11
1976	68	21	11
1980	66	24	10
1984	67	21	12
1988	65	25	10

Proposal: A series of four regional primaries to be held in different weeks in June during presidential years

Year	Good idea	Poor idea	No opinion
1982	44	33	23
1984	45	30	25
1985	40	34	26
1988	51	32	17

SOURCE: *Gallup Report,* March 1988, 10-11.

The adoption of a national primary law would represent the sharpest departure from the current system. It would favor well-known, well-financed candidates and would hurt outsiders—those lesser-known candidates who gain visibility and momentum through a win or an impressive showing in an early primary or caucus state. Inevitably, a national primary would have a destructive impact on the political parties, eliminating them from any role in the selection of presidential candidates. Austin Ranney writes:

> [The] clear gainers in influence from the dismantling of the party organizations would be the national news media—the national television and radio networks, the major newspapers, and the wire services. . . . [Their] interpretations of the state primaries and caucuses, especially the early ones, already have a powerful influence on who

wins or who loses. . . . In a national primary . . . the only preelection
facts relevant to who was winning would be public opinion polls and
estimates of the sizes of crowds at candidate meetings. The former
are scientifically more respectable than the latter, but neither constitutes hard data in the sense that election returns do. And hard data of
that sort would be available only after national primary day. Thus, a
one-day national direct primary would give the news media even
more power than they now have to influence the outcomes of contests
for nominations by shaping most people's perceptions of how these
contests were proceeding.[47]

The Media, the Presidential Nominating Process, and the Parties

It would be hard to exaggerate the importance of the print and broadcast
media in shaping the presidential nominating process. Not surprisingly,
media influence is as controversial as it is pivotal.

Critics charge that the media are preoccupied with the competitiveness, or "horse race," aspects of the presidential campaign while giving
too little attention to the candidates' records and issue positions. Complicated policy questions tend to be ignored by television and even by much
of the print media. By contrast, horse race stories are easy for journalists
to write, easy for television reporters to portray, and easy for the public
to understand. These stories have a standard format: they tell where the
candidates have been and where they are going; how their strategies have
emerged; how crowds and organized groups are responding to them; how
politicians evaluate them and their campaigns; how they have dealt with
events and mistakes; who has endorsed them; and most important, who is
winning and who is losing. What the campaign is all about is ordinarily
lost in horse race accounts.

Numerous studies have shown that more than half of all stories on
presidential campaigns have a horse race theme.[48] During the crucial
first half of the 1988 presidential nominating season, 80 percent of the
network news airtime was devoted to horse race stories and 20 percent to
substantive issues. One of the campaign's early casualties, Robert Dole,
had these observations on campaign reporting:

> What I witnessed generally on my own campaign plane was an
> aircraft filled with reporters who became each other's best audience.

It was an ultra-insider's game of gossip and nit-picking that turned presidential campaign coverage into trivial pursuits. It was a daily spin from the experts on the state of the campaign, whether it came from a reporter who had been on board for one month, or one stop. . . . Preconceived notions, prewritten stories and premeditated clichés were all confirmed regardless of the facts. And if there was a nice soap opera campaign story out there, it would be kept on the spin cycle for a good week or so. All the while, reporters' necks were craned in the rear of the plane scanning the campaign staff up front for smiles or frowns, or seating arrangements that would somehow reveal the inside story. Meanwhile, the issues disappeared somewhere over Iowa airspace. . . . I just wish I was hounded on the federal deficit as I was on my staff. I just wish I was interrogated about American agriculture as I was about fund-raising. I just wish my voting record was as thoroughly scrutinized as were my wife's personal finances.[49]

Another feature of media coverage of nominating campaigns singled out by critics is the practice of focusing on front-runners at the expense of providing information on other candidates' campaigns. The early public opinion polls provide the initial impetus to prepare press and television stories on the front-runners. Thin on evidence, these early and speculative stories nevertheless generate additional coverage of the leaders, even before the first caucus or primary is held. In natural progression, the candidates who win or place well in the Iowa precinct caucuses, the New Hampshire primary, or both become media darlings and gain even more coverage. A narrow win can sometimes emerge as a lopsided victory in the next day's news. An unexpectedly strong showing by a little-known candidate may vault him into national prominence—that is the essence of "surprise journalism."[50] Additionally, William G. Mayer writes:

Not only does a win in New Hampshire bring lots of publicity; the publicity is almost entirely positive. The victorious candidate is portrayed as popular, exciting, confident, in control: in short, a leader. His poll ratings are increasing; his organization is growing; his message is catching on; his crowds are large and enthusiastic. His opponents, by contrast, are dead, dying, or in disarray.[51]

The media's role is particularly important in the early phase of the presidential nominating process. Television and press journalists sort out the candidates (ranking them as "the hopeless, the plausible, and the likely, with substantial differences between the three in the amount and quality of coverage" [52]), establish performance expectations, boost some campaigns while writing off others, and launch the bandwagons. Their evaluations create winners and losers. Candidates who capture the media's attention are rewarded out of proportion to the significance of the contests and perhaps to their shares of the vote as well. Early winners and surprise candidates gain momentum in this system of "lotteries driven by media expectations and candidate name recognition." [53]

The media also play a critical role in publicizing the factional appeals of candidates in primaries and caucuses. Increasingly, presidential candidates have eschewed coalition building while seeking to mobilize narrow ideological, religious, ethnic, or sectional followings. The more crowded the field, the greater the probability that an active, passionate, well-organized faction can keep the candidate in contention from one Tuesday to the next in the crucial early weeks of the season. Through extensive coverage of the campaign, the media help the candidates to attract, instruct, and mobilize their distinctive factional followings.[54]

Campaign schedules, speeches, and statements all revolve around the media. Candidates fly from one airport tarmac to the next, from one television market to the next, in their quest for press attention and free media time on local television stations. Nothing may be more important than free media time. Brief stops are the order of the day. During the 1988 nominating campaign preceding "Super Tuesday"—when most of the action was concentrated in the South—some candidates visited five or six states (or more accurately, assorted airports in these states) in a single day, not to see crowds of voters but to secure a few seconds of exposure on the local evening news (and, with luck, a snippet on the network news).

The influence of the media on the presidential nominating process obviously is pervasive. But two broad effects stand out. The first is that the media have undercut the position of party elites. As almost every candidate could testify, free media time and paid advertising are a much more effective means for influencing mass electorates than working through party leaders and party organizations. The media also provide an excellent opportunity for candidates, tutored by media consultants, to raise campaign money by gaining public attention. Impressive televised speeches sometimes produce a flood of campaign contributions. It is not far from the truth to suggest that the media are now used to "deliver" votes and money in a way that state and local politicians did a generation ago. What is more, political consultants and handlers are at least as important as any party professional in shaping campaign decisions.

Second, the media have played a key role in the transformation of the national party convention. They did this by becoming the vehicle by which candidates and candidate organizations distanced themselves from the party organization. Today's conventions are run by candidates and their organizations; the influence that party and elected officials wield is a function of their affiliation with candidate organizations. The vast majority of the delegates arrive at the convention committed to a candidate, and the convention meets to ratify the voters' choice, expressed in primaries and caucuses, as the presidential nominee. Typically, the nominee is known long in advance of the convention. The old "deliberative" convention, marked by high-stakes bargaining among party leaders, with the nomination in suspense, is all but extinct.

In virtually every phase, the new party convention is a media event. Activities are scheduled at times that will produce maximum television audiences. Deals are struck to avoid controversy. Politics is sanitized. Celebrities are properly celebrated. Speeches are kept brief. Trivial events and "news" are magnified by television reporters scurrying around for interviews. Orchestration and entertainment pervade the convention agenda as leaders strive to showcase their candidates, enhance the party's image, and hold an audience notorious for its short attention span. Elaborate efforts are made to avoid boring the viewers. National party conventions have turned into spectacles because they no longer actually choose the candidates, because they are trying to stay in business in a mass-oriented political system, because they are driven by the entertainment imperative, and because the media control the interpretation (and thus shape the politics) of the preconvention season. Not a great deal is left for the convention to decide. That at least has been the experience of the last several decades.

Notes

1. Does a hard fought, divisive primary hurt the party's chances in the general election? Politicians and political observers tend to believe that it does—that supporters of the candidate or candidates who lost in the primary will switch

their allegiance or decline to vote in the general election. Although the question is not settled, the preponderance of evidence suggests that conflictual (or competitive) primaries do have an adverse impact on the parties' chances for victory in the general election. The candidate who survives a primary battle is not as likely to win in November as a candidate who had little or no primary opposition. Support for this interpretation appears in Patrick J. Kenney and Tom W. Rice, "The Effect of Primary Divisiveness in Gubernatorial and Senatorial Elections," *Journal of Politics* 46 (August 1984): 904-915; and Robert A. Bernstein, "Divisive Primaries Do Hurt: U.S. Senate Races, 1956-1972," *American Political Science Review* 71 (June 1977): 540-545. But for a study that finds the relationship weak, see Richard Born, "The Influence of House Primary Divisiveness on General Election Margins 1962-76," *Journal of Politics* 43 (August 1981): 640-661. The "carryover effect" has also been studied in presidential elections by Walter J. Stone. He finds a strong carryover effect among partisan and committed activists; that is, activists who supported candidates who lost the nomination were less active in the general election. See his article, "The Carryover Effect in Presidential Elections," *American Political Science Review* 80 (March 1986): 271-279. For additional evidence on the importance of the carryover effect, see Kenney and Rice, "Presidential Prenomination Preferences and Candidate Evaluations," *American Political Science Review* 82 (December 1988): 1309-1319. For the most recent studies of the effects of divisive primaries, see Kenney and Rice, "The Relationship between Divisive Primaries and General Election Outcomes," *American Journal of Political Science* 31 (February 1987): 31-44; and Patrick J. Kenney, "Sorting Out the Effects of Primary Divisiveness in Congressional and Senatorial Elections," *Western Political Quarterly* 41 (September 1988): 765-777.

2. This discussion of closed and open primaries rests largely on an analysis by Craig L. Carr and Gary L. Scott, "The Logic of State Primary Classification Schemes," *American Politics Quarterly* 12 (October 1984): 465-476. Also see Malcolm E. Jewell and David M. Olson, *American State Political Parties and Elections* (Homewood, Ill.: Dorsey Press, 1978), 127-131; and David E. Price, *Bringing Back the Parties* (Washington, D.C.: CQ Press, 1984), 127-131.

3. The closed primary states, listed from least to most restrictive in terms of the length of time necessary to change party affiliation, are: Iowa, Ohio, Wyoming, South Dakota, Oregon, Kansas, North Carolina, Delaware, Massachusetts, West Virginia, Pennsylvania, Florida, Colorado, Arizona, New Jersey, Nevada, Oklahoma, Maine, Nebraska, New Hampshire, New Mexico, Maryland, Connecticut, Kentucky, New York, and California.

4. Do members of the U.S. House of Representatives from closed primary states have higher party support scores than members elected from states with less restrictive, or more open, systems? The answer is that closed primary states do tend to produce more partisan officeholders; their partisanship, however, appears to be a function of party strength and other attitudes toward parties present in the state rather than the result of a closed primary nominating system. See Steven H. Haeberle, "Closed Primaries and Party Support in Congress," *American Politics Quarterly* 13 (July 1985): 341-352.

5. *Tashjian v. Republican Party of Connecticut,* 107 S. Ct. 544 (1986). See a comprehensive analysis of the *Tashjian* decision by Leon D. Epstein, "Will American Political Parties Be Privatized?" *Journal of Law and Politics* 5

(Winter 1989): 239-274.

6. The states with the purest form of open primary are Hawaii, Idaho, Michigan, Minnesota, Montana, North Dakota, Utah, Vermont, and Wisconsin.

7. The "crossover" voting data are drawn from Ronald D. Hedlund and Meredith W. Watts, "The Wisconsin Open Primary, 1968 to 1984," *American Politics Quarterly* 14 (January-April 1986): 55-73. Also see Ronald D. Hedlund, Meredith W. Watts, and David M. Hedge, "Voting in an Open Primary," *American Politics Quarterly* 10 (April 1982): 197-218; David Adamany, "Communication: Cross-over Voting and the Democratic Party's Reform Rules," *American Political Science Review* 70 (June 1976): 536-541; and James I. Lengle and Byron E. Shafer, "Primary Rules, Political Power, and Social Change," *American Political Science Review* 70 (March 1976): 25-40.

8. *Democratic Party of the U.S. v. LaFollette*, 101 S. Ct. 1010 (1981).

9. The observations made in this paragraph are based mainly on an analysis by Charles D. Hadley, "The Impact of the Louisiana Open Elections System Reform," *State Government* 58, no. 4 (1986): 152-157. Also consult Thomas A. Kazee, "The Impact of Electoral Reform: 'Open Elections' and the Louisiana Party System," *Publius* 13 (Winter 1983): 132-139; and, for a general analysis of factionalism, see Earl Black, "A Theory of Southern Factionalism," *Journal of Politics* 45 (August 1983): 594-614.

10. Laws in a few states make provisions for the parties to hold preprimary conventions for the purpose of choosing the organization slate. The candidates selected by these conventions will usually appear on the ballot bearing the party endorsement. In the great majority of states, however, slating is an informal party process; the party depends on its organizational network and the communications media to inform the voters which candidates carry party support.

11. These themes appear in Frank J. Sorauf, *Party Politics in America* (Boston: Little, Brown, 1980), 220-224.

12. V. O. Key, Jr., *American State Politics: An Introduction* (New York: Knopf, 1956); William H. Standing and James A. Robinson, "Inter-Party Competition and Primary Contesting: The Case of Indiana," *American Political Science Review* 52 (December 1958): 1066-1077; and Malcolm E. Jewell, "Party and Primary Competition in Kentucky State Legislative Races," *Kentucky Law Journal* 48 (Summer 1960): 517-535.

13. See Harvey L. Schantz, "Contested and Uncontested Primaries for the U.S. House," *Legislative Studies Quarterly* 5 (November 1980): 545-562.

14. Denis G. Sullivan, Jeffrey L. Pressman, and F. Christopher Arterton, *Explorations in Convention Decision Making* (San Francisco: Freeman, 1976), 17.

15. Sullivan, Pressman, and Arterton, *Explorations in Convention Decision Making,* 20-21.

16. See an instructive analysis of the caucus-convention system by Rhodes Cook and Dave Kaplan in the *Congressional Quarterly Weekly Report,* June 4, 1988, 1523-1527.

17. Changing from one system to another has unanticipated consequences. Richard W. Boyd has shown, for example, that frequent elections depress turnout. Thus, states that switch from caucus-convention systems to direct primaries to select candidates and convention delegates will have a lower general election turnout. See his article, "The Effects of Primaries and Statewide Races on Voter Turnout," *Journal of Politics* 51 (August 1989): 730-739.

18. *Congressional Quarterly Weekly Report,* February 27, 1988, 532.

19. Turnout in presidential primaries tends to be highest in those states distinguished by high levels of education, facilitative legal provisions on voting, and competitive two-party elections. Interestingly, high turnout is not associated with high levels of campaign spending. See Patrick J. Kenney and Tom W. Rice, "Voter Turnout in Presidential Primaries: A Cross-Sectional Examination," *Political Behavior* 7, no. 1 (1985): 101-112. In terms of participation in presidential primaries, there is little or no difference between Democrats and Republicans. See Jack Moran and Mark Fenster, "Voting Turnout in Presidential Primaries," *American Politics Quarterly* 10 (October 1982): 453-476. Candidate strategy does influence turnout. See a study of how the number of candidates in the opposition party and the intensity of campaigning in the presidential party influence aggregate turnout levels: Barbara Norrander and Gregg W. Smith, "Type of Contest, Candidate Strategy, and Turnout in Presidential Primaries," *American Politics Quarterly* 13 (January 1985): 28-50. Turnout for first-tier caucuses is heightened by the presence of significant ideological choice among candidates, although no relationship exists between ideological range and turnout in primary states. See Steven E. Schier, "Turnout Choice in Presidential Nominations," *American Politics Quarterly* 10 (April 1982): 231-245.
20. *Congressional Quarterly Weekly Report,* July 9, 1988, 1892-1897.
21. See an analysis of the decline of success-minded professionals in party conventions and the growing "principle mindedness" of national convention delegates by John R. Petrocik and Dwaine Marvick, "Explaining Party Elite Transformation: Institutional Changes and Insurgent Politics," *Western Political Quarterly* 36 (September 1983): 345-363.
22. *Congressional Quarterly Weekly Report,* March 17, 1990, 849.
23. William J. Crotty, *Political Reform and the American Experiment* (New York: Crowell, 1977), 255-260.
24. *Congressional Quarterly Weekly Report,* August 25, 1984, 2092.
25. Operating under its primary-caucus hybrid system, Michigan Republicans in August 1986 elected about ten thousand precinct delegates to attend first-round caucuses in early 1988.
26. See William C. Adams, "As New Hampshire Goes...," in *Media and Momentum: The New Hampshire Primary and Nomination Politics,* ed. Gary R. Orren and Nelson W. Polsby (Chatham, N.J.: Chatham House Publishers, 1987), 42-49.
27. Are the voters who take part in presidential primaries ideologically unrepresentative? Evidence offered by Barbara Norrander indicates that they are not. See her article "Ideological Representativeness of Presidential Primary Voters," *American Journal of Political Science* 33 (August 1989): 570-587. Also see an article by John G. Geer, "Assessing the Representativeness of Electorates in Presidential Primaries," *American Journal of Political Science* 32 (November 1988): 929-945.
28. William R. Keech and Donald R. Matthews, "Patterns in the Presidential Nominating Process, 1936-1976," in *Parties and Elections in an Anti-Party Age,* ed. Jeff Fishel (Bloomington: Indiana University Press, 1978), 216.
29. This observation and the previous three are drawn from F. Christopher Arterton, "Campaign Organizations Confront the Media-Political Environment," in *Race for the Presidency: The Media and the Nominating Process,* ed. James David Barber (Englewood Cliffs, N.J.: Prentice Hall, 1978), 5.

30. *Congressional Quarterly Weekly Report,* August 23, 1986, 1999.
31. Nelson W. Polsby, *Consequences of Party Reform* (New York: Oxford University Press, 1983), 67.
32. David L. Paletz and Robert M. Entman, *Media Power Politics* (New York: Free Press, 1981), 36.
33. Arterton, "Campaign Organizations Confront the Media-Political Environment," 10 (emphasis added).
34. Arterton, "Campaign Organizations Confront the Media-Political Environment," 9.
35. Voters in primary and caucus states do not respond to exactly the same forces. A study of the 1984 Democratic party primaries and caucuses found that sociodemographic groups (in particular, blacks and labor) and general economic circumstances (levels of unemployment and income) were the major factors in influencing candidates' vote shares. Their vote shares in caucus states were heavily influenced by the sociodemographic makeup of the population and by levels of campaign spending. Candidates have very little control over the dominant factors in primary states, but they have considerable control over the major factor of campaign spending in caucus states. T. Wayne Parent, Calvin C. Jillson, and Ronald E. Weber, "Voting Outcomes in the 1984 Democratic Party Primaries and Caucuses," *American Political Science Review* 81 (March 1987): 67-84.
36. See an analysis of the factors that affect turnout in presidential primaries by Lawrence S. Rothenberg and Richard A. Brody, "Participation in Presidential Primaries," *Western Political Quarterly* 41 (June 1988): 253-271. Short-term factors, such as the closeness of the election and the presence of a hot contest, are particularly important in fostering participation.
37. These figures on participation are derived from several sources: Austin Ranney, *Participation in American Presidential Nominations, 1976* (Washington, D.C.: American Enterprise Institute for Public Policy Research, 1977), 15-20; *Congressional Quarterly Weekly Report,* July 5, 1980, 1869; June 2, 1984, 1315-1317; July 7, 1984, 1618-1620; and July 9, 1988, 1892-1897.
38. But see a study of the 1980 presidential primaries by Barbara Norrander that finds that voters made little use of candidates' issue positions in deciding how to vote. The most frequent correlates of vote choice are the qualities of the candidates. "Correlates of Vote Choice in the 1980 Presidential Primaries," *Journal of Politics* 48 (February 1986): 156-166.
39. *New York Times,* July 17, 1988.
40. *USA Today,* August 15, 1988; and *New York Times,* August 14, 1988.
41. For additional data on the delegates, see issues of the *New York Times,* July 17 and August 14, 1988.
42. Few contributions of the major parties are more likely to be criticized or ridiculed than the party platforms. Commentators have found them meaningless, irrelevant, and nearly useless in charting the direction of the government by the winning candidate and party. The truth is something else. Platform pledges tend to be adopted by the parties once they take control of government. Recently, about two-thirds of all platform promises have been fulfilled in some measure. See Gerald M. Pomper and Susan S. Lederman, *Elections in America* (New York: Longman, 1980), especially 161-167; and Alan D. Monroe, "American Party Platforms and Public Opinion," *American Journal of Political Science* 27 (February 1983): 27-42.

43. An exception to this rule occurred in 1956 when Adlai Stevenson, the Democratic presidential nominee, created a stir by declining to express a preference for his vice-presidential running mate. Left to its own devices, the convention quickly settled on a choice between senators Estes Kefauver and John F. Kennedy. Kefauver, who had been an active candidate for the presidency, won a narrow victory. Kennedy came off even better—he launched his candidacy for the presidential nomination in 1960.

44. The preference of party professionals for a balanced ticket grows out of their instinct for the conservation of the party and their understanding of the electorate. In the view of party professionals, the ticket should be broadly appealing instead of narrowly ideological or sectional. The factors that ordinarily come under review in the consideration of balance are geography, political philosophy, religion, and factional recognition.

45. Does balancing a ticket geographically make a difference? Specifically, does it increase the vote for the ticket in the vice president's home state? The answer is that it makes some positive difference if the candidate is from a small state, but "it is the presidential candidates who dominate the nation's politics." See Robert L. Dudley and Ronald B. Rapoport, "Vice Presidential Candidates and the Home State Advantage: Playing Second Banana at Home and on the Road," *American Journal of Political Science* 33 (May 1989): 537-540. Also see an earlier study by Michael S. Lewis-Beck and Tom W. Rice, "Localism in Presidential Elections: The Home State Advantage," *American Journal of Political Science* 27 (May 1983): 548-556.

46. A variation of this regional plan would require all states to hold a presidential primary.

47. Austin Ranney, *The Federalization of Presidential Primaries* (Washington, D.C.: American Enterprise Institute for Public Policy Research, 1978), 36-37. This monograph provides a comprehensive analysis of the proposals discussed in this section.

48. Doris A. Graber, *Mass Media and American Politics* (Washington, D.C.: CQ Press, 1989), 219-221.

49. U.S. Congress, Senate, *Congressional Record,* daily ed., 100th Cong., 2d sess., April 26, 1988, S4734-4735. The data on horse race versus issue airtime are taken from a study commissioned by *USA Today,* as reported in the issue of April 22, 1988.

50. Michael J. Robinson and Margaret A. Sheehan, *Over the Wire and on TV* (New York: Russell Sage Foundation, 1980), 89-90.

51. William G. Mayer, "The New Hampshire Primary: A Historical Overview," in *Media and Momentum,* 14.

52. Mayer, "The New Hampshire Primary," 16.

53. Henry E. Brady and Richard Johnston, "What's the Primary Message: Horse Race or Issue Journalism?" in *Media and Momentum,* 128.

54. Nelson W. Polsby, *Consequences of Party Reform,* 67.

chapter four

Political Parties and the Electoral Process: Campaigns and Campaign Finance

POLITICAL CAMPAIGNS are difficult to describe for one very good reason: they come in an extraordinary variety of shapes and sizes. Whether there is such a thing as a typical campaign is open to serious doubt. Campaigns will differ depending upon the office sought (executive, legislative, or judicial), the level of government (national, state, or local), the legal and political environments (partisan or nonpartisan election, competitive or noncompetitive constituency), and the initial advantages or disadvantages of the candidates (incumbent or nonincumbent, well known or little known), among other things.

The standards by which to measure and evaluate the effectiveness of campaigns are not easy to discover because of the vast number of variables that intrude both on campaign decisions and on voter choice. Does the party that wins an election owe its victory to a superior campaign or would it have won in any case? Data needed to answer the question are elusive. What is evident is that strategies that are appropriate to one campaign may be less appropriate or even inappropriate to another. Tactics that work at one time or in one place may not work under other circumstances. Organizational arrangements that satisfy one party may not satisfy the other. Campaigns are loaded with imponderables. Neither the party organizations nor the candidates have any control over numerous factors in a campaign. Moreover, parties and candidates cannot develop an immunity against campaign mistakes. Even so, in most cases it is not immediately clear when a miscalculation has been made, how serious it may have been, or how best to restore the damage.

Despite the variability and uncertainty that characterize political campaigns, a few general requirements are imposed on all candidates and parties. The candidate making a serious bid for votes must acquire certain resources and meet certain problems. Whatever his perspective of the campaign, the candidate will have to deal with matters of organization, strategy, and finances.

Campaign Organization

Very likely the single most important fact to know about campaign organization is that the regular party organizations are ill equipped to organize and conduct campaigns by themselves. Of necessity, they look to outsiders for assistance in all kinds of party work and for the development and staffing of auxiliary campaign organizations. A multiplicity of organizational units is created in every major election for the promotion of particular candidacies. Some businesspersons will organize to support the Republican nominee and other businesspersons will organize to support the Democratic candidate. And the same will be true for educators, lawyers, physicians, advertising executives, and even independents, to mention but a few. At times these groups work in impressive harmony with the regular party organizations (perhaps to the point of being wholly dominated by them), and at other times they function as virtually independent units, seemingly oblivious to the requirements for communication or for coordination of their activities with those of other party or auxiliary units.

The regular party organizations share influence not only with citizen groups but also with political action committees (PACs) of interest groups. Among the best known are the American Medical Association Political Action Committee, the Realtors Political Action Committee, The National Rifle Association Political Victory Fund, the AFL-CIO Committee on Political Education, and the National Congressional Club. Like other campaign groups, these committees raise funds, endorse candidates, make campaign contributions, and spend money on behalf of candidates. In 1988 PACs contributed $148 million to candidates for Congress, roughly one-third of their total expenditures. In addition, some 180 PACs and assorted groups spent more than $21 million independently on federal elections—two-thirds of it focused on the presidential candidates and one-third on congressional races. In the presidential contest, groups' independent spending overwhelmingly favored the Republicans: roughly $13 million to $600,000.[1]

At the top of the heterogeneous cluster of party and auxiliary campaign committees are the campaign organizations created by the individual candidates. Virtually all candidates for important, competitive offices feel they must develop personal campaign organizations to counsel them on strategy and issues, to assist with travel arrangements and speeches, to raise money, to defend their interests in party circles, and to try to coordinate their activities with those of other candidates and campaign units. The size of a candidate's personal organization is likely to vary according to the significance of the office and the competitiveness of the constituency. The member from a safe district, for example, habituated to easy elections, has less need of an elaborate campaign organization than a candidate from a closely competitive district. Some congressional districts are so safe (at least for the candidate, if not the party) that were it not for having to attend certain district party and civic rites, the incumbent could easily skip campaigning and remain in Washington.

In some campaigns the regular party organization is reduced to being just another spectator. Candidates commonly employ professional management firms to direct their campaigns instead of relying on the party organizations.[2] Most facets of American politics today come under the influence of public relations specialists and advertising firms. Possessing resources that the party organizations cannot match, they raise funds; recruit campaign workers; develop issues; gain endorsements; write speeches; arrange campaign schedules; direct the candidate's television appearances; and prepare campaign literature, films, and advertising. Indeed, they sometimes create the overall campaign strategy and dominate day-to-day decision making. Their principal task is to build images of candidates by controlling the way they appear to the general public. An adviser to Richard Nixon's 1968 presidential election campaign made the point in this observation:

> [Nixon] has to come across as a person larger than life, the stuff of legend. People are stirred by legend, including the living legend, not by the man himself. It's the aura that surrounds the charismatic figure more than it is the figure itself that draws the followers. Our task is to build that aura.[3]

Few if any features of American politics have changed more dramatically than the way in which candidates contend for office. Barbara G. Salmore and Stephen A. Salmore write:

> The role of the party boss has been taken over by the political consultant, that of the volunteer party worker by the paid telephone bank caller. Most voters learn about candidates not at political rallies but from television advertising and computer-generated direct mail; candidates generally gather information about voters not from the ward leader but from the pollster. The money to fuel campaigns comes less from the party organizations and "fat cats" and more from direct mail solicitation of individuals and special-interest political action committees. In short, candidates have become individual entrepreneurs, largely set free from party control or discipline.[4]

Campaign Strategy

The paramount goal of all major party campaigns is to form a coalition of sufficient size to bring victory to the candidate or party. Ordinarily, the early days of the campaign are devoted to the development and testing of a broad campaign strategy designed to produce a winning coalition. In the most general sense, strategy should be seen as "an overall plan for acquiring and using the resources needed for a campaign."[5] In developing a broad strategy, candidates, their advisers, and party leaders must take into consideration a number of factors. These include (1) the principal themes to be developed during the campaign; (2) the issues to be emphasized and exploited; (3) the candidate's personal qualities to be emphasized; (4) the specific groups and geographical areas to which appeals will be directed; (5) the acquisition of financial support and endorsements; (6) the timing of campaign activities; (7) the relationship of the candidate to the party organization and to factions within it; and (8) the uses to be made of the communications media, particularly television.

To the casual observer, there appear to be no limits to the number of major and minor strategies open to a resourceful candidate. However, important constraints serve to shape and define the candidate's options. For example, campaign strategy will be affected by the political, social, and economic environments that are present. Among the factors that intrude on campaign strategy are the competitiveness of the district, the

Television Advertising and the Voters

Candidates for major offices typically spend well over half of their budgets on television advertising. Is the money well spent? The results of a recent national survey by the Times Mirror suggest that it is—that TV ads have a significant impact on voter decisions. Here is what the voters had to say:

Statement	Completely agree	Mostly agree	Mostly disagree	Completely disagree	Don't know
I often don't become aware of political candidates until I see their advertising on television	17%	45%	28%	7%	3%
I get some sense of what a candidate is like through his or her TV commercials	9	49	30	8	4
I like to have a picture of a candidate in my mind when I go to vote for him or her	21	53	14	6	6

Which gives you a better idea of where a candidate stands on issues: news reports on TV or candidates' TV commercials?

News reports	74%
Candidates' TV commercials	17
Don't know	8

Which gives you a better idea of what a candidate is like personally: news reports on TV or candidates' TV commercials?

News reports	65%
Candidates' TV commercials	26
Don't know	9

SOURCE: *The People, the Press, and Politics 1990* (Washington, D.C.: Times Mirror Center for the People and the Press, 1990), 133.

NOTE: Percentages may not total to 100 because of rounding.

nature of the electorate, the quality and representativeness of the party ticket, the unity of the party, the presence of an incumbent, the election timetable (for example, presidential or off-year election), and the predispositions and commitments of political interest groups. Although difficult to weigh its significance, the temper of the times will also affect the candidate's overall plan of action. "In eras of general complacency and economic well-being," V. O. Key has written, "assaults against the interests and crusades against abuses by the privileged classes seem to pay small dividends. Periods of hardship and unrest move campaigners to contrive strategies to exploit the anxieties of people—or to insulate themselves from public wrath." [6] Whatever the impact of these constraints on campaign strategy, most of them are beyond the control of the candidate; they are simply conditions to which the candidate must adjust and adapt. The overall strategy that the candidate fashions or selects must be consonant with the givens of the campaign environment.

Opportunities and constraints vary from campaign to campaign and from candidate to candidate. Although this results in great diversity, the three overarching strategies that serious candidates usually follow can be depicted. The most important is for the candidate to *get supporters out to vote.* A great many elections are won or lost depending on the turnout of the party faithful. Minority party candidates probably would win most elections if they could increase the rate of turnout of their own supporters (assuming turnout for the major party candidates remained the same). The second general strategy is to *activate latent support.* Successful campaigns often turn on the ability of the candidate to activate potential voters among the groups that ordinarily support his party. For the Democratic candidate, this means that special effort must be directed to involve such segments of the population as Catholics, Jews, blacks, blue collar workers, union members, and urban residents; for the Republican candidate, this rule prescribes a similar effort to activate Protestants, whites, suburban and rural residents, and professional, business, and managerial elements. Efforts may be made to catalyze powerful single-issue groups, such as those in the prochoice and prolife movements. The third general strategy is to *change the opposition.* [7] In recent years this strategy has been spectacularly successful. A large number of Democrats, for example, voted for Dwight D. Eisenhower in the elections of 1952 and 1956, and a large number of Republicans bolted their party to vote for Lyndon B. Johnson in 1964. Similarly, in 1972 Democrats in great numbers abandoned their party's candidate,

George McGovern, to vote for Richard Nixon (though it is probable that they were not so much attracted to Nixon as repelled by McGovern). In 1980 about one-fourth of all Democrats voted for Ronald Reagan, and in 1984, about one-fifth. Fifteen percent of all Democrats voted for George Bush in 1988. Party switchers have played a crucial role in recent Republican victories.

Myths and facts are mixed in about equal proportion in the lore of campaign strategy. Strategies are not easily devised, sorted out, or tested. Indeed, it is scarcely ever apparent in advance which strategies are likely to be most productive and which least productive or even counterproductive. However disciplined and well managed campaigns may appear to those who stand on the outskirts, they rarely are in reality. As Stimson Bullitt has observed:

> A politician, unlike a general or an athlete, never can be invincible, except within a constituency which constitutes a sinecure. Furthermore, a candidate cannot even be sure that his campaigning will change the election result. . . . [A] politician must act on his hypotheses, which are tested only by looking backward on his acts. A candidate cannot even experiment. Because no one knows what works in a campaign, money is spent beyond the point of diminishing returns. To meet similar efforts of the opposition all advertising and propaganda devices are used—billboards, radio, TV, sound trucks, newspaper ads, letter writing or telephone committee programs, handbills, bus cards. No one dares to omit any approach. Every cartridge must be fired because among the multitude of blanks one may be a bullet. . . .
>
> A common mistake of post-mortems is to assert that a certain event or a stand or mannerism of a candidate caused him to win or lose. Often no one knows whether the election result was because of this factor or despite it. Spectacular events, whether a dramatic proposal, an attack, or something in the news outside the campaign, are like a revolving door. They win some votes and lose others.[8]

Campaign decisions may be shaped as much by chance and the ability of the candidate to seize on events as by the careful formulation of a broad and coherent plan of attack. Consider the decision of John F. Kennedy in the 1960 presidential campaign to telephone Coretta Scott King to express his concern over the welfare of her husband, the Rev. Dr. Martin Luther King, Jr., who had been jailed in Atlanta following a sit-in in a department store. There is no evidence that Kennedy's decision—

The Democratic Party's Dilemma

The Democratic party is the nation's majority party. It maintains a continuing advantage in voters' party identification—though its lead has slipped—and regularly controls Congress, a majority of state legislatures and governorships, and virtually all major cities. Presidential elections are another matter. The party's ability to win this office is often frustrated by its failure to hold its own partisans. The record shows that Democratic voters play a decisive role in the election of Republican presidents.

Party identification	Voting behavior							
	1972		1980		1984		1988	
	D	R	D	R	D	R	D	R
Democrat	67%	33%	69%	26%	79%	21%	85%	15%
Republican	5	95	8	86	4	96	7	93
	Nixon wins, 62% to 38%, over McGovern		Reagan wins, 51% to 41%, over Carter		Reagan wins, 59% to 41%, over Mondale		Bush wins, 54% to 46%, over Dukakis	

SOURCE: Developed from data in the *Gallup Report*, November 1988, 6-7.

NOTE: In 1968 George C. Wallace received 14 percent of the vote of Democratic identifiers and 5 percent of the vote of Republican identifiers. In 1980 John B. Anderson received 4 percent of the vote of Democratic identifiers and 5 percent of the vote of Republican identifiers. Even when Jimmy Carter won in 1976, 18 percent of all Democratic identifiers voted for the Republican nominee, Gerald R. Ford.

perhaps as critical as any of the campaign—was based on a comprehensive assessment of alternatives or possible consequences. Instead, according to Theodore H. White, the decision came about in this way:

> The crisis was instantly recognized by all concerned with the Kennedy campaign. . . . [The] suggestion for meeting it [was made by] Harris Wofford. Wofford's idea was as simple as it was human— that the candidate telephone directly to Mrs. King in Georgia to express his concern. Desperately Wofford tried to reach his own chief, Sargent Shriver, head of the Civil Rights Section of the

Kennedy campaign, so that Shriver might break through to the candidate barnstorming somewhere in the Middle West. Early [the next] morning, Wofford was able to locate Shriver . . . and Shriver enthusiastically agreed. Moving fast, Shriver reached the candidate [as he] was preparing to leave for a day of barnstorming in Michigan. The candidate's reaction to Wofford's suggestion of participation was impulsive, direct, and immediate. From his room at the Inn, without consulting anyone, he placed a long-distance telephone call to Mrs. Martin Luther King, assured her of his interest and concern in her suffering and, if necessary, his intervention. . . . The entire episode received only casual notice from the generality of American citizens in the heat of the last three weeks of the Presidential campaign. But in the Negro community the Kennedy intervention rang like a carillon.[9]

Congressional campaigns and election outcomes carry few surprises. Candidates win where they are expected to win and lose where they are expected to lose. Incumbent House members who lose in their bids to retain office are almost as rare as some entries on the endangered species list. Senators have more reason to worry over what the voters will deal to them, but they, too, campaign from a position of strength. Congressional campaigns go as expected for two major reasons. One is that incumbents enjoy overwhelming advantages. Among other things, they have a public record to which they can point, resources that permit them to assist constituents with their problems, the franking privilege, generous travel allowances, a staff and offices, and steady access to campaign funds—especially from PACs. Voters are more familiar with them than with their challengers. By contrast, congressional challengers cannot bank on a large and attentive public audience. No matter how tirelessly they transmit their messages, much of what they say is lost on a public preoccupied with other things.

Second, members of Congress campaign year-round. Constituent problems are handled by their staffs, and members return home weekend after weekend. Everyone in the member's entourage knows that reelections are won in nonelection years:

I have the feeling that the most effective campaigning is done when no election is near. During the interval between elections you have to establish every personal contact you can, and you accomplish this through your mail as much as you do it by means of anything else. At the end of each session I take all the letters which have been received on legislative matters and write each person telling him how the legislative proposal in which he was interested stands. Personally, I will speak on any subject. I am not nonpartisan, but I talk on everything whether it deals with politics or not. Generally I speak at nonpolitical meetings. I read 48 weekly newspapers and clip every one of them myself. Whenever there is a particularly interesting item about anyone, that person gets a note from me. . . . [You] cannot let the matter of election go until the last minute.[10]

You can slip up on the blind side of people during an off-year and get in much more effective campaigning than you can when you are in the actual campaign.[11]

The reason I get 93-percent victories is what I do back home. I stay highly visible. No grass grows under my feet. I show that I haven't forgotten from whence I came.[12]

Campaign issues are of two basic types: positional (or substantive) and "valence." Positional issues involve the candidate's stance on such questions as the environment, national defense, or taxes. Valence issues center on the personal qualities of the candidate—integrity, trustworthiness, capacity for leadership, and the like.[13]

The development of positional issues is not necessarily of great importance in designing campaign strategy. For one thing, voters frequently are unable to identify the positions of the candidates—this is particularly true in congressional elections.[14] For another, although some voters are sensitive to the specific issues generated in a campaign, many others are preoccupied with the candidate's image, personality, and style. Candidates are often judged less by what they say than by how they say it, less by their achievements than by their personality. Voters' perceptions of a candidate's character are highly important—perhaps especially in presidential contests. Scandals in government typically have a major impact on the strategies of subsequent campaigns, serving to heighten the significance of the candidate's alleged personal virtues— particularly those of honesty and sincerity—and to diminish the significance of positional issues. "I don't think issues mean a great deal about whether you win or lose," observes a U.S. senator. "I think issues give you a chance to [demonstrate] your honesty and candor."[15] And along the same line, a Democratic media consultant contends: "I don't think inflation is an issue. Who's for it? . . . The real issue is which of the two candidates would best be able to deal with [it]."[16]

According to ABC News exit polls in 1988, voters supporting George

Bush and Michael S. Dukakis gave sharply different reasons for their choices. Those who supported Bush stressed his experience, leadership, and the belief that "he can be trusted in a crisis." For Dukakis voters, the main reasons were that the candidate "cares about people like me," "is honest," and "can get things done." Perceptions of each candidate's personal qualities were clearly of major importance in voters' decisions.[17]

Dramatic changes have taken place in the way television covers presidential campaigns. A 1968 study by Kiku Adatto shows the average "sound bite" (or interval of uninterrupted speech) for presidential candidates was 42.3 seconds. Candidate statements of more than a minute's duration were common. By 1988 the average sound bite had slipped to 9.8 seconds[18]—an impossibly brief period for the development of even the simplest argument. In an era of videopolitics, issue development is subordinated to staged events and to conveying messages through the presentation of striking images, such as the 1988 Republican ad on Massachusetts' "revolving door" furlough program. Adatto's analysis is particularly instructive:

> In the last twenty years, the politicians, assisted by a growing legion of media advisors, have become more sophisticated at producing pictures that will play on television. The networks, meanwhile, have been unable to resist the temptation to show the pictures. Vivid visuals make good television, and besides, the networks might argue, if the candidate goes to Disneyland [Bush] or rides in a tank [Dukakis], does not covering the campaign mean covering those events? Even as they film the media events and show them on the evening news, however, television journalists acknowledge the danger of falling prey to manipulation, of becoming accessories to the candidate's stagecraft. One way of distancing themselves from the scenes they show is to turn to theater criticism, to comment on the scenes as a performance made for television, to lay bare the artifice behind the images. The problem with theater criticism, or image-conscious coverage as a style of political reporting, is that it involves showing the potent visuals the campaigns contrive. Reporters become conduits for the very images they criticize.[19]

Campaign Money

Of all the requirements for successful campaigns, none may be more important than a strong infusion of money. Campaign costs have risen

---

Media-driven Politics . . .

"Television has established itself as the prime medium of political communications. The most significant point to be made about television, as compared to printed media, is that it is personality dominated. It deals with political figures, not political institutions. . . . Political parties as such have almost no role in television's portrayal of the political drama."
—David S. Broder

"The media stand in a position today, especially in the nomination phase, where the old party bosses used to stand."
—John Sears

"In effect, Boss Tube has succeeded Boss Tweed of Tammany Hall, Boss Crump of Memphis, and the Daley machine in Chicago. Television brings politicians right into the living room and lets voters form their own impressions, rather than voters having to depend on what local party bosses, union leaders, church spokesmen, or business chiefs say. . . . [The] modern campaign is mass marketing at its most superficial. It puts a premium on the suggestive slogan, the glib answer, the symbolic backdrop. Television is its medium. Candidates must have razzle-dazzle. Boring is the fatal label. Programs and concepts that cannot be collapsed into a slogan or a thirty-second sound bite go largely unheard and unremembered, for what the modern campaign offers in length, it lacks in depth, like an endless weekend with no Monday morning."
—Hedrick Smith

---

steadily over the years. In 1952 expenditures for the nomination and election of public officials at all levels of government came to about $140 million. By 1968 this figure had climbed to $300 million. Candidates and parties spent approximately $425 million in 1972, $540 million in 1976, $1.2 billion in 1980, $1.8 billion in 1984, and $2.7 billion in 1988.[20]

Most of the cost of American elections is borne by private individuals and groups. In presidential elections, however, public financing is available. Under amendments adopted to the Federal Election Campaign Act (FECA) in 1974, candidates for the presidential nomination can qualify for matching public funds. Once the nominations have been settled, the candidates can elect to receive full federal funding in the

... *in a Television Age*

"The mark of a good day on the campaign trail is measured by the time devoted to the candidate's activities that gets on the air. A sound bite added to the picture is an extra elixir."

—Marvin Kalb

"Disdain for politicians as unprincipled power-seekers permeates the national media."

—S. Robert Lichter, Stanley
Rothman, and Linda S. Lichter

"This new relation, between image-conscious coverage and media-driven campaigns, raises with special urgency the deepest danger for politics in a television age. This is the danger of the loss of objectivity—not in the sense of bias, but in the literal sense of losing contact with the truth. It is the danger that the politicians and the press become caught up in a cycle that leaves the substance of politics behind, that takes appearance for reality, perception for fact, the artificial for the actual, the image for the event."

—Kiku Adatto

SOURCES: David S. Broder, "Of Presidents and Parties," *Wilson Quarterly* 2 (Winter 1978), 109-110; Sears quoted in Albert R. Hunt, "The Media and Presidential Campaigns," in *Elections American Style*, ed. A. James Reichley (Washington, D.C.: Brookings Institution, 1987), 54; Hedrick Smith, *The Power Game: How Washington Works* (New York: Random House, 1988), 36, 693; Kalb quoted in Kiku Adatto, *Sound Bite Democracy: Network Evening News Presidential Campaign Coverage, 1968 and 1988* (Cambridge, Mass.: Barone Center on the Press, Politics and Public Policy, 1990), 2; S. Robert Lichter, Stanley Rothman, and Linda S. Lichter, *The Media Elite* (Bethesda, Md.: Adler and Adler Publishers, 1986), 115; and Adatto, *Sound Bite Democracy*, 6.

general election campaign. Even so, private money dominates the financing of political campaigns at all levels of government.

The spiraling costs of running for office result from a number of factors. The steady increase in the general price level is one reason: inflation affects campaign costs as well as everything else. The growth in population and the enlargement of the electorate also make campaigning more expensive. The utilization of new techniques, such as computerized mailings, has proved costly. The substitution of presidential primaries for caucus-convention systems appears to have increased campaign expenditures. Considerable sums are spent by candidates in hiring political consultants to direct their campaigns. And the availability of private

The Public's Role in Financing Political Campaigns

Did you use the one-dollar checkoff on your federal income tax return to make a political contribution this year?

Yes	25.5%
No	67.5
Don't know	7.0

Did you give money to a political party during this election year?

Yes	5.9%
No	94.1

Did you give money to an individual candidate running for public office this year?

Yes	5.7%
No	94.3

Did you give any money to any group that supported or opposed candidates?

Yes	4.1%
No	95.9

SOURCE: These questions are drawn from the 1988 presidential election survey, National Election Study, Center for Political Studies, University of Michigan.

money in large quantities, particularly from the political action committees of interest groups,[21] encourages candidates to add to their campaign treasuries. Congressional incumbents believe that the best way to discourage challengers is to amass a large campaign fund well in advance of the next election. Thus it is common for members of Congress to solicit and accept PAC funds even when they have no serious competition. Some members use surplus funds to make contributions to the campaigns of colleagues.

Singled out in particular, however, for driving up campaign costs is broadcast advertising. Television, critics contend, is the real culprit.

Selecting Congressional Candidates for Campaign Contributions: Factors in PAC Decisions

1. *Incumbency status.* The rule is simple: Reward your friends, based on past support, and recognize that incumbents are going to win anyway. Recently, about $5 out of every $6 contributed by political action committees (PACs) to congressional candidates has gone to incumbents.
2. *Ideological compatibility.* For distinctively liberal or distinctively conservative groups, political philosophy is sine qua non.
3. *Risk avoidance.* Steer clear of losers who will hurt the organization's batting average.
4. *Risk avoidance.* Avoid alienating probable winners by not contributing to their opponents.
5. *Risk avoidance.* Think twice about offering funds to candidates who are in crowded or difficult primaries.
6. *Networking.* Recognize viable contenders—candidates who are on the "right" lists, having been endorsed by other (key) PACs.
7. *Networking.* Recognize viable contenders—candidates who have been targeted for support by the national parties.
8. *Reward pilgrims.* Give money to those challengers who make the pilgrimage to Washington (PAC City) to ask for it—if their policy stances are appropriate, if they have a credible campaign strategy, if they appear to have a reasonable chance of winning, if they have demonstrated they can raise money at home, and if they are not palpable nerds.

SOURCE: These propositions are fashioned from the observations of various PAC managers interviewed by Congressional Quarterly. See *Congressional Quarterly Weekly Report,* March 22, 1986, 655-659.

David Broder estimates that U.S. Senate candidates allocate 70 to 80 percent of their funds to paid television, turning them, as one senator put it, into "bag men for the TV operators." [22] Frank Greer, a Democratic media consultant, contends that 75 to 80 percent of the budgets in competitive campaigns is earmarked for television. The television industry itself estimates that television and radio advertising amounted to only 21.6 percent of campaign spending in 1986 and, for television alone, only

8.4 percent of total spending (federal, state, and local) in 1988. Herbert E. Alexander, who believes that television costs in overall political spending are not as great as critics contend, points out that only about one-half of the candidates for the U.S. House of Representatives ever purchase television time. What everyone concedes is that the unit cost of television advertising in prime time has grown rapidly.[23]

Because of the restrictions placed on contributions to presidential campaigns, perhaps the best way to begin the analysis of money in national political campaigns is to examine the sources from which congressional candidates secure funds. Several features of the money hustle of the 1988 election (covering the two-year election cycle and including primary, runoff, and general elections) stand out (see Table 4-1). First, the contributions of individuals represent the major source of campaign money for congressional candidates. And because FECA limits individual contributions to $1,000 per election, these gifts arrive in relatively small sums. In 1988 private contributions made up nearly 50 percent of the funds received by House candidates and more than 60 percent of the funds raised by Senate candidates. Second, PACs are also a major source of congressional campaign funds. Indeed, they have become critical in the campaigns of House incumbents, making up 47 percent of their total receipts (both parties) in 1988. Although not as dependent on interest groups, Senate incumbents nevertheless raised 29 percent of their funds from PACs. Third, congressional campaign fund raising is, purely and simply, an incumbent-dominated system. Challengers do not fare nearly as well in the PAC sweepstakes (see Table 4-1).

Overall 74 percent of all PAC funds in 1988 were given to incumbents, 12 percent to challengers, and 14 percent to candidates for open seats. The average House incumbent received $199,000 from political action committees, while challengers averaged only $27,000. Forty-eight House incumbents each accepted more than $350,000 from PACs; Speaker Thomas S. Foley (D-Wash.) reported PAC gifts of $560,000, while Minority Leader Robert H. Michel (R-Ill.) took in $556,000. Among senators, Lloyd Bentsen (D-Texas) easily led the way with PAC gifts, exceeding $2.3 million; forty-one Senate candidates each accepted more than half a million dollars from political action committees.[24]

The two parties' congressional candidates fare differently in raising PAC money. Democratic challengers and incumbents both do better than

TABLE 4-1 The Sources of Funding for 1988 Congressional Candidates

	Individual contributions	PAC contributions	Party contributions	Candidate contributions and loans	Other receipts
House					
Incumbents	45%	47%	1%	1%	6%
Challengers	52	19	3	23	3
Candidates for open seats	47	20	2	28	3
Senate					
Incumbents	65	29	1	1	4
Challengers	70	14	1	10	5
Candidates for open seats	54	21	1	19	5

SOURCE: Calculated from data in press release, Federal Election Commission, October 31, 1989.

NOTE: PAC = political action committee. This analysis includes primary, runoff, and general election funds of all candidates running in the November 1988 general election.

their Republican counterparts. In 1988, for example, all Democratic candidates for the House received 42 percent of all their funds from PACs, as contrasted with 30 percent for all Republican candidates. Figured separately, House Democratic incumbents garnered an extraordinary 51 percent of their funds from PACS. PACs contributed 40 percent of the funds amassed by House Republican incumbents (see Table 4-2).[25]

The overall growth of PAC contributions has been sizable (see Table 4-3). PACs contributed almost three times as much money to House and Senate candidates in 1988 as in 1980. The numbers themselves are instructive: a total of $55 million was contributed in the 1980 election cycle and $148 million in the 1988 election cycle.

Political action committees target their contributions carefully, taking into consideration incumbency, party, and legislative position. In 1988 labor PACs contributed $33.9 million to congressional candidates, with 93 percent given to Democrats. Corporate PACs gave $50.3 million to congressional candidates, of which 62 percent went to Republicans.[26] Committee chairmen and party leaders are major beneficiaries of interest group largesse. Committee membership is also taken into consideration. Members of the tax and commerce committees, for example, invariably

TABLE 4-2   Congressional Candidates' Reliance on Political Action Committee (PAC) Funds, 1984-1988, by Party and Incumbency

	Proportion of total receipts from PACs		
	1984	1986	1988
House			
All Democratic candidates	38%	39%	42%
Democratic incumbents	46	49	51
All Republican candidates	29	28	30
Republican incumbents	38	38	40
Senate			
All Democratic candidates	17	22	23
Democratic incumbents	29	28	30
All Republican candidates	17	20	24
Republican incumbents	22	26	28

SOURCE: Data from press release, Federal Election Commission, February 24, 1989.

receive more PAC money than members of the judiciary or foreign policy committees. The pattern of contributions is illustrated by these observations:

> The main goal is to support our friends who have been with us most of the time. (An official of the UAW)
>
> The prevailing attitude is that PAC money should be used to facilitate access to incumbents. (The director of governmental and political participation for the Chamber of Commerce of the United States)
>
> We're inclined to support incumbents because we tend to go with those who support our industry. We are not out looking to find challengers. Our aim is not to change the tone of Congress. (A spokesperson for the Lockheed Good Government Program)
>
> We're looking especially for members who serve on key committees, and people who help us on the floor. (A spokesperson for the Automobile and Truck Dealers Election Action Committee)[27]

Political action committees spread money around. Parties as well as candidates now depend on them. In 1988 the two major parties collected assorted PAC gifts totaling $14.2 million, up from $10.4 million in 1984.[28] Putting those numbers in perspective, for every one dollar that PACs gave to the party organizations they gave ten dollars to candidate organizations.

TABLE 4-3   The Contributions of Political Action Committees (PACs) to
Congressional Campaigns, 1980-1988

✳	1980	1982	1984	1986	1988
Total PAC contributions	$55.2	$83.6	$105.4	$132.7	$147.9
House campaigns	37.9	61.1	75.7	87.4	102.3
Senate campaigns	17.3	22.5	29.7	45.3	45.6
PAC percentage of all funds raised by					
House candidates	26	29	34	34	37
Senate candidates	17	16	17	21	23

SOURCE: Data from press releases, Federal Election Commission, May 16, 1985; February 24, 1989; and April 9, 1989.

NOTE: Dollar figures are in millions.

In addition to making direct contributions to candidates, PACs are permitted to make *independent* expenditures, spending for or against candidates. No limits govern the amounts PACs may spend, but they are prohibited from consulting candidates concerning these expenditures. In 1988 PAC independent expenditures totaled $21.1 million.[29] The biggest PACs now hire media consultants and polling experts to make their independent aid as effective as possible. In 1986 the American Medical Association (AMA) budgeted $300,000 to support the opponent of Rep. Andrew Jacobs, Jr. (D-Ind.), who had incurred the AMA's wrath for urging House colleagues, in a debate on Medicaid, to "vote for the canes, not for the stethoscopes." [30] Despite AMA opposition, Jacobs was reelected by a comfortable margin. Under the Federal Election Campaign Act, direct PAC contributions to any candidate in any election are limited to $5,000. Independent spending is thus a way of circumventing this restriction.

So popular is the PAC idea that many members of Congress have created their own political action committees to raise and disburse campaign funds. The thrust of some member PACs is simply to help to reelect partisan or ideological allies. But for most member PACs the dominant purpose appears to be self-promotion. The most active congressional PACs are those created by members with aspirations for the presidency, the speakership, and a range of other positions, such as floor leader, whip, or committee chairman. These leadership PACs distribute campaign funds to members (and occasionally to challengers) as a way of building good will and creating support. For presidential hopefuls in particular, having one's own PAC is invaluable in meeting the expenses of political travel necessary to capture public attention or to campaign for other congressional candidates. Probably the best known member PAC is North Carolina Republican senator Jesse Helms's National Congressional Club. Among the other influential member PACs are Campaign America (Sen. Robert Dole, R-Kan.), Fund for a Democratic Majority (Sen. Edward M. Kennedy, D-Mass.), and America's Leaders Fund (Rep. Dan Rostenkowski, D-Ill.). Of no particular surprise, most of the money contributed to member PACs come from other PACs.[31]

The availability of PAC money makes life easier for incumbents. They and their aides understand the PAC network, know how to curry favor with PACs (or at least how to avoid their enmity), know how to solicit funds from them, and know how to respond to their initiatives. Members are largely comfortable in this world of organization money even though they resent the amount of time required to raise funds and worry over possible obligations to their benefactors. Nonetheless, access to PAC money is not the most important advantage of incumbents. Their main advantage is simply the opportunities and resources that are attached to holding congressional office: the franking privilege; a public record; name recognition; generous travel allowance; opportunities to make news; opportunities to take credit for "pork" brought into the constituency; and, perhaps most important of all, a large staff (many of whom are assigned to the district or state). "The Hill office," writes David R. Mayhew, "is a vitally important political unit, part campaign management firm and part political machine." [32] The office is a political unit financed by the Treasury, and the contributions to incumbents are substantial. Michael Malbin estimates that House incumbents enjoy perquisites of office, supporting constituent contact, worth at least $1 million over the period of a two-year term ($400,000 for constituent-service staff; $400,000 for district office expenses, travel, phones, computers, and the like; and $250,000 for unsolicited mailings to constituents).[33] Hence the heavy support of political action committees is simply icing on the cake—double-rich.

Raising campaign money is a relentless pursuit for members of Congress and their aides. House and Senate rules permit each office to have at least one staff member assigned to receive campaign contributions. Additionally, many members hire professional fund raisers who advise them on the techniques for soliciting money (to ask for the "right" amount—not too much, not too little) and who travel around the country with them to court contributors. Increasingly, the money hunt has prompted members to seek funds from sources outside their home states. Fund-raising events at Washington watering holes occur night after night (cost of admission: usually $500 on the House side, $1,000 or more on the Senate side), attracting lobbyists and assorted contributors who know that gifts are acknowledged with the promise of access. Members solicit and accept out-of-state political money, first, because it is readily available and, second, because it is easier than asking their own constituents and perhaps offending them.[34]

The third most important source of campaign funds for congressional candidates is the political party. The party's role is limited, however, by the Federal Election Campaign Act, both in terms of how much money it can contribute directly to candidates and how much it can spend on their behalf. In making direct contributions to House candidates, national party committees (national committee and congressional campaign committee) face the same limitation as PACs—each is limited to a contribution of $5,000 per candidate per campaign. Candidates for the Senate can receive up to $17,500 in direct contributions from the national committee and the senatorial campaign committee, combined, in a calendar year. State and local committees can also make limited contributions to congressional campaigns. Much more important are national party expenditures made on behalf of congressional candidates—so-called *coordinated* expenditures. Permitted only in the general election, coordinated expenditures are made by the party committees alone, though they may consult with the candidates' organizations to decide how the money is to be spent. Based on state voting-age populations, the amounts permitted are sizable for Senate campaigns in populous states. In California, for example, each party in 1990 could spend $1.1 million on behalf of its senatorial candidate; in New York, $684,000; in Texas, $605,000; in Pennsylvania, $462,000; and in some dozen relatively small states, $50,000. For House candidates in 1990, coordinated expenditures were limited to $25,000 (except in states with only one representative, where the limit was $50,000).[35]

In addition, fortified by a Supreme Court ruling,[36] a state party committee can transfer its spending authority to the national committee, which effectively doubles the expenditures the national party can make on behalf of its candidates. These agency agreements have been a boon to the spending plans of the Republican party in particular.

Party support for congressional candidates has been growing.[37] In 1988 coordinated expenditures totaled more than $14 million for the Republican party and about $9.5 million for the Democratic party. Gary C. Jacobson estimates that national party committees can supply one-fourth of the money necessary for a serious House campaign and, in some states, up to half of the funds necessary for a full-scale Senate campaign.[38] Nevertheless, the parties do not stack up well in comparison with PACs. If the behavior of officeholders is influenced by campaign money, as Herbert E. Alexander has observed, the parties do not have a particularly strong claim for preference, especially in view of the contributions to legislators by individuals and political action committees.[39]

Spending campaign money intelligently is problematical at the least. Candidates spend as heavily as they do because neither they nor their advisers know which expenditures are likely to produce the greatest return in votes. Lacking systematic information, they jump at every opportunity to contact and persuade voters—and every opportunity costs money.

Political money is not a subject that lends itself to easy analysis. Tracing exactly how it is raised and how it is spent is far from simple. In a federal and fragmented system campaign money is collected and spent by a multiplicity of competing political actors and institutions. If there is fashion at all, it is helter-skelter. In addition, the effects of money on elections, political behavior, and public policy are not fully understood. One point about which there is substantial agreement, however, is that campaign spending has grown dramatically in recent years.

Congressional campaigns provide a good example. They are expensive. In 1976 House and Senate candidates collectively spent about $100 million.[40] In 1984 they spent about $374 million, and in 1988, about $459 million. The consumer price index, by contrast, "merely" doubled between 1976 and 1988. Inflation obviously does not account for the lion's share of the increase.

Expenditures by winning congressional candidates have grown at an unusually rapid rate. Data on House and Senate spending by winning candidates from 1976 to 1988 are presented in Figure 4-1. Over this period, expenditures by successful House candidates increased by almost 500 percent and those by successful Senate candidates by 600 percent.[41]

Spending by winners and losers in 1988 House elections suggests several conclusions (see Table 4-4). First of all, the most expensive races

FIGURE 4-1   Total Spending by Winning Congressional Candidates, 1976-1988

Millions of dollars

SOURCE: Press release, Federal Election Commission, October 31, 1989.

NOTE: Spending is for all campaigns, including campaigns for the primary, runoff, and general elections. An election cycle is for two years, the election year and the year preceding.

involve incumbents who think or know they are in trouble with the voters. Half-million dollar campaigns are common for apprehensive House incumbents. At the same time, incumbents who expect to win and do win easily spend less than anyone except hopeless challengers. But even for safe incumbents (some of whom faced no opposition) the median expenditure in 1988 was $287,000. Second, with relatively few exceptions, incumbents outspend their challengers, many of whom are severely underfinanced. About half of all challengers in 1988 spent less than

TABLE 4-4   The Expenditures of Winners and Losers in U.S. House Elections, Shown in Relation to Electoral Margins, 1988

	Winning with 60 percent or more of vote		Winning with 55-59.9 percent of vote		Winning with less than 55 percent of vote	
Median expenditures of winning						
Incumbents	(353)	$287,996	(30)	$640,539	(23)	$581,888
Challengers	(1)	516,737	(1)	385,402	(5)	600,114
Candidates for open seats	(10)	453,913	(4)	515,266	(13)	569,830
	Losing with 45 percent or more of vote		Losing with 40-44.9 percent of vote		Losing with less than 40 percent of vote	
Median expenditures of losing						
Incumbents	(3)	$1,069,699	(2)	$723,638	(1)	$696,301
Challengers	(13)	378,469	(27)	355,016	(230)	44,205
Candidates for open seats	(8)	489,937	(6)	463,725	(11)	80,675

SOURCE: Data from press release, Federal Election Commission, October 31, 1989.

NOTE: Number of House candidates in each category shown in parentheses.

$50,000 on their campaigns. Third, spending in campaigns for open seats (no incumbent) is nearly always high, averaging more than $500,000 for winners in 1988. Fourth, the costs of some House campaigns border on the scandalous. One Tennessee Republican spent more than $2.5 million in 1988 while losing to her Democratic opponent who spent $1.8 million. Fifty House candidates spent more than three-quarters of a million on their campaigns.

In several Senate races in 1988, spending was nothing less than spectacular. Pete Wilson spent $13 million in California to defeat his Democratic opponent, who spent $7 million. The two major party candidates in Ohio spent a total of $17 million. Altogether, twelve Senate candidates spent in excess of $4 million on their campaigns. For winning Senate candidates, the average expenditure was about $3.75 million. The all-time record for expensive Senate campaigns is held by Jesse Helms (R-N.C.), who spent $16.4 million to win reelection in 1984. Plainly, congressional campaign politics is not a poor man's game, at

The Money Chase
in the 1988 Congressional Elections:
PACs, Incumbents, and Challengers

Allocation of PAC Funds

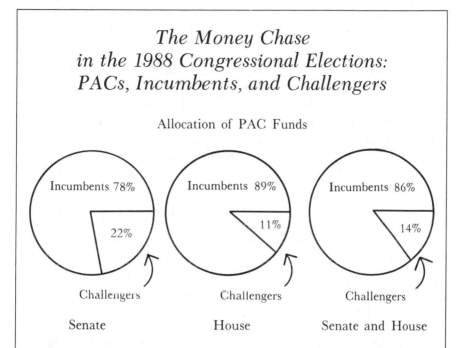

Of the $128.9 million given by political action committees (PACs) to congressional incumbents and challengers for the 1988 elections, $110.9 million was given to incumbents. Often ignored by PACs, challengers spend their own money and scrounge for individual contributions and loans. Both parties' incumbents excel in the PAC money chase, as these data show:

	Total receipts from PACs	Percentage	Average per incumbent
Senate incumbents			
Democrats (15)	$15,256,672	53	$1.0 million
Republicans (12)	13,422,457	47	1.1 million
House incumbents			
Democrats (248)	53,356,704	65	215,000
Republicans (164)	28,822,871	35	175,000

SOURCE: Calculated from data in press release, Federal Election Commission, October 31, 1989.

NOTE: PAC contributions to candidates for open seats are not included in this analysis. Number of incumbents is shown in parentheses.

least not for candidates who want to be taken seriously.

Of all the issues raised concerning campaign finance, none seems to stir more interest than the role of PACs, particularly in congressional campaigns. The national press frequently focuses on their contributions. Common Cause has prepared dozens of studies over the years, and their findings point to the dangers of the PAC movement.[42] Even Congress itself occasionally becomes exercised over the "PAC problem"—the growing reliance of members on interest group money and the suspicion that these gifts undermine the independence of members. Are members' votes influenced by the PAC gifts they receive? On certain narrow economic issues, such as dairy price supports and cargo preference, a relationship between contributions and voting behavior has been found.[43] Nonetheless, influence is hard to establish: Does money follow votes or votes follow money? Not surprisingly, members evaluate PACs in sharply different ways, as the following observations show:

> It is fundamentally corrupting. At best, people say they are sympathetic to the people they are getting money from before they get it; at worst, they are selling votes. But you cannot prove cause and effect. I take the money from labor, and I have to think twice in voting against their interests. I shouldn't have to do that. (Rep. Richard L. Ottinger, D-N.Y.)

> There's a danger that we're putting ourselves on the auction block every election. It's now tough to hear the voices of the citizens in your district. Sometimes the only things you hear are the loud voices in the three-piece suits carrying a PAC check. (Rep. Leon E. Panetta, D-Calif.)

> PAC money is destroying the electoral process. (former senator Barry Goldwater, R-Ariz.)

> I don't worry about being bought, because I'm not for sale. The truth is I am proud of the PACs and the people who support me. (Sen. Phil Gramm, R-Texas)

> If you're not able to fund your campaign and keep your responsibility to the people who send you here, you don't belong in office. (Rep. John D. Dingell, D-Mich.)

> PACs facilitate the political participation of hundreds of thousands of individuals who might not otherwise become involved in the election of an individual. (Sen. John W. Warner, R-Va.)[44]

Bills to curtail PAC influence in campaigns have been introduced frequently in Congress over the last decade. Among other things, these proposals have sought to place a cap on the total amount of PAC funds that congressional candidates can accept; cut the size of their contributions (usually from $5,000 to $3,000); limit their independent spending for or against candidates; and close a loophole in the law that permits them to receive individual contributions, bundle them together, and pass them along to candidates in the PAC's name but without falling under the limitations on spending. In a sharp departure in 1990, Senate Republicans proposed that federal PACs be eliminated altogether, and Senate Democrats countered with a proposal to prohibit PAC contributions to Senate candidates while preserving their right to contribute to party committees. (Congressional Democrats have had considerably more success in raising PAC money than Republicans.)

Access to PAC funds represents a major advantage for incumbents over their challengers, and whether members will be willing to give it up remains to be seen. Yet if PAC contributions continue unabated, the intensity of this special interest issue will also grow. Whatever the reality of PAC influence on decision makers, PAC power is an issue made in heaven for good government groups, reformers, certain insiders, and the media. At some point, probably sooner than later, members may feel compelled to impose restrictions on PAC contributions. Severe restrictions would likely be tested in the courts as a violation of the First Amendment's protection of free speech.

The Regulation of Campaign Finance

Public restiveness over the role of money in American politics has long been present. Dissatisfaction focuses around three main complaints. The first is simply that campaign costs have risen to such an extent that candidates with limited resources are seriously disadvantaged in the electoral process. The doubt persists that some talented people never seek public office because they lack financial support or are unwilling to solicit funds from others because of the risk of incurring political indebtedness and of compromising their independence. Moreover, the high cost of elections may mean that the public hears only one side of the campaign, that of the candidate with access to large sums of money.

The second complaint is that the individuals, families, and groups that contribute lavishly to parties and candidates are suspected of buying influence and gaining preferments of some kind in return for the money they channel into campaigns. Whether this is true may not be as important as the fact that the public believes it to be true. In some measure, public suspicion about campaign financing contributes to public suspicion of government.

And finally, as a result of the Watergate exposé, a heightened awareness exists of the potential for corruption and abuse when huge sums of money are collected and spent for political purposes.

To deal with a variety of maladies associated with the financing of federal political campaigns, Congress passed the Federal Election Campaign Act of 1971. This act, the first serious attempt since 1925 to reform campaign financing, is of unusual importance. Adopted prior to the Watergate incident, the act anticipated public financing of federal election campaigns by providing that taxpayers could earmark one dollar on their personal income tax returns for use in the 1976 presidential election. Of at least equal importance, the act provided for rigorous disclosure requirements concerning campaign contributions, expenditures, and debts. Finally, a provision to stimulate private contributions to political campaigns was placed in the act. Under a tax-incentive system, taxpayers were permitted to deduct small campaign contributions from their tax obligations. In retrospect, the extraordinary dimensions of the 1972 presidential election scandal would not have been uncovered without the disclosure requirements for political contributions and expenditures contained in the law.

Crisis is often a spur to legislative action. Largely in response to Watergate, Congress in 1974 passed comprehensive amendments to the Federal Election Campaign Act. Designed to curtail the influence and abuse of money in campaign politics, these amendments placed tight restrictions on contributions, expenditures, disclosure, and reporting. Most important, the 1974 legislation provided for at least partial public financing of presidential primaries, elections, and nominating conventions. The constitutionality of the provisions relating to the presidential electoral process was promptly tested in the courts. In *Buckley v. Valeo*,[45] decided in 1976, the Supreme Court held that the act's limitations on individual expenditures (either those of the candidate[46] or those of individuals spending independently on behalf of a candidate) were unconstitutional, since they interfered with the right of free speech under the First Amendment. Political money, in a sense, is political speech.

The Court upheld the limitations on contributions to campaigns, the disclosure requirements, and the public-funding provisions for presidential primaries and elections. The main features of the nation's campaign finance law are included in Table 4-5.

The leading characteristic of the campaign finance law is its focus on the presidency. No provision is made for the public financing of campaigns for Congress. For those who believe that what is good for the goose is good for the gander, the observations of Senator Kennedy are especially appropriate:

> Abuses of campaign spending and private campaign financing do not stop at the other end of Pennsylvania Avenue. They dominate congressional elections as well. If the abuses are the same for the presidency and Congress, the reforms should also be the same. If public financing is good enough for presidential elections, it should also be good enough for Senate and House elections.[47]

Many members of Congress have become weary of the struggle to raise campaign funds:

> To raise $4 million [required for an average winning Senate campaign in 1988] means that for every single week for six years without exception a member of the Senate would have to figure out how to raise $15,000 in campaign contributions. (Sen. David L. Boren, D-Okla.)[48]

> The present system does not even allow the incumbents with new ideas to get them into place. We are too busy out engaging in the money chase. We cannot be here in the committees, we cannot be here on the floor doing our work. . . . We are kept so busy out there knocking on doors all over the country, seeking money, asking for money, begging for money, getting on our hands and knees for money, we do not have time to give thought to new ideas and to be putting them into creative legislation. (Sen. Robert C. Byrd, D-W.Va.)[49]

> I have been introduced into 21st century campaigning and I don't like it. All of a sudden you have to hire a fundraiser, a media consultant, a press attaché, a mailing specialist. (Rep. Sidney R. Yates, D-Ill.)[50]

Numerous attempts to overhaul the nation's election finance law have been made since the late 1970s, but thus far unsuccessfully. Reform proposals invariably have become entangled in partisan politics. On the

TABLE 4-5   Major Provisions for the Regulation of Campaign Financing in
Federal Elections

I. Contribution Limits
   A. No individual may contribute more than $1,000 to any candidate or
      candidate committee per election. (Primary, runoff, and general elections
      are considered to be separate elections.)
   B. Individual contributions to a national party committee are limited to
      $20,000 per calendar year and to any other political committee to $5,000
      per calendar year. (The total contributions by an individual to all federal
      candidates in one year cannot exceed $25,000.)
   C. A multicandidate committee (one with more than fifty contributors that
      makes contributions to five or more federal candidates) may contribute no
      more than $5,000 to any candidate or candidate committee per election, no
      more than $15,000 to the national committee of a political party, and no
      more than $5,000 to any other political committee per calendar year.
   D. The national committee and the congressional campaign committee may
      each contribute up to $5,000 to each House candidate, per election; the
      national committee, together with the senatorial campaign committee,
      may contribute up to a combined total of $17,500 to each Senate candidate
      for the entire campaign period (including a primary election).
   E. Political action committees formed by businesses, trade associations, or
      unions are limited to contributions of no more than $5,000 to any
      candidate in any election. No limits apply to their aggregate contributions.
   F. Banks, corporations, and labor unions are prohibited from making con-
      tributions from their treasuries to federal election campaigns. Government
      contractors and foreign nationals are similarly restricted. Contributions
      may not be supplied by one person but made in the name of another
      person. Contributions in cash are limited to $100.

II. Expenditure Limits
   A. Candidates are limited to an expenditure of $10 million each plus COLA
      (cost-of-living adjustment) in all presidential primaries. (In 1988 each
      candidate could spend up to $23 million in all presidential primaries.)
   B. Major party presidential candidates may spend no more than $20 million
      plus COLA in the general election (a total of $46.1 million each in 1988).
   C. Presidential and vice-presidential candidates who accept public funding
      may spend no more than $50,000 of personal funds in their campaigns.
   D. Each national party may spend up to two cents per voter on behalf of its
      presidential candidate.
   E. In addition to making contributions to candidates, the national committee,
      together with congressional and senatorial campaign committees, may
      make expenditures on behalf of House and Senate candidates. For each
      House member—in states with more than one district—the sum is
      $10,000 plus COLA. For each Senate candidate the sum is $20,000 plus
      COLA or two cents for each person in the state's voting-age population,
      whichever is greater. (Under the second formula, party committees could
      spend $1.1 million on behalf of a California Senate candidate in 1990.)
      State party committees may make expenditures on behalf of House and
      Senate candidates up to the same limits.

F. As a result of the *Buckley v. Valeo* decision, there are no limits on how much House and Senate candidates may collect and spend in their campaigns (or on how much they may spend of their own or their family's money).

G. Also in the wake of *Buckley v. Valeo,* there are no limits on the amount that individuals and groups may spend on behalf of any presidential or congressional candidate so long as the expenditures are independent—that is, not arranged or controlled by the candidate.

III. Public Financing

A. Major party candidates for the presidency qualify for full funding ($20 million plus COLA) prior to the campaign, the money to be drawn from the federal income tax dollar checkoff. In 1988 the Democratic and Republican nominees each received $46.1 million in campaign funds. Candidates may decline to participate in the public funding program and finance their campaigns through private contributions. Candidates who accept public funding may not accept private contributions.

B   Minor party and independent candidates qualify for lesser sums, provided their candidates received at least 5 percent of the vote in the previous presidential election. New parties or parties that received less than 5 percent of the vote four years earlier qualify for public financing after the election, provided they drew 5 percent of the vote.

C. Matching public funds up to $5 million (plus COLA) are available for presidential primary candidates, provided that they first raise $100,000 in private funds ($5,000 in contributions of no more than $250 in each of twenty states). Once that threshold is reached, the candidate receives matching funds up to $250 per contribution. No candidate is eligible for more than 25 percent of the total available funds. The maximum amount of matching funds available to any candidate in 1988 was $11.5 million.

D. Presidential candidates who receive less than 10 percent of the vote in two consecutive presidential primaries become ineligible for additional campaign subsidies.

E. Optional public funding of presidential nominating conventions is available for the major parties, with lesser amounts for minor parties.

IV. Disclosure and Reporting

A. Each federal candidate is required to establish a single, overarching campaign committee to report on all contributions and expenditures on behalf of the candidate.

B. Frequent reports on contributions and expenditures are to be filed with the Federal Election Commission.

V. Enforcement

A. Administration of the law is the responsibility of a six-member, bipartisan Federal Election Commission. The Commission is empowered to make rules and regulations, to receive campaign reports, to render advisory opinions, to conduct audits and investigations, to subpoena witnesses and information, and to seek civil injunctions through court action.

Senate Campaign Reform Bills ...

Senate Democratic Version: Spending Limitations and Public Funding

1. Spending limits established for each state, ranging from $950,000 for general elections in the least populous states (Alaska and Wyoming) to $5.5 million for California. Funds raised in amounts of $100 or less from home-state voters would be partially exempt from spending limits.

2. Candidates qualify for public funding (pegged at 70 percent of a general election campaign) by adhering to spending limits, spending no more than $250,000 of their own money, and raising funds in small amounts (half to come from residents of their own state).

3. Provision of government vouchers to purchase prime-time television slots for longer ads (one to five minutes) and requiring broadcast stations to make longer time periods available for such ads. Candidates required to appear at conclusion of broadcast to take responsibility for the ad. (Objective: to undercut 30-second, negative attack ads.)

4. Contingency money: If spending limits are exceeded by a candidate, his opponent would receive public funds equal to the amount spent beyond this limit.

5. Political action committees (PACs) barred from contributing to candidates but could continue to contribute to party committees, with certain limitations.

6. Individual contributions to state party committees and to PACs increased as well as those to federal candidates (from $25,000 to $30,000 for all federal candidates).

7. Candidates opposed in independent campaigns that pay $10,000 or more for television ads become entitled to public funds to respond to these ads.

8. Restrictions on the use of state party "soft money" (money spent on such activities as get-out-the-vote drives, voter "education," or voter registration) to help state and federal candidates. Federal limits and disclosure would apply to soft money raised by state parties.

... *Introduced in the 101st Congress*

Senate Republican Version: Party-Centered and PAC Elimination

1. Eliminates federal political action committees.

2. Eliminates restrictions on the spending of national parties for organizational activities including research and get-out-the-vote drives. Limitations on party expenditures for candidates on television advertising and certain other activities would remain.

3. Substantially increases contribution limits for individuals—from current maximum of $25,000 in annual contributions to all federal candidates to $85,000. Maximum contribution to a candidate from a person who is not a resident of the candidate's state reduced to $500.

4. Tax-exempt organizations, such as labor unions, would be barred from taking action ("electioneering") for or against specific candidates. (Their role in campaign funding would be eliminated under the general ban on federal political action committees.)

5. Parties would be permitted to match, up to $100,000, money raised in-state by candidates challenging incumbents.

6. Opponents of candidates spending or lending more than $250,000 of their own money would be permitted to raise funds in $5,000 amounts (instead of $1,000) from individual contributors and, at a certain point, to raise unlimited amounts of money and to benefit from unlimited spending on their behalf by their party.

7. Candidates would be permitted to buy the best television time slots in a broadcaster's schedule at the cheapest price offered anyone for that time period.

8. Members would be restricted in their use of the franking privilege for mass mailings during an election year and prohibited from transferring campaign funds to their office accounts.

9. Restrictions on the use of state party "soft money" on ticketwide activities if a federal candidate is on the ballot.

SOURCE: Developed from analyses in *Congressional Quarterly Weekly Report,* May 5, 1990, 1322-1323.

whole, Democratic members have favored public financing of congressional campaigns and relatively strict limits on spending; Democrats are particularly united on the need to impose spending limits. For their part, Republicans see proposals for public financing as designed to protect incumbents—which translates into the safeguarding of Democratic majorities, especially in the House. Prospects for the Republican party, they reason, are better under the present system of private financing. For the same reason, Republicans also show little enthusiasm for spending limits. As Senate Republican leader Robert Dole has observed, "An absolute, fixed cap on campaign spending is nothing more than a prescription for incumbency protection." [51] Most Republicans put great stock in the findings of political scientists, such as Gary Jacobson, that money spent by congressional challengers has a much larger effect on election outcomes than money spent by incumbents.[52] Hence, placing a limit on Republican challengers' spending diminishes their chances of winning (and the party's chances of regaining the majority in Congress).

Whatever the motives that underlie members' attitudes toward campaign finance reform, it is plain that this issue bears peculiarly on congressional careers. The temptation is strong for members to evaluate all proposals for reform in personal and political terms, favoring or opposing legislation in light of its probable impact on their electoral security and the welfare of their party. At the same time, members feel pressure to do something in view of the runaway costs of recent years and the heavy involvement of PACs in campaign spending.

Despite the partisan deadlock that has smothered campaign finance legislation in recent years, Congress unlikely has written its last word on the subject. Members of both parties, for example, profess the need to reduce out-of-state fund raising and to diminish candidates' excessive reliance on PAC money. And there is broad support on both sides of the aisle for legislation that would cut the costs of television time for candidates and require broadcasters to make available for campaign ads the best time slots in their advertising schedules. Whatever changes ultimately are made, one should expect the legislation to contain key provisions that benefit the members who wrote and adopted it.

At this point it is useful to take stock of what has happened since the adoption of the Federal Election Campaign Act and its subsequent amendments. Experience with the campaign finance law for nearly two decades provides support for a number of observations concerning its impact on citizens, parties, candidates, and the political system:[53]

1. *The campaign finance law and its amendments have encouraged citizen contributions to the parties and candidates.* Until recently, only about 10 percent of the electorate had contributed money to political parties or individual candidates in election campaigns. As a result of the adoption of income tax checkoff provisions at the federal and state levels, financial participation has increased significantly. Slightly more than one-fifth of the electorate now takes advantage of the checkoff option, but the proportion has been declining. This type of contribution is a relatively low-cost activity, since it does not increase the individual's tax liability; its cumulative impact is nevertheless enormous in financing presidential preconvention and general election campaigns.[54] Altogether, about $159 million in federal funds were distributed to presidential candidates in these election phases in 1988 (with another $18 million allocated for funding the parties' conventions).[55] Direct contributions by citizens are also made. In 1988 about 15 percent of the public contributed money to either a party, individual candidate, or political action committee.[56] Plainly, political parties no longer dominate the organization and funding of campaigns.

2. *The campaign finance law has aided the parties in some respects and weakened them in others.* Among the provisions of the Federal Election Campaign Act that benefit the parties are these: (a) individual contributors can give more money to the parties ($20,000) than they can to candidates ($1,000); (b) each national party can spend money on behalf of its presidential and congressional candidates (coordinated expenditures); (c) both national and state party committees can make direct contributions to House and Senate candidates; (d) public funds are available to defray the costs of presidential nominating conventions; and (e) under a 1979 amendment, state and local parties can spend unlimited sums on campaign materials, voter registration, and get-out-the-vote drives in presidential elections—so-called party-building activities.

Other features of the law, however, do not serve the party interest. The parties' impact on presidential elections has been diminished. The public funds made available in the nominating and election phases go directly to the candidates instead of to the parties; each major party candidate received $46.1 million in 1988. In this major feature, the law is plainly candidate-centered. Moreover, the parties are limited in the amounts they can contribute to their candidates and in the amounts they can spend on behalf of them. Many observers believe that the limits are

Public Subsidies in Presidential Elections, 1976-1988

Presidential elections have been publicly financed since 1976 under the terms of the Federal Election Campaign Act. Presidential candidates who agree to observe spending limits in primary and general elections are eligible for public funds. The data presented in the table below show the funds made available and the number of recipients in each election since passage of the act. Third party and long-shot candidates find it relatively easy to qualify for matching funds in the primary/caucus season (simply by raising $5,000 in sums of $250 in each of twenty states). Unless more voters decide to support public financing by checking off a dollar for the fund on their income tax returns, the fund faces a deficit by the 1996 election.

	1976		1980		1984		1988	
	Amount	Recip- ients	Amount	Recip- ients	Amount	Recip- ients	Amount	Recip- ients
Prenomi- nation period	$24.8	13D/2R	$ 31.3	4D/6R	$ 36.1	9D/1R/ 1C	$ 67.2	8D/6R/ 1NA
National conven- tions	4.1	1D/1R	8.8	1D/1R	16.2	1D/1R	18.4	1D/1R
General election	43.6	1D/1R	63.1	1D/1R/ 1NU	80.8	1D/1R	92.2	1D/1R
Total	$72.5		$103.2		$133.1		$177.8	

SOURCES: U.S. Congress, Library of Congress, Congressional Research Service, *Campaign Financing in Federal Elections: A Guide to the Law and Its Operation* (Washington, D.C.: U.S. Government Printing Office, 1989), 24; and *Congressional Quarterly Weekly Report,* September 9, 1989, 2326-2329.

NOTE: D = Democrat, R = Republican, NU = National Unity, C = Citizens, NA = New Alliance. Dollar figures are in millions.

too stringent, and some believe they should be abolished altogether. PACs and individuals can spend unlimited amounts on federal campaigns (opposing as well as supporting candidates) as long as these expenditures are made independently—that is, made without consulting the candidate or the candidate's organization. And, as noted, direct contributions by PACs to candidates for Congress have increased substantially in recent years. On the whole, the campaign finance law has increased the influence of nonparty groups in American politics. No one apparently planned for that to happen.

3. *Spending in congressional and senatorial primaries and elections has increased dramatically.* The 1976 ruling of the Supreme Court in *Buckley v. Valeo* that restrictions on the personal and total expenditures of candidates for Congress were unconstitutional led to an explosion of spending. Winning candidates for the Senate in 1976 spent a total of $20.1 million; in 1988 they spent $124 million, about six times as much. Winning candidates for the House in 1976 spent a total of $38 million; in 1988 they spent $171 million, four and one-half times as much. In 1988 thirty-nine Senate candidates spent more than $2 million on their campaigns. Twenty-two House candidates spent more than $1 million.[57] And as a result of the *Buckley* decision, it is not unusual today for a candidate to spend half a million dollars or more of personal funds in a campaign. A few spend much more than that. The sky is the limit. Whatever can be raised can be spent. The overall spending record belongs to North Carolina, where the two Senate candidates in 1984 spent in excess of $25 million. The most expensive campaign in 1988 took place in California, where the two Senate candidates spent about $20 million.

4. *Interest group involvement in campaign funding is greater than in the past.* The impact of interest groups is especially pronounced at the congressional level. In 1974 political action committees made campaign contributions of about $12.5 million to congressional candidates. In 1988 their contributions totaled $147.9 million—a dozen-fold increase. Currently there are about 4,200 political action committees, about seven times as many as in 1974.

5. *Although the Federal Election Campaign Act places certain restrictions on the parties in raising and spending funds, their role in campaigns is nevertheless growing—particularly in the case of the Republican party.* According to Federal Election Commission studies, Republican party committees at national, state, and local levels raised about $267 million in 1988, while corresponding Democratic committees raised $135 million. Ten years earlier, for the 1977-1978 election cycle, Republican committees had raised $85 million and Democratic committees $26 million.[58] Although the Republican party is still much more effective in overall fund raising, the gap between the parties has narrowed (see Figure 4-2). For every one dollar raised and spent by the

FIGURE 4-2   Party Money Spent on Congressional Candidates

Millions of dollars

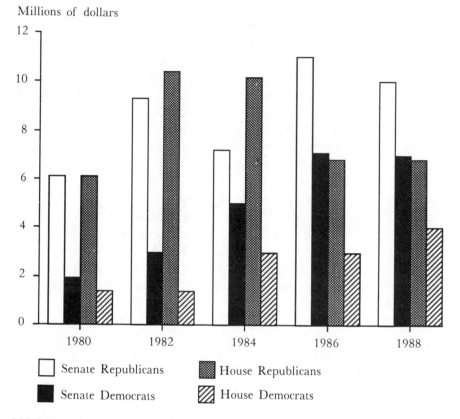

SOURCE: *Congressional Quarterly Weekly Report*, April 1, 1989, 717, based on data drawn from studies by the Federal Election Commission.

NOTE: This spending reflects contributions to candidates and coordinated expenditures made on their behalf.

Democratic party in 1988, the Republican party raised and spent two dollars. The parties secure the great bulk of their contributions from individuals, but contributions from PACs have been growing, particularly on the Democratic side.

6. *The direct influence of fat cats (wealthy contributors) on electoral politics has declined, at least at the national level.* The contributions of an individual to federal candidates are limited to $1,000 for each election and to a total of $25,000 in a calendar year. This, however, is not a stringent limitation. Wealthy individuals, like PACs, can spend an unlimited amount of money to help elect a candidate if the money is

spent independently. In 1988, $9.7 million was spent independently by individuals and PACs in support of the Bush campaign, while $519,000 was spent on behalf of Dukakis. Independent funds are also used in campaigns to defeat candidates; in 1988, negative spending came to $3 million against Dukakis and $75,000 against Bush.[59] In addition, wealthy candidates can give $5,000 to state parties (all fifty if they like), knowing that this money will help the overall ticket. Thus it is a myth that private money is excluded from the presidential campaign and that strict limitations govern contributions to federal campaigns. Only direct contributions to federal candidates are effectively limited.

7. *The importance of raising large amounts of money in small sums has become apparent to all candidates, and particularly to those seeking the presidential nomination.* As provided by the Federal Election Campaign Act, matching federal funds become available for presidential primary and caucus candidates who first raise $100,000 in small sums— by obtaining $5,000 in contributions of $250 or less in each of twenty states. Once a candidate has reached the $100,000 threshold, the government matches the first $250 of any gift. In the preconvention campaign of 1988, sixteen candidates (eight Democrats, six Republicans, and the presidential candidate of the New Alliance party) raised about $214 million, with two-thirds of it received from individuals and most of the remainder from federal matching funds (about 31 percent).[60] One result of the new emphasis on small gifts is that firms that engage in direct-mail solicitations, working with computerized mailing lists, have assumed even greater importance in the fund-raising efforts of candidates. In fund raising, as in certain other respects, the party organizations now face major competition from other quarters.

8. *Opportunities for persons to engage in corrupt practices in the use of money in federal elections have been constricted.* The risks of detection are greater as a result of timely and comprehensive disclosure provisions, requirements for centralized accounting of contributions and expenditures, curbs on cash contributions, and the existence of a full-time agency—the Federal Election Commission—to administer the law and to investigate alleged infractions of it. Every major presidential candidate organization has numerous accountants and lawyers to analyze and monitor the candidate's financial activities. Bookkeeping has thus become a major feature and expense of campaigns for federal office, congressional as well as presidential.

9. *While paying lip service to the finance law, both parties have*

nevertheless searched imaginatively for ways around its restrictions—and they have been successful. As noted earlier, the finance law limits the amount of money that national party committees can give directly to candidates and the amount that party committees can spend on behalf of candidates—coordinated expenditures. Actually, these restrictions are not taken seriously. Under regulations of the Federal Election Commission, a party is permitted to collect checks from donors that are earmarked for specific candidates, bundle them together, and pass them on to designated candidates. These sums do not count against FECA party limits. And bundling is only part of the problem. Other controversies have arisen concerning party solicitation of contributions from corporations to pay for a national television address by the president on the eve of the election, misuse of "soft money" (limited to party-building activities such as paying for campaign headquarters or get-out-the-vote drives) for the promotion of candidates, and the explosion of PAC independent spending, effectively bypassing the limits on direct contributions to candidates. At a minimum, the parties and PACs are now skirting, if not violating, the law. New techniques for raising and allocating funds, combined with unprecedented spending, seem likely to place new pressures on Congress to revise the basic law.

10. *Adoption of the Federal Election Campaign Act (and its 1974, 1976, and 1979 amendments) has not by any means solved all the problems of financing American elections.* Inequities, confusion, and uncertainties persist. Have campaigns become too costly? Some close observers argue that they are underfinanced.[61] Should congressional as well as presidential campaigns be publicly financed? Thus far, Congress has said no. And if public financing of these campaigns is adopted, should spending limits also be established? And what of interest groups, now spending with a vengeance and undoubtedly gaining improved access to policy makers or securing questionable preferments? Should new limits on PAC direct and independent expenditures be imposed? How much regulation will the Supreme Court permit? And if tighter limits on PAC contributions are adopted, will PACs be encouraged to make even heavier independent expenditures? Is it realistic to think of passing new campaign finance legislation that makes elections more competitive by diminishing the advantages of incumbents over their challengers? As it stands, the massive advantages of office for incumbents, who are benefited additionally by one-sided PAC campaign support, ordinarily leave challengers with no more than an outside chance of

winning, particularly in House elections. And in some years Senate challengers find their prospects equally bleak. Both law and practice have combined to build a comprehensive incumbent-protection system. Can campaign finance legislation be designed to strengthen the parties, and should this be a public policy goal? Should party committees be permitted to contribute larger sums to House and Senate candidates and to spend more on their behalf or on behalf of presidential candidates? These are some of the questions that will inform debate on campaign finance and its reform. Answers to them are not easy to fashion. The consequences of change, moreover, are not easy to anticipate. Protecting the status quo is the best single safeguard against the unanticipated outcomes that invariably accompany change.[62]

The manner in which political campaigns are financed has long been a source of controversy. Devising acceptable public policy on the subject has proved to be difficult, as it usually is on complex questions. But the objectives of regulation have been clear: to increase public confidence in the political process by curbing the abusive uses of political money, to enhance the opportunities for citizens to participate in politics by running for public office, and to reduce the vulnerability of candidates and public officials to the importunings and pressures of major benefactors. The campaign finance law has contributed in varying measure to the achievement of these objectives. It has also created new problems, accentuated certain old ones, fostered uncertainties, conferred advantages on some politicians and disadvantages on others, and, arguably, done more to weaken the parties than to strengthen them.

Notes

1. Press release, Federal Election Commission, May 19, 1989. Nearly one-fourth of the groups' independent expenditures in 1988 was devoted to negative spending—that is, spending to defeat candidates. This was the highest level of negative spending since 1982.
2. For an analysis of the new style of campaigning, particularly in terms of the role of campaign management firms, see Robert Agranoff, *The New Style in Election Campaigns* (Boston: Holbrook Press, 1972).
3. Quoted by Joe McGinniss, *The Selling of the President* (New York: Trident Press/Simon and Schuster, 1968).
4. Barbara G. Salmore and Stephen A. Salmore, *Candidates, Parties, and Campaigns* (Washington, D.C.: CQ Press, 1989), 215-216.
5. David A. Leuthold, *Electioneering in a Democracy* (New York: Wiley, 1968), 3. Leuthold's study of congressional campaigns shows that "the problems of

acquisition are more significant than the problems of using the resources. As a result, the decision on making an appeal for the labor vote, for example, will depend not only on the proportion of the constituency which is labor-oriented, but also on the success that the candidate has had in acquiring such resources as the support of labor leaders, the money and workers needed to send a mailing to labor union members, and information about issues important to labor people."

6. V. O. Key, Jr., *Politics, Parties, and Pressure Groups* (New York: Crowell, 1964), 464.
7. Lewis A. Froman, Jr., "A Realistic Approach to Campaign Strategies and Tactics," in *The Electoral Process,* ed. M. Kent Jennings and L. Harmon Zeigler (Englewood Cliffs, N.J.: Prentice Hall, 1966), 7-8.
8. Stimson Bullitt, *To Be a Politician* (Garden City, N.Y.: Doubleday, 1961), 72-73.
9. From Theodore H. White, *The Making of the President, 1960* (New York: Atheneum, 1961), 322-323. For analysis of the major models of campaign decision making, see Karl A. Lamb and Paul A. Smith, *Campaign Decision-Making: The Presidential Election of 1964* (Belmont, Calif.: Wadsworth, 1968).
10. Charles L. Clapp, *The Congressman: His Work as He Sees It* (Washington, D.C.: Brookings Institution, 1963), 332.
11. Clapp, *The Congressman,* 331.
12. *Congressional Quarterly Weekly Report,* July 7, 1979, 1350.
13. Salmore and Salmore, *Candidates, Parties, and Campaigns,* 112-113.
14. Salmore and Salmore, *Candidates, Parties, and Campaigns,* 113.
15. "Campaign Consultants: Pushing Sincerity in 1974," *Congressional Quarterly Weekly Report,* May 4, 1974, 1105.
16. Salmore and Salmore, *Candidates, Parties, and Campaigns,* 113.
17. *Washington Post,* November 9, 1988.
18. Kiku Adatto, *Sound Bite Democracy: Network Evening News Presidential Campaign Coverage, 1968 and 1988* (Cambridge, Mass.: Joan Shorenstein Barone Center on the Press, Politics and Public Policy, 1990), 4.
19. Adatto, *Sound Bite Democracy,* 7.
20. See Herbert E. Alexander, *Financing the 1980 Election* (Washington, D.C.: CQ Press, 1983); William J. Crotty and Gary C. Jacobson, *American Parties in Decline* (Boston: Little, Brown, 1980), 816-823; and Frank J. Sorauf, *Money in American Elections* (Glenview, Ill.: Scott, Foresman/Little, Brown, 1988), 186-221. The estimate for total expenditures in 1988 was made by Herbert Alexander, as reported in U.S. Congress, Library of Congress, Congressional Research Service, *Campaign Financing* (Washington, D.C.: U.S. Government Printing Office, 1990), 3.
21. The development of political action committees represents a major change in American electoral politics. See an article by Frank J. Sorauf that examines the organizational lives of PACs, the role of donors to PACs, and PAC accountability: "Who's in Charge? Accountability in Political Action Committees," *Political Science Quarterly* 99 (Winter 1984-1985): 591-614. Also see the studies of PAC goals, organization, and decision making by Theodore J. Eismeier and Philip H. Pollock III, "An Organizational Analysis of Political Action Committees," *Political Behavior* 7, no. 2 (1985): 192-216, and "Strategy and Choice in Congressional Elections: The Role of Political Action Committees," *American Journal of Political Science* 30 (February 1986): 197-213. The authors distin-

guish three PAC roles: *accommodationist* (seek access in Congress through gifts to incumbents); *partisan* (basically financial auxiliaries of the major parties); and *adversary* (seek to defeat members whom they regard as hostile to their interests).

22. *Washington Post,* June 15, 1987.
23. See an article, "Spend, Spend, Spend," in *National Journal,* June 16, 1990, 1450-1452.
24. Press release, Federal Election Commission, October 31, 1989.
25. Press release, Federal Election Commission, February 24, 1989.
26. Press release, Federal Election Commission, October 31, 1989.
27. *Congressional Quarterly Weekly Report,* April 8, 1978, 850-851; and November 11, 1978, 3260-3262.
28. Press release, Federal Election Commission, March 27, 1989.
29. Press release, Federal Election Commission, May 19, 1989.
30. *Wall Street Journal,* September 9, 1986.
31. *Congressional Quarterly Weekly Report,* August 2, 1986, 1751-1754.
32. David R. Mayhew, *Congress: The Electoral Connection* (New Haven, Conn.: Yale University Press, 1974), 84.
33. *Wall Street Journal,* September 24, 1986.
34. See an interesting account, "Don't Look Homeward," in *National Journal,* June 16, 1990, 1458-1460.
35. Press release, Federal Election Commission, February 16, 1990.
36. *Federal Election Commission v. Democratic Senatorial Campaign Committee,* 454 U.S. 27 (1981).
37. For a study that finds that national party contributions to congressional candidates enhance their party loyalty, see Kevin M. Leyden and Stephen A. Borrelli, "Party Contributions and Party Unity: Can Loyalty Be Bought?" *Western Political Quarterly* 43 (June 1990): 343-365.
38. Gary C. Jacobson, "Party Organization and Distribution of Campaign Resources: Republicans and Democrats in 1982," *Political Science Quarterly* 100 (Winter 1985-1986): 611.
39. Herbert E. Alexander, "Political Parties and the Dollar," *Society* 22 (January/February 1985): 49-58.
40. Norman J. Ornstein, Thomas E. Mann, Michael J. Malbin, Allen Schick, and John F. Bibby, *Vital Statistics on Congress, 1984-1985 Edition* (Washington, D.C.: American Enterprise Institute for Public Policy Research, 1984), 65-70.
41. Press release, Federal Election Commission, October 31, 1989.
42. According to Common Cause, 80 percent of the 248 House members who voted to weaken federal gun control laws in 1986 had received campaign gifts (averaging more than $4,000) from the National Rifle Association (NRA), while the 176 members who voted against the NRA position received no funds. Press release, Common Cause, May 1986. This evidence, however, does not prove anything conclusively about PAC influence on voting. Those who believe that PAC influence has been exaggerated can point out that PACs give money to members (or candidates) with whose policy positions they are in agreement. This is the argument that "money follows votes," and not the reverse.
43. For studies of the relationship between PAC contributions and congressional floor votes, see John R. Wright, "PACs, Contributions, and Roll Calls: An Organizational Perspective," *American Political Science Review* 79 (June 1985): 400-414; W. P. Welch, "Campaign Contributions and Voting: Milk

Money and Dairy Price Supports," *Western Political Quarterly* 35 (December 1982): 478-495; Henry W. Chappell, Jr., "Campaign Contributions and Voting on the Cargo Preference Bill: A Comparison of Simultaneous Models," *Public Choice* 36, no. 2 (1981): 302-312; and James B. Kau and Paul H. Rubin, *Congressmen, Constituents, and Contributors* (Boston: Martinus Nijhoff, 1982).

44. These observations on PACs by members of Congress are drawn respectively from *Congressional Quarterly Weekly Report,* March 12, 1983, 504; *Time,* March 3, 1986; *Congressional Quarterly Weekly Report,* January 11, 1986, 99; December 7, 1985, 2568; March 12, 1983, 504; and *Washington Post,* December 5, 1985.

45. 424 U.S. 1 (1976).

46. Struck down by the Court were provisions that limited the spending of personal funds by candidates ($35,000 for Senate candidates and $25,000 for House candidates) and those that limited total expenditures. Senate candidates were to be limited to total expenditures of no more than $100,000 or 8 cents per eligible voter (whichever is greater) in primaries, and $150,000 or 12 cents per voter (whichever is greater) in general elections. Fund-raising costs of up to 20 percent of the spending limit could be added to these amounts. House candidates were to be limited to no more than $70,000 in primaries and $70,000 in general elections (plus fund-raising costs of up to 20 percent of the spending limit).

47. *Congressional Quarterly Weekly Report,* October 12, 1974, 2865.

48. U.S. Congress, Senate, *Congressional Record,* daily ed., 101st Cong., 1st sess., May 11, 1990, S 6037.

49. U.S. Congress, Senate, *Congressional Record,* daily ed., 101st Cong., 1st sess., May 11, 1990, S 6038.

50. *Congressional Quarterly Weekly Report,* June 30, 1990, 2023.

51. *Congressional Quarterly Weekly Report,* May 26, 1990, 1662.

52. What campaign money buys for nonincumbents is voter recognition. See Gary C. Jacobson, "The Effects of Campaign Spending in Congressional Elections," *American Political Science Review* 72 (June 1978): 469-491; Jacobson, "Money in the 1980 and 1982 Congressional Elections," in *Money and Politics in the United States: Financing Elections in the 1980s,* ed. Michael J. Malbin (Washington, D.C.: American Enterprise Institute for Public Policy Research, 1984), 60-63; Jacobson, "The Effects of Campaign Spending in House Elections: New Evidence for Old Arguments," *American Journal of Political Science* 34 (May 1990): 334-362; and Donald P. Green and Jonathan S. Krasno, "Rebuttal to Jacobson's 'New Evidence for Old Arguments,' " *American Journal of Political Science* 34 (May 1990): 363-372. Also see Scott J. Thomas, "Do Incumbent Campaign Expenditures Matter?" *Journal of Politics* 51 (November 1989): 965-976. Thomas argues that incumbent expenditures do make a difference: "the principal effect of incumbent spending is to win back voters who would have voted for the incumbent in the absence of the receipt of challenger (negative) advertisements." Quotation on p. 973.

53. For a discussion of some of these themes, see an insightful essay by F. Christopher Arterton, "Political Money and Party Strength," in *The Future of American Political Parties,* ed. Joel Fleishman (Englewood Cliffs, N.J.: Prentice Hall, 1982), especially 116-122.

54. See Ruth S. Jones and Warren E. Miller, "Financing Campaigns: Macro Level

Innovation and Micro Level Response," *Western Political Quarterly* 38 (June 1985): 187-210; and Ruth S. Jones, "Campaign Contributions and Campaign Solicitations: 1980-1984" (Manuscript, Arizona State University, 1986). These studies rest on data drawn from the National Election Study.

55. *Federal Election Commission Record* (Washington, D.C.: Federal Election Commission, February 1989), 7.
56. National Election Study, 1988, Center for Political Studies, University of Michigan.
57. Press release, Federal Election Commission, October 31, 1989.
58. Press release, Federal Election Commission, October 31, 1989.
59. Press release, Federal Election Commission, May 19, 1989.
60. *Federal Election Commission Record* (Washington, D.C.: Federal Election Commission, October 1989), 11. George Bush and Pat Robertson each raised more than $30 million in their campaigns for the Republican nomination, while on the Democratic side, Michael Dukakis raised about $28 million and Jesse Jackson about $20 million. New Alliance party candidate Lenora Fulani raised about $2 million.
61. Alexander, "Political Parties and the Dollar," 49-58.
62. For insight into the reform question, see Michael J. Malbin, "Looking Back at the Future of Campaign Finance Reform: Interest Groups and American Elections," in *Money and Politics in the United States*, 232-270.

chapter five

Political Parties
and the Electorate

IT IS A nagging fact of American life that for a large proportion of the population politics carries no interest, registers no significance, and excites no demands. A vast array of evidence shows that the political role of the typical citizen is that of spectator, occasionally aroused by political events but more often inattentive to them. However tarnished this commonplace, it comes close to being the chief truth to be known about the political behavior of American citizens. Much less certain, however, is what this means. Whether it is necessary to have greatly interested and active citizens to have strong and responsible political institutions is by no means clear. No neat or simple formula exists for assessing public support for political institutions. Does the presence of a large nonvoting population reflect substantial disillusionment with the political system and its processes, or does it reflect a general satisfaction with the state of things? The answer is elusive.[1]

Whatever the consequences of low or modest turnouts for the vitality of a democratic political system, it is obvious that some American citizens use their political resources far more than others. Their political involvement is reflected not only in the fact that they vote regularly but also in the fact that they participate in politics in various other ways— perhaps by attempting to persuade other voters to support their candidates or party, by making campaign contributions, or by devoting time and energy to political campaigns. The net result of differential rates of participation is that some citizens gain access to political decision makers and can influence their decisions, while other citizens are all but excluded from the political process.

An important element in understanding the political behavior of the active members of the American electorate is the political party. More than any other agency, the party provides cues for the voters and gives shape and meaning to elections. Some voters elude party labeling, preferring the role of the independent. Even though their importance cannot be minimized, especially in presidential elections, their consistent impact on politics is less than that of party members. The reason for this is partly a matter of numbers: about two out of three voters classify themselves as members of one or the other of the two major parties. Before examining the behavior of partisans and nonpartisans, however, it is appropriate to consider the broad characteristics of citizen participation in politics.

Turnout: The Diminished Electorate

Few facts about American political behavior stand out more sharply than the comparatively low level of citizen involvement in politics. And there are clear signs that popular participation is declining.

Atrophy of the Electorate

In presidential elections during the last quarter of the nineteenth century, turnout was regularly high; in the presidential election of 1876, for example, more than 85 percent of the eligible voters cast ballots (see Figure 5-1). Beginning around the turn of the century, however, a sharp decline in voting set in, reaching its nadir of 44 percent in 1920. A moderate increase in turnout occurred during the next several decades, with participation hovering around 60 percent during the 1950s and 1960s. But participation declined again in the 1970s, dropping to 54.3 percent in 1976 and to 53.2 percent in 1980—its lowest level since 1948. In the 1984 election between Ronald Reagan and Walter F. Mondale, turnout rose only fractionally, to 53.3 percent.[2] In 1988 turnout declined further, with only 50.16 percent of the voting-age population casting ballots. Thus for the last two decades, only slightly more than half of the eligible voters have taken part in presidential elections.

Although these data on American voting participation are far from

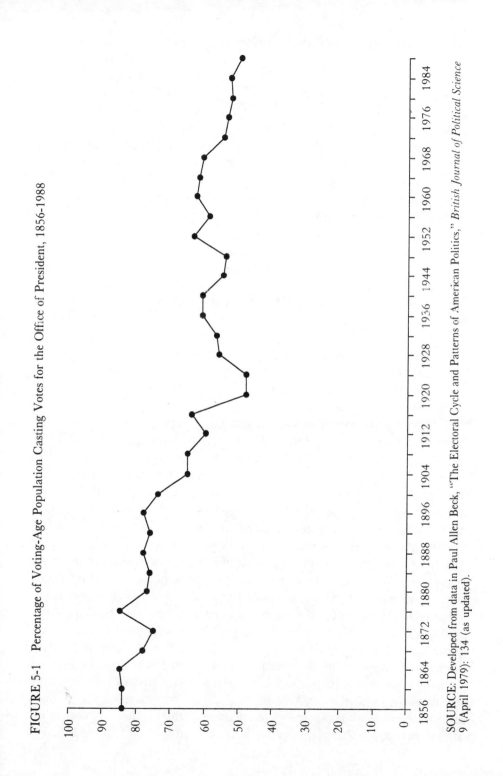

FIGURE 5-1 Percentage of Voting-Age Population Casting Votes for the Office of President, 1856-1988

SOURCE: Developed from data in Paul Allen Beck, "The Electoral Cycle and Patterns of American Politics," *British Journal of Political Science* 9 (April 1979): 134 (as updated).

impressive, they may conceal more of the problem than they uncover. The hard truth is that turnout is much lower in nonpresidential elections. In off-year congressional elections from 1950 to 1970, turnout percentages ranged between 41 and 45 percent of the eligible voters. In the midterm election of 1974, turnout dropped to 36 percent; in 1978, it fell to 35.1 percent. In the midst of a marked economic slump in 1982, the turnout percentage rose to 37.7 percent. But it eased off to 33.4 percent in 1986. It rose slightly in 1990, to about 36 percent. More than 60 percent of all eligible voters do not take the trouble to vote in off-year elections (see Figure 5-2).

A survey of the turnout percentages in the fifty states in the 1988 presidential election shows that the highest turnout rates were achieved in certain western, upper midwestern, and New England states (see Figure 5-3). Minnesota led all states with a turnout of 66.3 percent, followed by Montana (62.4), Maine (62.2), Wisconsin (62.0), North Dakota and South Dakota (61.5). Most of the states with unusually low participation rates were southern. Only 38.8 percent of the voting-age population voted in Georgia; next lowest was South Carolina (38.9). The populous states of California and New York had turnout rates of 47.4 and 48.1, respectively.

Turnout in state and local elections is more of the same story of widespread citizen indifference. An analysis of voting for the office of governor, for example, supports three main generalizations. First, the states differ sharply in their turnout patterns. The relation of region to participation is shown by the higher voter participation rates in midwestern, western (especially plains and mountain), and New England states, and the lower rates of participation in most southern states. Second, those states that elect governors in presidential years (about one-fifth of the total) nearly always have higher turnouts than those in which gubernatorial elections occur in off years. Third, notwithstanding major variations among the states, overall citizen performance is disappointing. The median turnout for the states that elected governors in the off-year of 1986 was only 39 percent. Leading the way were South Dakota (58 percent) and Idaho (56 percent). Only 27 percent of Georgia's voters bothered to vote, while 29 percent turned out in Kentucky and Texas.[3]

The low point in participation is ordinarily plumbed in primary elections—a total primary vote of only 20 to 25 percent of the eligible electorate is not unusual. In certain southern states, however, participation in primary elections—often the real election in that region—is about

FIGURE 5-2 Voter Turnout in Off-year Elections, 1946-1990

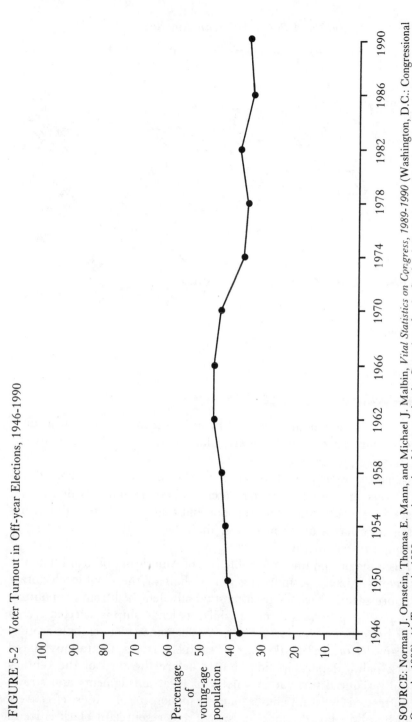

SOURCE: Norman J. Ornstein, Thomas E. Mann, and Michael J. Malbin, *Vital Statistics on Congress, 1989-1990* (Washington, D.C.: Congressional Quarterly, 1990), 46. Turnout in 1990 was estimated at 36 percent by the Committee for the Study of the American Electorate, as reported in the *New York Times*, November 11, 1990.

FIGURE 5-3   Voting Participation Rates in 1988 Presidential Election

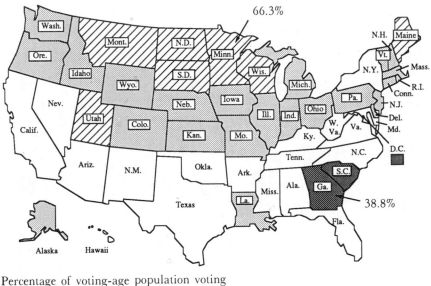

Percentage of voting-age population voting

☑ 60 percent and over   ☐ 40-49.9 percent

▨ 50-59.9 percent   ▮ Under 40 percent

as high as it is in general elections.[4] Primary turnout is highest in states where primaries are open (and particularly high in blanket or nonpartisan primaries), where the parties are most competitive, where presidential primaries coincide with other primaries, and where higher educational levels are present among voters. There is some evidence that closeness of election stimulates turnout and that incumbency diminishes it. Each state has a different mix of these factors, thus contributing to variations in turnout rates.[5]

It is a major and uncomfortable fact of American political life that a great many citizens—comprising almost half of the eligible electorate even in presidential years—are almost wholly detached from the political system and the processes through which its leadership is selected. What reasons help to account for the poor performance of twentieth century American electorates? In the case of southern states, limitations placed on black political participation shortly before the turn of the century drastically reduced turnout. A variety of legal abridgments and strategies, buttressed by social and economic sanctions of all kinds, effectively disfranchised all but the most persistent and resourceful black citizens.

The ingenuity of southern white politicians during this era can scarcely be exaggerated. Poll taxes, literacy tests, understanding-the-Constitution tests, white primaries,[6] stringent residence and registration require- ments, and discriminatory registration administration—all were con- sciously employed by dominant elites to maintain a white electorate and thus to settle political questions within the white community.

Another prime reason for the sharp contraction of the active elector- ate stems from the advent of one-party politics throughout large sections of the country. Democratic domination of the South began shortly after the Civil War Reconstruction governments were terminated. Neverthe- less, even in the 1880s, the Republican presidential vote was at least half of the Democratic vote in all but a few southern states. The election of 1896, one of the most decisive elections in American history, culminated in the virtual disappearance of the Republican party in the South and in a precipitate drop in Democratic strength in the North. E. E. Schatt- schneider's analysis of this election is instructive:

> The 1896 party cleavage resulted from the tremendous reaction of
> conservatives in both major parties to the Populist movement, a
> radical agrarian agitation that alarmed people of substance all over
> the country. . . . Southern conservatives reacted so strongly that they
> were willing to revive the tensions and animosities of the Civil War
> and the Reconstruction in order to set up a one-party sectional
> southern political monopoly in which nearly all Negroes and many
> poor whites were disfranchised. . . . The northern conservatives were
> so badly frightened by the [William Jennings] Bryan candidacy that
> they adopted drastic measures to alarm the country. As a matter of
> fact, the conservative reaction to Bryanism in the North was almost
> as spectacular as the conservative reaction to Populism in the South.
> As a result the Democratic party in large areas of the Northeast and
> Middle West was wiped out, or decimated, while the Republican
> party consolidated its supremacy in all of the most populous areas of
> the country. The resulting party lineup was one of the most sharply
> sectional political divisions in American history. . . . Both sections
> became more conservative because *one-party politics tends strongly to
> vest political power in the hands of the people who already have
> enormous power*. Moreover, in one-party areas (areas of extreme
> sectionalism) votes decline in value because the voters no longer have
> a valuable party alternative.[7]

The smothering effect of a noncompetitive environment on partici- pation can be seen in election turnouts following the realignment of the

1890s. Consider this evidence: between 1884 and 1904, turnout in Virginia dropped 57 percent; in Mississippi, 51 percent; and in Louisiana, 50 percent. Part of the explanation for these drop-offs undoubtedly can be associated with the success of southern efforts to disfranchise blacks, but one-party politics also had a decisive impact on the electorate. In the first place, the drop in participation was too large to be accounted for merely by the disappearance of black votes. And, in the second place, the impact of the new sectionalism was not confined simply to the South. Despite their growing populations, some fourteen northern states had smaller turnouts in 1904 than they did in 1896.[8]

The lower rate of turnout in the South in the twentieth century is partially attributable to diminished competition between the parties. If the outcome of an election is predictable, voters have scant inducement to pay in time, energy, and other costs that voting requires. Changes in the turnout of southern voters, however, are under way. Today, elections in the South (especially presidential) are substantially more competitive than they were a generation ago, and voter turnout rates have been increasing, here and there dramatically. The elimination of legal barriers to registration and voting (such as the poll tax and the literacy test) has also contributed to the expansion of southern electorates. In presidential elections, voters in some southern states now participate at a level only marginally lower than voters in other parts of the country.

Still other reasons have been advanced for the decline in mass political involvement in this century. One concerns woman suffrage. Although women were given the vote in 1920, large numbers of them were indifferent to their new right and did not use it immediately. In subsequent decades, a significantly larger proportion of women entered the active electorate; today, their rate of participation is about the same as that of men.

In the past, stringent registration laws served to keep many citizens away from the polls. During the latter part of the nineteenth century, when turnout was regularly between 75 and 85 percent of the eligible electorate, in many parts of the country voters were not required to register or automatic registration was in effect. During the early twentieth century, registration laws became much more restrictive, making voting more difficult. Provisions were adopted, for example, requiring voters to register annually in person, purging voters' names from the registration rolls if they failed to vote within a particular period, and requiring that voters reside within a state at least a year (and sometimes two) before becoming eligible to register. In addition, poll taxes and literacy tests were used, particularly in the South, to disfranchise prospective voters. The effect of these legal barriers was to diminish turnout.

Major changes in the 1960s and 1970s, however, greatly relaxed registration laws. Poll taxes and literacy tests were eliminated. Periodic registration gave way virtually everywhere to permanent registration. As a result of an act passed by Congress in 1970, the residency requirement for federal elections is now limited to a maximum of thirty days before the election; moreover, for other elections, only a handful of states have closing dates earlier than thirty days. In about one-third of the states, registration is possible up to twenty days before the election. Finally, all states must now meet certain minimum national standards for absentee registration.[9]

Although states vary in their registration requirements, their laws today are not generally burdensome. Nonetheless, a study by Steven J. Rosenstone and Raymond E. Wolfinger found that if all states had registration laws as permissive as those present in the most permissive states, turnout would increase. If permissive laws had been in effect everywhere in the 1972 presidential election, turnout would have been about 9 percent higher.[10] A 1987 study found that turnout in presidential elections would be increased by six million to seven million voters if all states adopted election-day registration.[11]

Late closing dates for registration have the largest impact on voting participation, according to Rosenstone and Wolfinger. Facilitative provisions for absentee registration also encourage turnout, as do provisions for registration during normal business hours, evenings, and Saturdays. What it comes down to is that in states where registration laws are permissive, the costs of voting in time, energy, and information are lower. It is simply easier to vote. Less restrictive provisions are particularly likely to increase the participation of persons with limited education and limited interest in politics.[12]

In the 1988 election there were 80 million nonvoters. A further relaxation of registration statutes doubtlessly would reduce the number of nonvoters, but by no means would it solve the problem. As Curtis Gans, director of the Committee for the Study of the American Electorate, points out, there are two nonvoting problems. One is *low* voter turnout, which is to some extent the result of registration barriers. The other is *declining* voter turnout. Although the country's voting laws have been liberalized in recent decades, turnout has fallen by 20 percent nationally and by more than 30 percent outside the South. For example, turnout in North Dakota, which has no requirement to register, has declined 16.5 percent since 1960. Obviously, registration statutes cannot be blamed for declining participation. The underlying explanation is *declining motivation* to vote.[13]

The evidence thus accumulates that legal barriers to participation no longer are a key explanation for low turnout in American elections. One reason for the overall poor voting performance is that the number of potential voters has increased as a result of lowering the voting age to eighteen. Younger voters have the lowest participation rate of any group in American society.[14] In 1988 only a little more than one-third of those persons between eighteen and twenty-one turned out at the polls.

Youthful insensitivity and indifference to politics, however, is only part of the story. Turnout rates have declined for most major demographic groups (see Table 5-1).

Nonvoters offer a variety of reasons for their failure to vote. A growing number of people do not take the trouble to register—typically the explanation offered by at least one-third of the nonvoters. People who change residence are required to sign up again, and many fail to do so. Since nearly one-third of the nation now moves every two years, a recent study shows, change of residence has become a significant explanation for failure to vote.[15] Other people do not vote because they disapprove of the candidates—usually about 10 to 15 percent in Gallup surveys of nonvoters.[16] And then there are those who are not interested in politics, those who find voting inconvenient, and those who have "no particular reason" for not voting.

California may or may not be a special case, but a 1990 poll by the *Los Angeles Times* found that the main reason people in that state fail to vote is that they are too busy doing other things to bother voting. This reason was given by an extraordinary 35 percent of the respondents. The next most frequent reason, cited by 8 percent, was a lack of interest in politics.[17]

A central explanation for nonvoting thus lies in the public's attitude toward politics and political institutions. It seems likely, for example, that participation has declined because an increasing number of citizens care less which party or which candidate wins, because they believe that their votes will not make much difference, because they believe that public officials are not concerned about what voters think, because they think that politicians cannot be trusted, and because they believe public

TABLE 5-1   The Decline in Voting in Presidential Elections, 1972-1988

Group	Percentage of persons reporting that they voted				
	1972	1976	1980	1984	1988
Nation	63.0	59.2	59.2	59.9	57.4
Men	64.1	59.6	59.1	59.0	56.4
Women	62.0	58.8	59.4	60.8	58.3
White	64.5	60.9	60.9	61.4	59.1
Black	52.1	48.7	50.5	55.8	51.1
Spanish origin	37.4	31.8	29.9	32.6	28.8
18-20 years old	48.3	38.0	35.7	36.7	33.2
21-24	50.7	45.6	43.1	43.5	38.3
25-34	59.7	55.4	54.6	54.5	48.0
35-44	66.3	63.3	64.4	63.5	61.3
45-64	70.8	68.7	69.3	69.8	67.9
65 and over	63.5	62.2	65.1	67.7	68.8
Metropolitan	64.3	59.2	58.8	a	a
Nonmetropolitan	59.4	59.1	60.2	a	a
North and West	66.4	61.2	61.0	a	a
South	55.4	54.9	55.6	a	a
Employed	66.0	62.0	61.8	61.6	58.4
Unemployed	49.9	43.7	41.2	44.0	38.6
Not in labor force	59.3	56.5	57.0	58.9	57.3

SOURCE: Derived from data in U.S. Bureau of the Census, *Statistical Abstract of the United States* (Washington, D.C.: U.S. Government Printing Office, 1990), 262.

NOTE: Actual turnout is lower than reported turnout.

[a] Not available.

officials are unresponsive.[18] It also seems clear that the overall decline in the strength of voters' party identification has played a role in the decline of electoral participation.[19] Indifference, alienation,[20] declining party loyalty, and a generalized distrust of government combine to cut the turnout rate in elections. Frequent elections also discourage turnout, particularly among the peripheral electorate—those people who easily lapse into nonvoting unless party and campaign organizations make a special effort to turn them out.[21] For many citizens, "voting simply isn't worth the effort." [22]

Voter turnout in the 1988 presidential election—50.16 percent—was the lowest since the early 1920s, when women were enfranchised. Voter

The People's Choice?

Most presidential winners have sought to portray their victory as a mandate from the American people. But even landslide victors in the nationwide popular vote have been the choice of barely one-third of the entire voting-age population.

The following chart compares the percentage of the popular vote that presidential winners since 1932 have received with the percentage of the entire voting-age population that their vote total represents. The latter percentage is based on voting-age population estimates updated each election year by the U.S. Bureau of the Census.

Year	Winner	Percentage of total popular vote	Percentage of voting-age population
1932	Roosevelt (D)	57.4	30.1
1936	Roosevelt (D)	60.8	34.6
1940	Roosevelt (D)	54.7	32.2
1944	Roosevelt (D)	53.4	29.9
1948	Truman (D)	49.6	25.3
1952	Eisenhower (R)	55.1	34.0
1956	Eisenhower (R)	57.4	34.1
1960	Kennedy (D)	49.7	31.2
1964	Johnson (D)	61.1	37.8
1968	Nixon (R)	43.4	26.4
1972	Nixon (R)	60.7	33.5
1976	Carter (D)	50.1	26.8
1980	Reagan (R)	50.7	26.7
1984	Reagan (R)	58.8	31.2
1988	Bush (R)	53.4	26.8

SOURCE: *Congressional Quarterly Weekly Report*, January 21, 1989, 137.

NOTE: D = Democrat; R = Republican. The votes cast for third party candidates are included in this analysis.

disaffection, meanwhile, may have been at its highest in 1988. According to opinion surveys of registered voters taken shortly before the election, about half viewed the campaign as boring. Sixty-two percent considered it to be more negative than positive, and two-thirds said they would have preferred another choice besides George Bush and Michael S. Dukakis.[23]

Turnout in other industrialized democracies averages about 80 percent of the eligible electorate, vastly higher than the average turnout in American presidential elections. A study by G. Bingham Powell, using aggregate and comparative survey data, finds that voter participation in the United States is "severely inhibited" by institutional factors such as voluntary registration (as opposed to automatic registration common in other nations), low levels of competition in many electoral districts, and weak linkages between parties and social groups (thus making the parties' task of voter mobilization more difficult). To approach the turnout levels of other democracies, Powell argues, the United States would need to adopt automatic registration laws and change the structure of party competition to mobilize lower-class voters.[24] Obviously, changing registration laws would be easier to accomplish than changing party character and party competition.[25]

The Regulation of Voting

As stipulated in the U.S. Constitution, states have control over suffrage. The basic reference to suffrage in the Constitution appears in Article I, Section 2, which provides that for elections to the House of Representatives "the electors [that is, voters] in each state shall have the qualifications requisite for electors of the most numerous branch of the state legislature." Until recently the major national intrusions involving suffrage came in the form of constitutional amendments. The Fifteenth Amendment (1870) forbade the states to deny citizens the right to vote on the grounds of race, and the Nineteenth Amendment (1920) provided that states could not deny citizens the ballot on account of sex. The Twenty-fourth Amendment (1964) outlawed poll taxes, and the Twenty-sixth Amendment (1971) lowered the voting age in all elections to eighteen.

In recent decades, the tradition of state control over suffrage has been significantly challenged by Congress through the passage of a series of civil rights acts (1957, 1960, 1964, and 1965). The acts of 1957 and 1960 were designed primarily to prevent discrimination against blacks seeking to register to vote. Individuals who were denied the right to register by local registrars could seek relief from the federal government through the attorney general and the federal court system. Where discriminatory practices affecting registration were found to exist, the court was empowered to appoint federal voting referees to enroll black

Participation in Elections: Comparing the United States with Twenty-seven Other Nations

Highest Turnout, Any National Election, 1968 to 1986 (in percentages)

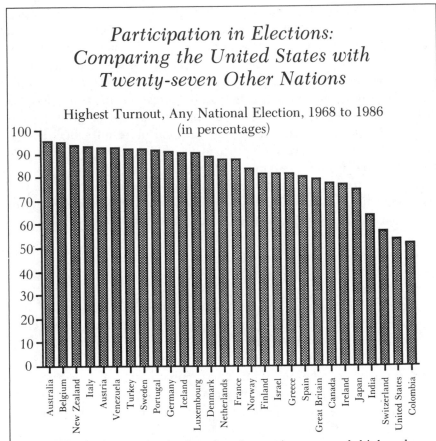

Why is turnout in elections in other nations so much higher than in the United States? One reason is that some nations, such as Australia and Belgium, have compulsory voting—laws requiring electoral participation. Another is that other nations commonly hold their elections on nonworkdays, a practice that encourages participation. A third major reason is that other countries automatically register all persons eligible to vote, instead of requiring the individual to take the initiative to register, as in the United States. Registration laws in the American states, on the whole, do little to facilitate voting. (The size of the electorate in all of these countries except the United States is the number of registered voters. In the United States it is the voting-age population as computed by the U.S. Bureau of the Census.)

SOURCE: Developed from data generated by the Congressional Research Service of the Library of Congress, November 1987.

voters. Although the overall impact of these early acts on black voting was marginal, due largely to the cumbersome procedural requirements involved in jury trials and in establishing patterns of discrimination, they were important for establishing the power of the federal government, through a legislative enactment, to intervene in state election systems.

Of much greater substantive significance has been the Civil Rights Act of 1964 and the Voting Rights Act of 1965. In its provisions concerning voting, the 1964 act made a sixth-grade education presumptive evidence of literacy and required that all literacy tests be administered in writing. In addition, registrars were required to administer registration procedures fairly and were forbidden to reject registration applications because of immaterial errors on registration forms.

With the support of strong majorities of both parties, Congress passed the Voting Rights Act of 1965. Under its terms, literacy tests or other voter qualification devices used for discriminatory purposes were suspended in any state or county in which less than 50 percent of the voting-age residents were registered to vote in November 1964 or less than 50 percent voted in the 1964 presidential election. Augmenting the federal government's power to supervise elections, the act called for the appointment of federal voting examiners with the authority to register persons who had been unable to register even though they met state requirements for voting. Finally, the act provided that if a state or local governmental unit decides to change its voting regulations, the U.S. attorney general or the U.S. District Court for the District of Columbia must first certify that the new rules will not serve the purposes of racial discrimination. In 1975 this act was extended for another seven years, with its coverage expanded to include "language minorities" (including Spanish-speaking populations, American Indians, Alaskan natives, and Asian-Americans). The extension also placed a permanent ban on voter qualifying tests. The most effective civil rights law ever adopted, the 1965 Voting Rights Act, was again extended by Congress in 1982.

In its most important respects, the regulation of voting is today as much a matter of federal law as it is of state law. Had the civil rights movement in the 1950s and 1960s not taken place, such fundamental changes probably would not have occurred in the regulation of suffrage. What has been the impact of the new role of the national government in protecting the right to vote? For black political participation, the results have been dramatic (see Table 5-2). In 1960 only 29 percent of the blacks of voting age were registered to vote in the eleven states of the

South; in 1986, 61 percent. In Mississippi, nearly fourteen times as many blacks were registered to vote in 1986 as there had been in 1960. The vast majority of these new voters in Mississippi and elsewhere were enrolled following the passage of the Voting Rights Act of 1965. In 1986 voters in the rural Mississippi Delta (Second Congressional District) elected the state's first black representative since the military occupation, or Reconstruction, following the Civil War.

Widespread black political participation is now a reality in southern politics. To be sure, registration and voting will not solve all the problems of the black citizen. But political participation does give blacks much greater leverage in the political system. Race-baiting campaign ploys by white politicians are a thing of the past. The number of black elected officials has increased dramatically in recent years, and particularly in the South. The southern state electorates of today are vastly different from those of the 1950s. And it is a certainty that whatever the future shape of southern politics, black voters and black politicians will play a more important role in political decision making than at any time since Reconstruction.

Forms of Political Participation

The act of voting is an appropriate point of departure for exploring the political involvement of American citizens, but it is not the only form of participation. A comprehensive survey of political participation in America by Sidney Verba and Norman H. Nie shows the range and dimensions of citizen activities in politics (see Table 5-3). Several findings should be emphasized. Perhaps of most importance, the only political activity in which a majority of American citizens participates is voting in presidential elections. Voting regularly in local elections follows as a rather distant second.[26] The survey discloses that as political activity requires more time, initiative, and involvement of the citizen—working to solve a community problem, attempting to persuade others how to vote, working for a party or candidate, contributing to political campaigns—participation levels drop even lower.

The impression most deeply conveyed by the data is that a relatively small group of citizens performs most of the political activities of the nation. There is obviously much more than a germ of truth to this. Yet, to some extent, the data underrepresent the political activity of citizens,

TABLE 5-2   Percentage of Voting-Age Population Registered to Vote in Eleven
Southern States, by Race, 1960 and 1986

State	1960		1986	
	White	Black	White	Black
Alabama	63.6	13.7	77.5	68.9
Arkansas	60.9	38.0	67.2	57.9
Florida	69.3	39.4	66.9	58.2
Georgia	56.8	29.3	62.3	52.8
Louisiana	76.9	31.1	67.8	60.6
Mississippi	63.9	5.2	91.6	70.8
North Carolina	92.1	39.1	67.4	58.4
South Carolina	57.1	13.7	53.4	52.5
Tennessee	73.0	59.1	70.0	65.3
Texas	42.5	35.5	79.0	68.0
Virginia	46.1	23.1	60.3	56.2
Total	61.1	29.1	69.9	60.8

SOURCE: Developed from data in U.S. Bureau of the Census, *Statistical Abstract of the United States* (Washington, D.C.: U.S. Government Printing Office, 1989), 261. The data for 1960 are drawn from the 1986 edition of the *Statistical Abstract,* 257.

since those citizens who perform one political act are not necessarily the same as those who perform another act. Verba and Nie indicate that, excluding voting from the analysis, less than a third of their sample reported engaging in no political activities.[27] Even so, this is a fairly large lump of the citizenry.

The evidence from a number of studies of political participation is that people do not get involved randomly in politics. Instead, there is a hierarchy of political involvement (see Figure 5-4).[28] Individuals who are politically active engage in a wide variety of political acts. A major characteristic of their participation is that it tends to be cumulative. The active members of a political party, for example, are likely to be found soliciting political funds, contributing time and money to campaigns, attending meetings, and so on. Individuals who are minimally involved in politics typically take part only in such limited activities as those grouped near the base of the hierarchy. At the very bottom are those persons who stand on the outskirts of the political world, scarcely, if at all, aware of the political forces that play on them or of the opportunities open to them to use their resources (including the vote) to gain political objectives.

Some portion of the explanation for the passivity of American

TABLE 5-3   A Profile of the Political Activity of American Citizens

Form of activity	Percentage of citizens
Report regularly voting in presidential elections	72
Report always voting in local elections	47
Acting in at least one organization involved in community problems	32
Have worked with others in trying to solve some community problems	30
Have attempted to persuade others to vote as they were	28
Have ever actively worked for a party or candidates during an election	26
Have ever contacted a local government official about some issue or problem	20
Have attended at least one political meeting or rally in last three years	19
Have ever contacted a state or national government official about some issue or problem	18
Have ever formed a group or organization to attempt to solve some local community problem	14
Have ever given money to a party or candidate during an election campaign	13
Presently a member of a political club or organization	8

SOURCE: Sidney Verba and Norman H. Nie, *Participation in America: Political Democracy and Social Equality* (New York: Harper and Row, 1972), 31.

citizens may lie with the parties and candidates themselves. They are not particularly active in clearing the way for popular participation. A recent Gallup survey found that only a small proportion of citizens are contacted by party or candidate organization workers in an effort to win their vote. During the 1988 election campaign only 11 percent of the public reported that they had been contacted by someone from the Bush organization and only 9 percent by someone from the Dukakis organization. The individuals most likely to come in contact with campaign electioneering activities are those with high socioeconomic status—in particular those with a college education, a professional or business background, and a high income. For most Americans the party organization, *qua* organization, is all but invisible.[29]

The Active and Passive Citizenry

A number of social, demographic, and political variables are related to the act of voting. The data in Table 5-4 provide a profile of those citizens

FIGURE 5-4   Hierarchy of Political Involvement

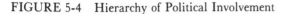

Holding public and party office	
Being a candidate for office	
Soliciting political funds	Gladiatorial activities
Attending a caucus or a strategy meeting	
Becoming an active member in a political party	
Contributing time in a political campaign	
Attending a political meeting or rally	
Making a monetary contribution to a party or candidate	Transitional activities
Contacting a public official or a political leader	
Wearing a button or putting a sticker on the car	
Attempting to talk another into voting a certain way	
Initiating a political discussion	Spectator activities
Voting	
Exposing oneself to political stimuli	

Apathetics

SOURCE: Lester W. Milbrath, *Political Participation* (Chicago: Rand McNally, 1965), 18.

who are more likely to turn out at elections and those who are less likely to turn out. Some of the characteristics are closely related—for example, high income, high occupational status, and college education. Nevertheless, the high rate of participation by citizens of higher socioeconomic status is not simply a function of status. The explanation lies in the civic orientations that are linked to upper-class status and environment. Upper-status citizens, for example, are more likely than citizens of lower status to belong to organizations and to participate in their activities, more likely to possess the resources and skills to be effective in politics, and more likely to be attentive to political problems and to feel efficacious in dealing with them.[30]

How much the factors that influence participation at the individual level can account for the differences among the states in voter turnout is not altogether clear. What is clear is that of all the sections of the

---

The American Voter: Orientations . . .

Interest in Politics

Would you say you follow what's going on in government and public
affairs most of the time, some of the time, only now and then, or
hardly at all?

Most of the time	22%
Some of the time	37
Only now and then	26
Hardly at all	15

Would you say that you were very much interested, somewhat interested,
or not much interested [in the 1988 campaign]?

Very much interested	28%
Somewhat interested	47
Not much interested	25

Ideology

We hear a lot of talk these days about liberals and conservatives. Here is
a 7-point scale on which the political views that people hold are
arranged from extremely liberal to extremely conservative. Where
would you place yourself on this scale, or haven't you thought much
about this?

Extremely liberal	2%
Liberal	5
Slightly liberal	9
Moderate, middle of road	22
Slightly conservative	15
Conservative	14
Extremely conservative	3
Don't know	4
Haven't thought much	26

---

country, the South ranks not only lowest in turnout but also lowest in
terms of family income, levels of education, and other measures of
economic well-being. Moreover, the legal structures (for example, elec-

... *toward Political Activity*

Political Efficacy

Sometimes politics and government seem so complicated that a person like me can't really understand what's going on.

Agree	77%
Disagree	23

Political Activity

During the campaign, did you talk to any people and try to show them why they should vote for or against one of the parties or candidates?

Yes	29%
No	71

Did you wear a campaign button, put a campaign sticker on your car, or place a sign in your window or in front of your house?

Yes	9%
No	91

Did you go to any political meetings, rallies, speeches, dinners, or things like that in support of a particular candidate?

Yes	7%
No	93

Did you do any work for one of the parties or candidates?

Yes	3%
No	97

Did you give money to a political party during this election year?

Yes	6%
No	94

SOURCE: These questions are drawn from the 1988 presidential election survey, National Election Study, Center for Political Studies, University of Michigan.

tion laws) in southern states typically do not encourage voting as much as those in northern states. The level of participation in southern states probably will increase as their sociodemographic characteristics change

TABLE 5-4   A Profile of the More Active and Less Active Citizenry

More likely to vote	Less likely to vote
High income	Low income
High occupational status	Low occupational status
College education	Grade school or high school education
Middle-aged	Young and elderly
White	Black and Hispanic
Metropolitan area resident	Small-town resident
Northern state resident	Southern state resident
Resident in competitive party environment	Resident in noncompetitive party environment
Union member	Nonunion labor
Homeowner	Renter
Married	Single, separated, divorced, widowed
Government employees	Private workers
Catholics and Jews	Protestants
Strong partisan	Independent

SOURCE: These findings were drawn from a large number of studies of the American electorate. For wide-ranging analyses, see Lester W. Milbrath, *Political Participation* (Chicago: Rand McNally, 1965); Raymond E. Wolfinger and Steven J. Rosenstone, *Who Votes?* (New Haven, Conn.: Yale University Press, 1980); and M. Margaret Conway, *Political Participation in the United States* (Washington, D.C.: CQ Press, 1991).

(for example, an improved economic position) or as their legal structures become more facilitative.

For all their interest, the distinctions drawn from the data presented in Table 5-4 cannot be taken at face value. The differences between voters and nonvoters are less apparent today than in the past. The participation rates of people who live in rural or urban areas are about the same today. Men and women now vote at about the same rate. Turnout in the South is on the rise, while it is decreasing in the North. A noticeable decline in voting by middle-aged persons has occurred.[31] What stands out most is that participation has declined along a broad demographic front.

The lower turnout of Protestants is also deceptive. It is undoubtedly due in part to the lower levels of participation of southern and of rural voters, who happen to be largely Protestant.

Finally, it should be stressed that the variables are not of equal importance. The best indicators of voting participation are those that reflect socioeconomic status: education, income, and occupation. And of these, education is the most important (see Table 5-5).

TABLE 5-5   Education and Voting Turnout in Recent Presidential Elections

Educational level	Percentage voting		
	1980	1984	1988
Grade school	58.6	58.0	41.7
High school	54.8	66.3	58.2
College	76.4	85.5	82.4

SOURCE: Adapted from M. Margaret Conway, *Political Participation in the United States* (Washington, D.C.: CQ Press, 1991), 22. As Conway points out, individuals who are more highly educated are also more likely to overreport voting.

Citizens who show enthusiasm for voting and who participate regularly in elections can be distinguished by their psychological makeup as well as by their social and economic backgrounds. The prospect that persons will vote is influenced by the intensity of their partisan preferences: the more substantial their commitments to a party, the stronger the probability that they will vote (see Table 5-6). Persons who have a strong partisan preference and who perceive the election as close are virtually certain to vote. Voters can also be distinguished by other indices of psychological involvement in political affairs. Survey research data show them to be more interested in campaigns and more concerned with election outcomes. They are also more likely than nonvoters to possess a strong sense of political efficacy; that is, a disposition to see their own participation in politics as important and effective. Finally, in contrast to nonvoters, voters are more likely to accept the norm that voting is a civic obligation. In sum, the evidence suggests that psychological involvement—marked by interest in elections, concern over their outcome, a sense of political efficacy, and a sense of citizen duty—increases the probability that a person will pay the costs in time and energy that voting requires.

Party Identification in the Electorate

Examining the distribution of party identification in the electorate from 1937 to 1990 is an interesting study in stability and change (see Figure 5-5). Throughout most of this lengthy period, the proportion of persons identifying themselves as Democrats remained relatively stable. In the

TABLE 5-6　Partisanship and Turnout in the 1988 Presidential Election

Party identification	Percentage voting
Strong Democrat	80
Weak Democrat	62
Independent Democrat	64
Independent-Independent	49
Independent Republican	64
Weak Republican	75
Strong Republican	89

SOURCE: Center for Political Studies, University of Michigan.

NOTE: Actual turnout is lower than reported turnout.

usual survey from 1950 to 1990, between 40 and 48 percent of the respondents identified themselves as Democrats, with the remainder reflecting changing divisions between Republicans and independents.[32] At certain intervals during the 1960s and 1970s (but not in recent years), Democratic identifiers outnumbered Republican identifiers by a margin of two-to-one. (Data showing the intensity of party identification over time appear in Table 5-7.)

Of greater interest are the changes that have occurred in party identification, particularly of late. According to Gallup polls, during the late 1970s only about 21 to 24 percent of the voters saw themselves as Republicans—the smallest proportion of Republican partisans since the first surveys were taken half a century ago. The election of Ronald Reagan was followed by a sharp increase in the number of Republican partisans, reaching 35 percent in early 1985 (to the Democrats' 37 percent), before settling back to 32 percent in 1986 (to the Democrats' 39 percent). In 1988, about the time of the election, the division between the parties was 42-30, with the Democrats still ahead. In 1990 Democratic identifiers led Republican identifiers by only 39 to 35 percent.

One of the most significant changes in party identification has occurred among younger voters. Since the mid-1980s, voters under thirty years of age have been more likely to identify as Republicans than as Democrats. The net result of changes in partisan preference is that the Republican party is now closer to parity with the Democrats than at any time since World War II.

An especially interesting change in partisan affiliation has occurred along racial lines. Since 1952 the commitment of black voters to the

FIGURE 5-5   The Distribution of Party Identification in the Electorate, 1937–1990

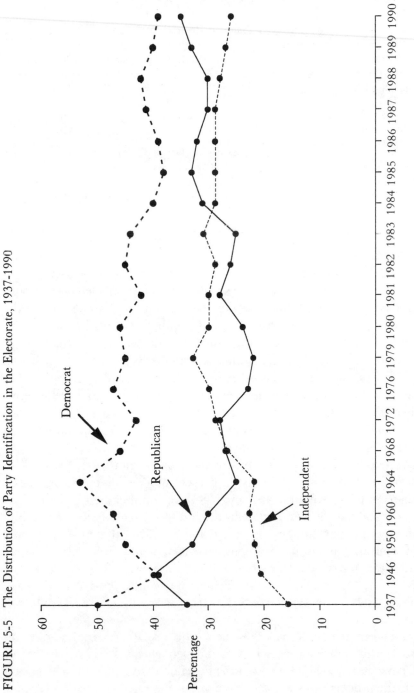

SOURCE: Developed from data in *Gallup Report*, various issues.

TABLE 5-7   Party Identification, Selected Presidential Years, 1952-1988

Party identification	1952	1964	1976	1980	1984	1988
Strong Democrat	22%	27%	15%	18%	18%	17%
Weak Democrat	25	25	25	23	22	18
Independent Democrat	10	9	12	11	10	12
Independent-Independent	6	8	15	13	6	11
Independent Republican	7	6	10	10	13	13
Weak Republican	14	14	14	14	15	14
Strong Republican	14	11	9	9	14	14
Apolitical	3	1	1	2	2	1

SOURCE: Center for Political Studies, University of Michigan.

NOTE: Columns may not add to 100 because of rounding.

Democratic party has grown markedly. Current surveys disclose that about 70 to 75 percent of all blacks see themselves as Democrats, with independents outnumbering Republicans about two-to-one among the remainder. The overall growth in Republican identifiers in recent years is due almost entirely to a shift of white voters, particularly in the South. As the data of Table 5-8 show, southern white strong Republicans number almost as many as southern white strong Democrats; black voters in the South, as in the North, identify overwhelmingly with the Democratic party. Indeed, the party identification configuration in the South increasingly resembles that of the nation as a whole.

The party identification of members of religious groups has also undergone change. In 1952 only 13 percent of Jewish voters considered themselves to be Republicans; by 1988 the number had grown to 18 percent (and it was even higher in the mid-1980s). For northern white Catholics the percentages were 23 and 28. But the most dramatic change of all has occurred among southern white Protestants, where Republican party identification doubled between 1952 (17 percent) and 1988 (34 percent). This latter change is congruent with the broad movement of white southerners toward the ranks of the Republican party.[33]

Another major change has been the growth in the number of persons who perceive themselves as independents.[34] In 1940 one out of five persons was classified as an independent; during the 1970s and 1980s the proportion was almost one out of three. Current surveys show

TABLE 5-8 Party Identification in the South, by Race, 1988

Party identification	Black Southerners	White Southerners
Strong Democrat	35%	16%
Weak Democrat	26	19
Independent Democrat	19	13
Independent-Independent	4	11
Independent Republican	7	15
Weak Republican	6	12
Strong Republican	3	14

SOURCE: Center for Political Studies, University of Michigan.

that independents ("leaners" and "pure") constitute about 27 to 30 percent of the electorate. The results of recent elections confirm the proposition that independents have been at the center of American elections, holding the balance of power between the major parties. Republican presidents in particular have benefited from the support of independents.

Declining partisanship can be detected throughout the electorate. The loyalty of older voters to the parties is not as firm as in the past. Of greater significance, many younger voters who entered the electorate as partisans have deserted their parties in favor of independence. But the most important factor in partisan dealignment has been the entry of new voters with low levels of partisanship. The new voters and the younger voters who have abandoned their partisan ties, one study shows, account for about 75 percent of the decline in partisanship in the electorate.[35] In sum, the broad picture is one of younger persons who are less partisan than their parents and hence more volatile in their voting behavior. As these younger voters succeed older ones, M. Kent Jennings and Gregory B. Markus observe, "the role of political parties in mass politics may be substantially redefined." [36]

The Significance of Party Identification

The distribution of underlying partisan loyalties in the electorate is plainly an advantage for the Democratic party. Over most of the last four decades, the Democratic party has launched each national campaign (including that of 1988) with at least 60 percent of all partisans affiliated in one degree or another with it. When the party has received relatively

The Voting Behavior of Independents . . .

	1956		1960		1964		1968	
	D	R	D	R	D	R	D	R
National vote	42%	58%	50.1%	49.9%	61%	39%	43.0%	43.4%
Independents	30	70	43	57	56	44	31	44

SOURCE: Developed from data in *Gallup Report,* November 1988, 6-7.

The American public is composed of partisans, independents, and apoliticals. The number of independents has grown significantly in recent decades. All candidates and political analysts take them seriously today, and much more is known about their behavior.

Independents are a varied lot. They are not simply civic misfits who reside on the outskirts of politics, as they have sometimes been portrayed. Like other citizens, independents are both attentive and inattentive to politics, involved in elections and indifferent to them, well informed and uninformed, ideological and nonideological. There are "pure" independents, whose voting behavior is especially volatile, and "leaners," who tilt toward one party or the other and whose voting behavior resembles that of partisans. Typically, almost one-third of the electorate classifies itself as independent, with leaners much more numerous than the pure variety. Whites are twice as likely to be independents as blacks.

Independents like winners, independents produce winners, or both. In seven of the nine presidential elections between 1956 and 1988, independents voted on the side of the winner and contributed substan-

strong support from those who identify themselves as Democrats and made a reasonably good showing among independents, it has won. The Republican party has faced a more formidable task. It has had to hold its own partisans, carry a major share of the independents, and attract a significant number of Democrats. One factor that has helped Republicans to win is that the turnout rate of Democratic partisans is always lower than that of Republicans.[37]

Despite its electoral disadvantage, the Republican party has done remarkably well in presidential elections, beginning with the election of Dwight D. Eisenhower in 1952. In 1956 one out of four Democrats and

... in Presidential Elections, 1956-1988

1972		1976		1980		1984		1988	
D	R	D	R	D	R	D	R	D	R
38%	62%	50%	48%	41%	51%	41%	59%	46%	54%
31	69	38	57	29	55	33	67	43	57

NOTE: D = Democrat; R = Republican.

tially to these victories. But in 1960 independents voted decisively for Nixon over Kennedy, and in 1976, decisively for Ford over Carter.

When the nation has favored a Republican candidate for president (and with no third party or independent candidates in the race), independents have voted for him emphatically—averaging about 7 percent more Republican than the national average (elections of 1956, 1972, 1980, 1984, and 1988). "Hidden" Republicans among self-identified independents are apparently more numerous than "hidden" Democrats. A majority of independents supported the Democratic presidential nominee only once (1964) between 1956 and 1988.

Independents are more likely than partisans to vote for a nonmajor party candidate. In 1968, 25 percent of all independents voted for George C. Wallace, presidential candidate of the American Independent party. In 1980, 14 percent of independents voted for the self-styled independent candidate John B. Anderson, a former Republican representative from Illinois who began his presidential quest in Republican presidential primaries.

three out of four independents joined a united Republican party to reelect Eisenhower by a comfortable margin. Following the Kennedy and Johnson interlude, Republicans again captured the presidency with Richard Nixon's narrow victory in 1968 and his decisive reelection in 1972. The predictive value of party identification suffered again in the presidential elections of 1980 and 1984, each won easily by Ronald Reagan despite the Democrats' superior position among party identifiers. The Democrats began the 1988 campaign with a 42-30 percentage advantage in party identification, but it could not be translated into an election victory. George Bush won with relative ease. The Republican party has won seven out of the last ten presidential elections and five out of the last six.

In three respects, party identification is less important today than it was several decades ago. First, fewer persons now choose to identify with a party. During the 1950s and early 1960s, nearly 80 percent of all persons classified themselves as either Democrats or Republicans. During the 1980s, the proportion hovered around 70 to 72 percent. Second, the proportion of strong party identifiers in the nation has declined, particularly in the Democratic party. For white voters during the 1950s and early 1960s, the percentage of strong Democrats ranged between 20 and 26 percent; the high point for this group during the 1980s was only 16 percent (1988). Strong Republicans are slightly less numerous today (between 11 and 14 percent from 1980 to 1990) than in the 1950s and early 1960s (12 to 17 percent).[38] Less than one-third of all voters now profess to be strong, rain-or-shine partisans. And third, the influence of party identification on voting is less pronounced, though it is by no means inconsequential. In 1988, for example, among white voters, 93 percent of strong Democrats voted for Dukakis and 98 percent of strong Republicans voted for Bush (see Table 5-9).

Although party identification is less significant today in explaining voter decisions, it is nevertheless an important factor in voting and in other respects.[39] First, party identification continues to be the best single explanation for the vote decision on candidates. Most voters support the candidates of the party with which they identify (see Table 5-10 for evidence covering the last two decades). In both 1984 and 1988, 81 percent of all voters were party-line voters in the presidential contests, while 12 percent were defectors (those who voted for the candidates of the other party). House elections have become increasingly candidate-centered, but 74 percent of the voters in 1988 were still loyal to their parties, while 20 percent were defectors. (The breakdown is about the same for Senate elections.) Democratic victories in congressional elections year in and year out are due in no small degree to the party's superior position in party affiliation. Second, party loyalty is closely associated with political involvement. Strong partisans are more likely than weak partisans or independents to be interested in political campaigns, to vote, and to express concern over election outcomes. Third, and most important, despite the overall decline in party identification, it continues to be salient for a great many voters, serving to orient them to

TABLE 5-9   Party Identification and the Vote: White Major Party Voters Who Voted Democratic for President, 1976-1988

Party identification	1976	1980	1984	1988
Strong Democrat	88%	87%	88%	93%
Weak Democrat	72	59	63	68
Independent Democrat	73	57	77	86
Independent-Independent	41	23	21	35
Independent Republican	15	13	5	13
Weak Republican	22	5	6	16
Strong Republican	3	4	2	2

SOURCE: Data for 1976-1984 are from Paul R. Abramson, John H. Aldrich, and David W. Rohde, *Change and Continuity in the 1984 Elections* (Washington, D.C.: CQ Press, 1986), 215. Data for 1988 are from Center for Political Studies, University of Michigan.

candidates, issues, and political events and to simplify and order their electoral choices.[40]

Party Identification and National Election Outcomes

Traditionally, presidential elections have been classified in broad contour by examining the relationship between election outcomes and the pattern of party loyalties present in the electorate. Three basic types of elections have been identified: *maintaining, deviating,* and *realigning.*[41] A maintaining election is described as one in which the pattern of party attachments in the electorate fixes the outcome; the winning party owes its victory to the fact that more voters identify with it than with any other party. A deviating election, by contrast, is one in which existing party loyalties are temporarily displaced by short-term forces, enabling the minority (or second) party to win the presidency. In a realigning election the majority party in the electorate not only loses the election but also finds that many of its previous supporters have abandoned their loyalties and moved into the ranks of the other party. So fundamental is the transformation of partisan affiliation that the second party becomes the majority party.

From a historical perspective, the most common form of presidential election has been that in which the party dominant in the electorate wins the presidency—that is, a maintaining election. The dynamics of a maintaining election are furnished by the majority party; the minority party loses because it has been unable to develop either issues or candidates sufficiently attractive to upset the prevailing pattern of party

TABLE 5-10   Party-Line Voting in Presidential and House Elections, 1972-1988

	Presidential election			House elections		
Year	Party-line voters [a]	Defectors [b]	Pure independents [c]	Party-line voters [a]	Defectors [b]	Pure independents [c]
1972	67	25	8	75	17	8
1974				74	18	8
1976	74	15	11	72	19	9
1978				69	22	9
1980	70	22	8	69	23	8
1982				76	17	6
1984	81	12	7	70	23	7
1986				72	22	6
1988	81	12	7	74	20	7

SOURCE: Norman J. Ornstein, Thomas E. Mann, and Michael J. Malbin, *Vital Statistics on Congress, 1989-1990* (Washington, D.C.: Congressional Quarterly, 1990), 65 (as adapted).

NOTE: Figures are a percentage of all voters. Percentages may not add to 100 because of rounding.

[a] Party identifiers who vote for the candidate of their party.
[b] Party identifiers who vote for the candidate of the other party.
[c] The SRC/CPS National Election Surveys use a seven-point scale to define party identification, including three categories of independents—those who "lean" to one or the other party and those who are "pure" independents. The "leaners" are included here among the party-line voters. Party identification means self-identification as determined by surveys.

affiliation. Most of the Republican victories during the last half of the nineteenth century and the first quarter of the twentieth century would be classified as maintaining elections. Recent elections of this type occurred in 1948, 1960, 1964, and 1976. The 1976 election is of special interest. After a period of party decline, party identification assumed much of its earlier importance, as a significantly larger proportion of party identifiers cast votes in accordance with their partisan predispositions. As Warren E. Miller and Teresa E. Levitan observed, "the 1976 election was as much a party election as those elections from the 1950s or early 1960s in which party was acknowledged to be a major determinant of voters' decisions." [42]

Deviating elections are those in which the party that occupies minority status in terms of electoral preferences wins the presidential office. Although the Republicans held an electoral majority in the early twentieth century, Democrat Woodrow Wilson was twice elected president—in 1912, when the Republican party was split between Theodore

Split-Ticket Voting and Split-Party Victories

Declining partisanship in the electorate is a paramount fact of contemporary American politics. Candidate organizations, rather than party organizations, now dominate most campaigns for office at all levels of government. Another result of the declining salience of party in the electorate has been an increase in split-ticket voting and split-party victories.

Year	Number of states electing governor and senator at same time	Number of states electing governor and senator of different parties	Percentage of split victories
1950	19	3	16
1952	20	6	30
1954	25	5	20
1970	23	11	48
1972	12	6	50
1974	26	11	42
1976	10	3	30
1978	24	10	42
1980	9	5	56
1982	22	6	27
1984	7	3	43
1986	26	11	42
1988	10	4	40
1990	25	14	56

SOURCE: Data drawn from Richard M. Scammon, ed., *America Votes 1* (New York: Macmillan, 1956); and various issues of *Congressional Quarterly Weekly Report*.

Roosevelt and William Howard Taft, and in 1916, when Wilson's incumbency and the war issue were sufficient to give him a slight edge. More recent examples are the elections of 1952, 1956, 1968, 1972, 1980, and 1984. Similarly, Democrats were clearly ahead in party identification in 1988 when George Bush defeated Michael Dukakis by a margin of 54-46 percent. Despite the appeal of the minority party's presidential candidate, the coattail effect rarely has been strong enough to give the candidate's party control of Congress. Hence, deviating elections are likely to result in control of the presidency by one party and control of Congress by the other.

Change and Continuity . . .

Almost 92 million individuals cast ballots in the 1988 presidential election. Their voting decisions were influenced by their independent judgments, political party affiliation, and membership in various groups.

The most important factor in voter decisions is political party affiliation. Although the impact of party identification on voting behavior is clearly less significant today than it was several decades ago, it is nevertheless true that about two out of three Americans still hold attachments to the Democratic or Republican parties. The great majority of these partisans vote in keeping with their identification. Party has declined but not disappeared in the voting calculus.

Group membership historically has also had a major effect on voting. Each party has been distinguished by group-based loyalties. The Republican party has carried special appeal for upper-income groups, while the Democratic party has appealed to the relatively disadvantaged in the process of assembling a coalition of minorities. Today, these loyalties are in flux. The accompanying graphs reflect the voting behavior of key groups in the Democratic and Republican coalitions over the last forty years. As a vote predictor, group membership, like party identification, is less reliable than in the past.

Social class does not explain much about voting behavior in the presidential elections of the current era. Voters from the ranks of the professions and business do not vote much more Republican than the national Republican average, while manual workers are less committed to the Democratic party.

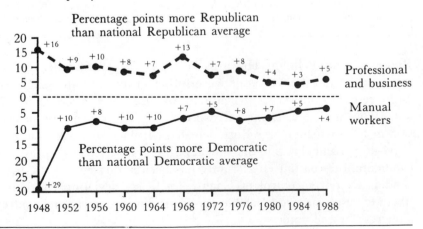

... in Voting Behavior

Nor does Catholic or Protestant religious affiliation. The voting behavior of Catholics and Protestants is becoming increasingly similar; Catholics much less Democratic in their preference, Protestants somewhat less Republican.

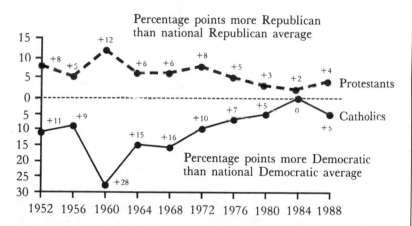

But blacks and Jews continue to have a distinct preference for Democratic presidential candidates.

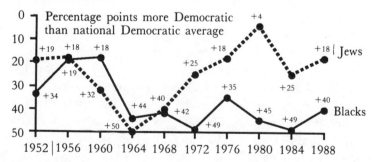

SOURCE: Calculated from data in *Gallup Report,* November 1988, 7; and *New York Times*/CBS News poll, as reported in *New York Times,* November 10, 1988. For social class vote in 1948, see Robert R. Alford, *Party and Society* (Chicago: Rand McNally, 1963), 352. Data on Jewish vote, for 1952-1968, drawn from Mark R. Levy and Michael S. Kramer, *The Ethnic Factor* (New York: Simon and Schuster, 1972), 103; for 1972-1980, Robert J. Huckshorn, *Political Parties in America* (Monterey, Calif.: Brooks/Cole, 1984), 214; and for 1988, *New York Times*/CBS News poll.

NOTE: In 1980, 14 percent of the Jewish vote was cast for John B. Anderson.

The familiar terrain of American politics is sharply changed as a result of realigning elections. Large numbers of voters move out of the majority party and into the minority party, switching not only their vote but their party allegiance. Major changes in public policy are likely to result.[43] The most recent examples of realigning elections are those of 1896 and 1932. In the former, a great many Democrats left their party following the financial panic of 1893, voted for William McKinley in 1896, and became part of the strong Republican majority that dominated the country until 1932. An even sharper upheaval in the electorate occurred in the election of 1932, when the normal Republican majority collapsed as a result of the Great Depression. Franklin D. Roosevelt was swept into office, and millions of Republicans shifted into the ranks of the Democratic party. And even more important, the new voters entering the electorate during the realignment era were predominantly Democratic.[44]

Based on party identification, the categories of elections currently are less useful in analyzing presidential elections than they are in analyzing congressional and subnational elections. In the first place, for many voters party identification has lost its saliency.[45] And second, voters' evaluations of presidential candidates have increasingly focused on personality characteristics rather than on parties or issues. Thus in judging presidential contenders, a recent study suggests, many people use broad categories, assessing candidates in terms of competence (political experience, ability, intelligence), integrity (honesty, sincerity, trustworthiness), reliability (dependable, hardworking, decisive), charisma (leadership, dignity, ability to communicate and inspire), and personal features (age, health, smile, religion, and the like). By far the most important of these dimensions is competence, followed by integrity and reliability.[46] For voters who use the personality mode of organizing information about candidates, in the process of making assessments of them, party identification is obviously of slight significance.

Voting in presidential and other elections can also be examined in terms of prospective and retrospective perspectives. In prospective voting, voters consider the platforms, policy positions, and promises of the candidates and seek to assess which one is closest to their own view of what is important and what should be done, and vote accordingly. In retrospective voting, a less demanding form of evaluation, voters simply judge how well things have been going—how well the party or incumbent has done in the past—and vote accordingly. Incumbents (or the parties or both) are rewarded if they have been successful and punished if they have been unsuccessful. Thus Jimmy Carter was defeated in 1980 primarily because voters evaluated his performance as largely unsatisfactory.[47] Ronald Reagan was reelected in 1984 primarily be-' cause of positive retrospective evaluations of his administration. George Bush's election in 1988 undoubtedly owed a great deal to the voters' favorable assessment of the Reagan administration; according to an ABC News exit poll, 93 percent of the voters supporting Bush indicated that they "wanted to keep to the Reagan course." [48] The evidence is persuasive that retrospective voting has played a major role in all recent presidential elections. Interestingly, partisanship is closely related to restrospective evaluations.[49]

The Voting Behavior of Social Groups

The role of social groups needs to be examined in explaining the behavior of the American electorate. It has long been known that the voting behavior of individuals is influenced not only by their personal values[50] and predilections but also by their affiliations with social groups.[51]

The most important conclusion to be drawn from a study of the relationships between social categories and voting behavior in the six presidential elections between 1968 and 1988 is that each party has enjoyed a set of relatively loyal followings within the electorate—at least until recently (see Table 5-11). In most elections since the advent of the New Deal, the Democratic party has received strong, sometimes overwhelming, support from the poor, members of the working class, union households, blacks, Catholics, Jews, voters with limited formal education, central-city voters, and younger voters. In contrast, the Republican party has received disproportionate support from the nonpoor, nonunion families, whites, Protestants, voters with college educations and professional and business backgrounds, white collar workers, older voters, and voters from outside central cities.[52] These party-group linkages have contributed to the stability of the political system.

But change is in the air. The Democrats' majority status in the electorate is much less imposing. Republican support among younger voters has surged. Independents are numerous. Split-ticket voting is widespread. An extraordinary number of voters ignore elections alto-

TABLE 5-11 Vote by Groups in Presidential Elections, 1968-1988

Group	1968 D	1968 R	Wallace	1972 D	1972 R	1976 D	1976 R	1980 D	1980 R	Anderson	1984 D	1984 R	1988 D	1988 R
National	43.0%	43.4%	13.6%	38%	62%	50%	48%	41%	51%	7%	41%	59%	46%	54%
Men	41	43	16	37	63	53	45	38	53	7	36	64	44	56
Women	45	43	12	38	62	48	51	44	49	6	45	55	48	52
White	38	47	15	32	68	46	52	36	56	7	34	66	41	59
Nonwhite	85	12	3	87	13	85	15	86	10	2	87	13	82	18
College	37	54	9	37	63	42	55	35	53	10	39	61	42	58
High school	42	43	15	34	66	54	46	43	51	5	43	57	46	54
Grade school	52	33	15	49	51	58	41	54	42	3	51	49	55	45
Professional and business	34	56	10	31	69	42	56	33	55	10	34	66	40	59
White collar	41	47	12	36	64	50	48	40	51	9	47	53	42	57
Manual	50	35	15	43	57	58	41	48	48	5	46	54	50	49
Under 30 years	47	38	15	48	52	53	45	47	41	11	40	60	37	63
30-49 years	44	41	15	33	67	48	49	38	52	8	40	60	45	55
50 years and older	41	47	12	36	64	52	48	41	54	4	41	59	49	51
Protestants	35	49	16	30	70	46	53	39	54	6	39	61	42	58
Catholics	59	33	8	48	52	57	41	46	47	6	39	61	51	49
Republicans	9	86	5	5	95	9	91	8	86	5	4	96	7	93
Democrats	74	12	14	67	33	82	18	69	26	4	79	21	85	15
Independents	31	44	25	31	69	38	57	29	55	14	33	67	43	57
East	50	43	7	42	58	51	47	43	47	9	46	54	51	49
Midwest	44	47	9	40	60	48	50	41	51	7	42	58	47	53
South	31	36	33	29	71	54	45	44	52	3	37	63	40	60
West	44	49	7	41	59	46	51	35	54	9	40	60	46	54
Members of labor union families	56	29	15	46	54	63	36	50	43	5	52	48	63	37

SOURCE: *Gallup Report*, November 1988, 6-7. Professional and business, white collar, and manual percentages for 1988 are from a *New York Times*/CBS News survey, as reported in *New York Times*, November 10, 1988.

NOTE: D = Democrat; R = Republican.

gether. And the Democrats' hold over the groups composing the New Deal coalition has eased substantially.[53] In the presidential elections of the 1980s, blue collar workers, members of labor union families, and Catholics became more supportive of the Republican party. The shift of white southerners to the Republican party, beginning earlier, has been nothing short of spectacular.[54] The extent to which these changes will endure in the 1990s remains to be seen, but it seems altogether unlikely that the traditional Democratic majority coalition can be restored intact.

Both loyalties and group ties to the parties have weakened, particularly in presidential elections. Longstanding religious, regional, and class differences between the parties have lost their vitality or vanished. Political affiliation for many voters is casual at best, and for some, simply irrelevant. An electorate characterized by stable, deep-rooted party loyalties no longer exists. Whatever else may be said about these conditions, they are fully consistent with a period of party dealignment and electoral volatility.

What do these changes mean for the future of American politics and parties? Is the nation now in the early stages of a critical realignment that will culminate in a major transformation of the party system and a period of sustained Republican dominance? Or is the present condition merely a state of dealignment that itself might persist on a long-term basis (and thus not necessarily serve as a precursor to a new and durable partisan alignment)?

These are hard questions to answer. But several general observations can be made. First, scholars themselves do not agree on the answers to these questions;[55] nor do politicians. Second, it helps to remember that "we cannot be sure realignment has occurred until after it has ended." [56] Third, although the Republican party has thoroughly dominated recent presidential elections, it has not been able to capture the House or to retain control of the Senate (which it won in 1980 and lost in 1986). And of most importance, it thus far has not made solid gains at the state and local levels. Typically, Democrats hold about 60 percent of all state legislative seats and between 55 to 60 percent of the governorships. In 1990 Democrats controlled three times as many state governments (both executive and legislative branches) as the Republicans. But the real winner, as usual, in a period of electoral party decomposition, was divided party government—the governorship and the legislative chambers split between the parties, a condition present in six out of ten states in 1990.

Group Basis of the 1990 Congressional Vote

The data presented below reflect the behavior of traditional party groups, groups worth noting, and groups that significantly exceeded the national average in support of Democratic or Republican House candidates in 1990. Although most groups followed their usual party inclinations, this off-year vote was not a carbon copy of the 1988 presidential vote. Blacks, Hispanics, and agricultural workers, for example, voted more Republican than they did in 1988; Catholics and Jews more Democratic than they did in 1988.

	Democratic			Republican	
Group	Percentage Democratic	Percentage points more Democratic than national average	Group	Percentage Republican	Percentage points more Republican than national average
Blacks	78	26	White Fundamentalist or Evangelical Christian	68	20
Jews	74	22			
Hispanics	69	17			
Low income [a]	66	14	High income [a]	61	13
Union members	65	13			
Teachers	59	7	White Protestants	57	9
Government employees	58	6	Agricultural workers	56	8
Easterners	58	6	Homemakers	55	7
Not high school graduates	58	6	Middle-aged men [b]	54	6
High school graduates	58	6	Income over $50,000	53	5
Catholics	57	5	White men	52	4
First-time voters	56	4	Professionals or managers	51	3
Blue collar workers	55	3	College graduates	51	3
			Midwesterners	51	3
Women	54	2	Whites	50	2

SOURCE: Developed from *New York Times*/CBS News exit poll data, as reported in the *New York Times,* November 8, 1990. For the vote of major groups in Senate and gubernatorial races in 1990, see the *Washington Post,* November 8, 1990.

NOTE: Democratic national average was 52 percent; Republican national average, 48 percent.

[a] Low income: under $15,000; high income: over $100,000.
[b] Middle-aged: 45-59 years old.

What the Republican party has demonstrated convincingly in the last two decades is that, in presidential voting, it stands a good chance of winning, irrespective of its minority position in the electorate.[57] But it has not become the nation's majority party, either by virtue of its lopsided (1980 and 1984) and comfortable (1988) victories or by virtue of a critical realignment. It has had a big advantage in presidential elections, but to award it a lock on the presidency would be premature. No durable voting alignment exists in a politics largely without omen. Probably the best guess about the future, or at least the near future, is for a continuation of dealignment—marked by loose ties between the public and the parties; voter ambivalence; and voting behavior that reflects ticket-splitting, a preference for incumbents in legislative elections, and an inclination to switch parties without giving it a second thought. Faithful to this pattern, voting decisions are likely to be heavily influenced by voter inferences concerning presidential candidates' qualities (competence, integrity, and reliability in particular) and their retrospective appraisals of the performance and success of presidents, administrations, and parties in promoting the nation's well-being.[58] Nothing in this picture suggests the emergence of tidy and predictable politics.

Notes

1. Among the studies that can be consulted on the meaning of modest rates of turnout are the following: E. E. Schattschneider, *The Semisovereign People* (New York: Holt, Rinehart and Winston, 1975), especially Chapter 6; Heinz Eulau, "The Politics of Happiness," *Antioch Review* 16 (September 1956): 259-264; Arthur T. Hadley, *The Empty Polling Booth* (Englewood Cliffs, N.J.: Prentice Hall, 1978); William H. Flanigan and Nancy H. Zingale, *Political Behavior of the American Electorate* (Boston: Allyn and Bacon, 1983), especially Chapter 1; and, of a different order, Everett Carll Ladd, Jr., *Where Have All the Voters Gone?* (New York: Norton, 1982).
2. Paul R. Abramson and William Claggett, "Race-Related Differences in Self-Reported and Validated Turnout in 1984," *Journal of Politics* 48 (May 1986): 413. The U.S. Bureau of the Census showed reported turnout in 1988 to be 57.4 percent, about 7 percent higher than the actual turnout.
3. The turnout percentages are calculated from data in the *Statistical Abstract of the United States* (Washington, D.C.: U.S. Government Printing Office, 1989), 253, 259.
4. The explanation for this is well known: often the only significant choice among candidates available to southern voters is to be found in Democratic primaries. As the Republican party gains competitive strength in the South, participation in general elections is virtually certain to increase.

5. Patrick J. Kenney, "Explaining Primary Turnout: The Senatorial Case," *Legislative Studies Quarterly* 11 (February 1986): 65-73. Also see Malcolm E. Jewell, "Northern State Gubernatorial Primary Elections: Explaining Voter Turnout," *American Politics Quarterly* 12 (January 1984): 101-116; and Malcolm E. Jewell and David M. Olson, *American State Political Parties and Elections* (Homewood, Ill.: Dorsey Press, 1982). Several studies deal with the question of whether election night forecasts decrease turnout: Raymond E. Wolfinger and Peter Linquiti, "Tuning In and Tuning Out," *Public Opinion* 4 (February/March 1981): 56-60; John E. Jackson, "Election Night Reporting and Voter Turnout," *American Journal of Political Science* 27 (November 1983): 615-635; and Michael X. Delli Carpini, "Scooping the Voters?: The Consequences of the Networks' Early Call of the 1980 Presidential Race," *Journal of Politics* 46 (August 1984): 866-885.

6. The white primary in southern states resulted from the exclusion of blacks from membership in the Democratic party, which was held to be a private organization. Since the real election at this time in most southern states occurred in the Democratic primaries, blacks had little opportunity to make their influence felt. After many years of litigation, the Supreme Court in 1944 held that the white primary was in violation of the Fifteenth Amendment. The Court's position in *Smith v. Allwright* was that the primary is an integral part of the election process and that political parties are engaged in a public, not a private, function in holding primary elections. After the white primary was held unconstitutional, southern states turned to the development of literacy and understanding tests, along with discriminatory registration systems, to bar black access to the polls.

7. Schattschneider, *The Semisovereign People*, 78-80.

8. Schattschneider, *The Semisovereign People*, 84.

9. Steven J. Rosenstone and Raymond E. Wolfinger, "The Effect of Registration Laws on Voter Turnout," *American Political Science Review* 72 (March 1978): especially 25-30. The most facilitative laws on closing dates, apart from North Dakota, which requires no registration, are those of Idaho and Vermont. Voters in these states may register up to three days before the election. Maine provides for eight days and New Hampshire for nine.

10. Rosenstone and Wolfinger, "The Effect of Registration Laws on Voter Turnout," 27-45. Also see their book, *Who Votes?* (New Haven, Conn.: Yale University Press, 1980); and M. Margaret Conway, *Political Participation in the United States* (Washington, D.C.: CQ Press, 1991), especially chapter 7.

11. Committee for the Study of the American Electorate, *Creating the Opportunity: How Changes in Registration and Voting Law Can Enhance Voter Turnout* (Washington, D.C., 1987).

12. Rosenstone and Wolfinger, "The Effect of Registration Laws on Voter Turnout," 31-36.

13. Curtis B. Gans, "A Rejoinder to Piven and Cloward," *PS* 23 (June 1990): 176-178.

14. See an article by Stephen D. Shaffer, "A Multivariate Explanation of Decreasing Turnout in Presidential Elections, 1960-1976," *American Journal of Political Science* 25 (February 1981): 68-93.

15. Peverill Squire, Raymond E. Wolfinger, and David P. Glass, "Residential Mobility and Voter Turnout," *American Political Science Review* 81 (March 1987): 45-65. The authors propose that change-of-address notices left with post

offices be modified to permit movers to shift their voting address (as well as their mail) to their new residence. Using these forms, registration officials would automatically reregister the individual at the new address. With mobility no longer a factor in turnout, according to the authors' estimate, participation would increase by 9 percentage points.

16. *Gallup Report,* November 1984, 11.

17. *Pittsburgh Press,* July 9, 1990.

18. See Paul R. Abramson and John H. Aldrich, "The Decline of Electoral Participation in America," *American Political Science Review* 76 (September 1982): 502-521.

19. Abramson and Aldrich, "The Decline of Electoral Participation in America," 504-510; and Shaffer, "A Multivariate Explanation of Decreasing Turnout in Presidential Elections, 1960-1976," 68-93. Also see James DeNardo, "Turnout and the Vote: The Joke's on the Democrats," *American Political Science Review* 74 (June 1980): 406-420; and Harvey J. Tucker, Arnold Vedlitz, and James DeNardo, "Does Heavy Turnout Help Democrats in Presidential Elections?" *American Political Science Review* 80 (December 1986): 1291-1304.

20. For a study that finds alienation to be a major factor in nonvoting, see Priscilla L. Southwell, "Alienation and Nonvoting in the United States: A Refined Operationalization," *Western Political Quarterly* 38 (December 1985): 663-674.

21. On the relationship between frequent elections and turnout, see the research of Richard W. Boyd, "Decline of U.S. Voter Turnout: Structural Explanations," *American Politics Quarterly* 9 (April 1981): 133-160; "Election Calendars and Voter Turnout," *American Politics Quarterly* 14 (January-April 1986): 89-104; and "The Effects of Primaries and Statewide Races on Voter Turnout," *Journal of Politics* 51 (August 1989): 730-739.

22. Richard A. Brody, "The Puzzle of Political Participation in America," in *The New American Political System,* ed. Anthony King (Washington, D.C.: American Enterprise Institute for Public Policy Research, 1978), 306.

23. *New York Times,* November 6, 1988; and *Congressional Quarterly Weekly Report,* January 21, 1989, 135.

24. G. Bingham Powell, Jr., "American Voter Turnout in Comparative Perspective," *American Political Science Review* 80 (March 1986): 17-43.

25. Why do close elections increase turnout? One explanation is that ordinary citizens are more likely to participate in close elections because they believe their vote will make a difference. A second possibility is that turnout increases because the closeness of any election prompts elites (candidates and their financial supporters) to focus on getting voters to the polls (thus stimulating campaign expenditures). A recent study by Gary W. Cox and Michael C. Munger finds that closeness of elections affects behavior at both mass and elite levels. "Closeness, Expenditures, and Turnout in the 1982 U.S. Elections," *American Political Science Review* 83 (March 1989): 217-231. Also see Kenneth D. Wald, "The Closeness-Turnout Hypothesis: A Reconsideration," *American Politics Quarterly* 13 (July 1985): 273-296.

26. Actual turnout is clearly lower than the voting percentages reported in Table 5-1. Survey respondents sometimes forget whether or not they voted or else exaggerate their participation.

27. The findings of these paragraphs are drawn from Sidney Verba and Norman

H. Nie, *Participation in America: Political Democracy and Social Equality* (New York: Harper and Row, 1972), 25-43.

28. Lester W. Milbrath, *Political Participation* (Chicago: Rand McNally, 1965), 17-21. The holding that political participation involves a hierarchy of political acts—under which the citizen who performs a difficult political act, such as forming an organization to solve a local community problem, is virtually certain to perform less demanding acts—can be overstated. See Verba and Nie, *Participation in America*, especially Chapters 2 and 3. Their general position is that "the citizenry is not divided simply into more or less active citizens. Rather there are many types of activists engaging in different acts, with different motives, and different consequences." Quotation on p. 45.
29. *Gallup Report,* November 1988, 17.
30. See Verba and Nie, *Participation in America,* 133-137.
31. See Hadley, *The Empty Polling Booth,* especially Chapter 1.
32. For an analysis of the phenomenon of independence in the United States, the various categories of independence, and what it means to be an independent, see two articles by Jack Dennis, "Political Independence in America, Part I: On Being an Independent Partisan Supporter," and "Political Independence in America, Part II: Towards a Theory," in *British Journal of Political Science* 18 (January 1988, April 1988), 77-110, 197-219.
33. *Public Opinion,* October/November 1985, 21-31; and September/October 1988, 34.
34. For a view that strengthened partisanship within the electorate depends on convincing people that the two parties are different in policy orientations and that these differences affect peoples' well-being, see Patrick R. Cotter, "The Decline of Partisanship: A Test of Four Explanations," *American Politics Quarterly* 13 (January 1985): 51-78.
35. Helmut Norpoth and Jerrold G. Rusk, "Partisan Dealignment in the American Electorate: Itemizing the Deductions since 1964," *American Political Science Review* 76 (September 1982): 522-537.
36. M. Kent Jennings and Gregory B. Markus, "Partisan Orientations over the Long Haul: Results from the Three-Wave Political Socialization Panel Study," *American Political Science Review* 78 (December 1984): 1000-1018 (quotation on p. 1016). See an analysis of young adults that suggests that they are active in adjusting their partisan affiliation to coincide with their views on preferred policies: Charles H. Franklin, "Issue Preferences, Socialization, and the Evolution of Party Identification," *American Journal of Political Science* 28 (August 1984): 459-478.
37. A disposition to participate in elections is related to high interest, information, and involvement. The Democratic vote regularly suffers because citizens who might be expected to vote Democratic—those in the lower socioeconomic strata—are often not sufficiently interested or involved in the election to turn out on election day.
38. Paul R. Abramson, John H. Aldrich, and David W. Rohde, *Change and Continuity in the 1984 Elections* (Washington, D.C.: CQ Press, 1986), 211-215.
39. For evidence on the significance of party identification for different offices over time, see Stephen D. Shaffer, "Voting in Four Elective Offices: A Comparative Analysis," *American Politics Quarterly* 10 (January 1982): 5-30.
40. See a study that finds that the American electorate is changing in three

significant ways: becoming more "ideologically constrained and sophisticated," more rational in behavior, and less stable in its behavior (or less consistent in its support of parties). Michael X. Delli Carpini, "Political Distillation: The Changing Impact of Partisanship on Electoral Behavior," *American Politics Quarterly* 11 (April 1983): 163-180.

41. Angus Campbell, Philip E. Converse, Warren E. Miller, and Donald E. Stokes, *The American Voter* (New York: Wiley, 1960), 531-538.

42. Warren E. Miller and Teresa E. Levitan, *Leadership and Change: Presidential Elections from 1952 to 1976* (Cambridge, Mass.: Winthrop, 1976), 211.

43. The major effect of a realignment, David W. Brady argues, is the creation of a unified majority party in Congress that is capable of bringing about significant changes in public policy. See David W. Brady, "A Reevaluation of Realignments in American Politics: Evidence from the House of Representatives," *American Political Science Review* 79 (March 1985): 28-49; David W. Brady and Joseph Stewart, Jr., "Congressional Party Realignment and Transformations of Public Policy in Three Realignment Eras," *American Journal of Political Science* 26 (May 1982): 333-360; and Barbara Sinclair, "Party Realignment and the Transformation of the Political Agenda: The House of Representatives, 1925-1938," *American Political Science Review* 71 (September 1977): 940-953.

44. James E. Campbell, "Sources of the New Deal Realignment: The Contributions of Conversion and Mobilization to Partisan Change," *Western Political Quarterly* 38 (September 1985): 357-376.

45. It is interesting to find that partisan defectors (those who identify with one party but vote for the other party's presidential candidate) are much more likely to cast a negative or anticandidate vote than persons who vote in keeping with their party identification. See Michael M. Gant and Lee Sigelman, "Anti-Candidate Voting in Presidential Elections," *Polity* 18 (Winter 1985): 329-339.

46. Arthur H. Miller, Martin P. Wattenberg, and Oksana Malanchuk, "Schematic Assessments of Presidential Candidates," *American Political Science Review* 80 (June 1986): 521-540. Interestingly, college-educated voters place particular emphasis on these characteristics. Party competence evaluations are also important in explaining the congressional vote. See Albert D. Cover, "Party Competence Evaluations and Voting for Congress," *Western Political Quarterly* 39 (June 1986): 304-312.

47. President Carter's relations with Congress were also unsatisfactory. See Charles O. Jones, "Keeping Faith and Losing Congress: The Carter Experience in Washington," *Presidential Studies Quarterly* 14 (Summer 1984): 437-445.

48. *Washington Post,* November 9, 1988.

49. See the analysis and evidence of Abramson, Aldrich, and Rohde, *Change and Continuity in the 1984 Elections,* especially Chapters 6 and 7; and Morris P. Fiorina, *Retrospective Voting in American National Elections* (New Haven, Conn.: Yale University Press, 1981).

50. For an analysis of the importance of friends and family in influencing voter decisions, see John G. Geer, "Voting and the Social Environment," *American Politics Quarterly* 13 (January 1985): 3-27.

51. Studies of electoral behavior that bear too heavily on the group as the unit of analysis may do some injustice to the individual voter, making him appear as an object to be managed by skillful propagandists or as the victim of social determinants (for example, occupation, race, or education). Preoccupation with

the gross characteristics of voters may lead the analyst to minimize the individual's awareness and concern over issues. V. O. Key, Jr., has argued that "the electorate behaves about as rationally and responsibly as we should expect, given the clarity of the alternatives presented to it and the character of the information available to it." By and large, in Key's study, the American voter emerges as a rational and responsible person concerned about matters of public policy, governmental performance, and executive personality. See V. O. Key, Jr. (with Milton C. Cummings), *The Responsible Electorate* (New York: Vintage Books, 1966), 7.

52. For an analysis of the characteristics of the Democratic and Republican party coalitions between 1952 and 1984, focusing on the importance of each group to the total party vote, see Robert Axelrod, "Presidential Election Coalitions in 1984," *American Political Science Review* 80 (March 1986): 281-284.

53. See an analysis of shifting group loyalties by Harold W. Stanley, William T. Bianco, and Richard G. Niemi, "Partisanship and Group Support Over Time: A Multivariate Analysis," *American Political Science Review* 80 (September 1986): 970-976. They conclude that "journalistic and party obituaries for the New Deal coalition appear harsher than the reality warrants. Native southern whites had a strong, prolonged decline in their incremental partisan impact, but the milder declines for most groups [such as Catholics and working-class members], coupled with the increases for females, Jews, and blacks, suggest the New Deal group basis of Democratic identification may not be dazzling, but is far from dead." Quotation on p. 975.

54. See the thesis of Edward G. Carmines and James A. Stimson that the rapid change in behavior of blacks and native southern whites in the mid-1960s constituted a racial realignment. "Racial Issues and the Structure of Mass Belief Systems," *Journal of Politics* 44 (February 1982): 2-20.

55. For instruction on the dealignment-realignment question, see James L. Sundquist, *Dynamics of the Party System: Alignment and Realignment of Political Parties in the United States* (Washington, D.C.: Brookings Institution, 1983); Paul A. Beck, "The Dealignment Era in America," in *Electoral Change in Advanced Industrial Democracies: Realignment or Dealignment*, ed. Russell J. Dalton, Scott C. Flanagan, and Paul A. Beck (Princeton, N.J.: Princeton University Press, 1984), 240-266; Herbert B. Asher, *Presidential Elections and American Politics* (Homewood, Ill.: Dorsey Press, 1984), 281-302; Abramson, Aldrich, and Rohde, *Change and Continuity in the 1984 Elections*, 281-305; Theodore J. Lowi, "An Aligning Election, A Presidential Plebiscite," in *The Elections of 1984*, ed. Michael Nelson (Washington, D.C.: CQ Press, 1985), 277-301; Raymond E. Wolfinger, "Dealignment, Realignment, and Mandates in the 1984 Election," in *The American Elections of 1984*, ed. Austin Ranney (Durham, N.C.: Duke University Press, 1985), 277-296; John E. Chubb and Paul E. Peterson, "Realignment and Institutionalization," in *The New Direction in American Politics*, ed. John E. Chubb and Paul E. Peterson (Washington, D.C.: Brookings Institution, 1985), 1-30; and Everett Carll Ladd, "On Mandates, Realignments, and the 1984 Presidential Election," *Political Science Quarterly* 100 (Spring 1985): 1-25.

56. Paul A. Beck, "Realignment Begins: The Republican Surge in Florida," *American Politics Quarterly* 10 (October 1982): 421-438. Quotation on p. 433.

57. The importance of Republican victories in presidential elections should not be exaggerated, writes Gerald M. Pomper. "It is possible that the presidency has

now become completely nonpartisan, individualized and distinct from the general political system, so that elections for the chief executive have no larger import." "The Presidential Election," in *The Election of 1984: Reports and Interpretations,* ed. Gerald M. Pomper (Chatham, N.J.: Chatham House, 1985), 86. See the evidence on electoral disaggregation by Morris P. Fiorina, "The Electorate in the Voting Booth," in *The Parties Respond,* ed. L. Sandy Maisel (Boulder, Colo.: Westview Press, 1990), 116-133.

58. The 1988 presidential election can be interpreted as a retrospective triumph for Reagan—"a triumph of popular satisfaction with his policies, with the general state of the world and of the nation as he left office, and with his performance." See an interesting essay by Warren E. Miller, "The Electorate's View of the Parties," in *The Parties Respond,* 97-115. Quotation on p. 113.

The Congressional Party and the Formation of Public Policy

THE TASKS that confront the American major party are formidably ambitious. From one perspective, the party is a wide-ranging electoral agency organized to make a credible bid for power. Here and there a party organization is so stunted and devitalized that it seldom can make an authentic effort to win office. Where it is not taken seriously, the party finds it difficult to develop and recruit candidates, to gain the attention of the media, and to attract financial contributors. Elections may go by default to the dominant party as the second party struggles merely to stay in business. But throughout most of the country the parties compete on fairly even terms—if not for certain offices or in certain districts, at least for some offices or in a state at large. Presidential elections are vigorously contested virtually everywhere. As electoral organizations, the parties recruit candidates, organize campaigns, develop issues, and mobilize voters. Typical voters get their best glimpse of the workings of party when they observe the "party in the electorate" during political campaigns.

From another perspective, the party is a collection of officeholders who share in some measure common values and policy orientations. In the broadest sense, its mission is to take hold of government, to identify national problems and priorities, and to work for their settlement or achievement. In a narrower sense, the task of the "party in the government" is to consolidate and fulfill promises made to the electorate during the campaign. How it is organized to do this and how it does it is the concern of this chapter. The focus centers on the party in Congress.

Congressional Elections

The two most important variables in the election of members of Congress are incumbency status and party affiliation. Congressional incumbents have numerous advantages in elections. The offices and staffs of members are basic units in their campaign organizations. Voters are much more likely to recognize the name of the incumbent than that of the challenger. Some voters will have benefited from the many services that members regularly perform for their constituents. The franking privilege permits members to send mail to their constituents at government expense. And of major importance, incumbents ordinarily find it much easier than challengers to raise campaign funds, particularly from the political action committees (PACs) of interest groups. Thus, it is not surprising that incumbents are frequently reelected. It is rare for less than 90 percent of all House incumbents seeking reelection to be successful; this happened last in 1974. Recently, the reelection successes of House incumbents has been spectacular: 98 percent in 1986, 98.5 percent in 1988, and 96 percent in 1990. Although Senate incumbents usually face stronger competition, they also win much more often than they lose. In 1988, 85 percent of all Senate incumbents running for reelection were successful; in 1990, 97 percent.

Party affiliation is also a key factor in congressional elections. In the typical state, some districts nearly always elect Democratic legislators and some districts nearly always elect Republican legislators. Some districts are so thoroughly dominated by one party that the second party has virtually no chance of winning. With few exceptions, for example, House districts in major cities are securely Democratic, irrespective of the incumbency factor. In other suburban, small-town, and rural districts Democratic candidates may face insurmountable odds in election after election.

Districts do not often switch from one party to the other. In no election from 1954 through 1990 did more than 13 percent of the 435 seats switch party control. In 1988 a mere 9 seats (2 percent) switched party hands.[1] In 1990, 21 seats (5 percent) changed from the control of one party to the other.

Incumbency and party combine to yield a great many one-sided elections, especially in the House. Nearly three-fourths of all House elections from 1970 to 1988 were won by margins of 60 percent or more (see Figure 6-1). By contrast, only 14 percent of all elections were marginal—that is, won by less than 55 percent of the vote. In 1988 an extraordinary 84 percent of all House elections were won by 60 percent or more of the vote; less than 9 percent were marginal.

Close elections sometimes carry large consequences for the parties and public policy. Increasingly, they have determined which party controls the Senate. In 1980 Republican senatorial candidates won nine of twelve Senate elections in which the winner received 52 percent or less of the vote and in the process captured the Senate for the first time in more than two decades. Some argue, with reason, that the "Reagan [policy] Revolution" turned on these Senate victories. In 1982 Republicans continued their Senate control by winning all six elections in which the winner gained 52 percent or less of the vote. From this set of very close elections in 1984, Democratic candidates won three of five. And in 1986 the Senate shifted back to Democratic control as Republican candidates lost nine of eleven races settled by a margin of 52 percent or less. The way the votes break is thus paramount. With a shift of only 28,000 votes in five states (Alabama, Colorado, Nevada, North Dakota, and South Dakota) the Republicans would have maintained control of the Senate for the last two years of the Reagan administration. Instead they suffered a devastating loss. In 1988 Republicans won four of seven of the closely contested Senate races. Each party won two of the four Senate races in 1990 decided by a margin of 52 percent or less.

Competition between the parties for congressional seats is now at about its lowest level in the twentieth century. A number of possible explanations exist for this. One notion is that Democratic and Republican state legislators increasingly cooperate to protect each party's incumbents: they draw congressional district lines (along with their own) in such a way as to create as many safe seats as possible. Never known for altruism in matters of elections, incumbents of both parties obviously prefer this solution when faced with redistricting. David R. Mayhew contends that incumbents have become more skillful in "advertising" their names, in "claiming credit" for federal governmental programs that benefit their districts, and in "position taking" on key issues of concern to their constituents. And they have large and talented staffs to help them cultivate their constituents.[2] Another study finds that information on the

FIGURE 6-1   Marginal and One-sided House Elections, 1970-1988

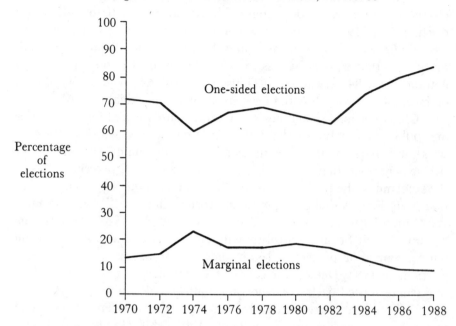

SOURCE: Developed from data in various issues of *Congressional Quarterly Weekly Report*.

NOTE: One-sided elections were won by 60 percent or more of the vote; marginal elections were won by less than 55 percent of the vote. All other elections fell in the 55-59.9 percent range.

candidates is an important factor. If it is not available on both candidates, voters "are likely to vote for incumbents, whom they already like and may have voted for, faced with challengers they know little, if anything, about." [3] The success of incumbents also seems to be promoted by the relative weakness of congressional challengers.[4] Finally, it may be that competition has declined because voters now attach more importance to incumbency than to party affiliation in casting their ballots; the electoral parties are plainly weaker today than in the past, hence less capable of providing voting cues for the public.[5]

The level of competitiveness for seats in Congress, and especially in the House, is not high. Safe seats abound, fostering a relatively stable membership. Exactly how public policy is affected by this condition is hard to say. Conventional wisdom holds that opportunities for major policy change are limited by a membership that remains largely intact election after election.

Party Representation in Congress

Two central conclusions emerge from a study of the parties in the congressional races from 1932 to 1990 (see Figures 6-2 and 6-3). First, with few exceptions since 1932, the Democratic party has held comfortable majorities in Congress. Second, the capacity of the Republican party to win presidential elections has not extended to Congress. The Republican party controlled the House by a slim margin from 1952 to 1954 and broke even in the Senate during the same period. Since then the party has controlled only the Senate—for six years during the Reagan presidency. Given the prevailing pattern of party allegiance in the electorate and the Democrats' continuing incumbency advantage, Republican presidents can expect to face Democratic majorities in one or both houses of Congress. The success of their legislative programs usually depends on their ability to develop effective biparty coalitions.

Seeking to strengthen its representation, the national Republican party has been unusually active in providing campaign money and services for all of its congressional candidates, not just for its most competitive contenders. But the results have been disappointing. Paul S. Herrnson writes:

> Party-focused television advertisements cannot overcome a candidate's image problems; party contributions, coordinated expenditures, and campaign services are no substitute for an effective candidate campaign organization; and there is little a party or candidate can do to defeat a highly popular incumbent or to win a seat in a district composed predominantly of people with strong loyalties to the opposite party. *These factors serve as reminders that congressional elections are principally local contests fought between individual candidates; it is the candidates who are ultimately responsible for the failures and successes of their campaigns.*[6]

Party membership is a major factor not only in determining who is elected to Congress but also in influencing members' behavior once they have taken office. The fact that party cohesion collapses on certain issues that come before Congress does not alter the general proposition that party affiliation is a major explanation of voting behavior. Party cues are not taken lightly by most members. They recognize that there are advantages to going along with the leadership and voting in agreement with their party colleagues. An examination of party voting follows an analysis of congressional party organization.

FIGURE 6-2 Democratic Strength in Senate Elections, 1932-1990

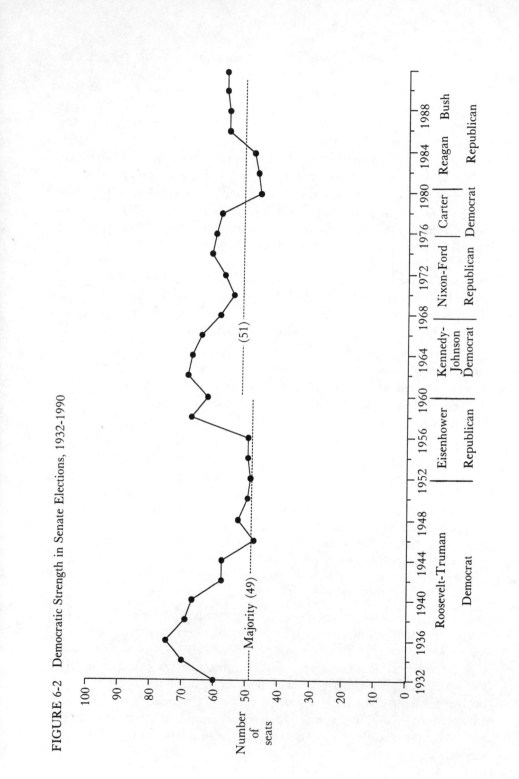

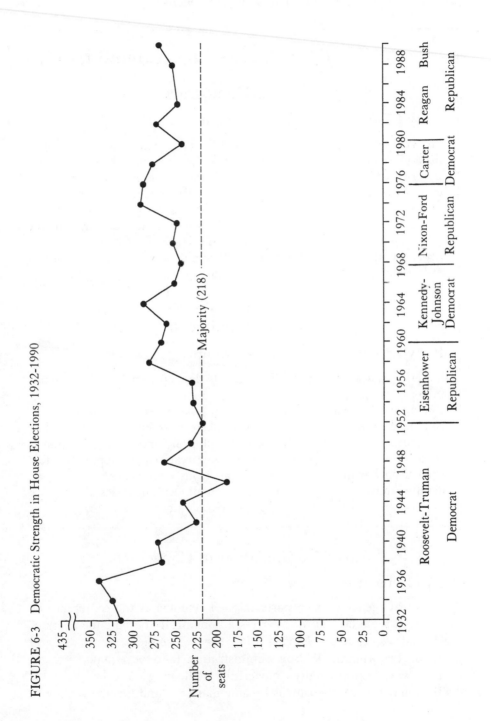

FIGURE 6-3 Democratic Strength in House Elections, 1932-1990

Party Leaders and Committees . . .

House Democrats

Party Leaders

Speaker
majority leader
majority whip
caucus chairman
caucus vice
   chairman
chief deputy whip
deputy whips
at-large whips

Party Committees

Steering and Policy: assigns Democratic members to committees and helps to develop party policy. Speaker serves as chairman, majority leader as vice chairman.

Democratic Congressional Campaign Committee: provides campaign support for Democratic House candidates.

Personnel Committee: supervises the party's patronage positions.

House Republicans

Party Leaders

minority leader
minority whip
conference chairman
conference vice
   chairman
conference secretary
chief deputy whip
deputy whips

Party Committees

Policy: helps to develop Republican policy positions.

Committee on Committees: assigns Republican members to committees.

National Republican Congressional Committee: provides campaign support for Republican House candidates.

Personnel Committee: supervises the party's patronage positions.

Party Organization in Congress

Party Conferences

The central agency of each party in each chamber is the conference or caucus. All those elected to Congress automatically become members of their party's caucus. During the early twentieth century, and particularly during the Wilson administration, the House majority party caucus was exceptionally powerful. Following World War I, disillusionment with the caucus became manifest, and members came to

...in 102d Congress (1991-1992)

Senate Democrats

Party Leaders

president pro tempore
majority leader
majority whip
conference chairman
conference secretary
chief deputy whip
deputy whips

Party Committees

Policy: helps to develop party policy and advises on the scheduling of legislation. Majority leader serves as chairman.

Steering: assigns Democratic members to committees. Majority leader serves as chairman.

Legislative Review Committee: analyzes legislative proposals and makes recommendations.

Democratic Senatorial Campaign Committee: provides campaign support for Democratic Senate candidates.

Senate Republicans

Party Leaders

minority leader
assistant minority
    leader
conference chairman
conference secretary

Party Committees

Policy: helps to develop party policy and advises on the scheduling of legislation.

Committee on Committees: assigns Republican members to committees.

National Republican Senatorial Committee: provides campaign support for Republican Senate candidates.

---

question the right of the caucus to bind them to a course of action. The power of the caucus declined sharply in the 1920s, and soon its functions were limited to the selection of party leaders such as the Speaker of the House, the floor leaders, and the whips.

For all intents and purposes, the caucus was moribund for the next half century. In 1969, after years of somnolence, the Democratic caucus began to hold regular monthly meetings to examine proposals for reforming the House. In the early 1970s, the caucus made several modifications of the seniority system, the most important of which provided for secret ballots on nominees for committee chairmen. A Steering and Policy Committee was created by the caucus in 1973 to formulate legislative programs and to participate in the scheduling of legislation for floor consideration.

The power of the Democratic caucus was dramatically demonstrated at the opening of the Ninety-fourth Congress in 1975 when, among other things, the caucus voted to remove three committee chairmen from their positions, transferred to the Steering and Policy Committee the power to make committee assignments from the Democratic members of the Ways and Means Committee, and made a number of changes involving nominations and subcommittee procedures. Included in these changes was a provision to empower the Speaker, subject to caucus approval, to nominate the Democratic members of the powerful Rules Committee. The key test in filling vacancies on this committee now appears to be the member's allegiance to the Speaker. Major disciplinary action by the Democratic caucus occurred again at the start of the Ninety-eighth Congress (1983-1984). In an unusual action, the caucus voted to remove a Texas representative from the Budget Committee because in the previous Congress he had worked closely with the administration in the design of President Reagan's budget strategy.

The revitalization of the Democratic caucus has weakened the hold of the seniority system and strengthened the positions of party leaders, particularly the Speaker. But to what extent can the caucus influence the behavior of party members on major policy proposals? Caucus power collides with the nagging reality of all legislative politics: the individual member's electoral security, and thus his primary interest, lies in the constituency. For many members of the House, the attractions of a cohesive party are not nearly so great as the attractions of independence, with all the opportunities it affords the legislator to concentrate on constituency interests and problems. Party leaders and committee leaders, moreover, usually take a dim view of caucus involvement in policy questions. As Speaker Thomas P. ("Tip") O'Neill, Jr. (D-Mass., 1977-1986), observed: "I don't like any of these [policy] matters coming from the caucus on a direct vote." A similar view was expressed by Richard Bolling (D-Mo.) during his long tenure in the House: "I think [members] would have an awful time if they tried [to set party policy in the caucus]. It's better left to the committee system." [7] The cards are stacked against centralized power in any form. The independence of today's members makes a return to the earlier days when "King Caucus" reigned over the House all but impossible.

The Speaker of the House

The most powerful party leader in Congress is the Speaker of the House.[8] In the early twentieth century, the Speaker's powers were almost beyond limit, the House virtually his private domain. It is scarcely an exaggeration to say that legislation favored by the Speaker was adopted and that legislation opposed by him was defeated. The despotic rule of Speaker "Uncle Joe" Cannon eventually proved his undoing. A coalition of Democrats and rebellious Republicans was formed in 1910 to challenge the leadership of Cannon. After a struggle of many months, it succeeded in instituting a number of rules changes to curb the Speaker's powers. He was removed from membership on the Rules Committee (of which he had been chairman), his power to appoint and remove members and chairmen of the standing committees was eliminated, and his power to recognize (or not to recognize) members was limited. Although the "revolution of 1910-1911" fundamentally altered the formal powers of the Speaker, it did not render the office impotent. Since then, a succession of Speakers—men disposed to negotiate rather than to command—has helped to rebuild the powers of the office. What a Speaker like Joseph G. Cannon (R-Ill., 1903-1911) secured through autocratic rule, today's Speakers secure through persuasion and the astute exploitation of the bargaining advantages inherent in their positions.

Each Speaker leaves his imprint on the office. Changes in the times and in the character of politics also help to shape the speakership. Speaker Tip O'Neill once observed:

> Old Sam Rayburn [Speaker for seventeen years between 1940 and 1961] couldn't name 12 new members of Congress, and he was an institution that awed people. Only on the rarest of occasions could a Congressman get an appointment to see him. And when he called the Attorney General and said, "You be in my office at 3 in the afternoon," that Cabinet officer was there at 3 in the afternoon. Politics has changed. I have to deal in dialogue, in openness; if someone wants to see me, they see me. And of course they're highly independent now. You have to talk to people in the House, listen to them. The whole ethics question has changed. Years ago you'd think

nothing of calling Internal Revenue and saying that this case has
been kicking around for a couple of years, and it ought to be civil
instead of criminal. You'd think nothing of calling a chairman of a
committee and saying, "Put this project in, put this dam in." Well,
you can't do that now.[9]

The Speaker's formal powers are wide ranging, though not especially significant in themselves.[10] He is the presiding officer of the
House, and in this capacity he announces the order of business, puts
questions to a vote, refers bills to committees, rules on points of order,
interprets the rules, recognizes members who desire the floor, and
appoints members to select and conference committees. He also has the
right to vote and enter floor debate. Ordinarily he exercises these rights
only in the case of major, closely contested issues.

Although difficult to delineate with precision, the informal powers
of the Speaker are far more impressive. As the foremost leader of his
party in Congress, he is at the center of critical information and policy-
making systems. No one is in a better position than the Speaker to obtain
and disseminate information, to shape strategies, or to advance or frus-
trate the careers of members. Perhaps the principal tangible preferment
the Speaker has at his disposal is the influence he can exert to secure
favorable committee assignments for members of the majority party.
Having the good will of the Speaker is important to members of his
party anxious to move ahead in the House. The following analysis by
Randall B. Ripley describes the structure of the Speaker's influence:

> His personal traits influence his ability to deal with members of his
> party. The one constant element is the importance of his showing
> trust in and respect for individual members of his party. A smile or
> nod of the head from the Speaker can bolster a member's ego and
> lead him to seek further evidences of favor. Being out of favor hurts
> the individual's pride, and may be noticed by his colleagues. Most
> Speakers have had an instinct for knowing their loyal followers on
> legislative matters. Others have either kept records themselves or
> made frequent use of whip polls and official records to inform
> themselves about the relative loyalty of their members. Speakers have
> been able to convey critical information to members on a person-to-
> person basis, often with the help of the Parliamentarian. They have
> also encouraged their floor leaders and whip organizations to become
> collectors and purveyors of information on a larger scale. Particularly
> useful to a number of Speakers has been an informal gathering of

intimates and friends of both parties to discuss the course of business in the House. Through such discussions, Speakers have been able to keep themselves informed of developments in the House and, at the same time, convey their desires to other members invited to attend.[11]

Another way of viewing the Speaker and other party officials is provided by Joseph Cooper and David W. Brady. Today's party leaders, they write, "function less as the commanders of a stable party majority and more as brokers trying to assemble particular majorities behind particular bills."[12] Similarly, David W. Rohde observes: "In their day, Speakers such as Reed or Cannon ordered and punished the members at will. But it is . . . inconceivable to think of this in the modern Congress. The members now tell the leaders what to do, and the leaders do it."[13]

The Floor Leaders

In addition to the Speaker of the House, the key figures in the congressional party organizations are the House and Senate floor leaders, who are chosen by party caucuses in their respective chambers. The floor leaders serve as the principal spokespersons for party positions and interests and as intermediaries in both intraparty and interparty negotiations. The floor leaders of the party that controls the presidency also serve as links between the president and his congressional party. Because floor leaders are obliged to play several roles at the same time—for example, representatives of both the congressional party and the president—it is not surprising that role conflicts develop. Serving the interests of their congressional party colleagues or perhaps those of their constituents is anything but a guarantee that they will be serving presidential interests.

Floor leaders have a potpourri of informal, middling powers. Their availability, however, does not ensure that they can lead their colleagues or strongly shape the legislative program. By and large, their influence is based on their willingness and talent to exploit these powers steadily and imaginatively in their relations with other members. They can, if they choose, (1) influence the allocation of committee assignments (not only rewarding individual members but also shaping the ideological makeup of the committees); (2) help members to advance legislation of particular interest to them; (3) assist members in securing larger appropriations for their committees or subcommittees; (4) play a major role in debate; (5) intercede with the president or executive agencies on behalf of members (perhaps to assist their efforts to secure a federal project in their state or district); (6) make important information available to members; (7) help members to secure campaign money from a congressional campaign committee or from the political action committee of an interest group; (8) campaign on behalf of individual members; and (9) focus the attention of the communications media on the contributions of members. Much of the influence of floor leaders, like that of the Speaker, is derived from informal powers, in particular from opportunities afforded them to advance or protect the careers of party colleagues. In solving problems for them and in making their positions more secure, floor leaders increase the prospects of gaining their support on critical questions. By the same token, floor leaders can in some measure hamper the careers of those members who continually refuse to go along with them. At the center of active floor leaders' powers is the capacity to manipulate rewards and punishments.

An important function and a major source of power for the majority floor leader, particularly in the Senate, is that of controlling the scheduling of bill consideration on the floor. In the House, the Rules Committee dominates the process of controlling the agenda. However pedestrian the scheduling function may sound, it is a surprisingly important source of power. The majority leader who fails to keep his lines of communication clear, who misjudges the sentiments of members, who neglects to consolidate his majority by winning over undecided members or by propping up wavering members, or who picks the wrong time to call up a bill can easily go down to defeat. Prospective majorities are much more tenuous and much more easily upset than might be supposed. Support can be lost rapidly as a result of poor communications, missed opportunities for negotiation and compromise, and bad timing. The effective leader builds his power base by tending to the shop, by ordering priorities, by having a sense of detail that overlooks nothing, by taking account of the demands placed on members, by sensing the mood of congressional opinion (especially that of key members), and by exhibiting skill in splicing together the legislative elements necessary to fashion a majority.

The principal power of the floor leader is the power of persuasion. As a former Democratic leader of the Senate, Lyndon B. Johnson (D-Texas), once observed, "the only real power available to the leader is the power of persuasion. There is no patronage; no power to discipline; no authority to fire Senators like a President can fire his members of Cabinet." [14] Jim Wright (D-Texas), former Speaker and former majority leader, expressed a similar view of the leader's role: "The majority leader is a conciliator, a mediator, a peacemaker. Even when patching together a tenuous majority he must respect the right of honest dissent, conscious of the limits of his claims upon others." [15] The current majority leader, Richard A. Gephardt (D-Mo.), described his view of the office in this way: "We've had huge turnover in the last ten years and they are not the kind of people who came here to take orders. [Ours] will be a leadership that will be engaged in lots of meetings." [16] Another dimension of the position is suggested in these observations by a House Republican leader: "Everyone has a different idea as to how the leadership is to operate. I think that's perfectly healthy. But I think everybody also understands that you can't please everybody on everything. To please the majority, you have to keep from going too far to the left or to the right." [17]

To be persuasive, a leader must know the members well, know what they want and what they will settle for, and what concessions they can make and what concessions they cannot make, given their constituencies. The critical importance of such information requires the leader to develop a reliable communications network within his party. But more than that, he requires good lines of communication into the other party to pick up support when elements of his own party appear likely to wander off the reservation. Members prefer to support their leader and the party position rather than the opposing forces. The task of the leader is to find reasons for them to do so and conditions under which they can.

The development of a legislative program requires the majority leader to work closely with the key leaders in his party, particularly the chairmen of the major committees. As Lyndon Johnson observed during his tenure as Senate majority leader, "You must understand why the committee took certain actions and why certain judgments were formed." [18] His successor, Mike Mansfield (D-Mont.), observed: "I'm not the leader, really. They don't do what I tell them. I do what they tell me. . . . The brains are in the committees." [19] The effective leader works with the resources available—in essence, the power of persuasion. Relations between the leader and the committee chairmen are never characterized by a one-way flow of mandates. On the contrary, the leader must be acutely sensitive to the interests of the chairmen, adept at recognizing their political problems, and flexible in his negotiations with them. Bargaining is the key characteristic of the relationships between the majority leader and the committee chairmen.

Party management in Congress has become increasingly difficult in recent years. Several reasons help to explain this situation. First, the adoption of "sunshine" rules in both houses has made Congress a much more "open" institution. For the most part, committee, subcommittee, and even party caucus meetings are now open to the public. Second, combined with the new visibility of congressional actions, the growing power of interest groups, stemming particularly from their campaign contributions, has made members more vulnerable to outside pressures and, at the same time, increasingly resistant to the influence of party leaders. Third, the weakening of the electoral parties has been accompanied by an extraordinary growth in candidate-centered campaigns. Members who are elected to Congress largely on their own efforts have less reason to concern themselves with party objectives, less reason to defer to the wishes of party leaders. Independence and freewheelingness have become the modus vivendi of many members of Congress. Finally, internal changes have contributed to the further decentralization of congressional power. Subcommittees have grown both in number and in independence.[20] The influence of committee chairmen has declined while that of subcommittee chairmen has grown. In addition, both chambers now limit the number of committee and subcommittee chairmanships that a member may hold, the effect of which has been to spread leadership positions (and thus power) among more members. The presence of a large number of specialized policy caucuses may also have made it more difficult for the parties to integrate policy making. Singly and in combination, these changes have diminished the capacity of the parties to build majorities and to mobilize their members for concerted action.

A prominent New York Democrat, Emanuel Celler, who served fifty years in the House (nearly twenty-five years as chairman of the Judiciary Committee), made these comments on the devolution of congressional power:

> When I was in Congress, we had strong chairmen. . . . They ruled the roost. . . . Then came along the so-called young Turks, insisting upon lessening the power of the chairmen. And you have all these youngsters clamoring for power and more power and more help, so that there's a tremendous proliferation of [staff] assistants to the subcommittees. And they are yammering and hollering for more and more power, which results in the combined efforts of Congress shouting and trying to make itself heard above the power of the president.[21]

The more individualistic Congress becomes, the more difficult it becomes for the party leadership to play a decisive role. Senate majority whip Alan Cranston (D-Calif.) has observed: "A lot of leadership is just housekeeping now. Occasionally you have an opportunity to provide leadership, but not that often. The weapons to keep people in line just aren't there." [22]

What has been said thus far suggests that several important constraints shape the position of the floor leader. The leader is not free to fashion his role as he might like to see it. The limited range of powers available to him, his personality, his relationship to the president, and his skills in bargaining—all affect in some measure the definition of his role. Moreover, no two leaders are likely to perceive the leader role in exactly the same light. In addition, the nature of the leader's position is strongly influenced by the nature of the legislative parties. Persistent cleavages present within both parties make it necessary for a leader to occupy the role of middleman. The leader is a middleman in the sense that he is more or less steadily involved in negotiations with all major elements within the party, and also in terms of his voting record.[23] In the passage of much legislation the test is not so much the wisdom of the decision as it is its political feasibility. A leader identified with an extreme group within his party would find it difficult to work out the kinds of compromises necessary to put together a majority. The leader is first and foremost a broker. Candidates for leadership positions whose voting records place them on the ideological edges of their party are less likely to be elected than those whose voting records fall within the central range of party opinion.

The Whips

Another unit in the party structure of Congress is the whip organization. Party whips are selected in each house by the floor leaders or by other party agencies. Many assistant whips are required in the House because of the large size of the body. On the Democratic side, for example, more than one-quarter of all members are now in the whip organization, making it a "mini-caucus every week." [24] Working to enhance the efforts of the leadership, the whips carry on a number of important functions. They attempt to learn how members intend to vote on legislation; relay information from party leaders to individual members; work to ensure that a large number of "friendly" members will be present at the time of voting; and attempt to win the support of those party members who are in opposition, or likely to be in opposition, to the leadership. The influence of the Speaker and the majority leader supplements the pressure of the whips. As described by the chief staff assistant to the majority whip, whips apply "the heavy party loyalty shtick. Then it's more personalities than issues. There are some members who can only be gotten by the Speaker or the majority leader." [25]

The central importance of the whip organization is that it forms a communications link between the party leadership and rank-and-file members. The whips are charged with discovering why members are opposed to certain legislation and how it might be changed to gain their support. The intelligence the whips supply is sometimes the difference between victory and defeat on a major issue. The decentralization of Congress has made the whip function indispensable to all efforts to achieve party unity.[26] On some issues no amount of activity on the part of the leadership can bring recalcitrant members into the fold. If the outlook for a bill is unpromising following a whip check of members' sentiments, the leadership will often postpone its floor consideration. Whip checks can thus protect the leadership from embarrassing losses.

Being in the whip system gives members access to information from the leadership and some small measure of status, as these comments by a deputy whip, Rep. Norman Mineta (D-Calif.), illustrate:

> Among my colleagues, I'm given some recognition for having some information, being connected. Like Ivy League eating clubs, . . . well, I'm part of the Speaker's eating club. . . . People say to me, "You're part of the leadership, what's going on?" And then I say, "Gee I don't know," and I go and find out. I think you're part of the inside track in asking questions.[27]

The Policy Committees

Few proposals for congressional reform have received as much attention as those designed to strengthen the role of political parties in the legislative process. The Joint Committee on the Organization of Congress recommended in its 1946 report that policy committees be created for the purpose of formulating the basic policies of the two parties. Although this provision was later stricken from the reorganization bill, the Senate independently created such committees in 1947. The House Republicans established a policy committee in 1949, though it did not become fully active for another decade.[28] Rounding out the list, the rejuvenated House Democratic caucus voted to establish a policy committee in 1973.

The high promise of the policy committees as agencies for enhancing party responsibility for legislative programs has never been realized. Neither party leaders nor rank-and-file members agree on the functions of the policy committees. The policy committees are "policy" committees in name only. The policy committees in the Senate "have never been 'policy' bodies, in the sense of considering and investigating alternatives of public policy, and they have never put forth an overall congressional party program. The committees do not assume leadership in drawing up a general legislative program . . . and only rarely have the committees labeled their decisions as 'party policies.' " [29]

It is not surprising that the policy committees have been unable to function effectively as agencies for the development of overall party programs. An authoritative policy committee would constitute a major threat to the scattered and relatively independent centers of power within Congress. The seniority leaders who preside over the committee system would undoubtedly find their influence over legislation diminished if the policy committees were to assume a central role in defining party positions. The independence of the committee system would be affected adversely, and many individual members would suffer an erosion of power. If the policy committees had functioned as planned, a major reshuffling of power in Congress would have resulted. To those who hold the keys to congressional power, this is scarcely an appealing idea. However attractive the proposal for centralized committees empowered to speak for the parties in Congress, these committees are unlikely to emerge so long as the parties are decentralized and fragmented, composed of members who represent a wide variety of constituencies and ideological positions.

Although the lack of internal party agreement prevents the policy committees from functioning in a policy-shaping capacity, it does not render them useless. Both parties require forums for the discussion of issues and for the negotiation of compromises, and for these activities the policy committees are well designed. Moreover, the staffs of the committees have proved helpful for individual members seeking research assistance. Most important, the policy committees have served as a communications channel between the party leaders and their memberships. The policy committees are an ambitious attempt to deal with the persistent problem of party disunity. If they have generally failed in this respect, they have nonetheless succeeded in other respects. As clearinghouses for the exchange of party information and as agencies for the reconciliation of at least some intraparty differences, they have made useful contributions.

Informal Party Groups and Specialized Congressional Caucuses

In addition to the formal party units in Congress, several informal party organizations meet more or less regularly to discuss legislation, strategy, and other questions of common interest. Among these organizations are the Democratic Study Group (DSG) (liberal), Conservative Democratic Forum, United Democrats of Congress (conservative), Republican Study Committee (conservative), and Wednesday Group (Republican, liberal). Formed to promote the policy positions of a faction within the party, these groups are major sources of information for their members. They focus primarily on the congressional agenda, drafting and introducing legislation and amendments as well as seeking to attract the interest and support of other members and outside forces. Extending their reach, some of these groups have sought to influence the content of party platforms. The largest and best known of these groups is the Democratic Study Group, formed in 1959 by liberal Democrats as a counterbloc to the southern wing of the party. Today the DSG has a membership of more than two hundred, an elected chairman and executive committee, a professional staff, and a whip system that functions on important legislation. Issuing fact sheets and weekly legislative reports, the DSG focuses its efforts on providing information for its members and in encouraging them to turn out for floor votes.

Informal party groups compete and cooperate with dozens of other specialized policy caucuses organized to advance particular interests. These relatively narrow-gauge groups are formed around geographic, economic, race, gender, and assorted concerns. Included in this far-flung policy network are such caucuses as the Steel Caucus, Coal Caucus, Textile Caucus, Travel and Tourism Caucus, Farm Crisis Caucus, Wine Caucus, Mushroom Caucus, Port Caucus, Human Rights Caucus, Black Caucus, Blue Collar Caucus, Hispanic Caucus, Sunbelt Caucus, Northeast-Midwest Congressional Coalition, Border Caucus, Congresswomen's Caucus, Rural Caucus, Suburban Caucus, Crime Caucus, Arts Caucus, and Drug Enforcement Caucus. Groups such as these have come to play a significant role in the policy process through problem identification, member mobilization, and coalition building. They are centers for information exchange.[30] At the same time, they reflect the fragmentation of power in Congress. Whether they enhance or inhibit the capacity of party leaders to control the policy-making process is an empirical question. But whatever the answer, it is not likely that these representative mechanisms will disappear.

Factors Influencing the Success of Party Leaders

The cohesiveness of the parties in Congress can never be taken for granted. The independence of the committees and their chairmen, the rudimentary powers of elected leaders, the importance of constituency pressures, the influence of political interest groups, and the disposition of members to respond to parochial impulses—all, at one time or another, contribute to the fragmentation of power in Congress and to the erosion of party unity. The member who ignores leadership cues and requests or is oblivious to them, or who builds a career as a party maverick, is far more common than might be supposed. Few weapons in the leadership arsenal can be used to bring refractory members into line.

Research on the Democratic party in the House by Lewis A. Froman, Jr., and Randall B. Ripley identifies a number of conditions under which leadership influence on legislative decisions will be either promoted or inhibited.[31] First, leadership success is likely to be contingent on a high degree of agreement among the leaders themselves. Ordinarily the Speaker, majority leader, and whip will be firm supporters of their president's legislative program; frequently, however, other key leaders, such as committee chairmen, will be allied with opponents. When unity among the leaders breaks down, prospects for success fall sharply. Second, leadership success in gathering the party together tends to be affected by the nature of the issue under consideration—specifically, whether it is procedural or substantive. On procedural issues (for example, election of the Speaker, adoption of rules, motions to adjourn), party cohesion is ordinarily much higher than on issues that involve substantive policy. Third, the efforts of party leaders are most likely to be successful on issues that do not have high visibility to the general public. In the usual pattern, conflicting pressures emerge when issues gain visibility, and the leaders must commit greater resources to keep party ranks intact.

Fourth, the visibility of the action to be taken will have a bearing on the inclination of members to follow the leadership. Not all forms of voting are equally noticeable. Roll-call votes on final passage of measures are highly conspicuous—the member's "record" on a public question is firmly established at this point. On the one hand, voting with the leadership on the floor may seem to the member to pose too great a risk. On the other hand, supporting the leadership in committee or on a key amendment is less risky, because the actions are not as easily brought into public focus. Fifth, and perhaps most important, members are most likely to vote with their party when the issue at stake does not stir up opposition in their constituencies. Party leaders know full well that they cannot count on the support of members who feel that they are under the thumb of constituents on a particular issue—for example, some southern members on certain questions relating to civil rights. Finally, support for the leadership is likely to be dependent upon the activity of the state delegations. Leadership victories are more likely to result when individual state delegations are not involved in bargaining with leaders over specific demands.

These conditions, then, constitute the background against which leadership efforts to mold their party as a unit are made. Party loyalty, it should be emphasized, is more than a veneer. By and large, members prefer to go along with their party colleagues. But they will not queue up in support of their leaders if the conditions appear wrong, if apparently more is to be lost than gained by following the leadership. Members guard their careers by taking frequent soundings within their constituencies and among their colleagues and by making careful calculations of the consequences that are likely to flow from their decisions.

National Party Agencies and the Congressional Parties

In theory, the supreme governing body of the party between one national convention and the next is the national committee, which is composed of representatives from each state. In the best of all worlds, from the perspective of those who believe in party unity and responsibility, close and continuing relationships would be maintained between the national committee of each party and fellow party members in Congress. Out of such associations, presumably, would come coherent party policies and a heightened sense of responsibility among members of Congress for developing a legislative program consistent with the promises of the party platform. The tone and mood that dominate relations between the national committees and the congressional parties, however, are as likely to be characterized by suspicion as by cooperation. Congressional leaders in particular are little disposed to follow the cues that emanate from the national committees or, for that matter, from any other national party agency.

Not only do national party leaders have a minimal impact on congressional decision making, but they are also largely excluded from the process of nominating congressional candidates. Although the National Republican Congressional Committee (NRCC) sometimes enters House primary fights, giving funds to the Republican candidate it prefers, the practice is not common. "We don't look for fights, which would do both us and [the candidates] damage," the NRCC campaign director said. "The thing we look for is whether a candidate has [local] support." The Democratic Congressional Campaign Committee does not make funds available to primary candidates.[32]

National party leaders seldom become involved in the congressional nominating process because state and local leaders are likely to resent it. Occasionally an intrepid president has sought to influence congressional nominations, as Franklin D. Roosevelt did in 1938. Disturbed by mounting opposition to his program in Congress, Roosevelt publicly endorsed the primary opponents of certain prominent anti-New Deal incumbent Democrats. As it turned out, nearly all of the lawmakers marked for defeat won easily, much to the chagrin of the president. Twelve years later President Harry S. Truman met the same fate when he endorsed a candidate in the Democratic senatorial primary in Missouri. The state party organization rallied to the other side, and the president lost. Although a few presidential "purges" have succeeded, most attempts have failed. The lesson seems evident: congressional nominations are regarded as local matters, to be decided in terms of local preferences.

The national party is concerned with the election of members who are broadly sympathetic to its traditional policy orientations and its party platform. In counterpoise, local party organizations aim to guarantee their own survival as independent units. Occasional conflict between the two is predictable. The principal consequence of local control over congressional nominations is that all manner of men and women get elected to Congress, those who find it easy to accept national party goals and those who are almost wholly out of step with the national party. The failure of party unity in Congress is due as much as anything to the folkway that congressional nominations are local questions to be settled by local politicians and voters according to preferences they alone establish.

Do the Parties Differ on Public Policies?

Party affiliation is the cutting edge of congressional elections. Ordinarily few surprises occur on election day: Democratic candidates win where they are expected to win, and Republican candidates win where they are expected to win. The public at large may continue to believe that each election poses an opportunity for the outs to replace the ins, but this happens infrequently. The chief threat to an incumbent legislator is a landslide presidential vote for the other party, one so great that congressional candidates on the winning presidential ticket are lifted into office on the strength of the presidential candidate's coattails. Even landslide votes, however, do not disturb the great majority of congressional races.

If party affiliation largely determines which men and women go to Congress, does it also significantly influence their behavior once in office? The answer for most legislators—for majorities within each party—is yes. Party affiliation is the most important single variable in predicting how members will respond to questions that come before them. Indeed, the key fact to be known about any member is the party to which he belongs—it influences his choice of friends, his membership in groups, his relations with lobbies, his relations with other members and the leadership, and, most important, his policy orientations. Party loyalty does not govern the behavior of members; neither is it a factor taken lightly.

The proportion of roll-call votes in Congress in which the parties are firmly opposed to each other is not particularly large. A study of selected congressional sessions between 1921 and 1967 shows that the number of "party votes" that occur in the House has declined markedly over the years. Between 1921 and 1948, about 17 percent of the House roll-call votes were party votes—votes in which 90 percent of the voting membership of one party opposed 90 percent of the voting membership of the other party. In the usual House sessions since 1950, party votes have numbered between 6 and 10 percent of the total.[33] The "90 percent versus 90 percent" standard is a rigorous test of party voting. If the standard is relaxed to "50 percent versus 50 percent," the proportion of party votes rises sharply. Between 1986 and 1989, for example, about 55 percent of all House roll-call votes and about 42 percent of all Senate roll-call votes found party majorities arrayed against each other. Divisions between party majorities in the House occur more frequently today than during the late 1960s or the 1970s. Partisan conflict is less contagious in the Senate.[34]

One of the main reasons that party voting is not greater is found in the behavior of the wings of each party. A study of voting patterns in the House from the Eighty-sixth Congress through the Ninety-first revealed not only a sharp decline in party voting but also a growing tendency for eastern Republicans to join forces with northern Democrats against an alliance of noneastern Republicans and southern Democrats. Throughout this period the majority elements of the two parties—northern Democrats and noneastern Republicans—steadily opposed each other on issues involving some degree of controversy. Defections among the minority segments of each party eastern Republicans and southern Democrats—are traced to a growing responsiveness among members to constituency preferences.[35]

Although the level of party voting in Congress is not particularly high, it is higher at some times than at others. What factors appear to promote partisan cleavage? Examining a recent thirty-five-year period, Samuel C. Patterson and Gregory A. Caldeira found that party voting in the House increases significantly when external party conflict is high—in particular, during periods when sharp differences exist between the national parties on central issues of the economy, labor-management questions, and the distribution of wealth. Interparty conflict also escalates when the presidency and House are controlled by the same party. In the Senate, where party voting is less common, presidential leadership is the key factor; specifically, when the Senate majority is of the same party as the president, party voting increases. Surprisingly, in view of conventional interpretations, the election of many new members does not lead to markedly greater increases in partisan cleavages.[36]

Whatever the extent of party voting in Congress, important issues are often at stake when party lines form. In general, Democrats have been much more likely than Republicans to support federal programs to assist agriculture, expanded health and welfare programs, legislation advantageous to labor and low-income groups, government regulation of business, reductions in the defense budget, and a larger role for the federal government. Recently, interparty conflict has become more common on certain kinds of foreign policy questions, such as aid to anticommunist guerrillas. Data in Table 6-1 depict how the parties lined

TABLE 6-1 Congressional Party Behavior: Key Differences between the Parties during the Bush Administration

| | | Party conflict | |
Legislation	Bipartisan[a]	Moderate[b]	Significant[c]
Nonmilitary aid to Nicaraguan contras	R-support (93%) D-support (61%)		
Adoption of 1990 budget resolution	R-support (63%) D-support (62%)		
Allow savings and loans to count "good will" as capital in restructuring	D-oppose (85%) R-oppose (67%)		
Reduce initial construction funds for superconducting supercollider	R-oppose (84%) D-oppose (74%)		
Reduce longer term commitment to produce B-2 ("Stealth") bombers	R-oppose (84%) D-oppose (54%)		
Repeal requirement that employers must prove their health benefit plans are nondiscriminatory, but deny favorable tax treatment to employee benefit plans that discriminate in favor of owners and executives	R-support (99%) D-support (87%)		
Repeal Medicare Catastrophic Coverage Act	D-support (94%) R-support (79%)		
Aid to Poland and Hungary	D-support (94%) R-support (79%)		
Across-the-board cuts in budget authority in all discretionary accounts of the government		R-oppose (95%) D-support (64%)	

Legislation	Bipartisan[a]	Party conflict	
		Moderate[b]	Significant[c]
Prevent federal law from preempting state laws on oil-spill liability, compensation, and cleanup		D-support (82%) R-oppose (57%)	
Phase out honoraria for members and raise salaries		D-support (66%) R-oppose (51%)	
Override President Bush's veto of minimum wage bill			D-support (89%) R-oppose (88%)
Decrease funds for strategic defense initiative (SDI)			D-support (85%) R-oppose (80%)
Restore deductibility for individual retirement accounts (in lieu of capital gains cut) and increase tax rates for the highest incomes			R-oppose (99%) D-support (75%)
Delete child-care provisions and replace with an expanded earned-income tax credit			R-support (91%) D-oppose (86%)
Permit use of federal funds to pay for abortions in cases of "promptly reported" rape or incest			R-oppose (77%) D-support (71%)

SOURCE: Developed from data in *Congressional Quarterly Weekly Report*, December 9, 1989, 3403-3405.

NOTE: R = Republican; D = Democrat. The data in this table show how the parties voted in the House (controlled by the Democrats) on sixteen major issues (designated as "key votes" by Congressional Quarterly) during the first session of the 101st Congress (1989-1990). On fully half of these key issues, bipartisanship prevailed. Only five issues produced sharp partisan conflict (minimum wage, SDI, tax rates, child care, and abortion). On key issues, partisanship was less important at the beginning of the Bush administration than during the second term of President Reagan.

[a] Bipartisan: majorities of both parties in agreement.
[b] Moderate party conflict: party majority against party majority.
[c] Significant party conflict: at least 70 percent of the voting members of one party aligned against at least 70 percent of the voting members of the other party.

up on major issues in the House during the first session of the 101st Congress (Bush administration).

The Parties and Liberal-Labor Legislation

The current policy orientations of the parties in Congress are not distinctly different from those they have held over the last half century. The positions of the parties (and the wings within them) on proposals of interest to the AFL-CIO in the 101st Congress are presented in Figures 6-4 and 6-5. A member voting in agreement with the AFL-CIO would have supported such measures as an increase in the minimum wage, restoration of individual retirement accounts (in lieu of a capital gains tax cut), revision of the Hatch Act to permit federal employees to campaign and to run for office, a ban on the transfer of certain technology to Japanese companies to build the FS-X fighter plane, the establishment of an emergency board to recommend a settlement of the Eastern Airlines labor dispute, equal representation of employees and employers on single-employer pension plans, favorable wage standards for companies with federal contracts, and a federal child-care program.

Inspection of Figures 6-4 and 6-5 will show two broad patterns of congressional voting on legislation of central interest to organized labor. First, the parties are not cohesive units in voting on liberal-labor legislation. Second, despite noticeable intraparty splits, substantial differences exist between the parties. The two largest groups in each house—northern Democrats and northern Republicans—view liberal-labor legislation from vastly different perspectives. The only Republicans who are found at the highest support level—voting in agreement with AFL-CIO positions between 76 and 100 percent of the time—are a few members from eastern states. Northern Democrats, by contrast, give overwhelming support to labor objectives. Only a handful of northern Democrats are markedly out of step, voting less than half the time with the AFL-CIO.

The strongest opponents of liberal-labor legislation are Republicans from anywhere but the East. Although southern Democrats are arrayed at all points, a strong majority in each house supports the objectives of the AFL-CIO. In recent years southern Democratic senators have had voting records on labor legislation that are almost indistinguishable from those of their northern colleagues. Southern

FIGURE 6-4   House Support for Labor Legislation by Party and Region, 101st Congress, First Session

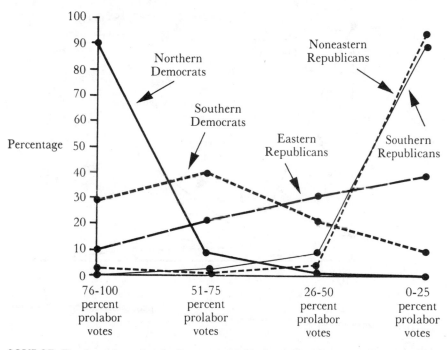

SOURCE: Developed from data in *Congressional Quarterly Weekly Report*, March 3, 1990, 706-707.

NOTE: House members are ranked by the percentage of votes they cast in accord with the positions of the AFL-CIO. The South is defined as the eleven states of the Confederacy plus Kentucky and Oklahoma. Noneastern Republicans are all northern members except those from eastern states.

Democrats and southern Republicans are anything but peas in the same pod.

Another way of looking at the policy orientations of the congressional parties is to examine the range of attitudes in the Senate in the 101st Congress, First Session, on issues deemed important by the liberal-oriented Americans for Democratic Action (ADA) and the conservative-oriented American Conservative Union (ACU) (see Figure 6-6). Senators are located on the diagram according to the percentage of votes that they cast in agreement with the positions of each political interest group. Senators Patrick Leahy (D-Vt.), Brock Adams (D-Wash.), Timothy Wirth (D-Colo.), Paul Simon (D-Ill.), and Tom Harkin (D-Iowa) emerge as the most liberal members of the upper house. At the conserva-

FIGURE 6-5   Senate Support for Labor Legislation by Party and Region, 101st Congress, First Session

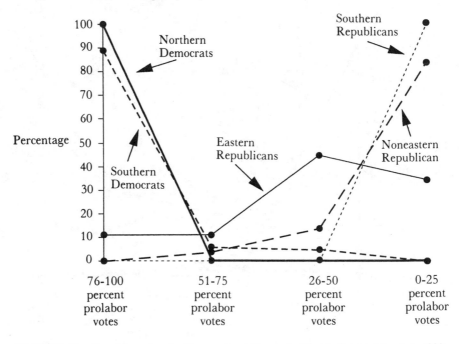

SOURCE: Developed from data in *Congressional Quarterly Weekly Report,* March 3, 1990, 705.

NOTE: Senate members are ranked by the percentage of votes they cast in accord with the positions of the AFL-CIO. The South is defined as the eleven states of the Confederacy plus Kentucky and Oklahoma. Noneastern Republicans are all northern members except those from eastern states.

tive pole are such senators as Malcolm Wallop (R-Wyo.), James Mc-Clure (R-Idaho), Phil Gramm (R-Texas), and William Armstrong (R-Colo.).

The data in Figure 6-6 reinforce the conclusions reached earlier. Despite the party-in-disarray quality that appears in the Senate scattergram, significant differences separate the majorities of the two parties. Nearly all of the Republican senators are found on the right-hand side of the diagram, indicating their agreement with the ACU, while most Democratic senators are lodged on the left-hand side, showing their agreement with ADA policy objectives. The deviant behavior of party members is largely confined to certain wings in each party—in particular, southern Democrats and eastern Republicans.

FIGURE 6-6   Support for Positions Held by Americans for Democratic Action
(ADA) and by American Conservative Union (ACU) by Each
Senator, 101st Congress, First Session

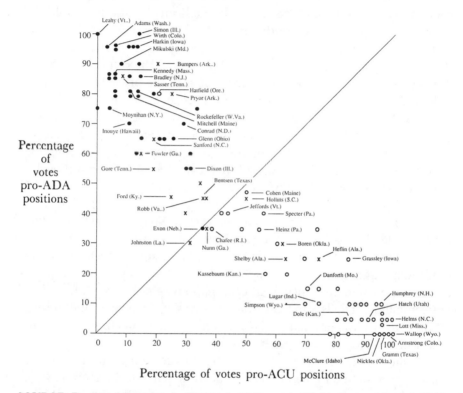

SOURCE: Developed from data in *Congressional Quarterly Weekly Report*, March 3, 1990,
705.

NOTE: • = Northern Democrats; x = Southern Democrats; o = Republicans.

Biparty Coalitions

Of all the problems that confront the legislative party, none is more
persistent or difficult than that of maintaining party unity. Some members assiduously ignore the requests and entreaties of leaders; others
cling tenaciously to constituency lines without pausing to consider the
requirements of party; still others seek to tailor party measures to the
specifications of those parochial interests to which they respond. The
party is a repository for divergent claims and preferences. Getting it to
act as a collectivity is no mean feat.

The disruption of party lines leads to the formation of biparty coalitions. The most durable biparty coalition in the history of Congress has been the so-called conservative coalition—an informal league of southern Democrats and northern Republicans. Data in Table 6-2 provide a statistical picture of the power held by the coalition since 1961, or from the Kennedy presidency to the Bush presidency. In recent years the coalition has appeared on about 10 percent of the roll-call votes held during a session—much less frequently than in the past. The coalition's success rate, however, continues to be impressive. In only two sessions since 1961 (the first two years of Lyndon Johnson's Great Society, 1965 and 1966) did the coalition win less than 50 percent of the roll calls on which it appeared. In twenty of the twenty-nine sessions, the batting average of the coalition exceeded 60 percent. Recently the coalition has won almost nine out of every ten appearances.

Although the conservative coalition is not as powerful as in the past, it is still a force to be reckoned with on certain kinds of issues. In 1989, for example, the coalition had thirty-three roll-call victories in the House and thirty-six in the Senate—involving such issues as school prayer, minimum wage, abortions, military aid, various weapons systems, defense appropriations, illegal aliens, capital gains tax cut, aid to anticommunist rebels, and antiflag desecration. Defense and foreign affairs issues now dominate the coalition's agenda much as civil rights issues did two or three decades ago.[37]

Some portion of the explanation for the declining influence of the conservative coalition may be that Democratic party leadership, particularly in the more partisan House, has become more effective in bridging regional differences and diminishing intraparty conflict. While there is some impressionistic evidence on this score, it is not the main reason for the changing behavior of southern Democrats. They have become more in tune with northern Democrats because the South itself has lost some of its distinctiveness. Since passage of the Voting Rights Act of 1965 blacks have entered southern state electorates in great numbers, and their participation in turn has driven Democratic incumbents and challengers to adopt more liberal positions on certain domestic policy questions. Black voters in southern Democratic primaries are now in a much better position to influence the behavior and policy stances of Democratic congressional candidates. In the same vein, economic development in the South has made that region resemble the North in many ways. The bottom line is simply that southern constituencies have changed, prompt-

TABLE 6-2   The Conservative Coalition in Congress, Appearances and Victories, 1961-1989

Year	Percentage of roll calls in which the coalition appeared in Congress	Percentage of coalition victories		
		Congress	House	Senate
1961	28	55	74	48
1962	14	62	44	71
1963	17	50	67	44
1964	15	51	67	47
1965	24	33	25	39
1966	25	45	32	51
1967	20	63	73	54
1968	24	73	63	80
1969	27	68	71	67
1970	22	66	70	64
1971	30	83	79	86
1972	27	69	79	63
1973	23	61	67	54
1974	24	59	67	54
1975	28	50	52	48
1976	24	58	59	58
1977	26	68	60	74
1978	21	52	57	46
1979	20	70	73	65
1980	18	72	67	75
1981	21	92	88	95
1982	18	85	78	90
1983	15	77	71	89
1984	16	83	75	94
1985	14	89	84	93
1986	16	87	78	93
1987	8	93	88	100
1988	9	89	82	97
1989	11	87	80	95

SOURCE: *Congressional Quarterly Weekly Report,* December 30, 1989, 3551-3555. For individual member scores, see *Congressional Quarterly Weekly Report,* January 6, 1990, 58-61.

NOTE: A "coalition roll call" is defined as any roll call on which the majority of voting southern Democrats and the majority of voting Republicans are opposed to the majority of voting northern Democrats. Congressional Quarterly considers these states in the southern wing of the Democratic party: Alabama, Arkansas, Florida, Georgia, Kentucky, Louisiana, Mississippi, North Carolina, Oklahoma, South Carolina, Tennessee, Texas, and Virginia. The other thirty-seven states are classified as northern in this analysis.

ing southern politicians to change. Constituency characteristics, in other words, really matter. The Democratic party is now more of a national party than at any time in its history.

Party "Loyalists" and "Irregulars" . . .

Democratic senators	High party loyalty — Votes cast with own party against majority of other party	Republican senators	High party loyalty — Votes cast with own party against majority of other party
Leahy (Vt.)	96%	Thurmond (S.C.)	98%
Cranston (Calif.)	95	Garn (Utah)	97
Sarbanes (Md.)	95	Nickles (Okla.)	96
Adams (Wash.)	94	McConnell (Ky.)	94
Mikulski (Md.)	94	Symms (Idaho)	94
Riegle (Mich.)	93	McClure (Idaho)	93
Metzenbaum (Ohio)	92	Burns (Mont.)	92
Burdick (N.D.)	90	Coats (Ind.)	92
Daschle (S.D.)	90	Lott (Miss.)	92
Kennedy (Mass.)	90	Gramm (Texas)	91
Moynihan (N.Y.)	90	Grassley (Iowa)	91
Dodd (Conn.)	89	Wallop (Wyo.)	91
Sasser (Tenn.)	89	Armstrong (Colo.)	90
Average Democratic senator	78	Average Republican senator	78

SOURCE: Adapted from data in *Congressional Quarterly Weekly Report*, December 30, 1989, 3546-3549, 3566.

The President and the Congressional Party

Presidential power appears more awesome at a distance than it does at close range. Although the Constitution awards the president a number of formal powers—for example, the power to initiate treaties, to make certain appointments, and to veto legislation—his principal everyday power is simply the power to persuade. The president who opts for an active role in the legislative process, who attempts to persuade members of Congress to accept his leadership and his program, runs up against certain obstacles in the structure of American government. Foremost among these is the separation of powers. This arrangement of "separated institutions sharing powers" [38] not only divides the formal structure of government, thus creating independent centers of legislative and

... in the Senate, 101st Congress, First Session

Limited party loyalty		Limited party loyalty	
Democratic senators	Votes cast in opposition to own party majority	Republican senators	Votes cast in opposition to own party majority
Heflin (Ala.)	61%	Hatfield (Ore.)	58%
Shelby (Ala.)	54	Jeffords (Vt.)	53
Boren (Okla.)	46	Heinz (Pa.)	49
Exon (Neb.)	46	Cohen (Maine)	48
Hollings (S.C.)	39	D'Amato (N.Y.)	46
Breaux (La.)	38	Specter (Pa.)	45
Dixon (Ill.)	38	Chafee (R.I.)	43
DeConcini (Ariz.)	35	Packwood (Ore.)	43
Ford (Ky.)	35	Durenberger (Minn.)	42
Average Democratic senator	20	Average Republican senator	20

NOTE: Members are ranked according to their behavior on party unity votes, which are defined as those recorded votes that split the parties, with a majority of voting Democrats opposing a majority of voting Republicans. Failures to vote lower both party unity and opposition-to-party scores.

executive authority, but it also contributes to the fragmentation of the national parties. The perspectives of those elements of the party for whom the president speaks are not necessarily the same as those for whom members of his congressional party speak. Policy that may suit one constituency may not suit another. Indeed, the chances are high that the presidential constituency and the constituencies of individual members of his party in Congress will differ in many important respects, thus making inevitable a certain amount of conflict between the branches.

The separation of powers is not the only constraint that faces the activist president who hopes to move Congress to adopt his program. The limited influence of party leaders on Congress, the insulation and independence of members that stem from the substantial staff and other office resources they enjoy,[39] the relative independence of committees and subcommittees, the difficulty of applying sanctions to wayward legislators, and the parochial cast in congressional perceptions of policy problems all converge to limit presidential influence. Moreover, electoral arrangements and electoral behavior may make executive leadership difficult. Off-year elections are nearly always more damaging to the president's party than they are to the out party. In off-year elections from 1926 to 1986, for example, the president's party gained seats in only one House election (1934) and in only three Senate elections (1934, 1962, and 1970). Losses are often severe. The Democratic party emerged from the 1966 election with forty-seven fewer seats in the House, and the Republican party lost forty-three House seats in the 1974 election. Following the first two years of the Reagan administration, the Republicans lost twenty-six seats in the House while holding their margin in the Senate. In 1986 the Republicans lost eight seats in the Senate but only five in the House. In 1990, when many incumbents of both parties won by smaller margins than usual, Republicans suffered a loss of eight House seats and one Senate seat. Over the sixty-four-year period from 1926 to 1990, the administration party had an average loss of thirty House seats in off-year elections. The president has every reason to fear the worst when these elections roll around; the next two years are certain to be more difficult.

Finally, the root of the president's legislative difficulties may lie with the voters themselves. The election that produces a president of one party may yield a Congress dominated by the other party or one influenced by a different ideological coloration. James Sundquist's analysis of John F. Kennedy's congressional miseries is informative:

> [It] is neither fair nor accurate to blame the failure of the Kennedy domestic program in the Eighty-seventh Congress primarily upon congressional organization or procedure—the power of the reformed House Rules Committee, the seniority system, or any other of Congress' internal processes. The failure of Congress to enact the Kennedy program is chargeable, rather, to the simple fact that the voters who elected Kennedy did not send to Congress enough supporters of his program. His razor-thin popular majority was reflected in a Congress formally Democratic but actually narrowly balanced between activists and conservatives. If the machinery of both houses had been entirely controlled by supporters of the Kennedy program, that in itself would not have changed the convictions of the members so as to produce a dependable administration majority. The machin-

ery might have been used more effectively to coerce Democratic congressmen into voting in opposition to their convictions—but that is another matter.[40]

A measure of the legislative success enjoyed by presidents from 1953 (the Eisenhower administration) to 1989 (the Bush administration) is presented in Figure 6-7. This analysis shows how frequently Congress voted in accordance with positions taken by each president during his administration. The highest rate of success of any of these eight presidents was achieved by Lyndon Johnson; in 1965 his position prevailed 93 percent of the time. The major reason for his success was undoubtedly that the Democratic party controlled both houses by such large margins that even the defections of southern members had minimal impact on outcomes. Ronald Reagan's 82 percent success rate in 1981 ranks third highest in the preceding thirty years. In the process of winning numerous legislative victories, Reagan received unusually strong support from Republican members in both houses, but especially in the Senate where his party held a majority. His overall party support scores were higher than those of any other president since 1953.[41] And, as expected, his support declined after the honeymoon period. During 1987 and 1988 Reagan's success rate slipped below 50 percent, a level lower than for any year of the Carter administration. In 1989 George Bush won only 63 percent of the roll calls on which he took a position; this was the worst first-year record of any president since the early 1950s.[42] When the opposition party controls one or both houses of Congress, presidential influence is typically constrained. Republican presidents understand this better than anyone. The last five Republican presidents—Eisenhower, Nixon, Ford, Reagan, and Bush—were steadily confronted by this nagging party problem.

So many words have been written about the role of the president as chief legislator that it is easy to lose sight of the fact that members of Congress have power in their own right. Although in recent decades the initiative for generating legislation has shifted to the president, Congress remains one of the world's most powerful legislative bodies. A good many conditions are inimical to presidential domination of Congress. Congress may adopt what the president proposes but in the process may change the accent and scope. Sometimes it merely disposes of what he proposes. Nothing in the president's plans is inviolable. No certainty exists that Congress will share his perceptions or succumb to his influ-

FIGURE 6-7   Presidential Success on Votes, 1953-1989

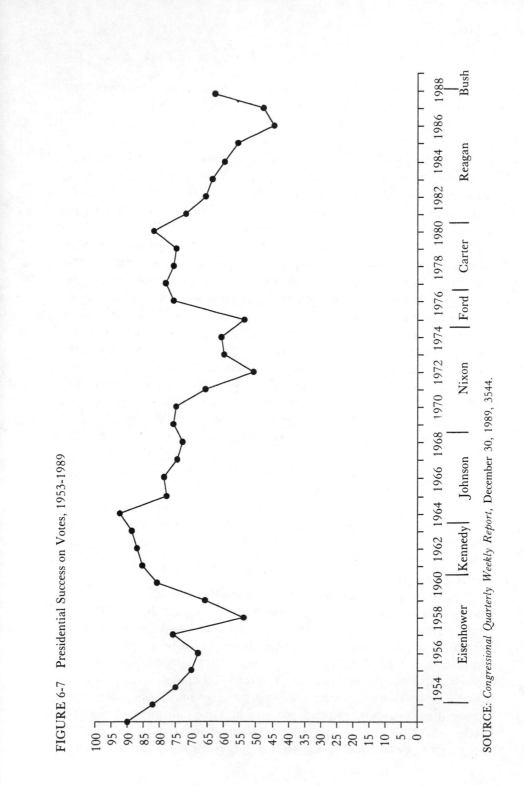

SOURCE: *Congressional Quarterly Weekly Report*, December 30, 1989, 3544.

ence. The careers of individual legislators are not tightly linked to the president's, except perhaps for those members from marginal districts, and even here the link is firm only when the president's popularity is high.[43] Indeed, some members of Congress have made their careers more secure through the visibility that comes from opposing the president and his program. Notwithstanding the worldwide trend toward executive supremacy, Congress remains a remarkably independent institution—a legislature almost as likely to resist executive initiatives as to embrace them.

The president and Congress get along as well as they do because of one element that the president and some members of Congress have in common: party affiliation. In substantial measure, party provides a frame of reference, an ideological underpinning, a rallying symbol, a structure for voting, and a language for testing and discussing ideas and policies. The member's constituency has never been the only valid criterion for assessing the wisdom of public policies. Legislators prefer to ride along with their party if it is at all possible, if the costs do not loom too large. Moreover, the president and his legislative leaders are not at liberty to strike out in any direction they feel may be immediately popular with the voters. They are constrained by party platforms, by previous policy commitments, by interest group involvement, and by the need to consult with party officials and members at all levels, particularly with those who compose the congressional wing. Consensus politics is the essence of party processes.

The President and Legislative Leaders

A study of majority party leadership in Congress indicates that many alternatives are open to the president and party leaders in Congress in structuring their relations with one another. Typically, when the president and the majority leadership in Congress are of the same party and the president assumes the role of chief legislator, relations between the two branches have been characterized by cooperation. Within this pattern leaders tend to see themselves as lieutenants of the president, of necessity sensitive to his initiatives and responsible for his program. However, even though his party controls Congress, the president may decline to play a central role in the legislative process. In this situation, relations between the president and congressional leaders tend to be mixed and nonsupportive. Collegial rather than centralized leadership usually emerges as Congress generates its own legislative program instead of relying on presidential initiative. Finally, when the president and the majority in Congress (at least in one house) are of opposing parties (a so-called truncated majority), relations between the president and congressional leaders are often characterized by conflict and opposition. Leadership tends to be highly centralized, but legislative successes are usually few in number. "The leader of a truncated majority has great room for maneuver in the tactics of opposition and embarrassment on the domestic front, if his followers are willing to go along with him, but he must necessarily remain partially frustrated by his inability to accomplish much of his program domestically." [44]

David Truman has described the relationship between the president and the elective leaders of his congressional party as one of "functional interdependence." There are mutual advantages in this interdependence. The president needs information to make intelligent judgments, and the leaders can supply it. Moreover, they can offer him policy guidance. At the same time, the leaders can do their jobs better if bolstered by the initiatives and leverage of the president. They have no power to give orders. They can only bargain and negotiate, and their effectiveness in doing this, in notable measure, is tied to the president's prestige and political assets. The nature of their jobs makes it important for the president's program to move through Congress. If the president wins, they win; if he loses, they lose.[45]

The Role of the Minority Party in Congress

A study by Charles O. Jones identifies a number of political conditions that individually and in combination help to shape the role that the minority party plays in mobilizing congressional majorities and in shaping public policy. Some of these conditions originate outside Congress; others manifest themselves inside Congress. The principal external forces are the temper of the times (for example, the presence of a domestic or an international crisis), the relative political strength of the minority party in the electorate, the degree of unity within the parties outside Congress, and the power of the president and his willingness to use the advantages that are inherent in his office. Conditions within Congress that affect minority party behavior are legislative procedures, the majority party's margin over the minority, the relative effectiveness of majority and minority party leadership, the time the party has been in a minority status (perhaps contributing to a minority party mentality), and the relative strength of the party in the other house.[46]

The important point to recognize about the behavior of the minority party is that the strategies open to it are determined not simply by the preferences of the leadership or the rank-and-file members, by idiosyncratic circumstances, or by opportunities thrust up from time to time. Rather, what it does is influenced to a significant extent by conditions of varying importance over which it has little or no control. By and large, the conditions most likely to affect the minority party's behavior and shape its strategies are, among the external group, party unity and presidential power, and among the internal group, the size of the margin and the effectiveness of party leaders in both parties. Although restrictive political conditions depress the range of alternatives available to the minority party, a resourceful minority leadership can occasionally overcome them, enabling the minority party to assume an aggressive, creative role in the legislative process. Among twentieth-century Congresses, however, this has been the exception, not the rule.[47]

The Party in Congress

It is about as difficult to write about congressional parties without revealing uncertainty as it is to pin a butterfly without first netting it. The party is hard to catch in a light that discloses all its qualities or its basic significance. Party is the organizing mechanism of Congress, and Congress could not do without it. It is hard to imagine how Congress could assemble itself for work, process the claims made on it, lend itself to majority coalition building, or be held accountable in any fashion without a wide range of party activities in its midst. Moreover, there are some sessions of Congress in which the only way to understand what Congress has done is to focus on the performance of the majority party. But that is only part of the story. In the critical area of policy formation, majority party control often slips away, to be replaced by enduring biparty alliances or coalitions of expediency. Party counts, but not predictably—hence the reason for the uncertainty in assessing the role of the congressional party.

Summary arguments may help to establish a perspective on the congressional parties. The indifferent success that sometimes characterizes party efforts in Congress is easy to explain. The odds are stacked against the party. In the first place, members of Congress are elected under a variety of conditions in a variety of constituencies: they are elected in environments where local party organizations are powerful and where they are weak; where populations are homogeneous and where they are heterogeneous; where competition is intense and where it is absent; where the level of voter education is relatively high and where it is relatively low; where income is relatively high and where it is relatively low; and where one or a few interests are dominant and where a multiplicity of interests compete for the advantages government can confer. The mix within congressional parties is a product of the mix within the nation's constituencies. It could scarcely be otherwise. The net result of diversity is that the men and women who make their way to Congress see the world in different ways, stress different values, and pursue different objectives. A vast amount of disagreement inevitably lurks behind each party's label.

In the second place, the salient fact in the life of the legislator is his career. If he fails to protect it, no one else will. The representative or senator knows that his party can do very little to enhance his security in office or, conversely, very little to threaten it. As a member of Congress puts it, "If we depended on the party organization to get elected, none of us would be here." [48] Each member is on his own. Whether he is reelected or not will depend more on the decisions he makes than on those his party makes, more on how he cultivates his constituency than on how his party cultivates the nation, more on the credit he is able to claim for desirable governmental action than on the credit his party is able to claim,[49] more on the electoral coalition he puts together or benefits from than on the electoral coalition his party puts together or benefits from. A sweeping electoral tide may carry him out of office. Though this is to be feared from time to time, he cannot do much about it. Hence, the typical member concentrates on immediate problems. He takes his constituency as it is; if he monitors and defends its interests carefully, he stands a good chance of having a long career in Congress, no matter what fate deals to his party.

The growing importance of party campaign expenditures on behalf of congressional candidates (coordinated expenditures) may ultimately increase the members' dependence on the party and, accordingly, be reflected in their voting behavior in Congress. But there is little evidence now that members vote one way or another in response to party pressures linked to financial aid in campaigns. Parties are in business to win elections, and each prefers the election of its own mavericks to the election of members of the opposition. The ability of members to attract sizable PAC contributions, moreover, gives them additional political space in which to maneuver, free from party controls. What interest groups may extract from them is another question.

In the third place, party efforts are confounded by the fragmentation of power within Congress. The seniority leaders who chair major committees and subcommittees are as likely to have keys to congressional power as the elected party leaders. Committees go their separate ways, sometimes in harmony with the party leadership and sometimes not. Powerful committees are sometimes under the control of party elements that are out of step with the leadership and with national party goals. No power to command rests with the party leadership, and there is not a great deal it can do to bring into line those members who steadily defy the party and oppose its objectives. Two former, well-known members of the House comment on the problems that confront party leaders:

> In order for the Speaker to twist arms he has to have power, and we haven't recovered from the revolt against Uncle Joe Cannon which stripped power from a dictatorial Speaker nearly 65 years ago. (James O'Hara, D-Mich.)

> We Democrats are all under one tent. In any other country we'd be five splinter parties. Years ago we had patronage. The Speaker doesn't have any goodies to hand out. The President can promise judgeships, public works and fly [members] around in the airplanes. There's nothing like having the White House.[50] (Thomas P. ("Tip") O'Neill, Jr., former Speaker of the House)

In addition, the party caucuses and the policy committees have never in any real sense functioned as policy-shaping agencies. "Parties" within parties, such as the House Democratic Study Group, bear witness to the lack of party agreement on public policy. Numerous specialized caucuses (steel, coal, textiles, cotton, sunbelt, New England, and the like) also contribute to the decentralization of power in Congress.

In the fourth place, the intricacies of the legislative process make it difficult for the parties to function smoothly and effectively. For the party to maintain firm control, it must create majorities at a number of stages in the legislative process: first in the standing committee, then on the floor, and last in the conference committee. In the House a majority will also be needed in the Rules Committee. Failure to achieve a majority at any stage is likely to mean the loss of legislation. Even those bills that pass through the obstacle course may be so sharply changed as to be scarcely recognizable by their sponsors. In contrast, the opponents of legislation have only one requirement: to splice together a majority at one stage in the decision-making process. Breaking the party leadership at some point in the chain requires neither great resources nor imagination. For these reasons, the adoption of a new public policy is immeasurably more difficult than the preservation of an old one. All the advantages, it seems, rest with those legislators bent on preserving existing arrangements.

Finally, the congressional party functions as it does because, by and large, it is a microcosm of the party in the electorate, beset by the same internal conflicts. The American political party is an extraordinary collection of diverse, conflicting interests and individuals brought together for the specific purpose of winning office. The coalition carefully put together to make a bid for power comes under heavy stress once the election is over and candidates have become officeholders. Differences ignored or minimized during the campaign soon come to the surface. Party claims become only one input among many the member considers in shaping his positions on policy questions. Not surprisingly, national party objectives may be disregarded as the member sorts out his own priorities and takes account of those interests, including his local party organization, whose support he deems essential to his election the next time around.

The astonishing fact about the congressional parties is that they perform as well as they do. One reason for this is the phenomenon of party loyalty—the typical member is more comfortable when he votes in league with his party colleagues than when he opposes them. Another reason is that most members within each party represent constituencies that are broadly comparable in makeup; in "voting their district" they are likely to be in harmony with the general thrust of their party.[51] A third reason is found in the informal powers of the elected leaders. Members who respond to their leadership may be given assistance in advancing their pet legislation, awarded with an appointment to a prestigious committee, or armed with important information. There are advantages to getting along with the leadership. Lastly, presidential leadership seems to serve as a unifying force for his congressional party. Members may not go along with the president gladly, but many of them do go along, and even those who do not, give his requests more than a second thought.

Notes

1. Norman J. Ornstein, Thomas E. Mann, and Michael J. Malbin, *Vital Statistics on Congress, 1989-1990* (Washington, D.C.: Congressional Quarterly, 1990), 42, 52.
2. David R. Mayhew, *Congress: The Electoral Connection* (New Haven, Conn.: Yale University Press, 1974), especially 49-77. For a sampling of other studies that bear on the decline of competitive seats, see John C. McAdams and John R. Johannes, "Constituency Attentiveness in the House: 1977-1982," *Journal of Politics* 47 (November 1985): 1108-1139; Glenn R. Parker and Suzanne L. Parker, "Correlates and Effects of Attention to District by U.S. House Members," *Legislative Studies Quarterly* 10 (May 1985): 223-242; Albert D. Cover, "The Electoral Impact of Franked Congressional Mail," *Polity* 17 (Summer 1985): 649-663; and Melissa P. Collie, "Incumbency, Electoral Safety, and Turnover in the House of Representatives, 1952-1976," *American Political Science Review* 75 (March 1981): 119-131.
3. Lyn Ragsdale, "Incumbent Popularity, Challenger Invisibility, and Congressional Voters," *Legislative Studies Quarterly* 6 (May 1981): 215.
4. See Gary C. Jacobson, "The Effects of Campaign Spending in Congressional Elections," *American Political Science Review* 72 (June 1978): 469-491.
5. See Warren Lee Kostroski, "Party and Incumbency in Postwar Senate Elections," *American Political Science Review* 67 (December 1973): 1213-1234; and Donald A. Gross and James C. Garrand, "The Vanishing Marginals, 1824-1980," *Journal of Politics* 46 (February 1984): 224-237.
6. Paul S. Herrnson, "National Party Decision Making, Strategies, and Resource Distribution in Congressional Elections," *Western Political Quarterly* 42 (September 1989): 301-323. (Emphasis added.)
7. *Congressional Quarterly Weekly Report,* April 15, 1978, 875-876.
8. For interesting studies of the congressional leadership, including patterns of leadership change, see Robert L. Peabody, *Leadership in Congress* (Boston: Little, Brown, 1976); and Garrison Nelson, "Partisan Patterns of House Leadership Change, 1789-1977," *American Political Science Review* 71 (September 1977): 918-939.
9. *New York Times,* April 5, 1977. In discussing President Carter's many difficulties with Congress, Speaker O'Neill observed, "Maybe the President ought to go the route I go. I just come into a congressman's office and get down on bended knees." *U.S. News & World Report,* June 11, 1979, 17.
10. The Speaker's formal counterpart in the Senate is the vice president, who serves as president of the Senate. His role is simply that of presiding officer, since he is not a member of the body, cannot enter debate, and is permitted to vote only in the case of a tie. His influence on the legislative process is ordinarily insignificant.
11. Randall B. Ripley, *Party Leaders in the House of Representatives* (Washington, D.C.: Brookings Institution, 1967), 23-24.
12. Joseph Cooper and David W. Brady, "Institutional Context and Leadership Style: The House from Cannon to Rayburn," *American Political Science Review* 75 (June 1981): 417.
13. *Congressional Quarterly Weekly Report,* December 30, 1989, 3550.
14. "Leadership: An Interview with Senate Leader Lyndon Johnson," *U.S. News & World Report,* June 27, 1960, 88. See also Ralph K. Huitt, "Democratic Party Leadership in the Senate," *American Political Science Review* 55 (June

1961): 333-344.
15. *Congressional Quarterly Weekly Report,* December 11, 1976, 3293.
16. *Congressional Quarterly Weekly Report,* June 10, 1989, 1377.
17. *Congressional Quarterly Weekly Report,* July 7, 1979, 1345.
18. "Leadership," 90.
19. *New York Times,* July 17, 1961, 11.
20. Changes in committee-subcommittee relations in the 1970s, including the adoption of a Subcommittee Bill of Rights, have had a major impact on decision making in the House. Subcommittees now have relatively clear-cut policy jurisdictions and, of more importance, substantial control over their own budgets, staffs, and agendas. Subcommittee chairmen commonly manage legislation on the floor. For analysis of the new role of subcommittees, see Norman J. Ornstein, *Congress in Change: Evolution and Reform* (New York: Praeger, 1975), 88-114; and David W. Rohde, "Committee Reform in the House of Representatives and the Subcommittee Bill of Rights," *The Annals* 411 (January 1974): 39-47.
21. *Pittsburgh Press,* September 23, 1978.
22. *Congressional Quarterly Weekly Report,* September 4, 1982, 2181.
23. Concerning the middleman role of the floor leader, see these studies: David B. Truman, *The Congressional Party* (New York: Wiley, 1959), 106-116 and 205-208; Barbara Hinckley, "Congressional Leadership Selection and Support: A Comparative Analysis," *Journal of Politics* 32 (May 1970): 268-287; and William E. Sullivan, "Criteria for Selecting Party Leadership in Congress," *American Politics Quarterly* 3 (January 1975): 25-44.
24. Burdett A. Loomis, *The New American Politician: Ambition, Entrepreneurship, and the Changing Face of Political Life* (New York: Basic Books, 1988), 175.
25. *Congressional Quarterly Weekly Report,* May 27, 1978, 1304.
26. See a study by Randall B. Ripley, "The Party Whip Organizations in the United States House of Representatives," *American Political Science Review* 58 (September 1964): 561-576.
27. Quoted in Loomis, *The New American Politician,* 177.
28. For a detailed study of this committee, see Charles O. Jones, *Party and Policy-Making: The House Republican Policy Committee* (New Brunswick, N.J.: Rutgers University Press, 1964).
29. Hugh A. Bone, "An Introduction to the Senate Policy Committees," *American Political Science Review* 50 (June 1956): 352. Also see Peabody, *Leadership in Congress,* 337-338.
30. Among the studies to consult on this subject are Susan Webb Hammond, Daniel P. Mulhollan, and Arthur G. Stevens, Jr., "Informal Congressional Caucuses and Agenda Setting," *Western Political Quarterly* 38 (December 1985): 583-605; Arthur G. Stevens, Jr., Daniel P. Mulhollan, and Paul S. Rundquist, "U.S. Congressional Structure and Representation: The Role of Informal Groups," *Legislative Studies Quarterly* 6 (August 1981): 415-437; Burdett A. Loomis, "Congressional Caucuses and the Politics of Representation," in *Congress Reconsidered,* 2d ed., ed. Lawrence C. Dodd and Bruce I. Oppenheimer (Washington, D.C.: CQ Press, 1981), 204-220; Arthur G. Stevens, Jr., Arthur H. Miller, and Thomas E. Mann, "Mobilization of Liberal Strength in the House, 1955-1970: The Democratic Study Group," *American Political Science Review* 68 (June 1974): 667-681; and Kenneth Kofmehl, "The Institutionalization of a Voting Bloc," *Western Political Quarterly* 17

(June 1964): 256-272. Of related interest, see Barbara Sinclair, "State Party Delegations in the U.S. House of Representatives: A Comparative Study of Group Cohesion," *Journal of Politics* 34 (February 1972): 199-222; Richard Born, "Cue-Taking within State Party Delegations in the U.S. House of Representatives," *Journal of Politics* 38 (February 1976): 71-94; and Jeffrey E. Cohen and David C. Nice, "Changing Party Loyalty of State Delegations to the U.S. House of Representatives, 1953-1976," *Western Political Quarterly* 36 (June 1983): 312-325.

31. See Lewis A. Froman, Jr., and Randall B. Ripley, "Conditions for Party Leadership: The Case of the House Democrats," *American Political Science Review* 59 (March 1965): 52-63.

32. *Congressional Quarterly Weekly Report,* November 1, 1980, 3235.

33. See Edward V. Schneier's revised version of a classic study by Julius Turner, *Party and Constituency Pressures on Congress* (Baltimore, Md.: Johns Hopkins Press, 1970), especially Chapters 2 and 3, from which certain data in this paragraph were drawn. Also see *Congressional Quarterly Weekly Report,* January 16, 1988, 103.

34. *Congressional Quarterly Weekly Report,* December 30, 1989, 3546-3549; and January 6, 1990, 55-57.

35. Barbara Sinclair, "Political Upheaval and Congressional Voting: The Effects of the 1960s on Voting Patterns in the House of Representatives," *Journal of Politics* 38 (May 1976): 326-345. Also see David W. Brady and Barbara Sinclair, "Building Majorities for Policy Change in the House of Representatives," *Journal of Politics* 46 (November 1984): 1033-1060.

36. Samuel C. Patterson and Gregory A. Caldeira, "Party Voting in the United States Congress," *British Journal of Political Science* 18 (January 1988): 111-131. The authors employ the "majority versus majority" concept of a party vote.

37. *Congressional Quarterly Weekly Report,* December 30, 1989, 3553-3555, 3567-3571.

38. Richard E. Neustadt, *Presidential Power: The Politics of Leadership* (New York: Wiley, 1960), 33.

39. See a particularly instructive discussion of the insulation of members from party and committee controls in Loomis, *The New American Politician,* Chapter 6.

40. James Sundquist, *Politics and Policy: The Eisenhower, Kennedy, and Johnson Years* (Washington, D.C.: Brookings Institution, 1968), 478-479.

41. *Congressional Quarterly Weekly Report,* January 2, 1982, 20-21.

42. *Congressional Quarterly Weekly Report,* December 30, 1989, 3540-3545, 3559-3563.

43. There is additional evidence that a member's support for the president's policy proposals is influenced by how well the president ran in his district. In essence, the stronger the president runs in the member's district, the more policy support he will receive from that member. Presidential elections thus do more than select winners; they help to shape support patterns in Congress for presidential initiatives. See George C. Edwards III, "Presidential Electoral Performance as a Source of Presidential Power," *American Journal of Political Science* 22 (February 1978): 152-168.

44. From Randall B. Ripley, *Majority Party Leadership in Congress* (Boston: Little, Brown, 1969), 175.

45. See Truman, *The Congressional Party,* especially 279-319. *The Congressional*

Party is required reading for an understanding of the role of party in the contemporary Congress. Its central conclusions continue to ring true. To examine congressional parties from other perspectives, see these recent studies: Keith T. Poole and R. Steven Daniels, "Ideology, Party, and Voting in the U.S. Congress, 1959-1980," *American Political Science Review* 79 (June 1985): 373-399; Sara Brandes Crook and John R. Hibbing, "Congressional Reform and Party Discipline: The Effects of Changes in the Seniority System on Party Loyalty in the U.S. House of Representatives," *British Journal of Political Science* 15 (April 1985): 207-226; Ross K. Baker, "Party and Institutional Sanctions in the U.S. House: The Case of Congressman Gramm," *Legislative Studies Quarterly* 10 (August 1985): 315-337; David W. Brady, "A Reevaluation of Realignments in American Politics: Evidence from the House of Representatives," *American Political Science Review* 79 (March 1985): 28-49; Burdett A. Loomis, "Congressional Careers and Party Leadership in the Contemporary House of Representatives," *American Journal of Political Science* 28 (February 1984): 180-202; David W. Brady and Barbara Sinclair, "Building Majorities for Policy Changes in the House of Representatives," *Journal of Politics* 46 (November 1984): 1033-1060; Donald A. Gross, "Changing Patterns of Voting Agreement among Senatorial Leadership: 1947-1976," *Western Political Quarterly* 37 (March 1984): 120-142; Jeffrey E. Cohen and David C. Nice, "Changing Party Loyalty of State Delegations to the U.S. House of Representatives, 1953-1976," *Western Political Quarterly* 36 (June 1983): 312-325; Charles S. Bullock III and David W. Brady, "Party, Constituency, and Roll-Call Voting in the U.S. Senate," *Legislative Studies Quarterly* 8 (February 1983): 29-43; Thomas H. Hammond and Jane M. Fraser, "Baselines for Evaluating Explanations of Coalition Behavior in Congress," *Journal of Politics* 45 (August 1983): 635-656; Robert G. Brookshire and Dean F. Duncan III, "Congressional Career Patterns and Party Systems," *Legislative Studies Quarterly* 8 (February 1983): 65-78; Richard A. Champagne, "Conditions for Realignment in the U.S. Senate, or What Makes the Steamroller Start?" *Legislative Studies Quarterly* 8 (May 1983): 231-249; William R. Shaffer, "Party and Ideology in the U.S. House of Representatives," *Western Political Quarterly* 35 (March 1982): 92-106; Thomas E. Cavanagh, "The Dispersion of Authority in the House of Representatives," *Political Science Quarterly* 97 (Winter 1982-1983): 623-637; Walter J. Stone, "Electoral Change and Policy Representation in Congress," *British Journal of Political Science* 12 (January 1982): 95-115; and Patricia A. Hurley, "Predicting Policy Change in the House," *British Journal of Political Science* 12 (July 1982): 375-384.

46. Charles O. Jones, *The Minority Party in Congress* (Boston: Little, Brown, 1970), especially 9-24.

47. This study by Charles O. Jones identifies eight strategies open to the minority party in the overall task of building majorities in Congress: support of the majority party by contributing votes and possibly leadership, inconsequential opposition, withdrawal, cooperation, innovation, consequential partisan opposition, consequential constructive opposition, and participation (this strategy representing a situation in which the minority party controls the White House and thus is required to participate in constructing majorities). Strategies may vary within a single session of Congress and from one stage of the legislative process to the next. Jones, *The Minority Party in Congress*, 19-24 and Chapters

4-8.

48. Charles L. Clapp, *The Congressman: His Work as He Sees It* (Washington, D.C.: Brookings Institution, 1963), 30-31.

49. For an analysis of the "credit claiming" activities of members, see Mayhew, *Congress: The Electoral Connection*, 52-61. The basic assumption of this remarkable little book is that reelection to Congress is the singular goal of members, and the relentless pursuit of it steadily influences not only their behavior but also the structure and functioning of the institution itself.

50. *Washington Post,* June 17, 1975, 12.

51. The typical northern Democrat is elected from a district with these characteristics: higher proportion of nonwhite population, lower owner-occupancy of dwellings, higher population density, and higher percentage of urban population. The typical northern Republican represents a district whose characteristics are just the opposite. Constituency characteristics undoubtedly have an important impact on congressional voting. See Lewis A. Froman, Jr., "Inter-Party Constituency Differences and Congressional Voting Behavior," *American Political Science Review* 57 (March 1963): 57-61.

The American Party System:
Problems and Perspectives

EXTOLLING the virtues of the American party system is something of
an anomaly in popular commentary and scholarship. A few scholars
have found merit in the party system, particularly in its contributions to
unifying the nation, fostering political stability, reconciling social conflict, aggregating interests, and institutionalizing popular control of
government. But the broad thrust in evaluations of this basic political
institution has been heavily critical. American parties, various indict-
ments contend, are too much alike in their programs to afford voters a
meaningful choice, are dominated by special interests, are unable to deal
imaginatively with public problems, are beset by a confusion of purposes, are ineffective because of their internal divisions, are short on
discipline and cohesion, are insufficiently responsive to popular claims
and aspirations, and are deficient as instruments for assuming and
achieving responsibility in government.

The Doctrine of Responsible Parties

The major ground for popular distress over the parties may be simply
that most people are in some measure suspicious of politicians and their
organizations. The criticism of scholars, meanwhile, has focused
mainly on the lack of party responsibility in government. The most
comprehensive statement on behalf of the doctrine of party responsibil-

281

ity is found in a report of the Committee on Political Parties of the American Political Science Association (APSA), *Toward a More Responsible Two-Party System,* published in 1950. The report, a classic document in political science, argues that what is required is a party system that is "democratic, responsible, and effective." In the words of the committee:

> Party responsibility means the responsibility of both parties to the general public, as enforced in elections. Party responsibility to the public, enforced in elections, implies that there be more than one party, for the public can hold a party responsible only if it has a choice. . . . When the parties lack the capacity to define their actions in terms of policies, they turn irresponsible because the electoral choice between the parties becomes devoid of meaning. . . . An effective party system requires, first, that the parties are able to bring forth programs to which they commit themselves and, second, that the parties possess sufficient internal cohesion to carry out these programs.[1]

Two major presumptions underlie the doctrine of responsible parties. The first is that the essence of democracy is to be found in popular control over government rather than in popular participation in the immediate tasks of government. A nation such as the United States is far too large and its government much too complex for the general run of citizens to become steadily involved in its decision-making processes. But this fact does not rule out popular control over government. The direction of government can only be controlled by the people as long as they are consulted on public matters and possess the power to replace one set of rulers with another set, the "opposition." The party, in this view, becomes the instrument through which the public—or more precisely, a majority of the public—can decide who will run the government and for what purposes. Government by responsible parties is thus an expression of majority rule.

The second tenet in this theory holds that popular control over government requires that the public be given a choice between competing, unified parties capable of assuming collective responsibility to the public for the actions of government. A responsible party system would make three contributions. One, it "would enable the people to choose effectively a general program, a general direction for government to take, as embodied in a set of leaders committed to that program." Two, it would help to "energize and activate" public opinion. Three, it would increase the prospects for popular control by substituting the collective responsibility of an organized group, the party, for the individual responsibility assumed, more or less inadequately, by individual office-holders.[2]

The responsible parties model proposed by the Committee on Political Parties is worth examination because it presents a sharp contrast to the contemporary party system. Disciplined and programmatic parties, offering clearer choices to voters, would replace the loose and inchoate institutions to which Americans are accustomed. The committee's report deals with national party organization, party platforms, congressional party organization, intraparty democracy, and nominations and elections.

National Party Organization

The national party organizations envisaged by the committee would be much different from those existing today. The national convention, for example, would be composed of not more than five hundred or six hundred members, more than half of whom would be elected by party voters. Ex officio members drawn from the ranks of the national committee, state party chairmen, and congressional leaders, along with certain prominent party leaders outside the party organizations, would make up the balance of the convention membership. Instead of meeting every four years, the convention would assemble regularly at least once every two years and perhaps in special meetings. Reduced in size, more representative of the actual strength of the party in individual states, and meeting more frequently and for longer periods, the new convention would gain effectiveness as a deliberative body for the development of party policy and as a more representative assembly for reconciling the interests of various elements within the party.

The most far-reaching proposal for restructuring national party organization involves the creation of a party council of perhaps fifty members, composed of representatives from such units as the national committee, the congressional parties, the state committees, and the party's governors. Meeting regularly and often, the party council would examine problems of party management, prepare a preliminary draft of the party platform for submission to the national convention, interpret the platform adopted by the convention, screen and recommend candidates for congressional offices, consider possible presidential candidates, and advise such appropriate party organs as the national convention or national committee "with respect to conspicuous departures from general party decisions by state or local party organizations." Empowered in this fashion, the party council would represent a firm break with familiar and conventional arrangements that contribute to the dispersion of party authority and the elusiveness of party policy. The essence of the council's task would be to blend the interests of national, congressional, and state organizations to foster the development of an authentic national party, one capable of fashioning and implementing coherent strategies and policies.

Party Platforms

Party platforms, the report holds, are deficient on a number of counts. At times the platform "may be intentionally written in an ambiguous manner so as to attract voters of any persuasion and to offend as few voters as possible." State party platforms frequently espouse principles and policies in conflict with those of the national party. Congressional candidates and members of Congress may feel little obligation to support platform planks. No agency exists to interpret and apply the platform in the years between conventions. There is substantial confusion and difference of opinion over the binding quality of a platform—that is, whether party candidates are bound to observe the commitments presumably made in the adoption of the platform.

To put new life back into the party platform, the report recommends that it should be written at least every two years to take account of developing issues and to link it to congressional campaigns in off-year elections; that it should "emphasize general party principles and national issues" that "should be regarded as binding commitments on all candidates and officeholders of the party, national, state and local"; that state and local platforms "should be expected to conform to the national platform on matters of general party principle or on national policies"; and that the party council should take an active role in the platform-making process, both in preparing tentative drafts of the document in advance of the convention and in interpreting and applying the platform between conventions. In sum, the report argues that party platforms and the processes through which they are presently formulated and implemented are inimical to the development of strong and responsible parties.

Congressional Party Organization

One of the most vexing problems in the effort to develop more responsible parties has been the performance of the congressional parties. The proliferation of leadership committees in Congress, the weakness of the caucus (or conference), the independence of congressional committees, and the seniority system have combined to limit possibilities for the parties to develop consistent and coherent legislative records. To tighten up congressional party organization would require a number of changes. First, each party in both the Senate and the House should consolidate its various leadership groups (for example, policy committees, committees on committees, House Rules Committee) into a single leadership group; its functions would be to manage legislative party affairs, submit policy proposals to the membership, draw up slates of committee assignments, and assume responsibility for scheduling legislation.

Second, more frequent meetings should be held by the party caucuses, their decisions to be binding on legislation involving the party's principles and programs. Moreover, members of Congress who ignore a caucus decision "should not expect to receive the same consideration in the assignment of committee posts or in the apportionment of patronage as those who have been loyal to party principles."

Third, the seniority system should be made to work in harmony with the party's responsibility for a legislative program. The report states:

> The problem is not one of abolishing seniority and then finding an alternative. It is one of mobilizing the power through which the party leadership can successfully use the seniority principle rather than have the seniority principle dominate Congress. . . . Advancement within a committee on the basis of seniority makes sense, other things being equal. But it is not playing the game fairly for party members who oppose the commitments in their party's platform to rely on seniority to carry them into committee chairmanships. Party leaders have compelling reason to prevent such a member from becoming chairman—and they are entirely free so to exert their influence.

Fourth, the assignment of members of Congress to committees should be a responsibility of the party leadership committees. "Personal competence and party loyalty should be valued more highly than seniority in assigning members to such major committees as those dealing with fiscal policy and foreign affairs." At the same time, committee assignments should be reviewed at least every two years by the party caucus. A greater measure of party control over committee assignments is essential, if the party is to assume responsibility for a legislative program.

Finally, party leaders should take over the function of scheduling legislation for floor consideration. In particular, the power held by the House Rules Committee over legislative scheduling should be vested in the party leadership committee. If the party cannot control the flow of legislation to the floor and shape the agenda, there is little chance that it can control legislative output, which is the essence of responsible party performance in Congress.

Intraparty Democracy

The achievement of a system of responsible parties demands more than the good intentions of the public and of party leaders. It requires widespread and meaningful political participation by grass-roots members of the party, democratic party processes, and an accountable leadership. According to the report:

> Capacity for internal agreement, democratically arrived at, is a critical test for a party. It is a critical test because when there is no such capacity, there is no capacity for positive action, and hence the party becomes a hollow pretense. It is a test which can be met only if the party machinery affords the membership an opportunity to set the course of the party and to control those who speak for it. The test can be met fully only where the membership accepts responsibility for creative participation in shaping the party's program.

The task of developing an active party membership capable of creative participation in the affairs of the party is not easy. Organizational changes at both the summit and the base of the party hierarchy are required. "A national convention, broadly and directly representative of the rank and file of the party and meeting at least biennially, is essential to promote a sense of identity with the party throughout the membership as well as to settle internal differences fairly, harmoniously, and democratically." Similarly, at the grass-roots level, local party groups need to be developed that will meet frequently to generate and discuss ideas concerning national issues and the national party program. The emergence and development of local issue-oriented party groups can be facilitated by national party agencies engaged in education and publicity and willing to undertake the function of disseminating information and research findings.

A new concept of party membership is required—one that emphasizes "allegiance to a common program" rather than mere support of party candidates in elections. Its development might take this form:

> The existence of a national program, drafted at frequent intervals by a party convention both broadly representative and enjoying prestige, should make a great difference. It would prompt those who identify themselves as Republicans and Democrats to think in terms of support of that program, rather than in terms of personalities, patronage, and local matters.... Once machinery is established which gives the party member and his representative a share in framing the party's objectives, once there are safeguards against internal dictation by a few in positions of influence, members and representatives will feel readier to assume an obligation to support the program. Membership defined in these terms does not ask for mindless discipline enforced from above. It generates the self-discipline which stems from free identification with aims one helps to define.

Nominations and Elections

The report's recommendations for changing nomination and election procedures fit comfortably within its overall political formula for strengthening the American party system. It endorses the direct primary—"a useful weapon in the arsenal of intraparty democracy"—while expressing preference for the closed rather than the open version. The open primary is incompatible with the idea of a responsible party system, since by permitting voters to shift from one party to the other between primaries, it subverts the concept of membership as the foundation of party organization. Preprimary meetings of party committees should be held for the purpose of proposing and endorsing candidates in primary elections. Selection of delegates to the national conventions should be made by the direct vote of party members instead of by state conventions. Local party groups should meet prior to the convention to discuss potential candidates and platform planks.

Three major changes should be made in the election system. The electoral college should be changed to give "all sections of the country a real voice in electing the president and the vice-president" and to help develop a two-party system in areas now dominated by one party. Second, the term of members of the House of Representatives should be extended from two to four years, with coinciding election of House members and the president. If this constitutional change is made, prospects would be improved for harmonizing executive and legislative power through the agency of party. Finally, the report recommends a variety of changes in the regulation of campaign finance, the most important of which calls for a measure of public financing of election campaigns.

The Promise of Responsible Parties

In the broadest sense, the publication of *Toward a More Responsible Two-Party System* was an outgrowth of increased uneasiness among many political scientists over the performance of the nation's party system and the vitality of American government. Specifically, the report sought to deal with a problem that is central to the overall political system: the weakness of political parties as instruments for governing in a democratic and responsible fashion. The report is not a study in political feasibility. It does not offer a blueprint depicting where the best opportunities lie for making changes in the party system. What it does offer is a set of wide-ranging prescriptions consonant with a particular model of political organization. If the model sketched by the committee were to come into existence, the American party system would bear only modest resemblance to that which has survived for well over a century. The key characteristics of the new parties would be the national quality of their organization, a much greater degree of centralization of party power, a tendency for party claims to assume primacy over individual constituency claims in public policy formation, a heightened visibility for the congressional parties and their leadership and for the president's role as party leader, and a greater concern over party unity and discipline.

To its credit, the report was not accompanied by the usual somnolence that settles over prescriptive efforts of this kind. Nor, however, did queues of reformers form in the streets, in the universities, or elsewhere to push for its implementation. What occurred instead was that the report gave substantial impetus to the study of American political parties and helped to foster a concern for reform that, in one respect or another, continues to the present.

The goal of advocates of party responsibility is to place the parties at the creative center of policy making in the United States. That is what party responsibility is all about. Voters would choose between two disciplined and cohesive parties, each distinguished by relatively clear and consistent programs and policy orientations. Responsibility would be enforced through elections. Parties would be retained in power or removed from power depending upon their performance and the attractiveness of their programs. Collective responsibility for the conduct of government would displace the individual responsibility of officeholders. Such are the key characteristics of the model party system.

How well responsible parties would mesh with the American political system is another matter.[3] Critics have contended that disciplined parties might contribute to an erosion of consensus, to heightened conflict between social classes, to the formation of splinter parties (and perhaps to a full-blown multiple-party system), and to the breakdown of federalism. Moreover, the voting behavior and attitudes of the American people would have to change markedly to accommodate to the model of centralized parties, since many voters are more oriented to candidates than they are to parties or issues. The indifference of the public to the idea of programmatic parties would appear to be a major obstacle to rationalizing the party system along the lines of the responsible parties model.

Responsible Parties and Party Reform

The reform wave of the last two decades has produced a number of organizational and procedural changes in the American party system and in Congress. Perhaps as much by accident as by design, a surprising number of these changes are largely or fully compatible with the recommendations of the APSA report.

Intraparty Democracy

Consider the steps that have been taken to foster intraparty democracy. No feature of the reform movement of the Democratic party, beginning with the guidelines of the Commission on Party Structure and Delegate Selection (the McGovern-Fraser Commission), stands out more sharply than the commitment to make the party internally democratic and more responsive to its grass-roots elements.

Commenting on the overall process by which delegates were selected to the 1968 convention, the McGovern-Fraser Commission[4] observed that "meaningful participation of Democratic voters in the choice of their presidential nominee was often difficult or costly, sometimes completely illusory, and, in not a few instances, impossible." For example, the commission found that (1) in nearly half the states, rules governing the selection process were either nonexistent or inadequate, "leaving the entire process to the discretion of a handful of party leaders"; (2) more than one-third of the convention delegates had, in effect, been chosen prior to 1968—well before all the possible presidential candidates were known and before President Johnson had withdrawn from the race; (3) "the imposition of the unit rule from the first to the final stage of the nominating process, the enforcement of binding instructions on delegates, and favorite-son candidacies were all devices used to force Democrats to vote against their stated presidential preferences"; (4) in primary, convention, and committee delegate selection systems, "majorities used their numerical superiority to deny delegate representation to the supporters of minority presidential candidates"; (5) procedural irregularities, such as secret caucuses, closed slate making, and proxy voting, were common in party conventions from the precinct to the state level; (6) the costs of participating in the delegate selection process, such as filing fees for entering primaries, were often excessive; and (7) certain population groups—in particular blacks, women, and youth—were substantially underrepresented among the delegates.

To eliminate these practices and conditions, the commission adopted a series of guidelines to regulate the selection of delegates for future conventions. Designed to permit all Democratic voters a "full, meaningful, and timely" opportunity to take part in the presidential nominating process, the guidelines set forth an extensive array of reforms to be implemented by state parties.

The initial step required of state Democratic parties was the adoption of a comprehensive set of rules governing the delegate selection process to which all rank-and-file Democrats would have access. Not only were these rules to make clear how all party members can participate in the process but they were also to be designed to facilitate their "maximum participation." In addition, certain procedural safeguards were specified. Proxy voting and the use of the unit rule were outlawed. Party committee meetings held for the purpose of selecting convention delegates were required to establish a quorum of not less than 40 percent of the members. Mandatory assessments of convention delegates were prohibited. Adequate public notice of all party meetings called to consider delegate selection was required, as were rules to provide for uniform times and dates of meetings.

The commission enjoined state parties to seek a broad base of support. Standards eliminating all forms of discrimination against the participation of minority group members in the delegate selection process were required. To overcome the effects of past discrimination, moreover, each state was expected to include in its delegation blacks, women, and young people in numbers roughly proportionate to their presence in the state population.

A number of specific requirements for delegate selection were adopted by the commission. For example, provisions must be made for the selection of delegates in a "timely manner" (within the calendar year in which the convention is held), for selection of alternates in the same manner as delegates, for apportionment of delegates within the state on the basis of a formula that gives equal weight to population and to Democratic strength, and for the selection of at least 75 percent of the delegates at the congressional district level or lower (in states using the convention system). The number of delegates to be selected by a party state committee was limited to 10 percent of the total delegation.

One of the most remarkable aspects of this unprecedented action by the national party was the response of the state parties. They accepted the guidelines, altered or abandoned a variety of age-old practices and state laws, and selected their delegations through procedures more open than anyone thought possible. And with "maximum participation" in mind, they produced a convention whose composition—with its emphasis on demographic representation—was vastly different from any previous one.[5] Whether for good or ill, the Democratic party had by 1972 accepted the main tenets of intraparty democracy.[6]

No evidence exists, however, that party democratization has contributed to the development of a more responsible party system. Indeed, the reverse is probably true: the greater the degree of intraparty democracy, the harder it is to develop a coherent program of party policy.[7]

Strengthening the Congressional Parties

Reform, like conflict, is contagious. Essentially the same forces that produced major changes in the electoral structure of the Democratic party have produced major changes in the Democratic congressional party, particularly in the House. The thrust of these changes is in line with the theory of responsible parties. Advocates of this theory have sought not so much to promote the formation of a new party structure in Congress as to breathe new life into existing party structures and procedures. The changes have been impressive. Long dormant, the Democratic caucus is now a more influential force in the affairs of the House, particularly in controlling committee assignments and in shaping rules and procedures. At the opening of the Ninety-fourth Congress (1975-1976), the caucus removed three committee chairmen from their positions, increased party control over the committee assignment process, brought the Rules Committee more firmly under the leadership of the Speaker, and established a requirement that the chairmen of the appropriations subcommittees be ratified by the caucus. These were not stylized or marginal alterations. They should be seen for what they were: as systematically conceived efforts to reshape the power structure of Congress by diminishing the influence of the seniority leaders (who have often been out of step with a majority of the party) and augmenting the power of the party caucus and the leadership. And there have been other demonstrations of caucus power in the 1980s. At the outset of the Ninety-eighth Congress (1983-1984), the Democratic caucus voted to remove a southern party member from the Budget Committee because he had played a key role in fashioning President Reagan's budget strategy in the preceding Congress. Although party disciplinary action is not often taken, it can occur if the provocation is severe.

Organization, Platforms, Nominations, and Elections

A potpourri of other recent reforms was anticipated by the APSA report on responsible parties. Among them were the reassertion of the national convention's authority over the national committee, the selection of convention delegates by direct vote of the rank and file, the allocation of national committee members on the basis of the actual strength of the party within the areas they represent, the use of closed primaries for the selection of convention delegates, the public financing of presidential elections, and the provision for holding a national party conference between national conventions.[8]

In sum, many of the reforms that have been introduced in the party structure and in Congress are consistent with recommendations carried in *Toward a More Responsible Two-Party System*. They touch far more than the outer edges of the party and congressional systems. Nevertheless, there is no good reason to suppose that responsible party government is around the corner—that these reforms will somehow result in the institutionalization of a durable, highly centralized, and disciplined party system. Traditional moorings throughout the political environment make change of this magnitude all but impossible. And the current trends in American politics have done more to disable the parties than to strengthen them.

Trends in American Politics

Office holding in the United States is dominated by the two major parties. The vast majority of aspirants for public office carry on their campaigns under the banner of one or the other of the two major parties. The most important fact to be known about the candidates in a great many electoral jurisdictions throughout the country is the party to which they belong, so decisive is party affiliation for election outcomes. Virtually everywhere, save in nonpartisan environments, the trappings of party—symbols, sponsorship, slogans, buttons, and literature—are in evidence. The parties and their candidates collect money, spend money, and incur campaign deficits on a scale that dwarfs their budgets of a generation ago. Party bureaucracies are larger than in the past. More than two out of three citizens continue to see themselves as Democrats or Republicans, however imperfectly they may comprehend their party's program or the performance of their party's representatives. Party-based voting decisions are common in numerous jurisdictions. These are the signs of party vitality. But in reality they are largely misleading. Major problems confront the party system. Moreover, the key trends in contemporary politics are essentially antiparty in thrust.

1. The loss of power by electoral party organizations.

At virtually every point associated with the recruitment and election of public officials, the party organizations have suffered an erosion of power. The reasons are many and varied. At the top of the list, perhaps, is the direct primary. "He who can make the nominations is the owner of the party," E. E. Schattschneider wrote some years ago, and there is no reason to doubt his observation.[9] Given that nonendorsed candidates may defeat party nominees in primaries, one may wonder whether, in some elections and in some jurisdictions, anyone except the candidates really owns the parties. The party label has lost significance as candidates of all political colorations, with all variety of relationships to the organization, earn the right to wear it by capturing primary elections. Most important, a party that cannot control its nominations finds it difficult to achieve unity once it has won office and is faced with the implementation of its platform. Candidates who defeat the organization may see little reason to subscribe to party tenets, defend party interests, or follow party leaders. Not only does the primary contribute to the fragmentation of party unity in office but it also divides the party at large.

> Primaries often pit party leaders against party leaders, party voters against party voters, often opening deep and unhealing party wounds. They also dissipate party financial and personal resources. Party leadership usually finds that it has no choice but to take sides in a primary battle, the alternative being the possible triumph of the weaker candidate.[10]

The weakening of the parties is nowhere more apparent than in the domain of presidential campaign politics. The spread of presidential primaries and the opening up of caucuses introduced a participatory system that undermined the role of party leaders and organizations in the presidential nominating process. Candidates for the nomination touch bases with party leaders as much out of courtesy as out of need, and while presumably leaders' endorsements help, they are surely not critical. The introduction of public funding for presidential campaigns has reduced the party's fund-raising role for this office. And it could be argued that the typical national convention is a party conclave in name only. As Byron Shafer has observed, the Democratic reforms "restricted, and often removed, the regular party from the mechanics of presidential selection."[11] Additionally, in the election of the president, the linkage between party and outcome is of no more than modest importance, if that.

Still other reasons may be adduced for the atrophy of the party's role in the electoral process. The great urban machines of a generation ago have practically disappeared. Employing an intricate system of rewards and incentives, the machines dominated the political process—controlling access to power, political careers, and, most important, votes. Their decline, due to a number of reasons, contributed to a growth of independence both within the electorate and among politicians.

Electoral party organization is simply not particularly important in the political lives of today's self-reliant candidates. Some members of Congress, for example, have created their own political action committees (PACs) for electoral purposes. Virtually all of them not only campaign continuously, using all the resources of their office, but also have their own campaign operations (including staff aides assigned to the district) and reelection treasuries. John McCartney quotes a field representative of a California member of Congress:

> I'm never through campaigning—except for one evening every two years. Election night there's no campaign. We have a victory party, I drink a lot of champagne, and I go home and go to bed. Next morning I begin campaigning all over again.[12]

Ambitious, issue-oriented, and media-conscious, the "new model" members of Congress exploit their office resources to the hilt in gaining publicity, advertising their names, and strengthening their reelection base. Some years before he became Speaker, Thomas S. Foley (D-Wash.) commented on the new style politician in Congress: "At worst, these guys say in effect, 'It doesn't matter. I am my own party,' [and] they emphasize their personal qualities." [13]

Finally, the easing of the party grip on the processes by which a person is recruited and elected to office is explained by a miscellany of reasons: the decline in the volume of patronage due to extension of the merit system, the decline in the attractiveness of patronage jobs, the steady growth of a better-educated electorate, the mobility of voters, the awesome costs of campaigns, the requirement for technical skills in the use of the mass media and in other innovative forms of campaigning, the emergence of the celebrity candidate, and the inability of the parties to capture the imagination and esteem of the voters.

The classic functions of party involve recruitment, nomination, and campaigning.[14] Today's parties are unable to dominate any of these activities, and often their impact is negligible. American politics in the media age is thoroughly candidate-centered. For most offices, major and minor, most of the time, candidates are on their own in making the decisions that count. No party organization or leadership tells them when to run, how to run, what to believe, what to say, or (once in office) how to vote. Candidates may tolerate party nudging on some matters while they welcome party money, technical assistance, and services. And they receive them, especially on the Republican side, where a well-developed national system is in place for raising funds and providing services to candidates and state party organizations. But it is unmistakably the candidates who decide what to make of their party membership and party connections—both in and out of government. And no one, including party leaders and party committees, can do much about it. In jurisdictions where American parties have more than ordinary importance, they are essentially facilitators, helping candidates who wear their label to do better what generally they would do in any case.

2. The decline of partisanship.

One of the far-reaching changes in American politics during the modern era has been the decline of partisanship in the electorate. For many voters, party no longer carries much weight. Although their number has declined somewhat in recent years, more than one-fourth of all voters describe themselves as independents (see Table 7-1). Southerners are becoming more Republican and more independent. To be sure, not all voters who perceive themselves as independents actually behave as independents; some are undercover partisans who stay with the same party in most or all elections. Nonetheless, as the proportion of self-styled independents rises, problems mount for the maintenance of a vigorous party system. The party stimulus is weakened all along the line, from the recruitment of candidates, through elections, to office holding. Party electoral prospects become harder to forecast. Voter independence is to party vitality what coalition legislative voting is to party responsibility—a relationship of conspicuous incompatibility.

Every election attests to the "departisanization" of the electorate. In the 1986 House elections, a mere 8.4 percent of all voters said that the candidate's party was the most important factor in influencing their voting choice. The most important consideration was the candidate's character and experience, according to 41 percent of the sample. For 23 percent, state and local issues loomed most important. And of unusual interest, in this *national* election, only 20 percent reported basing their decision on *national issues*.[15] The stark fact is that personality factors and parochialism often dominate American elections.

The prevalence of ticket splitting is further evidence of party decomposition. Nearly six out of ten people now cast split ballots in presidential elections, and in elections for local offices the proportion is

TABLE 7-1   Party Identification in the Nation and in the South, 1960 and 1990

	Democrat	Republican	Independent
Nation			
1960	47%	30%	23%
1990	39	35	26
South			
1960	59	22	19
1990	39	35	26

SOURCE: The 1960 data were taken from *Gallup Opinion Index*, August 1970, 3. The 1990 data for the nation appeared in *Gallup Poll News Service*, May 16, 1990, 2, while the 1990 data for the South were furnished by the Gallup Organization.

even larger.[16] This behavior is not surprising since an overwhelming majority of the public believes that "the best rule in voting is to pick the best candidate, regardless of party label." [17] Ticket splitting has major ramifications for the control of government, as can be seen in an examination of the vote for presidential and congressional candidates within congressional districts. Table 7-2 includes data on the number and percentage of congressional districts with split election results— districts won by the presidential candidate of one party and by the congressional candidate of the other party—from 1920 to 1988. The data depict a more or less steady increase in split elections for these offices. A high point was reached in 1972, when 44 percent of all House districts split their results, due largely to the voters' rejection of George McGovern, the Democratic presidential nominee. The proportion of split results was almost as high in 1984 as voters everywhere voted for Ronald Reagan and Democratic House candidates. More split election outcomes occurred in the six elections between 1968 and 1988 than in the twelve elections between 1920 and 1964. Party now provides less structure to voting, in the sense of shaping the choices of voters, than in the past.[18]

Evidence that the party linkage between voters and government has atrophied can also be found in the contrast between presidential votes in the nineteenth and twentieth centuries. In the sixteen presidential elections from 1836 to 1896, only the election of 1872 was of landslide dimensions—that is, an election in which the winning candidate received 55 percent or more of the two-party vote. By contrast, eleven of twenty-three presidential elections from 1900 through 1988 were decided by landslide margins. Party switching from one election to the next has

TABLE 7-2 Congressional Districts with Split Election Results: Districts Carried by a Presidential Candidate of One Major Party and by a House Candidate of Other Major Party, 1920-1988

Year and party of the winning presidential candidate	Number of districts	Number of districts with split results	Percentage
1920 R	344	11	3.2
1924 R	356	42	11.8
1928 R	359	68	18.9
1932 D	355	50	14.1
1936 D	361	51	14.1
1940 D	362	53	14.6
1944 D	367	41	11.2
1948 D	422	90	21.3
1952 R	435	84	19.3
1956 R	435	130	29.9
1960 D	437	114	26.1
1964 D	435	145	33.3
1968 R	435	141	32.4
1972 R	435	193	44.4
1976 D	435	124	28.5
1980 R	435	141	32.4
1984 R	435	191	43.9
1988 R	435	148	34.0
Total	7,278	1,817	24.9

SOURCE: Milton C. Cummings, Jr., *Congressmen and the Electorate* (New York: Free Press, 1966), 32 (as updated).

NOTE: R = Republican; D = Democrat. Presidential returns for some congressional districts were not available between 1920 and 1948.

become increasingly common, and the party-oriented voter of the last century has been displaced by the volatile, candidate-oriented voter of this one. Consider the recent past. Democrats by the millions deserted their party's presidential nominee in 1952, Adlai E. Stevenson, to vote for the Republican candidate, Dwight D. Eisenhower. Similarly, Republicans in droves cast their ballots for Lyndon B. Johnson in 1964 instead of for Barry Goldwater, thus contributing substantially to the landslide Democratic vote. Even more massive switches occurred in 1968 and 1972. In the latter election, one-third of all Democrats voted for the Republican presidential nominee, Richard Nixon. Even in 1976, an election in which party affiliation again surfaced, nearly one out of five

Democratic identifiers voted for the GOP presidential candidate. A major reason for Ronald Reagan's victory in 1980 was that fully one-fourth of all Democrats voted for him, and his support among Democrats was almost as great in 1984. Fifteen percent of all Democrats voted for George Bush in 1988.

Departisanization of the electorate contributes significantly to the insularity of politics and elections. John R. Petrocik and Dwaine Marvick describe this nexus:

> State and local candidates find their fate almost unrelated to the success of the national ticket. With the decline in party loyalty among voters and the development of skills and resources that increase the individuality of any given candidate, only a notoriously weak national ticket seems able to influence congressional, state legislative, or city council elections.[19]

3. The steady weakening of group attachments to the Democratic party in presidential elections.

Since Harry S. Truman's election in 1948, the Democratic party has won only three of ten presidential elections—in 1960 (Kennedy), 1964 (Johnson), and 1976 (Carter). Among the explanations for the party's weakness, two stand out. One is that Democratic presidential candidates have been rejected by independents. Between 1952 and 1984, the Democratic presidential candidate gained a majority of the vote of independents only in 1964, a landslide Democratic year. In recent elections, this large group of voters has strongly supported the Republican candidate. Sixty-seven percent of independents voted for Reagan in 1984 and 57 percent for Bush in 1988. Independents represent about 25 percent of the turnout.

But a more important reason is that the Democratic coalition, which emerged during the presidency of Franklin D. Roosevelt, has lost much of its potency. In election after election from the 1930s to the mid-1960s, Democratic presidential candidates received strong, sometimes overwhelming, support from Catholics, blacks, southerners, blue collar (especially union) workers, ethnic minorities, big-city dwellers, and young voters. A dramatic shift in support among these groups has occurred (see Table 7-3). The changes among Catholics, white southerners, and younger voters are particularly striking. In 1960 and 1964 about three out of four Catholics voted for John F. Kennedy and Lyndon

TABLE 7-3 Shifting Groups and Changing Party Fortunes: Major Democratic Losses among Demographic Groups since 1960

Demographic group	Percentage Democratic					Percentage point loss by Democrats from 1960 to 1988
	1960 (Kennedy)	1964 (Johnson)	1976 (Carter)	1984 (Mondale)	1988 (Dukakis)	
Catholics	78	76	57	39	51	27
Age 18-29	54	64	53	40	37	17
Southerners	51	52	54	37	40	11
Manual workers	60	71	58	46	50	10
Whites	49	59	46	34	41	8
Men	52	60	53	38	44	8
High school graduates	52	62	54	43	46	6
Southern whites	a	a	47	28	33	a

SOURCE: Developed from data in *Gallup Report*, November 1988, 6-7; and in *Public Opinion*, December/January 1985, 4, and January/February 1989, 34.

[a] Not available. Note that Democratic presidential support from southern whites has dropped 14 percentage points since 1976.

Johnson. Support among Catholics for Jimmy Carter was also relatively high. Even though Michael S. Dukakis attracted many more Catholic voters in 1988 than Walter F. Mondale did in 1984, the proportion was still well below earlier levels. Younger voters are much more likely to vote Republican today than formerly. A mainstay of the traditional Democratic coalition, southern whites have abandoned the party in droves: a mere 28 percent voted for Mondale and only 33 percent for Dukakis. For the Democrats, group defections have become the norm.

The groups that have remained staunchly Democratic are few. Heading the list is the black community, which votes overwhelmingly Democratic in election after election. The black vote for Mondale and Dukakis was about 90 percent. Also, about two out of three Jews, Hispanics, and unemployed voted for the Democratic candidates in 1984 and 1988.[20]

Republican support, by contrast, has surged. Ronald Reagan received 72 percent of the vote of white Protestants, and George Bush received 66 percent. Bush received an extraordinary 81 percent of the vote of evangelical Christians, while Reagan received 78 percent. White

Protestants and evangelical Christians made up more than half of the voting public in 1988. About two out of three upper-income voters ($50,000 and over) supported the Republican candidates in 1984 and 1988.[21]

The erosion of the Democratic coalition does not necessarily presage an endless stream of Republican victories. Events and policy failures can undermine administrations and the party in power. Voters who have shifted away from the Democratic party can shift back. The stability of the Republican coalition will be tested—with George Bush, not Ronald Reagan, at the head of the ticket. And presidential popularity and party popularity are not the same thing. Nevertheless, it seems improbable that the Democratic coalition fashioned during the Roosevelt era can be restored. Too many changes have taken place. The dilemma is that the New Deal (and its successors) turned many "have nots" into "haves" and reduced the saliency and appeal of the party's traditional economic issues. The New Deal, in effect, sowed the seeds of its own destruction. Key elements in the party's traditional following, with their status changed, their confidence in the economy heightened, have found fewer reasons to vote as they did in the past. Switching to the Republican side has not been all that difficult for them. The intriguing question asks what these groups will do in the future.

4. The growth of racial polarization in voting.

Historically, the great divide in racial voting occurred in the 1960s, beginning with a massive shift by blacks in 1964 and continuing with a sizable shift by whites in 1968. In broad outline, this is what happened: Under the leadership of President Johnson, a bipartisan majority in Congress passed the Civil Rights Act of 1964, the most significant civil rights legislation since Reconstruction. The Republican National Convention shortly chose as its presidential nominee Barry Goldwater, a militant conservative, an exponent of states' rights, and one of the main opponents of the 1964 act. With the lines clearly drawn, blacks voted overwhelmingly (94 percent) for Johnson in November (see Table 7-4). Of the six states carried by Goldwater, five were in the Deep South, where his states' rights/civil rights stance undoubtedly was attractive to white voters. Following Johnson's landslide victory, a top-heavy Democratic Congress passed an even more important civil rights bill: the Voting Rights Act of 1965. This landmark legislation paved the way for

TABLE 7-4   Growing Racial Polarization in Voting in Presidential Elections

	1956	1960	1964	1968	1972	1976	1980	1984	1988
Percentage of electorate voting Democratic	42	50	61	43	38	50	41	41	46
Percentage of whites voting Democratic	41	49	59	38	32	46	36	34	41
Percentage of blacks voting Democratic [a]	61	68	94	85	87	85	86	87	82
Racial differential: percentage point difference between black and white Democratic vote	20	19	35	47	55	39	50	53	41

SOURCE: Developed from data in *Gallup Report,* November 1988, 6-7.

[a] Technically, this is the nonwhite vote. If the black vote were completely separated from other nonwhite votes, the black Democratic proportion would be several percentage points higher. In 1988, for example, the black vote in the *New York Times* survey was 86 percent, while ABC exit polls reported it as 90 percent. See the *New York Times,* November 10, 1988; and *Washington Post,* November 9, 1988.

blacks to enter fully into the nation's political life.

By 1968, as a result of movement by white voters, black-white voting divisions intensified; 85 percent of blacks but only 38 percent of whites voted Democratic. With a southerner, Jimmy Carter, at the head of the ticket in 1976, more whites (but less than a majority) voted Democratic than in either of the previous two elections. But this election was merely a blip—a modest exception to a profound trend. Today there are no signs that racial cleavages are ebbing, and the current split is particularly sharp. In 1988 roughly nine out of ten blacks voted for Michael Dukakis, while six out of ten whites voted for George Bush. The division of the races along party lines, grounded in economic policies as well as civil rights, is one of the outstanding facts of contemporary American politics.[22]

5. The emergence of distinctive spheres in party office holding, reflected in the election of Republican presidents and Democratic congressional majorities.

National elections of the last several decades have usually turned on a form of "branch" politics. Republicans regularly win the presidency, while Democrats regularly win Congress (though Republicans held the Senate for six of eight years during the Reagan administration). Republicans have won five of the last six presidential elections and seven of the last ten, often by huge margins in the electoral college (see Figure 7-1). The party's electoral college advantage stems largely from its firm regional bases in the South (once the "solid" Democratic South) and the West. States in these fast-growing regions have consistently supported Republican candidates in recent elections. The Democrats are simply no match for the Republicans in having predictable regional or state support in presidential elections. That is the root of the party's problem.

The Democratic party is the nation's "legislative party," invariably winning the House and ordinarily winning the Senate. From the Ninety-first (1969-1970) through the 102d Congresses (1991-1992), the Democrats won an average of 60 percent of the House seats and 54 percent of the Senate seats. Democratic legislative successes, especially in the House (controlled continuously by the party since 1955), stem largely from four factors, the first three closely related: substantial ticket splitting, growing candidate-centered voting accompanied by defections among Republican partisans, heightened significance of incumbency in elections, and gerrymandering by Democratic-controlled state legislatures. Split-ticket voting has become increasingly frequent. A common pattern shows voters supporting a Republican candidate for president and a Democratic candidate for the House (see the winning combinations in Table 7-5). Voters may prefer a Republican in the White House, but to minister to local needs they lean toward Democratic House candidates. It strains the imagination to learn that almost twelve million persons who voted for George Bush in 1988 did not vote for a Republican House candidate. By contrast, Democratic House candidates garnered nearly two million more votes than their presidential candidate, Michael Dukakis.

Massive split-ticket voting is perhaps the best evidence that party-centered elections have been displaced by candidate-centered ones. And as partisanship has ebbed, the number of party identifiers who vote for the candidate of the other party has grown. Currently, about 20 percent of all party identifiers defect in House elections to vote for the candidate of the other party.[23] And at least three-fourths of these defections take place in the challenger's party, thus strengthening the reelection bids of incumbents.[24] For this and other reasons, incumbents are extremely difficult to defeat; in election after election 90 percent or more of all

FIGURE 7-1 Republican Dominance in Presidential Elections, 1952-1988

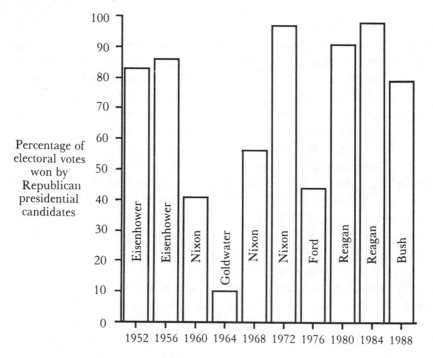

House incumbents on the ballot (98 percent in 1988 and 96 percent in 1990) are reelected. Long dominant in the House, the Democratic party is the main beneficiary of the voters' decisive preference for incumbents. Put another way, the current successes of Democratic incumbents are derived from their past successes. When incumbency reigns, victories beget victories.[25]

Gerrymandering of congressional districts is the final piece of the puzzle. These district lines are drawn by state legislatures, where the Democratic party typically controls between two and three times as many chambers as the Republican party. Following the 1988 election, for example, Democrats held majorities in sixty-eight state chambers as contrasted with twenty-nine for the Republicans. Democrats controlled both chambers in twenty-eight states while Republicans controlled both in only eight.

Party control of the legislature is an invitation to draw district lines to serve the interests of party candidates. Leaders of both parties know their way around in gerrymandering, but the weakness of the Republi-

TABLE 7-5   Election Outcomes in Voting for President and House Members in
1988: Party Unity and Party Splits in 435 Congressional Districts

	Number	Percentage
Bush and Republican House candidate	162	37
Bush and Democratic House candidate	135	31
Dukakis and Democratic House candidate	125	29
Dukakis and Republican House candidate	13	3

SOURCE: *Congressional Quarterly Weekly Report,* July 8, 1989, 1710-1711. Split-party outcomes occurred in 52 percent of all districts in the South, 31 percent in the East and the Midwest, and 15 percent in the West.

cans at the state legislative level has limited their ability to manipulate district lines for partisan purposes. The Democratic party has been notably successful in getting the most from its electoral support. The evidence lies in the ratio between the national House vote and seats won (see Table 7-6). In 1988 the Democratic party won 54 percent of the nationwide House vote but nearly 60 percent of the House seats—a profit margin to which the party has grown accustomed. This persistent imbalance prompts national Republican leaders to argue that gerrymandering has given the Democrats at least twenty House seats that "belong" to the Republicans. Democratic gains in 1990 gubernatorial and state legislative elections promised to make redistricting struggles even more difficult for the Republicans.

Voting patterns are not static. Although the Republicans have held a House majority for only four years since 1931 (1947-1948, 1953-1954), the party's long-haul prospects may be somewhat brighter. In the first place, Republican strength in southern congressional races has grown significantly in the last twenty-five years. Second, when a southern Democratic House incumbent dies or retires, the odds are reasonably good (about four out of ten from 1952 to 1974) that his successor will be a Republican.[26] Two out of three southern representatives today are Democrats; three out of four were Democrats in the 1970s. And finally, the Supreme Court's new position on gerrymanders, making flagrant ones subject to invalidation, generally will serve Republican interests more fully than Democratic ones.[27]

TABLE 7-6 The Relationship between Nationwide Party Vote Totals and Seats
Won by Parties, U.S. House of Representatives, for Presidential
Election Years 1972-1988

	1972	1976	1980	1984	1988
Nationwide vote for Democratic House candidates	51.7%	55.9%	50.4%	52.1%	54.0%
House seats won by Democrats	55.9	67.1	55.9	58.2	59.8
Nationwide vote for Republican House candidates	46.4	42.0	48.0	47.0	46.0
House seats won by Republicans	44.1	32.9	44.1	41.8	40.2
"Unearned" increment of seats gained by Democrats	4.2	11.2	5.5	6.1	5.8

SOURCE: Developed from data in *Congressional Quarterly Weekly Report,* March 31, 1979, 575; April 13, 1985, 687; and May 6, 1989, 1063.

As for the other party sphere, the presidency, there is no reason to believe that the Republican party has a lock on it. This is a highly competitive office. Hence the durability of the two-tiered (executive-legislative) electoral system remains to be seen. In the short run, it is more likely to be disrupted by a Democratic presidential victory than by a Republican sweep of both houses of Congress.

6. The escalation of interest-group activity.

The growth in the number and influence of interest groups is one of the key developments in American politics in recent years. Members of Congress have become acutely sensitive to the power of lobbies. To quote former senator Abraham Ribicoff (D-Conn.): "Lobbying has reached a new dimension and is more effective than ever in history. It has become a big computerized operation in which the Congress and the public are being bombarded by single-issue groups." [28]

The increasing influence of interest groups has contributed to the weakening of the parties. Parties and interest groups compete for the same political space. When legislators are more concerned with satisfying interest-group claims than with supporting party positions and leaders, the vitality of legislative party organizations is sapped. When party lines collapse, collective responsibility for decisions is diminished. Increasingly, individual members are on their own, crowded and pressured by groups intent on getting their way. Rep. David R. Obey (D-

Wis.) said: "It's a lot more difficult to say no to anybody because so many people have well-oiled mimeograph machines." [29] Or, in the grimly blunt words of Sen. Edward M. Kennedy (D-Mass.): "We have the best Congress money can buy. Congress is awash in contributions from special interests that expect something in return." [30]

The current controversy over interest groups focuses on their campaign contributions to candidates for office. Political action committees have become a dominant force in financing congressional campaigns, especially for House seats. Overall, PAC contributions to House and Senate candidates in the 1988 election reached $148 million, an increase of $43 million over 1984 contributions. Forty-seven percent of all campaign funds received by House incumbents in 1988 came from political action committees. The average House incumbent accepted nearly $200,000 from assorted PACs, almost eight times as much as PACs gave to the average House challenger. Currently, about 30 percent of all campaign funds collected by Senate candidates is derived from PACs. For forty-one Senate candidates in 1988, PAC contributions amounted to more than $500,000.[31] The data on funding point in the same direction: congressional candidates have become increasingly dependent on interest-group money. And it is not unreasonable for writers, politicians, public interest groups such as Common Cause, and the public to wonder whether those public officials whose campaigns are heavily financed by PACs find their independence compromised in the policy-making process. Legislation to reduce PAC contributions in congressional campaigns has become a persistent item on the congressional agenda, and prospects for adoption have increased.

Another dimension of the interest-group problem is that of single-issue groups.[32] Their issue is *the* issue; their position is the one on which legislators are to be judged. The compromises that occur naturally to practical politicians seldom carry much weight with the leaders of single-issue groups; members are either for or against gun control, abortion, tax reductions, equal rights, nuclear power, environmental safeguards, prayer in the public schools, or any of a number of other issues including certain foreign policies for which there are active domestic constituencies. Insistent groups gather on each side of each of these troublesome questions. And legislators do not find it easy to hide from these groups, especially since decision-making processes have become increasingly open as a result of the reform wave of the 1970s.

Weakened parties provide slim protection for the harassed legislator in a free-for-all system. Middle-of-the-road politicians find themselves in trouble. Public service itself becomes increasingly frustrating in a politics of tiptoe and tightrope. Shortly before he was defeated for reelection in 1978, a northern Democratic senator observed:

> The single-interest constituencies have just about destroyed politics as I knew it. They've made it miserable to be in office—or to run for office—and left me feeling it's hardly worth the struggle to survive.[33]

The "special cause" quality of much of contemporary politics is also reflected in these comments by a leading official in Minnesota's Democratic-Farmer-Labor party:

> Frankly, there are very few of us in the party leadership now whose primary goal is the election of candidates committed to a broad liberal agenda. Most of the people in control are there to advance their own special causes. From the time we spend on it, you would think the most important problem in the world is whether there should be speedboats on six lakes in northern Minnesota.[34]

The arrival of narrow issue politics has changed the American political landscape. Pragmatic politics has been diminished and compromise has declined as a way of doing business. In forming their positions on certain inflammatory, high-principle issues, members believe that there is a reduced margin for error. A wrong vote can cost them electoral support and produce new challenges to their reelection. And not in a few cases members believe they are faced with a no-win vote—where a vote on either side of a controversial, high-visibility issue appears likely to damage their electoral security.

7. The public's declining confidence in political institutions.

The confidence of the American public in its social and political institutions is substantially lower today than it was two or three decades ago. Nevertheless, it is not as low as it was in the mid-1970s.

Popular disillusionment concerning politics and political institutions did not simply emerge as a result of the revelations of Watergate. This trend began earlier (see Table 7-7). The disclosures of criminal activities by leading officials of the White House, and President Nixon's role in the coverup, merely accentuated it.

No simple explanation exists for the decline of trust in government.

TABLE 7-7 Popular Trust in Government, 1964-1988

Response	1964	1970	1972	1974	1978	1980	1984	1988
Always	14%	7%	5%	3%	3%	2%	4%	4%
Most of the time	62	47	48	34	27	23	40	37
Some or none of the time	22	44	45	62	68	73	54	58
Don't know	2	2	2	1	2	2	2	1
N [a]	1,445	1,497	2,279	2,499	2,288	1,606	1,921	1,768

SOURCE: National Election Studies, Center for Political Studies, University of Michigan.

NOTE: Question: How much of the time do you think you can trust the government in Washington to do what is right—just about always, most of the time, or only some of the time?

[a] NAs excluded.

Many factors have been at work, probably the most important of which centers on public dissatisfaction with policy outcomes—involving urban unrest and riots in the 1960s, the Vietnam War, and the government's inability to solve certain social and economic problems. The public's negative evaluations of the performance of several presidents also likely contributed to the erosion of public confidence in government.

Whatever the explanation, many voters have a cynical view of government. About six out of ten people now believe, for example, that "government is pretty much run by a few big interests looking out for themselves." And about half of those surveyed agree with the proposition that "public officials don't care much what people like me think" (see Figure 7-2).

Declining trust in government has affected the party system. Though the evidence is elusive, the loosening of ties to party (as manifested in the large number of independent voters and the increase in ticket splitting), the influx and successes of celebrity candidates, the preponderance of candidate-centered campaigns, the popular fascination with anti-establishment candidates, the apparent success of negative campaigns, and the preoccupation with party reform probably all bear a relationship to the depletion of popular good will toward government and to the generalized skepticism concerning political institutions.

Nothing about this condition of declining trust is immutable. Changes in political leadership, reorientations in governmental policies

FIGURE 7-2   Evidence of Public Alienation from Government

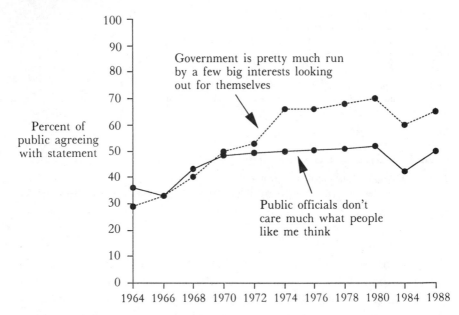

SOURCE: Data drawn from National Election Studies, Center for Political Studies, University of Michigan.

leading to amelioration or resolution of nagging problems, successful new policy ventures, and the more complete fulfillment of popular expectations could strengthen trust in government.

8. The growing importance of professional campaign management firms and the media in politics.

One of the principal facts to be known about the party system today is that American party organizations no longer dominate the process of winning political support for the candidates who run under their labels. The role of party organizations in campaigns has declined as professional management firms, pollsters, and media specialists—stirred by the prospects of new accounts and greater profits—have arrived on the political scene. Indeed, so important have they become in political campaigns, especially for major offices, that it often appears as if the party has been reduced to the role of spectator. To be sure, the parties continue to raise and spend money, to staff their headquarters with salaried personnel and volunteers, and to seek to turn out the vote on election day. What they do matters, but much less so than in the past.

The center of major political campaigns now lies in the decisions and activities of individual candidates and in their use of consultants, campaign management firms, and the mass media—not in the party organizations or in the decisions of party leaders. Modern political campaigning calls for resources and skills that the parties can furnish only in part (more so on the Republican than Democratic side). Public opinion surveys are needed to pinpoint important issues, to locate sources of support and opposition, and to learn how voters appraise the qualities of the candidate. Electronic data processing is useful in the analysis of voting behavior and for the simulation of campaign decisions. For a fee, candidates with sufficient financial resources can avail themselves of specialists of all kinds: public relations, advertising, fund raising, communications, and financial counseling. They can hire experts in film making, speech writing, speech coaching, voter registration, direct-mail letter campaigns, computer information services, time buying (for radio and television), voter analysis, get-out-the-vote drives, and campaign strategy. Fewer and fewer things are left to chance or to the vicissitudes of party administration. What a candidate hears, says, does, wears, and possibly even thinks bears the heavy imprint of the specialist in campaign management.

Campaign consulting is a growth industry. Consultants whose candidates win upset or overwhelming victories are celebrated by politicians and the media alike. They are hot commodities, and candidates vie to purchase their services. Folklore develops that the right consultant is the key to victory.

A seemingly endless variety of services are made available to candidates by management firms. The Campaign Communications Institute of America (CCI) has an arrangement under which a candidate low on cash can charge services on his American Express card. A glimpse of other services CCI provides may be gained from this account:

> Under a middleman arrangement with some 35 manufacturing and service firms, [CCI] has produced a swollen bag of personalized vote-getting tricks. There are the routine items—bumper stickers, buttons, litter bags, matchbooks, posters, and flags. But there is also a $19.95 tape-playing machine that enables the candidate to carry his inspirational messages into the homes of voters over the telephone. There

are Hertz rental cars equipped with bullhorn sound systems. And there is a $39.95 portable projector that flashes slogans, pictures, and platforms on anything from a living-room wall to the side of an office building. "Our job," the board chairman of CCI has said, "is to enable the low-budget candidate to get the most votes for his bucks."

For well-heeled candidates, CCI will also arrange mass telephone campaigns at a cent and a half a call, state-wide voter polls (sample prices: $4,000 for Vermont, $9,000 for New York) and direct campaigns through Western Union Services or New York's big Reuben H. Donnelly Corporation. . . . "Whenever and wherever people elect people, we'll be there," says the CCI board chairman. "That's our market." [35]

The coming of age of the mass media, technocracy, and the techniques of mass persuasion has had a marked impact on the political system.[36] A new politics has emerged that is dominated by image makers and technical experts of all kinds—organizations and persons who know what people want in their candidates and how to give it to them. Consider these views and prognoses for an issueless, pseudopolitics:

It is not surprising . . . that politicians and advertising men should have discovered one another. And, once they recognized that the citizen did not so much vote for a candidate as make a psychological purchase of him, not surprising that they began to work together. . . . Advertising agencies have tried openly to sell Presidents since 1952. When Dwight Eisenhower ran for reelection in 1956, the agency of Batton, Barton, Durstine and Osborn, which had been on a retainer throughout his first four years, accepted his campaign as a regular account. Leonard Hall, national Republican chairman, said: "You sell your candidates and your programs the way a business sells its products." [37]

Day-by-day campaign reports spin on through regular newscasts and special reports. The candidates make their progress through engineered crowds, taking part in manufactured pseudo events, thrusting and parrying charges, projecting as much as they can, with the help of makeup and technology, the qualities of youth, experience, sincerity, popularity, alertness, wisdom, and vigor. And television follows them, hungry for material that is new and sensational. The new campaign strategists also generate films that are like syrupy documentaries: special profiles of candidates, homey, bathed in soft light, resonant with stirring music, creating personality images such as few mortals could emulate.[38]

In all countries the party system has folded like the organization chart. Policies and issues are useless for election purposes, since they are too specialized and hot. The shaping of a candidate's integral image has taken the place of discussing conflicting points of view.[39]

[Party] organizations find themselves increasingly dependent on management and consultant personnel, pollsters, and image-makers. The professional campaigners, instead of being the handmaidens of our major political parties, are independent factors in American elections. Parties turn to professional technicians for advice on how to restructure their organizations, for information about their clienteles, for fund-raising, and for recruiting new members. Candidates, winning nominations in primaries with the aid of professional campaigners rather than that of political parties, are increasingly independent of partisan controls. The old politics does not rest well beside the new technology.[40]

If we get the visual that we want, it doesn't matter as much what words the networks use in commenting on it.[41]

If you're not on television, you don't exist.[42]

No matter what happens, the national political parties of the future will no longer be the same as in the past. Television has made the voter's home the campaign amphitheater, and opinion surveys have made it his polling booth. From this perspective, he has little regard for or need of a political party, at least as we have known it, to show him how to release the lever on Election Day.[43]

9. The increasing nationalization of politics.

So unobtrusively has the change come about that a great many American citizens are unaware of the extent to which sectional political alignments have been replaced by a national political alignment. The Republican vote in the South in the 1952 presidential election was, it turns out, more than a straw in the wind. Eisenhower carried four southern states, narrowly lost several others, made the Republican party respectable for many southern voters, and, most important, laid the foundation for the development of a viable Republican party throughout the South.

From the latter part of the nineteenth century until recently, the main obstacle to the nationalization of politics was the strength of the Democratic party in the South. Presidential, congressional, state, and local offices were won, as a matter of course, by the Democrats. No longer is this the case. Republicans now dominate presidential elections in the South. In the three elections of the 1980s, for example, among southern states only Georgia (in 1980) voted for the Democratic presidential candidate. To recapture the South, popular wisdom suggests, the Democrats may have to nominate a southern candidate. A southern vice-presidential candidate on the ticket (Lloyd Bentsen in 1988) is not sufficient.

Republican gains in southern congressional elections have also been impressive (see Table 7-8). The Republican statewide percentage of the vote for representative has grown more or less steadily since the 1950s. About one-third of all House members elected in the South from 1984 through 1990 were Republicans. Vigorous two-party competition occurs even in the states of the Deep South (Alabama, Georgia, Louisiana, Mississippi, and South Carolina). In the 1950s, by contrast, the Republican party rarely even nominated candidates for the House of Representatives in these states. And throughout the South Republican candidates for the Senate now compete much more effectively than in the past. A strong breeze of Republicanism has been coursing through southern electorates.

The movement from parochial to national politics has not been limited to the South. No matter what its history of party allegiance and voting, no state is wholly secure from incursions by the minority party. The vote in presidential elections[44] now tends to be distributed more or less evenly throughout the country; fewer and fewer states register overwhelming victories for one or the other of the major parties. One-party political systems dwindle. "It is probably safe to say that in national and state-wide politics we are in the time of the most intense, evenly-spaced, two-party competitiveness of the last 100 years." [45]

The sources for the growing nationalization of American politics are both numerous and varied. Social changes, rather than conscious party efforts to extend their spheres of influence, have provided the principal thrust for the new shape given to American party politics. Among the most important of these has been the emergence and extraordinary development of the mass media in political communications. Through the electronic media, national political figures can be created virtually overnight, national issues can be carried to the most remote and inaccessible community, and new styles and trends can become a matter of common knowledge in a matter of days or weeks. Insulation, old loyalties, and established patterns are difficult to maintain intact in the

TABLE 7-8   Republican Percentage of the Statewide Major-Party Vote for the
U.S. House of Representatives, Selected Years, Southern States

State	Republican statewide percentage							
	1950	1952	1968	1978	1982	1984	1986	1988
Alabama	0.7	5.4	30.8	42.9	32.9	27.3	33.0	37.4
Arkansas	0.0	14.3	53.0	66.1	47.6	21.0	41.5	41.7
Florida	9.6	25.9	42.8	41.7	40.8	48.9	44.4	53.0
Georgia	0.0	0.0	20.5	32.6	33.8	28.3	37.9	33.3
Louisiana	0.0	8.7	18.8	50.0	a	a	a	a
Mississippi	0.0	2.5	7.5	36.9	42.0	38.5	47.3	33.6
North Carolina	30.0	32.2	45.4	35.9	44.3	47.6	43.3	44.2
South Carolina	0.0	2.0	32.8	37.6	45.5	48.4	42.4	44.4
Tennessee	30.3	29.8	51.1	47.3	37.8	44.8	49.2	38.9
Texas	9.5	1.3	28.1	40.6	32.4	42.3	50.9	40.3
Virginia	24.9	31.0	46.4	50.2	53.1	55.8	54.0	57.3

SOURCE: Developed from data in *The 1968 Elections* (Washington, D.C.: Republican
National Committee, 1969), 115-116; and *Congressional Quarterly Weekly Report*, November 9, 1974, 3084-3091; November 11, 1978, 3283-3291; November 6, 1982, 2817-2825;
April 13, 1985, 689-695; November 8, 1986, 2864-2870; and May 6, 1989, 1074-1080.

[a] In Louisiana, House candidates run on a nonpartisan ballot in the September primary. If no
candidate receives a majority in the district, the top two (irrespective of party) face each other
in November. Candidates who receive a majority in the primary are considered to be elected.

face of contemporary political communications. Consider these observations by Harvey Wheeler:

> Eisenhower was himself a newcomer to party politics. . . . He was
> heavily financed. He employed expensive and sophisticated mass
> media experts. "Madison Avenue" techniques were devised to project
> a predesigned "image." A new kind of electoral coalition was formed,
> composed largely of urban, white-collar people dissociated from the
> grass roots traditions of the agrarian past. His campaign cut across
> traditional party lines to orient itself about the personality of the
> candidate rather than the machine or the party. The new coalition of
> voter groups was socially and geographically mobile. The new politics required image manipulators rather than ballot box stuffers. The
> new organizations were ad hoc affairs created overnight by national
> cadres of advance men. The presidential primary overshadowed the
> party convention. This was to be the wave of the future. Television
> truly nationalized campaign communications and undermined the
> federal structure of the old machines. Party politics gave way to
> personality politics.[46]

Growing Republicanism in the South

	Republican party performance in southern states					
	1948	1952	1964	1968	1984	1988
Presidential						
Percentage of two-party popular vote	36	49	47	53	63	59
Percentage of white popular vote	a	a	a	a	72	67
States won	0	5	5	7	13	13
Electoral votes won	0	65	47	74	155	155
Percentage of electoral votes	0	45	32	51	100	100
Congressional						
Percentage of House seats held following election	3	8	15	26	36	34
Percentage of Senate seats held following election	0	4	15	27	46	35
Gubernatorial						
Percentage of governorships held following election	0	0	8	38	15	46
State legislative						
Percentage of chambers controlled following election	0	0	0	0	0	0
Percentage of lower house seats held following election	5	6	9	16	24	27
Percentage of upper house seats held following election	4	5	8	15	19	23
Party identification						
Percentage Republican overall	a	a	15	17	36	34
Percentage of white southerners						
Strong Republicans	a	4	8	5	11	14
Weak Republicans	a	7	7	8	13	12
Independent Republicans	a	3	6	12	15	15

SOURCE: The data are drawn from a variety of sources, including *Congressional Quarterly Weekly Report, Statistical Abstract of the United States, Book of the States,* and *Gallup Opinion Index.* The data on the party identification of white southerners are from the Center for Political Studies, University of Michigan, some of which are reported in Raymond E. Wolfinger and Michael G. Hagen, "Republican Prospects: Southern Comfort," *Public Opinion* 8 (October/November 1985): 9. Also see *Public Opinion* 12 (January/February 1989): 34.

[a] Not available.

For all their importance to the changes under way, the electronic media have not by themselves transformed the face of American politics. Changes in technology, the diversification of the economic bases of the states, the growth of an affluent society, the higher educational attainments of voters, the mobility of the population, the migration of black citizens to the North, the enfranchisement of black citizens in the South, the illumination of massive nationwide problems, the growth of vast urban conglomerations, and the assimilation of immigrant groups have all contributed to the erosion of internal barriers and parochialism and, consequently, to the strengthening of national political patterns. Whatever the complete explanation for this phenomenon, one thing is clear: the forces for the nationalization of politics are far more powerful than the forces for localism and sectionalism. A changing party system is the inevitable result.

10. A continuation of party competition based on meaningful policy differences between the parties.

The American parties are often criticized for being Tweedledum and Tweedledee—for being so similar that even attentive voters can miss the alternatives they present. This criticism has limited merit. Consider, first of all, the ideology and policy attitudes of Democratic and Republican elites—in this case, delegates to the 1988 party conventions (see Figure 7-3). Sixty percent of the Republican delegates described themselves as conservatives, as contrasted with a mere 4 percent of the Democratic delegates. At the other ideological pole, the differences are also striking: liberals made up 39 percent of the Democratic delegates but only 1 percent of the Republican delegates. Neither party elite, it should be stressed, accurately reflected the ideological position of average party members: Democratic delegates were more liberal than the average registered Democrat, while Republican delegates were more conservative than the average registered Republican.

Differences in ideological perception and in political philosophy translate into differences in public policy views and differences on the proper role of government. Fifty-eight percent of the Democratic delegates, for example, thought that government should provide more services; only 3 percent of the Republican delegates held this view. Ninety percent of the Democratic delegates were in favor of increased federal spending on education, as contrasted with 41 percent of the Republican

FIGURE 7-3   The Ideology of Democratic and Republican National Convention
Delegates, 1988, Contrasted with the Ideology of Rank-and-File
Democrats and Republicans

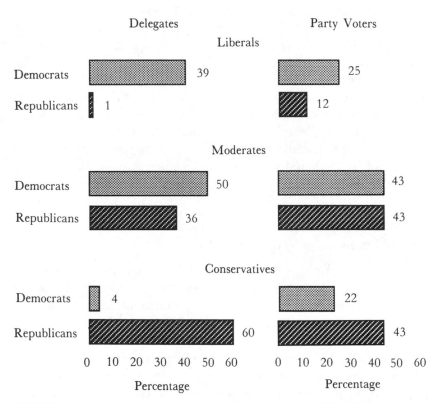

SOURCE: Adapted from various surveys published by *New York Times*/CBS News. See the
issues of the *New York Times* of July 17, 1988, and August 14, 1988.

NOTE: Ideological positions are based on self-classification. Party voters are self-identified
Democrats and Republicans who reported they were registered to vote. Percentages do not add
up to 100 because some respondents were unclassified.

delegates. In terms of the federal role in day care and after-school care
for children, 87 percent of the Democratic delegates but only 36 percent
of the Republican delegates favored increased program funding. Democratic delegates were much more likely to be prochoice than Republican
delegates, while Republican delegates were much more likely to be
prodefense than Democratic delegates.[47] The differences between the
activists of the two parties are important and unmistakable: one set is
clearly liberal, the other is clearly conservative.

Party conflict in Congress also occurs along liberal-conservative lines. Over the years most Democratic members have supported labor-endorsed legislation, measures to provide for government regulation of business, social welfare bills of great variety, civil rights legislation, federal aid to education, and limitations on defense expenditures. By contrast, Republican members have generally favored business over labor, social welfare programs of more modest proportions, private action rather than government involvement, state rather than federal responsibility for domestic programs, the interests of higher-income groups over those of lower-income groups, and a greater emphasis on national defense. When viewing the economy, party members typically focus on different problems: Republicans are more concerned about inflation, Democrats more concerned about unemployment.[48] During the Reagan presidency, party conflict in Congress was particularly intense over the defense budget, arms control, and the administration's support for guerrilla movements opposing leftist regimes.

The important point to recognize is that the parties' weaknesses—particularly apparent in the electoral process—have not clouded the ideological differences between their leaders. Meaningful differences separate the parties in Congress (or at least majorities of the two parties). Even larger differences divide the parties' national convention delegates. Quite plainly, Democratic and Republican party elites do not evaluate public problems in the same light. Nor are they attracted to the same solutions.

Differences between the parties can also be examined from the perspective of the public. The survey data in Table 7-9 show the internal differences within the electoral parties as well as the broad differences between them. Obviously, neither party is monolithic, in the sense that its members share a common set of beliefs. On certain social issues, such as prayer in the public schools and abortions, certain Democratic and Republican subgroups share the same political space—one broadly defined in this Times Mirror study as intolerance for particular personal freedoms. Nevertheless, differences between the voters of the two parties appear to be more important. In their attitudes toward social justice, most Democratic partisans are easily distinguished from most Republican partisans. Democrats are aligned on the side of egalitarianism, social spending, the disadvantaged, and racial equality. They are much more likely than Republicans to favor increased spending on programs that assist minorities, the homeless, the unemployed, and the elderly. Repub-

TABLE 7-9 Party in the Electorate: The Views of Democratic and Republican Voters on Major Social and Economic Issues

Position	Democratic groups				Republican groups	
	'60s Democrats	New Dealers	Passive poor	Partisan poor	Enterprisers	Moralists
Favor constitutional amendment to permit prayers in public schools	52%	83%	83%	81%	69%	88%
Favor mandatory drug testing for government employees	39	78	77	69	58	80
Favor changing laws to make it more difficult for a woman to get an abortion	26	54	47	38	40	60
Favor increased spending on programs that assist minorities	50	39	57	60	12	21
Favor death penalty	53	79	78	66	78	85
Favor cutbacks in defense and military spending	69	49	58	57	31	31
Favor increased spending on:						
programs for the homeless	77	73	82	83	38	62
programs for the unemployed	40	49	62	68	11	30
improving the nation's health care	76	80	85	84	42	68
improving the nation's public schools	80	70	77	77	56	65
aid to farmers	62	69	72	70	29	60
social security	62	76	81	85	29	57
programs for the elderly	79	84	84	87	44	71

SOURCE: Developed from data in *The People, the Press and Politics* (Los Angeles: Times Mirror, 1987), *passim*.

NOTE: '60s Democrats: well-educated, upper-middle class, tolerant on personal freedom issues, mainstream Democrats, committed to social justice. New Dealers: aging, traditional Democrats, blue collar, union members, less tolerant on personal freedom issues, moderate income. Passive poor: aging, poor, less well-educated, uncritical, disproportionately southern, committed to social justice. Partisan poor: firmly Democratic, very low income, poorly educated, urban, disproportionately black, concerned with social justice issues. Enterprisers: affluent, well-educated, white, suburban, probusiness, antigovernment, tolerant on personal freedom issues. Moralists: middle-aged, middle income, white, disproportionately southern, suburban, small cities and rural areas, regular church-goers, anticommunist, prodefense.

lican voters tend to be dubious of big government, fiscally conservative, probusiness, anticommunist, and prodefense spending. Divisions within Republican clusters are less serious than those found on the Democratic side. The profound point is that the policy views of the parties' affiliants differ from one another in significant respects. Put another way, the parties do stand for something in the minds of many voters.

Other evidence on the public's general awareness of party positions is available. Gallup poll survey data presented in Figure 7-4 show the distribution of voters on the recurrent question of which party best represents certain interests, for example, labor or business. Prior to the Reagan administration, the typical survey findings showed that at least one-third of the voters saw no difference between the parties or had no opinion. Since then, the lines between the parties have been drawn more clearly. The Democratic party has consistently emerged as the party of the working class, while the Republican party has been viewed as the party most responsive to the interests of business and professional people as well as white collar workers in general. These perceptions of interest-group orientations form a classic distinction in American politics. They are salient for many voters, helping them to organize political information and to evaluate candidates. Hence in the policy orientations of their elites and in the public mind, the parties do stand for something—almost surely for more than they are given credit.

11. An era of party and governmental reform.

Ordinarily, changes in American politics do not come easily. No democratic political system anywhere rivals the American system for the number of opportunities present to prevent or delay the resolution of public problems or the adoption of new forms and practices. American politics is slow politics. Nonetheless, during the current era many large-scale reforms have found their way into the party structure, into Congress, and into public policies that shape and regulate the political process. In the main, these changes took shape and were adopted during a time in which the political system was in substantial disarray. In the midst of an unpopular war, challenged on all sides, President Johnson withdrew from the presidential election campaign of 1968. Robert F. Kennedy was assassinated. The 1968 Democratic convention, meeting in Chicago, was an ordeal of rancor, tumult, and rioting. And then came the Watergate affair—an assault on the political process itself. Public

FIGURE 7-4   The Public's Perception of the Party Best for Unskilled Workers,
Business Owners and Professional People, and White Collar
Workers, 1947-1984

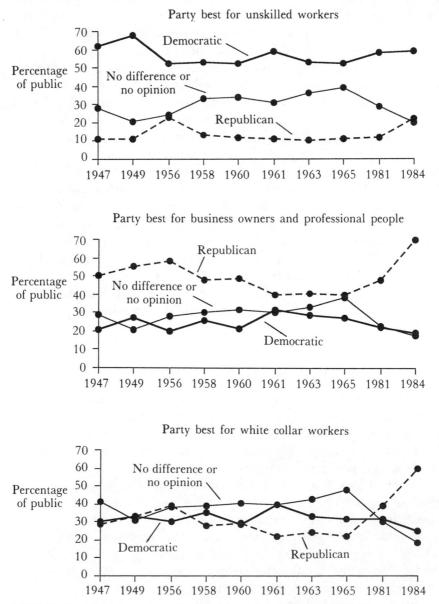

SOURCE: Developed from data in *Gallup Report,* November 1981, 29-45, and January/
February 1985, 21-34.

alienation from the political system, which had been building for years, reached a high point. The stage was set for reform. The success of those who brought it about was due to their ability to seize upon these unusual and transitory circumstances to develop new ways of carrying on political business.

From almost any perspective, the changes were remarkable. More reforms were adopted between 1968 and 1974 than at any time since the early nineteenth century.[49] The power of national party agencies to set standards for state party participation in national nominating conventions was established—and the Supreme Court added its imprimatur to this development. The first national party charter was adopted by the Democrats. At the state level, a number of presidential primary laws were adopted to broaden political participation, and caucus-convention systems were opened up—thus contributing to the democratization of the nominating process. Nor was Congress immune to change. The seniority system was modified by providing for secret caucus ballots on nominees for committee chairmen, thus increasing the responsiveness of these leaders to fellow party members. Committee power itself was dispersed as subcommittees and their chairmen won new measures of authority. The filibuster rule was revised, making it easier for a Senate majority to assert itself. The party caucus took on new roles and new vigor. To reduce the influence of private money and big contributors in political campaigns, the Federal Election Campaign Act was adopted, with its provision for public financing of presidential campaigns. In sum, numerous new choices and opportunities were presented to politicians and public alike.

For the most part, the party reforms of the modern period were designed to democratize political institutions and processes. Concretely, reformers set out to reduce the power of elites (that is, party leaders or "bosses") and to augment the power of ordinary citizens. And they were successful, at least on the surface. But as Nelson W. Polsby has shown, the reforms led to numerous other, unanticipated consequences, particularly on the Democratic side: state party organizations were weakened; party elites lost influence to media elites; candidate organizations came to dominate the presidential selection process; presidential candidates were encouraged to develop factionalist strategies (in seeking to differentiate their candidacies) rather than to build broad coalitions; and the national convention fell under the sway of candidate enthusiasts and interest-group delegates as its role in the presidential nominating process shifted from candidate selection to candidate ratification.[50] These changes are truly momentous.

In evaluating the party reforms, it is easy to lose sight of their relationship to the strength of American parties. As David B. Truman observed recently, the McGovern Commission reforms "could not have been accomplished over the opposition of alert and vigorous state parties. The commission staff exploited the limitations and weaknesses of the state parties; they did not cause them." [51] The reforms, in other words, weakened an institution already in more than a little trouble.

Party reform is thus not the same as party strengthening. A more open political process, for example, does not necessarily contribute to the increased participation of the general public, to a heightening of political trust, or to popular acceptance of the parties. A demographically representative national convention, a central objective of the Democratic reforms, has not led to the selection of candidates who can best represent the party, unify it, or be elected. The public financing of presidential election campaigns has not by any means solved the problem of money in politics, as the spiraling costs of elections and the growing power of PACs show. Changes in party-committee relations in Congress have not altered congressional behavior in significant ways—Congress remains an institution whose members have an unusually low tolerance for hierarchy in any form. The adoption of a national party charter has not diminished the prevailing federalism of American politics or reduced the autonomy of state and local parties on most matters that count.[52]

The reform of the party system must therefore be taken with a grain of salt—for a reason obvious to anyone who began reading this book in advance of this page. American parties are to an important extent the dependent variable in the scheme of politics, more the products of their environment than the architects of it. The only governmental system the parties have known is Madisonian, marked by division of power and made to order for weak parties. Federalism, the separation of powers, and all manner of structural arrangements and election laws (for example, direct primary, candidate-oriented campaign regulations, nonconcurrent terms for executive and legislature, nonpartisan elections, and staggered elections) militate against the development of strong parties. And by diminishing party control over the presidential nominating process, the reforms weakened the only national institution fully empowered to represent the party's constituent elements. The massive use of television for political campaigns, the increasing power of special-interest groups, and the arrival of public relations, media, survey, computer, and fund-raising experts have also contributed heavily to the current candidate-centered system that stresses personality over party and, frequently, style over substance. And for an American public that has never had much enthusiasm for parties, their current desuetude is not likely to be cause for popular concern.

12. A growing effort to professionalize and strengthen party organization.

In this era of overall party decline, there is one bright spot: the increasing strength of parties in organizational terms. Evidence of professionalization and organizational strength is varied. It appears, for example, in the significant growth of permanent and professional party staffs at both national and state committee levels. The national committee's functions have been broadened and diversified, as the committee has shifted from an exclusive preoccupation with presidential matters. The Republican National Committee (RNC) has become heavily involved in a range of party-building activities that include serious efforts to promote party fortunes in state and local election campaigns. Operating budgets for the national committees have grown markedly. The capacity of the national parties to raise funds, particularly in direct-mail campaigns, has improved dramatically—in this respect, the Republican party again led the way, but the Democrats have been gaining ground. On the Democratic side, national party authority has been substantially enlarged through the development of rules for state party participation in national nominating conventions. While the Democratic party has increased the legal authority of its national organization, the new importance of the national Republican apparatus has stemmed from successful fund raising that permits it to offer extensive services to state party organizations and candidates.[53]

The strength of state party organizations, a recent study finds, is partly a function of the party-building activities of the national party organization, leading to greater national-state party integration. State party organizational strength is reflected in matters of program, recruitment, and bureaucratization; specifically, it appears in services to candidates, headquarters' staff size and complexity, newsletters, voter mobilization programs, public opinion polling, headquarters accessibility, candidate recruitment, issue leadership, leadership professionalism, and money contributions to candidates. Many Republican state party organizations score high on these indicators. Virtually without exception, Democratic state organizations are substantially weaker than their Republican counterparts. Nonetheless, the weaker Democratic National Committee seems to have had more success than the stronger RNC in adding to the capabilities of its state party organizations, perhaps because any addition in resources for a weak organization renders it more effective. For the most part, national-state party integration (or influence) is a one-way street, since most state parties rank low in the degree to which they are involved in (and thus influence) national committee affairs.[54]

Professionalism of the parties is clearly on the rise. At the national level, the parties' financial strength never has been greater. Staff development has been impressive. The parties, through their staffs, have become sophisticated in the use of modern campaign technologies that involve computers, electronic mail, television, marketing, advertising, survey research, data processing, and direct-mail solicitations. And of considerable interest, influence generally flows from the national level downward, a distinctly different pattern from the state-dominated party structure of the past.[55]

Intriguing to consider is whether the structural changes and other developments have arrested the parties' downward slide and strengthened their capacity to function as parties. Are they better able to discharge the traditional functions of party involving recruitment, nominations, campaigns, and control of government? Specifically, how strong is party performance today in grooming and recruiting candidates, controlling nominations, managing campaign resources (money, manpower, expertise), electing candidates and controlling a range of offices simultaneously, mobilizing voters, stimulating competition, maintaining effective coalitions and inhibiting factional conflict, illuminating issues and fashioning policy alternatives, representing and integrating group interests, making public policy, enforcing discipline, providing public instruction, winning public acceptance and loyalty, and providing voters with a means for keeping government accountable? Exactly what a resurgence of the parties would consist of is hard to say, but it would seem to require them to conduct these activities, or at least most of them, reasonably well. National fund raising and provision of services aside, the reality is that the parties are unable to do most of these things much, if any, better than in the past. And in certain key respects, the parties seem to be doing substantially worse.

In the old-fashioned sense of party organization as a network of individuals that does grass-roots party work, as Byron Shafer observes, the parties are in "precipitous decline." [56] Unquestionably, the party-in-the-electorate has never been weaker.[57] Partisanship is at low ebb. Candidates and incumbents dominate the electoral system. Party coalitions, the quintessence of American parties, have atrophied. Control over nominations, the sine qua non of strong parties as E. E. Schattschneider and others have argued, is thin and insubstantial at all levels.[58] (And in an ecumenical spirit, but only 5-4, the Supreme Court recently opened the door for independents to vote in party primaries, if the parties approve.)[59] Split-election outcomes and divided government are the norm in nation and state. Party control over government continues to be uneven and unpredictable, and programmatic responsibility, which is occasionally impressive, is typically elusive and erratic. The influence of the media and interest groups in key phases of politics has probably never been greater. Indeed, in the presidential selection process, the media have simply supplanted the parties. The overall condition of American parties thus leaves a great deal to be desired. All things considered, and despite their heightened professionalism and enhanced bureaucratization, the parties are in about the same shape as observers have long known them, which is to say that, at best, they are no more than moderately successful in some of the things they do.

The Prospects

The American party system has been shaped more by custom and environment than by intent. Indeed, in broad contour, the parties of today resemble closely those of previous generations. For as long as can be remembered, the major parties have been loose and disorderly coalitions, heavily decentralized, lacking in unity and discipline, preoccupied with winning office, and no more than erratically responsible for the conduct of government and the formation of public policy. There is, of course, another side to them. They have performed at least as well as the parties of other democratic nations—and perhaps far better. Democratic politics requires the maintenance of a predictable legal system; institutionalized arrangements for popular control of government and the mobilization of majorities; methods and arenas for the illumination, crystallization, and reconciliation of conflict; and means for endowing both leaders and policies with legitimacy. To each of these requirements the parties have contributed steadily and often in major ways.[60]

A truism of American politics is that it is invariably difficult to cut free from familiar institutions. Old practices die hard. Conventional arrangements hang on and on. Change arrives incrementally and unnoticed. Most Americans are habituated to weak parties, and the parties themselves are accustomed to the environment in which they function. It would seem that prospects for the development of a system of responsible parties are thin at best. But the matter deserves a closer look.

On most counts the parties have lost ground in recent years. The electoral party organizations have been weakened. Their control over the nominating process, once a virtual monopoly, has gradually slipped away. Primary battles for major offices appear to occur more and more frequently. So-called independent candidates seem to be more numerous and more successful than in the past. Indeed, many candidates use the party label "in the same spirit that ships sail under Liberian registry—a flag of convenience, and no more." [61] More voters have come to regard themselves as independents than ever before—occasionally independents outnumber Republicans (though not since early in the Reagan administration). The power of local party leaders probably never has been less than it is today. The media, public relations consultants, campaign management firms, and political action committees are now as much a part of campaigns as the party organizations—at least when important offices are at stake. In sum, American parties compete within the political process but do not dominate it. In some jurisdictions they are all but invisible. A great deal of contemporary politics lies outside the parties and beyond their control.

The weakness of the parties makes the prospects dim for the development of a full-blown responsible party system. Too many obstacles—constitutional, political, and otherwise—stand in the way. But this is not to say that responsible party performance in government is unattainable. The way in which parties govern is far from dependent upon the strength and vitality of the electoral party organizations or upon the way in which men and women are elected to office. The party-in-the-government, it is worth remembering, is both different from the party-in-the-electorate and largely independent of it.

The essence of a responsible party system is not to be found in party councils, closed primaries, demographically representative national con-

---

What Would "Strong" Parties Look Like?

In the electorate:

1. Public perception of parties as legitimate and fair.
2. Party electioneering, broad electoral appeal, and well-established "mainstream" constituencies.
3. Sufficient power to limit fragmentation by keeping the nomination stage from becoming a free-for-all among numerous candidates.
4. Sufficient resources (for example, money, manpower, expertise) to perform their functions adequately.

In the government:

5. Power associated with responsibility: the capacity to govern through distinctive cooperation and cohesion among fellow partisans in the policy process.

In electorate and government:

6. The presence of sufficient rewards and incentives to induce support and secure compliance among activists and officeholders.
7. Capacity to limit disaffection and conflict among groups that compose the party coalition.
8. Capacity to adapt in response to changes in the political environment.

SOURCE: This is a modest adaptation of a list of attributes developed in David E. Price, *Bringing Back the Parties* (Washington, D.C.: CQ Press, 1984), 123.

NOTE: Do the parties meet these broad requirements? In my view, the answer is "hardly at all" in the case of 1, 2, 3, and 6 and "moderately at best" in the case of 4, 5, 7, and 8.

---

ventions, off-year party conventions, government financing of elections, or intraparty democracy. Instead, the key idea is represented in party responsibility for a program of public policy. Such responsibility requires, in the first place, a strong measure of internal cohesion within the party-in-the-government in order to adopt its program and, in the second place, an electorate sufficiently sensitive to party accomplishments and failures that it can hold the parties accountable for their records, particularly in the case of the party in power. At times, neither requirement can be met to any degree. Nevertheless, occasionally American political institutions function in a manner largely consonant with the party responsibility model.

A responsible party system at the national level demands a particular kind of Congress—one in which power is centralized rather than dispersed. Over long stretches of time, Congress has not been organized to permit the parties, *qua* parties, to govern. The seniority system, the independence of committees and their chairmen, the filibuster, the weaknesses present in elected party positions and agencies, and the unrepresentativeness of Congress itself have made it difficult for party majorities to assert themselves and to act in the name of the party. These barriers to party majority building have been notably diminished in recent years.

Every so often the congressional party comes fully alive. Consider the first session of the Eighty-ninth Congress (1965)—"the most dramatic illustration in a generation of the capacity of the president and the Congress to work together on important issues of public policy":

> In part a mopping up operation on an agenda fashioned at least in spirit by the New Deal, the work of the 89th Congress cut new paths through the frontier of qualitative issues: a beautification bill, a bill to create federal support for the arts and humanities, vast increases in federal aid to education. . . . [The] policy leadership and the legislative skill of President Johnson found a ready and supportive response from a strengthened partisan leadership and a substantial, presidentially oriented Democratic majority in both houses. A decade of incremental structural changes in the locus of power in both houses eased the President's task of consent-building and of legislative implementation. Yet Congress was far from being just a rubber stamp. On some issues the President met resounding defeat. On many issues, presidential recommendations were modified by excisions or additions—reflecting the power of particular committee chairmen, group interests, and bureaucratic pressures at odds with presidential perspectives.
>
> [The lessons of the Eighty-ninth Congress] proved that vigorous presidential leadership and sizable partisan majorities in both houses of the same partisan persuasion as the President could act in reasonable consonance, and with dispatch, in fashioning creative answers to major problems. The nation's voters could pin responsibility upon a national party for the legislative output. If that partisan majority erred in judgment, it could at least be held accountable in ensuing congressional and presidential elections.[62]

Party responsibility came to the fore again in the Ninety-seventh Congress (1981-1982). President Reagan was the beneficiary of the highest party support scores received by any president over the last three decades. His legislative proposals received unusually strong support in Congress. During the first session of the Ninety-seventh Congress, Senate Republicans voted in agreement with the president 80 percent of the time and House Republicans 68 percent of the time.[63] At session end, Republicans could reasonably claim that their party had moved the nation in a new direction. The major elements of their program consisted of major budget cuts, sizable reductions in individual and business taxes, the largest peacetime defense appropriation in the nation's history, a significant cutback in federal regulations, and a moderate reordering of federal-state relations that gave the states greater discretion in the use of funds provided through federal aid. Consonant with the party responsibility model, the performance of the Reagan administration was the overriding issue in the off-year election of 1982, in which Republicans lost twenty-six seats in the House while holding Democrats to a standoff in Senate races. In sum, presidential leadership, in concert with Republican congressional leaders and bolstered by party imagination and discipline, characterized the Ninety-seventh Congress (especially the first session) almost as much as it had the Eighty-ninth. From the perspective of the president, these were halcyon days, but they passed by quickly. Conflict between the branches intensified, the president's legislative successes declined, and legislative assertiveness during the latter stages of the Reagan administration, and particularly during the One-hundredth Congress (1987-1988), became manifest.

Government by party was conspicuously absent during the first two years of the Bush administration. For one thing, the president's agenda was limited. And equally important, both houses of Congress were dominated by the Democrats. Interparty conflict increased somewhat in the House, while continuing its decline in the Senate. In 1989 fewer "party votes" (majority against majority) took place in the Senate than at any time since 1970. Relatively few measures bore a partisan stamp of any kind. "We have a coalition government now," Sen. Tom Daschle (D-S.D.) observed. "It only works when both sides are on board." [64]

No one should expect party-oriented Congresses to be strung together, one following another. The conditions must be right: a partisan majority in general ideological agreement (or an effective majority, such as the Republican-led conservative coalition in the House during the

The Missing Link in the Party Responsibility Model: An Informed, Attentive Public

Do you happen to know which party had the most members in the House of Representatives in Washington before the election?

> Findings: 41 percent didn't know or selected the wrong party (Republican).

Do you happen to know which party had the most members in the U.S. Senate before the election?

> Findings: 46 percent didn't know or selected the wrong party (Republican).

Would you say that you have generally agreed with the way [your congressperson] has voted on bills, agreed and disagreed about equally, generally disagreed, or haven't you paid much attention to this?

Agreed	17%
Agreed and disagreed about equally	13
Disagreed	3
Haven't paid much attention	67

SOURCE: These questions are drawn from the 1988 presidential election survey, National Election Study, Center for Political Studies, University of Michigan.

Ninety-seventh Congress) and a vigorous president are essential. A long or innovative policy agenda may also be required. In any case, the point not to be missed is that, under the right circumstances, the deadlocks in American politics can be broken and the political system can function vigorously and with a high degree of cooperation between the branches of government. Party responsibility can thrive even if unrecognized and unlabeled. The evidence of these Congresses suggests that the first requirement for government by responsible parties—a fairly high degree of internal party agreement on policy—can, at least occasionally, be met.

The second requirement—an electorate attuned to party performance in government—is a different matter. This is the point at which the total system of responsible parties tends to break down.

What the public knows about the legislative records of the parties and of individual congressional candidates is a principal reason for the departure of American practice from an idealized conception of party government. . . . The electorate sees very little altogether of what goes on in the national legislature. Few judgments of legislative performance are associated with the parties, and much of the public is unaware even of which party has control of Congress. . . . Many of those who have commented on the lack of party discipline in Congress have assumed that the Congressman votes against his party because he is forced to by the demands of one of several hundred constituencies of a superlatively heterogeneous nation. In some cases, the Representative may subvert the proposals of his party because his constituency demands it. But a more reasonable interpretation over a broader range of issues is that the Congressman fails to see these proposals as part of a program on which the party—and he himself—will be judged at the polls, because he knows the constituency isn't looking.[65]

Experiments with forms of party responsibility, like fashion, will perhaps always possess a probationary quality—tried, neglected, forgotten, and rediscovered. The tone and mood of such a system will appear on occasion, but without the public's either anticipating it or recognizing it when it arrives. More generally, however, the party system is likely to resemble, at least in broad lines, the model to which Americans are adjusted and inured: the parties situated precariously atop the political process, threatened and thwarted by a variety of competitors, unable to control their own nominations or to elect "their" nominees, active in fits and starts and often in hiding, beset by factional rifts, shunned or dismissed by countless voters (including many new ones), frustrated by the growing independence of voters, and moderately irresponsible. From the vantage point of both outsiders and insiders, the party system ordinarily will appear, to the extent that it registers at all, in disarray. And indeed it is in disarray—more so than at any time in the last century—but not to a point that either promises or ensures its enfeeblement and disintegration.

Notes

1. All of the proposals for reforming the party system cited in this section, along with quoted material, are drawn from the Committee on Political Parties of the

American Political Science Association's report, *Toward a More Responsible Two-Party System* (New York: Holt, Rinehart and Winston, 1950). The longer quotations appear on these pages of the report: 1, 2, 22 (definition of party responsibility), 61-62 (seniority), 66 (intraparty democracy), and 69-70 (party membership).

2. For a comprehensive development of the themes of this and the preceding paragraph, see Austin Ranney, *The Doctrine of Responsible Party Government* (Urbana: University of Illinois Press, 1954), 10-16.

3. There are a number of excellent analyses of party responsibility. See Austin Ranney, "Toward a More Responsible Two-Party System: A Commentary," *American Political Science Review* 45 (June 1951): 488-499; T. William Goodman, "How Much Political Party Centralization Do We Want?" *Journal of Politics* 13 (November 1951): 536-561; Evron M. Kirkpatrick, "Toward a More Responsible Two-Party System: Political Science, Policy Science, or Pseudo-Science?" *American Political Science Review* 65 (December 1971): 965-990; Gerald M. Pomper, "From Confusion to Clarity: Issues and American Voters, 1956-1968," *American Political Science Review* 66 (June 1972): 415-428; Michael Margolis, "From Confusion to Confusion: Issues and the American Voter (1956-1972)," *American Political Science Review* 71 (March 1977): 31-43; and David S. Broder, "The Case for Responsible Party Government," in *Parties and Elections in an Anti-Party Age,* ed. Jeff Fishel (Bloomington: Indiana University Press, 1978), 22-32.

4. The recommendations of the commission are found in *Mandate for Reform* (Washington, D.C.: Commission on Party Structure and Delegate Selection, Democratic National Committee, 1970).

5. The price of these reforms was high. Delegates of the new-enthusiast variety were far more numerous than party professionals. Moreover, the ideological cast of the delegates was markedly different—that is, much more liberal—from that of the general run of Democrats. And fewer delegates belonging to labor unions were present than is ordinarily the case. In some respects the new rules produced a most unrepresentative convention. The candidate it nominated, George McGovern, was overwhelmingly defeated in the election—due in part to the defection of party moderates and conservatives. Ironically, though it was expected that the quota system for blacks, women, and youth would increase support among these groups in the election, nothing of the sort occurred. Blacks and youths supported the 1972 Democratic presidential candidate in about the same proportion as they did the 1968 candidate. Support among women voters declined notably. See Austin Ranney, *Curing the Mischiefs of Faction: Party Reform in America* (Berkeley: University of California Press, 1975), 153-156, 206-208.

6. To achieve a system of responsible parties, according to *Toward a More Responsible Two-Party System,* "The internal processes of the parties must be democratic, the party members must have an opportunity to participate in intraparty business, and the leaders must be accountable to the party." Committee on Political Parties of the American Political Science Association, *Toward a More Responsible Two-Party System,* 23.

7. See the analysis by Kenneth Janda, "Primrose Paths to Political Reform: 'Reforming' versus Strengthening American Parties," in *Paths to Political Reform,* ed. William J. Crotty (Lexington, Mass.: D.C. Heath, 1980), especially 319-327.

8. In addition, though tangential to this account, certain major recommendations of the report have been met through action by the federal government. A number of barriers to voting were eliminated as a result of the passage of the Voting Rights Act of 1965 and the adoption of the Twenty-sixth Amendment to the Constitution in 1971.

9. E. E. Schattschneider, *Party Government* (New York: Holt, Rinehart and Winston, 1942), 64.

10. Frank J. Sorauf, *Political Parties in the American System* (Boston: Little, Brown, 1964), 102.

11. Byron E. Shafer, *Quiet Revolution: The Struggle for the Democratic Party and the Shaping of Post-Reform Politics* (New York: Russell Sage Foundation, 1983), 529.

12. This quotation appears in Burdett A. Loomis, *The New American Politician: Ambition, Entrepreneurship, and the Changing Face of Political Life* (New York: Basic Books, 1988), 187.

13. Quoted by Loomis, *The New American Politician*, 10.

14. David B. Truman, "Party Reform, Party Atrophy, and Constitutional Change: Some Reflections," *Political Science Quarterly* 99 (Winter 1984-1985): 167.

15. These data are derived from a *New York Times*/CBS News poll, as reported in the *New York Times*, October 7, 1986.

16. Martin P. Wattenberg, *The Decline of American Political Parties, 1952-1984* (Cambridge, Mass.: Harvard University Press, 1986), 21.

17. See Jack Dennis, "Public Support for the Party System, 1964-1984" (Paper delivered at the annual meeting of the American Political Science Association, Washington, D.C., August 28-31, 1986), 19; and Wattenberg, *The Decline of American Political Parties*, 22.

18. See an analysis that finds ideology supplanting party as the primary structuring agent in presidential elections: George Rabinowitz, Paul-Henri Gurian, and Stuart Elaine Macdonald, "The Structure of Presidential Elections and the Process of Realignment, 1944 to 1980," *American Journal of Political Science* 28 (November 1984): 611-635.

19. John R. Petrocik and Dwaine Marvick, "Explaining Party Elite Transformation: Institutional Changes and Insurgent Politics," *Western Political Quarterly* 36 (September 1983): 350.

20. See the exit interview data assembled by the *New York Times*/CBS News poll, as reported in the *New York Times*, November 10, 1988; and the ABC exit poll, as reported in the *Washington Post*, November 9, 1988.

21. *New York Times*, November 10, 1988.

22. For analysis of the voting patterns of blacks and whites, see Harold W. Stanley, William T. Bianco, and Richard G. Niemi, "Partisanship and Group Support over Time: A Multivariate Analysis," *American Political Science Review* 80 (September 1986): 970-976; and Edward G. Carmines and James A. Stimson, "Racial Issues and the Structure of Mass Belief Systems," *Journal of Politics* 44 (February 1982): 2-20.

23. Norman J. Ornstein, Thomas E. Mann, and Michael J. Malbin, *Vital Statistics on Congress, 1989-1990* (Washington, D.C.: Congressional Quarterly, 1990), 65.

24. Thomas E. Mann and Raymond E. Wolfinger, "Candidates and Parties in Congressional Elections," *American Political Science Review* 74 (September 1980): 620.

25. The success of incumbents is high, but they are no safer today than they were in the 1950s. The key to incumbent survival is to maintain "an image of invulnerability" to discourage activists of the other party from mounting a major challenge. Steady attention to the district is essential in this strategy. See Gary C. Jacobson, "The Marginals Never Vanished: Incumbency and Competition in Elections to the U.S. House of Representatives, 1952-82," *American Journal of Political Science* 31 (February 1987): 126-141. And on the general subject of legislative-constituency relations, see David R. Mayhew, *Congress: The Electoral Connection* (New Haven, Conn.: Yale University Press, 1974); and Richard F. Fenno, Jr., *Home Style: House Members in Their Districts* (Boston: Little, Brown, 1978). As a general rule, college students majoring in political science should not be permitted to graduate, or at least not with distinction, until they have read these books.

26. Richard G. Hutcheson III, "The Inertial Effect of Incumbency and Two-Party Politics: Elections to the House of Representatives from the South, 1952-1974," *American Political Science Review* 69 (December 1975): 1399-1401.

27. *Davis v. Bandemer,* 106 S. Ct. 2797 (1986).

28. *Time,* August 7, 1978, 15.

29. *Time,* January 29, 1979, 12.

30. *U.S. News & World Report,* January 29, 1979, 24.

31. Press release, Federal Election Commission, October 31, 1989.

32. See a discussion of single-issue and ideological PACs in William J. Crotty and Gary C. Jacobson, *American Parties in Decline* (Boston: Little, Brown, 1980), 117-155.

33. *Washington Post,* September 13, 1978. The comment was made by Sen. Wendell R. Anderson (D-Minn.) to columnist David S. Broder.

34. *Washington Post,* September 13, 1978.

35. *Newsweek,* April 29, 1968, 76. For a comprehensive study of the public relations person in politics, see Stanley Kelley, Jr., *Professional Public Relations and Political Power* (Baltimore: Johns Hopkins Press, 1956).

36. See an analysis by Benjamin Ginsberg, "Money and Power: The New Political Economy of American Elections," in *The Political Economy,* ed. Thomas Ferguson and Joel Rogers (Armonk, N.Y.: M. E. Sharpe, 1984), 163-179.

37. Joe McGinniss, *The Selling of the President* (New York: Trident Press/Simon and Schuster, 1968), 27.

38. Robert MacNeil, *The People Machine: The Influence of Television on American Politics* (New York: Harper and Row, 1968), xvii.

39. Marshall McLuhan, as quoted by McGinniss, *The Selling of the President,* 28.

40. Dan Nimmo, *The Political Persuaders: The Techniques of Modern Election Campaigns* (Englewood Cliffs, N.J.: Prentice Hall, 1970), 197.

41. Comment by a Bush adviser quoted in *Time,* November 14, 1988, 66.

42. An unnamed gubernatorial candidate quoted by Barbara G. Salmore and Stephen A. Salmore, *Candidates, Parties, and Campaigns* (Washington, D.C.: CQ Press, 1989), 139.

43. Harold Mendelsohn and Irving Crespi, *Polls, Television, and the New Politics* (Scranton, Pa.: Chandler, 1970), 310-311.

44. The evidence of a recent study by Laura L. Vertz, John P. Frendreis, and James L. Gibson suggests that some offices are much more influenced by national forces than others. They find that presidential elections have become nationalized and that congressional races remain localized. "[If] factors such as

the *national* media are irrelevant to a race, as is usually the case with congressional elections, then the electorate responds to the more constituency-related, localized forces." "Nationalization of the Electorate in the United States," *American Political Science Review* 81 (September 1987): 961-966 (quotation on p. 965).

45. Frank J. Sorauf, *Party Politics in America* (Boston: Little, Brown, 1980), 48.

46. Harvey Wheeler, "The End of the Two Party System," *Saturday Review*, November 2, 1968, 20.

47. See the evidence on these and other policy views held by Democratic and Republican delegates in the *New York Times*, August 14, 1988.

48. Concerning this point, see Edward R. Tufte, *Political Control of the Economy* (Princeton, N.J.: Princeton University Press, 1978), especially Chapter 4. See a study of presidential elections from 1948 through 1984 that finds that the *state of the economy* is an even better predictor of election outcomes than the *candidates' popularity* (or the voters' relative liking of them). Robert S. Erickson, "Economic Conditions and the Presidential Vote," *American Political Science Review* 83 (June 1989): 567-573.

49. Ranney, *Curing the Mischiefs of Faction*, 3.

50. For an elaboration of these themes, see Nelson W. Polsby, *Consequences of Party Reform* (Oxford, England: Oxford University Press, 1983), especially Chapter 2.

51. Truman, "Party Reform, Party Atrophy, and Constitutional Change: Some Reflections," 169.

52. Apart from its provisions concerning intraparty democracy, the Democratic party charter boasts very little that is new. The midterm party convention that adopted the charter in 1974 rejected numerous provisions designed to centralize the party and to alter its federal character, including a dues-paying membership, a mandatory national party conference every other year, an independent national chairman elected for a four-year term (to reduce the presidential nominee's influence over the chairman), an elaborate regional party organization, and a strong national party executive committee. Few changes were made in the major organs of the party: the national convention, the national committee, and the office of the national chairman. The vast majority of the compromises reached both prior to and during the convention were struck on the side of those who wanted to preserve a party system notable for its decentralization. See an interesting account of the convention's issues involving centralization versus decentralization by David S. Broder, *Washington Post*, December 1, 1974.

53. Cornelius P. Cotter and John F. Bibby, "Institutional Development of Parties and the Thesis of Party Decline," *Political Science Quarterly* 95 (Spring 1980): 1-27. For a close analysis of the services made available to congressional candidates by national party committees, especially those of the Republican party, see Paul S. Herrnson, "Do Parties Make a Difference? The Role of Party Organizations in Congressional Elections," *Journal of Politics* 48 (August 1986): 589-615.

54. Robert J. Huckshorn, James L. Gibson, Cornelius P. Cotter, and John F. Bibby, "Party Integration and Party Organizational Strength," *Journal of Politics* 48 (November 1986): 976-991.

55. For the development of these and cognate themes that point to a political rebirth of the American party system, see Xandra Kayden and Eddie Mahe, Jr., *The Party Goes On: The Persistence of the Two-Party System in the United States*

(New York: Basic Books, 1985). And also of interest, see Xandra Kayden, "The New Professionalism of the Oldest Party," *Public Opinion* 8 (June/July 1985): 42-44, 49.

56. Byron E. Shafer, "The Democratic Party Salvation Industry," *Public Opinion* 8 (June/July 1985): 47. And see the analysis of Michael Margolis and Raymond E. Owen, "From Organization to Personalism: A Note on the Transmogrification of the Local Political Party," *Polity* 18 (Winter 1985): 313-328. For a finding that local parties have not become less active and less organized in the current era, see James L. Gibson, Cornelius P. Cotter, John F. Bibby, and Robert J. Huckshorn, "Whither the Local Parties?: A Cross-Sectional and Longitudinal Analysis of the Strength of Party Organizations," *American Journal of Political Science* 29 (February 1985): 139-160. In addition, see Barbara C. Burrell, "Local Political Party Committees, Task Performance and Organizational Vitality," *Western Political Quarterly* 39 (March 1986): 48-66.

57. No study documents and explains this better than Wattenberg, *The Decline of American Political Parties.*

58. E. E. Schattschneider, *Party Government,* 64ff.

59. *Tashjian v. Republican Party of Connecticut,* 107 S. Ct. 544 (1986). Political scientists are divided on the *Tashjian* case. See an analysis by Leon D. Epstein, "Will American Political Parties Be Privatized?" *Journal of Law & Politics* 5 (Winter 1989): 239-274.

60. To explore the literature that defends the American party system, see in particular Herbert Agar, *The Price of Union* (Boston: Houghton Mifflin, 1950); Pendleton Herring, *The Politics of Democracy* (New York: Norton, 1940); Arthur N. Holcombe, *Our More Perfect Union* (Cambridge, Mass.: Harvard University Press, 1950); and Edward C. Banfield, "In Defense of the American Party System," in *Political Parties, U.S.A.,* ed. Robert A. Goldwin (Chicago: Rand McNally, 1964), 21-39.

61. *Time,* November 20, 1978, 42.

62. Stephen K. Bailey, *Congress in the Seventies* (New York: St. Martin's Press, 1970), 102-103. Among the other major accomplishments of the first session of the Eighty-ninth Congress were the passage of bills to provide for medical care for the aged under Social Security, aid to depressed areas, the protection of voting rights, federal scholarships, the Teacher Corps, immigration reform, and a variety of programs to launch the War on Poverty.

63. *Congressional Quarterly Weekly Report,* January 2, 1982, 20-21.

64. *Congressional Quarterly Weekly Report,* December 30, 1989, 3540; evidence on party unity appears on 3546-3550.

65. Donald E. Stokes and Warren E. Miller, "Party Government and the Saliency of Congress," in *Elections and the Political Order,* ed. Angus Campbell (New York: Wiley, 1966), 209-211.

Index